ALSO BY JAY CANTOR

FICTION

The Death of Che Guevara

Krazy Kat

ESSAYS

On Giving Birth to One's Own Mother

The Space Between: Literature and Politics

GREAT NECK

Alfred A. Knopf

New York

2003

GREAT

NECK

A NOVEL

JAY

CANTOR

THIS IS A BORZOI BOOK
PUBLISHED BY ALFRED A. KNOPF

www.aaknopf.com

Library of Congress Cataloging-in-Publication Data
Cantor, Jay.
Great Neck : a novel / Jay Cantor.— 1st ed.
p. cm.
ISBN 0-375-41394-4
1. Great Neck (N.Y.)—Fiction. 2. Jews—New York (State)—Fiction.
3. Baby boom generation—Fiction. 4. Civil rights workers—Fiction.
5. African Americans—Fiction. 6. Peace movements—Fiction.
7. Mississippi—Fiction. 8. Friendship—Fiction. 9. Radicals—Fiction. I. Title.
PS3553.A5475 G74 2002
813'.54—dc21   2002067123

The author would like to thank the
John D. and Catherine T. MacArthur Foundation for its
generous support during the writing of this book.

Manufactured in the United States of America
Published January 20, 2003
Second Printing, February 2003

For the Graces

Contents

1

1978: SIDEBAR

On the morning of his thirtieth birthday, Arthur Kaplan—nicknamed Arkey by his brother-in-law and transformed to **OurKey** in the Billy-Books series *Tales from the Kabbalah*—bounced nervously in a taxi, bumping along on an Israeli jockey's Island City route to the courtroom. Asleep or awake, in long reveries and fleeting images, Arkey Kaplan was given to dreaming, mixtures of memory and longing that transformed and commanded him. Today, a sentient corpse ordered him to pat his jacket pocket to make sure he had his checkbook—in case he needed to pay his childhood friend Beth Jacobs' bail for not showing up for trial in Chicago nearly a decade before. Or for setting bombs throughout this great land of ours. Or for God knows what else.

Can you actually pay bail with a personal check? Distracted, Arkey forgot to tell the cab driver to take the bridge. *Too late.* The Israeli jockey had thrust them into the line for the Holland Tunnel—that insecure Dutch dike against the river, that clammy, oppressive place, that long, tight ceramic tomb.

Ghouls and coffins were much on Arkey's mind. Perhaps they always had been, but a year and a day ago, Arkey had had his second operation for skin cancer at the Beth Israel Hospital in Boston. "Happy Birthday," his surgeon had said as Arkey lay nauseous in the recovery room, dreaming of the time he'd opened a mojo hand's rolled scroll and so put a curse on himself. "The margins were very good," the doctor had said. "We got it all." His savior had looked down at his chart then and had added, mildly, "Probably."

Arkey wore his long-sleeved shirt buttoned to the top so the sun couldn't tickle his weak-willed skin. He had a white scarf around his neck and a Panama on his head, and he even kept his hands in his pockets. Moisture bloomed under his arms, formed a fragrant acid-and-roses river with the Guerlain cologne he wore to mask his continual sweating. How had Billy Green managed to predict *that* in his comic books?

And how much longer would this damn tunnel go on for? Any dark enclosed space made Arkey feel already trapped in his grave. *How long,* each bump said, *how long, how long?* This fucking tunnel ends in Pardes, Arkey dreamt, and the cab would take him to join the person he had most respected, his grandfather Abraham, the shop steward, now one month in his own tomb. The word reminded him of the Tombs, where Beth waited, just as Granddad had predicted, Avraham having found strength to denounce her, among others, before he died, this allrightnick's Eleventh—and scrupulously observed—Commandment being *Thou shalt criticize others.* "She was never part of the world she supposedly wanted to save, Arthur. She acted without guidance from any class organization. No discipline. No solidarity."

"They had solidarity, Granddad. With the Third World."

"Baloney!" Abe's once strong voice was now a harsh whisper. "A fantasy," he gasped—magisterially. His finger, skinny but for the swollen knuckles, tapped a temple. "She and her pals really served their own meshuginah psychologies. That's *it!*"

Thank God, Arkey had thought, *I've always remained faithful to long dead socialist organizations*—for avoiding Abe's poking finger had been, since childhood, Arthur Kaplan's Eleventh Commandment. And Abe's approval? *That* miracle was reserved for the great—the greatly moral, observers of the mitzvahs, heroes of labor. I.e., *not Arkey,* who was merely a historian of the movement, not a participant.

His grandfather had coughed, the ratchets of his lungs grinding on each other. A claw reached toward the night table for Kleenex, scattering bottles, letters, flowers, capless ballpoints. Arkey had knelt to pick things up, bobbed up and down by the bedside, trying to arrange things by category, with the long black box of the nurse's call button in front.

"Thank you," Avraham said. "You are a pillar for me, Arkey."

Well, Arkey tidied, Arkey loved, but on the whole Avraham didn't make much distinction between Beth Jacobs, for example, and the rest of Arkey's generation, including the grandson himself. "It was *never* a revolutionary situation in this country," Avraham had said, that visit. "She was putting on a show for herself and her friends with those bombings. America is a stage set for her psychodrama. The audience stops watching, boychick, she'll get bored and surrender."

Apparently true. Anyway, according to Jesse Kelman, at least Arkey and his friends had nothing to worry about from Beth's trial. The State, he said, didn't know anything more than before about the MIT bombing—or anyway, it couldn't *prove* anything—so long as Michael Healy didn't talk. And as for what Beth might have done *after* that, well, whatever it had been, other parts of the Weather Underground—known as the Eggplant, at least in their own frenetic, whimsical imaginations—had gotten wrist slaps when they'd surfaced: suspended sentences, probation, tiny morsels of county time. Mark Rudd had—in Eggplant patois—*inverted* a year before Beth. He'd gotten off with a two-thousand-dollar fine and some probation time. Only Cathy Wilkerson, Jesse said, might get more—her parents had owned the town house, which put her in legal possession of the dynamite. But all the government could hang on Beth Jacobs was being there. Or so Jesse Kelman had said. And, as always, his friends had rested themselves in Jesse's quiet certainties, his *You're home now, I'll take care of you* tone. Thus his nom de BillyBooks: **The Defender**, with its overtones, rare for Billy's work, of Campbell's Soup and Mom.

Special Agent Olson, still especially piqued with Beth, had managed to delay her bail hearing a week with jive about a vast international terrorist network still crouching in the American night. But even Olson couldn't jerk off to that fantasy for long. Beth's hearing this morning, Jesse said, would be brief and pro forma. She would probably walk out with them this afternoon, bored with setting bombs, ready for a new life; the final bow of the Weathermen—with most of the audience already at their summer houses.

But when a brusque guard stopped Arkey in the courthouse lobby and passed a metal detector's curved rods over the legs of his seersucker suit and into his sweaty crotch, Arkey knew there'd been a glitch. Jesse had got it wrong. Maybe Beth had been heedless again, suffering from a masochistic desire for a restrictive, punishing authority (her psychoanalyst father's theory) or just from an upper-middle-class certainty that the world would once again conform to her fantasies.

A Hispanic TAC Squad officer holding a rifle with a curved clip stood next to the guard. He glared at Arkey as he walked past him into the courtroom, probably able to tell from Arkey's long nose that he was a friend of the guard's hated enemy, the defendant, the notorious comic book star Beth Jacobs, i.e., **Athena X**, or **Ninja B.**, or (in the *Justice* series) **Deborah, AKA the Prophet**. The guard muttered something. A curse?

Arkey loosened his scarf as he walked to the front of the court and took a seat next to his friend Jeffrey Schell. The guard, Arkey knew, wanted him to die. He needed wood to knock on, to stop new tumor cells from sprouting. *This must be the throne room of Zargon, or of the devil himself! Only concrete everywhere!* Arkey tapped his own head lightly, clearly wood through and through, Avraham often said. Arkey knew superstitions meant religion had failed him; or he'd failed it, Arkey fitfully observant only for the last six months and lacking the hefty Abe-style moral greatness that might provoke God's protection. Besides, old habits die hard; probably after the person, even. Had he been this bad, he wondered, before the melanoma?

"Yeah," Laura had said, last time he dragged this subject up. He'd always been a wood knocker, she said, a crack skipper. A penny swallower. Laura usually wore stylish versions of peasant things, thickly textured, many different-colored threads—but both a little more intricate and more muted, this peasant's patron Saint being Laurent. In fact, Laura, in consultation with her dressmaker, designed her own knockoffs, gathered her fabrics for her kimonos moderne, her très riche Irish milkmaid cloaks, Laura a multiethnic tribe unto herself. That day for an amiable lunch—croque mesdames in the faded Bauhaus of the Brasserie—she'd worn a straight, long tweed skirt, a woven forest-garden.

"Wood knocking," Arkey had said, "that's ordinary kid stuff, you ask me." He'd hoped still that Laura might make love again even if only for old times' sake; pity even. Touching someone pushed death away—for a moment anyway.

"Arkey, darling," Laura said, with a mock shake of her head, "you have to spin around every time someone mentions sausage. You have to tie your hair in knots and rip the knots out at one in the afternoon and one at night. We won't even talk about the dropped-coin thing, or that you can't even listen to 'Take Me to the River' because someone you knew who died once listened to it, all right? None of that is ordinary, dear. You're more like a tribe of your own."

Him, too? "You know, I think it was Billy's sixth-grade school report that traumatized me. I had to come up with magic spells to keep the Nazis away from Great Neck."

Laura had laughed at that explanation. Insufficiently Oedipal, probably. "Well, thanks for your effort. It seems to have worked."

"Yeah. *So far.*" He took another forkful of fried bread and cheese. Join the Jews for a Larger Tribe and Better Spells? Not that *theirs* had worked so very well against Germans. Or even Babylonians, for that matter.

Then, just as he was imagining Laura's bow-shaped lips, his dream became reality and Laura Jaffe—AKA **SheWolf**, and **Dr. Fantasy** in Billy-Books—walked into the crowded courtroom, in a short black skirt—

more professional today than haute couture peasant—a short-sleeved, white scalloped shirt and small pearls, and a cane topped with a silver wolf. The lawyers, as if on cue, started to gabble at each other in excited voices. The whole thing, Arkey thought, must have sounded to Laura like a murderous argument at her family's dinner table. After all, Robert Brown, the government's lawyer, was the handsome nephew of her family's maid, and the defense counsel was played today by Jesse Kelman, her first lover—and still, Arkey suspected bitterly, the champeen.

Laura glanced at Arkey—the not-quite-father of the child she hadn't had—and she smiled almost warmly at him (or was it at her best friend, Jeffrey Schell?)—but the seat she decided on was across the aisle from them. A *snub*. Arkey couldn't help himself; he tucked his leg under his bottom so he'd look taller.

Laura, as if responding, put her right hand under her long black hair and lifted it over her blouse collar, a gesture that seemed to Arkey, like everything she did since they'd split up two years ago, both enticing and dismissive.

Though what Laura actually felt that morning was anxious—like *she'd* suddenly become the one on trial here. She liked being looked at, loved being wanted, but she didn't cotton to being divided, used up, found wanting, and she sat now in a courtroom with Jesse Kelman, a handsome boy who, in girl-times, she'd deeply loved; Arkey Kaplan, a lover in penny loafers who'd always wanted too much from her; and Bobby Brown, a man with whom she'd already, in fantasy, started to make love. So she touched her hair to reassure herself, anxiety being most certainly not good for her under-siege myelin. *How important could this case be*—she said to herself to mock her own desire—*if the Justice Department has sent a thirty-year-old lawyer to try it?*

Still, she couldn't take her eyes off Robert Brown, who, with an expertly controlled lawyer's death-voice that without inordinate volume could push you into the corner of a room and beat your brain black and blue, now said that Laura's dear friend Beth Jacobs had, to the government's certain knowledge, participated in several bombings over the last ten years. The government would show that during the course of these conspiracies the defendant had seriously wounded at least one man. And those were just the felonies the government could be certain about. The government soon would present evidence of other, even more destructive, crimes and conspiracies, some of them just at the point of explosion. The defendant had jumped bail before, he said, and would undoubtedly flee again when she realized how desperate her situation really was, coldly indifferent as always to the effects of her actions on her community and her family. Robert Brown nodded his head toward Beth's parents, and the strength in Brown's muscular body, his numen of banked power and anger, or so Laura dreamt him, gave the downward tilt of his large head an expressive force, as if this strong man was simply overcome with righteous sympathy for these wronged old people, whose dearest wish, he knew, was that their cruel daughter should be denied bail. Laura couldn't help herself, she became a little wet for square-jawed Bobby Brown, could feel his arms pulling her toward his chest. *(Too square, too large? What would children of his look like?)*

Then Harrison Baker, the other of Beth's lawyers, smiled, showing wolfishly long, Chesterfield-patinaed teeth, and whispered a question in Jesse's ear. Arkey had told her he felt confident their friend could pass the Talmud's test for a lawyer's ability to try a capital case: that he could elaborate sixteen reasons why it was all right to eat snake, even though Leviticus expressly forbade it.

Jesse rose in an ill-fitting gray suit and shook his curly black–haired head with sad surprise at Bobby Brown's "unreasonable cruelty." In slow, soft tones that made him sound like a weary father correcting an obtuse, obstinate child, Jesse said that the State's claims were a government fantasy to clear the books at this poor woman's expense, for if the State had evidence of supposed conspiracies why had no other Weathermen ever been charged in them? Beth had surrendered voluntarily, and this huge, nonsensical show of force—metal detectors, pat searches, police riflemen inside the courtroom—was the State's unconscionable attempt at intimidation, its way of substituting innuendo for argument, trying to convince the judge that Beth was a dangerous character, when, in truth, she never had been a violent threat to anyone and her parents' dearest wish was only that she be returned to them and to Great Neck, Long Island, the town where she was born and still had deep roots. Surely the court could give some consideration to how much this family had already suffered?

Was Beth a threat? Laura wondered. Beth had spent two weeks hiding out in Laura's studio apartment, while Jesse negotiated her surrender. She'd been meek, bewildered, and obviously bored. Does a terrorist spend her afternoons watching *Family Feud*? Nights, they'd eaten take-out Kung Pao Chicken together, and Beth had never once mentioned the violent overthrow of the government. The only secret communiqués she'd received had been love notes from her boyfriend, Snake, scrawled on torn magazine pages.

But if she wasn't dangerous, then what made Beth worth even this charade of force? Did they hope for heavy bail as a present for Special Agent Olson—his lips set tightly but his eyes shining, Laura imagined, with dreams of finally imprisoning Beth in a box she'd never escape from. Olson had somehow known about Beth's part in the MIT bombing from the first moment he'd interrogated Laura about the explosion, had already badly wanted to nail Beth then. But *still*? Why would even he want to make an example of her? For what audience in this wide, indifferent world? Beth had maybe been briefly notorious in 1968, when her father, Dr. Leo Jacobs, camp survivor and media favorite, had published a famous essay in *Commentary* on her misguided generation, a bunch of sadomasochists undone by fantasies—a hook for *Life* magazine to make his daughter a Symbol, and himself famous among the parents worried that their children might follow Che Guevara's or Herbert Marcuse's piping right into the ground. But by now, Laura would bet that only adolescent comic book readers cared about Beth Jacobs, or someone kind of like her, called **Ninja B.**, or **Deborah, AKA the Prophet,** or whatever tawdry new marketing gimmick Billy Green had thought of to make her multicolored, big-breasted antics ripe for geekoid consumption.

And consume they did! Two years before, Laura had sold a silly picture book Billy had done for her when he was twelve to a twenty-year-old Chinese American with bad teeth and a nasty smile, netting more than enough to pay for her abortion. Billy Green, he told her as he'd wrapped the hand-sewn pages in cellophane, was the greatest American genius since Herriman, whoever that was, and Beth the greatest heroine since Wonder Woman (though she was sure that wondering was pretty much all this boy had ever done about women). Only people like that cared about the real Beth Jacobs anymore, Laura was sure, and only because she was Billy's character.

Her father cared mightily, though—and probably still thought of Beth as *his* character. He sat with his wife on the other side of the courtroom from their daughter, and their two small bodies rocked forward and back when hers did, as if they wanted to seize any possible link with her. Dr. Jacobs' face turned longingly toward Beth as they swayed, and his eyes behind thick lenses looked scoured—as they usually did, actually—by a long weeping. But Beth wouldn't look at her small, sad-eyed parents, or at any of her friends; she only stared downward, at the wooden defense table.

The two lead lawyers, doing their steps in the jail minuet, approached the bench. Robert Brown, Arkey imagined, gave the judge a smile meant to say, There'll be plenty of evidence soon, so trust us, Your Honor—if you cut her loose, we'll see that Beth Jacobs is the *Daily News* boner of the day for you:

NINNY JUDGE SETS COMIC BOOK STAR NINJA B. FREE!
She and the Joker Start Unfunny Gotham Terror Wave!

Meanwhile, as the lawyers gabbled, Beth, in short-sleeved blue denim prison dress, slumped even lower at the counsel table, the neon-passion color of her fingernails seemingly the only defiant thing about her. A thin leather cord went around her neck and under long black hair in back. A leather packet hung from the cord, and lay on the table right in front of her. In 1964, just before he'd been murdered, Laura's brother, Frank, had sent Beth that flat, embroidered pouch from Mississippi, calling it an African custom re-told in the new world, "a nation sack." Beth must have given the prison officials her unblinking organizer's stare and a torrent of words to convince them that her pouch had constitutionally protected religious significance, her equivalent of tefillin, the black leather boxes attached to leather thongs that Arkey himself had just learned to wind criss-cross around his arm and circled about his head when he recited morning prayers, the boxes containing, by sublime tautology, the fragment of the Torah that said to wear the boxes. Arkey was also pretty sure that the sack contained one of the letters that Frank had mailed from the Lovette jail. Or, according to some folk, from the grave.

Beth, probably feeling she was just the legal system's McGuffin, sunk a little farther forward with each sentence of the lawyer's wrangle. She pillowed her head on her pale, bare arms. Her body looked wan—but, Jesus, Arkey whispered to his companion, was that a pale green snake tattoo curling out from under the edge of her sleeve?

"Beth's like a work of found art," Jeffrey Schell whispered into Arkey's waxy ear. "Sculpted by the history ocean, smoothed and shaped until she's been cast up in this courtroom for us to stare at. And it needn't be beautiful if it's fascinating, charismatic, even."

What the fuck was he talking about? If anyone on God's earth was beautiful, Arkey had known from the time he was eleven and she'd given him a painful afternoon-long boner, it was Beth Jacobs with her thick black hair, green eyes, a straight if down-turned nose, and already amazing, intimidating, breasts.

But truly Jeffrey just wanted to riff on his beloved, he always having been the one perhaps *most* crazy about crazy Beth, an artwork, an opera star, the woman, perhaps, that he would have wanted to be. "Maybe whatever fixes the attention is called art by us morally indifferent moderns," Jeffrey murmured with seductive knowingness, while the lawyers continued to blow wind into the judge.

Jeffrey was all soft musing *maybes*—the reverse of the bully labor historians and ideologues (his grandpa Abraham included) that Arkey usually apache-danced with. An Ichabod Crane of a man, Jeffrey had a large Adam's apple, thinning blond hair, and the largest nose of the group. And, a reverse miracle by Great Neck standards, he had uneven teeth—the sadism of his father having denied him the sadism of the orthodontist. He had nearly translucent skin, too, the tracery of every vein visible beneath. Jeffrey looked vulnerable, slightly morbid. And yet *he* managed to make the package appear dandyish—like he'd intentionally stitched himself from such ungainly parts. Arkey tasted something almost erotic about his initial distaste, as if such a strange-looking person must be in touch with secrets it would be worthwhile to know.

But the bailiff didn't think so. He glared at them both. A courtroom, apparently, was the wrong place for a seminar. Arkey looked at the rifles—*they* really fixed his attention. Did that make them art? He whispered to Jeffrey to shut up. But hypnotized by Jeffrey's art-dealer voice, Arkey took another look at Beth, like he was deciding whether or not to acquire *her* for his nonexistent collection. The tattoo on her arm showed a snake surrounded by blue Arabic-looking letters worked into a red-and-green design, and it felt unclean to Arkey even to look on it, to be joined to it by the eyes. It excited him and made him queasy, like a cock ring or a pornographic stage show, a tattoo being forbidden, Arkey had learned in his Talmud study group just the week before, not by good taste and class decorum only but by Law (Leviticus 19:28); the body to be returned to the Creator as delivered (minus, for men, that one crucial snip, a sacrifice that made you worthy of God's attention). Still, Arkey yearned to draw the letters over with his finger, for he had always dreamt there was a magic to touch, and he imagined that contact with Beth's skin would give him entry into Beth's hidden world, the underground rivers of passion and violence that had fed her Eggplant existence. Those were waters that he feared and despised, adrenaline rivers for adventurist junkies, a particularly disastrous drug (he could hear his grandfather say) for the working class. Just look what happened to that boychick Healy! Yet Arkey still longed to feel the turbulence of Beth's heart's blood for a moment.

"Sit up, Miss Jacobs," the judge said, peering between the lawyers to see Beth more clearly. A fifty-year-old man, he still wore a Marine's crew cut in 1978—a retro-coiffure, which couldn't, Arkey thought, bode well for his friend's case. "You'll have plenty of time to sleep later."

Beth's back rose slowly from the table, but her head still slumped toward the earth. Billy Green's pencil moved along the large sketchbook page on his knees, following, Arkey imagined, the line of defeat in Beth's bent shoulders, probably drawing the Alphaville courtroom for the next ish of *Girls with Guns*. In BillyBooks, Billy Green (who'd lost a tiny bit of hearing in the upper registers) had become a character called Billy Bad Ears, a boy who'd gone grandly deaf weeping for the world's pain and so gained the power to hear other men's hearts. As "The Super Hero Who Draws Himself" Billy was famous among the can't-dance adolescents and adults who worshiped comic books. Well, why not? After all, hadn't Arkey and his friends themselves once worshiped Billy, a rite that had helped make *them* into self-deluded isolates with their own dating—and legal—troubles?

Arkey saw tears in Billy's eyes, and maybe not only for suffering humanity this time. Michael Healy had been a stand-up guy, but during his trial the courtroom had been crowded with spectators who gave the judge the power salute and oinked whenever he rose from the bench. The NLF's envoy to Cuba had called Michael "a hero of the Vietnamese people." But that was 1970. In 1978, Arkey imagined, a girl might want to make a deal to avoid jail time that nobody cared about anymore—even in Cuba or Vietnam.

But not **Ninja B.!** who had already stood shackled (in *Girls with Guns*, Ish. #46) in a "courtroom" whose gray cement and dark wooden benches signaled it was also one of Zargon's control centers, the walls covered with video screens that showed any place in the world—for in this parallel reality your home TV was a double agent that also scanned you, providing instantly updated computer readouts of when your eyes widened with desire (Hey, look, he doesn't know he likes the beefcake better than the babes!) or blinked with fear, matching the scan with your charge card receipts, your mail orders for pornography, and so revealing, by Psycho-Spectral Marketing Analysis, the kinks by which every consumerzen could be manipulated, to his bliss and your profit. **Ninja B.** (Beth's name depending on what comic book series she was in, who her enemy was) wore heavy Bobby Seale chains at the waist and feet and a straitjacket (for in comics things are never bad enough); and her mouth—watch out for the Death Scream!—was gagged. Beth was only a year older than Billy, but like a stone her father had sent skimming across a lake, she'd skipped on two more grades ahead of them, into college and its initiation, they'd all dreamt, into subtle sexual mysteries. She was Billy's older woman, teasing him for weeks, fucking him rarely—making Billy a Skinner-box pigeon, Arkey thought, on a random reinforcement schedule—so he'd paid continual court to her (who knows, push a lever—or set a fuse—and this might be your big day, little pigeon), which meant **Ninja B.**'s premier skill was to make people her mind-slaves. Today the chains and straitjacket kept her from using her psyche-controlling arts, or the voodoo hand jive that could (in the kind of pun that comics thrive on) manipulate the weather, bringing tornadoes as disturbing as a teenager's desires down upon her enemies; and she couldn't shake her body with the esoteric martial arts techniques (the snake, the slow grind, the bump) whose vibrations could mambo a man to bloody pieces.

But those eyes, those lips, those breasts! The Judge wants to kiss **Ninja B.**—perhaps because Billy himself, or someone else in the courtroom whose feelings Billy received on that psychic radio he can't jam, had yearned for Beth Jacobs' full, slightly down-turned mouth, thinking that its touch would let him join with her power, her underground existence.

The Judge orders her brought to him.

He strips off his own robes to reveal his 346 suit

—for in BillyBook world most people wore futuristic costumes—skateboarder's knee pads and colored codpieces for women and short kilts for young men, who also wore neck braces as fashion accessories—but the ORG.'s minions almost always wore blue Brooks Brothers suits.

The foolish lovesick Judge orders Ninja B. ungagged—

and Beth unleashes the Death Scream—a sound rawer than any soul singer's throaty yell!

It turns the Judge into her zombie puppet!! He orders the Imperium's soldiers—trained in the neo-samurai code of absolute, hypnotic obedience—to point their guns at their own heads and kill themselves!!! And he puts a gun to his own temple!!!!

Blood spatters the television screens!!!!!

But what would become of **OurKey**, Arkey wondered, that fussy, nervous, ancient historian, whose kabalistic spells brought the mutants the wisdom to see their enemy's plans, though he hadn't, in his real-life Clark Kent identity as a graduate student in labor history when **OurKey** first appeared in *Girl Guerrillas*, #12, known any kabala besides what Billy Green himself had taught them when he was fifteen. And what of Jesse—the Defender—or Jeffrey Schell, known in BillyBooks as **Jeffrey the Sophist**, master of faulty logic and empty rhetoric, super con man of the dread Band of Outsiders? Or of Laura, who was far from being an analyst when Billy first drew her as **SheWolf**, a lithe magician, who can show her victims hologram hallucinations of their screaming fears and va-voom desires, visions that make her enemies flee out windows, or run forward toward her claws? (Actually, *had* Billy predicted those things, or just drawn them into one of the endless revisions called The New, or The True, or The New True, Never Before Revealed Origins of the Band of Outsiders?) Would **Ninja B.** give the Death Scream to her former comrades now—that commanding, enchanting sound that would force her aboveground supporters who had fertilized her underground Eggplant existence with an old sweater or a bus ticket to purge themselves for their weakening commitment to world revolution? Probably someday soon the panel Billy drew would fill with *their* blood, too.

A book of Beth, Arkey thought, could be called *The Woman Brought Up On the Opera*, Arkey remembering Leo Jacobs' program of special Euro-education for his Valkyrie daughter. *That* was the whole problem. Or had the problem started when she'd spurned the Met and become *Undone by Rhythm and Blues: The Story of the Girl Who Wanted to Be the Scream from James Brown's Mouth.*

Maybe that's what he should do for his next book—a book of Beth that would really be a book about all of them, written in a hectoring way that his late grandfather and the Brandeis Tenure and Promotion Committee might approve of. Possible title: *Jews with Money*—an outtake title from his first book, the one that had been a rewrite of his thesis on the Jewish labor movement, telling the story of their grandparents' and parents' rise (but was it a rise?) from the Lower East Side ghetto to the mink-lined one.

Arnie Golden, a Jew who already had lots more money than Arkey ever would, strolled into court with a yachtsman's rolling walk, taking a seat right in front of FBI agent Olson. It was Arnie who had saved Arkey's first book from the *JWM* title with an irony to it as bitter as the mounds of cocaine Arnie had passed around to the guests on his leather-covered couch in his all-white Beverly Hills living room. "Yes," he'd said disgustedly, "it *was* a rise. For God's sake, think about your malarkey, Arkey-Barkey. Wide lawns, good schools, no tuberculosis. Don't be an asshole. Of course it was a rise." And he'd shepherded Arkey toward writing a popular (with the Jews, anyway) story of Jewish triumph, *Our Brilliant Careers,* a book mostly purged of his beloved grandfather's gravelly voice, the radical cutter and cloakmaker's Yiddish harangues rich with the Prophet Isaiah madness that said *this success is no success,* and that even Arkey's near best-seller was bupkis—for he hadn't helped realize Justice for All. Abraham's son and his grandson and all their wealthy friends had made nothing but houses of sugar that the rain of Righteousness would surely someday wash away.

But "yes," Arkey's father, Isaac Kaplan, had said, reconciled to his son's life by the same book that glorified his own, "yes. My father has always been a fool. But my son has gotten it right. *This* is the Promised Land." Meaning Great Neck. Moses, a few millenniums previously, had mistakenly turned left to Jerusalem instead of right toward Long Island, causing no end of trouble, the Jews probably having been destined, just as his Israeli cab driver must have suspected, not for the unfortunate weather of the Middle East but for endless summer afternoons by the country club pool, good delicatessens, fine public schools, and minor skirmishes with the tough Italian kids in Little Neck.

Taking his seat, Arnie Golden smiled at them with grand, tanned well-being, pleased with a world that had someone like him in it, certain that a little sugar-melting rain would only be a cooling, comfortable change after so much lovely beach sun. A thin, beautiful blond woman sat cuddled next to him with a clipboard on her lap, their legs touching. Both of them wore deep blues you could drown in, draped silks and linens whose tailoring Arkey genuinely admired, though linen was an unkosher fabric for all but Cohenim, Arkey had already *lerned,* giving a moral meaning to his envy—for as rich children, Arkey and his friends had felt certain that they starred in a fairy tale, while poorer Arnie Golden had grown rich making fairy tales. *So there's a movie in Beth,* Arkey thought, *or Arnie Golden wouldn't be here.* He had heard, too, that Arnie had been in touch with Michael Healy in jail, probably trying to option his life rights for the screen. *That* would probably be more seductive to Michael than the time off the feds had once offered. And if Michael ever sold his story, some of his friends might be arrested too, which was probably the cream of the jest for Arnie, angry that they had never let him into their teenage clique—an omission that was, Arkey suspected, probably an unconscious class prejudice; Arnie's parents were high school teachers, Jews with less money. Or maybe it was just Arnie's precociously developed cynicism that had blackballed him; Arnie already the kind of kid who wouldn't clap to save Tinkerbell, let alone someone already dead and buried, like Frank Jaffe.

Mostly, though, Arkey wasn't scared of Arnie or guilty toward him; he was *competitive*. Arnie would infallibly know whether irony toward their dreams was hip and enticing (as it was in a late-night comedian, like Arnie's client Jimmy Benjamin) or impious and disfiguring (as it would have been in a history of the Jews). Arkey tried to scan his friends' faces more deeply into himself, tried to experience their souls the way Billy seemed able to—so *he* could write the book before Arnie could option their lives. And he felt for a moment the residue (like grains of sleep on the eyelids after you awake) of what he'd sometimes felt in Laura's bedroom listening to Frank's letters when high on teenage sublimity (which had to be, he thought, the strongest and stupidest drug in the world, secret fuel for all the world's armies), that his life had been covered with the dark wing of History's grandeur and terror. He had been called to help Frank Jaffe, who suffered in his grave. How? By healing the world, doing justice.

But Arkey didn't know anymore what justice meant, what the fuck he was supposed to do to rescue the dead Frank: Bring the working class to power? Make sure all swords got beaten into plowshares? Help Beth? Or maybe keep *her* from doing any more damage? And who, he wondered, could he even ask about any of it? He couldn't talk about it to any friend, rabbi, or psychiatrist; he'd never even talked about it with any lover but Laura, because she'd been part of it, too—and even they had hardly whispered to each other that they'd once thought they had actually received letters transmitted from her brother *after* he'd died— "which," Laura had said one night, "we might have realized was unlikely. I mean, how can communication from the dead possibly come through the U.S. mails? They can barely manage to deliver a supermarket circular!" the MIT bomb having supposedly blown a belief in those letters out of her long ago.

There had been three of those, postmarked from Lovette, Mississippi. The first had said, *I am dyed, I am done, I am dead*, in a broken childlike script, not (Beth and Laura said) like Frank's own precise, angular handwriting. Jesse thought that was maybe because the deputy sheriff of some little Mississippi town had again smashed Frank's hand in the jail door, making his fingers stumble forming words, and that he meant he couldn't take any more of "jail, no bail." The second letter said, "*I am still in pain. If anything, the pain is worse. How long, how long, how long? Oh God, what if this is hell?" The pain is worse,* Jesse said, must mean his hand hurt more. *How long?* Maybe that meant he was thinking of staying past August—which would give his parents a conniption fit. He wasn't going to graduate school or return to his family until . . . until when? *How long?* Well, how long until the Negroes in the South had their freedom, or at least the vote? So, by *hell,* they had thought that he meant Mississippi.

Except for Billy Green. When Beth had finished reading the first letter, his little voice floated up from the floor. "He's dead," he said. "He's been murdered. And he's forced someone's living hand to move, to write to us."

Which, Jeffrey Schell had said immediately, had to be crap. Billy, he pointed out, already drew for his father's comic book company. Naturally he wanted to turn life into a horror story! But then, when a lot of other things Billy said about what had happened to Frank turned out to be true on the front page of the *New York Times,* they had decided that the letters had been written by Frank himself *before* he died, the way Jesse had said, but still when Billy had touched them he'd known that Frank had *already* been murdered by the Lovette sheriff, which made him eerily psychic—and *that* meant, in a blind feedback loop, that if someone as psychic as Billy said so, then maybe the letters *had* come from the grave. Billy had become their leader—or maybe something more, something like their suburban wonder rabbi.

So maybe Frank was just the way Billy also said, alive-yet-not-alive in his box, like a coma victim–cum-zombie, and his pain in the grave would be endless (*how long?*) unless his friends, as Billy instructed, helped him out, doing holy actions that would raise his soul-spark back to its source. He should have called the *Enquirer*:

MIDGET JEW GURU REVEALS IN-GRAVE HORRORS!
Fucks Up Friends' Lives with Pointless Quest to Help Corpse!

Anyway, making justice, Arkey had to admit now, was a job he'd been a lot more sensitive to fourteen years ago in Laura's bedroom, when he'd listened avidly to Billy's high, excited, earnest voice and had grown dazed by a strong mixed drink made up of: one jigger of the letters and Billy's stories about them; two parts the sweet, syrupy whiskey that Jeffrey Schell finagled for them from older men; and many, many tumblers of the close proximity of 2Girls2, Beth and Laura, beautiful members of the opposite sex with whom Arkey had secrets (if what Billy said was true anyway) that linked him almost more intimately than sex could have—and that would certainly, he'd hoped, tumble over into sex with at least one of them.

Drunk on all that, he'd felt like a great hand had swiftly lifted him up toward heaven and shown him the Big Picture, given him a chance at greatness—a high they'd maybe all chased after for the next fourteen years, in violent actions, in art, in drugs and sex as orgiastic as they could make it given their physical and moral limitations, chased after though they should have felt from the first that they were being fools for sure if they believed in such overstuffed melodramatic furniture as *giant hands*. Yeah, Arkey thought. But the thing was, *they did believe.*

Or used to.

Probably the letter Beth carried around her neck was all that was left of those fragments. Billy had given each of them pieces to save, and each of them, except for Beth, had, he knew, contrived to lose them, misplace them, leave them at home in the pages of a *Little Lulu* comic book hoarded since childhood, half knowing that the letter and the whole comic book collection would be swept into the trash when their parents cleaned out the attic.

They really needed to bail Beth out, Arkey thought, go someplace calm, like that very same bedroom of Laura's, with its views of the wide back lawn and the double rows of Dr. Jacobs' dogwood trees, and bend together over the most opaque of texts, the one most difficult to tell the truth about, the story of their lives. They needed to discuss their memories of Frank's "special" letters, be like Talmudists in reverse, and move from the letters' supposed laws back not to Moses and Sinai but to a crazy mistake they'd all made together, led astray by their tiny magus, Billy Green, alias Billy Bad Ears, the Super Hero Who Draws Himself.

Though before the spring of Mr. Hartman's sixth grade class in 1960, all Arthur Kaplan had ever valued about Billy Green was his height, Arthur thanking God and knocking on wood each September when they lined up in size places and he found that Billy was still the smallest student, boy *or* girl, at Arrandale, the gloomy secondary school of worn brown bricks, a relic of Great Neck Before the Jews Arrived, and so sadly different from Cherry Lane, their enlightened windows-everywhere primary school, with its pleasantly bogus poetic name, bright pink bricks, and (no doubt for good educational reasons) musky, dark forest along the side filled with sewer-smelling skunk cabbage, where a boy could defy his fear by making others fear his wildness, playing boisterous running games of keepaway whose art was to throw the stolen object—a tan windbreaker, a Yankees cap, the right to practice medicine—tauntingly just over the head of its rightful owner, who was, often enough, little Arthur or even littler (thank God!) Billy Green.

By sixth grade there was only one pretty blue-eyed girl between Billy and Arthur, Arthur's wall to keep back an ocean of shame called Smaller Than *All* the Girls!, Laura Jaffe, who had a tiny scar on her wrist that scared Arthur, as if he couldn't or shouldn't love her because she was marred, though he also dreamt he might touch her scar and be deliciously linked with her. But if he tried, he knew she would laugh dismissively at him, the thing he feared most in the world.

Anyway, without Laura between them in the class photo Arthur imagined he'd be ever more humiliatingly married with Billy Green because they were both small and sickly, and because neither of them could kick the mottled red ball out of the infield, and because both of them were suck-a-thumbs through the second grade, though Billy did it shamelessly in public, while Arthur discreetly hid himself in the bathroom for time with his special friend.

One day in the fourth grade, Johnny Ryan, the graceful, heedless kickball star and keepaway aficionado, had urged him to slug Billy, and ashamed that he hadn't understood a dirty joke Johnny had told them earlier (about a woman and Houdini, who couldn't escape from a scumbag), ashamed, most especially, of his body, its sickness and its negligible size, he'd hit Billy on the side of the head as a way to please Johnny Ryan and to say *I'm not like him* about Billy Green. Billy threw himself at him, and they rolled around in the grass next to the asphalt playground, staining Arthur's specially tailored white Saks Fifth Avenue shirt. The other kids gathered in a ring, screaming with excitement, while Arthur and Billy cried and batted at each other with skinny open hands and almost straight arms, not understanding how to cock their fists for a punch. "Come see the Battle of the Midgets!" Jimmy Benjamin shouted, and Johnny Ryan screamed, "Come on, Tiny, break his beak." But who was Tiny, and which beak did he mean? Had his mentor abandoned him? Billy got on top, and Arthur was terrified that he and Billy would be joined now in everyone's mind, even kind of mixed together, like he might get called by Billy's name. He lost heart for the fight, and just cried and spit and gasped for breath as if the warm weight of the body on his chest were monstrous, though really Billy's skinny body was more like sixty-one damp washcloths.

Billy rolled off, and lay beside him, and though he was the victorious one, Billy wept, too, and smiled quizzically at Arthur, as if they must both be bewildered to find themselves lying in the dirt. "Wait," Billy gasped. "Please." But Arthur got up and ran away, humiliatingly beaten by someone who didn't even care about beating him.

In the two years since that fight Arthur had hardly ever spoken to Billy, even on the way to Sunday school, for their mothers, and Jimmy Benjamin's doting mama, carpooled together, though Mrs. Green wasn't born Jewish, which meant, Arthur's mother said, that Billy wasn't really kosher—like Arthur maybe dreamt of *eating* some of Billy! Every Sunday, Billy looked toward Arthur expectantly, as if this time they were going to be friends because they were linked by the way their bodies had once touched, but Arthur, pressing his legs together so his thighs wouldn't make contact with Billy's, turned away and looked out the window, even though Billy's father published comic books.

This whole Billy thing was driving Arthur crazy, because when he even said anything to him in the car, like "did you see last night's *Twilight Zone*," he felt like Billy was a starving space monster with long sucker-arms that would leave hickeys all over his legs. And he laughed so hard when Arthur told a stupid moron joke that he looked like that fat man on television going *hardy har har*—like maybe he hadn't really gotten the joke, which was impossible, it was a moron joke!

It wasn't just Arthur who thought Billy was creepy. Every day, Billy sat alone in the corner of the cafeteria, eating his brown bag lunch (probably queer medicine foods), rocking back and forth, humming to himself. Once Arthur had walked by accidentally-on-purpose to hear what was going on. "Mr. Sandman, send me a dream," he heard Billy sing quietly. "Someone to buy me vanilla ice cream, Someone who likes pizza and never feels blue. Mr. Sandman, tell me it's you . . . One, two, three, look at Mr. Lee, four, five, six, pick up sticks, seven, eight, nine, oh, I must not whine." Arthur was pretty sure those weren't the right words. Billy looked over and smiled at Arthur, he even maybe batted his eyes at him! And then, as if Arthur had asked for an encore, Billy had his brain damage Arkestra play a little number called "I married Joan, what a whirl what a twirl what a swirl what a girl what a pearl what a merle, what a furl, what a churl, what a curl, what a . . . ," and on and on. Arthur had to run away before anyone could think Billy had been singing to him. Thing was, Billy had taken over his mind; even in the bathroom, he still heard *whirl twirl swirl girl,* round and round, like it meant something. When it *didn't.* Except that Billy was creepy.

Other days Billy creepily forgot to eat lunch, and just sat rubbing his eyes for a half hour at a time, the ball of his thumb making a slow repetition in the socket that looked positively painful. Once, Jimmy Benjamin had even said, "Look, he's playing with himself," and everyone had laughed. Billy looked up bewildered, like he hadn't known there was anyone else there; then, of course, he started to cry, making a river of snot run from his nose. Jesus, why *would* Arthur *ever* want to talk with such a weirdo, such a *tiny* weirdo? Arthur was even careful not to throw at Billy in dodgeball, though he would be an easy, badly coordinated target and the kiss of the well-aimed ball would have raised a satisfying red welt on his pale, skinny arm, a sweet tribute mark, like the painful Indian rope burn a bully summer camp counselor had once given Arthur when he was seven and in tenderfoot bunk.

That spring in Mr. Hartman's sixth grade class they were each to give their reports on the countries of Europe. The morning before, Arthur had marched to the front, his bowels twisting inside him, and standing before the blackboard, right beside Mr. Hartman's huge gray metal desk, he'd read from five-by-eight cards that were too large for his small hands about Rembrandt, Vermeer, and the history of the Netherlands, which

was surrounded by dikes, which were walls that kept the ocean back—
or the Dutch would all drown because they were *under* the ocean, really
(and so, Arthur dreamt, the Dutch were scared to death every waking
moment of their lives).

Billy's country was France, and Arthur worried that showed how
much more Mr. Hartman liked Billy, for he had given him what Arthur
suspected was Mr. Hartman's personal favorite, a country with a lot of
history, which meant a long entry in the encyclopedia that all school
reports were rewritten from, for basically a school report, his older sister, June, wise in the ways of academe, had explained to him, was a matter of changing enough words from the encyclopedia article so that your
essay wasn't called "plagiarism" (though Arthur's childhood, outside
class reports, was often a matter of repeating sounds from the huge
Encyclopedia of Adulthood—like "scumbag" or "justice" or "love"—
which he didn't understand and couldn't possibly put into his own
words).

Mr. Hartman had given each student an eleven-page mimeographed
list of all the great artists and writers of the countries they were going to
study, and France had won the genius Olympics, though Holland had
done well, too, Arthur thought—partisan now of the doughty Dutch as
of the mighty and reliable New York Yankees—for such a little country.
The sharp-smelling blue-on-white lists also contained Mr. Hartman's
personal ratings of the importance of each thinker on a scale of one to
five stars, and you were supposed to say something about all of the fives
from your country in your report. Arthur had decided to memorize the
non-Dutch part of the list too, because the list was important to Mr.
Hartman, and Mr. Hartman was important to Arthur, so different from
his stocky, balding father, who was kinder, Arthur could tell, naturally
both more powerful and more gentle than Mr. Hartman, yet too concerned, his mother implied, about money, the factors, the goniffs, the fall
line, and not—Arthur thought, though his mother didn't say this—about
truly precious treasures, like genius, "the cultural wealth"—Abraham
told him—"that would someday be the common inheritance of all the
world's people." Arthur felt these lists were an important clue to a grand
future he would begin to make by memorizing all the names and rank-
ings on the list, as if training in being a genius was to recognize other
geniuses and give each one the right number of stars, and he was frighteningly certain that Mr. Hartman's grades for geniuses—or for Arthur—
would be accurate.

. . .

Arthur's awe of Mr. Hartman's judgment would have comforted the teacher, who, like the Dutch, was scared every moment of his life. Age twenty-eight, overqualified for Arrandale and ill at ease in Great Neck, where there seemed almost to be zoning laws against homosexuality, Mr. Hartman taught this suburban sixth grade because it gave him many opportunities to display the stern educational protectiveness that Arthur found so attractive. The work also offered him precious free time to work on his poems, and a job that was close to his analyst's suburban office, but most of all it gave him children to mold—children he didn't entirely *like,* with their wailing for no reason, when there were, if they but knew it, so many good reasons. The children were the subjects he used, Dr. Jacobs had told him, to embody his own confusions before they choked him inside, though he'd explained to Dr. Jacobs that he didn't use the students to ease his own psyche; his severity would educate these spoiled children who were the same age as he was when he was saved; hidden; abandoned. For Mr. Hartman's parents hadn't loved him, or they wouldn't have sent him away; if they hadn't miraculously contrived to send him away from the transport camp at Drancy, he knew, he would have been murdered along with them; they had sent him away because they loved him so much. He envied his charges for their sheltered lives, and confused himself with his parents in his desire to protect them and to hurt them *for their own good,* for sheltered as they were, no protection, he must teach them day by day, would ever be enough, and one wrong answer could lead to their murder. His uncle in Queens thought Great Neck was the Promised Land, and Hartman the handmaid to children who bathed in warm milk and frolicked with honey. But he washed them in cold water, and he washed their clothing in cold water, and gave the rags back to them to wear.

Arthur could hear that, like him, adults, too, thought Mr. Hartman was different and special. Mr. Hartman had been raised by an uncle, in Queens, New York, because his real parents were from Austria, like the Kaplans' neighbor Dr. Jacobs, but they had moved to France, and stayed there, which was strange; they had *never* come to the United States, his mother said meaningfully (and out of such half-understood hints—for Arthur, for example, feared "jack's boots," and "creamertoria" though he didn't exactly know what they were—Arthur formed some of his nightmares). Living in so many countries was why Mr. Hartman had a strange accent, one that Arthur heard as lovely and distinguished, though his parents thought it might be too hard for children to understand. Mr. Hartman looked different, too; his clothes were loose on him—something Arthur's mother would never have allowed, for she made the tailors at Saks measure Arthur all over, even, embarrassingly, what the tailor called his seat and his crotch. His black hair, even in the age of the crew cut, was too closely cropped against his skull, which made him look self-denying, unsparing. And his short hair made his large brown eyes seem, to an eleven-year-old uncertain about percentages and fractions, fervid and inquisitorial—and certainly he'd be as likely to punish Arthur as himself. When the other teachers, mostly women, bunched together during recess Mr. Hartman stood apart, because, Johnny Ryan said, Mr. Hartman was a homo, and Billy Green was a homo, too, you could tell because they both had long eyelashes, and maybe that was why, Arthur thought jealously, Mr. Hartman might like Billy more than him, and had given him France to report on. Maybe he should become a homo, too?

Still, all the parents thought Mr. Hartman was really smart, for he'd heard his mother and Jimmy's talking about the teacher. Mr. Hartman had the children put hand-drawn maps of the world on the classroom wall—which was, they said, more grown-up and challenging than cutting out colored pictures of native costumes, like the other classes did—a pedal-go-logical advance that came from Mr. Hartman having a teaching degree from Columbia, and an advanced degree, too, an M.A. in French literature. His father said there must be something wrong with Mr. Hartman if he had an M.A., and all that meant was that he could teach sixth grade, even in Great Neck with its superb schools, something wrong with him or with M.A.'s in French literature. Yet his father, too, Arthur thought, respected Mr. Hartman, and sounded like he was beating something back with his words, as if he were trying to destroy the world Mr. Hartman stood for in Arthur's mind. Arthur would have a difficult time telling his father what that world was (or what Grandpa Abe's socialism meant) except that they were places where people remembered the achievements of those on Mr. Hartman's list, so it was worth doing something like they had, because you would go on the list and be remembered. Arthur felt his father respected Mr. Hartman's list, wished he had his name on it; he criticized Mr. Hartman to discourage Arthur from doing what he hadn't had the courage, or the chance, or the ability, to do himself, the way he had discouraged Arthur's mom, who had been working for her M.A. in economics when his father had met her at a Temple dance and said, "I'll make you a different kind of MA." Maybe now his father didn't want that bargain criticized, while his mother praised Mr. Hartman's degree as a way to accuse his father of denying her such a wonderful distinction by saddling her with an Arthur and a June to mold instead of an economy.

Mr. Hartman, too, though his eleven-year-old admirer didn't suspect it, hated M.A.'s and the sorts of things they studied, even his own poems, especially his own poems, with far more ferocity than Mr. Kaplan could, for the differences between him and the cloak-and-suiter included Mr. Hartman's gift for hatred. Mr. Hartman lived for the art he dreamt of making (and despised); for he, too, imagined joining his own list of those who had made objects worthy not just of interest but of adoration (as if such objects mattered)! He crossed Middle Neck Road by the train station in his badly fitting black suit, its jacket pocket sagging from the books he'd carried there. He imagined his bohemian costume would gather other bohemians—but then why did he choose to live where there were none, choose Great Neck, where the bourgeoisie would ostracize and protect him? He was on the way to Kuck's, the German's empty delicatessen, for his nightly roast beef sandwich, and he felt terribly exposed. His uncle had said that as he grew up the world would grow smaller. It hadn't. It had grown larger. God, he knew, had zimzumed himself to leave empty space where creation might take place. But so much empty space! And all without God!

"... and with plenty of mayonnaise," he said to the broad-faced, surly owner behind the high glass counter. Why had this man come to a Jewish suburb to live? Mr. Hartman wondered. What choking internal conflict did *he* make these burghers embody?

I'm not a Jew of faith, he thought, on his way back to his room, as he imagined the suburban householders who crowded Squire's Jewish delicatessen were, *or rather my faith* is *culture,* like (he liked to think) Freud's faith, or Kafka's or Proust's or Walter Benjamin's, all the old Talmudic fervor now focused on secular texts, literary masterpieces made almost holy by the longing and the burning regard of the acolyte.

Only *almost* holy, Kafka prompted from his imaginary chorus. What a terrible swindle art was, what always disappointing idolatry to worship art! For Mr. Hartman found his beloved endlessly enticing, endlessly disappointing. As he watched the opening credits of a movie at the Squire or the Playhouse, the two theaters facing each other on Middle Neck Road where he went regularly twice a week to watch whatever they had playing; or as he stripped the cellophane from a new long-playing album; or gave a hard crack to the spine of a new book of poems; he always felt that *this* would be the longed-for friend, *this* would be his transformative angel; and he was, of course, forever disappointed.

Culture, popular or esoteric, was insufficient as compensation for what he'd lost, and it was part of his faithful love to the parents who saved him to find it so. And as transcendence, a world elsewhere for him to live in, culture was more ineffective than a weekend at Grossinger's (where he'd often gone with his single uncle); the repetition of the movie, the aria, the poem, never translated his torso into poetry, his limbs into fire that fed on air. No, he remained abandoned in the third row on the aisle and still alone in his rooms near the train station, listening to Callas records, eating his sandwich with dollops of consoling mayonnaise, growing forgetful of himself, not like one teased out of thought but like one made so infinitely small that he almost had to look at his wooden tag to discover his name. This Jew of Culture loved art and felt always, like the prophet Isaiah, on the point of cursing it, and those who studied it, and those who created it; even himself; especially himself; his prominent ears; his queer heart; for Johnny Ryan was right, he was homosexual—at least that. He is his dead mother; he is him, his father who he lost—was lost by. His sister stayed—was *left*—and he had to find her, too, inside himself. The world was gone; he must bear them. And all their eyes looked out behind his, making a terrible pressure in his skull that caused him to hate his large, pursed lips; his too wide nose; his clumsy words; his ugly accent, for while Arthur found his speech beautiful, Mr. Hartman thought himself robbed of all language, each word battling another with an equal claim to be his mamaloshen, an equal reason to be hated by him, until any sentence he spoke seemed mangled by sharp shadows and sounded like gnashing and wailing. We are digging the pit of Babel, the archangel Kafka had said. But Mr. Hartman was sure he lived there.

And Arthur was right, the French words that tormented him in that pit were the most loved, and the most despised, the most darkly shadowed. The French had produced works Mr. Hartman helplessly adored above all others; they had conspired with the Nazis to murder his parents and to murder him. If France could have done that, then culture meant nothing, language could order anything, murder could happen anywhere to the accompaniment of Bizet, of Ravel, of Berlioz, by men whom music made feel noble and sentimental as they slaughtered the innocent. And France had done that; murder could happen anywhere; art meant nothing. He knew that. But he could think of nothing else to want in this whole overly large world. So Mr. Hartman kept beautiful shapes and murderous deeds apart in his mind by force of a continually overstretched will, which made, he knew, his poems difficult to write, impossible to read, an endless, clunking series of insipid oppositions, without form, without vitality, without a reason to live or a will strong enough to die.

But Arthur didn't know any of that when he counted France's golden 5's, or when Mr. Hartman spent yesterday afternoon lovingly telling them how the artists and thinkers of France had invented liberty, equality, and fraternities, without a word for Arthur's efforts on behalf of Holland. And Mr. Hartman even got out from behind his desk and stood in front of them in his baggy brown suit, displaying large reproductions of Renoir paintings, sweet women swathed in wide red dresses, that Mr. Hartman had himself pasted on white oaktag backings—something he hadn't done for Arthur's Rembrandt, though Arthur had to admit that the women made Arthur feel soft inside, like when his sister stroked his hair at night so he could sleep (though it didn't help him sleep) while Mr. Rembrandt's photos made him feel scared and helpless. Mr. Hartman so loved France he had even taught them to say *l'etoile,* and *non,* and *oui,* and *I, my name is,* in French.

When they got back from the cafeteria and recess, Mr. Hartman looked down at the black assignment book open in front of him on his desk and gave the closed-lip smile that made Arthur feel ashamed of himself. "Billy Green," he said, and Billy trod slowly to the front, his upper body swaying, and he made small sharp gasps as he walked, the departing winds of a tear storm. Maybe, Arthur thought, Billy's scared to give his report, though he should know *that* wasn't something that would make Mr. Hartman relent. School was far too important for such childish considerations! Billy carried a pale brown reversible windbreaker in his right hand, as if he planned to run away, and a wad of five-by-eight cards in his left. His bright blue short-sleeved shirt was unevenly buttoned, his khaki chinos hung on him like the hospital johnny Arthur had worn for his tonsillectomy, and his arms looked like knobby sticks. Maybe he shook because he was faint from hunger. Maybe he was wasting away. Maybe, Arthur imagined, moved by a murderous jealousy, Billy had just learned he had *a fatal disease*!

Billy's head bobbed from side to side, like it was on a spring. "Wait," he said. "Please. I know I shouldn't cry. I know I'm ruining things." He put the note cards and the jacket in the same hand, then separated them again, then used his mouth to hold the jacket so he had both hands free to put the cards in the right order—but then his jacket dropped to the floor.

"Bozo the student," Jimmy Benjamin, the class clown, said, letting Arthur laugh away the nervousness he'd started to feel on Billy's behalf.

Billy bent to pick his jacket up with his left hand, stood up, and leaned against the chalk well of the blackboard.

"Now suck your thumb for us, Rabbit Mouth," Johnny Ryan said, and Arthur put his own hands under his thighs.

"Begin," Mr. Hartman ordered, sick of the boy's clumsiness and his horrid little sobs. Mr. Hartman had hardly slept the last two days, his arms waking him as they unconsciously crossed over his head trying to ward off the air that might reduce him to nothing; he could not teach his hands to sleep. This boy must stop his disgusting whining, worse than nails scraped on blackboard, so Mr. Hartman could let his attention rest on an inner darkness, as it usually did during these pointless class reports.

Billy told the class that his father had just gotten an encyclopedia of Jewish history, eighteen heavy volumes, and so Billy had looked in that encyclopedia for information about France (which represented both a tremendous scholarly innovation on Billy's part and an unfair advantage, adding to Arthur's anger at him). Billy said he hadn't understood a lot of the words in the new books. Arthur thought it was so very like him to admit he had used an encyclopedia, thus giving away everyone's chief resource (instead of simply pretending that you had *always* known about Holland so as to not raise in the teacher's mind the copying possibility) and to admit, too, that he hadn't understood something, as if he had given up trying to protect himself, or maybe he thought being simply true would protect him, that modesty would be more winning to Mr. Hartman than braggadocio. This genius that was either before or beyond ordinary strategy made Arthur want to work on Billy's little arm until it burned with red welts.

Billy said that according to his father's new encyclopedia France wasn't always good to the Jews who lived there. "During World War II, the people that ran France even agreed with the Germans and didn't like the Jews, or maybe it was all the ways they had hated them before, coming out again," Billy said, though it was difficult to understand him because each of his words had a foggy halo of exhalation. In those days, Billy told them, anyone who had two Jewish grandparents was considered Jewish. "So I'm Jewish in France," Billy said and his head stopped bobbing like a spring toy, he snuffled mucus back from his lips, and he smiled at the class. "And in those days *we* Jews weren't allowed to be in the government. Or to be in the army. Or to be on television."

Arthur noticed immediately that Billy had made a mistake: there wasn't any television in those days! He raised his hand and waved it about, but Mr. Hartman stared at the class with large empty eyes, as if he weren't paying attention to them but to something inside himself, like a stomachache or a daydream. Maybe he was sick, too? Or, why would he let Billy get away with this? Where were the 5's, the painters and the poets? Could Billy and Mr. Hartman have arranged this in advance, Arthur wondered—for Arthur examined Mr. Hartman's actions or his restraint the way he did the gestures and silences of his grandfather; the way later he would attend to his psychoanalyst; and then to the Omnipotent God. Confused, Arthur put his hand down. Also, he didn't entirely want Mr. Hartman to stop Billy. This story was about *him*. He wanted to know more, the kinds of things his parents hadn't told him and June about, but had sometimes, as if they couldn't help themselves, hinted at.

"And in France," Billy said, "Jews couldn't be in movies, or newspapers, or in shows. And we weren't allowed to be bankers anymore, or to sell antiques, like, you know, Mrs. Jaffe does, and Jews couldn't run newspapers, and we weren't allowed to have most jobs, except for things like sweeping floors. And Jews couldn't become doctors either," Billy said, "like Dr. Strauss, or lawyers, like Mr. Jaffe, and if we had stores we had to put up signs that said we were Jewish, and if we owned factories, like Arthur's father and Jesse's father, we had to give our business to a Frenchman who wasn't Jewish. And the Jews who had just come to France from other countries and they didn't have much money, they had to go to special prison camps. And a lot of people died when it got cold there, because they didn't have any warm clothing."

This game of keepaway played with the life of the Jews pushed Arthur against the sharp fragments that he'd gathered from his parents' dinner table talk, and as the shards scraped at his side, he began to calculate: if the French who had so many geniuses, and had invented liberty, had camps where they sent Jews, then *any* country might have camps. He pretended to rub his cheek, so Johnny Ryan wouldn't see him removing the moisture from his eyes. This wasn't fair, Arthur thought angrily. Why did Mr. Hartman let Billy scare them? But then Arthur began his calculations—for when, at age eleven, he heard about a plane crash, or the threat of a nuclear war, he figured that he lived far enough from New York to avoid the fireball, or that he and his family would have been sitting in the safe back of the plane, where his father always placed them. Billy had said it was foreign Jews who were put in the camps, but Arthur had been born in America, and his parents were born here, too; and he saw now why his parents boasted about being second-generation Americans: it was life or death. So he concluded: *we aren't foreigners* but had been gathered into the American family because he had been born here and so had his sister, and his parents had been born here, too.

But not his grandparents! So were *they* safe? Was *he* really safe? Where could he find out how many generations you had to be from here before you were from here? He became scared again, and reasoned further that even if they weren't from here *they had money.* Yes, thank God, *they had money,* and Billy had said it was the poor who had to go to the camps, so *they* wouldn't have to go, it's an awful thing, but *they wouldn't have to go!*

And Jimmy Benjamin figured that his mother said he was going to be a star and that's better than money (for Jimmy's family wasn't as rich as most in Great Neck), *because everyone loves stars.*

While Laura Jaffe reasoned that her parents knew Senator Hubert Humphrey, and they knew John Kennedy, and one of them, she reminded herself forcefully, was *about to become president of the United States!* Laura smiled, reassured.

And Larry Strauss remembered that his father already was a *doctor*—and knowledge, his mother often said, was something they could never take away from you, so his father could *always* earn a good living.

Billy, meanwhile, put his brown jacket back in his mouth, turned some cards, then took his jacket out of his mouth, decorated with spit and teeth marks. "And then after they arrested the poor foreigners, the French police arrested the Jewish lawyers in Paris and some Jews who were famous."

That made Jimmy Benjamin turn his head to the side in open-mouthed wonder, for Billy was saying that fame *wouldn't matter,* and that wasn't possible (was it?) or his mother wouldn't care so much about it—or about him. He shook his head *non* at Billy.

"Yes, really," Billy said in a high-pitched voice, like he was begging Jimmy to believe him. "The police even made a list of all the Jews and everything they owned and where they lived, and every Jew over six years old had to wear a yellow star wherever he went." Billy's face muscles became rubbery, his eyes, cheeks, and mouth all pushed together toward his nose, and he began to sob again, not fitfully, as he had been doing all along, but wholeheartedly, and Arthur, from his seat in the second row, could see dirty tears streaming down Billy's feverish face. "I know I have to stop crying! Wait, please!" His sobs subsided, and he wiped the snot from his nose with his windbreaker, but Arthur knew from Billy's ferocious crying that the stars must be a terrible thing. *L'etoile,* he thought, and, in an unknown kinship with Mr. Hartman, he clamped his jaws angrily shut because he knew *their* word.

"You had to wear the star over your heart," Billy said, "and Jews had to wear the star everywhere they went so that people would know you were a Jew and stay away from you." Billy took a Pez dispenser from the pocket of his windbreaker and jabbed himself repeatedly in the cheek with the joker-faced cap. "And Jews weren't allowed in swimming pools." (*jab*) "And Jews couldn't go to the Squire, or the Playhouse." (*jab*) "And Jews couldn't eat in restaurants." (*jab*) "And Jews couldn't go to the library." (*jab*) "And Jews had to ride on the last car on a train." (*jab*) "And they could tell who was a Jew by his yellow star and if someone thought you were a Jew because you had a big nose like my father does, and you weren't wearing your star, he could call the police and the policeman would arrest you because you weren't wearing your star and put you in the prison camp. And Jews," Billy said, weeping again. "And Jews." He paused. "Jews," he said quietly. And "Jews," he whispered. "Jews. Jews." Then he stopped, and just stared at them while he rhythmically smashed the peaked cap of the dispenser's green joker head in and out of his flesh, raising a red sore on his cheek and transfixing Arthur with the mechanical savagery of the pistonlike motion of his arm and the dazed, indifferent look on his face. *Would he poke through the skin? Would there be drops of blood?*

"My head hurts," Billy said. "It's hard to see. I make mistakes."

He looked down at his note cards. "And then," he said, "they decided to collect more Jews for the prison camp, rich Jews and poor Jews and foreign Jews." He turned his head to the side like a swimmer and mouthed some air. "And French ones, too, who had nearly always lived there, and a lot of French Jews didn't even run away when the policemen and the firemen came for them, because they thought the French police wouldn't do anything bad to them and they went along quietly, and they didn't know where they were going." Then Billy tried to change a card with his jacket still in his hand, and dropped his dispenser and all his five-by-eights.

He squatted to pick them up, turning his back to the class, making the seat of his pants clownishly large and his pants legs pool around his sneakers, while Arthur remembered the Great Neck policemen who had twice given him rides in their cruisers, their guns making him feel princely, for they were broad-shouldered and strong, yet they had driven him home to 42 Frog Pond Lane, the house with the pillars in front, as a tribute to his own big-nosed father, who was older and smaller but somehow controlled them. But did his father know that they had the address and they might turn against him someday and arrest his entire family?

Billy rose and leaned against the blackboard again, abandoning his Pez dispenser. "Some families," he said, "stayed away from home and they went into hiding to avoid the police."

Yes, Arthur thought, *his father would hide them!* It wouldn't matter that the police knew their address! And Arthur dreamt of the forest behind the Cherry Lane school, though his mother and his sister would hate the stink from the large-leafed plants. At night Arthur would sneak back to their kitchen and get them food.

But Billy said, "And the police watched the forests where Jews hid and they found them when they came out to look for food. Other families put their children in hiding places to keep them away from the police."

Yes, Arthur thought, *thank God,* my *father would do that.*

"But the French police knew all the places that the Jews had hidden their children, and they went there to drag them all away."

Not all, Mr. Hartman thought, for though he didn't look at the sixth graders or at the boy speaking, he found himself listening to Billy, and he grew angry with the little boy, for Mr. Hartman knew that before August 1942 you could sometimes arrange for the necessary bribes to ransom a child, even from Drancy, if, by some miracle, you chanced on a sympathetic French guard; and sometimes a convent or a French family could be found courageous enough to hide a Jewish child if he didn't cry too much. It was sentimental to hate the world more than God did, as this boy and his encyclopedia seemed to do. Would the boy get to Drancy? Mr. Hartman wondered, as if he had simply to wait helplessly to see. The family that once had hidden him had threatened to turn him over to the PQJ if he didn't stop his bawling, the way some other family at some other time would have talked jokingly about the Bogey Man or the Scissors Man; now the sound made him weak and mute, he couldn't bear it or stop it or comfort someone who made it. So the boy's yowling blanked Richard Hartman's eyes and forced him inside himself. To say stop (arret? alt?) was impossible; speaking would mean raising heavy, hateful foreign words—and all words were foreign words to him—a thousand miles upward toward the classroom. Yet he dreaded, too, that Billy might stop crying and go on to speak of Drancy, the darkest place in Mr. Hartman's inner world, the place where he had lost his parents, the place he had been rescued from and would never leave. What could this child know about how things were *there?* He almost laughed at this farce: he was listening to his own history being recounted by a weeping suburban boy who could not possibly understand what he was talking about, even the words he used, a boy who uncomprehendingly repeated passages from some adult encyclopedia, as they all did. Yet how odd, he mused, almost calmly, that this should happen to him, here in this protected place, even *here* where they knew nothing of history, and he and Dr. Jacobs were, he thought, the only *geheimnistragers,* the bearers of secrets.

"And they marched us to the train stations and put us in boxcars that were really cars for cattle and the cars had straw on the floor and a carton of books that the YMCA had put there, and you had to pee on the straw," Billy said—but the class didn't giggle, feeling tightly packed together in a cattle car, bodies pressed tighter than the crowd jamming the exit at a ballpark. *Not me! I'm not like them!* each one wanted to shout, but the words wouldn't rise between them; they were touching so closely that they were like each other forever now, and their shared smell was so thick around them that they breathed each other in like animals they'd visited at farms during summer camp. But now, in their imaginations, *they* were the animals.

"The trains took all the Jews to a prison camp in Drancy" (which Billy sounded out to rhyme with "Nancy"). "That's a suburb of Paris, and in the camp they only had a small bowl of cabbage soup and a piece of bread each day." Billy said that for the last few weeks he had eaten only bread and soup. (And, though Billy hadn't told anyone, he'd also hidden the bowls of soup and the pieces of bread in his desk drawer until filaments of gray mold had covered them, which might make him suffer, Billy hoped, as the people in the camps had suffered.) He told the class that he had lost a lot of weight, and he felt dizzy when he walked.

Arthur could see now that Billy leaned against the blackboard to keep from falling over, and his cheeks were too red, and Mr. Hartman didn't even look at him! Why hadn't Billy's parents noticed that he was growing smaller instead of larger? Why were all the adults abandoning them? Arthur wanted to shout at the teacher to help Billy, but he dreamt that if he woke him, Mr. Hartman would be an empty-eyed monster, like in one of Billy's father's comic books.

"The trains left from that suburb to go to the big concentration camps in Poland," Billy said. "The Germans didn't want the French to send the children to Poland. They wanted to leave us in the suburb. But the French said oh, *non,* the children are too hard to take care of, and they wanted to send us. But the Germans said not yet, not yet, and the Germans really ran things and they left the children behind." Billy stopped. He'd gathered some of his note cards in the wrong order and was bewildered to be back to the racial laws. He began to re-sort them, but he dropped his windbreaker; a few notes tumbled after, and he watched them flutter slowly down and down onto his jacket, like falling angels.

But Mr. Hartman—not realizing that Billy would have seen things through if he hadn't lost his precarious grip not on history but on some oversized pieces of cardboard—felt compelled to speak. There were things Mr. Hartman *had* to tell these children, some important corrections to Billy's report. For example, that the children whose parents hadn't hidden them, or ransomed them even at the last minute and sent them away during the first roundups (for in later ones even that was no longer possible), weren't simply *left* in that suburb outside Paris. As if this were a fairy tale with such a happy ending! The things he must say would raise red welts on the children's pale psyches, but those bruises, too, were necessary—and causing them pain, he dreamt, would also, happily, make him more powerful, would ease his anxiety at being all alone in this enormous room.

"At the camp the children were forever and ever separated from their families," Mr. Hartman said in a soft tone. "Then, after the children were taken from their parents—and how the children screamed and held on, pleading not to be left behind—the parents were sent to Poland to be murdered."

Arthur felt slapped, and tears welled up behind his eyes, making a terrible pressure. For he had kept back a tiny little hope that Billy was mistaken or crazy or lying, that this hadn't all really happened, or wasn't as bad as he had said, as awful as Arthur had guessed long ago from his parents' hints. Now Mr. Hartman said it was true like he was angry with Arthur for having ever, even with small hopes, doubted it (perhaps because at Arthur's age, he too had hoped, for to believe then that his parents had been murdered was to go mad).

"The children at Drancy lived in wooden barracks," Mr. Hartman went on, speaking from behind his desk because he didn't want to get too close to these children anymore, with their tears and their dripping noses and their runny asses, but he wanted to make sure that this story was properly finished, that they knew about the place where he would have died if his parents, from love of him (and because, he dreamt confusedly, they, too, couldn't stand his crying at night), hadn't sent him away. They had to know there was nowhere safe from the muck and blood and the mean-spirited pettiness of life. There was no translation to a better realm—the way art deceivingly promised. Billy had this afternoon once again reminded him how paltry culture was—a realm he confused for the moment with France itself, its seeming civilization, its murderous betrayals—so he turned on it with an angry, destructive fervor. "In those French barracks there were a hundred children to a room and those rooms were much smaller than this classroom. Many of the little prisoners were too young to get all the way downstairs to the bathrooms, so buckets were left on each stair landing for the children to use as toilets. Remember, they had only cabbage soup to eat for weeks and weeks, as Billy told you, and it gave them all diarrhea, and they soiled everything, their straw-filled mattresses and their clothing. They had to wait naked while their older sisters rinsed their underwear in cold water. But they were just sick little children like you, they couldn't help it, they couldn't run to the landing, and they and their clothes had to be cleaned over and over with icy water."

Mr. Hartman's soft accents promised the children that they were protected from the awful world he described, for this was just a dreamy story, but his insistent voice said, too, that adults wouldn't always be there to protect them, so they must know these secret things, and guard against these things, that he was, even by his dreamy voice and his empty eyes, telling them there'd be no way to guard against. And *he'd* become one of those things, Arthur having heard tones a lot like Mr. Hartman's before, when the camp counselor had talked to him in a sleepy, insistent voice as he rotated his big hands back and forth, chafing Arthur's bare arm, heating it like kindling, saying he was a sweet stupid little boy, he deserved to be punished. Arthur wanted to run downstairs to the bathroom to get away from this voice, but he couldn't, they were pressed too tightly together, he was too nervous, the bathroom was too far away. *Why was Mr. Hartman doing this to them?*

"Some of the little children were so confused, and so hungry, and so scared that they couldn't remember their own names anymore. A sister had to tell them who they were." And Arthur dreamt he heard June saying, *You are Arthur Kaplan of 42 Frog Pond Road, Great Neck, New York,* while Mr. Hartman said, "But they were children and they would soon forget what their sisters had said. So the sister might write the boy's name on a small wooden tag, and the children wore the tags around their necks. These children cried all night long. Many of the children weren't strong enough for such a difficult place, they died in the camp."

Then Billy said, "So I'm already dead," in a sleepy small voice, like a child hearing a bedtime story who, in this imagining, had already entered the enchanted forest that is inside, so he drifts into himself and off to sleep, perhaps calling out one last time to the adults by his bedside, which is also the edge of the musty foliage their voices had created in him. Billy stopped his small crying sounds and began to breathe normally, as if his announcement had comforted him, and it added to the uncanniness of Billy's performance that while he had made Arthur more and more frightened, he had grown calmer, if weaker, by accepting even to the end the end Arthur feared. And Arthur also dreamt that Billy had said, "I know I'm the smallest person here, I know that's why you choose me last for kickball games, and that that's why Arthur doesn't want to be my friend," and Arthur felt that it wasn't just Billy's being weak, but the way Arthur had acted about it (his *don't talk to me* in the backseat of the car, his *don't even let your skinny thigh touch mine*) that had led to Billy's death at Drancy, though he knew at the same time that this was a silly confusion, for there was the little boy in front of him, he hadn't died! Still, the more that Billy wouldn't in his imagination protect himself, the more strongly Arthur dreamt he wanted to rebutton Billy's shirt properly, and put the back of his hand against Billy's forehead, the way his mother did for him, touching his sickly body, even his snotty nose. He imagined announcing to the class that Billy was burning up, the report must stop, school was less important than the health of this child! when his reverie was interrupted by Jimmy Benjamin's nasal voice: "Hey, Billy, you say you're already dead, but you're still talking!"

Billy just smiled, leaning against the blackboard again, and announced, "Yes, I'm still talking," as if he, too, were surprised.

Unrelenting, Mr. Hartman ignored them. "Soon they sent all the surviving children in the trains," he said, his voice not dreamy anymore, but clipped, hard, final, for the children's interruptions had made him realize what he'd done to this pointless but secure job by what Dr. Jacobs would soon call his "acting out"; yet he felt in the grip of something strong that transformed his limbs into fire; *he* was now the implacable one, the being-above-human, not this boy, not the Nazis, not his parents; he would finish this properly, he would teach them the hidden things. "They sent the children to the death camps in Poland, where they murdered them, just like their parents."

The class sat silently for a few moments, sullenly hating Mr. Hartman. They all felt that he had wanted to hurt them, and they felt, too, that he thought it was "for their own good," which made him all the more terrifying, for pain done for your own good seemed to have no foreseeable end, you need so much good done to you. Arthur, as if he'd absorbed some of Mr. Hartman's own gift, hated the teacher so ferociously, so utterly, that it made his body ache with a need to hurt him.

"Wait," Billy said, "I forgot something." He dropped his five-by-eight cards on the gray Formica floor, and using both hands he unfolded the light brown windbreaker he'd clutched throughout his report. He had pinned a yellow star on it, made from construction paper, with "Juif" written across it in black magic marker, which was, he said, the French for "Jew." The star scared Arthur, made him ashamed to be Jewish.

"You don't know what you have done . . ." Mr. Hartman said, putting his palm over the star, to block it from view, the children thought, for they wanted him to remember to protect them. Really, though, he was measuring its size. "Do you?" His last words contemplative, rather than angry, as if the fact that the star was as large as a man's palm meant, ridiculously enough, that Billy did perhaps have some supernal knowledge more important than the job he'd just seduced Mr. Hartman out of, some communication meant especially for him, to tell him that having an M.A. didn't matter (as his meager employment, anyway, had taught him, as he knew better than Billy ever would), that culture, no matter how accurately assessed and assiduously worshiped, didn't matter. For Billy's report was for all of them, even the teacher, a long subtraction so insistent that it seemed almost holy, as in some Everyman story that goes, you have money, *but it doesn't matter,* you are smart, *but it doesn't matter,* you have fame, *but it doesn't matter,* you are a king with three daughters, *but it doesn't matter,* you are beautiful (except for a small scar on your wrist, perhaps), *but it doesn't matter.* That story was wrong, of course (wasn't it?), those things would matter very much in these children's lives (wouldn't they?); yet for a little while they also went on thinking that Billy was right, and that anxiety formed sometimes a mild shadow over their often grand prosperity.

At dinner that night in the Kaplans' grand dining room with its marble floors, cream-colored bas-relief French court scenes on the ceiling, and pictures of milkmaids on the wall, Arthur's parents asked him what he had learned in school that day.

Arthur, sitting on his legs to reach the table—which he preferred to the more childish pillows and phone books he had once used—replied as the Haggadah of childhood dictates, "Nothing," for he knew that something had gone badly awry in school that involved his Mr. Hartman. The teacher shouldn't have spoken to them the way he did, and probably not about those things, he shouldn't have let Billy go on swaying like that, so sick that he could barely stand up. He might have permanently hurt Billy's health, and he had certainly hurt the rest of them, and Arthur was sure that he'd *meant* to hurt them. He felt angry with Mr. Hartman, but he wouldn't betray him to his parents, he wasn't ready to give up what Mr. Hartman had come to mean to him, he would protect Mr. Hartman, though Mr. Hartman hadn't protected them.

But others did speak, and for the last two weeks of the term they had a substitute teacher, an irritable old woman who had them spend most of their day reading to themselves; and Arthur felt guilty toward Mr. Hartman, as if the child had abandoned the adult, Mr. Hartman having fed them the black milk of his imagined failure toward *his* parents, killed at Auschwitz. But then he remembered Mr. Hartman taking such evident pleasure in frightening them, saying, "They sent the children to the death camps in Poland, where they murdered them, just like their parents." Fear and anger flooded Arthur, drowning his guilt.

Arkey would know lots more people like Mr. Hartman when he got to graduate school, students and teachers who worshiped an imaginary Europe: England at first—nothing could be sweeter, after all, than to drink tea and eat strawberries by the banks of the Cam in the other Cambridge; then a France of black clothes and blacker theories about the impossibility of anyone understanding anyone. Arkey realized, though, that Mr. Hartman—when Arkey occasionally thought of him— had worshiped *his* imagined kingdom more desperately, with a virtuoso self-hatred that precluded smugness, unlike the graduate students, professors, and minor poets Arkey disdained. After all, Hartman had accepted work in the sixth grade in order to work on his poems. "Poems," one biographer wrote shortly after Hartman's suicide, "that became extraordinary once they began to examine their own demonic will to engorge and name and judge the world. His lyrics then described how the poet's very desire for truth also marked a complicity in the cruel world of Drancy, how he wished to assassinate with his poems," making Arkey wonder if Mr. Hartman, too, sometimes remembered that day when he'd wanted to hurt those sixth grade children, though it would be only one brief episode, according to his poems, in a long litany of those he'd hurt—or tried to hurt. "Recognizing his own intention to use his history to cause pain helped make his poems come alive, made the oppositions matter. Hartman's hatred of the world, he thought, gave rise to the poems that were supposed to be his refuge from the murderous world. But how could art bring peace, when it, just like the world, was made out of hatred? Good and Bad no longer lived in separate houses. So over and over," this critic wrote, "his poems questioned their own, and the poet's, right to be; and left the question open, his honesty and his anger directed against his faith in culture. And, one night, apparently, against himself."

After all, if he wanted to feel more powerful by having power over another, shouldn't that other, in all honesty, be his own body, Hartman having written the poem about killing himself before he actually did it, his parents in the poem pleading with him, saying wait, please don't cry, don't ruin things, isn't it better, dearest child, to go about with empty eyes than to have them closed forever? And in the poem, he grows even more furious with himself for hating them, for hating everything that had made him and was now part of him—his many languages, his parents—and ends his life.

"Richard Hartman left us, though, extraordinary work," the critic wrote. "He is our American Celan. Writing in a language that he feels will never be truly his makes Hartman a particularly American poet," the critic wrote, "where the conflict of heritages that cast us out from Europe—and so also saved us—made our speech in this big, unforgiving country sound like a clamorous wailing for protection in a haunted, dangerous wilderness.

"So America claimed Mr. Hartman for those poems that with meticulous concrete images made the reader experience an absence so total and cold—his lost parents? his hidden God?—that it sucked the light and warmth from the room where you read them" (as the yellow star pinned to a child's brown windbreaker had, Arkey thought, one day swallowed the world for him). "But then there was, magically, an exhalation, something was returned to us to cling to, and it was—as if the moment of inhalation and exhalation could be identical—*this very same poem.*" Or so the critic wrote. And Arthur sometimes thought he even felt it—or something like it, anyway.

A few years after that, Arthur Kaplan sat in the pulmonary ICU at Mount Sinai and listened to the wheeze of the hardworking pump that breathed for his grandfather. *I know how you feel,* he said to the oscillating pistons. *I've spent my life breathing for him, too,* caught up in struggles with long dead Communists who tried to use Abe's union as cannon fodder in a fight with Trotskyites, all of them now equally dumped in the dustbin of history. Arkey had breathed for him, too, when he continued Abraham's fight with his son, Arkey's father, life becoming a long Passover dinner at Bubbie's, the gefilte fish exuding pus long after the fish had died—like the politics of the past—his grandfather Abraham arguing with his friends, turning the story of slaves in Egypt into workers in the U.S. Neat trick, until you saw him do the same thing to the Army-McCarthy hearings, or Koufax versus Don Larsen.

Arkey tried to gabble like that with his grandfather this morning, but the old man, his brain fritzed from pain pills and lack of oxygen, hadn't understood, hadn't even known that Arthur was his grandson—let alone the savior of the radical cutters of the past, dreaming him instead a fellow slave who'd wandered into his room from Egypt—where he seemed to think Mount Sinai Hospital had been relocated today. Arthur felt lonely—Abe, after all, his judge and his comrade, damn near the last member of *his* imaginary internationale.

So moral greatness got you nothing? This was what all Abe's mitzvahs and his organizing come down to—a place with no one to negotiate you a better deal; and the One Big Union is death. *Which is right inside me, too*—Arthur giving a sidelong glance to the electrical plug. One pull and he wouldn't have to watch this horror anymore. Or listen to Abe, if he ever became lucid and started criticizing his book again.

Horrified by the world and himself, Arthur turned for a few minutes to Richard Hartman's poems—not for relief, really, but to deepen, expand, and clarify a vast, hungry emptiness that, for the moment, felt like all that mattered.

That day in the spring, Mr. Hartman thanked Billy for his report, then had them do a silent reading period, though they felt fretful till the time came for the busses to transport them home. *Could you trust a fireman, a policeman, a bus driver?* Someone said something about how they should have straw so they could pee in the bus. But the joke scared even the one making the joke, and the driver noticed how strangely quiet they were on the ride home, down the long tree-lined hill of Middle Neck Road, into Kings Point and the large houses with wide lawns. On the bus Arthur sat next to Billy but didn't talk to him. Billy rested his forehead against the cool glass, but he didn't have the strength to hold his neck steady, and Arthur watched Billy's head go bumpty-bump all the way home, like the jab, jab, jab of the Pez dispenser. So Arthur got off with Billy at the Kennilworth stop, and he walked alongside of him, though Billy's house was in the wrong direction, inside the rough brown stone gates to Kennilworth, while Arthur's (though just as nice!) was outside, at 42 *Frog Pond Lane.* He was worried that Billy would fall down. *Little Guys Must Stick Together,* he thought to himself, and it seemed more funny than painful. "The Midget Brigade," he said to Billy, the way one uses some curse oneself to take the curse off. And Billy replied, "Two Tiny Tykes," and Arthur began, "Two Tiny . . . ," thinking of another curse, a clever rhyme he found he couldn't speak, so instead he said, ". . . Jews." Billy smiled, but didn't say anything. Arthur kicked a stone, and said something about maybe trading comics, but Billy didn't say anything to that either, and Arthur wasn't sure anymore that Billy even knew he was there. At the driveway of his family's tree-sheltered house, a place with levels and turrets made of white stucco crossed with flat, broad pieces of weathered brown wood, Billy said, "Thank you. Wait, please. You know I have a lot of comic books. . . ." Arthur patted him on the shoulder, but that made Billy start to cry again, and he turned and walked down the path, under a roof of overhanging branches. Arthur forgot-on-purpose to give Billy the Pez dispenser that he'd rescued for him from the classroom floor and that he gripped tightly now in the pocket of his pants.

The next Sunday Billy didn't come to Temple with them because he had pneumonia. Jimmy said Billy's report showed how he would do anything for attention—as if they were competitors, as someday they would be, for the entertainment dollar (for Jimmy's failed joke, the moral rebuke he had felt from the class that day, rankled in memory, became a small spur in his search for an implacable irony new to stand-up comedy that would leave no one able to make him responsible for his own remarks, endlessly uncertain if what he had done—insulting women, peeing onstage—was meant to be funny, if the audience had been insulted if they had believed in his fantasies, or if he had only insulted himself, until they slumped before their screens in pleasant bewilderment). "And did you see the tricky way he pulled that jacket out at the end?" Jimmy said. "He's a show-off." Jimmy's loopy mother nodded her inevitable complete agreement with her dopey son.

Arthur touched the Pez dispenser in his pocket and felt disdain for Jimmy Benjamin, that mama's boy. "Well, *you* ought to know about show-offs," he said, for he and Billy were friends now, *not like* this selfish jerk Jimmy Benjamin, *not like* that savage, Johnny Ryan. He and Billy (Arthur dreamt) knew how bravely to bear suffering, for they'd been made a lot like each other when their bodies had touched.

That same Sunday afternoon Nathan Green, owner of Green Co. Comic Books, sat beside his son's bed and tried to practice drawing with him, a game to help Billy forget the pain in his ears, the gravity in his lungs, Nathan feeling a companion pain in himself, the guilt of wondering how he and his wife couldn't have seen that their son had been losing weight, that he'd eaten only bread and soup for weeks—as Laura Jaffe had told her mother, who had told Elizabeth "as a way, can't you see, to say what a rotten goyish mother I am."

Well, maybe they were bad parents. Maybe they left him alone with the inattentive maid too much, maybe that was the problem. But thank God Yvonne *hadn't* noticed all the Coca-Cola Billy drank from the bar-tap in the finished basement, or she might have tried to stop him from ruining his appetite. Then he wouldn't have gotten *anything* to eat! Nathan smiled sadly. Billy definitely imagined a very American concentration camp—one where the thin soup was accompanied by Coca-Cola. Or maybe his addiction to cola drinks was stronger than his neurosis?

And was it *neurosis*? Looking at his son, under the thick blankets he demanded, foam rubber pillows piled up behind him (for Billy was over-sensitive to down, to pollen, to mold, to dust, and now, apparently, to history), Nathan couldn't help feeling that Billy was in this pickle not from mental illness precisely, but from piety—like if they really cared about the fate of the Jews, he and Elizabeth would also eat only camp rations. And drink Coca-Cola.

He felt guilty for smiling. How could they not have seen that their already too small son had been growing smaller? How could they not have known about his interest—or was it an obsession?—in the Holocaust? Billy had often sat with him in his study during the weeks when he must have been losing weight, reading a comic book while Nathan drew, but he was so quiet Nathan hardly noticed him, was sometimes startled to look up and find his son peeking over the pages of his comic book, smiling at him, his teeth bucking out from his many years of assiduous thumb-sucking. The doctors had said this babyish habit was bad for his ears, drew mucus into the canals, but Billy had refused to give it up until the second grade. A thumb, he'd said to his mother, never leaves you. Could his son have calculated the pathos of that remark, the effect on his mother? Could he have been that smart, that manipulative?

When Nathan was at home, Billy rarely left his side. Since he was two, he would play quietly on the floor while Nathan fiddled with the red and yellow wires for the hi-fi or stand for hours watching while Nathan perched on the stool in his study sketching story pages. But until this sickness Billy had barely tried to draw himself, had always fumbled when he did, undone probably by poor hand-eye coordination and weak small-motor skills, his fingers an unmanageable group of rebellious provinces that forced the center to surrender in tears. Always the tears! Dear God, Nathan prayed as they began the lesson, don't let him cry again today. And this morning Billy did a bang-up job on some simple drawing exercises. So maybe, Nathan concluded, his previous clumsiness hadn't been caused by bad coordination, but by anxiety gumming up the works. Maybe pneumonia acted like Miltown; it didn't leave his son enough extra oomph for fear.

Billy clasped Nathan's arm with his left hand, as his right formed a line on the page, Billy's fear having never exactly been about screwing up a drawing but more about the disaster that would lead to—disappointing his dad, who would leave him alone with his illness and his mother. What chance would he have then?

It had been a dream of being linked with his father that had led Billy to the volumes of the Jewish encyclopedia, books he could barely lift, filled with long double columns and hard words. But Billy had felt something good pour into him from the pages, something that would make him more like his father, closer to him, and maybe to his father's father, and to all the fathers before who, Billy dreamt, bent over the world. So the volumes pressed against his thighs, weighing him down outwardly and inwardly, *not* like the sadness when his father was disappointed in him and his body felt stupid and weak, but reassuringly, like the weight of blankets at night.

In the encyclopedia Billy learned about the fairy-tale kingdom of France, where Jews had once been accused of murdering gentile children to get blood for their matzos, blamed for poisoning wells and starting plagues, and were slaughtered or chased from their homes. And then, if a survivor had money for bribes, he might be allowed to return to be murdered or sent away again. In his imagination his dad carried him as they fled, wrapped in thick blankets, pressed to his side, and as they ran it was like something from his dad flowed into Billy, a thick, bitter, nourishing liquid, like a black milk that would tell him how to be a man, how to be a Jewish man. When he stopped reading, though, *that* Jewish father disappeared, like the morning dust Billy brushed from his eyes; or maybe he wasn't worthy of that father; wasn't sufficiently *like him*.

But now Billy had found *drawing*—something that was his father in the way that morning prayers and the kosher laws just weren't. *This* would be the best way ever to bind his father to him. But it was dangerous, too. Billy might screw up, fail his dad—so fierce with bushy brows and thick tufts of nose hair like a lion's whiskers. That's why he'd always grown clumsy when he'd tried to draw with him before. If he goofed, his dad would suddenly remember something else he had to do, he'd give him back to his mother. And *she* couldn't possibly protect him.

Though Elizabeth, who had just arrived with a bowl of freshly made chicken soup (carefully skimmed by repeated applications of paper towels over the top to lift the endless goddamn fat), thought she was a pretty tireless and efficient protector herself, taking him from doctor to doctor, the immunologist, the endocrinologist (for shouldn't he be larger than some of the girls by now?), and the top ENT man at Mount Sinai, the one who had examined Mao's ears!—the Jews apparently believing it an honor to be sick if such a talented, educated, famous person as Mao's doctor would consequently condescend to place his otoscope in your ear canal. She was the one who arranged for the bimonthly audiometer tests where Billy was locked away from her in a wooden booth, and she could see him but not talk to him, his ears muffled by large headphones receiving the tones whose disappearance signaled his inevitable hearing loss. She'd even taken him to Minnesota to visit the Mayo Clinic, where frost covered the high, lead-valenced windows and the doctors had bent their gray warlock heads and recommended radium implants for his ear canal, something too science-fiction for Elizabeth to agree to, though she worried she'd sacrificed the upper part of his audible scale to her ignorance, her superstitious fear of that glowing magical metal that just might have melted the bacterial frost around his ears.

And this new horror, had this been all her fault? Why had he sobbed so in class when he knew it was bad for him? Why this obsession (*she* was sure what to call it) with the Holocaust? Was it because she'd been raised tepidly Protestant—had that gotten all mixed up for Billy with what her husband called her coolness, the same distance that she knew

Nathan had married her for, an attractive challenge to his ardor and a relief from Sophie, who mostly referred to her daughter-in-law, Elizabeth heard (hand over the extension mouthpiece), as the "blonde." As in: "How's the blonde doing today? What clothes did the blonde buy? What did the blonde make you for dinner?"

Elizabeth loved her son, but was it so wrong of her to wish sometimes that she didn't have to devote her life to his ears, to wish that she'd had a kid who wasn't so "special," so self-dramatizing, who didn't have to show how compassionate he was by crying all the time, the mucus pooling up and providing a little internal petri dish for bacteria to grow in and migrate to their land of opportunity, his middle ear. Was it too much to ask of God to give him a growth spurt, change him into a standard-issue son who wasn't as sensitive and small as a girl, and who had a stronger immune system, so that an ordinary earache didn't so often turn into a respiratory tract infection and then pneumonia?

They were just wishes anyway. They passed. Did that make her a monster? They were all against her, and it was *so* unfair. Maybe she sometimes pushed her husband away, but she never felt the least bit distant from her son, yearned to speak fondly to him when he was locked away in that booth, wanted to comfort him now, when he so clearly preferred his father, the two of them concentrating so hard they didn't even seem to notice her. She wiped up a puddle of Coke on the night table, put the soup dish down, and quietly left the room.

Nathan made another grid on the big pad he held for Billy, and Billy, piece by piece, drew the upside-down drinking glass that they'd placed on the blanket by his feet, the reversal meant to estrange the glass, make Billy see it as pieces, not worrying about anything beyond the specific segment, trusting the grid to reassemble it into a working Coca-Cola container. He did a swell job, too, even getting some glints on the glass.

Then, after ten minutes or so, Billy let the pencil drop to his chest and fell asleep almost in the middle of a downward stroke. Nathan put the glass on the veneered-wood bedside table, an easy-wipe surface for Billy's many spills, and pressed his fingers against a forehead much smaller than the back of his hand. Nathan was short, broad, and hale, his wife was tall, lean, constantly active, yet they'd had this sickly, changeling son, whose head was still warm, but less feverish certainly than even four hours before, so at least the vector—knock on veneered wood—was maybe going in the right direction.

· · ·

When he woke, Billy asked his mother if he could see his father again; he wanted "to get back to work." That made Nathan feel buoyant, like if he could pull Billy back from the darkness by the thread of the boy's new interest, he wouldn't have to feel so guilty for all he hadn't noticed about him before. He called New York and reassigned a few titles to other artists, so that the cognoscenti of comics detected that July 1960 marked a decided falling-off in *Rubber Man*'s artistic quality, the issue lacking the piquancy of an all-curves, extruding-man whose limbs moved across the panel-quanta like an arm that snakes across the almost equally inviolable barrier between a boy and his date at the movies, flesh transformed by desire till it was able to slink around angles and make right turns, the law of the panel's grid (and the father's prohibitions) violated. Nathan Green's stylistic quirks (for real fans knew his name even before comic books were signed) were absent from that month's issues, to his admirers' disappointment but to Billy's joy and later to the cognoscenti's own, when Billy's education concluded and his career began.

For it was a month of miracles at the Green home, Nathan spending the next four weeks sitting by his son's bedside, teaching, sometimes impatiently, but usually with pleasure in Billy's growing power and health, and especially in his considerable talent. Billy's gift, Nathan saw with mingled joy and regret—the most intense sweet-and-sour dish he'd ever tasted—was greater than his own, an imagination and a line that was freer with all the regular grids than his, not defiant or ironic but playful. Perhaps as an artist, Billy would find that his dangerous softness—the way he took everything hard, like the other kids' moods when they got angry with him, or their bacteria, or the fights between Nathan and his wife, or the history of the Jews—might work for him. Billy, he thought, pressed the world deeply into his heart, then gave it back transformed, while Nathan knew he himself was a squared-off, bluff, Fearless Fosdick cutting across the ocean of other people's feelings, pushing people away or overpowering them. He just had less inside him to work with. So his son might become the unhappier man, but he *might* be the better artist—which meant that Nathan's best work could be Billy himself. Not an entirely happy thought. Still, for a few months he gave himself over to the job of Billy-formation, thinking it might entertain him anyway, give him some relief from the crisis in his life and marriage, the feeling of time misused and slipping away from him, without point, without joy. It made him want to scream. He bore down on Billy—pedagogically, mind you—with all his rage at the way his hair now grew thickly from his nose and sparsely from his head, at his not-quite-large-enough talent, at the adult world's disdain for comic books, at his wife's indifference to his flabby, pale body. Should he risk an affair? No, the woman was a master counterspy. So teaching Billy wasn't much compensation, but it was better than the alternative: namely *nothing;* it surely didn't stop the scream his life made slipping away from him, but it quieted it a little.

And over the next month Nathan never felt so fatherly, so generative—in a confined, nearly impotent way—as when he was instructing his long-lashed, impressionable son, feeling most masculine those days as Billy's teacher, like when his wife gave in to him—for surrender, rather than collaboration, was definitely what lovemaking felt like with his Elizabeth, and when she looked away from him at the end, he couldn't help feeling there was defeat in her face instead of satisfaction. But Billy-times were better than that, too; he never looked away, just gazed up to him from the pile of pillows, wanting to learn more.

Billy felt how he was now both the page and the pencil held between his father's hand and his own. It was still painful to be corrected by his father, but *this* anger didn't cast him out anymore but bound him more tightly to his dad, like the sting of his correcting him, once it was re-assembled by some grid inside him, was revealed to be just love seen upside down. For a while Billy felt like each thing he learned brought him nearer to the father he'd dreamt about, the one who would definitely protect him. But then, as Billy began to feel the size of his own talent, even how that contributed to his dad's anger, he understood how the sideways shading of his pencil took him further away from that imaginary man and closer to a father he might encounter later, a smaller man, one maybe who couldn't draw as well as he could! So who would take care of him then? But Billy couldn't think about that now; he was having too good a time.

Billy would be the third generation of artists in the Green family, counting from the day in the winter of 1931 when Nathan's father, Joseph, guided by the Angel of Whimsy, had taken the Sunday comic supplement, folded it neatly into fours, cut it, stapled it, made a booklet of it, delighting five-year-old Nathan, the original test market. So Joseph's first "comic book" had been manufactured from Sunday discards bought up cheaply or rag-picked on Monday and sold as books for a penny each on Tuesday, not quite a feat requiring superpower but something that would take him and his family beyond Green Street, from which he'd borrowed his name. Then, throughout the thirties, Joseph added some characters drawn by himself, though his draftsmanship, compared to his son's or his grandson's, was clumsy, and he became more of a producer to other artists than one himself, a conductor, he liked to think, of their fantasies—rather than the meddling, stingy man they imagined him.

Well, too bad for them. Joseph Green had had to be tough. Comics ain't the movies. It was a low-margin business. And he'd never asked anyone to work harder than he did. But after the first risk of buying up old newspapers, he knew he'd lost a lot of his courage and inspiration. He'd even, Nathan told his son as they drew together, passed up a chance to acquire Siegel and Schuster's excluded-from-ordinary-life-yet-perfect hero, Superman. Can you imagine that? No doubt that was why in Nathan's comics Superman was often referred to by the other characters not as if he were a person, but as a kind of nuclear weapon, a sword of world, or, anyway, comic-book-business, domination. Then, when Billy took over the helm, the Man of Steel was addressed as "Soup," or "Noodle." And Soup, in the gospel according to Billy, had become a power deployed by the rogue government against the BillyBook heroes, his x-ray vision and acute hearing only a super version of the phone taps and surveillance cars that would be used to track Ninja B. and the mutant Band of Outsiders who worked tirelessly to stop the ruling cabals from subverting democracy. Superman, never directly represented (for even Rubber Man can't cross the lines of copyright law), became sicklied o'er with tragedy in BillyBooks; a version of the hidden Jew growing up in disguise in Middle America, having fled the ghetto of Krypton with eons of pent-up energy and Talmud-honed intellect. Yet he only wanted to use his superpowers to . . . to be a mensch; not to make new law for himself like the Nietzschean over-man, but to enforce ever more perfectly the old law; until, in one famous BillyBook (Feb. 1977), "Matzo Ball," with his back turned toward the viewer—but that stupid squared-off haircut! who else could it be?—confesses to Billy Bad Ears himself that he mourns for how his love of law has led to *this,* his serving a ruling class who are not, as he'd once thought, guardians of a City on a Hill, but flawed men and women. "They just want more and more power, while I have power—superpower. And I want justice!" And no doubt, if we could see his face, he wore a sad smile. "But let's be realistic," he says to the mal-oreilled one, "what other world is there, until the Messiah comes?"

Nathan Green, without Superman (and Girl, and Boy, and Dog), didn't have the biggest sellers, but his company (first called Federal, then Green Co. Comics) did have some steady-selling titles, with a slightly odder angle to them than DC's cleancuts, enough to take his family from a small house in Queens to this large home, an oak-shadowed Tudor mansion in Great Neck, twelve rooms built on two charming V-tilted acres, with the house sited in the declivity and climbing up both ways, so that several rooms had to have steps within them, an eccentric construction appropriate to Nathan Green's own sense of space, Green Co. Comics having a similarly askew feeling, which extended to a sideways or low-angle blocking to a picture (film noir for comics) or long, thin rectangles for frames, or a whole book where the story was told within separate puzzle-shaped pieces.

In addition to these odd angles, Green Books' originality came from their having a little more gore and a lot more underwear than the majors had. Then, after the Comics Code censorship, Nathan and his crew of inkers and letterers, and his five or six staff artists and writers (two or three on their way to better-paying jobs at the larger companies, two geezers left over from Joseph's shop and there for a life sentence, and all of them living, really, within Nathan's now tiring imagination), had to become even more inventive in their perversity, sublimating and disguising the characters' psychic tiltings as skillfully as any dream censor. His company's characters were, Nathan and Billy thought with pride, deeper than those of the majors, the heroes' personalities a little more inwardly and outwardly distorted—as who wouldn't be?—by having superpowers. A Green Company hero had sour depressions during which he felt arrogant, bitter, and contemptuous, hated the "herd" for rejecting him and despised them for needing him. Ordinary men and women wanted the super ones to save them from nuclear destruction and evil genius after evil genius, oh, sure, but they were always turning them down for dates! And the superheroes would have preferred to mate with the ordinary, the nonchosen (the gentile, perhaps?) rather than with another mutant; they didn't want to hang out socially with other super-club members who would just remind them of their own strangeness, something caused by mutagenic genes or a radioactive snakebite; or puberty; something, anyway, that gave them powers that made them *not like others*. And so able to show evildoers their dreams and terrify and entice them (as Laura Jaffe, AKA SheWolf, AKA Dr. Fantasy, would); or move more decisively, quickly, and violently than others (like Beth Jacobs, AKA Athena X, Ninja B., or Deborah, AKA the Prophet, who could give a ululating cry that would drive her followers to frenzy); or the gift to con the malcontents from some evil intent (like Jeffrey Schell—the Sophist—whose skinny life-size counterpart would someday use the same charm to close mega-deals for Harry Hennessy's paintings); powers that made them outcasts, wailing with adolescent angst, consigned only to date other freaks. Especially because in BillyBooks the hero always had an unexpected and unattractive physical symptom that came along with his power, like a need to urinate thirty times a day, a ravenous appetite for sugar, a permanent runny nose, nails that grew too fast, hair loss, or terrible body odor.

Still—as the heroes would someday tell their psychiatrists—they wouldn't have it any other way. The character's power might begin with terrible pain, like a nervous breakdown, or headaches, or muscles suddenly jumping about like she had multiple sclerosis—or as if someone else's dreams controlled her central nervous system. But when the super-hero sees how she can make her parents' TV explode right in the middle of yet another boring visit from Topo Gigio on *The Ed Sullivan Show,* she had to admit to the doc that she'd thought, borrowing a phrase from Mikey, the cereal pitch-boy, *"I like it! I like* it! I *want* it." I *want* to go faster than they do. I *want* to know them better than they know themselves, to feel their thoughts, to see more clearly, more deeply, to hurt them if I must (do I actually *hope* I must, Doc?) for their own good with my marvelous powers.

So superpowers might leave the queer heroes dateless, yet they still won't surrender them when the doctor at the Mayo Clinic offers to cure them. For their power—whose premonitory and embarrassing pains may never go away—is, they feel, all that makes them worthwhile, all that might lift their sadness from them; though that same power, on the exhale, is what causes the sadness that it lifts them from, the deep blue loneliness at prom time.

That May, Billy began to learn how very much he, like his future super-heroes, wanted *his* power, too, such as it was, even if—as he romantically imagined—his talent might make him look stranger to others than being turned upside down would. Or maybe they wouldn't be able to see him, here, anymore at all. He felt less vivid, less interesting, empty almost, could feel the color leaking out of him onto the page. Still, if that was the deal, he *wanted* it. For the slight movements of his small hand shaving the wood with a razor blade to reveal more of the magical lead, or a stroke properly made, a shadow melded in by using the wider side of the pencil point, took him farther from his body, where he'd spent so much of his childhood listening to the pain in his ear. When he drew he was here in Great Neck, of course, he knew *that,* but he was kind of *there,* too, within the drawing in a way, powerful, vital—momentarily free from discomfort and shame.

As long as he was drawing, anyway. After all, drawing a superhero didn't make him into one, didn't even clear his ears or his lungs; after the pencil stopped moving and the frame was finished his body was still stuck in bed.

Toward the middle of that first marvelous May, as Billy felt a little stronger, the length of the lessons with his father chased the expanding sunlight hours, went on for almost an afternoon at a time, interrupted only by toast and chicken soup painfully made to his grandmother's exacting recipe. Billy, looking down at the latest issue of *Rubber Man,* said he wouldn't mind having some Soft Serve ice cream like the cone on the back cover for dessert, actually a sly request that his father might get some Carvel for him at the stand in Little Neck.

Billy told his father he often dreamt of having the things pictured on the back of comic books, stuff you could buy or get if you sold a billion issues of *Grit,* like bicycles, binoculars, or a device that would throw your voice. At night, he'd sometimes look at the pictures, concentrate and stare till his eyes blurred, thinking that if only he got his mind right perhaps the thing would appear. Wasn't that crazy? But drawing reminded him of that. Maybe the artist had wanted a Soft Serve cone, too, and had drawn a picture of it. But concentrating or drawing didn't produce the cone. (This whole story, though true, was mostly meant as a way to get his wish across to his dad: *go to Little Neck now, bring back ice cream for me.*)

Nathan got the point, teased his kid by pretending to be obtuse. "Maybe," Nathan said, "one day the pen accidentally pricks his finger and blood drops into his ink bottle. And when he makes drawings using that ink, they become real."

"Drawings of ice cream," Billy said. "Soft Serve. The good kind. Like from Carvel. In Little Neck."

"Yes, ice cream," Nathan said, smiling. "He begins as a child, so he has silly childlike desires. He only thinks about drawing ice cream for himself."

"Then later, he draws a stupid Rolls-Royce," Billy said, "like Alan King's," for one of their neighbors was the famous Vegas comedian, owner of a white Phantom, calling it stupid because his father, Billy suspected, coveted that car as much as Billy wanted ice cream, which he knew his father knew.

"And then he uses his powers to get out of jams, to make devices to capture villains."

"The ones," Billy said, sleepy again, "that killed his parents," thinking of the trains, the deportations, and what Mr. Hartman had said, and feeling guilty that he hadn't thought about that in a while.

Nathan paused. Billy heard the quiet but sharp intake of breath. Did his father think Billy wanted to kill *him? Did* he want to kill him? For there were other hints at the dinner table, ones not about history but about Eddie Puss. Was his father angry? Billy felt pressed into the bed by that imagined fury—exhausted, hopeless, helpless, unholy and blue. He had to explain himself. "Maybe the boy was very lonely and tried to draw a playmate for himself."

"And he succeeded," Nathan said. "But an evil scientist learns of it and uses his spells to get control of the Golem."

"Golem?" Billy smiled, happy that his father would still play with him.

"It's a monster, like Frankenstein. It's an image come alive. You know, the playmate."

"The evil neighbor wears suits with baggy pockets," Billy said. "He has glaring eyes, and he wants the powers of the boy's father, the secret formulas the father keeps in a special encyclopedia, eighteen big books in his laboratory. Because, you know, the boy's father is a very powerful magician." He smiled at Nathan, winningly, he hoped. "So the evil scientist hypnotizes the playmate and uses him to kill the boy's parents."

It marked a turn in Nathan's work—or was it Billy's work?—a deepening, for the hero was at least implicated in the world's disaster; *he'd* made the playmate, after all. The boy in this early story was Nathan, was Joseph, was now Billy, "all those who worshiped graven—okay, lithoed—images, stories told in little pictures," wrote the Chinese-American critic who had bought Billy's proto-books from Laura. "That ardor for drawings violates a commandment more powerful than the frames that Rubber Man crossed. So the hero who broke the commandment against worshiping images was implicated in his parents' death, and he has to avenge them in order to redeem his guilt. But, really," he concluded melodramatically, "nothing will redeem his guilt."

And the evil scientist—*the neighbor*—was that, Nathan wondered, the psychoanalyst they'd just hired, Dr. Jacobs? For during the third week of his recuperation, Billy had moved to the "master bedroom" during the days—a place where Nathan never felt the master—so he could have the big TV while Elizabeth and the maid gave a thorough cleaning to Billy's musty room. Elizabeth had opened Billy's desk drawers, not cleaning but prying, looking for some clue to what had caused her son to sob so in class, terrifying the other students, terrifying her, not believing it could be just an encyclopedia article about France. Rifling his desk drawers, she'd found two bowls of soup and bread covered with black and green iridescent mold. Had he not eaten at all? Or had he eaten *this*: moldy soup, poisoned bread? Did her son want to die? Her hand shook, spilling slime on the carpet.

She had wondered if she should call a psychiatrist. It was unheard of, really, to consult a psychiatrist about your child, even here, though this science was supposed to be something that especially belonged to the Jews. One of her neighbors in Kings Point, Dr. Jacobs, was a famous analyst, literally a student of Freud's; and he was a Holocaust survivor, too. Would that be good for Billy, or would it reinforce his obsession? Would Dr. Jacobs say she'd made him neurotic? Had she let him suck his thumb too long? Should she have breast-fed him? Was she too distant? Had her hatefulness made him want to eat moldy soup and die? To punish herself she'd imagined Billy in a straitjacket, locked away in a booth where she could see him but not speak to him, wires put to his head for electroshock. Had she condemned him to that by calling his trouble mental illness instead of piety? Or had she finally done something halfway sensible that might save his life?

Dr. Jacobs had seemed so sallow and reserved when Elizabeth saw him out walking, a short man, incongruously strolling in a blue business suit and vest, as if, Elizabeth thought, he didn't understand what "stroll" meant, what ease was. But he had been friendly and reassuring to her on the phone. He'd even offered to come to the house to talk to Billy the next day. Surely the other Jews in Kings Point would think it okay, an honor even, to be head-sick if a student of Freud's would make a house call for you!

And Billy had seemed to like the man whose hawk nose took up so much of his small face, the schnozz supporting glasses so thick that his goggly eyes looked like, well, a cartoon character's—a sour one, though, like that fellow in Li'l Abner with the cloud over his head and the vowelless last name.

Yet here he'd reappeared as an evil scientist—or so Nathan thought, misled by his own jealousy of his son's doctor, missing the clue of the ill-fitting brown suit, telltale sign of Mr. Hartman's still-living heart. Nathan felt wickedly pleased by Billy's seeming ambivalence toward Dr. Jacobs, the appearance in their lives of the tiny self-contained doctor with the deep-set judge's eyes seeming a symptom of a son permanently marred. Maybe if Billy didn't like him that also meant he didn't need him, because this was all just a stage he would outgrow without anyone's help. Yet Nathan was scared for his son, too, hated himself for his jealousy, his feelings curving back on his love like filaments of mold. "What's the boy's name?" he asked.

"Johnny," Billy said, for he worried that he'd hurt Johnny Ryan's feelings with his report about Jews and France, made him feel left out. Now he could make it up to him, make him the hero of his comic book.

"And where do they live?"

"I don't know," Billy said. "In Gotham? You know, with Batman?"

"Well, I like to put my heroes in the suburbs. Most of our readers live there, and there isn't enough magic in the suburbs, is there? So let's put their houses in . . . Scarsdale. And doesn't the boy have to do something about his playfellow too? Teach him how to behave?" Nathan imagined Hebrew school for the Golem, Talmud class.

"Yes. He has to kill him," Billy said, smiling. Then his lips fell, shocked by what he'd said. "I mean he feels guilty doing it, he was his friend, and he'd made him, the Goolem—"

"Golem," Nathan said, then prayed his priggishness wouldn't stop the flow of his son's invention.

"The Golem didn't know what he was doing when he killed Johnny's parents. But it's too dangerous to let him live. He has to get rid of him. The Golem can tell that Johnny's going to kill him. So Billy, I mean Johnny, he makes a grid and does an exact copy of the Golem. The Golem's eyes are blank, you know, no pupils, he's paying attention to something inside himself while Johnny draws, you know, like he has a stomachache or he's daydreaming, because he knows he's going to die and his best friend is going to kill him. But the Golem knows that it's the right thing to do. Johnny finishes the drawing."

"Right. He was a drawing of Johnny's," Nathan said, "now he has to erase him."

"Yes. Johnny shouldn't make any more people. He has to remain lonely."

"Right." Nathan roughed out sketches as they talked. "There must be no more images brought to life by our idolatrous love," Nathan said, "our mixtures of memory and longing."

When Billy woke up, Nathan offered him the prize he'd seized from the Carvel stand in Little Neck, where the black-jacketed Brando poseurs with their motorbikes had made his stomach clench. After all, what if they weren't poseurs? Hitters, they'd called guys like that on Green Street, the name still resonant for Nathan with the possibility of being, well, hit. "A present for you."

"What? A what?"

Was he fuzzy with sleep? Had Nathan spoken too softly? Or had his deafness gotten worse?

"You know you mustn't cry so much, right?" Nathan said, thinking of the doctors' impossible-to-fulfill injunction to keep a sensitive little boy from weeping. Nathan was thinking, too, of Dr. Jacobs, who was supplanting him, taking over the chief role in his supposedly greatest creation. His son was a smart boy. Why use this psychiatric hunting around? Why not just speak directly to Billy? Just tell him it was all right to care but not all right to cry. He had to learn not to take things so hard. "It's bad for your ears."

But his father's direct speech felt like a criticism to Billy. He took it hard, dreaming his dad would leave him in bed, alone, unable to feed himself. So he began to cry.

Nathan put the pint of ice cream and the bowl and spoon he'd brought on the bedside table, next to Billy's rocket-ship lamp. "Maybe we could make up a character who cries too much," he said, hoping to distract Billy into drawing a version of himself. Like play therapy?

"He has bad ears, too," Billy said, rubbing his hand across his face.

"What shall we call him?"

"Billy," Billy said, smiling again. This time he'd be able to escape into the character for sure, he thought, though it wouldn't be much of a refuge if the character was screwed up the way he was.

"Okay. Billy it is." Nathan picked up the sketch pad from the bed and sat down in the small hard-backed chair from Billy's desk. "Billy who has bad ears."

And, as you know, fellow Band supporters, in episode after episode, Billy Bad Ears cried and cried often, sometimes for himself, but more often (because it's comic books we're talking about here) he wept for others, even those who'd lived long ago and died horrible deaths. Because of his exposure to radiation, he produced lots more snot than most kids when he wept, glowing mucus collected in his ear canals, so they became infected again and again. Billy Bad Ears knew as he began to cry that his ears would become infected, both his parents having been told by the Top Man at Mount Sinai that the drum would be scarred with thin lines like the tear streaks that often crossed BBE's face, and that those scarrings, if they got thick enough, would destroy his hearing. Billy Bad Ears was flooded with the hurt other people felt, the fear from dying people poured into him, and the tears formed like other eyes behind his eyes. Billy Green had a slight deficiency in his right ear, but

Billy-in-the-comics, Billy Bad Ears, had it lots worse ('cause remember, it never gets worser enough in comics); the crying caused by the world's violence deafened him completely.

But in the comics this heightened his sense of empathy, the very sense that had originally, by causing his compassionate tears, also caused his deafness. Billy Bad Ears' empathy became positively superpowered, supernatural; BBE knew what people were feeling, people whose faces he'd never even seen. He could tell what suffering, what love (not a heck of a lot, alas), and what evil (plenty of that—this is comics, after all) lurked in the hearts of men. How is Bad Ears to keep from endlessly crying at the misery of the world? Only by bringing relief, bringing justice! BBE *feels* the plans of evildoers even before they act, and thwarts them, weeping transformed into the endless housekeeping of putting the bad behind bars. (But what if he starts weeping for the evil ones as well? Then what in G-d's name would he do to stop his annoying sobbing?) To heighten his powers still further, he sometimes fasts, or nearly, eating only bread, soup, and Coca-Cola for a week. Even power-amplified, though, he cannot do justice quickly enough, and often enters a dark frame where he is overwhelmed by the enormity of his task. And then Billy Bad Ears, like Holmes with his cocaine, takes to his room, stays up all night drinking tea—no drugs allowed in comics—simply weeping. After all, what more harm can it do him?

Nathan wasn't sure if BBE had been his idea first, and Billy had intuited it, or if it had come from Billy—it had a boatload more pathos, after all, than Nathan usually allowed through the comic canal—and he'd simply drawn to his son's dictation. And Billy didn't know who the credit belonged to either, never did, really. *Is that my feelings or their feeling?* he would sometimes wonder in later life, lost in Beth's or Helen's or Leo Jacobs' or his father's bewilderments.

That month in 1960 he didn't worry about that, or about what *his* plans would be when—as Nathan promised, feeling a little guilty for nabbing his son's inventions—he inherited Green Co. He didn't wonder if he even really wanted to make comic books for his living, or if *that* was Nathan's idea, and maybe moved not by his own desire but by love for his father, his need for his protection, he had enthusiastically agreed. On that particular day he just felt happy to be at one with his balding father.

By the time they finished the first Bad Ears comic (a steady seller from then on, though not the most popular of BillyBooks until Billy himself took over the line), Billy had stopped crying. He and Nathan laughed with delight at each new invention, and at Billy's growing skills, the two collaborating on a comic book hit. Better: Nathan saw a future where he could market Billy, a kid who draws comic books for kids. The teen-turnips would love it! Billy and his books could be his *Superman*!

The two of them looked over at the pool of ice cream on the bedside table, the melted goop slithering to the edge like a Rubber Man pseudopodia, dripping onto the confetti-colored carpet, adding its chocolate to the blue, white, and red. How Elizabeth would complain! Nathan/Billy, as if they'd also collaborated in being messy children together, a sin particularly annoying to their wife/mother, giggled about that, too, dipping their fingers together in the chocolate blob.

"Women!" his dad said. "Can't live with 'em—"

"Can't make them come alive from comic book drawings," Billy said—with that odd precociousness, Nathan thought, that was at once so eerie and would be—he was sure—so profitable.

Provided that psychoanalyst didn't cure him of his talent.

The next week, Laura Jaffe's mother put her handkerchief back in her small black purse as the thrilling nasal voice behind her said, "I believe Billy Green's pneumonia has cleared up."

Dr. Jacobs' patient for close to a decade, Ellen Jaffe knew that each of the doctor's sentences—even the few that might *seem* very casual— were undoubtedly filled with special instruction for her. This one, she concluded, must mean that her daughter should invite Billy Green to go sailing on the *Ellen and Jackie II.* She felt a twinge of jealousy—well, more like a rotten flash of murderous rage—toward the little boy, but what better way to ease that pain than (as always, with her father and her brothers) actually to aid Dr. Jacobs; to be, that is to say, the good, helpful daughter? She smiled at herself.

And what harm could it do?

That same day in the middle of June, Beth Jacobs, on the way to the kitchen window seat with her copy of Rilke, tiptoed by the oddly half-open door to her father's consulting room and joined Arthur Kaplan, Ellen Jaffe, Nathan and Elizabeth Green, in the hot tar pits of Billy Green envy. *I'm a jealousopuss,* she whispered, remembering herself, age six in front of her parents' bedroom mirror, arms akimbo on her flow-ered nightgown, her mother behind her softly brushing her hair. "Ann," Beth had declared, "you have the ugliest color hair," when really she'd always thought her mother had the most beautiful, thick, long, womanly red hair, so much better than her own drab black. Her father, laughing, had named his new animal "the jealousopuss." Maybe this little boy, who her father said had a gift for such trivialities, could draw the creature.

Had she really even been jealous, age six, she wondered now, or had she just said those things to please her father—for she knew he *wanted* her to snap at her mother, to prove that she was a normal Oedipus, even though in every other way her father had contempt for the ordinary. That's why she'd broad-jumped over two grades, and, next September, at age thirteen, would start ninth grade—thus showing *tout Great Neck* that she was the very special child of *un père très spécial*. She stepped to a coign of vantage, just behind the door, to listen and peek through the hinges. She didn't look forward to working on her soliloquy anyway, had had such trouble sitting still this summer, like she was maybe losing one of her best attributes, her *sitzfleisch*. But what if he asked her to recite the poem about the panther at dinner tonight while her mother nervously busied herself collecting the dishes, not looking at Beth as she paced around the table in cramped circles, like a ritual dance around a center. Ann didn't approve of these tests by her father. But she'd be pleased if Beth did well—or maybe just relieved that she hadn't made her father unhappy. Anyway, Beth knew she had to work harder on it, just in case.

Soon, though. Not quite yet.

And was that why he'd left the study door ajar? Did he want her to see him with this boy—as a rebuke for her not concentrating well? But she hadn't failed him yet, had she? He didn't know about her trouble sitting still?

Or was he thinking about that minute-that-was-an-hour three months before after the first Wagner she'd ever heard, a performance she and her father had spent weeks preparing for, *Grove* entries, essays by Nietzsche, and even a book she had most definitely not understood by Theodor Adorno, Professor Marcuse's friend. She'd gotten, though, that Wagner's music might be seemingly beautiful yet hide a destructive core, and had made herself stiffly *en garde*. But then, when the conductor brought his baton down, the amazing sounds had lulled her, taken her over so that the winged women rising in her waking reverie had been like figures woven from and riding the roar that had always—she realized then—been right inside her. She had wanted it to go on and on and on. What did that say about *her*? She knew she shouldn't love Wagner unambivalently. Did she have something rotten in her also? Was that why she was so much taller than her parents? (Thank God she was near-sighted like them!) When she'd finally been able to look away from the Valkyries, her dad had been facing the floor, his palms pressed into his eyes.

In the dark Cadillac, gliding home, he asked her what she'd thought of the opera, a test of her sensibility always, of why she should be in the car with him instead of Ann. She'd stumbled, "I . . . I mean, I don't know what to think of it exactly . . ." Had the music made him very unhappy? Or very bored—too lacking in rigorous structure, which was what she thought Mr. Adorno had said. The dashboard lights left her father and herself half in shadows, so that someone seeing the glowing light skimming by could just make out two people in that private world called Passing Through and not know what they might be to each other. That night had been ruined for her. She had wanted to be alone with her feelings. She had kept quiet, and he hadn't pressed her, just sat silently the rest of the trip home, probably thinking to himself how very *ordinary* she was, all their study together wasted.

The next time he'd suggested a trip to the Metropolitan Museum, Beth hesitated, worried that she would fail him and tired of worrying; she wanted some time to herself. He heard her silence, and said maybe it wasn't a good idea right now, he had so much work. She knew she'd hurt his feelings, but she just needed some time off to regain her strength.

Perhaps now he thought she was too dull; he had to find someone else to teach to do the things the world needed done. After all, the boy *couldn't* be there for analysis, because her father had already told her that Anna Freud had been wrong, children *didn't* benefit from analytic insight, their egos—not *hers,* he said, but the others'—were too weak.

Or had he changed his mind about that? If he hadn't, why had he gone to the boy's house to visit him when he was sick? What made him *that* important? She edged just a little closer to the wall, but the hum of the air conditioner that her father set so deliciously cool masked their words. Or were they sitting silently, the boy probably unable to think of anything to say? They faced each other, her father in his leather high-backed chair appearing wonderfully somber in a dark blue suit, vest, and tie, while Billy—in tennis shorts, canvas docksiders, and a shirt with one of those ridiculous alligators on it—most certainly looked a *très ordinaire* Great Neck boy.

Then her father rose from his chair, took off his suit jacket, folded it carefully over the back of his chair, rolled up the sleeve of his white shirt, *and held his forearm out to the boy.*

"Oh, that this too too sullied flesh would melt," Beth whispered, clutching the Rilke to her chest.

Had she said that out loud? Thank God the air conditioner would keep them from hearing her! But it *was* so unfair! She'd seen her father's bare arm only a few times in her whole life—and he'd never *meant* to show it to her. He'd come out of the shower not knowing she was in his bedroom once, or met her in the hall late at night, not wearing his white pajama top. So why was he letting Billy Green see *that,* what could *he* ever have done to deserve it, when Beth was the one who had read books about Dachau, about Auschwitz? Had he been able to tell that it all felt distant to her, that she couldn't take it inside herself? Had he thought maybe she *did* have a rotten core, was a cold, unfeeling person? Is that why he wouldn't talk to her about the camps? But that wasn't fair! More than anything in her life she wanted to have been *there* with him—she just couldn't be, even in her imagination, until she heard the story in *his* words, in *his* voice, heard how it had felt to *him*, the most precious person in the world to her.

But when she asked him questions, he put her off, like she was Innocent Ann. Had he heard something naïve or callous in her voice when she'd asked about Block Eleven the last time they'd gone to the Metropolitan Museum, something she hadn't understood, she had said, in an Italian writer's book about the camps.

But he'd said, "Oh, darling, you don't want to know about that." Then, because she'd hurt him by asking, he'd walked quickly down the high corridor.

He'd stopped, then, and waited a little ways down the hall, pretending to look at a painting, but really too sad, she was sure, to see it. She'd run to catch up, the hall suddenly stretching endlessly in front of her as she ran, her body growing smaller and smaller—until, thank God, he'd turned and smiled at her, and she became her own size again, and could easily come toward him. They'd walked down a favorite corridor then, where it became Paris in 1880.

"Why would such a genius," he'd wondered aloud finally, "care so much about women's fashions?" Was that a test? Or was he saying that *she'd* started to care too much about how she dressed—which was why she'd chosen a plain blue jumper today, for when he would find her reading Rilke in her kitchen nook. Still, the beautiful forms made his voice sweeter, and he'd spoken to her then about his friend Herbert Marcuse and his faith in the future, the best part of this story being that her father sounded less burdened when he told it, and closer to her, treating her like an adult, really—no, something better than that, a friend, a comrade. Professor Marcuse said that there'd be a vast change in the economic system soon. "No more oppression," her father repeated, "no more competition." She'd taken his hand, the knuckles so damaged by beatings, swollen forever. She concentrated on sending warmth to his hands, a healing force that would be transmitted directly to his joints as the two of them walked down the hallway together, like this place was their own castle.

"Humanity will transform its work," he said, "to make it pleasurable. Like what Renoir did. Good for others, yes, but fun for him, too, don't you think? Like an infant playing with his feces." Such pleasurable work would join people to their society, and to each other. "They'll cherish their lives then." Which was Beth's cue to gaze at her father, her head to the side, face composed just so: a little surprised to discover that a great artist was like a baby playing with his poop, but not *too* shocked, either, because Professor Marcuse's ideas were meant to be her dreams too, even though she couldn't put the ideas into her own words yet, only repeat them, like the Torah passage she'd learned to sound out at Hebrew school. Her father chanted, too, when he told her this story, reciting quickly, in a singsong voice, as if he might forget some part of *his* portion. And he often forgot things lately, like where the car was parked, and even once, last week, as he filled out a school form for her, her middle name, which had made her feel as if she had a gaping hole in her chest. Or maybe he had that singsong sound because he really couldn't believe that people would *ever* cherish human life again; perhaps her task was to show him that that really was possible, even after all he'd seen. *The time is out of joint,* she'd thought. *O cursed spite, that ever I was born to set it right.* So Beth was like Hamlet in a way—she and the prince both had missions their fathers had given them, though she'd never understood what she was supposed to do about hers exactly. Maybe write something. But what? Everybody giving pleasure to each other made her think of a pack of dogs, each one licking another's anus, and *that* couldn't be right.

He'd stopped by one of her favorite paintings then, a beautiful woman swathed in red, like the color of her clothes had come from within, the beautiful pink of her cheeks having grown more intense as it moved outward into the cloth, the color making everyone at the outdoor café in the painting look at her the way Beth herself did, their hearts filled by what the woman spread out before them: *herself,* a beautiful woman with full breasts, like her own would soon be, and her eyes filled with gay knowledge that made Beth want to lay her head on the woman's chest, press herself against her and be comforted about all the confusing things that were happening to her body. And at the same time she wanted to wear a red dress like that herself.

Just the week before, Professor Marcuse and his tall wife, the beautiful doctor Inge, in a tight red dress, had visited her family again, both of them dignified but not somber, their long, thin faces filled with humor and mockery. Beth felt that they didn't care about anyone's opinion, which made everybody want to please them—even her father. They were Jews, she thought, yet they were aristocrats.

They'd even pretended to chastise her father! Why didn't he let Beth play more with her friends? All these violin lessons, French lessons, Italian lessons, museums and operas, did he think that would turn Great Neck into Vienna? What kind of life was that for a teenage girl, an *American* teenage girl?

But I like my violin lessons, Beth thought, or liked playing Mendelssohn for her father at night anyway, his "sentimental favorite" he called it, as he sat with his eyes closed on the couch, saying finally, "Lovely, Beth. You *are* a wonder."

"Why don't you write again yourself, Leo," Inge had said, "instead of force-feeding her like a goose. Isn't that what you're doing? Trying to make *her* into a writer, so she'll do your work?"

"Ah," her father had said, "I've written enough." He put his hand on Beth's head, his fingers feeling to her like they were charged with static electricity. "Besides, my daughter's far more brilliant than I am, a fine musician, writer, actress. Who knows what she might do?" Beth felt proud when he said that, but terrified, too, like she had a school assignment due tomorrow that she didn't understand. What was she supposed to tell the world? About how pleasure would tie people together so they wouldn't hurt each other anymore? Eros, she'd said, mostly seemed to make boys think she was just a pair of breasts! Professor Marcuse had laughed openheartedly at that, like he was certain the world would be amused by what amused him. "It's like I have these magnetic rays that come out of my chest that make boys bump me when I'm putting books in my locker, you know, all very accidentally-on-purpose." Inge and Herbert had both smiled at her again, and she'd seen that her father saw them smile. She'd felt giddy.

The first time the Marcuses had visited she'd been only six years old, and her father had said then that he didn't write because his wife didn't want him to; she was afraid it might call attention to him, they'd find out about his past. He pointed to her mother. "She wouldn't want me to risk everything."

Professor Marcuse had laughed. "Maybe, Leo, you wouldn't want to either?"

Inge had turned to her husband. "These are very nice things to risk, Herbert," she'd said mockingly. "*Much* nicer than ours, I think."

They'd come with another friend from the old country, a short round Fizzyits named Hans, who squinted always, as if the dim dining room light hurt his eyes. He knocked over his glass, held it up to show everyone the chip. "Yes, these are very nice things. Such thin glasses."

He'd smiled at his own clumsiness, shyly, apologetically, which had made him look like Mole in *The Wind in the Willows*. His veal swam helplessly in a puddle of red wine.

The Fizzyits had said he'd gotten a letter from the man who knew how the universe worked. *Is it happening again?* Einstein had wondered. Then they'd begun to talk about Edgar Bergen's dummy. The Fizzyits had said he had a high-pitched singsong tone, just like the other one. "Look what's happened to Oppenheimer. What had he ever done wrong?"

"So you hide here, Leo," Herbert said to her father, "in this lovely bunker, yes, with these wonderful neighbors." His voice had gotten louder, like a teacher's. "But you see, Leo, even in very nice places the police may turn against you, not because you're Jewish this time, perhaps, but for other reasons."

"Exactly," her father had said, smiling with his lips closed. "That's why I hide."

"He's sensible, Herbert," Inge had said, doing something Beth's own mother would never have dared—laughing at her husband. Her father had smiled.

Still, Beth could see he'd been glad when his friends had left. "When I see him now," he'd said, "I long for him to go, and a day after he leaves, I long to hear what he's thinking about!" Her father had stood in the doorway for a moment more, but away from the porch light—looking to see, he told her, if anyone had followed his friends.

At six, she'd thought that he meant her father's first wife. The Marcuses had known her, the one he'd left in the police station in Vienna. They'd sat on a wooden bench against a stone wall, waiting to be interrogated. Anna Freud, his friend David Weiss had told them, had reported for interrogation the day before, and the same afternoon the American chargé d'affaires had obtained her release. His wife had said, "I'm well connected and gentile. They'll ask me about my politics, my friends will intercede, they'll let me go. But you must leave." She'd pushed him to the edge of the bench. "Now, Leo! No waiting today. No thinking some more about it, no analysis. Just go!" Beth thought her father had been very courageous to walk out of a police station without permission.

He'd smiled. "No," he'd said. "I was just following orders."

But he and his wife had miscalculated. She'd been sent to Dachau— for having married a Jew, for having been, her father had said, "so infuriatingly rich and left wing—a Bolshevik plutocrat." But her father had said that special friends of his had protected her in Dachau, which was a concentration camp then, not yet a death camp. She'd survived the cholera; and her relatives in the States had ransomed her. She wasn't impure, her father had said, just contaminated. He pursed his lips tightly, making Beth dream that contact with Jews covered gentiles with dirt, infected them with a hidden virus. "Anyway," he'd said, "they just wanted us out of the country then, not out of the world."

He'd fled to Paris, with David Weiss; and then, when the Germans came, they'd taken a train to the French Alps, the Italian zone of occupation. It was, her father had told her, a very pretty place. And then?

He wouldn't tell her, not about France, not about what had happened after. When the camps were liberated, he'd said, skipping over so much she wanted to know, his friends in the U.S. State Department had miraculously found him in a displaced persons camp, and they'd arranged for him to come here. But he and his first wife couldn't be together anymore; they reminded each other of what they'd each suffered, how they'd each changed. "Up until the transport to Auschwitz," he'd said once, when Beth was eight, "I was one person, then I wasn't that person anymore."

"Who are you now, Daddy?" she'd asked, touching the swollen knuckles. He took too many aspirin, her mother said. He'd give himself an ulcer, which was like a sore in the stomach. "Are you the person you were before the camps again?" A foolish thing to say, she saw even then, but less than what she really wanted to ask: *have I helped you, nourished you? restored you?*

"Sometimes I'm the same," he'd said, smiling with his lips tightly shut—which meant, *I said that to please you, so don't believe me or I'll never trust or respect you again.*

And now, with this boy, was he becoming *another person* again, was that why he'd been able to show him that tattoo? Was Billy Green, in his tennis shorts, part of a new life?

Well, would that be so awful? Maybe it would be a good thing for her if the little boy went to museums with her father for a while. Let's see how *he* does on the Wagner test. And perhaps she could try some of the things the other kids in her school did, like bowling or ice-skating, or just standing by the swings in the Grace Avenue park, where she'd seen the boys circling on their bicycles, the girls turning toward each other, laughing. Trivial things, she knew, ones she was embarrassed even to mention to her father. Still, it had looked like it might be fun to drink Coca-Cola mixed with aspirin like those teenagers she'd seen in a *Life* magazine at the dentist's office, and then she might even do "the Twist"; it didn't seem to have any steps really, she wouldn't need a brother or a

friend to teach her, she could just imitate what she saw on Huntley/
Brinkley. She might enjoy doing that for a while—though probably once
would be plenty. After all, how interesting could it be? You could finish
Life magazine in a few minutes. Like American culture, it had no depth
at all! Still, it could be like a vacation for her—a little time apart from
her father to let her brain rest. Then, when he saw how insipid this little
American boy was, she could return and work with him even harder
than before.

She stepped in front of the door, and shut it slowly, so her father
would see her and know she'd seen them, seen the boy seeing his arm.
Wasn't that a jealosopuss thing to do, she thought. She tried to smile—
but as soon as she shut the heavy, soundproofed door, she wanted to
open it again, run inside even and throw her arms around her father. No,
that would be far too childish. No matter how she felt about the boy, he
and her father were in the middle of a session!

Leo, glimpsing Beth's black hair and her blue jumper as the door clicked
closed, decided that she must have walked by his study on the way to the
kitchen and seen his open door. Then, with her usual consideration for
his work, she'd quietly shut it for him. But perhaps, he thought, there
was another message in that gesture, too—that she meant to shut a door
on *him* in a way, on a stage of her life. He'd felt the restiveness in her for
a while, her mind elsewhere when they went to a museum or the opera.
After all, as Herbert had said, Beth was a teenage girl, an *American*
teenage girl. She must be feeling the changes in her body—that longing
to run, to reach up, to pull down. Naturally, she feared them. He smiled,
remembering what she'd said to Herbert, about the boys bumping into
her, with an accidental purpose. Still, she was no hysteric; she would also
want what those feelings so obscurely promised, that almost nameless
thing—and not to be tied to a dead man anymore. No doubt that was
why the last few times he'd suggested a trip to the city, she'd said yes so
hesitantly.

He looked down then at his arm and the boy's finger. Why do she
and the boy make such a fetish about the numbers, he wondered, as if
they weren't written all over his body? He'd warned the boy, too, told
him what he'd always told his daughter, "you don't want to see that. It
will make you a *geheimnistrager*, like the ones who stirred the bodies."
But unlike his daughter, the boy had said, "I do, please," and then over
these last few weeks he'd asked several times more, annoying, really,
both heedless and selfish. Billy didn't care how he might hurt himself, or,
oddly, how he might hurt Dr. Jacobs; odd, because in other ways he

cared far too much about his elders' feelings. Hartman had said that during his class report, too, the weeping boy had acted implacably, as if he thought himself one of God's angels—the avenging variety, naturally, the only kind of celestial being, Hartman said, that he believed in anymore. Which meant the boy could be cruel, perhaps, and certainly neurotic, but also for some reason—a malign one, probably, and consequently reliable—he did want to know. Should Leo tell him that this tattoo made him feel he wasn't human anymore, but animal? No, instead he said, "In the camps, only the Jews got tattoos, an especial affront, a violation of Mosaic law." (Only the Jews? What about their brothers, the Gypsies? He couldn't remember.) "Always on the left forearm. You had to show your numbers to get your bowl of soup. Fewer calories in the soup than you expended each day." Should he test him? *At what point would a man of one hundred kilos become too weak to work efficiently, ready to be culled from the herd*—the kind of algebra problem he'd sometimes used to distract himself. Billy sat down again and cried—a hysterical symptom really, for what was Leo to him yet—though he nonetheless felt a little touched by it, shivered pleasantly from the cold, and watched the boy cry, a small yellow-green glob just forming under his nose. He offered him a box of Kleenex, then rolled down his sleeve, put on his suit jacket. The boy took the Kleenex, but his tongue went up anyway, to get the delicious snot ball from his upper lip. *That* was the sort of thing a child would do. Ah, perhaps he'd misjudged him?

His Beth, though, was different; so bright, so fresh in her perceptions, so observant, so beautiful. When she was three they'd sat on the floor, building with smooth wooden blocks in the West Side apartment, knowing that there's only the whirl and swirl of chance, yet his daughter's dark hair, her large eyes, made him feel for a moment that if existence could produce someone as miraculous as her—putting that finishing arch on her car-house-plane—then there must be an underlying order to it all. Ridiculous! He knew there was only chance, of course; God hadn't intended Beth and wouldn't protect her; all that stood between her and smelly gnomes, beady-eyed witches, and men with outlandish racial theories who would batter her head against rocks were his own best efforts, which wouldn't be enough, no matter how immoderately he loved her. Still, she cheered him, so proud of herself as they talked about paintings together or she recited Shakespeare, Goethe, Rilke, for him. He had to be very careful that he didn't monopolize her time, didn't become one of those survivors who feel that they've suffered so much that they're entitled to use others, their daughters, even, when no one is entitled to that.

And her beauty? He could almost hear Freud's voice—a rare appearance among his usual throng of clamoring ghosts—*why did you mention* that? *Do you want so much from your daughter because of her youth, her beauty?*

Leo thought of Freud and his daughter, Anna, his Antigone, whom the master had sealed in the cave with him during that wildly inappropriate analysis. But he would do better than Freud this time; he would surrender his far more attractive daughter to junior high dances and pimply Minotaurs at skating rinks. *Must it be?* he thought, and smiled. *Yes, it must be.* Her thinking, her desires, should be encouraged. They were normal.

While except for his taste for his own mucus, there was little that was normal, it seemed, about this pale, endlessly crying little boy. What more should he tell him about his life? He could talk about the restaurant in Talloire, perhaps, the one owned by his "benefactor," the fat man who wanted to murder him. What was his name?

Early in his career in America he had occasionally used the story about the restaurant owner; it established his reliability. But the name had been washed under long ago. Always the same problem: "let their names be blotted from history for all time" and "we must never forget."

Still, he would try to dredge it up for this patient. In a case like this, it was crucial to gratify the patient in small ways at the beginning of the treatment, to make a therapeutic bond. Later, of course, he would have to be frustrated, and *not* told things, so he could find he could separate himself from the protection of older men, give up his almost preternatural, homosexual ability to mingle himself with their purposes.

Alas, Leo couldn't tell him much else anymore. So much he'd forgotten—and not just about the camps. His mother's maiden name, for example. The name of the doctor who'd convinced her not to abort him, telling her, "He'll become a famous doctor and take care of you in your old age." His memory had been eaten away by the carbolic weariness of his stale marriage in this pretty place where he narcotized himself by strolling between rows of trees named for that comic strip character, when he should be . . . where? doing what? writing another essay about Herbert's Imaginary Erotic Internationale. *That* was surely what Marcuse had in mind, more words to glorify Herbert's own work.

Anyway, he thought, he should turn down the air conditioning for the boy's sake. But as he walked across the thick carpet a small confusion troubled his mind, made him forget where he was going. Could he really have said that other thing to the boy, said *the ones who stirred the bodies?* From the middle of the floor, he looked over at his oldest companion—the fountain pen gone, the *Ba* lost, Weiss dead—the heavy dome-shaped brass clock on his desk, a gift from Smerless. Fortunately, it said their hour was over.

A good friend, that oval brass clock, Leo thought as he walked between his double rows of dagwood trees that evening, and the only useful thing that had come from his empty hours with his first American analyst, Arnold Smerless. Leo looked about at the flowers and a stately bronze chestnut tree, his backyard truly a pleasant place to stroll when he could forget that his next-door neighbor and longest analysand, Ellen Jaffe, was undoubtedly spying on him from her kitchen window, turning his slow, anxious shuffle into a dance number performed for her special instruction.

Arnold Smerless, though, had been no analytic Astaire, had he? Not that Leo was—except in Ellen Jaffe's fantasy—but at least, he hoped, he wasn't a Consul of the Unconscious, either, whispering thunderously, "No admittance to your own mind till *I* stamp your papers!" How could *anyone* talk to a man like *that*? Smerless had wanted Leo to say that his distant manner that said *to have feelings is petty; to be godlike is to die to life* was just like Freud's, when truly Freud had been *avid*. Even in dream interpretation, he had hardly waited for Leo's associations before telling Leo what his own hat meant. Analysis with Freud had been filled with the heat of his excitement at his newest theoretical discoveries, and his almost erotic desire to enlist Leo in his cause. But he couldn't afford to tell that to Smerless, or he might not finagle him through the requirements for an American license. In any case, it felt impossible to talk frankly to a man who didn't know that really to die to life meant wasted muscle wrapped in ashen dry skin and, more, who didn't *want* to know, either. A survivor, after all, reminded these American Jews how they, too, could be humiliated beyond measure.

Leo took a small white branch from one of his trees, laid it against his cheek, and continued walking—the whole sequence no doubt puzzling Ellen Jaffe, who watched crouching on the floor by the window, her head just peeking over the edge, so Leo wouldn't see her—though she would confess the whole thing tomorrow. Well, if he saw her, she wouldn't have anything to confess, would she? and that was the real point, the erotic warm shame, telling the fantasy father that for once she'd been a very bad girl. He smiled, probably making Ellen Jaffe wonder if that was in memory of some witty remarks she'd made about Menachem Cutberg that morning, Ellen Jaffe not such a fool after all, gifted with numbers, able to understand business like a man. She

claimed—and Leo believed her—that she'd given Cutberg some pointers. "The key is," she told Leo one morning, "always use other people's
money. Borrow it to buy companies with undervalued assets, then sell
off some pieces, pay the banks back, keep the rest of the company for
your swag," Leo not understanding much, but saying—of course—
hmmm-hmmm. "Then the new companies' earnings get added to your
conglomerates and are valued at your high p/e ratio. Your stock sky-
rockets, and now you don't need the banks anymore. You can use your
shares to buy even more companies." Was she actually trying to sneak
him investment advice—*tips,* they were called, like what you would give
a waiter. He knew, too, that Ann wanted him to take them. Impossible,
of course. After all, what would Freud's ghost say?

That evening, Leo Jacobs turned the air conditioner up in his and his
wife's bedroom.

"Cold enough for you?" Ann said, intentionally using an idiom she
knew he wouldn't understand, a pointless irony. Her husband wanted
cold because he dreaded his own sweat—his dirt, his smell—but she
couldn't help feeling peeved that it meant *she* was forced to wear flannel
even in the spring. And, in fact, it was *never* cold enough for him now,
though when they'd first met, she remembered, it was heat he'd craved,
heavy wool coats from Brooks Brothers; thick sweaters from Ireland;
her embrace. Now he turned up the air conditioner in the house but
wore wool suits for his walks, as if that costume made his body disappear. But the wool also made him sweat, so the suit ended up reminding
him that he still carried one of those awful things with him everywhere.
He'd have to scrub and shower for forty minutes, making his flesh red
and raw, and all the more present to him. How he made the world impossible for himself! Well, that was his own choice. But he didn't even
notice her heavy nightgown, didn't see that he made the world difficult
for her, too. "I've been speaking to one of my patients," Leo said, as he
got back into bed.

"Yes? Investment advice, I hope?" She laughed, though she hadn't
been joking. The morning's *Times* had said that Cutberg stock had sky-
rocketed, and everyone at the Kennilworth pool knew that Menachem
Cutberg, the man who'd invented the conglomerate, was the Jaffes' best
friend, which meant the Jaffes must be filthy rich now, too, so why not
Leo's family? Wouldn't Mrs. Jaffe *want* to tell her beloved doctor what
stocks to buy, make him "comfortable" too—the sort of vulgar word
that family might use. Actually, the money didn't matter to Ann. Let the
Jaffes grub—in truth the only thing Ellen Jaffe had that Ann envied was

height. As for money, she and Leo had enough, and she would inherit more from her family. She just wanted Leo to succeed in a way that the whole world, and her parents in particular, couldn't deny, prove to them that he wasn't "damaged," that Ann hadn't made a mistake in marrying him. But Ann knew Leo would *never* get investment advice from a patient, *it was against the rules.* Not the kosher laws or the tax laws; they broke those just like everyone else. But Freud's rules—the only ones that mattered.

"No, not about stocks," he said. "About the camps."

Ann was silent for a moment. It was a delicate matter. "Good," she said, lifting herself on an elbow, stroking his cheek. At least tonight he didn't move away, as if even her fingers on his cheek might mean the unthinkable: that she wanted to make love to him. That *was* what they meant, but in this case his paradoxical rule was: he couldn't make love to her unless she wanted him—but it made him too uneasy to know she wanted him, so then he couldn't make love. "I often think about those long silent hours of yours. You know, when we're at a dinner party, I mean even for half an hour, and I don't say something, I feel like I've disappeared." She smiled. "I don't see how you do it." He turned and stared at her, and she felt foolish, his silence—just like her own analyst's—making her say stupid things. Perhaps that was the point, for both of them: Pin the Tail on the Patient. Or the wife.

And as with her analyst, there was always that little delay before he replied to her, so he could analyze his response; adjust the volume, not tell her how much he disdained her, hated himself, loathed his life—though he told her, of course, with each second he delayed his response.

But finally, this time, he spoke! "He's very young," he said, "the patient, but very curious."

"Is he?" Was he saying that he finally wanted to talk to her, really? If only *she* were more curious?

"I think it's crucial to tell him a little. To form a bond. Nothing too brutal, of course."

"Good," she said again. "You need to talk about it."

"Not for me," he said. "For him."

"Of course."

He smiled his infuriating non-smile, the fatal sign that meant, *You've gone too far, noticed too much, disobeyed my double injunction: you must give me special treatment; and you must not notice that I require it.*

She adjusted her foam pillows. An adept analysand herself, she observed her own shiver of jealousy toward this unnamed patient, maybe the one she'd seen here, the Greens' little boy. Well, Beth didn't seem to help him anymore, maybe it would be good for him to speak about himself even the little that analysis allowed, and even to a boy. Strange, that when he was still closest to the camps, he'd been most filled with appetite and interest, seemed at peace with sweat and dirt and bodies, interested in everything—especially her and her body, her sweat, her menstrual flow, the liquid of her cunt, a word she'd actually had to teach him, maybe because it was American, or because it was so vulgar. And she'd been proud of that, her strange boldness with a man far more cultured and experienced than any she'd met before; and she was proud, too, of the pleasure she'd given him, dreamt it was like medicine for him to make love to her, that she made his body and his spirit stronger. Of course she'd wanted to know everything that had happened to him, hadn't she, all he'd suffered? He'd told her about his many romances, but he hadn't wanted to tell her about *that,* afraid to "contaminate her." She hadn't known how to break that spell, maybe hadn't really tried, a young girl to him then, America, hope, a new start. And *citizenship,* her mother had added, worried that a survivor would be damaged goods, a world of problems; "unstable," her father said; and "not a reliable means of support," her mother added, "given what he's gone through." Which all had made Ann want to nurse him the more. Well, they hadn't—bless them—seen her role in life as taking care of others, or not in that way, or not others who weren't *them.* "But you're so much more beautiful than him," her mother had said, seeing only a short man with a gnomish face, not knowing how sympathetic he could be, how he could join his heart to hers.

Anyway, she'd understood before her mother said it that Leo wanted to stay in America, that a green card might be part of her attraction. But so what? She'd thought of it as her dowry, something to make up for the vast imbalance in their experience, their wisdom. He'd already had an article written about him in the *New York Times,* "The Student of Freud's Who Survived Auschwitz by Studying It," though he'd seemed mostly embarrassed by that kind of talk; modest, she'd thought, loving him the more for that. And then she'd become pregnant—less jelly in the diaphragm, or perhaps—she honestly couldn't remember—no diaphragm at all. Leo had seemed both pleased and bewildered, surprised, he'd said, that he could generate new life. So mixed with her shame at her underhandedness, she'd also felt proud of what she'd done, proving him wrong—in that way at least. They'd married—which was what she'd intended, she supposed, and really what he must have wanted, too, for love, she hoped, as well as for citizenship. And none of it so much as a plan, or a thought on anyone's part; really more just like one thing following another.

Then, soon after Beth was born, it had suddenly become too late to try to tease him into speech about the past. First she'd had to look away from him; she had to keep their child alive, didn't she, and no man appreciated how much labor was involved in that, not even a survivor; it seemed such a common miracle. She'd worried he might wander off, find another woman, having had a reputation in Vienna, Inge Marcuse had told her once, as a Romeo. "Women of all heights," she'd said, smiling fondly, "found him very attractive. We heard about him as far away as *Berlin.*"

"When he was married, too?" Ann had asked, and Inge had nodded, lifting her brows, sorry she'd begun this probably.

But *that* hadn't been Ann's problem; instead he'd grown depressed when she looked away toward her child, withdrawn to a place inside himself where she was forbidden to follow—even if she'd had the energy. She'd prayed something might help him, not an affair, precisely, but . . . what? Then, her prayer had been answered: the other woman turned out to be their daughter, Leo always having time for her; well, not to change her diapers perhaps, but once she'd brought Beth from animal to human, he'd read to her, taught her to read; taught her to add; taught her French, Italian, the fundamentals of psychoanalysis, taught her, taught her, taught her. But Beth seemed to like it, and Ann had been grateful. Ann knew all mothers thought their children beautiful, but the world concurred this time, terrifying her the way strangers would stop, other mothers exclaim almost against their will. The beautiful child with those large, supernaturally bright hazel-green eyes had drawn her husband back into life, and she'd smiled to see the two of them sitting on the floor in the evenings, playing happily with blocks, her daughter in a T-shirt and big-girl pants, her husband wearing a three-piece suit, a perfect picture for the next *Times* article, "The Analyst Educated by Suffering," about the doctor who made his patients feel their quotidian neuroses were as important as what had happened to him in the camps. She'd loved that piece. He didn't have to be rich, being famous was even better, something her father didn't have for all his money; something that certainly proved Leo wasn't damaged goods! But the *Times* profile had made Leo deeply uneasy, so there'd been no pictures, perfect or otherwise. He hadn't even spoken to the reporter himself, from modesty, yes, a sense of unworthiness that only added to the writer's admiration; but something more than that, she knew by then: he was *hiding.* She'd married a Communist, a disaffected *former* Party member, but a Red nonetheless. Still, the *Times* article had told the truth: she'd met patients of his, ones powerfully moved by his concern, illuminated by his insight, helped by his surprising, educated heart. So why couldn't he spare some compassion for himself, help her reach to him through the sadness that was already again like a heavy water filling the house, and only his daughter seemingly able to lift him above the waves for a moment, like—who was it? That comic book thing? Supergirl! Well, good, she'd thought, when Beth had been a toddler; it was hard enough caring for a child without having to turn her tired soul to saving her husband, too, a man who clawed at her face when she tried, who maybe truly wanted to drown. And the attention was bound to be good for Beth, wasn't it? She'd grow up a confident girl, not undercut or ignored by her father the way Ann had been. Beth more utterly, eerily beautiful now, too, even than she'd been as a child.

And by the time Ann had turned into a—what did he call it?—a jealosopuss about her own daughter, it was far too late, her husband hiding in his office from her every night, but all too eager to take Beth to see dinosaurs or paintings or operas, her daughter lost to her, too, now, disdainful, contemptuous. Innocent Ann, her daughter called her! How *dare* she say that!

Jealous, hurt, but what could she do about it? She couldn't come between them, Leo was too wily, too formidable an opponent. He'd analyze her motives for saying "such blind, hurtful things," enough truth to his words always that she knew she wouldn't be able to see to the bottom of them, would feel bewildered, lost inside her own internal devastation. Worse: he would act like she'd added to his pain, driven him closer to the never mentioned always-present possibility, his suicide. So it was far too late now, the silence between them had gone on too long, the distance between them had grown too wide, the lovemaking too rare, too hurried; and even something so simple as touching his cheek led to endless misunderstanding.

She looked at his sad, nearly blind eyes, still wearing their thick spectacles, just staring up toward the ceiling now, and she lost hope. *Nothing will help him anymore,* she thought. Not her, not his tall, beautiful daughter with her amazingly straight nose, her shining green eyes. (Thank God she needed glasses, or Ann would have been sure she was a changeling.) And surely not this little boy, either. She remembered a joke her mother had made to her at her father's funeral. "We got a Jewish divorce. Married for forty years, then he died of cancer." *Yes,* she thought, rolling over to face the wall. *I can't leave Freud's patient, the*

Angel of Auschwitz, the Man Who Survived the Death Camps by Study-
ing Them. So I have a Jewish divorce to look forward to instead. And
then she smiled—in a tight-lipped way.

The next day, Leo looked at Billy in the big leather chair, his upper lip
protruding, thumb-lust having once been the reliable alternative to the
yearned-for mother. Billy tucked his legs up under him tightly, and Leo
could feel the agitation rising in his bony frame. Perhaps today Leo
should fill the silence, tell him a little more about the Savoie and about
Clerc. Clerc! That was the name! Well, there were no bodies to be stirred
in this part of the story. And, really, what harm could Leo's words do to
Jews who amused themselves by falling down mountains with barrel
staves strapped to their feet, to Jews who went sailing?

Such rich tourists had made up Clerc's usual clientele. "Clerc was a
collaborator, his son a leader in the Milice. Yet when he heard there was
a student of Freud's in Talloire, a master of 'the Jewish science,' he
sought me out for therapy."

"Why would you help *him?*" Billy asked.

There; the story had worked again. "Well, for the food, first of all.
We had no ration books, and Clerc gave me two meals a week at his
restaurant, better than any I'd ever eaten in my life. And I did it, too,
because he'd asked." The patient could see that if Leo would help a
monster simply because he'd requested it—which was more or less
true—then he could be certain the doctor would always see him.

"What did he want you to help him with?"

Leo smiled. He knew the boy wasn't curious about *that,* really; he
wanted a very special reassurance. "You know I can't tell you."

"But he was an anti-Semite. I mean, you said he wanted to kill you."

"Yes. But he was also my patient. And I would never talk to anyone,
ever, about what any patient told me."

Leo was sure he detected the boy's small inward smile.

Actually, Leo had tried to help Clerc—but only by making a delicate
partial adjustment to the psychic mechanism—not so much that he
could infallibly fuck again. He wanted Clerc to need him; he wanted the
wonderful meals to continue.

"Clerc wanted everything *just so* at those meals," Leo said, the next
week, offering another morsel of his life in return for Billy's dreams,
Billy's fantasies. "He thought that if everything about the dinner was
sumptuous, then there'd be no pound of flesh—that's how he put it—for
me to exact later." He could almost hear the man's deep, reedy voice

again, his big hands crossed over his strumpot of a belly, the fingers drumming, making the voice quaver comically. "Jews," Clerc had said, "don't appreciate good cooking. Jews hate the physical world because they're all as blind and ugly as you."

Billy then, as Leo had hoped he would, admitted he really thought he was maybe an ugly thing himself, probably a little deaf, weak and pale. "Nothing," he said oddly, "to write home about." He lifted up his tennis shirt. "Look, you can see my ribs." So he was afraid to take showers with the other boys in gym class. "They'll see how dirty I am."

"Dirty?" Why had he said *that*? Could he be that preternaturally attuned to others?

"Well, I guess I meant how skinny," Billy corrected himself.

Afterward Leo filled his notebook with material from this session—a good feeling. Still, he thought he'd better take the train today. He didn't trust himself driving, that material having come just a little too close to his friend, David Weiss, and his silly feathered hat. The two of them, on the days that Clerc didn't provide Leo's lunch, had walked to local farms, Weiss carrying a string basket they hoped to fill with things from the black market. But Weiss had felt too sorry for the farmers, had been a dreadful negotiator who would trade a pair of good leather shoes, say, for a few cucumbers. Openhearted, kind, David had been Leo's only real friend in Vienna, where the other analysts had directed a ferocious jealousy toward him because of his rich gentile wife, and the small fame of his two essays on the new "Internationale" of sex: "Uncivilized Sexual Morality" and "The Psychology of the Orgy." And most of all, of course, because of his relationship with Freud.

The conductor shouted Douglaston, startling Leo. When the train jolted forward again, he put his head back, tried to return to Vienna, where David listened intently to Leo's theories, the candidates meeting together in their cramped imitation of the senior analysts' sessions. And Weiss had given him that same sly smile when after those meetings they drank burnt coffee together in a working-class place and Leo called Freud an unwitting tool of the bourgeoisie. Everyone saw that Freud had chosen to grapple Leo to his breast, to give him the best milk, and Weiss knew Leo's cavilling to be the shrillness of the child who resists an overwhelming, almost castrating, attachment to his father. But dear Weiss, he was always too kind to say such things. He talked instead about Leo's other interest, the Leninist party, which was, the genial Weiss said, too exclusive a club for him even to consider joining.

"Broadway!" a voice shouted from another world, but Leo let the word, with its overtone of vulgar style, remind him of how foolish Weiss had looked in the ridiculous feathered Tyrolean hat he'd worn in Talloire as they trudged from farm to farm. "Do you really think everyone fucking each other will bring world peace?" he'd asked. "Or was your orgy essay meant to *épater les bourgeois*? By which I mean," he added, eyebrows raised, "*pour épater* cher Doctor Freud."

"*Du même,*" Leo had replied, smiling.

"Oh, God, not the toothless smile," Weiss had said, throwing up his hands in mock horror. "Tick, you switch it on. Tock, it's switched off." Standing at attention, Weiss had done his own mechano-version. "Do you think I can be a good analyst without that smile? I think it's beyond me."

The train arrived at Penn Station. Leo thought for a moment about leaving his eyes closed, just touching his fingers on the suit jacket of the man ahead of him, let him lead him off the train. What nonsense! He opened his eyes, walked off the car onto the dark, dirty, fuming platform. The subway, he thought, would be unbearably crowded. Maybe a cab would be appropriate today? To celebrate the good session he'd had with Billy Green that morning.

"Couldn't you have gone over the mountains, to Switzerland?" Billy asked later that July. A good sign—his concern for Leo was so strong now that he didn't notice the implied criticism in his question.

"Yes," Leo said, smiling. "Weiss and I considered it. But the Swiss had promised the Nazis they wouldn't take us. The Swiss made exceptions, of course, but only for the rich."

Then that August, as a reward for Billy's courage in going swimming with his new friends at the Kennilworth pool, Dr. Jacobs told him more of the story. "Soon Vichy," he said, "decreed that there'd be no more exit visas for Jews *and* no more residence permits for foreigners."

"It can't sit, it can't stand, it can't lie down," Weiss had said to him—the Yiddish proverb that meant *it doesn't exist*. Or won't.

"Before, they just wanted us gone from here," David had said. "Now, no residence permits and no exit visas: they want us nowhere." Weiss had let his hand flutter and rise. Could it really have been like smoke going up a chimney?

Billy said, "What did you do?"

"Well, the town's baker rented us a tiny place no one else wanted. There was only a sink to wash in."

"Not having a bath," Weiss had said. "How will you stand it, you're so . . ."

Weiss had paused. Leo had smiled, wanly. "Fastidious?" admitting to a certain overscrupulousness about hygiene, being a good sport, keeping the peace.

"Anal, Leo, for God's sake. You're the very type Abraham wrote about, always looking down your nose at all of us, like you're smelling someone's shit."

Close quarters. Great fear. He and Weiss were getting on each other's nerves. "Hygiene," Leo said, probably too precisely, "is the difference between us and the animals."

"Beware the man who insists there's a great lot of difference between us and the animals!" Weiss replied. Still, the man couldn't help laughing. "And you, especially! I thought you wanted us to rut like the beasts of the field."

"No, David." Leo smiled. "Animals only enjoy coitus in season." Weiss had a jolly way about him that made their murderous desires toward each other pass quickly—before Auschwitz, anyway. "Human sexuality should exfoliate widely, permeate all our activities. That's another difference between us and the animals."

"As is priggishness," Weiss said. "So few pigs are allrightnicks." Meaning Leo, of course.

Well, no need to tell Billy Green any of that.

"The baker was a good neighbor," he said instead. "He sold us bread at a fair price, even though we foreign Jews had no ration books. It was wrong, the baker said, to profit from others' misery." Leo paused, trying to remember the taste of the hot bread. "People like that are rare," he said, surprised at his little greeting card.

So in Talloire, Leo had his good neighbors—his good enough neighbors, Winnicott would have said—his familiar guardian mountains behind him still, and lovely dagwoods.

"Dogwoods," Billy said.

"Not like the comic strip? Like the canine?"

"Yes."

It was a hot August afternoon. Leo, pleased with himself, walked over to turn the air conditioning up. For three months now, he'd doled out his tale of Talloire so the boy would trust him with *his* secrets, his maimed sense of self, and, most of all, his rage about that fantasized maiming. And already, he thought, his patient *was* changing, for when they'd begun their work, Leo sitting beside Billy's bed, the boy would never have offered even that mild botanical correction. Then he'd expressed his aggression only in pictures (and he did seem to have a great gift there, even if he used it, so far, in a vulgar American way), afraid that if he showed his anger directly he'd kill his parents with the magical force of a twelve-year-old's volcanic fury—as if it were one of those ridiculous "superpowers" the boy's father peddled! He smiled at Billy, still curled like a cat in the leather chair. "Our hour's up."

When he left Dr. Jacobs' house that day the white tips of the pink dog-wood leaves were snow to Billy; Great Neck was surrounded by mountains; and the Long Island Sound, where Billy and Laura and Arthur would go sailing again, had become Lake Annecy.

Then, at the end of a row of trees, he was surprised by Beth Jacobs in shorts and a white blouse.

"Do you think I could go with you guys today?"

Beth, a head taller than Billy, had bright, commanding green-brown eyes and strong-looking legs. She had to know—he couldn't wait to tell her—that she could have absolutely anything from him that she liked. He wanted to put his arm around her and lead her to the Kennilworth docks. He wanted to rest his head on her breasts. He wanted to tell her how truly beautiful she was and give her a drawing of ink mixed with his own blood that would make her down-turned lips smile at him. "Yes," he finally managed to stammer out. "That would be great."

Beth walked uneasily under the leafy trees toward the dock. Beth had passed tests that these children couldn't imagine and knew secrets about the world's horror that they couldn't even suspect, but as she watched Billy run on ahead, his sweater tied around his waist, that all suddenly seemed less important than the words to that silly Twist song! Laura Jaffe had probably already done that dance a lot. She probably already had a real boyfriend. Would it be okay, Beth wondered, to wear Bermuda shorts on her boat?

Laura had her back to them as they walked down the dock toward her. She dropped bread crumbs in the water, her arms and legs tan. She wore red Bermuda shorts herself—thank Gott—and smiled when she turned around. A small-featured face, like an amiable cat, Beth thought, but she still made Beth's tongue tie up, so she ended up sounding like a fool, saying, "I request if I could come on your boat." My God, Laura might think English wasn't her native language. Which *was* her problem in a way, wasn't it? If she'd never done the Twist, then it was like America still wasn't her native country.

But what Laura Jaffe heard was that Beth Jacobs was, as she'd always suspected, someone from a grander place and a better time, probably an aristocrat. Beth only a year older maybe, but two grades ahead already, with beautiful breasts and lovely even teeth, too, so she didn't have to wear the hideous braces that made Laura's gums ache, and Billy's, and practically everyone else's she knew. Beth wore dark green glasses that made her look sophisticated, like Laura's brother, Frank, and she probably even already had *real* boyfriends—not just little pals. But best of all, Beth was Dr. Jacobs' daughter, the man whom Laura's mother quoted every night at dinner to make Laura understand why she'd been mean to her mother. She even used Dr. Jacobs to criticize Laura's father, acting really kind of contemptuously toward him, though her father was, Laura reminded herself, a truly powerful man—more powerful, anywhere but in his own dining room, than Beth's dad was. For God's sake, he was a friend of John Kennedy and Hubert Humphrey, and now even of Martin Luther King Jr.—the man who her father said was "the true moral leader of this nation." Still, that didn't help Laura feel better—or not nearly so much as that Dr. Jacobs' very own daughter requested to come on her boat.

On the *Ellen and Jackie II,* Billy told the others the fragment of Beth's father's story that he'd heard that morning, maybe mixed with a few things he'd read, and probably some things he'd added, Beth thought, from his father's comic books, which were, her father had told her, an even more pernicious kind of American schlock than television, if such a thing were possible, a mishmash of homoerotic fantasies and hyperbolic defenses that made immature American teenage boys think that their acne had magical powers, and that men in red-white-and-blue tights could solve all the world's problems. Which meant that Nathan Green's son couldn't possibly understand what he was talking about! Beth stared at Laura and Arthur Kaplan's intent, sunburned faces. She'd heard about Billy's famous sixth grade class report. Apparently, Arthur and Laura couldn't get enough of Billy's horror stories! Why had she ever let this business with Billy get started, why had she even hesitated when her father had suggested going to the Met again? Still, she felt glad he hadn't asked her to memorize more passages of Shakespeare or Rilke for a while. She was mostly enjoying her "vacation." Just a little more time like this, and she'd be ready to have him send this boy home. For now, she turned her face up to the sky, so she wouldn't have to look at Billy Green.

Still, she had to admit Billy didn't do the thing she hated most in the world, making his voice all quavery, sensitive, and fake-sad when he talked about the Holocaust. She could see, too, the way his words tugged at the others, pulled their bodies toward him; and when he said "ration book" or "residence permit" he even worked his grade school trick on *her,* made her feel a cloud had run across the sun. Arthur Kaplan pushed his arms against his sides to warm himself. Laura, working the sails, said, "What if we couldn't live in America anymore? What if we didn't have any place where we could land?"

It was a sunny day with a good wind. Beth and Arthur helped Laura raise more sheet. Beth took her life preserver off, and Billy took his off, too, probably to show them all that he wasn't a sissy. Then Arthur Kaplan had to demonstrate that he was just as heedless, though without his Mae West he was clearly terrified by the boat's slightest motion. Why had he done it? Beth wondered. *Was it because of her?*

Something about this boat being in the middle of the ocean made Beth giddy. She did a little experiment, just turning her body away from Billy and Arthur—a kind of slow-motion Twist, perhaps. Bingo! Both boys' heads moved toward her chest, as if strong cords went from her body to theirs and she could tug them about just by throwing her weight from shoulder to shoulder. In the huge dark halls of Great Neck North, she never felt like she could control what boys did, the way they pretended to fall against her, or actually brushed her chest with their hands when they went by. Now she was pretty sure her leaning back made the little boy who'd stolen her father's secrets into her puppet.

She closed her eyes, turned her face back up to the warmth. Anyway, her father probably hadn't said anything really valuable to him, her father seeing that an American like Billy Green, the son of a comic book maker, couldn't possibly understand about dialectics, or that paint was like poop, and all the things they'd have to do to help Eros vanquish the kingdom of Death. *Eros?* She wondered what the two boys were doing now? Were they still staring at her chest? She flushed, ashamed of her ridiculous actions, pretending to pull them about. She turned toward the ocean, to hide her face.

And opened her eyes to the spangled light. The boat approached the dock at mostly gentile Sands Point, the place from which Daisy's green light had beckoned to Gatsby. They'd dock and get clams *frites* and the insipid *vin de pays* the little boy loved so much, Coca-Cola.

"Soon," Leo told Billy, who would repeat it all on the boat that September, "the SS checked papers on trains, arrested Jews in Lyon and Marseilles"—Leo offering this to fix a blockage in Billy's flow, the boy having seen him look toward the low window as he'd told about a soccer game. He needed to show Billy that he trusted him with his life; or his life story, anyway. "And when the Nazis had begun to take

Frenchmen for work gangs in Germany, even the baker wanted us gone. He was angry that the Jews had been spared the 'real deportations.'

"Mussolini fell," he went on, "and the Italians withdrew toward Nice. Weiss decided to march with them," Leo not trying, really, to persuade him to stay, suspicious of his own lassitude, unsure if it was dangerous to follow the Italians or if he just felt lulled by the sight of his small wooden table; his precious bird-nosed figurine Freud had given him, an Egyptian "Ba"—"a symbol," Weiss had said, "of Freud's soul begging for entry into your body"—his marbled blue Waterman pen; and the notebooks for a memoir of his greatest distinction, that his intricate sick mind had been worth Sigmund Freud's ministrations.

But in August 1944 the Germans had come to Annecy.

There was a long silence. "What are you thinking?" Dr. Jacobs asked.

Billy knew the rules. Dr. Jacobs trusted him with the story of the terrible things that had happened to him, so he had to trust Dr. Jacobs and tell him whatever he was thinking, without censoring it. "I thought that maybe you wouldn't be arrested. The baker's boy might warn you that the Germans are coming. He could take you back up to a cave where you could hide. Then, you know, each day he would sneak past the troops, carrying bread for you. Then maybe one day they capture him . . ." He was silent.

"Yes. What would happen if they captured him?"

"They'd maybe strip him naked. They'd, you know, they'd put him in a booth, and put headphones on him, and play tones that make him deaf. It would be *really* awful. Blood might seep from his ears and mouth. But he wouldn't tell anyone where he'd hidden you. You could be saved."

Leo immediately noted the perverse sexual nature of the comic book fantasy: feeling pain was meant both to protect the father and to be a sexual relationship with him. Billy must learn that self-sacrifice is not the way to merge with the father, gain the father's protection. Unanalyzed, this fantasy could have severe consequences for Billy's later development and produce a classic sadomasochist, a person who loved the father's prohibitions too much—a pure culture of the death instinct.

So to advance Billy's therapy, Dr. Jacobs reminded him that no, in truth, he hadn't been saved from the deportation. "They took foreign Jews from hospitals," he said, "and they dragged the old Jews who'd been too weak for the trek to Nice from the Foreigners' Reception Center." They'd also arrested the one younger Jew still in town, even though he'd known Freud, threw him with the others on the tile floor of the town hall with the old people and the sick. The Milice, in their black uniforms with silver fishhook crosses on the lapel, had stood by the door, rifles pointed down at them. He didn't tell Billy, though, how Clerc had come to see his doctor off. "You should remember, Jew," he'd whispered, "nothing is more infuriating to a man than being fully understood!" Clerc had flicked off Leo's glasses and crushed them with his fat foot. "And your fucking Jewish magic is worthless," he'd said. "I'm still embarrassed." Without his glasses, Leo's terror had been complete.

He did tell Billy, though, that he'd been deported from Drancy, on September 12. "It's odd, isn't it? It's the same date as today." There'd been eighty Jews with him, in a sealed cattle car filled with stinking straw and an iron pail for a toilet. He felt humiliated telling that to the boy, but also a little lighter. He added, "We were, you see, menschen no more. Not to our captors. And soon, worst of all, not always to ourselves." Then he heard Weiss's ghost say, "Leo, dear, the Unspeakable doesn't become more speakable just because a boy wants you to talk about it."

Leo didn't say anything more. The two of them—and Weiss, of course—sat silently until the hour ended.

That fall Arthur and Beth walked to Hebrew school silently, listening to Billy Green tell more of Dr. Jacobs' story. Laura strolled just ahead in a carefully chosen pleated blue skirt. She'd watched the way Beth had made Arthur and Billy sway toward her whenever she wanted, knew she'd never have breasts like that, Laura bound to end up looking like her own mom, long and flat. But now her body had lengthened wonderfully; she had "dancer's legs," like her mother's. She took extra-long strides. Then she felt how ridiculous that must make her look. Probably they weren't admiring her. Maybe they were even laughing at her. She *really* didn't want them to say anything to her about her legs anymore or about anything else, didn't want them even to notice her; she just wanted to disappear. She wished she'd at least worn tights!

Then that winter they went ice-skating together, and Laura wore costumes that had tights for her legs with a snowflake pattern that showed her skin but only in places, which was okay, and besides she was always moving around, which felt good, too, like they were all seeing her; then not. And the next spring they played tennis—which meant tennis skirts—on the fenced-in red clay court in Laura's backyard, sheltered by tall shade trees. In May they started to sail again on Laura's boat, renamed *Freedom* since her father had become an advisor to Martin Luther King.

And sometimes now Jesse Kelman, the son of Arthur's dad's partner in Kel-Kap, joined them, drawn by Laura's legs and what—in algebra class anyway—seemed to him like her *knowingness,* Jesse thinking he definitely needed someone who *knew* what they could do together, or he might fumble for hours with the girl's bra, probably come in his pants, or really and truly, like the asshole in one of Johnny Ryan's jokes, just sit there, staring, not knowing where to put it.

Usually, though, Jesse felt smarter than most other kids, like they needed his help. That's why this girl thing blindsided him. Not that the other kids were slow, but they were *heedless,* like they might play in traffic. Which was exactly what his older brother had done. An accident—except that the driver swore Morris had seen him coming, had even walked toward the car instead of stepping aside, like he was daring him, the man desolate that he couldn't stop in time. Jesse knew that *I dare you* look, Morris holding the cat off the roof, one eyebrow cocked questioningly, Jesse wailing. *It's your choice. Catch it if you want. I don't care.* Of course, Jesse had been only five then, the memory uncertain. It might not have happened. Or it might have been his snuggly cat, Nesselrode. Morris *had* been smirking, though, that way he had of raising one eyebrow like he knew a secret. Which was what? That he was willing to kill the cat? That he wouldn't mind dying himself? Jesse had tried to tell his parents how crazy Morris had become—not to tattle, but like they should help his brother. Instead, his father had grounded Morris.

"Or you might worry your brother was sad because your parents loved you more than him?" Dr. Jacobs had said to him, the once he'd seen him. *Of course they loved me more,* Jesse had thought. Morris had been a hateful person, liar, devourer of ice cream not his, torturer of pets or snugglies. Who wouldn't love Jesse more? Sometimes Jesse tried to push one brow upward the way his brother had, but otherwise he didn't think about Morris much anymore, his brother become a cloud of half-remembered, half-understood shouts and blows. And he would never talk about Morris or the visit to the shrink to anyone.

Except, maybe Laura. She was different. Laura was *the best,* he thought, not quite knowing what he meant by that, but sure it had to be absolutely true. Looking at her long legs in her Bermuda shorts, the socks leading to her thighs and the things you couldn't see in *Playboy* gave him a hard-on that made his bathing suit stick out. He hoped she couldn't see, unless that would be a good thing, make her like him? But how could it?

And then in July, Jeffrey Schell, in pristine white docksiders, wheedled his way on board, thinking that a place where boys and girls—misfits, for sure—talked together about stuff like hiding out from the Nazis and death camps might be comfortable for him, the right place, or the right Wrong Place, for Jeffrey with his Bad Acne, and More Height Than He Knew What to Do With, like his father said, the rare times his father bothered to notice him. Plus, of course, that Other Thing, this Awkward Stage he was going through where he wanted to touch and be touched by boys, an urge that got stronger now with each inch he grew, maybe like a fever coming to a head. How much bigger did he have to get, he wondered, before he outgrew it?

Though at the same time—now that he'd begun to meet friends of his parents, modern artists who made him feel that maybe he wasn't Awkward, wasn't odd, wasn't *queer*—he wasn't sure anymore he even wanted to outgrow this stage. If he did outgrow it, he wouldn't be so much like Andy Warhol anymore, the man who'd thought of silk-screening pictures of Coke bottles; which made him, Gaston Weil, the dealer's assistant, said, a Genius, not the screening, really—though the color palette, the painterly qualities, were *far more interesting* than people realized *yet*—but just the thinking of it; Andy thinking really to *think* about what people thought about all the time without thinking. Warhol himself hadn't said much to Jeffrey yet, but last week he'd looked at him as Jeffrey got out of the swimming pool in their backyard, looking in a *certain way,* not at his body, or anything, but into his eyes, Andy's head turned to the side. His mother had said that Andy always looked like Death Warmed Over in his black turtleneck and jeans and piss-stained shoes that looked like he kept them in a cat box. But he'd looked great to Jeffrey, Andy giving him a shy, amused, kindly smile as the water dripped from Jeffrey's baggy tan trunks onto his big feet. They hadn't said anything, maybe, but *a lot* had been communicated just by how long they had looked at each other without either pair of eyes glancing off. A few seconds, really, but that was a *long* deep contact for eyes, wasn't it? It made Jeffrey feel altogether okay, like Andy Warhol knew about him, and what he knew was definitely All Right with the artist, maybe more than all right, because it meant that long looks could Say a Lot to Jeffrey, without anything actually being said; so he and Andy had like almost telepathic powers to communicate with each other that *ordinary* people didn't have, and that were connected with who they were, you know, and that they liked boys. It was almost sad, really, that that stage would be over for Jeffrey soon. Would Andy know it had ended and not like him anymore then? But he was scared to like ASK ANDY that, putting it in CAPITALS in his mind because that made it Bigger, which was how it felt to him, but funnier, too, so it was less painful, less *serioso.*

Anyway, Andy's look had given him the courage to get on this boat with everyone, though his knowing artists like Andy, more even than his Altitude, his Acne, or his Urges, made Jeffrey odd to his new friends. And when Jeffrey's father paid two thousand dollars for a "picture" of a bull's-eye—which had got the whole family on the cover of the *New*

York Times Magazine—he'd become positively weird to them, like sur-rounded by a Gardol shield. The *Times* had opined that the "painting" wasn't precisely a painting, because—be sensible!—what made it differ-ent from any other target? Gaston had thrown the magazine down on their breakfast table, right on top of the slices of nova, and in front of the THING that Jeffrey called Dad/NotDad. (It had been Gaston's idea to place the papier-mâché Schells around a "real" breakfast table along with their fleshy counterparts, and the *Times* photographer had *loved* that idea.) "Jesus," he'd said, "couldn't they see *that* was precisely what you were actually supposed to think about!" *If* they could *think* they might *learn* something about Art and about Reality; and the grammar—*grah-mah* was how Gaston said it—of how the two fit together.

Or didn't, maybe. Like Jeffrey and girls? Or these other kids and Jef-frey, who still turned out to be oddest-man-out even here with this crew of smart misfits, because the target and the *Times* had made him a Celebrity, and made his parents (all their parents probably said) into idiots, worse than the Sculls, their *kopfs* emptier than their papier-mâché kounterparts.

"Look, the target," Jeffrey told the other kids on the boat, "it was, you know, like just thrown in with some other things we were buying."

Though after a few more weeks with Gaston, Andy, and the other artists who came to see his parents, he could almost admit to himself that he'd been lying to his friends. Since he was three, and he and Johnny Ryan had pulled down their pants together, he'd loved boys; and he was almost as fascinated by the Target/Not a Target as he was by boys' bodies. And his friends should be, too. Not that the artists came on to him or anything (and he certainly wouldn't have wanted it, would he?—except for Gaston, maybe), but the artists talked in a way that made him feel more and more that both things (sex and targets) were All Right, and also maybe mixed up with each other, which made them both even better than All Right. So if you liked the paintings *and* liked men too, then you definitely knew something that these kids didn't know about themselves yet, something about the way things like bodies *really* fit together and why; something about the lies people—like most boys—made up about themselves, too; the secrets hidden since the beginning of time; the grah-mah of the world.

So the artists said. And they knew Jeffrey had been standing near their pool chairs listening, he was pretty sure, like they were saying it to help him.

"Anyway, I don't know why everyone makes such a big deal about it," he said to the sprawling kids on the boat, meaning the painting, not penises. "It's just a target. I mean, a painting of a target." He smiled, and looked out Meaningfully over the ocean. Let them think about *that* for a while!

Laura, Jesse, Billy, and Beth and their parents all saw the painted Cokes and targets that summer when Jeffrey's parents had *tout* Great Neck over for a fund-raising party for a civil rights organization, the Student Non-Violent Action Program, the colorful paintings covering the walls of the ranch house, making the place seem grand and important, Jesse Kelman thought, like the stairs at Radio City Music Hall, and making his own long-necked mother look especially glamorous, her black hair pulled back on her head and a single strand of pearls around her neck. He saw his father lean toward her, probably saying something to her about how, for Christ's sake, these weren't like the old masters. Even a child could do this!

Billy, naturally, stared at a canvas that looked like a piece of a comic where a pretty woman threw a glass. The painting even had a speech bubble. "I can't allow that!!!" she shouted, if exclamation points meant shouting.

Maybe there was a guy somewhere who had just reached out and touched her breasts, the way he wanted to touch Laura's about a thousand times a day. He could feel himself getting stiff just thinking about it. The guy tried to unhook her bra, maybe, but he hadn't done the job quickly enough. That probably turned girls off. *And, Christ, what was he going to do with this boner?*

Probably Billy liked the painting, 'cause it was a comic?

"No. It's not," Billy said, sounding whiny. "It's just a panel, you know. I don't know. It's like it's saying that what my father does isn't really good, because you're supposed to think *this* isn't a real painting, it's like a comic book. So then how good is a comic? You know."

Jesse didn't. "I wonder what happens next," Jesse said.

"Yeah, well, I'll bet the guy who did this, he doesn't know that. Because he's the one who's not a real artist. I mean a comic book artist."

Billy started to touch the painting, but his father appeared, like instantly, and put his hand on his arm. "You *can* touch a comic book," Billy said to Jesse.

"Well, this isn't one," his father said sharply. Jesse could see that Billy's parents always had their eyes on their son, probably concerned he might hurt himself or something. Jesse felt he should try to keep an eye on Billy, too.

Billy looked at a man in a short white jacket who was standing behind a long rectangular table with every kind of drink on it, even big bottles of soda. He asked his father if he could have some Coke. Then Billy's mother said something to Mr. Green about the Schells having hidden their maid for the day, and they both laughed.

Jesse saw his own parents with Mrs. Schell. He prayed that today would be all right for his mother, that she wouldn't end up sitting on the Schells' silky-looking couch weeping. His parents were trying "to mend things." They were "healing—for the children's sake." His father, that meant, had done something with one of the Kel-Kap models—he had this image that his father had hurt her, maybe pushed her down accidentally, sprained her ankle; though, really, he knew it was more serious than that. Anyway, he'd had to get her out of trouble, and he'd made himself and everyone else miserable. But his father didn't seem like a bad person to Jesse, more like someone playing blind man's bluff who smashed into models, furniture, marriages. When his mother lay on the couch crying, he'd try to comfort her, or at least keep his little brother quiet. But he could do so little for them, not knowing what words to say; and they were so careless, got distracted too easily, said they wanted one thing, then did the complete opposite. Simple things they could have done to get along better, why couldn't they manage them? Like he'd tell his father to get his mother something nice for her birthday, but he couldn't do even that; he brought home a vacuum cleaner! *That* had been a tears and couch day.

Jesse went to the kitchen to get away from them, hoping Laura would be there. She wasn't, but there were the funny plaster casts of Jeffrey's parents and his sister, all of them seated at a real glass breakfast table. Jimmy Benjamin, the joker, stared at the casts, like he was really waiting for them to talk.

"Do you think this is where they actually eat?" Jimmy said. He could make his eyes seem to stick out of his head, like they were on springs. "You know, like Jeffrey comes down and every morning he has to figure out which one's his real father?" That was a joke, maybe, because everyone knew Jeffrey and his father didn't get along.

"Yeah," Jesse said. "I don't know." He could never find his footing with Jimmy. "I mean, but they could damage the statues, get coffee on them or something, right? So probably they don't eat with them."

Jimmy wasn't listening anymore, just staring, dumbstruck with wonder. "I wish they were my parents."

"The Schells?"

"No. The statues," he said in this flat way, like he really meant it.

Jesse laughed, maybe because it seemed cruel. Besides, he thought Jimmy *liked* his parents, didn't he? *He had to,* his mother was so crazy about him.

Jimmy turned toward him, noted the laugh; like he'd just learned something useful about the world. "See, I could say, hey, can I have the car, Dad? Don't say anything if the answer's yes."

But what could Jimmy do with a car? They weren't allowed to drive yet! To get away from Jimmy, Jesse went to look at an enormous painting of policemen beating Negroes, the picture made up of photos jumbled all on top of each other, like in a riot. And then there was a creepy empty electric chair, and a sign that said SILENCE over it. Next to the chair there was a blue panel, just blue; nothing else.

"Like death, maybe?" he said to himself, the word making him feel distinguished.

But Jeffrey had come up next to him. "No. He told me he did it to make the painting bigger, you know. So he could charge more for it." He smiled.

"Unh-huh," someone said. *It was Andy Warhol.* Odd white hair, and the palest skin Jesse had ever seen. He looked smaller than the photos of him, like he might break.

A red-haired man in a short white jacket came by offering a plate of tiny crustless sandwiches.

"Nnnnh-Nnnh," Warhol said, looking kind of ashamed.

"He only eats candy," Jeffrey told Jesse, like Warhol wasn't really there, or couldn't talk for himself. Jeffrey sounded fond, though, like Andy was a baby.

Warhol peered at Jesse. "Wow, you have lovely lashes. Like a girl almost."

Jesse felt queer. What was he supposed to say? "Thanks." A lot of what people said to him didn't make sense to him; and not to themselves either, he was pretty sure.

"Would you like a print? You know, like a Marilyn or something?"

"Sure. I guess."

Warhol nodded. "Great. Great. That would be great, thanks," like Jesse was giving him the gift. He gazed at Jesse for a moment, then over his shoulder. "Holy Cow, there's your mom and dad, Jeffrey," Warhol said, in breathy amazement—like he was surprised they were here, in their own house. "Do you think I could sell her another painting? Wouldn't that be great, Jeffrey?" He bounded off.

Jesse hated himself for not actually having said anything to Andy Warhol. He could have asked him if he'd read Albert Camus' essay on the death penalty, or something.

"I don't think he reads much," Jeffrey said. "But you should talk to him when he's done with my mom. He really likes you, I could tell. Whenever he meets someone he likes, he offers them a present." Jeffrey looked at the floor.

Well, not liked—thought was handsome, really. But if Jeffrey tried to tell Jesse *that,* his voice would probably crack. *He* really *liked* Jesse, too, with his deep, dark eyes, curly black hair, and the longest eyelashes Jeffrey had ever seen. Jesse mostly wore dark blue clothes, because he was color-blind and afraid of making mistakes, and that made it look like he had a signature, a costume, a role. Hero, probably. Jesse was tall, too, but his body looked all in the right proportion, like a movie star. Maybe he didn't know it, though. He didn't seem stuck on himself, anyway, didn't try to overwhelm you with how strong he was or how cool; or, like the other kids who went sailing with Laura, with how smart he was. Okay, he *liked* Jesse in *that* way. What did *that* matter, and why did there have to be two different ways to like people, anyway? Was that grammar, something that had to be or the world wouldn't fit together? Anyway, he'd never tell Jesse how he felt; and he could see Jesse would never figure that out for himself, even if Jeffrey risked looking into Jesse's dark eyes and didn't glance away.

Jesse, though, wanted to find Laura, and he walked by two tall men playing chess on a glass table in the living room while people with plastic flutes of champagne walked around them on their way out to the deck, where the adults in their long dresses and blazers stood in little clumps by the pool. Jesse looked down at the game. Maybe he could say something clever to them, make up for the chance he missed with Mr. Warhol? But there was no board under the wooden pieces. Were they really playing, or just kidding around? No one could really play chess without a board, could they?

The one with the broader face looked up at him. "Extraordinary," he said to the older man, as if Jesse weren't there.

"Juif?"

The broad-faced man raised his eyebrows. "Je ne sais pas."

Didn't that mean Jewish? But it didn't sound nasty when the old man said it. Or appraising. Or *anything.* Just a fact, like, it's sunny today. Jesse realized he'd never heard it said that way before.

"This is my friend Jesse Kelman," Jeffrey said, coming up next to him. That was nice of him, Jesse thought. Sometimes people surprised him that way.

The broad-faced man looked up again with a mild, inquiring look. "We don't occupy the same space," he said very slowly, "do we, Jeffrey?"

Jesse saw Jeffrey's eyes fill with tears. So the remark had been like a slap? Like he maybe meant Jeffrey was a spoiled collector's kid, and he was an artist. Or Jeffrey was a child and the man was an adult? Or, of course, Jews and gentiles—that was possible, too. Or something else, something really profound, that Jesse just wasn't getting?

Then the man looked away from them, back at the man with the long, thin face. "Different spaces," he said, musingly. "That always excites desire or aversion, doesn't it? But every space is also different, each in its own way?" He looked back at Jeffrey. "Our kind—or rather, this kind, because it isn't ours, others might occupy these spaces, too, that's what makes them spaces—our kind of space doesn't communicate. So desire and aversion will be very strong, but eventually, of course, turn to boredom." He looked down at the glass table again. "I'm sorry, Marcel. I've forgotten the board."

"As I did three moves back," the older man said, smiling. "I was just waiting for you to notice that my last few moves didn't make any sense." He made his face blank. "In relation to your moves, anyway."

Jeffrey put his arm under Jesse's, maybe needing reassurance, and led him a step away.

"You okay?" Jesse said. He thought Jeffrey had been the one insulted.

"Me? Sure." He asked the man in the short white jacket for a Coke. "It's supposed to be, you know, not personal what they say. Like science. He and this other painter we collect, Johns, they're trying to figure out *how* things fit together, you know, so they make sense. I mean, like grammar, verbs fit with subjects. Or something. Gaston says he's not really trying to say or paint a particular thing, but to show us what you need in order to paint *anything*. You know, like grammar." Then Jeffrey realized he'd repeated himself and shook his head.

"I don't get it," Jesse said.

Jeffrey laughed. "You know what makes you so really great, Jesse? You're like the *only* person I know who would *ever* say you don't get something." He looked down at his soda. "I don't get it either. Not really. Maybe it's all just crap. Like you take something everybody knows and you say it very v-e-r-y s-l-o-w-l-y, so that people think you *must* be saying something deep."

"Say it slow," Jesse sang, "and it's almost like praying."

"Yeah. Or like thinking. Like once, at an art auction, he said to me, 'The game is...won...by the team...which scores...which scores...the most...points.' Is that true here, too? Is art, then, a game?" He put the glass down on the long table. "It seemed like really smart to me."

"Yeah," Jesse said, "you know, I can see that." He smiled. "Sort of."

"Right, now you see it, now you don't."

Jesse laughed.

Jeffrey, in his own space, was in heaven. Then he dropped his Coke on the floor, and his father shouted. "You little putz. Get the fuck away from my paintings," his father laughing then, like it had all been a big joke. But it wasn't. His father wished, really, that Jeffrey wouldn't even look at the paintings, like his eye beams contaminated them. Artists could be sissies, sons should be...dead. Thank God, everyone filed in from the patio to the living room then, finding places on couches and folding chairs. Henry Waxman, the young rabbi with the candid face from their temple, introduced Mr. Joshua Battle, a Negro man with thick brows. He and his comrades from SNAP, the rabbi said, were going to register Negroes to vote in Mississippi. Rabbi Waxman reminded the people holding champagne and canapés on little napkins almost as thick as cloth that Jews and Negroes shared a heritage: they both remembered what it was to be slaves. Today, in Mississippi, Joshua Battle, like their own Joshua, worked to lead his people to freedom.

Mr. Battle looked at his hands embarrassedly as the rabbi talked, and when he stood up to speak, his voice was so quiet Jesse had to lean toward him to hear, Mr. Battle just standing very stiffly upright, looking directly in front of him, but not as if he even saw any of them. He said that the Negroes in Mississippi might not be slaves anymore, but their lives still belonged to others. If they tried to exercise the most basic right of American citizens, the right to vote, they got beaten and jailed. And if you then went to ask about your friend in jail, the police would pummel you until you passed out. But if the Negro people of Mississippi didn't try, if they didn't stand up to this terror, they would never own their own lives. He hoped the people here in the North would support them when they tried to stand up to the terror and make justice in Mississippi.

Jesse definitely wanted to stand with them. He thought of the Gran Sport bicycle he'd asked his dad for. Maybe he could tell his father to give the money for that to Mr. Battle? But that felt phony to him. He knew they'd still have enough money to buy him the bicycle anyway.

Meanwhile, Laura Jaffe, in her space, prayed that Joshua Battle might look at her; and that he absolutely wouldn't look, too, because what if he did, and then looked away because he didn't find her interesting enough in her stupid blue skirt and white cotton blouse? Her blood felt heavy, and she thought she would faint from how much she wanted to feel his hand on her cheek. He had the most beautiful hands she'd ever seen, his full lips were so soft-looking, and his thick eyebrows looked so powerful. It was almost painful the way the blood felt in her body when he stopped talking and looked down at his hands, like his short speech had tired him out.

Laura saw that her mother and several people watched Dr. Jacobs, wanting to see if he agreed with what Mr. Battle had said. And maybe Mr. Battle saw that as well, because as soon as he finished he went over to speak to Dr. Jacobs, the two of them standing by a painting that looked like a lot of tiny pictures of Mrs. Schell, the same as one the Sculls had, but not as good, Jeffrey had said. His mom had made Andy put in more pictures of her, and that had ruined it.

Laura moved as close to them as she dared, wanting to hear what they talked about, wanting just to be near Joshua Battle, his thick legs, his low voice. They both spoke so quietly though, almost whispering, that it was hard to hear what they were saying. Besides, her own blood beat so loud in her ears, she was actually afraid she might faint, though maybe that wouldn't be so bad. He'd have to pick her up and carry her to the white couch then, wouldn't he?

Mr. Battle told Dr. Jacobs that he could see the people in the audience hadn't believed him. "They wonder *if it's so bad, why are you alive?* So it couldn't be so bad."

Dr. Jacobs actually smiled, not just raising his lips, either. His teeth were all mottled. Maybe that was why he didn't let people see them. "Yes," he said, "they don't understand you don't have to kill everyone. Terror is enough to make people into . . ." but Laura didn't get the last word.

"That's what we called the walking dead," Dr. Jacobs said. "The resigned. The ones who would die soon." Dr. Jacobs added something then about a man with an Italian name who'd written that the death camps, too, had been built by racism.

Mr. Battle whispered, "You must tell them that."

"Me?" Dr. Jacobs said. "No, they wouldn't listen to me."

Mr. Battle shook his head wearily. Was that possible? Was he *dismissing* Dr. Jacobs?

Mr. Battle turned away, walked over to Jeffrey's parents, and in an almost inaudible voice thanked them for their consideration. Andy Warhol came up to them, and she heard him offer Mr. Battle a print to take with him back to Mississippi. Joshua Battle smiled, and said something she couldn't make out. She walked a little closer to their circle, then realized she would look like she was following them, like a little dog. She turned back. Dr. Jacobs stared at the floor sadly. Then he looked around, probably for Beth, who was speaking to Laura's brother, Frank, the two of them laughing together. Laura wished Frank would stop talking to her. She wanted to tell Beth how she'd felt, nearly fainting and all. Maybe, she thought, she would actually run off to Mississippi to work with Joshua Battle. Boy, would that amaze Beth—Laura ahead of her for the first time!

The next day Frank, to Beth's utter amazement, joined them on the family boat, even though everyone there was four years younger than he was, and he'd actually start college in the fall—Columbia University, which was in the Ivy League. Frank had beautiful long fingers that did everything, Beth saw, quickly, gracefully, perfectly, and his tortoiseshell glasses showed just how serious and penetrating his mind must be. He had this *decided* manner, certain in every thing he did, like when he grasped the lines of the boat, or opened his hands, gesturing, telling them about the civil rights demonstration he'd actually been arrested at in Maryland. So Frank had the courage to break the laws, to rebel—but that just made him more truly moral than all the ordinary, orderly, obedient ones, the "good Germans." Frank was four years older than his sister, but really he was *decades* ahead of her, of all of them, intellectually and spiritually.

At home that night, Beth had kicked the thin cotton blanket off her legs. What if Frank didn't come to the boat next day, was bored by Billy's endless stories? He probably thought they were such kids, hadn't seen yet how alike the two of them were, both knowing that the world *must* change.

Still, the next morning she had put on a blue-and-white sailor shirt that fit perfectly, Bermuda shorts, knee socks, and her new white Keds, just in case.

And there he was, in a T-shirt and jeans—standing by the dock with his sister, rubbing her head affectionately with his beautiful hands! The wind was too slight for sailing that day, but thank God Billy thought of going out in his Boston Whaler, a present his parents had bought for him, probably because her dad was making him better—*normal,* Beth thought to herself, *ordinary*—which is what he always really had been. The Whaler was a small, clumsy, flat-bottomed skiff, but Billy had made his parents get an oversized blue Evinrude outboard motor for it that Beth made roar now, turning the boat in a sharp arc and kicking a spray over her head whose separate droplets glistened magically, like her ecstasy had been woven into a pearly shawl. *Possible phrase for a poem?* Little Arthur Kaplan grabbed the sides of the boat with *ragged claws,* afraid probably that Beth would tip the boat over, drown them all in an *acid ocean.* She turned the engine up even farther, and smiled at Frank. Droplets of cool water pattered on her head, but not enough to ruin her hair.

Frank had this glow around him, a moral intensity, and his bare legs were so strong-looking, steady, reassuring, and she was just about certain he was attracted to her, too. That had to be why he came out with them on this ridiculous boat, he could see what she had inside her, that she had the same ferocious desire to make justice that he did. He would be the activist, she would . . . would what? Maybe write an epic poem about the Holocaust, like *Paradise Lost,* but *not* justifying God's ways to man, because her father had shown her *there is no God.* Or: *God is dead.* Or: *God is the roar of an engine.*

But then, why should people heal the world—or so she wondered when Billy Green lurched toward her. To make him jump she throttled the engine up just one more notch, *the roar making her thoughts stop, so it was like quiet to her.* Jeffrey Schell watched her in wonder, and Arthur Kaplan looked like he might actually cry. That made her laugh. Vibrations traveled through her arm and she relaxed her grip on the stick for a moment.

The Whaler bucked upward. Her arm turned, and the boat swept around in a tight arc, tilted on its side. Her stomach lurched. Then the boat and her stomach came down with a slap that pitched Billy Green overboard.

Arthur screamed. Billy's little arms beat against the water, his face twisting in terror, crying. He went under. Laura fell forward, her head crashing against the gunwale. Billy bobbed up again. Jesus, did he even know how to swim? Crying like that, he might drown! Roar, claws, and God all went out of her head, and she let go of the rudder, screaming. The boat swung in a wide circle. Maybe she could lean over, scoop Billy up, make it like this hadn't happened.

He went under again.

Jesse jumped in the water, and the front of the boat swung over his head. Beth screamed. The motor might go right into him, cut him in half! She grabbed the stick again, set the boat moving straight ahead. Jesse disappeared for a few seconds, then came up with Billy in his arms, the two of them bobbing in the water, Billy clawing at Jesse's cheeks.

But the boat circled away from them. Beth turned the prow back, Laura shouting at her and crying, blood on her forehead; Jesse, gripping Billy's body with one arm, back-stroked toward the boat, the flopping extra weight making him veer this way and that. Finally, he was close enough to reach out for the Whaler's sides, but Beth lost control again and the boat spun away from him. Jesse's reaching hand went down for a moment and into the engine. She thought she heard a small click, like a stick or a piece of seaweed had got caught in the blades. Jesse screamed, and a stream of blood swirled in the water. Laura shouted, "Jesus, Beth!" and pushed her in the chest, away from the engine. "For Christ's sake, you have to turn it off!" Laura took the throttle and cut the engine. The boat flapped forward, rocking slightly from side to side.

Jesse lifted Billy over his head, blood streaming down his arm over his face, and pushed him into the boat, Frank dragging Jesse up after, leaving him splayed on the floor, his body rippling now with small tremors, while Frank stripped off his T-shirt, knelt beside him, putting his head in his lap, saying, "I know how you feel, don't worry, we learned about this before the demonstrations, it's going to be all right." He twisted the shirt tightly round and round Jesse's hand, saying, "It's going to be all right, it's going to be all right," while the blood still dripped down, definitely not all right, soaking through Frank's shirt onto the floor of the boat, mixing with the water, slopping on Beth's Keds, staining them forever.

Beth sat down on one of the thwarts, stunned, and put her finger in the blood on her sneakers. She touched it to her tongue—salty, deadly. Jesse's face looked like it was going white. Was he going into shock? Oh, dear God, what if he died! Could that happen, could a person actually die like that? Laura headed the Whaler for shore and gunned the engine, Beth weeping uncontrollably. Frank must be thinking she was a complete fool, and all the worse for crying like this, but she couldn't stop. *What had she done?*

Still, they all continued to play together, and weekends when they couldn't sail anymore they went to the bowling alley, where Jeffrey saw Jesse—when he thought no one was looking—stare positively ravenously at Laura Jaffe, who was taking extra-long strides for Jesse on her way to releasing the ball. Jeffrey saw Jesse, who sometimes dared a light blue shirt now, rub the stump of his missing finger, like it was his cock, because after all, he told himself, *the outsider sees everything.* Then Jeffrey used his x-ray eyes to see the boner in Jesse's pants—which admittedly didn't require superpowers, being actually the Boner Visible from the Moon. Laura's ball guttered, and she turned to Jesse with a clumsy-little-me smile, probably having the same view of the digit-that's-not-there that Jesse had, that it meant He's the Kind of Cowboy Who Keeps His Word, Jesse proud of the wound rather than furious with Beth. But would Jesse *ever* actually *do* anything about Laura? No, he could rescue a drowning man, Jeffrey thought, but he wasn't ready to come on to a long-legged girl.

And if Jeffrey had not, you know, come on to Jesse, but even told him that he was interested in boys—okay, interested in *him,* okay, interested in sucking him off, Jesse would probably have run screaming like he'd put his hand, or his dick, in something lots worse than a propeller, wouldn't he? Jeffrey actually liked to sail and to bowl—though he pretended he found it all pretty boring. He liked his friends. But he knew he could never tell him who he *really* was now that he was sure that boys weren't like a phase for him, but a *fate.* Or a FATE. A *FATE.* **A FATE.** *A FATE.*

"It's your turn," Jesse said to him.

"Turn for what?" Jeffrey said, though of course he knew.

"To bowl." Jeffrey wasn't *that* dense, Jesse thought, but in a world overly full of stupidity he still seemed to think it funny to pretend he was.

"Go ahead," Jeffrey drawled, "you do it for me."

Jeffrey dipped a cardboard French fry in ketchup and felt lonelier and lonelier. If he couldn't tell any of them what mattered most about him right now, what kind of friends could they be, really?

Then, that December, all of them lonely inside their own teen spaces, they started ice-skating again at the big Quonset hut rink near West Shore Drive. The day before, Beth had been bas-mitzvahed by Rabbi Waxman, the young rabbi of Temple Sinai, and though her father said he was proud of her, still Beth had to understand that he couldn't attend the ceremony, couldn't welcome anyone into the community of Jews. She understood. He'd given her a beautiful marbled fountain pen, told her it was for the essays she'd write someday, and she'd felt proud but bewildered still. Essays about what? Anyway, she'd done it for her mother really, and she hadn't wanted to have a party in a circus-size tent, or on a yacht that held two hundred, or at the Metropolitan Museum, or as a trip to Israel for fifty, just some coffee and cake and cold-cut platters from Squire's wrapped in tawdry red-and-blue cellophane. The only guests had been her mother's relations—businessmen, doctors, accountants, journalists—ordinary compared to her father's family, whose infinite absence had caused her father's absence from the Temple, making her too ashamed to invite her own friends. Were they even really her friends? Except for Frank, what did they understand about her, about how she was someone who had to work absolutely *ceaselessly* to make human life valuable again?

"Now we're both bas mitzvah," Laura said. They leaned against the rail of the skating rink, watching the endless circles, drinking ersatz vending machine cocoa from the paper cups.

"Yeah." She knew Laura wanted her to explain why she hadn't been invited to the party, but the cocoa made Beth's throat close.

"We could be called the Bas Mitzvahs," Laura offered. "You know, like a girl group?"

"Girl group?" Once again, she realized that Laura was the one who had the knowledge about how to get along with boys, secrets hidden in all those songs that Murray the K played, that just sounded so insipid and stupid to Beth, the thing about her brother suddenly not mattering enough, and anyway, they'd hardly kissed.

"Like, you know," Laura said, "the Ronettes. High heels and"—she put her hand a foot above her head—"high hair, too. Higher than Jackie's." Beth had no idea what Laura meant about the groups, the hair, but she nodded anyway.

And Frank told her the girl groups Laura liked were nowhere, vapid, colorless, "white stuff." The real music, he said, the sounds that could tell you something, they came from what he called the deep river of Negro music that started with the blues. And while they waited for the movie to start, Frank told her again how the blues came out of a life where Negroes got treated like they were worthless.

"Like the Jews," Beth said, then looked around the Playhouse movie theater at classmates like her, on dates in chinos and dresses. "In the camps, I mean," not wanting to make him sad but wanting to remind him that she was connected to something powerful too.

"Right. It's like we have to make life valuable again."

She could hardly believe he'd said that, it was so great! Should she say that maybe the way to do that was to make life more pleasurable for people, the way Professor Marcuse said? But he might take that the wrong way. Still, it was so exciting that Frank understood that you had to change things.

"Like you almost don't deserve to live if you don't try," he said. "I know that sounds extreme and all, but that's how I feel sometimes." He let his arm go out across her shoulders but looked straight ahead like he didn't know what his arm was doing. Still, that was okay. "We have to do it, though, without being either victims or executioners." He turned to her. "That's from Camus."

"I know, Frank."

"Right. I forget how much you've read."

She smiled again. Then *Pillow Talk* started, and while the credits rolled, he kissed her a different way than she was pretty sure Laura had ever experienced from anyone. Had Beth ever heard a song that mentioned it? That might teach her what she should do back?

That winter, Laura's family, as if they thought the two girls really were a group, invited Beth to come with them to ski in Switzerland, which was a part of Europe, her real native land, a place infinitely more profound, more textured, and more murderous than America, with those vapid girl groups Laura liked.

Beth could hardly believe it: *she* was drinking clumpy, bitter European cocoa at a café on the side of a glacier near Gstaad, watching the skiers schuss theatrically to their stops. Her father's horseradish voice in her head tried to ruin it. *What kind of people find it amusing to fall down a mountain on barrel staves?*

Me, she said back. *His daughter* was that kind. *She* loved it, maybe because Frank had been such a good, patient teacher, not all anxious-making tests, so she didn't feel self-conscious, could already schuss back and forth, he said, like a pro. She added more sugar cubes to the Swiss chocolate that her father had never had the courage to cross the border and taste—which had been something she'd had to learn about her own father from Billy Green's stories. But that was all right, *he* could take care of her father, while she explored this brave new world that had such creatures in it, meaning Frank, of course, who waved to her now from the lift line, leaning on his poles so nonchalantly. He was the real reason she'd stood up to her father's contempt about skiing. Frank looked beautiful in his black stretch ski pants, his knit cap; she'd been yearning toward him all along, really; *he* had been, she thought, what had been obscurely promised her when her body had changed, Beth sensing that someone as wonderful as Frank would come into her life if only Billy

Green might take care of her father for a while. And this thing he wanted so much, he said she wouldn't be missing anything anymore if she did it. She would understand better what she and her father had talked about, what would bind people together someday, *Eros,* a force Billy Green didn't know anything about. Her father had never talked about *that* with him, the boy too immature, too unsophisticated to understand. Beth just had to leave Laura's side and tiptoe down the hall to Frank's bedroom, the way they'd talked about, well, *he'd* talked about; in fact, it was all he talked about anymore, not the civil rights movement or Camus, just how wonderful this would be, and she'd see that he'd still be there for her, she could trust him. And she did trust *him*—it was herself she wasn't sure about, the whole thing felt so overwhelming, did *she* really want it, or was it just him? And what if she did it and she disappointed him? She felt like a spaz when she danced, probably even kissed badly, both their eyes open, her tongue going into his mouth at the movies that first time, shock, maybe even disgust, in his eyes, she'd been sure. And where was the *pleasure* in it? My God, what if she was a hysteric, like Dora? But the one person she could talk about *that* with was definitely the one person she knew she couldn't talk to about that. Which made her feel lonely, the snow look implacable, the people at the café or on the slopes like a hateful excrescence to be wiped away to restore the purity to the scene.

Frank looked off toward the top of the mountain, pulled his goggles up over his eyes, then looked back to her, a halo around him from the snow glare. He waved his black glove to say she should join him on the line. Didn't he realize that was the lift for the intermediate run, much steeper than the baby slope he'd had her practicing on yesterday? Was she ready? She let the last big drops of sweet mud slide down her throat, then bent over and slowly flicked each buckle on her boot in time to a song Frank had played for her in Great Neck, *please, please, please,* the insistent rhythm giving her courage, the music like an emissary from him, a promise, because all that harsh, throaty pleading, it just had to be for something more than what she'd known so far, more than the French-kissing even or his stroking her between her legs with her slacks • still on. If they did this thing, he said, she'd really feel more comfortable with her body, and that's what the music promised, too. Frank said she just needed to take the plunge, like at the top of a ski run, or when James Brown sang and they danced together, her body would take care of the rest, everything would be all right.

She got up on her skis and poles, and suddenly felt off balance, terrified of what she *maybe* was going to do. Would it hurt? She stuck her arm out, got her balance back, imagined her and Laura on the junior slope tomorrow morning. *If* Beth did this, then she'd be a little bit ahead of Laura forever. Laura's eyes would cloud up, she'd try to hide inside herself, afraid to tell Beth how scared she was about a boy really touching her. But when they got back home, maybe the two of them would choose someone for Laura, like Jesse Kelman. She'd play Laura some *good* music, the soul music Frank had taught her about, like James Brown. He'd help Laura feel her body, give her courage to move it.

Beth shook her head with weary sadness. What could you do with people who were terrified to be alive, who talked about Eros but were ashamed of their own bodies? Was *she* going to be someone like that? Now was the time to decide.

She pushed off then through the soft powder, toward Frank and the lift line, her stomach suddenly lurching again, maybe from all the sugar she'd spooned into her cocoa.

That New Year's Eve, while his daughter slept beneath Frank Jaffe's duvet, Leo opened his desk drawer and looked at his blue-black Luger, so like the one he'd had in Talloire, so like a thumb, so much more reliable than a mother. He heard Smerless in an imaginary consultation for which he definitely hadn't asked. "Talking to this boy has helped both of you, hasn't it?" Smerless, in his fantasy, had scattered more and more American Indian artifacts on pedestals and shelves around his West Side consulting room, in pathetic imitation of Freud's antiquities.

"Helping *me*?" Leo asked, disingenuously. Leo had his imagination throw even more Indian peace pipes over every available surface, making Imaginary Smerless' office look like an obsessive's closet.

"Look," Smerless said proudly, "surely you can see that your nonsense about this gun is over?" And like monkeys eventually typing a Shakespeare play, Imaginary Smerless had, indeed, gotten something right, the nighttime trip to the drawer had become a memorial to his depression, not a real possibility to end possibility. He slid the drawer shut. He should get this thing out of the house.

"Mein Gott, when did you become so critical?" Leo asked. "That's not how I remember you."

"You were just out of Auschwitz, for God's sake," Smerless said, "so I babied you. But you don't need a maternal introject anymore, Leo. Things are better for you, I think."

"I can't talk to him about Auschwitz, though," he told the air.

"Do you need to?" Smerless replied. He picked up one of the precious long wooden pipes with feathers hanging down and filled it with tobacco from a maroon humidor. He ripped a page from the *International Journal,* rolled it loosely to make a spliff to light his pipe.

"For my sake? No. But do we have a strong enough therapeutic bond yet?"

Smerless smiled. His pipe, as always, went out.

"His ego's too weak for neutrality, too young, too fragile. When I don't respond, he's bereft. The once we tried the couch, he had a panic attack."

Imaginary Smerless patted him on the back, their hour over. "Well, I'm sure you'll make the right choice."

Then, a few weeks later, Billy asked if Leo knew what had happened to Dr. Weiss, which was something he most certainly couldn't talk about to the boy. But once again the silence crushed Billy, tears forming that might leave marks on his middle ear. "We were herded off the train in the middle of the night," Leo said, falling, like so many of his own patients, into the liar's trap, talking too much about the wrong subject, hoping his interrogator would be misdirected. He looked down, pretending to make a note, remembering the train had reduced him to a person who couldn't bear his own smell, one who felt that he had fecal matter stuck to the hair of his anus, until strand by strand he'd ripped it all out, leaking blood. Auschwitz had been like a chemical agent that reduced him to the core from which his personality had grown, his crucial symptom, his diagnosis.

Leo had barely been able to see, but the stench, the shouts of "Women and children to the right. Men to the left," the beatings from the butt end of rifles, had made clear that weak animals—a woman, a child, a nearsighted man—would be killed immediately. He touched the tips of his fingers to another man's shirt and found his way forward.

A shadow demanded what he'd done for a living. "Doctor," he'd said. A mark was made; the delousing he received had been fit for cattle; and Leo thanked not the nonexistent God who'd allowed Auschwitz in a fit of absentmindedness, but the real abortionist who'd put him on the path away from the showers when he'd refused his mother's business, saying, "He'll become a famous doctor and take care of you in your old age," though his mother, as it turned out, wouldn't have an old age. And it wasn't, truly, the reluctant abortionist who had saved him. Many days, David told him soon enough, the guards whimsically let the Jews get off higgledy-piggledy. Then they murdered whoever chose the left side. But not this day. Why? *For no reason.* The orderly-looking universe, David had learned in Auschwitz, is chance all the way down.

Luck then that for two saving hours each day he had been stopped from breaking rocks, had been sent to a wooden barracks to make the agar mediums for petri dishes for Mengele. If he held the materials close to his eyes, he could do the work.

"Weiss was there," he said to the boy, all liars—and all dream displacements—returning to the subject they most want to avoid. "A miracle, eh?" He looked down, the mixture of ironies in the word *miracle* had made him sick. "Working in what they called a laboratory."

"Where are your . . ." this blurred Weiss who couldn't be Weiss had begun to say. Other inmates had looked over. Fortunately Weiss had noticed, stopped talking, guided Leo unobtrusively around the barracks lab, finding him a spoon, and later, keeping others from taking his bread, even helping Leo to steal food from *muselmanner*—the ones who were about to die anyway—or, Weiss said, smiling slyly, "a nearly blind man like you wouldn't be able to steal from them."

Leo, in Great Neck, recalled Smerless' injunction then, and kept silent with Billy, remembering only for himself how he and Weiss had added to their diet by taking a few bits of beef sent to make broth for the cultures.

"From *parfait de foi d'oie au Heres* to *this*," David had said.

Then one day the Nazis had provided bits of sinewy human muscle for the agar, and Weiss started to say something to him. This time Leo had touched his finger to his lips. Another inmate had come then to pick up the stacks of prepared cultures and, thinking no one could see, had taken out his spoon, fished up a thin strand of muscle from the broth. This time, Weiss had put his finger to Leo's mouth.

The inmate had swallowed his meal, gone about his business.

Overcome with an attack of idiocy, Leo had insisted that they take the few remaining pieces of muscle outside and kick dirt over them. Weiss stood by the earth, furious with Leo for his sham piety, his sentimentality. After all, if a guard saw them, if the day's shortage was detected . . .

Still, Weiss had led him back inside the barracks. Later that night he'd even helped Leo steal spectacles from a dying man who lay helplessly on his bunk watching the vicious shadows. His lenses had made the world into obscure but manageable shapes.

Billy smiled, though he'd clearly been bewildered by Dr. Jacobs' long silence. He put his fingers out toward him in delighted surprise. "Dr. Weiss, he was alive too!"

"Yes," Leo said. "And our hour is up."

. . .

That night Leo lay down heavily next to his sleeping wife. He'd been right: Adorno, Celan, and Weiss' ghost had been right, one cannot ever speak of those things, the little bits of stories that he'd told Billy certainly not the truth, even though every word was true, of course. But they had become *stories,* anecdotes with beginnings, middles, ends, plots even ("A Friend Saves My Life"; "In Dreams a Mother Becomes Meat"). Auschwitz hadn't been so formally complete, fear having worked its own reduction, shattering every sentence, word, and letter. "We never see death purely," Freud had said, unfolding his near-Wagnerian structure to him among the suffocating Egyptian tchotchkes. "Thanatos is always bound up with some tincture of Eros, like the aggression in the surgeon's knife, or the soldier who kills for the motherland." But Freud had been wrong; such a thing—the black bottle filled with death—is possible. Well, how could he show the boy *that,* Billy Green of Great Neck, wearing a woolly sweater with a snowdrop design, his legs tucked up under him to make himself look taller, his face mobile with childish pity for Leo. And why would he *want* this pale young boy to feel as anxious as an obsessive—an anal type, say—deprived suddenly of his hand washing, his toilet paper, his showers, his kosher laws, his tefillin, his phylacteries? In the name of truth? Or was it that he had been so humiliated he wanted power over this boy, to make satisfying red welts on his psyche?

He and Richard Hartman used to talk of the techniques that have to be invented to tell the truth about the camps, pleasant analytic hours like literary seminars on Celan. "Nouns become verbs, adjectives become nouns—torsions meant to show what couldn't be said."

"Twisted, mangled sentences. In pain, perhaps?"

"Like my hands?" Leo had held them up, to remind Hartman, he was afraid, that Richard hadn't been there. He'd been ransomed, hidden.

"No," Hartman had replied. "After all, can a poem be starved, beaten?" Though it was clear Richard thought a poem could be, perhaps, a necessary insanity for a poet.

"Well, erased, there's that," Leo had said, smiling.

"So Celan tells the truth," Hartman had concluded, "but in a way that no one can understand. What good is that?"

They'd laughed, both pleased when they could convince themselves that defeat had been woven into the fabric of things.

With Billy, Leo had from time to time tried a few declarative sentences. That had failed. Or worse: *the boy probably thinks he understands something. But what he understands is a mistake.* Billy, Leo was sure, wanted Auschwitz to be redemptive. Like the *Times* reporter who'd profiled him, like Joshua Battle, all of them eager that Leo's life be filled with helpful lessons for the present. End racism. Join the human family. Recognize the murderer in all of us, etc. Bend Auschwitz to some good end, and it wouldn't be so, well, *sad.*

But there are no lessons here, he wanted to shout at them. Except this, perhaps: a train line had led from the cities and countryside of the past *to* the camps. And *from* the camps?

Nothing. No world; no time; no history.

No, *that* felt wrong too; a sentimental piety, like his burying the sinew; or maybe like a narcissistic anger that the world could go on after what had happened to him. After all, it did go on, and *after all.* It had become Billy's world and his daughter's; palpable indeed; satisfying surely, with sailboats, skating rinks, tennis courts, barrel staves.

All right, then, say this, perhaps: the two worlds, this one and that, they don't fit together. All history that tries to bring them together becomes like a mistake in grammar, tenses not agreeing. So how do we speak at all in a world that doesn't have a past anymore? No wonder he often couldn't remember his daughter's middle name. No wonder art becomes that Coke bottle "painting" the Schells had tacked on their wall—the thing almost an insult, really, flat, intentionally meaningless, all present, no past, no tragedy, no Auschwitz.

"Let their names be blotted from history for all time"; and "We must never forget." Forget what? No one could say. Future essay: "Our Choice: The Coke Bottle, or the Black Bottle Filled with Death."

Leo looked at his wife's still lovely breasts under her thin nightgown and cackled sadly. Ann stirred at the sound.

"Are you all right?" she asked, as she did a hundred times a day.

"Yes," he said. "I'm all right, darling."

Had he said *that,* Ann wondered, in that way? Said *darling*? She lay awake for a moment, her fingertips just touching the side of his long, muscular leg. All that walking, crisscrossing Great Neck every day, out to the Point, from Old village to New and back again. What did the neighbors make of him, she wondered, the wandering Jew in his blue pin-striped suit?

What did she?

That night, Billy Green lay awake reading, one hand pushing a pencil point rhythmically into his thigh. Of course, Billy had read lots of books on the Holocaust before, hiding them behind dustcovers from *The Fireside Book of Baseball* or *Ten Ever-Lovin' Years with Pogo,* so his par-

ents wouldn't worry. But the stories and the pictures had always seemed
far away; he couldn't find the secret route to take them inside himself.
Now the few words from Dr. Jacobs this morning became the magical
drop of blood; the books and pictures became *Dr. Jacobs' story,* his
friend who stood with him outside Block Eleven, the punishment block,
next to the wooden boxes where *it can't walk, it can't sit, it can't lie
down,* but has to bend over like the hunchback Jew until its spine cracks,
it suffocates and dies. They watched snow fall on another apathetic victim's indifferent cap. The other inmates . . . *no,* he and Dr. Jacobs,
because the man in this book, he'd said something Billy was sure Dr.
Jacobs had wanted to tell him: *a man is capable of anything, even the
worst thing, just to live another minute.* They poured freezing water
over the *muselmann*'s head until his body probably tremored slowly, like
Jesse's had when Frank had dragged him back onto the boat.

Long ago, reading that big encyclopedia, Billy had dreamt his father
would carry him. But then he'd learned to draw, and—he became frightened even thinking this—he'd become the stronger one of them. Then
once upon a time, he'd maybe been like a little boy, thinking Dr. Jacobs
would look after him. Now he knew that Dr. Jacobs couldn't even protect himself. Still, Billy might have *company.* He could witness another
man's suffering—and Dr. Jacobs might see Billy's.

The guards would laugh at them. During the night, the *muselmann*
would sicken, ready to be chosen for special treatment; or he'd save the
Nazis the trouble of killing him and die. Billy heard his father walking
down the hall *in Great Neck.* He pushed the book underneath his blanket, saw his father's outline in the door, the light from the hall seeming to
fade as it neared his body. Billy squinched his eyes shut; his father's lips
brushed his cheek, bringing him back to the bed.

The next day the boy asked Dr. Jacobs if he'd ever been punished.
"There, I mean. In Block Eleven?"

Hadn't his daughter asked him about this, too? Why this particular
curiosity? Leo wondered. Did it make things seem more ordinary—as if
the punishment block in Auschwitz meant that the rest was . . . what?
Not punishment? Well, perhaps it wasn't. Not punishment, not forma-
tion or training; annihilation only. He must wean him now, not talk
about his life anymore. "No," he said, perhaps too sharply.

And just as he'd told his imagined Smerless, the boy's face fell inward on itself, unable to bear his doctor's silence. Perhaps it would help
Billy to know that he'd once shared some of Billy's own fears, if he
told him how each week their bastard *kapo* had ordered them to lie

facedown on their bunks so he could inspect their feet. Nowhere to wash, yet Jews who the man decided had too much filth between their toes had to run in circles in the freezing courtyard. Leo had once been one of those dirty animals, feeling weakness and confusion spurt up in him as he talked—the child's shame at his own dirt mixed with the inmate's fear as he got weaker and weaker with each turn, the office floor falling away from him. Thank heavens this hour was over! Still, as Billy tied his sweater around his waist, Leo rallied himself to provide a moral. "But here I am." He smiled to say, *So you'll probably survive gym class.*

"Well, that's my point in a nutshell," Weiss said, as Billy closed the door. "Misunderstanding piled on mistake, until Auschwitz becomes a homily: Great Neck *kinder* needn't worry about displaying their genitals to other boys in the high school showers—because Leo Jacobs survived the death camps!"

Leo gave Billy a few minutes to get down the driveway, before beginning his own stroll through his dagwoods. *Well,* he said to Weiss, *at least I left out the things that I most need to say.* Meaning—Weiss knew best among all the dead and the living—that the next morning Leo had leaned against his wooden bunk exhausted from his exercise, spitting up rust-colored sputum. The SS man had pointed his walking stick at him.

Not wanting to die at that moment, Leo had extended his arm, and the trailing *kapo* had written down the number. Leo, who'd been sure he'd never in his life believed there was a God, had whispered, as if surprised, "There is no judgment, and there is no Judge."

The clean officer had smiled at him with tight lips that said, *But there is, Jew. I am.*

Leo sat down on the ground, leaned against the thin tree trunk in Great Neck, securely among the living—which was *his* innermost and very suburban hell. The prisoner-clerk who'd collated the *kapo*'s numbers had been a comrade from Leo's cell in the Austrian CP. One cold night in Vienna, Leo had missed dinner before a cell meeting where the speaker had spoken with certainty about the Agenda of History. Afterward, desperately hungry and wanting company, he'd bought coffee and pastry for this comrade—one who didn't have a rich wife—a gentile later arrested for his politics, sent to Auschwitz. With the express purpose on the deity's part that he save Leo Jacobs? No, Accident had saved Leo—a missed meal, a long speech, an immoderate need for sugar—and *not* the Almighty's right hand, because there are no such hands, neither left nor right.

And someone else had been sent to be murdered that day instead of

Leo, who had been put in the infirmary of paper bandages, had recovered because he recovered.

When he returned to the lab, Weiss had "wandered off." The man who'd forgiven Leo his pathetic specialness as Freud's son had perhaps been the very one sent to the gas chambers instead of him, Weiss not realizing until that moment, perhaps, how very special Leo was. *But had it been Weiss?* He remembered asking a wraith in his work group what day Weiss had left them. The man's emaciated face, his hollow eyes filled with as much fury as he still had strength for. These were things dangerous to talk about, and pointless and sentimental to boot.

If only he'd been able to recruit Weiss for the Party, he thought. If only he hadn't been so amiable, so easily worked on by Leo, and had fled over the mountains to Switzerland.

"Or if only I'd married a rich woman, the way you did," a ghostly Weiss said, the Weiss of the mountains on his way to a farm to barter for poultry, wearing that stupid Tyrolean hat. Weiss smiled, fully, like they'd just found a plump chicken for dinner. "Or if only I hadn't been born a Jew. And then, of course, another of your *if onlys.*" He stopped, pushed his hat back over his bald spot.

"Look, Leo, the chamber was crammed full of bodies that day, Polish Jews, some Gypsies. It could have been any of a thousand people who died instead of you."

That was no help at all. *Someone* had filled out the quota, someone had died instead of him. And sometimes, Leo admitted, it felt to his unconscious as if each one who'd died had died instead of *him.*

"Leo, darling," Weiss said with fond annoyance, "can't you see how well Freud had you pegged?" He squatted beside him now, in his camp stripes, his face as Leo had last seen it, bones barely held together by taut skin. "You're much too eager to feel guilty," Weiss said musingly. "You know, I always thought you actually liked your guilt just a little too much. The rest of us, we were free in our bourgeois pleasures. But that meant we were such pointless, whimsical creatures compared to Leo Jacobs. He had to justify his life, account for his salvation from the abortionist, save the whole world!" Weiss stopped. "Have you seen my hat?" He looked about him, bewildered. "Oh, well, your guilt's been useful to you," he continued, "hasn't it? Days it didn't keep you in bed, it gave you a little extra impulsion for your essays—where you can dream the nattering voice of guilt gets drowned out by the orgy."

Leo felt his face flushing.

"And now, it has to be that *everyone* in the Shoah died instead of Leo Jacobs. Or maybe that isn't enough for you. After all it was your membership in the CP that saved you, so let's add Bukharin, the Doctor's Plot, and the gulag, shall we?"

"Or look, David," Leo said, "perhaps I'm just being clever, accusing myself with crimes so general as to be vacuous, because it's better than the specific truth?" This reversal—Leo as prosecutor of Leo, the ghost as defender—was traditional with them, almost comforting. "After all, you know German accounting methods, David. On that day, the substitute had to come from our work group."

"For God's sake, what does it matter?" the ghost said, exasperated as always. "Stop this ridiculous game of this one rather than that one. The Germans are the ones who murdered me." Weiss lifted his face up to the blue, indifferent, suburban sky. "Not you. Me and six million more. I might have died then, instead of you. I'd certainly have died later."

And as always, Weiss' exasperated forgiveness just made Leo feel worse. "Not necessarily, David. I didn't."

And to that David—as always—said, "*Hmmm*. A good point. Who knows? It's all accident, after all."

Leo smiled, thinking that maybe this had been David's malicious plan all along: act the kindly father and make Leo feel all the guiltier. Then say, as if won over by Leo's arguments, that if it hadn't been for Leo, well, yes, he might have survived.

But Weiss hadn't. Because Communists contrived that others died instead of their comrades, all loyalties only tribal, Leo thought, Communists protecting Communists, Jews—and how rarely we can do it!—protecting Jews. And what keeps a tribe together, what even makes it a tribe, but enemies to despise—to murder?

No, that must not be anymore. Or so he'd vowed once—no doubt another pointless piety to Weiss, leading mostly to homilies to his daughter about Marcuse's idle notions, the "Internationale" of the human race. Did he think that if she believed, then he might believe that humanity could find a wider connection, an erotic, playerful ... no, playful ... erratic ... oh, empty rhetoric! He noticed a sickly sweet smell all around him from his trivial ideas. Or from something called cocoa mulch that the gardener had put down here. Is this what they made that wretched "soft drink" from? He stood up and carefully brushed the back of his blue pin-striped pants. Brown flecks stuck to his fingers. He had lain in a field of chocolate! *Eros Macht Frei*, he thought, and almost smiled. What, he wondered, would Ellen Jaffe, spying from her kitchen window, make of all this?

· · ·

On the *Freedom* that May, Billy, in white tennis shorts and a cotton shirt, told his friends the little that Dr. Jacobs had told him and the much more that he'd learned from books. But really that was from Dr. Jacobs too, wasn't it, so it was all right to tell everyone that he'd told him those things, Billy's words tumbling over each other, because he was uncertain it *was* all right to talk about *any* of this after the last terrible session, Dr. Jacobs sitting there silently for what seemed like hours before he told him that story about the *kapo*. What if Dr. Jacobs wouldn't accompany him anymore? He sputtered to a stop.

But not before his words had made Beth Jacobs sick to her stomach, her father having told her that he couldn't talk about Auschwitz because he couldn't ever tell *anyone*. So he must think the boy spiritually superior to her—and probably because he was a boy. She stared at the water, her anger just wearying her, even then knowing that she'd long ago swallowed her father whole, and that the withering disdain she wanted to direct at Billy Green and her father would have been done with her father's tight-lipped smile.

For relief, she looked to her lover squatting by the sail in his black bathing suit, and his beauty transformed her anger into fear for him; his body could be broken, too, his sinews could become nutrients for broth. Her bowels tightened. That night, she swore, she'd stroke his legs until he was stiff, and then she'd do something for him they'd talked about but never done—namely, take his dick into her mouth. She trailed her hand in the cool water, imagining his face going taut, his mouth open in wonder as he came. She almost forgot what had worried her. After all, look at him so lithe, strong, handsome—Billy's nonsense had made her foolish. Frank Jaffe of Great Neck, New York, wasn't about to die, for God's sake! No, he was about to have the time of his life.

Ann served Leo some salad from the wooden Dansk bowl, just enough greens for two, her daughter having gone to a movie with Frank Jaffe, a boy certainly too old for Beth, but what could she say—after all, she thought ruefully, they'd been so proud of how precocious she'd been in other ways. And if Ann tried to stop them, they'd just sneak around behind her back anyway—the way *she* would have at Beth's age. Besides, she was actually glad to have dinner alone with her husband— what even a year ago would have been an almost intolerable hour. Now he was often again the brilliant, kind, attentive man she'd married. It was an age of miracles, a camp survivor turned into an almost ordinary uxorious suburban husband, one who could even remember where he'd left the car. Still, they had to face facts about Beth. Ann needed to talk to her about birth control. But each time she'd brought that up with Leo he'd been blinded by . . . whatever it was that blinded fathers. Baboon possessiveness? They'd been walking by the dock, about to meet the kids returning from their sail, the sun nearly set, the air feeling cool to Ann in a flowered sleeveless Lilly Pulitzer, but her husband, alas, still in his Brooks Brothers uniform, his white shirt and plain maroon tie. A sweaty burgher here—especially compared to the lovely New World children now bobbing and waving to them from the edge of the float where they'd moored Laura's sailboat. His patient, sporting a ridiculous-looking pompadour, wore blue jeans, and an alligator over his heart. He looked sick to see that his doctor ever left his consulting room—as Ann, she had to admit, would have herself, if it had been her doctor. His analysand's daughter wore a brightly patterned shirt, Bermuda shorts, and knee socks, reminding her husband of lederhosen. "Great Neck wandervogel, eh?" Frank Jaffe, a handsome boy, had on tight red bathing trunks that showed the outline of his genitals. He rowed the dinghy toward the dock and her daughter that much closer to unwed motherhood. They *had* to deal with birth control immediately, she'd said the week before, but Leo had analyzed her worry away, Frank's attraction to Beth being nothing more, he said, than an aberration of transference, Leo suddenly blind to how beautiful their daughter was, her full breasts, her long, straight black hair, her even teeth, and her green eyes. And—special dispensation from God—she'd had maybe one pimple since she had entered puberty. Ann imagined telling that to Leo, God indifferent to Auschwitz but concerned about zits, about as much sense as his theory that Frank was just being oedipally competitive, wishing to deflower the daughter of his mother's therapist, his surrogate father. That way Frank could also take revenge on behalf of his actual, seemingly weak father, the one Leo had supplanted, etc., etc. "She'll see that none of it," he'd concluded, "is truly about her."

Nonsense—or anyway a matter of indifference to Frank's sperm. But she had waited till now to bring up birth control again.

"He's an admirable boy, really, isn't he?" Leo said. "A leader in the civil rights group at his college." He smiled. "A fond, foolish nonviolent warrior."

He's reconciling himself to the inevitable, Ann thought, and decided not to say, *So what? He still has a penis, doesn't he?* She passed Leo his salad plate. He stayed up to wait for Beth every night, heard her version of *oh, nothing, oh, nowhere,* and got a good-night kiss. Something—Frank perhaps—had come between them, but they still loved each other.

Leo worried that the Jaffe family's awe of Dr. King and his nonviolence might lead the boy, and perhaps his own most precious treasure, into underground rivers of passion and violence they couldn't possibly navigate. "After all, I know what racists might do, eh? I know Gandhian protest will *not* matter to men without a conscience." Still, it was his fault too, he said, all his talk about changing the world, when what he wanted her to do, really, was simply to survive, find work she loved, have children perhaps. Too late to say that now, though.

But not too late, Ann said finally, to have Beth fitted for a diaphragm.

Tonight he nodded, ate some salad, the two of them looking at their plates, feeling their age probably, and the loss of their little girl, the one running out of that funny little red preschool—Mrs. Tucker's Progressive—to hug her father.

"You know," her husband said, finally, "I have a patient who wears earrings made from cattle bones?"

"Do you?"

"Do you think my stories are like those earrings? It makes him feel more important to hear them?"

"You mean Billy Green?" The little boy again. She wondered how much he'd been telling him?

Leo nodded.

"Perhaps they give a suburban boy his connection to the Void, to death? Is that why he forces me to talk about it?"

"Does he force you, darling?" She smiled. "I can't imagine anyone forcing you to do things." She paused. Perhaps that compliment had been a mistake. Once, after all, he'd been forced to do many things.

Leo smiled, but fully, the whole tilting set on display—as if he could actually see a joke on himself. "So why do I think he *needs* to learn these things?"

Ann turned her salad fork about, careful not to spear any of the greens. She didn't want to say the wrong thing. Her husband talking to her frankly now, intimately, but a tine put falsely could make him think her unfeeling.

"What will it protect him from?" Leo asked himself. "For God's sake, his life is all barrel staves and sailboats!"

Ann raised her eyebrows. That should be all right. It's what her analyst would have done.

"Yet it's like he has an old soul."

Again, Ann fell back on what she remembered her analyst doing. "An old soul?"

That seemed to work. Leo stared up at the ceiling and went on talking. "Is the boy's sorrow just the result of bad ears or neurosis?"

You bet it is, Ann thought to herself. She'd heard about him from his own mother: the class report; the moldy soup. But she lifted her eyebrows again in what she hoped was a neutral, inquiring way.

"It's as if he somehow already knows that life is often monstrous, unjust crimes."

"And if he does?" Which was utter nonsense to start with. A boy was a boy, after all, snakes and snails and puppy dog tails, no "old souls." Billy Green was just a child, filled with a typical Great Neck kid's *"look at me."*

"Well, if he senses how awful life can be, then he must think he's insane, all this Great Neck noise in his ears, this continual bar mitzvah party. All sugary harmonies, no dissonance." Leo smiling as if to mock himself, say he couldn't quite mean this, though he did, Ann knew. "Perhaps he needs someone to tell him some of the worst," Leo said. "Reassure him, actually, that the world is a little the way he's always sensed with his inner ear." He ate a forkful of salad and smiled. "Not like Great Neck." A green leaf stuck to a front tooth that jutted slightly toward her.

What twaddle! Still, Ann felt jealous, and decided not to tell him about the ridiculous green spot on his tooth. But it wasn't *just* jealousy; she had her own experience of analysis, too. "Are you sure," she said, "this is good for the boy?" Then, she nearly trembled at what she'd done: calling her allrightnick husband wrong.

His eyes, staring through goggle-sized glasses, terrified her. Why had she done it? What did she care what happened to this little boy? And what if this era of good feeling came from telling a little of his past to this kid? Unlikely, but why risk it? She didn't want his sadness back, crushing everyone.

What, Leo wondered, looking at Ann's lovely green eyes, could this beautiful red-haired woman possibly see in him? "Perhaps you're right," he said quietly. He'd formed a bond with the Green boy. He had to be on guard now; anything more he said might well be only his own self-indulgence. And in any case, it would just bring him closer to Weiss, and perhaps something worse for him even than his guilt about that: namely, the Communist Party. He'd give it a rest.

"Darling," his wife said, putting her finger to her front tooth, "you have a little something there."

. . .

A few weeks later, when Billy Green asked him yet another question about Auschwitz, Leo blinked at the undersized boy who had on a blue V-necked sweater, the sort Leo would see in magazines in the twenties. He took off his glasses, rubbed his eyes like a man waking from a dream. Ann had been right. He'd be quiet now, say nothing more about the camps to a boy who couldn't possibly truly understand, shouldn't understand. After all, why would a doctor want to shatter inwardly a patient he'd sworn to make whole? Besides, Leo had looked again at Herbert's book that very morning, *Eros and Civilization*—where the primal words, *Karl Marx,* courageously appeared absolutely nowhere. If Herbert remained that reticent, then clearly it was all still dangerous to talk about. At least, Leo thought, he hadn't blown this boy's head full of wind, the way he'd once inflated his poor daughter's *kopf,* repeating Herbert's fantasy that Eros would someday blend so powerfully with death that it would transform our evil urges. Why had he told her all that nonsense when he'd long ago stopped believing it himself? Freud had known better, had offered us only two choices: death made external is the bomb and the camps; death internalized is the body imprisoned by guilt.

Or *formed*? Maybe only death can make the amorphous monstrous hive of our appetites into a human form—a mensch. Or was that just more talk? After all, for a man of his generation, being without ideology made one feel naked, speechless, like an infant, or an animal. Or maybe he just wanted to distract himself from this nearly crying boy who, desperate to get Leo to talk again, said, "What about the man in the funny feathered hat?" probably hoping that if he put it that way his doctor might answer him.

Leo smiled. "We need to talk about you now, Billy, not me or David Weiss." He sat silently, raised his brows inquiringly. Billy bent over, a child with a stomachache, seemingly devastated when he so utterly lost the intuitive vein that linked him to his doctor. Oh, he should definitely have weaned the boy earlier! Now, for the analysis to succeed—let alone for his own self-protection—he had to fail Billy by not talking to him, no matter how much the boy had come to expect it.

Or maybe he should gratify him just a little bit more, tell him about David's death? No, neither of them could bear that. Besides, Billy might tell the other children, someone would find out how Leo had survived, they'd find him here, in Great Neck. As Herbert had said, even in very nice places the police may turn against you.

So, when you're at a loss, Leo thought, follow the rules; that's the meaning of *a profession*. He couldn't bring himself to say, "Why do you ask?" like some psychoanalytic joke, so he would just be silent—and pray to Freud that that would be the best course.

Billy put his arms across his chest. Maybe the baker's boy, he dreamt, had gone to the camps with Dr. Jacobs, even though the boy could barely hear. The baker's boy would be terrified all the time that a *kapo* standing behind him would shout an order when Dr. Jacobs would be unable to lean down to him and say the order into his ear. It would get just too wearyingly hard to survive.

"What are you thinking?" Dr. Jacobs asked.

Should he tell him? *No.* Dr. Jacobs wouldn't talk to Billy anymore, had made it clear that there was so much more that Billy couldn't help him with, couldn't even hear about because he was a weak and worthless kid. *Inconsiderable.* Okay, then he'd show Dr. Jacobs that he didn't need his help, either. He wouldn't tell him that in the camps the baker's boy had put himself ahead of Dr. Jacobs, protecting *him* this time as his former protector coughed up blood-tinged sputum. As he was led to the gas chamber, the boy saw Dr. Jacobs' eyes fill with sorrow, with guilt, with love.

"Nothing," Billy said. "I wasn't thinking anything." He smiled at Dr. Jacobs with his lips still shut, meaning, *I'll never trust you again if you believe me now.*

But no time left that Friday to find out if Dr. Jacobs could be trusted again; their hour was up.

The next Sunday, the universal "maid's day off," Leo and Ann ate at Squire's Delicatessen. Leo watched the other burghers' sharp, even teeth tear at pieces of chicken in the pot, flanken, whitefish. Their comfort foods. More Eastern European than his *mittel* memories.

"I took your advice," he said. "I stopped talking to that patient I told you about. You were right. It's time for him to be weaned."

Ann felt anxious (did *he* still need the boy?), but flattered, too. "I'm sure you did the right thing."

He picked up another sour pickle, imagining a whisper of surprise in the eyes of the middle-aged woman at the next table who'd actually shaved off her eyebrows, then painted a thin, even line above her eyes. Did she know him? Well, they *all* did. The man who was in life but not of it anymore, who should live on air—not dilled cucumbers. "The Christians," he said to Ann, "have their saints. The Jews have us." He took another bite. "But they don't know what to do with us."

"Us, dear?" she asked disingenuously, dreading where this sourness might lead him. Lately, though, he talked to her about the wonders of guilt, and didn't seem so weighed down by it anymore. And what did he have to feel so guilty about? She rooted around discreetly, the way her analyst would, but the more she asked, the more abstract Leo became, all about the beauty of feeling bad, not whatever it was he actually felt bad about. "The rabbis saw the value of guilt," he'd told her. "Only a life lived intimately with death is worthy of God's attention." He laughed. "Or Freud's." He'd even bought himself a beautiful new gold-nibbed Waterman pen—his bar mitzvah present, he called it—for an essay he planned to write, his ode to guilt. But what was really on his mind? That the world hadn't done enough for the survivors? Hardly his style. No, something else must be hidden in this vacuous general confession. A pair of glasses stolen from Weiss, perhaps, something like that, she couldn't remember, that he'd talked about only once, and long ago. It had been something everyone who survived must have done, and probably the ones who died, too. Anyway, the tune had certainly changed from when they'd met sixteen years before, when he'd piped song about pleasure tying humanity together. At least he was piping again, that's what mattered. They'd probably even make love tonight, Ann thought, imagining a new holiday in their honor, with the menorah of the long—and could it be actually happily?—married: every candle marking a time the couple had sex in one week!

"Once the tattoos meant we weren't human, but animals," he was saying now. "Now: not human, but angels."

The amiable fat waiter brought their sandwiches, stared disapprovingly at the pickle. "Don't spoil your appetite, Doctor," he said. The New York deli style, Ann thought. Much fake chiding of customers. Many dollops of false, brusque maternal care. Like analysis in that way. Leo smiled at the waiter and pointed with his pickle at the empty bowl. Sol balanced the bowl like a mock chalice in his fat palm and padded off. Their little secret, Ann thought. Since the camps, free food sang siren songs to Leo. Sol plopped another bowl down. Leo made a spectacle of himself at her family weddings, any buffet, psychoanalytic society banquets even. Here he devoured three full bowls of half-sours with every sandwich.

Ann paused, her pastrami in midair, and waited till Leo looked down again. He was her husband—but it was still hard to eat a dripping sandwich while a saint watched, even one who freeloaded pickles.

"Okay, I admit I'm an angel to some of them only," Leo said. He slathered mustard onto his warm brisket with the teeny white spoon. "The ones who want to be tough, they dream I've been humiliated beyond their imagining. They can't stand to look at me. But the rest of them imagine my suffering has made me a special kind of doll, the Sickly Lamedvovnik. Like a Bettie Wettie."

Ann couldn't help herself, these chances came so rarely. "Betsy Wetsy."

"They can do a good deed if they say hello to me, or bring me pickles or . . ." He smiled at her, fully, maliciously, like he was about to say, *or if they fuck me*. He had another nibble of pickle. "They think I've seen so much violence I could never harm anyone." He took a big bite out of his sandwich and smiled at her. "Don't tell on me."

She put her hand on his, delighted by the way he seemed to accept all this now, to laugh at them and at himself. "I promise, darling. I promise."

"There's so much about me that they must never know," he said, but he was smiling. Pity they'd never had his teeth fixed. "They'd be so disappointed in their Angel of Auschwitz!"

Years later, at Beth's bail hearing, Laura looked over as Mrs. Jacobs put her arm around her weak, seemingly dependent husband, the man who had survived Auschwitz by studying it, the man who broke ranks with the psych establishment to tell us about the wonders of guilt, the essay that had made him famous. "Some guilt is overblown," he wrote—or something like that. Laura, after all, had read it fourteen years ago—the winter before Frank died—lying facedown on her bed in Great Neck, her feet on the pillow and the daunting double columns of *Commentary* magazine on the floor beneath her. "But there's also an order to the whirl and swirl that every day creates and re-creates us. There might not be an external Judge to punish us if we wound that order, yet our hearts still insist that we must heal it."

Thinking about it now, it seemed like a Hallmark card, like *Happy Mother's Day, Dear Universe, I feel terrible for how I've fucked you over*. Still, a safe bet that reading it in Great Neck had probably made her cry—everything did in those days. (And now? Well, after a kabillion years of analysis, not *quite* everything.) He'd said that there's always a core to the patient's guilt that marks a task, and maybe psychoanalysts, instead of analyzing and denigrating guilt, should help the patient find that core, a notion Laura had occasionally thought about, sitting opposite some vet who'd torched a village, or heard about it, or been in the same army that had done it, though her patients' task, she thought, was to stop shooting smack and get a fucking job. Was there actually some career for him that would help make up for the burnt village, when with stagflation there were no jobs at all, and if there were, vets who were addicts and Zippo masters scared the shit out of future employers. Or her, for that matter, like the client she'd seen just yesterday, with his Mohawk, tattoos, muscles out to here, a red self-made plastic codpiece over his genitals, and a surgical mask around his mouth, the costume of one of BillyBooks' equivocal villains, the Haunted Desperado (formerly a blood-drinking greyhound of Athena X), art become reality with a gun collection in this case, a man who must *never* find out that his therapist was *actually* SheWolf. That could only lead to Desperado dreams that he might carry her off for a romantic afternoon at the Singularity, the Outsiders' fortress, forever protected by a MyKill beam that placed it outside the Continuum—or the laws of the State of New York.

What had she actually understood of Dr. Jacobs' essay when she'd read it at sweet sixteen. Or now, for that matter? Anyway, she could see that Leo Jacobs had come a long way from his early articles—ones she'd recently checked out of the institute archives—fantasies about orgies and paint as poop, a utopia where people pleased themselves and each other so much they didn't even *dream* of hurting anyone. Dr. Jacobs had gotten young Beth to believe in that Erewhon, then—like a hippie become an Orthodox investment banker—he'd returned to the rabbis, left her with her tie-dyes and a pelvic inflammatory disease. So his new gospel, *We Must Tend the Whole,* had made Beth furious. She felt betrayed.

"We must tend the asshole," she'd screamed the week the *Commentary* article came out, she and Laura on their way to a wild Greenwich Village night (i.e., coffee and nosh at the Hungry Bagel and a late train trip home).

The word *asshole* made the other people on the train look at them —or so they imagined, their stares being one of the pleasures of the adventure.

"Really," Beth had said when she calmed down that evening, "my father always loved regret most of all, eh?"

Laura had shrugged, turned her head to the side. Even then, she'd sensed you didn't want to take one side of a person's ambivalence. Outside the window, the driving range at Douglaston went by, like childhood.

"Shame, sadness, and death, that's what my father likes best, I think. After all, what can Eros mean," she'd said, "to a man who can't even take off his cabana jacket at the pool?"

That's because of the numbers, Laura had thought. *You know that,* but Beth was on a tear, talking in full paragraphs, her voice choked— angry but also bewildered by her own enduring love.

Soon she'd begun to cry. Laura had put her arm around her, rested her head against her shoulder.

How do you think Billy Green feels now about Leo Jacobs, the Prophet of Guilt? Laura asked imaginary Smerless. Needing a shoulder to lean on herself to get her through this hearing, she fantasized about the analytic hour to come this afternoon.

Smerless stayed clammed up, of course, even in fantasy.

But she could hear his pen scratching on his notebook page. The imaginary sound reassured her, made her feel he was paying attention, and that she, like a fine work of art, was *fascinating.* She gazed at a peace pipe then, its drab, faded feathers dangling down defeatedly from the bowl, while her mind imagined *her own* article on Billy Green appearing in the double columns of the *IJOP.* Abstract: The destructive effects of a too strong, unanalyzed countertransference. "He used Billy," she would say emphatically this afternoon.

"Hmmm?" Smerless would reply, which Laura knew she'd probably translate into mad curiosity. "How?"

"Billy Green was an avid, pious, teenage boy, Doctor. He was ripe for the plucking. Doctor Jacobs had a fantasy about him, made him into someone special who needed to hear what Doctor Jacobs so badly wanted to tell him. Billy was a sucker for that. It made up for being a Little Guy."

Laura hoped Smerless—distinguished head of the training analysts at the New York Psychoanalytic, and, even more nobly, Her Mother's Analyst's Analyst—would hear the Hidden Message in her criticism of Leo Jacobs, namely, implied praise for his more classical, utterly with- holding, technique. "I've tried to get Billy to see you," she would say, offering the acoustic ceiling tiles a lovely ortho-corrected smile. "He just needs to see someone good, have himself analyzed again. But *soon—* before he does something really meshugah. He's talking about going to Israel. Actually, he wouldn't last a day in Israel, would he?" *Actually,* why did she think her doctor would know the answer to *that* question?

But when she'd even hinted to the real Billy, fantasy member of the Israeli Defense Force, about a new analysis to cure him of his soldier boy fantasy, he'd put his breadstick down on the white tablecloth, and his eyes filled with his endless supply of personal holy water. "I'm not going to complain about him to another doctor, Laura," he'd said, "a guy who actually knows him."

Still, looking at Dr. Jacobs now, his wife stroking his lined cheek, as if there were no one else in the courtroom, Laura thought she might give him a reduced sentence due to mitigating circumstances. After all, Billy Green really wasn't one who could ever deal with a *real* analysis and its desert-like silences, or even with a dinner table companion going to the ladies' room. Dr. Jacobs probably had responded to Billy's questions almost reluctantly at first, to keep him from disintegrating in the chair. Then—she could imagine this slippery slope so easily, *not* with the Haunted Desperado wanna-be, for God's sake, but there *were* others, you know—the doctor might have occasionally given in to his own need (not that *she ever* had), like a man who comforts a grieving widow (or a grieving veteran?) and finds it almost imperceptibly turns into lovemaking; the problem with *this* affair being that when the doctor ends it and shuts up, the patient feels devastated.

Then fantasy Smerless' imagined silence began to trouble her. She pulled one of his Navajo blankets over her bare legs to warm herself. God, she'd been stupid! Smerless had analyzed Dr. Jacobs, it had to feel to him like if she criticized Jacobs' handling of Billy's case, she was attacking Smerless' most successful son, the one who'd become truly famous, Dr. Jacobs' guilt shtick having moved him right out of the educational TV ghetto and into the *Times Magazine* by the sixties, when she and her friends, her parents thought, had lost all restraint, the old folks not seeing that it was probably guilt for not stopping the war, for not healing the world so Auschwitz would never happen again, that had actually driven the kids mad in the first place.

Meanwhile, that morning in court, the famous expert on suffering, guilt, and child-rearing leaned his head on his still beautiful wife's shoulder, had his cheek soothed by Ann Jacobs, whose long, lovely bones held her face taut, her own large eyes gleaming with tears. A little zaftig maybe, but she still had a figure. Laura hoped she'd look that good when she was sixty-five, even if she had to look that sad. But that would be the defendant's happy fate, not hers.

She looked away from the grieving couple to where Billy made a big X through the picture he'd been drawing. Maybe a picture of Jacobs? But Laura felt guilty just for thinking it. She most certainly wouldn't say *anything* about *any* of this to the real Dr. Smerless that afternoon.

But in 1963, before either of them had been on talk shows, Billy Green didn't want to draw an X through his doctor. No, he wanted *Harold's* purple crayon, so he could redraw the vein that had connected them, the one that made his doctor trust him and provide nourishment for him almost like he couldn't help himself. He wanted Dr. Jacobs to stop just sitting silently opposite him for days on end, not really answering Billy's questions—though Billy kept asking, of course, sure that Dr. Jacobs wanted him to show that he really wanted to know, and that Dr. Jacobs' refusal didn't hurt him so much anymore that he would let his heavy body stop him from asking. Billy tried talking about David Weiss in different ways, even saying stupid things, like "He was a doctor too, right?" the kind of questions a child asks that show he hasn't been listening, questions that are answered irritably but *are* answered. Or he asked about other things, even ones he knew the answers to from his reading, though he felt embarrassed to think his doctor would conclude he hadn't done any reading, didn't know anything—like what *geheimnistrager* meant.

But no matter what he did, Dr. Jacobs wouldn't talk to him about his life. Today he even said, "Billy, I want to thank you for listening to me," which made Billy shrink inside himself. Dr. Jacobs shouldn't be thanking him, like they were *friends* and he wouldn't take care of Billy anymore— or no more than Arthur Kaplan did. "You've really helped me, Billy," Dr. Jacobs said, and the space between them grew. "I even think I might write something again. And someday, perhaps, in your art, you will do something about all this, too. Something better than I can do, because you won't be so pressed against the fence of the actual." He smiled more fully than Billy had ever seen before, showing uneven brown stumps, and he bent toward Billy's chair as if he wanted to put his hand on Billy's arm. Billy leaned away. "But we've talked enough about me," Dr. Jacobs said. "Next time we have to concentrate on you." He gestured toward the door with a slight shake of his head. "But for today our hour is up." He stood and reached out his arm, like he meant to shake Billy's hand. Billy knew he mustn't put his hand in the doctor's or Dr. Jacobs wouldn't protect him anymore. But brain didn't get the message to arm fast enough, he could already feel the doctor's misshapen knuckles, the dry skin. Billy had thought his doctor's touch would be weird, magical, but it was ordinary, warm, all too human. Worst of all, the handshake meant: *equals*. And equals meant abandonment.

Had he failed Dr. Jacobs? What did Dr. Jacobs want him to do? Why wouldn't he talk to him anymore and help him figure that out? Billy passed the Jaffes' tennis courts, headed down the hill toward home. Should he draw cartoons about the camps? But you couldn't tell that story in the same words that Americans used to order pizzas, let alone in little pictures.

Besides, he thought, already bitter at his doctor's sudden prolonged silences, what if that wasn't what *he* wanted to do, his mind keeping him awake all night recently with his own ideas for stories, like something with a woman hero, and not just a Super/Bat/girl thing?

He started running then, the hill carrying him forward and through the brown stone gates. He wanted to get away from Dr. Jacobs now. If he wouldn't talk to him anymore about his life, then Billy wanted to have his own thoughts, like maybe doing something with Beth Jacobs, making her really powerful and wise, a girl who knew secret ways to destroy people just by touching them. His dad said that with the new code you could only show her cleavage, but he bet he could still make Beth look really sexy. After all, he'd never even seen her breasts, and she made him hard all the time. Maybe the Beth character could even team with Billy Bad Ears. How would Dr. Jacobs feel about that? Well, who cares? What would Johnny Ryan say? He'd say that Dr. Jacobs could go fuck himself, that's what!

He stopped ten houses from home. *Wait,* he wanted to tell his doctor, *that's not real,* or only Johnny Ryan would say that, not *him.* Billy really wanted to do what Dr. Jacobs wanted, knew that Dr. Jacobs would be really sad if he didn't do something that helped him not to be sad about the world, maybe try to change the world even. But without Dr. Jacobs' help he just didn't know what he should do to change it. Couldn't Dr. Jacobs see that? And that thought made Billy furious again.

For months after that, Dr. Jacobs still wouldn't talk to Billy. Billy's anger must have made Dr. Jacobs sick. Billy had always known that would be the problem, that once Dr. Jacobs realized what he was like inside he'd be disgusted with him, throw him out of their room, or just sit silently, unwilling to trust him anymore. So Billy told him things about school, or skating, or comic books he was working on, but now that Billy knew Dr. Jacobs had seen into him, knew his fury, his hatefulness, he knew it wouldn't work; he couldn't win him back. *It's all become a stupid waste of time,* he thought, walking home after a session, picking up acorns to crush between rocks. He snuck past his father sitting in the sunken living room, so he wouldn't have to tell him that things with Dr. Jacobs were going Nowhere, Billy feeling more and more sick of himself, of his own smell, which was, he knew, worse than shitty, like an animal's, yes, but not the way Dr. Jacobs' had been, no, more like the stench of one of the angry murderers, the Nazis. No wonder Dr. Jacobs hated Billy now and wouldn't help him become someone he wouldn't hate.

"To become a mensch," Rabbi Meltzer, the sour leader of the Nassau Synagogue, said to Billy when he went to him for advice about his repellent fury, "means to bind one's anger, to offer it as a sacrifice," and those words felt completely right, the key to the lock. Billy still went to Dr. Jacobs once a week to tell him silly things about gym class or sit silently across from his silence, but he eagerly went to learn with Rabbi Meltzer—and to follow as best he could the 613 rules of the Orthodox. He would obey the Law, and that would mean he would no longer be like one of the murderers.

Lately, Judaism had been burnished up in Arthur Kaplan's eyes, too, in his case by his sister June's potential fiancé, Specs (né Ralph Waldo) Mangione, who was also a possible new convert to the faith.

But convert or not, should the guy be allowed to marry June? That was the debate topic just about every night at the Kaplan family dinner table: IS RALPH A GOOD MAN?

For the affirmative, Arthur Kaplan, positive that Ralph was the best kind of man—one who could get tickets for Yankees games.

Once again, though: how does he get those tickets? Does he still *know* Mafiosi?

"Have you ever met his family?" Arthur's father asked the star of this dinner theater, the red-haired June Kaplan. "The boy sounds like an orphan."

"He *is* an orphan, Dad," June said, not looking up from the slice of cantaloupe the maid had just plopped down in front of her. "You know, like his parents are both dead."

Arthur's mother turned her searchlights on the Sullen Princess. "But have you met *any* of his family, dear?"

June continued to stare mutely at the orange-colored melon.

"You say his parents are gone," his mother said, like maybe Specs had lied, had them stashed in New Jersey, ready to pop up at the wedding. "But doesn't he have any aunts and uncles? Is he ashamed of his family?"

"Not half as much as I am of mine," June said. Unweepy. Nice controlled delivery, kind of Joey Bishop deadpan.

His parents talked about Specs marrying this comedienne like June was the Grand Prize in the Marriage Sweepstakes. After all, his mother said, June was thin, pretty. She knew how to dress. She could dance. She had a new and improved nose. *And* she was attending college—though that, Arthur suspected, was maybe not as big a deal anymore as his mother (Hunter College, '35) thought.

Besides, if it was such a great honor to marry his sister, why did his parents also sound like a June Kaplan was goods with a short shelf life, more like meat than cloth? Their words said *Is he good enough for our daughter,* but the undertone sounded desperate to Arthur, keening, sweaty, like *Is this the best deal we can make for her before she begins to rot?* After all, dance and dress and beauty aside, their daughter was already twenty years old!

June had met Ralph Mangione at a country club dance, a party for her father's factor, the guy who sometimes bought Kel-Kap's accounts receivable for a percentage on the dollar in the winter so they could buy cloth to run up the fall line. "We all know *he* uses their dirty money," his father had said. "But what can you do? They're all like that."

"It's a curse," his mother had said, "like in a fairy tale. We should never have let those people into our lives." She meant the factor, and the guys in the parking lot who sold the Kel-Kap workers cigarettes off the trucks, and the shylocks who loaned them money. Arthur smiled, remembering when he'd thought that meant people with antisocial hair, not guys who lent money at *ruinous* rates. But he knew a whole lot more about the world now.

He'd gotten hints that his father and Jesse's dad also forked over something called "protection money" to the mob. Arthur imagined the Puerto Rican guys jockeying their racks down the street with Italian guards running alongside them, like Musketeers.

"They keep our guys from being robbed, right?" Arthur said the next afternoon as he and Specs played a little catch in the backyard.

"Because maybe the cops don't always do their job? Maybe the cops are on the take?"

Specs laughed. "Arthur," he said, "they're not armed guards. The people they're protecting your father from are them."

Specs got down in a catcher's squat. He'd been teaching Arthur how to throw a curveball, which Arthur imagined would make him the greatest player in the history of Great Neck North Junior High, maybe ready for Triple A even. "I guess it's true, you could say they keep other wise guys away," Specs said, waggling him the two-finger signal for the new pitch. "But mostly they're saying, 'Pay us, and we won't steal your stuff ourselves.' "

No way for Arthur to pretend he'd really known *that,* that he'd just been kidding. But Specs didn't make him feel like a jerk. Like you didn't already have to know things with Specs; you could learn them. "Anyway," Arthur said, "mostly Mom thinks you're the greatest." Arthur felt a little guilty for lying. But he couldn't help himself, afraid Specs might back out of the June Derby if he knew his family didn't trust him. "I mean, I think she just wishes Dad and Mr. Kelman had stopped the wise guys"—use it once and it's your own—"from moving in on their workers."

Specs shrugged, flipped the ball back. "Yeah? Like what could they have done?"

Arthur felt he had to defend his dad, like he'd already been disloyal by working for the marriage before his parents had decided it was okay. "My dad's pretty tough."

Specs waggled one finger, which meant the fastball, what Specs called the Heat. Arthur knew it wasn't his strongest pitch. Actually, Arthur also knew he didn't have any strong pitches, that he'd never make the pros, would never even be on the team, should probably take up golf. But it was fun to pretend.

"He could go outside, you know, say, 'Get out of my parking lot.' "

"Yeah. I can see that. Your dad is the greatest. But, Arthur, I can also see him shot." He winged the ball back. "It's just not worth it to keep guys from borrowing money they want to borrow anyway."

Okay, so Specs knew about this stuff; that didn't make him part of it. "But how," his mother had wondered, "are they ever going to find out? You can't just ask a man if his family are mobsters!"

Then that night, as they sat in the living room before dinner, Specs said, "Yeah, my granddad, he was one of the Moustache Petes," bringing it up before anyone else had even begun the hinting. The name made Arthur think of the Looney Tunes character with the long drooping moustache who spewed saliva when he talked. When he shot off his big pistol, he always missed the rabbit. So how dangerous was that? "My father, though, he became a tax lawyer. He knew people because of Granddad and all. But that was it. He never asked anyone for favors. You have to pay too much for their help." He looked meaningfully at Arthur's dad. "And he'd been family, so they left him alone."

Specs smiled—not apologetic, just kind of giving Arthur's father a chance to join him as a man of the world. After all, Arthur thought, whatever Specs' grandfather had done, it was so long ago it wasn't a crime anymore, right? More like a legend of the Old West.

Arthur's father just stared at the thick, unaccustomed highball glass in his big hand, like he was thinking, *What do you do with this stuff?*

"My father died of cancer," Specs added, kind of out of the blue, probably a way to say his dad had the kind of conventional death from the big C that Arthur's parents talked about at dinner all the time—nothing exciting, nothing mob-related.

Arthur's parents gave a sad, respectful, *may he rest in peace* nod.

Anyway, Specs wasn't going to die of bullet wounds, for God's sake! The man was a trader with Goldman Sachs! And by the next week, Arthur's father had had friends check into that, too, and had sounded positively proud when he'd told the family that Ralph—who was only twenty-eight years old—already controlled millions of dollars of Other People's Money. "They say he has a gift, too, like they've never seen before. Usually a man specializes in one thing," he'd said to his daughter at dinner, "stocks, or bonds, or foreign exchange. Your Ralph, he does all of it, combines it, even, issuing bonds in Japan to take advantage of low interest rates, investing the net in dollar notes, and . . ."

Fortunately June interrupted before her dad reached the limit of his understanding. "I know, Dad. We talk about it all the time."

They did? Everyone looked at June with new respect. She could understand *this?*

Arthur felt the parent tide turning in Specs' favor.

Who had also been Ralph, un-nicknamed once upon a time, a thin, sickly kid (which, looking at him now, was another one of the really great things about him). So his friends had called him Specs even though he never wore glasses. Something about the money markets had always fascinated him, he explained to Arthur's parents at dinner the next week, so he used to lie in his parents' bed, twelve years old, sidelined with his second bout of pneumonia, propped up by pillows so he could breathe better, with the *Wall Street Journal* spread out around him. He'd done hours of research, filled marbled black notebooks with calculations of book value versus equity. "Graham and Dodd were like Ravi and Hillel to me," he said, smiling round the table. "There's always one key marker that tells you if a stock's kosher: when book value gets greater than equity value. When you can make more selling off the pieces of the company, then it's undervalued. It's bound to come back."

Arthur's dad grinned back. *That* he could follow.

Specs' own dad "gave me, like, pretend money to speculate with, keeping score. Then he gave me some real money. I started doing more complicated things then, selling warrants short, and going long on stocks."

Arthur's father leaned over for that and poured more Asti Spumanti in Ralph's glass. "Whoa, now!" Specs said jovially, like he was actually instructing horse-Nathan. The Asti foamed over, and Specs brought it quickly to his lips, trimmed it like an ice cream cone. The extra Asti had to mean something, like his dad really wanted Specs to marry June. "I dreamt I'd grow up to be like John Maynard Keynes," Specs said. "Lie in bed every day until noon, earning my living before I got up for the opera. Actually, now I have to wake up in the middle of the night to follow the foreign markets." He turned to his intended, smiling. "But one part of my dream has come true. June is my beautiful ballerina." Arthur didn't get what he meant by that. The Lindy sure, even the tango; but June had given up ballet at six.

The next day he took his bicycle to the library to look up Keanes. (Or was it Keenes? Khenes?) And the day after that, as they played catch, Arthur asked if Specs, like, had gone on playing the market all through prep school. He must be like a millionaire now!

"Nah, I had too much work to do at Andover. I put aside the market for medieval history."

"Yeah? My mom says they throw Jewish kids into the pond at Andover. That's why I'm going to the John Dewey School." Could he have gotten into Andover? He would never know, which felt like he'd been rejected.

"Yeah. They threw me in, too," Specs said while they played catch. "Just about every morning my first year." He smiled. "Thank God, they waited till after breakfast, so at least I got something to eat!" Specs laughed, and not in that phony "who cares" way that Arthur had used after those keepaway games near the skunk cabbage.

"It's kind of hard to imagine."

"That's because I started lifting weights at Andover."

Now he had humongous muscles. Specs had worn a maroon alligator shirt that day, and his arms actually made the sleeves look too small.

Arthur even got kind of scared when he looked at Specs' muscles for too long.

"But by the time I had arms, you know, the kids I wanted to get even with had graduated. What were they good for? I mean, I could throw other kids into the pond, that's about it."

"Did you?"

"Yeah, once." Specs stared at him a little too long, something more he wanted to say.

"A Jewish kid?"

"Yeah, I got to admit it was. I wanted to fit in, I guess."

"That's okay," Arthur said, like Specs had been asking for forgiveness—which made Arthur feel big. But he threw the ball back hard before Specs could squat down, giving the guy his best shot on behalf of his people.

"Whoa, big fella," Specs said, pretending to stagger backward. "You really got an arm on you. I gotta put a sponge inside this thing."

It was hard to imagine Specs picking on a Jewish kid, though—Specs who knew who all the Jewish writers were, and comedians, and senators, who knew more about Jewish history than Arthur did. "Yeah, it's always interested me. My father's Jewish friends used to say that maybe I really had a Jewish soul trapped in a gentile body."

Specs squatted in the sun. "Of course that wasn't exactly an honor in our neighborhood, you know, where 'Jew' meant 'Christ-killer.' "

Specs had what Arthur's mother called a Roman nose, which was big, like Arthur's own was suddenly getting to be, and as far as Arthur was concerned, big was big. So maybe the nose was a sign that he really *was* one of them. He already knew about the kosher laws. He was learning Hebrew, though no one was making him. Specs even worked for one of the Jewish firms on Wall Street.

"You probably know your way around the menu," Arthur's dad said that night at Squire's. "I saw Cutberg at the pool and he tells me you have a lot of Jewish friends, real go-getters," his dad maybe wanting to boast to Ralph, telling him he knew Cutberg.

Specs ordered pastrami, really lean. "Can you do that?" Specs said, sounding like Arthur's cousin Eddie, the newsman, if Eddie had had really big muscles that could send a man directly to hell.

"I don't know," Fat Sol said. "You are positively the first person who's ever asked for it that way." He waddled off.

Specs said again that he was thinking very seriously about converting, which really thrilled Arthur's parents. "Being Jewish makes a person very special," his father said to Arthur as he stuffed another pickle in his mouth, his dad sounding teary, like he did once a year, on Passover, when he drank too much Manischewitz. "But it has great dangers attached to it, too, you know. So not many people want to join us."

"Yeah," Arthur said. "It's like the Mafia." Sometimes he couldn't help himself: see joke, make joke, June looking like when they got home she'd murder him slowly. Specs was the only one who laughed.

His father turned to his wife. "He'd be showing a real commitment to this family if he did that. To what we stand for."

Arthur hadn't realized the Kaplan family stood for something, like the flag in the pledge of allegiance. What was their creed? That knock-offs are as good as the real thing! But he didn't make any more jokes.

After Andover, Specs had gone to Princeton, and had been instantly shunned there by people he'd thought had been his friends at Andover. So most of his pals at college, he told Arthur's parents, had been Jews.

Arthur beamed. These were definitely more pluses for Specs: Princeton was definitely good; and that he was shunned was good, too. And after Princeton, he'd gone to Harvard Business School and Harvard Law School! More than anything, he said, his grandfather and his father had both wanted him to get degrees.

Arthur could see that his parents were in heaven now. MBA + LLD = MD²!

"My father and grandfather both thought knowledge was the best thing, the only real protection—better than the guns Granddad had once used."

Arthur's parents nodded solemnly, like they, too, had just recently laid down their six-shooters for books. Arthur smiled. This was definitely a done deal. Ralph, great at picking stocks, might become a Jew and could hit a golf ball three hundred yards. Specs, they'd decided, was a really good deal for their Rotting Princess!

Besides, June wanted it, and really, what exactly were his parents going to do? Send her to France again, the way they had when she fell for the guy they'd been sure was a *fagalah*? Wouldn't work this time. Specs was no *fagalah*, he would just get on an airplane and carry her back to his castle on the East Side. Besides, if June even wanted a dress at Bendel that she knew her mother would scream at her for buying, let alone something as cool as Specs, she'd just charge it, have it shipped, listen to the screaming. If she wanted an A in a course, and she didn't have time to study, she'd cheat. Somehow, if her desire was strong enough, the thing she'd do to get it didn't even seem wrong to her; more like an unfortunate necessity that a confused world had mistakenly forced on her, when if they really knew how much she wanted to go out on this dynamite date, they would never have scheduled a test for the next day. He remembered her sneaking out of the house one November night in high school on her way to roar down the road with a jerk on a motorcycle, Arthur standing at the top of the stairs in his pj's, padding to the bathroom. She'd just laughed and coolly blown him a kiss, not nervous about her parents finding out, and definitely not afraid of her own conscience.

Billy Green crouched outside Rabbi Meltzer's study, terrified of his conscience. He had canceled his bar mitzvah at Temple Beth-El, where his family's rabbi, Henry Waxman, would have performed the ceremony with Billy *as is*. Rabbi Meltzer at the Great Neck Synagogue would set Billy harder tasks. "Well, shouldn't the Law be hard?" Rabbi Meltzer said today. Billy must be formed and re-formed by that God-given discipline that makes a bundle of greeds and furies into a mensch. "A thousand slights give rise to anger each day," the rabbi concluded, "but anger must continually re-learn its limits in Torah Law."

The Law demanded a fuller knowledge of Hebrew and of Torah; a cleansing immersion in a stone mikvah in the holy land of Brooklyn (not three blocks, his father, Nathan, noticed, from Green Street of not-so-blessed memory). And hardest (therefore best) of all, Meltzer declared that the Law meant that Billy must be made truly clean and acceptable in God's sight before he could be bar mitzvah. Pains like that would take care of his dirt, Billy dreamt, his pride and anger. Such a *big* pain must mean that there would finally be an unbreakable connection for him with the Jews. He would be like his father, and not only his father, but all the patriarchs; they wouldn't ever cast him out the way Dr. Jacobs had. They couldn't protect him, but they would still at least always suffer *with* him.

Specs had made Arthur Kaplan proud to be Jewish, and he felt additionally grand to be part of such a serious business as Billy Green's bris. Since he'd already been bar mitzvah he could count as one of the minyan, witnesses, standing at the mikvah with Billy's father and Jeffrey and Jesse and Frank Jaffe, who'd wrapped himself in a beautiful blue-and-white prayer shawl that had belonged to his grandfather, may he rest in peace, and six Orthodox men in dark suits. Arthur dreamt that if they looked too long at him those men might x-ray that he couldn't chant the prayers, only nod and daven, and that he hadn't, before Billy told him, even known the name of the ceremony. *Hatafat Dom B'rit*, he repeated to himself, though no one was asking. *Hatafat Dom B'rit*. He rolled some strands of his hair from the right side of his head between thumb and forefinger and tied them into a knot. If these holy men figured out that he was ignorant of the Law, then they'd spit him out—though he also kind of suspected that the men were actually dentists and doctors and the owner of the store where Arthur and his mother bought his Stride Rite shoes, and today, over their fringed garments—called, what?—they wore blue Brooks Brothers 346 suits. Jesus, what were they called? Tallit? Tallis? He wouldn't pull the knot out of his hair, he decided, until the ceremony was over. That should protect him.

It was a big day for Arthur, too. He couldn't wait to tell his friends about his new name, "Arkey," given him by Specs, which made the moniker in Arthur's—that is, *Arkey's*—opinion the best kind of nickname, the Italian kind, *the kind a gangster might have*. Not that Specs even *knew* gangsters.

Or did he? He looked over at Ralph, who stood discreetly off to the side, with a serious and respectful look on his face, like he maybe actually wanted to join them, get to wear an official yarmulke on his curly black hair. After the bris, Specs was going to take Arkey and Billy to a Yankees game, and Arkey had left his mitt in the car, just in case a ball got aimed their way. How, his father had wondered admiringly, had Specs snagged primo seats on the first-base line? Arkey smiled to himself now, thinking, well, maybe he's *connected*. Or then again, maybe, like he'd said, he got them from a friend in the Wall Street investment bank where he worked. In any case, he had everyone's blessing for his marriage to June now. And if Arkey liked to pretend sometimes that the gangster thing was an open question, well, that was like Santa Claus: fun to pretend.

Near the mikvah, Rabbi Meltzer went on droning in Hebrew, while the moil unpacked an ominous-looking black case. Was that a knife? Rabbi Meltzer, one eye traced with frightening bloodshot veins, said the prayers bound Billy to the rock and blessed him for submitting willingly to his bonds. Bonds? Arkey looked over at Specs. Did he know about *this* part of becoming Jewish? Specs looked thoughtful, though, not disgusted. Moved, even.

Rabbi Meltzer went on in his cicada voice, and the moil took up a leather case, carefully extracted a long needle. Suddenly it seemed to Arkey a great thing to have a Jewish mother, even one as annoying as Arkey's own; that meant hospital work was good enough for God—which was like getting a special discount, he thought, buying wholesale. The moil dipped a cotton swab in alcohol and ran it along the needle. Billy came out then, wrapped in a prayer shawl.

Hatafat Dom B'rit, Arkey repeated to himself nervously, *Hatafat Dom B'rit.* He made another quick knot in his hair. Then the moil actually touched Billy's penis. Arkey tied one more knot. The moil was a man, for God's sake, and he was actually holding Billy's dick in his large, hairy right hand, while he chanted in a high-pitched singsong. No one, he thought, was ever going to do that to Specs, were they? How was he going to become a Jew, then, marry June? Would this queer the deal?

The moil put the long needle to the side of Billy's modern-style penis, the foreskin snipped, long ago, and without ceremony, in the hospital where Billy had been born, and drew one glistening drop of blood, which made Arkey, tying two knots at once, want to throw up. The moil soaked up the magic juice with some cotton. Then all ten of them dreamt and imagined and thought in unison that Billy was a Jew, and they also thought that that must be true because ten men from the community all said so and pronounced—or, in Arkey, Jeffrey, and Jesse's case, nodded to—the blessing.

And it was for just such blessing lessons that Billy had spurned Rabbi Waxman, the broad-faced, close-shaven leader of Temple Beth-El, whom he admired much more than Rabbi Meltzer. Rabbi Waxman had gone on the Freedom Rides, "singing," he told the congregation, "with the others, to keep up my courage as the bus moved toward Jackson, Mississippi." They'd sung a new version of "Day-O," "Freedom's coming and it won't be long." But what Waxman had seen in *his* mind wasn't freedom—which looked like what? limbo dancers?—but the mob that *was* much more surely coming to meet them, as they had the busses two weeks before, men armed with clubs, pipes, bottles, ax handles, garden tools, baseball bats. Thoroughly terrified, he'd whiled away the last hundred miles listening to Willard Cane—nicknamd Sugar—a very intense CORE worker, tell the story of how firebombs had been tossed into the busses on the last ride, the fire meaning (a) *stay*—and burn or (b) *leave*—and let us whump you to death. Looking for a solution on that trip, some of the riders had thrown themselves on the floor to find air, but that answer was wrong, too; they got dragged out anyway, taken down alleys, where their faces, Cane said, got beaten into tomato paste, while the Alabama cops had been, alas, at home, or so Sheriff Bull Connor said, visiting with their mothers on their very special day—the mothers, that is, who weren't already at the bus station demanding that their sons git them niggers. Then Cane had bounced down the aisle of their bus reminding each of them again how to go limp, that they must cover their heads and remember that the man who beat them into paste was also *like* them, a fellow sinner who would one day see what his hands had done and weep with shame. This man would be an excellent preacher, Waxman had thought, lifted for thirty seconds from his terror by this moment of collegial admiration, though there was a worrisome contrast between Cane's obvious pleasure in scaring the crap out of them and his pious concern for the souls of the terrifying racist bastards. Something priestly about Sugar Cane, too; uncomfortable in his own skin, he made Waxman uncomfortable with his own. Like Sugar disapproved of himself first in relation to God, and then of *you,* in relation to *him.* Turned out that Sugar had thought he would be a minister once upon a time. Might still be, he said, if he got out of this. Then Sugar had had them all make out their wills.

"The Freedom Riders dared all this for the right to sit in a waiting room," Rabbi Waxman boomed to the congregation, "the right to use a bathroom or drink at a water fountain. They risked all this for simple justice!"

Segregated bathrooms, busses, housing blocks, water fountains. Leo Jacobs, making a rare visit to the Temple for this story, thought how right he'd been to warn his daughter about the insanity of nonviolence. What this Cane had said to the riders about the murderers' being "fellow sinners" was dangerous Christian nonsense. Leo crossed his arms in front of his chest and rocked with fear and anger.

Beth sat beside him, furious herself. Her father hadn't been able to go to her bas mitzvah but managed to sit on the padded wooden benches of the Temple for Rabbi Waxman's umpteenth retelling of his Mississippi adventures. Still, her mind flowed into every part of the scene—the brave riders and the furious strong arm that held the angry ax handle that would beat them down. Oh, Lord!

Rabbi Waxman said then that he particularly wanted to tell them about the man he'd sat next to on the bus, a handsome well-dressed Negro named David Watkins. It was, in truth, the rabbi told the congregation, the first time he'd ever really had a conversation with a Negro. How many of *them,* he asked with reflective false wonder, had ever really talked to Negroes other than the maids who cleaned their homes? How many of them had ever had Negroes over to their houses for dinner? This Negro of good family—his father, in Indianapolis, was a doctor, his mother a schoolteacher—had told Waxman that the mobs hated the few white Freedom Riders most of all, because *they* made it a matter not of black and white but of right and wrong. Rabbi Waxman (though he didn't mention it to his congregation) found himself once again very ambivalent at being one of a chosen people. Also, he'd wondered why Watkins was telling him this? Were he and Cane trying to get at him, see how terrified they could make him, because he was white? Couldn't they see that Waxman was about to weep?

"Some of the Negro riders," Watkins had said, "actually believe they might be carted off to Parchman Prison Farm and then killed."

Waxman had said, "No, this is America. Nothing here is as bad as *that*."

Watkins had laughed. People like Rabbi Waxman's companion— good friend, he called him by this point—David Watkins came from families just barely into the middle class, like Waxman's own, come to think of it. His seersucker suit was impeccably tailored, his oxford-cloth shirt buttoned down, and he wore a tie at all times. Martin Luther King had called them *exaggerated Americans*. But he was willing to risk his dearly won hold on middle-class status and go to jail like a common criminal to gain real equality for all his people. "Look at all the Negro has riskcd," Rabbi Waxman said again, gazing out at his congrcgation in their blue business suits, button-down shirts, and Saks Fifth Avenue dresses. "What will *we* risk," he asked, "for justice in America?"

Actually, David Watkins had so utterly terrified Waxman he thought he'd pee in his pants. "Maybe the rabbi didn't know what he'd gotten into," he said. "This ride was so dangerous that even King didn't want to go."

David Watkins had also shocked Waxman by calling King "De Lawd" in a high voice, but he wouldn't tell his audience *that*. Herbert Jaffe, a powerful member of his congregation, advised Martin Luther King. Jaffe was also the lawyer to Menachem Cutberg, the immigrant who'd invented the conglomerate, who belonged to that zealot Meltzer's congregation. But one day soon, Waxman was sure, Cutberg would grow tired of that man's squealing harangues. He'd want to find a Temple more in step with the Enlightenment world where he made so damn much money. Jaffe, King's lawyer, could put in a word for Waxman then—which meant there'd be no careless mockery of King from his pulpit.

Instead he moved on to when they'd reached Mississippi and the riders had sung "We are not afraid," because, Watkins had told him, in case he'd forgotten, "we *are* afraid, aren't we?" And they sang "Hallelujah, I'm a'travelin' / Hallelujah ain't it fine / Hallelujah I'm a'travelin' / down freedom's main line," which had buoyed Waxman's spirits even though freedom's main drag seemed to be lined with people screaming, "Go back to Africa!" Waxman had tried singing louder and louder so as not to think about what he was doing here, all he maybe didn't know about this business and what might happen in America. And then they'd seen a huge mob of whites outside the bus station, and he knew if he *didn't* sing he would probably faint, but if he *did* go on singing all the air would go out of him, and he was sure he'd faint.

Then the doors opened with the popping *whoosh* of an expiring vacuum, and the mob shouted, "How does it feel? Tell us how does it feel?" because as it turned out, the crowd had mostly been reporters.

Waxman didn't tell his congregation, but most of the riders—all but David Watkins and Willard Cane, really—had gone nuts then, even though they were safe, or *because* they were safe. Two black men fell down outside the bus and twitched like epileptics. A thin white woman rider pulled out great clumps of her own hair. Another black woman screamed an ugly sound of disappointment and anger that wavered in the air like oily blue-black water. A Negro man hit his head against the brick side of the station until he bled. And Waxman had thrown up on the tarmac, his stomach rippling like a cat expelling a hair ball. David Watkins held him up.

"I was ready to die," Waxman had gasped.

Watkins had patted him. "Yes, indeed," Watkins had said soothingly—a little pompously, too. "We've all been kind of *cheated*."

"But I don't want to die."

"Really?" David Watkins had said, laughing. "Not at *all*? Then what the hell are you doing here?"

When Waxman finished throwing up, Watkins went back to the others. Willard Cane led David and a few other Negroes toward the Whites Only bathroom. Captain Ray had shouted to his men to arrest all the nigger lovers and the niggers, and when Cane had said loudly, "I'm not a nigger, sir. I am a Negro," a dozen cocked police revolvers had pointed at his head. Cane, my God, had *smiled*. And all of this had been photographed, so the Beth-El congregation had seen their rabbi on TV, standing near a Negro with a dozen revolvers pointed at his temple, the beginning of a fame for Waxman that would continue for many years and lead to the rabbi's knowing almost as many powerful people as Herbert Jaffe did, including his new and generous Temple member Menachem Cutberg; also Hubert Humphrey and Lyndon Johnson, who would choose Waxman to be one of his election overseers in South Vietnam—which ended forever Beth's and Arthur's and Billy's and Jesse's admiration for him, replacing it with an unforgiving hatred that found spots of commonness in all the courage they'd once admired, until they decided, finally, that Waxman had, in fact, gone South maybe not to make justice but to become famous.

"And we sang at Parchman," he said, "where the jailers took our mattresses away as punishment for singing." Willard Cane had turned out to be an impressively dedicated, focused man. Waxman couldn't help feeling the Negro had the right to judge him. Cane had refused to surrender his mattress, had been dragged off clinging to it, had bravely gone on singing as Pee Wee, a fat "trusty" of Parchman, had done what a guard ordered and beat time on the side of Sugar's head. Pee Wee cried as he did it, but he did it. "I'm gonna tell God how you treat me," Sugar sang as he disappeared down the hall, "I'm gonna tell God how you treat me, one of these days."

As Waxman spoke, he felt how he placed himself at the center of the Negro's story, a small white spot in the black field to catch the eye, to give a perspective point: I am a man like you, and I suffered, I was there. In Parchman. For forty days, and forty nights, I, *a man like you,* ate molasses and hard biscuits and drank watery coffee. I slept in my T-shirt and my tiny pea-green shorts on the cold metal bunk, while the guards left the lights on to keep us awake. He knew he probably shouldn't make himself the center this way, but as generations of Hollywood producers would when they came to these tales, he told himself that it was necessary: for the story to work, the audience needed a character they could identify with, and that couldn't, naturally, be a black man.

In Parchman, Waxman and the two other rabbis prayed together, morning and evening. Crying to Him Who had made him reassured Waxman, for the length of the prayer anyway, that *he'd* been made by a God Who had given him an eternal unchanging soul, and so he couldn't be remade by the guards. But he knew, too, though he didn't tell the congregation this, that if he'd spent much more time in jail, he'd have melted, been a wax man. "This is Black Maria," a guard had said their first day, cracking his whip, "and Black Maria is gonna write her name on your back." He'd believed him. There had been all those terrifying rows of cotton, nothing but white all the way to the horizon, and prisoners in striped pajamas who leaned down to hack at the weeds around the cotton plants while one overseer, on horseback, cradled a rifle, looked down on them all, as if he were their . . . owner. All that empty space . . . and what if it were all without God? Then *they'd* make him, they'd write their name on him, tell him what to want and how to keep safe, and he'd want it, he'd do it, he'd beat time on Sugar's head. He'd probably cry as he bonked him, but he'd do it all the same, just the way Pee Wee had.

. . .

Meanwhile, the next week Billy listened as a few blocks away Rabbi Meltzer, in the pulpit of the Orthodox synagogue, a brick building with a lower ceiling, thundered—as best he could, given his misfortune of a voice—that Jews shouldn't have gone South for others. They would only endanger the Jews who lived in the South. Those Jews, in Mississippi and Alabama, would be left behind when the Freedom Riders left. *Those* were the Jews who'd feel the hatred, the curses, the ostracism. And meanwhile, the "Freedom Riders" from Great Neck would be safely tucked back in their suburban beds.

Yes, Rabbi Meltzer said, the Jews did have a mission to sanctify life, and not just on grand occasions but every day, in the synagogue, at the dinner table, even in the marriage bed. But this work could only be done *within* our community, by the laws of our Torah. "Always there are Jews who think they can throw off the yoke of the Torah. So they leave us. They go into politics. They embrace millennial movements—like communism, like this civil rights movement—chimeras that promise justice for all. Why do they do it? *Because they don't want to look too Jewish!* They become exaggerated goyim, *sacrificing* themselves, the way they think Christians do, for all humanity. Though they think they have left us, really they are still part of yiddishkeit, they still hold to the deepest Jewish aspiration—to *sanctify life!* But that task *can't* be done outside the Book. It cannot be done in Mississippi!"

After Parchman, when Rabbi Waxman *had* returned gratefully to his bed in Great Neck, David Watkins, the rabbi's friend from the bus, hadn't left Mississippi. Oh, he *had* gone back to Howard University as soon as he could, to wash the stench of Parchman from him with beautiful words, but sitting in his library carrel, in the middle of writing his senior thesis ("Blake and the Bible: Political Revolution Thwarted Becomes Spiritual Revolution"), he realized that he couldn't even stop writing to go to a Kappa party, that he'd been given a little extra push, a little extra impulsion to choose this subject and no other when his jailer had given him a Bible in Parchman—the only book allowed for prisoners, meant, in the jailer's hermeneutics, to make the colored man recognize himself as a son of Ham, cursed by God. David would show them otherwise, white trash though they were, and not likely to read his thesis on Blake. And *so* he realized that he'd never left Mississippi. Not in the evenings, when he was unable to sit still for a card game; not at night, with its sweats and terrors. That Freedom Ride had been the single worst, most terrifying, most horrible experience of his short life. He would never get over it. *Mississippi is hell,* he thought, *nor am I out of it.*

So David Watkins would have to go back to Mississippi because Parchman had nearly destroyed him (only nearly? he sometimes wondered), *but* the remedy for the cringe in his soul, the Mississippi in his bones, was to face down the power that had made him parade around in those fucking baggy pea-green shorts, that had fed him slop, put him in a tight wooden sweat box for singing freedom songs, and tried to make him its animal. For a long time, he'd been playing a game called "*so and but*": *so* (you did this to me), *but* I overcame (when I did this despite you), which had commenced, he thought, really, when he was born, but whose official beginning was in 1960 when he saw photographs of the young men sitting at the lunch counter in Greensboro, North Carolina, and had been so excited by their sullen determined looks that he'd wanted to jump clear out of his old self. These men weren't going to *swallow it,* they weren't going to play it cool, they weren't going to bottle up, they weren't going to *for God's sake restrain themselves.* He dreamt he'd seen the solution to the problem that was sucking the marrow right out of his bones: how to be a man in America, a Negro man, for these *were* certainly men, with all the righteous emotions a man was entitled to, *but* only, he felt, for as long as they defied the world that said they weren't.

When he told his father about this game of "so and but," the old man barked that *that* foolish notion meant his whole life would just be stupidly reactive; if ignorant whites said *yes* he'd have to say *no,* and what kind of "freedom" was that? "Why do you have to go to Mississippi?" his broad-shouldered father said, smiling mirthlessly. "Can't you find anyone in Washington to call you nigger?" David knew his father was furious to protect him, because that obscenity was small change at his frat, but he'd rarely heard it from his father.

His father, David also knew, thought that David couldn't see the tragedy in his bent shoulders, couldn't see that it was perhaps as hard for a Negro man in Indiana to become a doctor, and president of the Indiana Boulé, as it was for a Mississippi black to chop a field or two of cotton. But the thing was, his father, and Boulé, they were part of the problem— that, and Professor Franklin Frazier's book, *Black Bourgeoisie,* that mockery of his father's club, his mother's sorority . . . and himself, like a poison in his blood he had to spit out before it choked him to death, the professor having the cheek even to make him ashamed of what a damn fine poker player he'd become. When David looked at the "Situation of the Negro," well, if he didn't believe it had been the work of a bastard God, then he *had* to think Hap ruled, like in that poem of Hardy's. And most of the time David lived with a sick feeling that he didn't have the strength to battle *that.* Hell, he even backed down from fights with his "brothers." But when he filled a straight, saw those suckers' broken faces, then *he* dominated, and not just them, but Chance itself—Watkins become Lord of the Whole Damn Whirl.

So fuck you, Frazier, that Negroes gamble some, engage in what you call "conspicuous consumption"! Doesn't that just mean we know how to play and have a good time? Maybe like the rich Jews Frazier compared them with, Negroes were just a little less puritanical than WASPs, could enjoy ourselves just a little bit more. David would see Professor Frazier sometimes walking on the campus, carrying a ripped, bulging briefcase, and he'd dream of grabbing him by the neck, shouting things in his smug face. So Negroes form secret societies—why call *that* aping whites. Doesn't it just mean we're human—hell, Professor, probably apes form them, too. After all, isn't any class, even the French aristocracy, formed by its traditions, its Jockey Club, its Boulé—its sense of right and wrong, its exclusions? So why was Proust's club worth studying, and theirs—according to Professor Frazier—just pretend? So we have no power outside the Negro community, no one else but blacks we can exclude, no one else—no one *white*—who wants to join us? Why should that matter to *us*? Why should wanting power over whites be the center of *our* being? Why should we want to associate with people whose souls are all inevitably disfigured by racism? And maybe David could pass that paper bag test, but that didn't mean *he* had to care about it!

Stop right there. That last thing, *it* rankled David. He imagined explaining to Professor Frazier about his family's past, the advantages it meant they'd had—not that the *color* mattered, mind you, but the education it showed his great grandfather had had, the distance from the fields. But the book's poison thickened his throat so the words wouldn't come out; worse, it made his arguments seem tawdry. That and the fact that no one from Kappa would even read the book. And that no one offered to join him on the bus ride, to show how wrong Frazier was and flush the poison from their system. Him and Dr. King, come to think of it, they'd have to do the job for the whole black bourgeoisie—the Reverend, mind you, having been in Jack and Jill himself, you could look it up in *Up the Hill*.

Maybe his dad had hit it when he'd said, "David, there's only Down South and Up South. If you have to play your little 'so and but' game, you don't need Mississippi." But once he'd told everyone at that Kappa poker game that he was going, David couldn't see any other way forward *but* to go on the Freedom Ride, and *so* Parchman had happened, and Parchman had changed him. The crap about Frazier, the boasting at poker games, all that ignorant youthful foolishness got knocked out of him the first time Pee Wee hit his kidney. He had always known, of course—Jack and Jill, it couldn't keep the poison out of his life, as much as his parents had tried. But this was something maybe not bigger, but starker, more virulent, something he couldn't distract himself from by staking some money on whether a diamond might—please Hap—turn up on the next card. Black Maria had written a letter on his back that said, *I got to let you live this one time only, so don't come back here, don't let the Mississippi sun set on your head.*

Obey *that*, though, and he'd be pulverized.

. . .

But a year and a half ago he'd returned to Mississippi, where the beast was out of hiding and in every white man's eye; sharp, painful, vivid, and true. He'd sought out Joshua Battle, who'd given up teaching rich Jews at the John Dewey School in New York and become famous among Negro students countrywide for what he'd risk without seeming to think it was a risk, and his small band of coworkers (many, like Susan Lems and Sugar Cane, from the North, via Parchman, a few, like Willie Baker, a thin young man with expressive shoulders, homegrown) who were walking shack to shack. David still, just as Rabbi Waxman remembered him, had worn his tie and long-sleeved white shirt those first few months in the hot Delta sun of Houganoush and Hellangone and Dead Indian Counties, searching for black people courageous and educated enough to register to vote. To try to register at least. To go down to the county courthouse and say, "Sir, I would like to take the test." To be refused altogether, or to be told by an illiterate registrar that they were too unschooled, to be told by an ignorant registrar that they'd failed the Special Examination on General Knowledge. (How many bubbles in a bar of soap?) To be pistol-whipped by the insolent registrar for questioning whether that had been a fair test. To say to the deputy who ambled over to "investigate" the beating: "I don't know any niggers. I know some colored people." And to pay the price for his black mouth being too smart: to be beaten again by the sheriff. By his deputies. By his Klan friends. To be beaten like a fucking drum!

Man, how David *feared* that. Not *just* the beating, but *the waiting* to be beaten, the knowing as they marched to the registrar's office that the beating was coming. He feared the waiting and the pain—which, by the way, he thought *might* kill him; and he also feared his own anger, 'cause he knew that if he did anything with it, his anger *would* surely get him killed.

But the cringe those beatings had made in David's own soul, he dreamt, might finally be cured by once again accompanying the few reluctant recruits to the courthouse—where he'd receive more beatings. So he and the other SNAP workers had walked, again, from shack to shack to plead with more folks to join them.

Most of them had just looked at the ground, though, and said, "Yes, sir," meaning, *please, go away. But* a few *had* been willing to try to register, and then a few more. *So* the police sent out their many Pee Wees, prisoners given leave from Parchman to work for Eastland, black pointer dogs who made friends and reported back, *so* the uppity shacks could be shot into and the malcontent workers run off the land. As for

David, they'd beaten him lots more, poked at his genitals with sharp sticks, pulled out their guns, and said, "Nigger, give me one good reason." A rat-faced deputy in Houganoush County had even spun the barrel and played Russian roulette against his temple. *So* David had lost consciousness—and part of his sanity—and woke up in a puddle of his own shit and vomit. The terror seeped back into the countrypeople's whipped bones, too, and *so* there were soon only a few who would even think about registering anymore.

But that summer the SNAPs had ridden it out—waiting for courage to return; "chopping wood and carrying water," Joshua called it, and that's the kind of thing they did while they waited—they carried someone down to the store, they put nails in a tilted shack. And by then David didn't wear a rooster tie anymore. He'd sworn that he wouldn't imitate Joshua and go around in overalls, but one day—so the country folk would stop looking at the dirt and docilely calling *him* sir—he had; he'd stopped being an exaggerated American, hell, he wasn't even an American anymore, and he wouldn't be again until America caught up to him and the SNAP workers (Battle's niggers, the whites called them) he walked beside, *but on the sidewalk,* and *but no* we won't step into the street for *you,* and *but no,* we won't put a handle on that and say *sir,* either.

So they beat them all for that, too, *but* the strength did come back to the black folk (and to them, too, though they didn't say that), because just withstanding the terror, just standing their ground, was a mighty political act in Mississippi. The SNAPs wouldn't run. You need not cower. Really? And for just how much longer would that be true for *him*?

Just three months before, on Christmas Day, Joshua's father had died, and David's dearest wish had been that the project would be ended by that.

Joshua had said, "I should help my mom care for Jacob."

Please, God, yes, David thought. "He a handful?" David said, with an alligator's sympathetic smile.

"No, but he needs looking after. He's sensitive, you know? He's asthmatic. Shy."

"Black," Sugar had said.

"That, too," Joshua agreed. "Kind of David's color, actually. But still, that, too."

When Joshua went back for the funeral, David walked the shacks with Willie, and fervently hoped Joshua would see his responsibility to his brother and stay Up South so David could get out of Mississippi.

Then a few days after he'd been wishing hard not to see him again, Joshua had fallen into step beside them as they walked. "My mom sent me back."

"That's one powerful woman," Willie said, "if *you* do what she tells you."

"She said she can care for Jacob. He'll have to make his way in a hard world, we can't be looking out for him all the time."

"True and true," David said. His legs were tired, and he couldn't deny what his heart felt. This was his Beloved Community; and he rejoiced that Joshua had come back to this shitpile because suddenly— for a moment anyway—he didn't want to leave Mississippi until they had beaten it and transformed it. Only that, he thought sentimentally, would heal his heart—and he could only help do that if Joshua were here, beside him, calling out to his better self.

"She said the work we're doing is important."

"Mrs. Battle said that? Your very own mother!" David couldn't help it. He laughed to hear how proud Joshua sounded, like he'd gotten the Nobel Peace Prize. Joshua stared at him; then he laughed, too. And Willie laughed.

Joshua Battle ("my parents meant just that," he said dryly, making sure no one would again add to their creation with a "Fit the" or some-such) was a broad-faced, quiet-seeming dark man who David could have sworn (if he didn't know it had to be impossible) actually relished standing up to terror, spooning it down like it was hot sauce. A graduate of a dinky Ohio college, with a master's in mathematics from Harvard, Joshua looked ashamed of himself at meetings when everyone else sang freedom songs and roared together in one blaze, and he sat staring down at his big hands, or holding them balled into fists by the sides of his head, eyes closed; singing didn't connect Joshua, only knowing that he was in danger for others did.

Because if *he* showed he could bear the pain, then the country-people, he told David, would see they would survive as he had survived, so his pain would yield—he actually said this to David—"marvelous fruit." Joshua probably actually dreamt that they were all magically *fed* by his suffering, he was like the pelican mother (encountered by David in so many Shakespeare lines) who stabbed her bosom to give blood to her young. That being *exactly* the kind of Christian-Buddhist cloak that Joshua loved to wear, for Joshua had spent a summer on a Friends service project in Japan, building steps down a cliffside for a Zen monastery.

"Con job," David said to him. "Slave labor."

"But I got as much from it as they did."

"Like what?"

"Like Roshi said, I learned if you want to build a stairway you do it one step at a time."

Fuck you, David wanted to say, but too late. He'd been made the ingenue, the straight man, the lesson.

Joshua loved to give lessons that told them all that they were *empty, void,* just plain *not*—it actually comforting Joshua to dream his *self* didn't exist, because his real, very actual self was just too sensitive—for everyone saw that when some cracker called him nigger, Joshua recoiled each and every time with half-closed eyes, as if his face had been slapped; while everyone noticed, too, that these slurs were nothing to David Watkins.

"That's because this garbage isn't David's kind of white people," Sugar said. "That's the advantage of being a snob."

"Yup," David said, "it protects one against the slings and arrows of outrageous white trash."

They all needed some comfort rags to wrap around themselves when the crackers beat on them, scraps of Buddhism like Joshua's; or Christianity for Sugar Cane, the impetuous, violently nonviolent warrior, and the most physically courageous of all of them. Chuck Taylor, the black Jew (wasn't *that* trouble redoubled!), he wound himself in fragments of Hebrew. And David might savor and mock all his colleagues' rich rhetoric, but he felt himself naked as a baby, having only some little pieces of poems to say to himself to stand for the (snobbish?) grandeur of the Great Literary Oversoul, tags he repeated to get his feet moving down to the courthouse and the beating he knew awaited him there. Well, they all had their rags and scraps and tags; but when the pain started, he thought, there was only the pain.

But in the summer of '62, with whatever mojo of comforts and enticements, a few more blacks in the Delta *had* gotten their feet moving and had even encouraged others to try. That damn few was way too damn many for the crackers, *so* this last winter the worst had happened: Lechien and Sunflower Counties had cut off the meager food relief the county had supplied to get the sharecroppers through the dead season, from *the settle*—where the owners' crafty count cheated the workers of the money they'd truly earned, which would have supported them in the dead season—until *the furnish* of seed for next spring's planting. The county meant to say to them that they shouldn't even dare to try to register, to teach them that the new cotton-picking machinery meant *you niggers are too many, so why don't you go away . . . or die, for all we care.*

But then out of the worst the best had come, out of the rock, honey. (Was it the story he was in, David wondered, that made him talk in corny biblical measures? Or was he just, in his recruitment efforts, going to too many country church services? Inside or outside Parchman, you come to Mississippi, he thought, and you *will* become an expert on the Bible.) Food and blankets had been trucked in by supporters up North, when David, in his growing despair, had hardly believed anymore that they had supporters anywhere, that anyone would care if they starved. Then Miles Davis—can you believe it? motherfuckin' *Miles Davis*—had had a benefit concert for them at Carnegie Hall. Dick Gregory had sent two tons of food by plane, and in just one day this last February six *thousand* poor sharecroppers had lined up outside a wooden chapel to receive something to eat!

Joshua never shone when they sang in church, and his eyes were not even so bright and seeing when he led a few people to register while he meditated step by step, David knew, on his Heart Sutra, his pleasing inward no-jewel of emptiness; but he looked ablaze that February day. Standing by a long trestle table, his eyes bugged with joy as he doled out parcels of lard, cans of beans, woolen blankets. It probably almost hurt Joshua to put himself forward like this, distributing presents like Mr. Bountiful—too self-aggrandizing, too ego-satisfying—but this chance was his undoing temptation: to feed others and be connected to them, as if *he was the food*. You know the drill: *take, eat, this is my body*.

David had looked at the crowd that February day and, meaning to bring Joshua down—he had looked so damned ecstatic while there was a green bile of fear and disappointment growing in David's soul that almost couldn't stand another's hope—he'd said, "They can't read, Joshua, they can't write, they can't take the voting test. *This* isn't going to help us"; not meaning, of course, that they shouldn't be fed, he just needed an outlet for his despair. And Joshua had said, "Ah, David, what does it matter? In the last eight months, we've only gotten fifty people to take the test." A despairing remark, too, in its way, but Joshua had smiled broadly as he said it, because he meant, really, *this is my joy*. And he went on handing out parcels of food and blankets, until they had no more and thousands of people had to be turned away.

But after that, a few people from the shacks did start coming to their rallies, then some more came, as many as a hundred at a time. They heard Sam Black put freedom to a calypso beat, and James Bevel say, "Don't let the white man do your children as he has done you," and Dick Gregory himself came to town wearing a cowboy hat and mouthing off to the cops as few black men in Mississippi history had maybe ever dared before—and lived, anyway—though no one hurt him, because everyone *loves* stars (and reporters follow them around). One action had seemed to simply follow another, which Joshua called *the universe actualizing itself as the movement toward freedom,* for the moral arc of the universe is long, but (as De Lawd said) it bends toward justice.

David, afraid to let even himself know that his cynicism about blacks and whites and Justice Department officers was beginning to lighten a little, called the same process "good luck" but secretly thought that it was *perhaps* like the way Miles had sounded to him sometimes when he listened on the edge of a second drink, as if through Miles' fingers the universe worked the valves of his trumpet—but then you either had to drink more, till you finally couldn't follow the music, or you had to sober up and it was just "My Funny Valentine."

But just two weeks before, on the first of March, two hundred and fifty people had heard Miles Universe's freedom tune, and walked into the chapel. Joshua had stood in the pulpit and said, "Now you see the world cares. Now you see the world is watching what they do to us. Let that be an inspiration. Do you want to be free? You have to vote to be free!" which was a very long speech for Joshua, but every word nourished the heart, for Joshua truly believed in democracy, though he had a mystical and silly idea, in David's opinion, of what it meant. Once, when they'd been walking in thick red clay, hard work to lift the legs, on their way out to some isolated shack where probably nothing would happen (and if it did happen, David was damn sure, it would happen very slowly), Joshua had said to David, "Democracy means we make each other."

Of course. How could it not? *Everything* meant that to JB. "We make each other, Joshua?" David had said. "You mean, like the registrar makes me? And the crackers in front of the pool hall? And the fucking High Sheriff? And every shitty thing in this world that I hate? *That* doesn't seem to me like a cause for celebration."

"I thought," Sugar said, "that democracy means the last shall be first. The black souls in these shacks will finally get what's coming to them."

But Joshua laughed, like the idea that we'd be made by each other was actually a great relief to him—like it meant he could relax, didn't have to make himself up single-handedly every day anymore. Fortunately, David thought, Joshua didn't show him his mystical comfort rags too often. He kept his eyes on the prize.

Still, it had made David wonder what *he* was doing in Mississippi, among these molasses-talking, nappy-headed, napkin-wearing, long-suffering Negroes; he was way *ahead* of them (he could read and write; he could even *type,* a skill that amazed Skinny Willie, making him raise his expressive left shoulder in his sign for bewilderment), or he was *behind* them (they knew how to suffer), but he was not quite *with* them.

On the first day of March, he'd looked at Joshua smiling down at them from the pulpit, his eyes filled with a light so intense it was almost dark. He loved Joshua Battle, he had to admit, and more than a little. Surely he belonged with *him*.

He wasn't alone: eleven days before, on March 3, 150 of the poorest came to register, *so* the registrar said I got no time for so many of you, you are too many. *But* they waited patiently outside his office. *So* the ham-faced registrar chose a few and said, "How do the dead talk to the living?" *So* they failed. *But* the rest waited outside, quietly, for their chance to try to answer. *So* the police said, "Now you ignahr'nt niggers listen. You go home. You niggers do like you're told now and go home."

But they didn't go home! The police rubbed their eyes in wonder. They had never seen this in Mississippi! They'd said, go home, niggers. And the niggers . . . no, *the colored people,* no, *the Negroes* . . . hadn't gone home, which astounded the cops and tilted David's spirit level back up.

So they sent night riders to shoot into Jimmy Branch's and Joshua Battle's Buick, nearly killing Jimmy. *But* that just made the people mad! The ministers said, *We're ready to wade in the water*—finally! You can use our churches for your registration classes. *So* a wooden church was burned in Lechien, and night riders shot into Willie Baker's car, *so* the sheriff said, "You shot up your own car, to get publicity," and *so* they arrested Willie and *so* they shot into Dewey Greene's house, 'cause his son said he'd follow Meredith to Ole Miss, and *so* they burned out the SNAP office.

But then (if their violence had been the call, this was the response, if their bullets were the furnish, well, this time, Lord, this was the settle), it was *this* new day, *the fourteenth of March,* and here were a hundred more of the poorest waiting in Wesley Chapel.

When David Watkins looked at the crowd of sharecroppers outside Wesley Chapel in Boisvert, Mississippi, he, too, wondered what more he would risk for justice, what more these people would wager for him and themselves, these men in patched overalls and women in thin cotton dresses, even sometimes in the flour bag shifts that David had once thought a costume worn only in his father's admonitory fairy tales, fathers and mothers of teenage children sometimes without shoes, living in shacks that had no indoor toilets and newspapers pasted on the walls to keep out the wind. Well, you get the picture. David compared them to a better-dressed congregation he'd known in Indiana, who still set his sartorial standard, men in dark blue suits and women wearing their Sunday best.

He forgot—having fed himself a trumped-up bitterness meant to protect him from false hope—that some of the people he saw now also had Sunday-best hidden away in their shacks, garments fine enough even for the Indiana AME. Still, though he tried not to expect too much, his body that March day was rigid with exhilaration and fear, astounded to see so many courageous (albeit badly dressed) black people so bravely upright in the Delta of Mississippi. Perhaps, he dreamt, SNAP's work in Mississippi would come to something. Perhaps he hadn't been jailed and beaten, and then, to vary the program, beaten and jailed, for absolutely damn-all.

Today David was so proud of his people (if not of their clothes) that he felt far behind them, because when they even walked down to this meeting they'd transformed themselves more mightily than he'd so far managed, the cringe had been deeper in their souls and the distance each of their steps covered was like a millennium long, while the beatings David had received over a year and a half in Mississippi hadn't (he had to admit) squeezed the slave out of him but had set him back, as if each lick maybe had restored him for a while, till like some mysterious scale, his soul-balance had gotten to a brimming point of pain and had started to go down again into a realm that marked defeat, nihilistic bitterness, and cynical hatred.

They assembled outside, and David wondered, as he looked at the crowd, if *he* had the courage to restore himself *now*, when an opportunity for a *victory* finally welled before them? What more would he risk for justice in Mississippi?

They sang *We are not afraid* (because they were afraid), and *We shall overcome,* because maybe this time, afraid or not, they would. Joshua said, "We're not stopping now. Let's go down to register." And Sugar said to him, "Listen, Joshua, the people can't just take tests, and wait to take tests. They need an outlet for their anger or they're gonna blow. Listen, let's march on city hall, and *de-mand* the police protect us." Sugar was nonviolent, yet Sugar craved confrontation. Sugar preached Jesus, but you could feel the fury that his thin body restrained, which meant Sugar hated himself either way things went. The man was *upset* incarnate—the outside agitator! Contagious, too: he could get a crowd jumping with his own roiling unease. Then he showed them a way to resolve it, got them marching right out the door. Not that it ever resolved anything for Sugar, the man uncomfortable in his skin not because it was black but because it was human.

David could see Sugar's demand annoyed Joshua, for Joshua believed so strongly in the purity of the vote that he thought that only that single just demand—*we are Americans, and we want to vote*—should be repeated until it wore away the rocks (which was *this* patient Joshua's idea of blowing down the walls). But this fourteenth of March, Jacob saw Sugar was right. He said quietly, "Okay, we'll walk by city hall *on the way to register,* and we'll *talk* to the chief of police."

When they got to city hall, David saw cops from Sunflower and Houganoush and Lechien and Whataloser Counties, those last holding attack dogs. Joshua said to the mayor, "I want to talk to the police chief," which in the language of whites means, *let the dogs loose.* The German shepherds bit the minister of Wesley Chapel in his flowing black robes, and ripped the leg off Joshua's overalls, and Joshua shook with fear, *but* he sang even as the dog's teeth took a bloody chunk out of his leg. The countrypeople commenced to screaming and running into each other, while the whites shouted, "Sic 'em," and "Kennedy is your God," which was, David thought even at the time as he tried to get through the flailing crowd to help Joshua, a *gross* misapprehension of their cosmology.

So the cops laid about them with their burr-head busters, *but* Joshua got his shaking under control—he was greatly afraid of dogs—while blood dripped from his leg, and he led the crowd back to Wesley Chapel in a raggedy line, telling people, "We'll get cars to go down to the court-house now." And the amazing truth was the cops and the dogs and the guns had just fired them up, and a lot of them were ready to go down again.

So the cops came back to the church with rifles, and arrested Joshua, and David, and Sugar and Willie and Jimmy, and Fannie Mae Carter, and Susan Lems, and all the leadership, and dragged them to the court-house.

So the judge said four months.

But Susan, David's one true love, gave him a look of grimmest deter-mination. On the spot, she said, "Jail, no bail." Joshua nodded—for they could all see that she'd played the right next note, which was to pack the damp jails full, *make* the federal government intervene—for the cameramen from CBS had been there, and the newspapermen, and maybe the Justice Department would have to do something, *finally* (for there's a town in Mississippi called Liberty, and there's a department in Washington called Justice) to protect their right to register.

So two weeks later, the first of April, David—the prize fool—sat in jail again, and he wondered, *Am I on my way back to Parchman?* which he *knew* he wouldn't survive, because his anger would undo him, he would mouth back to a guard and be shot or put in a sweat box alone, crouched over until his despair leeched the life from him and he either became their creature or murdered himself. *But* David had comforted himself as best he could by seeing that Joshua didn't worry, that Joshua was as happy as he'd been the days he'd handed out food, Joshua even stood by the bars and sang, when the Lord (and everyone in the movement) knew that Joshua wouldn't sing, or, at least, really, *shouldn't.*

And it had worked! The federal government—April Fools!—had decided to represent them at tomorrow's hearing, and Joshua sang with joy, while the thieves and drunks said, "Tell it!" and Joshua (with a sad attempt at a little note-bending soulful melisma) called out, "Do you want your freedom!" And the jailbirds responded, "You know we do!" And Joshua called, "Are you ready to go to jail?" And a prisoner replied, "This *is* jail, brother, look 'round you." Making Sugar and David laugh with pleasure, for they would surely win protection in the federal courts for the registration marches, and then they could go about their business and teach people to read and write and pass the voting test (how much soap can one man eat? how much land does one man need?). And justice, David dreamt, would come to Mississippi.

But not, David realized that November in Washington, D.C., right soon. For seven months later he sat not in a Boisvert jail, or a Parchman sweat box, but in a classroom at Georgetown University, in the funereal city of Washington, the SNAP Voting Rights Project having gone out of state to gather in council so they wouldn't tempt some Klansman to get it over with by murdering them all at once. They'd mourned again for the schoolchildren in Birmingham and for Medgar, while *this* town buried its prince. David couldn't but sorrow a little with the beautiful woman and her little children, but he could hardly weep fulsomely for a fallen leader whom SNAP had known mostly as a temporizer, a compromiser, a gay betrayer—which suited David's mood, bitter now that he couldn't even share the country's bitterness, he couldn't do *anything* anymore with the rest of America, he couldn't even mourn with it, because since April SNAP had been utterly abandoned in Mississippi.

He tuned out Sugar's high, implacable voice and thought about how disaster had come to them in the form of a victory, all the *but*'s became *so*'s, the honey turned right back into rocks. *So* on April 2, Boisvert had caved in to federal pressure, and suspended their sentences, *but* really that meant abandonment, for the federal government then withdrew, unwilling to bring a case that would make Mississippi stop harassing registrants, *because Kennedy was afraid to win it*; he'd have to send in federal marshals to force Negro civil rights on the South (which was SNAP's dream and Kennedy's nightmare). *So* the Delta counties *let* the food aid be restored (*but* the federal government would pay for it). *So* there were no more beatings for a while, *but* Dick Gregory and the reporters left town, *so* their mass meetings were only attended by a few again, *but* the county let black people come down to the courthouse and try to interpret one of the 272 articles of the Mississippi constitution and answer questions of general knowledge ("why don't you kiss my ass?" and "why is the speed of light the constant in the theory of relativity?"), which of course any white Mississippi voter could easily answer. *So* they'd brought one thousand five hundred people to register, *but* fifty were chosen, proving (1) the Mississippi registrars could, or so the feds said, be left alone to do their jobs and (2) that in the next election in Lechien County, which was majority Negro, there would be ten thousand white voters and three hundred blacks. QED: Votes, O Subhuti, are no-votes. Freedom, O well-born ones, is not-freedom.

Sugar was talking now, attacking David for suggesting white people be allowed to come to Mississippi for a final gamble, a summer drive to register voters, a freedom summer—but Sugar was really shouting at Joshua *through* David (for everyone knew that David spoke for Joshua), going on at *him* because later, ferocious as Sugar was—and a Sugar-lashing was a terrifying thing—he still wouldn't be able to touch Joshua. But Joshua hadn't declared himself yet. Joshua waited; perfect in patience. Joshua would give everyone a chance to speak, as if he didn't want to use his charisma to sway anyone, though of course that *not doing* was *doing, was* his charisma. They all sensed Joshua's banked-down numinous power, all the force he had to use to restrain his power and *let* them speak. Goddamn if Joshua wasn't the aristocrat here, in a way that David could never be: namely, he made you *want* to guess what he'd have you say, so you could say it, please. David had seen him fatally work that trick on Amos Jones, saying quietly, "It's your choice." So Amos Jones had overcome a lifetime of cautious accommodation and had gone forward toward Joshua and justice, telling the feds how he'd seen state legislator Hall murder Claude Hays. *So* the feds had done nothing; and *so* last week, for Halloween, night riders had murdered Amos Jones—the man positively set up for it by Joshua's no-action that was action, which made your best self march forward for him . . . and get murdered.

Or maybe just endlessly savaged verbally by Sugar in that high, nearly womanly voice of his, the way David was getting beat up tonight, Sugar combining Gandhian nonviolence with a nearly race separatist line. Strange brew: you were enjoined to save savage, hateful, and clearly unsavable white souls by letting them beat on you! Saint Sugar seemed to groove on the scene; like he wouldn't do it himself, but almost felt joy in the movement of the arm that struck him. David felt a mighty power in Sugar, physical as much as spiritual. He envied *that*. David, since he'd turned ten, had always worried he wasn't tough enough on the football field, in his frat, or here. Sugar intimidated him doing the one violent thing he *could* do in this classroom, namely demolishing David's blindness with words, words, words.

Sometime tonight, when they all yearned for it enough, Joshua would finally speak; quietly, of course, so they'd all have to bend toward him. He'd say, "Let's break this down," and it would feel like he simply poured his arguments into their ears, as if they weren't arguments at all, but simply the clearest x-ray of the truth, showing them not just the facts of the world, but what produced those facts. But for now, David thought irritably, all that meant was that while they waited, Sugar—knowing the still small voice that was coming to blow him down—laid into David the harder, as if David were, despite his overalls, a traitor to his race.

David still wore his overalls, the SNAP monk's uniform, he thought (and unconsciously his hand brushed Susan's knee). Willie, who was from the shacks so he didn't need to dress like it, wore jeans and a clean work shirt; Jimmy (who was ditto) wore a white button-down and corduroys; Sam (likewise) wore a sport jacket and chinos; and Fannie, who'd picked cotton since eight years of age, wore a flowered dress— and they, who had been born in Mississippi, sat at the student desks, upright, while Sugar and he and Chuck and Susan and the other outsiders sat on the floor in farm clothes, *their backs against the wall.* Indeed. For since the press left, the Klan was everywhere, indistinguishable from the cops, a paramilitary wing of the White Citizens' Council, and the terror lapped all day at everyone's feet. When you said good-bye to a friend in the morning you couldn't stop yourself from hearing *Oh, this may be the last time, I don't know,* and you dreamt of his corpse being pulled out of the Yazoo River that night. Before you started your car, you checked for dynamite. At night you kept the lights off, stayed away from windows, and when you lay you down to sleep, you prayed to God or Brahma or Miles Davis—though David felt that all creation was now in league against him, a veil of false promises and deceptive hopes and murderous traps, and Mr. Davis, his fingers twiddled by the Universe no doubt, was playing a blues. So they chopped wood furiously and tirelessly carried water while they waited for courage to return, but this time David felt sure that it wouldn't, and soon there wouldn't be even a few who tried to register, and soon, too, the countrypeople wouldn't even want the SNAP workers there anymore; they would maybe hate themselves for it, but still they would dream that if "the outside agitators" left, the terror would diminish. Not stop. It would never stop. And really, though the countrypeople couldn't see it yet (David was ahead of them on this one), the terror would slowly get worse—for the whites had machines to harvest the cotton now, they didn't need so many blacks, and *that* need was the only bulwark that had ever kept the horror from becoming unbearable. Soon the whites would *want* to make it unbearable *so* the blacks would leave—and slowly, David knew, they would.

He rubbed his stubbly cheeks, trying to wake himself and grasp the thread again. They'd been up for a mighty long time now, two days straight. Mississippi was a sore they couldn't stop poking, as if, when they weren't there, they had to take over tormenting themselves. They wept in the middle of their own speeches. They would hit each other soon. "Sugar, we stand for black and white together," Fannie said. "One community. We *can't* be a blacks-only movement." They needed the white students' help for a Freedom Summer: To walk door to door. In overalls if they wanted. To go down with people to register at the courthouses of Mississippi. To teach older people how to read and write and answer the questions (who shaves the barber? what was your face before you were born?). To teach the people how to overcome the daily terror of being black and young and living in Mississippi, a subject on which the white teachers would spout pieties, as maybe David himself once had, before he learned (blow by blow, broken promise by broken promise) how empty the instruction of religion was and how hollow the law. For where was the judgment, where was the Judge? There was no Judge in Mississippi.

"Listen, David," Sugar said, "they can come organize here. But we can't go into their suburbs. Let *them* integrate first. This is our movement now. Listen, when they come, we'll be the invisible men."

My movement, my ivory, my intended, David, the former English major, thought; instead of living a Bible story, David was back in the Wasteland, comforting himself with fragments shored against his movement's ruin. (What would T. S. Eliot think of "the organic community" of white Mississippi? Probably, David feared, he'd admire it.) Sugar meanwhile was damn near calling him a house nigger, and he saw himself woolly-haired, in a brocade vest, a costume from the movies, his big broad nose stuck into a crack in the parlor door, watching the master's family reading their . . . *Four Quartets* or reciting "Dover Beach" to each other. Sugar, he thought, you West Indian bastard, *you* went to the Bronx High School of Motherfucking Science! He wanted to hit Sugar for putting him in that costume.

"No," Sugar said. "We need to free ourselves."

In truth David shared Sugar's uneasiness. The white students would come. They would, he knew, be so self-confident as not even to know that it was self-confidence, it was just their world, their ivory words, to be scattered about because they were so rich they wouldn't even need to hoard. And Willie chimed in with Sugar saying what they all felt, that *they* wouldn't let *us* talk. Yes, Sam said, they would be overbearing. Indeed, David knew that these white anti-racists would be racists, and they would look even at David Watkins (summa cum laude, child of a respected doctor and a beloved teacher) and they would see someone *who needed their help*. And the worst thing was, he *did,* they all did, not because they couldn't talk—*God knows* they could talk. They could break things down. But they couldn't get whites to *hear* them talking. They could be beaten, they could be shot at, they could go into the river two by two, like this one and that one, and it wouldn't even make the news when their bodies washed up on the banks. They needed the white kids to bring down the journalists and the television cameras, and make the FBI *come by here* and watch them (for *all* whites were stars!) while *they* were beaten and shot. It was the only way to expose to America the truth about Mississippi. Like generations of Hollywood producers, SNAP needed a spot of whiteness to make a perspective point, to hold the attention of the whites in the North and *their* government. So David said, We should let whites come because we're an integrated movement, but really (he thought) we want the whites here because racism is the given; whites up North will only care for whites, they will *never* care about us. Yes, he didn't entirely want these whites to come, but if there wasn't something more to try, if every blow he had borne in the Delta came to nothing, then David would feel a harsh, cynical despair beyond his bearing, he might take the policeman's power into his own hands, put a gun in his own mouth, play Russian roulette, let Miles Universe pull the trigger and accept his punishment for being black and standing up. Or then again, he might just shoot some white man.

"Let's wrap this up for tonight," Susan said. She had deep bags under her eyes. "Let's sing and then get some sleep." But they had to stay in dormitories, so he wouldn't get to spend the night with her warmth, her slow, insistent touch—which was about the only thing that brought him peace anymore.

"Go fuck yourself," Sugar said, as if Susan, or sleep itself, were the enemy.

"Fuck you!" David said, reflexively, defending his woman, not that Susan needed that from him. And *Temper, temper!* David thought, hearing his mother's voice. *Is this your best self?* his father asked. But his best self, he thought, had gone to sleep two days ago. Now they all either made no sense when they talked, or too much sense because they said what they meant.

Finally Joshua started to speak, quietly as always, and they all grew quiet, as always, ready to interrogate his words and his silences. They even stopped moving their legs about like restless children whose bones were weary from not having moved for so long.

"Let's break this down," he said, sitting upright, against the wall. "Look, the whites in the Delta are outnumbered. It isn't a black-white thing," he said, and Sugar snorted. "All right," he corrected himself. "But it isn't *just* a black-white thing. We are asking the whites of the Delta to do what no other elite has ever done willingly, which is that they give up power to the less well educated. Democracy in Mississippi will be a *revolution.*"

Joshua spoke in a low, hushed voice, looking down at his large hands, but his round face was radiant from just speaking his sacramental word. "And unless *every* black person can vote," Joshua said, "we are only gaining privileges for ourselves, for the Negro elite. The white ruling class will give middle-class blacks opportunities rather than give the black masses power over them. So do we identify with the masses or with the elites?"

They knew all this, of course. Still, it felt a little different when Joshua said it, for he *was* his faith, he truly yearned to be fairly made by others, democratically made, his union label. Which made his simple question enter David's heart like an arrow, and he was (because of Joshua's purity and his own exhaustion) overwhelmed not by the democratic beauty that Joshua had revealed, or the impossibility of its ever happening, but by the obvious meaning of *universal suffrage,* of one man, one vote, which felt tonight like a great implacable weight rolling over *him,* remaking him by crushing him. He'd thought, *I will help the*

*ignorant masses. I will speak for them. Because I'm like you, but won-
derfully different, more knowledgeable, more educated, more* . . . But
Joshua had revealed the truth. The masses would spurn him *because* he
was different; they would rule over *us,* and *they* was the uneducated
blacks in their overalls, undisciplined ignorant people who had never
known indoor plumbing or read a newspaper, let alone a poem of
William Blake's, while *us* was . . . who? white people surely, and . . .
him, too. He looked down at his denim-clad legs, but inside that denim,
he thought, is a man with a B.A., a head filled with T. S. Eliot, Blake's
Albion, and the history of . . . England! David smiled at that, but he
began to weep as well from sheer defense-destroying fatigue. He'd
labored so long for them, he wept, and they abandoned him in a cowardly way. He'd dreamt he would bring them to *his* level, when they
wanted only the right to vote as he did, have power, as he did, so they
could rule over *him* according to *their* ways. And after all this time in
Mississippi he didn't know what their ways were. Maybe they didn't see
him as the goal of human evolution. Maybe they had something else in
mind that he didn't have the ear for, something he should have heard
in their mumble-mouthed moaning songs, their funky dirges. So David
Watkins would be retold in the mouths of people who couldn't (or
wouldn't) understand anything about himself that he treasured; he
would be remade in their image, with their slow drawl, their vulgar
jokes, their endless, plaintive, harmonically crude singing.

"Do we identify with the black masses," Joshua said again, "or do
we really want privileges only for ourselves? Look, they will give us that.
We can go to universities. But the black people on the Delta can't even
read and write. If they don't get power now, then schools will never be
built for them. We have to demand one man, one vote, which means
black rule, and I don't see how we, alone, can push black rule down the
throats of white people. And, look, it will have to be *pushed* down their
throats. We need—" He stopped suddenly.

So David picked up, though he was still weeping. "We need whites
to come down and be beaten. So their families can see it on TV."

"Listen to me, David," Sugar said, standing over him, feet spread
apart, hands made into fists, "those careless, foolhardy, heedless white
children that you lead down to Mississippi won't just be beaten. They
will be shot. They *will* be killed. They will surely, surely die."

And *that* was the stone-cold truth; they all felt it soon as Sugar said
it. And they remembered, too, that Joshua *hadn't* said it, though Joshua
must have already seen it. It was *so* bad that the far-seeing, truth-telling

Joshua Battle had hoped they wouldn't see it, wouldn't say it; and the shock of that stunned them.

Sugar sat down again, and they agreed on the one thing they could still agree on, that they all needed to sleep. Weeping still, David went back to his dorm room. He watched Willie get undressed, and he took off his own overalls. He wanted to compare their arms, their legs, their chests. Were they the same? Willie looked at him looking at him as David stared first at Willie's skinny leg, then looked down at his own calf, his own thigh. Willie hunched his left shoulder quizzically, and David, without thinking, did the same. *Willie is darker than me,* David thought. *He will rule over me,* though David had a B.A. in English literature, though David had *their* culture—that magic bleaching cream!—their language, their confidence, their ease . . . their looks. No, not that, not never that, however well he did on that fucking paper bag test! Had he always dreamt that *he* (his beautiful soul, his cultured mind) was far *inside* his body because too many days he loathed *this* body, his lips; his clumsy words; the smell coming off him. Wait, he didn't loathe his body when Susan's lips touched it, that way she had, kissing him all over. But, Mr. Bones, what about high school, some "mixed group," like when he spoke at the Model UN? *Did* he sweat then? *Did* he hate his smell?

So did he *really* dream that the line of spiritual evolution was nigger, colored, Negro, and then . . . white? He imagined his white great-great-grandfather (who he'd never seen even a picture of) and his white relations (who did not even know he existed) as the family spread red-checked tablecloths in the meadow for a picnic—but God forbid David Watkins might sit down in that meadow with them! Is *that* why this Negro dreams of communion? he thought disgustedly. Christian communion, or the universe as a big band improvising together under the direction of Jelly Roll God, to make all people one—so the whites would *have* to admit they were related? Why the fuck should he care? Wasn't culture open to all, and hadn't he sat down at that feast? But he *did* care, goddamn his soul, and every bite he'd eaten at that culture-feast, he felt as he stood naked in the narrow dorm room, had really been like the Mississippi blows that made him feel momentarily better on one side of his soul and far more helpless and hopeless and excluded on some other.

He knew then that he could on any day tip over into hating himself for being black, and then he hated himself for possibly hating himself, a pain in his midriff like the worst beating he'd ever had. Hello, Pee Wee, he said to himself.

Willie looked over at him from under his thin blue cover. "Why are you calling me Pee Wee?"

David, standing alone in the middle of the room, had forgotten
Willie was there. He couldn't bear, then, to have Willie see how ugly,
how spiritually ugly, he was, so he ran outside in the cold, not noticing
the freezing air lapping around him until he found himself hugging one
of the trees in the courtyard for warmth and comfort. He rested his
cheek against the bark and commenced to throw up, remembering all
the pious civic lesson lies he'd told Willie and people like him in Mississippi, remembering, too, the rabbi he'd held as he vomited after the Freedom Ride, and the foolish metaphysics David had spoken then, wanting
to impress the Jew with his philosophical depth *simply because the fool
was white.* David's stomach had nothing in it to bring up but harsh acid
from coffee, from self-hatred, from lies, but he couldn't stop his long,
wrenching convulsions, because it is hard to change a dream. Is this
what Joshua wants? he wondered. To have no self? So he can finally stop
throwing his self up, *his ugly, bad, black self?*

When he finished with the bile and straightened up, he saw, like Adam,
that he was naked, and ran back into the dormitory, to the toilet at the
end of the hallway. But he *wasn't* finished; it would probably take his
whole life to get this acid out of him, and he couldn't stand upright yet,
couldn't overcome the cringe that came not just from beatings the racists
who hated him had given him, but from the deeper beating he'd first
received in the name of love, and then had gone on giving himself. He
splashed some cold water on his lips—his big lips. *I know my enemy
now,* he thought, *the one inside me.* He walked slowly down the hall to
bed, thinking that his parents had surely meant the best for him when
they had started him out to hate himself, his appetites, his impulses, his
body, for one wrong step and you slide down into the gutter, and the
cops are waiting for you and they say, *sorry boy, shouldn't lose your
temper,* and *boy, what are you doing outside naked, you just rape someone?* and the gutter runs straight to Indianola, which is Parchman,
which is San Q, which is all the sewers the white world has for what it
thinks of as its *refuse* . . . and you shout, *wait, I'm David Watkins, and I
think that the river is a strong brown God,* but they can't hear you (no
ear for your poetry because your blubber lips mangle the language) and
they think, *what's the mewling sound?* and they think, *it's my job to fill
the jails,* so *any nigger will do.* That was why his parents had said no to
Count Basie, no to Louis Jordan, no to Bobby Blue Bland, no to Little
Richard, and forget James Brown who looked like a gangster—those
sounds were too *exciting,* they might get his body moving, he might cry
out too loudly when he was hurt. So David began to weep again, and he

heard his parents say, *please don't cry, don't ruin things, because isn't it better, dearest child, to go about with empty eyes than to have them closed forever?* The honey of their sweet, protective love, which oiled his every muscle, had gotten all mixed up with the corrosive self-hating acid inside him, the love of parents who knew that being black in a racist white world could be a death sentence, so keep it down, keep it cool, *swallow it.* To squeeze the slave out of himself might be to take the love out of himself too. So, *must it be?* It must be, he thought, running again, down the hallway, back to his bed. *I am ready for the harder struggle, for the mental fight. . . .* But that made him laugh maniacally because "mental fight" was a phrase from Blake, and he realized that the most vivid words he had to speak his predicament in were the enemy's most precious treasures!

"You all right?" Willie asked as he slipped under his covers.

"Yeah," David replied. "Yeah, just something I ate." Something big, he thought, and sweet, and rotten, and white.

The next day they decided to stop talking and vote, because they were weary, and they needed to get back to their projects in Mississippi, each to his county; and besides, they couldn't stand one another anymore.

David Watkins said he was for Freedom Summer, one man, one vote—though most of them only heard an ally of Joshua's and not what he had been through: confessing to a tree. Except maybe for Fannie, who'd seen him naked in the cold, hugging that bark for dear life, and maybe wondered today how come he said so little—smart David who didn't usually lack for words?

Sugar talked again of the movement being taken away from them. And others, again, joined him. And he said, again, that the whites would be killed. "Listen, we aren't inviting them to a blues party. Listen, we are inviting them to die."

"That's not up to us," Sam said. "That's up to the Klan. Maybe they will *just* be beaten, maybe they won't die."

Sugar laughed like a pirate. "Listen, Sam, we're talking about black men and white women. *There will be deaths.* Black deaths for sure."

"We got *that* already," David said, and Fannie murmured amen. David wanted to put some steel into Joshua, whose restraint this morning felt soft, docile, confused, unbearable. "Like Amos Jones," he said quietly, so Joshua would hear him say: *who you helped to tell the truth. Who you helped murder.*

Joshua's hands went to the side of his head, and pressed, David imagined, until his temples hurt, and he looked around the room. His face looked fixed like a mask, and his eyes went wide. And Joshua told David and Chuck Taylor later how he'd looked around at all of them, saw all the things that had happened to them, and how they'd been changed by it, Fannie Mae Carter so worked over by cops that her body had grown callused and hard as wood; and even when she healed and grew soft again she would never bear children. Wouldn't she grow unbearably bitter when she realized what she'd given up for nothing? And Joshua looked at David, a finely calibrated, sensitive man, who'd soon be locked squatting in a Parchman sweat box, lifting his arms up to the light that came through the cracked wood ceiling, his sinews stretched as taut as in a drawing by his friend William Blake, until he couldn't bear the tension anymore and would maybe do some killing and die. And Joshua *saw* Willie, or so he said, who would not much longer turn that other cheek either, and he saw Susan Lems, on the phone at SNAP headquarters, her lips curled around her teeth, her almond-shaped eyes angry and terrified. The cracker on the other end offered her a neat riddle: *If you stay inside, we'll burn you up. If you go outside we'll shoot you.* And he remembered Jimmy falling into his arms, blood spurting from his neck while Joshua felt for the brake pedal. He'd wondered that day, he said, if he should bring it all to a halt. *They* could leave before they all went mad from the fear, or were killed. But the terror in the Delta wouldn't stop. "You have to feel the world cares," a Holocaust survivor had said to Joshua at some suburban fund-raiser, "or all the lines that hold you in life are severed. Then your desire to die, this death inside you, it takes over, and you just walk into the oven." Joshua had been smiling as he told them this, drinking beer at a juke in the Delta. "Well, haven't we all seen the slow shuffle of the poor black people in Mississippi?" he said. "Going toward each day's dishonest settle, bearing all of it from fear or Christian charity, and *because no one cared what happened to them.*"

"Your eyes," Chuck said, "they bugged right out of your head, you know that?"

"Did they? Well, I felt burdened, no doubt about it. 'Cause I could *see* this thing, and I knew it meant the end of me, I mean all that I had ever thought I was. I *saw* that it was gonna take deaths, white deaths, to make the world care about Mississippi. And I was gonna work to bring that about."

So that day in Washington, hardly knowing he was talking—for that was often why Joshua sounded so quiet to them, he was only murmuring to himself—Joshua had said it. "We can't protect ourselves. We can't protect our own. We must have white lambs of sacrifice."

. . .

In the years when he no longer talked to whites and his attention turned from England to Africa, David Watkins learned from Chuck Taylor the Yoruba word for what he'd maybe seen that morning in the classroom in Washington. Chuck (now called Baba) said Joshua's eyes had bugged out like that from *ashe*. Joshua had been *ridden*. A god had put his body on; and he'd looked about grandly, his eyes *bulging,* a thing they both swore to—because there were, Baba said, other eyes behind his, the eyes of the god who looked inward and outward, at the present and into the future. Or maybe that's what Chuck liked to think, African glory rags—supernatural approval for what they'd decided to do then. Anyway, they'd both felt the same thing when Joshua died, that he'd seen his own death, and even felt satisfied by it—like some crazy Buddhist-Christian alchemy would make his spilt blood flow into the veins of the black god, and through him into the black people of Mississippi.

Well, maybe it had, David Watkins thought, in his law office in Jackson, Mississippi, twelve years later, on the anniversary of Joshua's death. *I can't see it 'cause I don't have his bulging eyes. But maybe it had.* Anyway, it helped get that Civil Rights Act passed for damn sure. Then, on that particular day, David set to work to recruit a young lawyer, Jesse Kelman, wanting him—or anybody, for that matter—to join him in working against the death penalty in Mississippi, help devise strategies to keep black murderers from being murdered by the State. "Because," David told Jesse Kelman that day, knowing frankness and tragedy combined would make the pseudo-sublime sticky syrup to catch *this* fly, "I've seen enough death for one lifetime. I even that once collaborated with the world to cause the death of your friend. A boy I liked, too, you know? He had this avid, sentimental dream about us—like all black men were nature's noblemen." And more, he thought—and to his mind a whole lot more—he'd helped cause the death of the man whose bulging eyes had seen, the man whom David Watkins had most loved in all the world.

That day in Washington, Sugar looked at Joshua looking at him, and he, too, felt *so it must be.* He said, "Okay. Listen, let's integrate death," though, as it turned out, they couldn't. When the time came, black and white had to be buried in separate but equal graveyards.

And Sugar, dear Gandhian Sugar, Fannie heard, maybe looked forward to those deaths, and maybe not like Joshua, for what the death would do, but for the sweetness of *their* finally dying, too. Maybe they all looked forward to that, and she murmured, "Yes."

And if they won't let them come to the picnic, David thought, maybe they could all meet up in Heaven. Or, of course, in . . . Mississippi. "Yes," he said, spitting out the sour whiteness inside him, "let them send us their most precious treasures."

Then one by one they all voted—Willie and Sugar, Diane, Sam, Joshua, and David—and they all voted *yes*, bring those white lambs down.

A little after that vote, in January of 1964, Frank Jaffe, the man that David would remember later for his flattering dream of black nobility, finished his study of Yoruba religion in—he'd have been ashamed to say, if anyone in Mississippi had ever asked him—an all-white class at Columbia University. *Ashe* was already a word that was as magical for him as it would be for Chuck Taylor or David Watkins, though they would think it a quality that their ancestors must have sometimes had, that they'd probably seen in Joshua, while for Frank Jaffe it was a power he yearned for, one that could scour a man clean and draw down into him the spirit of prophecy, but that *he'd* probably never feel, for he thought there were no more prophets among the Jews—and anyway (just in case modesty was one of the requirements), he wanted the appropriate Committee to know that he knew he wasn't worthy to be one.

Frank told Laura and Beth and Arkey and Jeffrey and Jesse and Billy what he'd learned about *ashe,* the shining quality of a human who bore one of the gods inside him; and by way of illustration he unrolled his most precious treasures for them on his tape deck, rare recordings of rural blues obtained (with his well-connected father's help) from the Library of Congress, or from the collectors' network. He planned to take this same tape deck with him to Mississippi, and he would record the blues sure to be thick on the ground there, in hidden jukes, at plantation parties, in front-porch meetings. For Frank dreamt that he'd heard *ashe* in the blues, and if he couldn't have a spirit in himself he could maybe, by following the track of this music down to Mississippi and the Freedom Summer project, at least be with those who were possessed by a cause, by History (for the moral arc of the universe was long, but Reverend King had said it bent toward justice), be with those, he fervently imagined, whose culture let them feel justice and dance and prophecy all buckled together as they did the stroll down to the courthouse to register; he could, that is, be with those who felt a whole bunch of things that weren't at Columbia University, or in this white culture, this beautiful Great Neck, this . . . prison.

Except in the voices from the dead that sang out in the suburban air in his bedroom, where Frank listened with his young friends, but sitting against the wall, looking at the door, as if Great Neck were dangerous— for he dreamt of release through a possession that would also be a fulfillment of himself, but he feared some nameless invasion from without, some danger to his person that he couldn't see. To make his bedroom a shrine to the blues, he'd hammered a "one-string" into the wall behind him, a broom wire stretched between two nails with a brick sliding under the wire to make it tight like that and—depending on where the bulge is placed as you pluck—change the wire's pitch. Frank knew that a skillful man could run a bottle neck across the string, make an almost-human wailing sound, but when he broke the Coke bottle to get that jagged ring, his scream was altogether human. He wrapped his hand quickly in a white Brooks Brothers shirt to keep the blood from dripping onto his shag carpet—where it would scare his mother with the damage to him, and to her house. Frank also had a washboard leaning against the wall, a comb and paper in his desk, a kazoo in his blue work-shirt pocket. But he couldn't play a note, and even humming through the paper he still sounded . . . like Frank.

So maybe he wasn't a band but a curator, a professor, and what he *could* do was *explain* to his little friends what he'd been taught, how the paper membrane in the kazoo was somebody's memory of the African ritual face mask's paper membrane.

Jesse and Billy and Arkey attended closely. Maybe, they thought, there was a clue in all this as to how you got a woman to sleep with you, the way Frank had seduced Beth.

"The mouthpiece changes the voice of the man possessed into the voice of the god whose mask he wears, because there's only a paper-thin membrane between the worlds," Frank told Arkey Kaplan—wondering why if the worlds were so close *he* never felt certain about who, or what, he should desire or who he truly was; the only certain thing to him, for the moment, being that there was a clue to the answers in the flatted third, the twelve-bar form, the repetition of lines, the long plaints, and the world where guitars spoke with almost human voices of an oxymoronic brand—not available in Great Neck—of joyous agony. The blue note drowned the world in a suffering that was lived all the way to the bottom, yet on exhalation, something was returned for people to cling to, and it was (as if the moment of inhalation and exhalation could be identical) *this very same note.*

Frank played them a tune by Bo Weevil Jackson, "who many collectors," he said pedantically, "thought was really Sam Collins." *I'm gonna write me a letter,* Jackson sang, *I'm gonna mail it in the sky / Mama, I know you will catch it when the wind goes blowing it by,* and Frank explained that meant "he can tell the future. He looks around the juke joint with big, shining eyes. His face becomes a smooth mask, and the pretty women can tell he's made the god. Now they want to have the god inside them, too."

It meant that? Arkey thought. The women do? Possession by a god sounded to Arkey then like something worth having—a marvelous version of the mythical *Spanish fly* that Johnny Ryan had once told him about, and which he was beginning to think was the only thing that might let him have what he wanted *almost* more than straight A's and admission to a good college.

For *that* prestigious deliverance Arkey's parents thought even Great Neck's schools no longer good enough, and Arkey now wearily left Great Neck every morning at seven in blue blazer and burgundy knit tie to travel on the LIRR with admen and brokers to the all-boys John Dewey School—where Joshua Battle, he told everyone proudly, had once taught algebra. The train left him exhausted, and the all-boys school left him socially backward and so ever further from his other yearning: to be inside a girl who wanted *him* inside her . . . or would even tolerate having him inside her. Did he need to find a god inside himself first, to be able to do *that?* Jesus—how did he go about that? He listened hard to Frank's songs and his lectures, but he didn't feel any closer to first base.

Frank's father heard only mortal danger in those scratchy transcriptions, knowing that Frank had the mad idea that he should follow those mumbling voices back to their source, to Mississippi and something called "Freedom Summer." So blame it on the blues. Or on Rabbi Waxman's pompous whines about the Freedom Rides. Or on Herbert's own sins— his own blessing. Herbert, who'd been one spud in a whole potato field of student socialists, had, like many other tubers, put aside such childish things to become a Wall Street lawyer, advisor to the Democratic Party, and counselor to Menachem Cutberg, builder of America's first conglomerate. Or, as he'd felt one fine day in '62, a dead soul in a natural-shouldered suit. The CEO of one of Cutberg's treasures, his five-and-dime stores, had announced through Herbert's own office that "we can't afford to sacrifice white business by letting Negroes in our Southern stores. It is simply an economic decision," when it had been Herbert's particular misfortune to hear on Robert Trout's radio report that same day a manager of the Jackson, Mississippi, store say, "We don't need nigger custom." Herbert Jaffe's sour ears heard those were different words from his firm's press release, just played to the same tune. That week a friend had brought the Reverend Martin Luther King to meet Herbert, and at the sight of the man's smooth face, his compassionate eyes, Jaffe had started weeping—some psychological crisis, he'd thought, even as he heard himself saying, "I'll make a statement to the press about Cutberg and resign from the firm."

King, thank God, knew that gestures like that generally evaporate well short of fulfillment and had asked him instead to stay where he was and help them "with the long hard work of making justice." Herbert had set up a foundation for King, so contributions for SCLC would be tax free. Herbert had given him legal advice. Herbert had arranged for meetings with federal officials. For these things his son actually admired him. And all a matter of very small sacrifices—a few dicey moments with the Kennedys, and maybe Hoover taping his phones.

Until *this*—like the gods wanted him to give his firstborn son! Herbert didn't trust SNAP. They were arrogant. They—he knew, despite Waxman's editing, probably on his behalf—mocked King as "De Lawd." And just a month ago, when King and he had visited Schlesinger to lobby him for a new civil rights act that would make fuller use of the interstate commerce regulations, Arthur had asked them, in turn, to do a favor for Johnson and put a stop to the Mississippi project. It had the fulsome potential to pointlessly embarrass the president. Besides, the whole shebang, Schlesinger had said, had been dreamt up by the National Lawyers Guild, a Commie front, the Reds influencing SNAP to put kids from well-known white families in the most dangerous places— *kids like Herbert's son*—to get them killed. But King wouldn't take orders from Schlesinger; SNAP wouldn't have listened to De Lawd anyway; and his own son actually laughed when he passed on the message from the White House.

Still, the message made Frank's mother wake at three every morning, nauseous with fear, as if, she thought, she had morning sickness again. Ellen had tried to teach her children to feel they were endangered as Jews so they would never risk themselves, but she'd also wanted them to feel they were just like others, regular Americans, which meant *safe,* had even let them have a small Christmas tree and exchange gifts. Well, not *exchange,* for the greedy children simply brought her huge lists to be filled. Now she cursed herself for the tree that implied they were actually Americans, protected wherever they went—like God would now punish her for aping the gentiles by taking her child away.

She got up and sat in the dark at the round glass breakfast table, her heart beating frantically. She tried to think of something to say that would stop Frank from going. That Dr. Jacobs had said Frank wanted the Jews to be better Christians than the Christians. That Moses had understood life better than the Baptist ministers when he'd written "Thou shalt not *murder,*" *not* "Thou shalt not *kill.*" For all created things, Dr. Jacobs said, and she repeated, have a right to defend their lives. That's where morality begins.

Frank drank his coffee irritably as she talked, and went on reading the *Times,* jealous on his father's behalf, she knew, to hear her imitation of Dr. Jacobs' nasal voice, as if, he said, she thought her doctor's suffering meant he possessed all the history, wisdom, and prophetic power of the Jews. "We can't let this stand, Mother," he said, getting up from the table. "We can't let Mississippi continue. We can't just be obedient, law-abiding, good Germans. I saw the thing Dr. Jacobs wrote: our guilt tells us we have to heal the world we've maimed, right? Well, this is how, goddamn it. This is the world that needs healing."

She followed Frank back to his room and sat on his bed in her quilted red housecoat, parroting Rabbi Meltzer's singsong voice she'd heard on a TV show called *Unto This Light.* She said okay, he may be right. But Dr. Jacobs said each person's guilt offers different instructions; each person has a particular task to do. And *this* was not our story, we must look to our own. She said, actually, whatever she could think of to denigrate Frank's politics. Frank said viciously that she did this because she cared more for money than for justice. He joked to her face that she was the only woman in the world who knew the price of a toll call to anywhere in the United States, that she knew not only the price of everything and the value of nothing, but that she was a meta-philistine, she even knew the price of values.

But in truth, Frank, her nearly blind, curly-haired, usually kindly and always overly dramatic son, was her most precious treasure, and she valued him more highly than her own life. He had—with the help of years of expensive orthodontia—the sweetest, the warmest, most welcoming smile she'd ever seen on a man. So she willingly made herself a mean-spirited, miserly bitch in his eyes (a Phyllis Stein, she thought wryly)—praying that it might save her son.

But he remained blind to the dangers. He had said—in an overly dramatic way—that he felt positively privileged to have the chance to work for justice, and he smiled, she thought, like a boy drugged by his youth.

Dr. Jacobs' secondhand carping, or Arthur Schlesinger's attempt to scare his father, only made Frank more certain he was right to go—for shouldn't all Jews be willing to sacrifice for justice, wasn't *that* the meaning of prophetic Judaism that Rabbi Waxman had taught him in the classes before his bar mitzvah (when he was listening, anyway)—not kosher laws but the spirit that Reform Judaism discerned behind even those odd injunctions; they were to make community, render justice. Freedom Summer, he told his mother, was precisely what his guilt told him to do. *And of course,* he told his dad, SNAP would put whites in dangerous places where they might be beaten, *that* was the point: to dramatize to the rest of the country the dangers of Mississippi. The strong drug of his youth made Frank ferocious, ready, he imagined, for *any* sacrifice to make justice. Any sacrifice? Even if it meant his death? He said *yes*—but he was confident that he was just talking to himself at the time. If only he knew a Babalawo, priest of the gods of Ifa, those angelic manifestions of the god Olodumare. A baba who understood *ashe* could cast the pine nuts for Frank, make him sure of his choice, take his terror away.

His grandmother feared an evil spirit had led Frank. She went to her rabbi, had Frank's name changed so the Angel of Death wouldn't be able to find him.

And the family's maid, Ruth Brown, worried he might die, too. A thin, sharp woman, she felt furious at Frank's stupidity, at what he was doing to his family, at his arrogant ways. She took down his diddley-bow while Frank watched, and threw out his brick and his washboard, and his comb and paper. "Supposing," she said, too angry to bottle up anymore, "I played you the sad little tune your grandfather hummed when the Cossack knocked his fur hat into the mud? Do you understand me? The one he went on humming when he quietly picked up his hat. Would *you* like to hear *that* tune?"

Truth was, she *did* like to hear the music on Frank's tapes, all of which she knew in one form or another, had even once made her living from. She stood by the door of the stuffy little room she'd started living in since her nephew had gone off to school in New York, a closet-size place of discarded masking-taped sofas and chairs. In the next room, while Frank played his tapes for friends, gave them pompous little lectures, Ruth let the music make a magical horseradish tonic for her, a little something purged of resentment but not without bitterness, that left her feeling stronger. Still, she was angry with Frank's entitlement, thinking *he* had the right to their stories and their songs; and she was furious with him, too, for hurting his loving, suspicious mother, who spent hours every day at the round glass "kitchen-nook" table keeping Ruth from her work so she could nod at Ellen's tale of problems with her husband and her psychiatrist, a hawk-nosed concentration camp survivor, who was her lover, Ruth could tell, even if he wasn't her lover, the way Ellen sorrowed for him all day long, Ellen talking to her like Ruth were either a mute or a pet who could never tell anyone her secrets—or maybe like her best friend in the world, though Ruth knew that Ellen Jaffe had once snuck into her "best friend's" room to see if she'd been the one who had stolen the missing silverware.

Well, that had been long ago, before they knew each other well. But Ruth was still angry that the unfilial son of a mother who had made her eat from separate dishes the first few years she'd worked there, that *this* boy thought he could play the great white savior, putting himself in danger for the poor Negroes. Yes, his family had learned better over the years with her, had several times given her the chance to meet the Reverend King, but did that mean their boy would *understand* that there have been other diasporas, other slower holocausts, ones that wouldn't be halted by a boy's grand gestures, his freedom vacation in Mississippi? She dumped his shit in the trash.

But later that day she forgave him; after all, she'd more than partly raised him and his sister while his mother and father had been away, because it was more important to know a fat old woman like Hubert Humphrey than it was to take care of their own children. She handed him a forty-five in a plain brown wrapper, "Cambridge Records" big and red on the label. "Remember Me," Ruth said, meaning the sweet song, a Gullah spiritual her great-grandmother had sung on Johns Island, which Ruth and the band had turned worldly as all get-out, making it a woman pleading with a man, while the tune and her voice gave her love-pleading unhappy transcendent shadows—after all, there was *so* much damn pain for love to compensate her for, what earthly man wouldn't finally disappoint?

Ruth meant, too, that Frank shouldn't forget her. "But don't tell anyone about this"—*this* being a song from another life, a time that had been filled with empty promise and sad-hearted disappointment, treasure receding as she chased it, leaving her ever more sullen to be cleaning houses for her living, yet with just enough money to send her nephew on partial scholarship to the John Dewey School in New York for his last few years of high school. Thank God the boy could run to get the rest of it! She'd moved away from Steamboat Road to this house so she could save a little more for his books and things, and packed off her most precious treasure to live with his grandmama so he could get to that school on time each morning.

Frank, astonished and moved by Ruth's gift, asked, "What can I give you? I mean, you know, to remember me?" He wanted to thank her, to make up to her for whatever offense he'd given with his diddley-bow, and he wanted, too, to be in Ruth's thoughts as he went to do something that filled him with terror. Ruth asked for the prayer shawl that lay unused on his closet shelf, because she'd known Frank since he was ten, a quiet, frightened boy who had become a handsome, wary, but kind man. She wanted something to remember him by, and even maybe to wrap herself in as she prayed for him—if, that is, she were moved to do so. "It was my grandfather's," Frank started to say, fearing impiety, and its punishment, hoping she'd let him give her something else. But Ruth's round, sorrowful eyes stung him. He had hurt her somehow with his one-string and his interest in her culture. Maybe giving her this piece of cloth would help make things right.

Ruth's surprising gift fed his fantasy that the Negro people were bearers of treasures of suffering and song, all their words and silences to be interrogated like the words of a poet, or the rests in music. That feeling, combined with the liqueur of his youth, had helped him look forward again for a moment to the pains he might suffer in Mississippi. He imagined that when he met Joshua Battle he would sing Ruth's song for him, and the song, he dreamt, would make Battle sing something in return. The scene was a fantasy, but imagining it let him overcome for a night the anxiety about Mississippi that he hadn't dared show to anyone, drifting to sleep in the narrow bed where his greatest fears before then had been that the meteoric baseballs of Little League games would fall directly on his forehead.

The next night Frank and Beth lay together on a blanket in the very cold field of a rich man's tax-loss farm. Beth feared that the full-throated cry that she sometimes tried in hopes it might help her to have an orgasm might stampede the cows, and that kept her from even halfway enjoying making love.

Which made Frank dream when *he* came that this night would taint Beth's memory of him as a lover. He remembered Ruth's song, thought how Beth was like the women there, bringing this intense, unfulfillable need to him—as if he could be compensation for all she'd given up. Namely her fantasy of her sainted father. Nobody human, Frank thought, could really be that important, valuable, satisfying. Or anyway, *he* couldn't. Hell, maybe that was part of why he was leaving Great Neck for Mississippi.

"Remember me," he said.

"Oh, darling, of course I will."

"I might have to stay in Mississippi until, you know, the job's done—one man, one vote."

She searched around in the cold grass for her glasses.

"Then maybe I'll like become a lawyer to make sure all men receive equal justice."

They'd just made love, and these grand plans sounded to Beth mostly like another abandonment, but she certainly didn't want to hold him back. What he was doing was *right:* she felt like he was her soldier—her Valkyrie; almost like she was sending him into battle. "Maybe soon I can join you," she said. "We can work together."

And until then, he promised, he would write her every day.

"I was not prepared for how luxurious the vegetable beauty of Mississippi is, even in February, or for how many people, including my coworkers, seem to hate me for being here," he wrote Beth several weeks later.

And then, after that, his letters to Beth didn't come daily or even weekly, because each day in Mississippi he did as Joshua Battle said and carried wood and chopped water, and his thoughts were jumbled by a fatigue and fear that made writing nearly impossible. The Klan had greeted the first trickle of white volunteers with a fire in the lane outside the local supporter's house where Frank stayed, a pale picture of Jesus above his narrow bed; and each night thereafter pickup trucks drove by the shack with their gun racks showing, their motors humming, *I'll be back, so just keep still.* He stayed away from the front room, as per Sugar Cane's instruction, "so that he might spare this good family when the shooting came," stayed off the streets after dark; and he fervently recited the S'hama, the one Hebrew prayer he still completely remembered, hardly believing that declaring the right number of gods would be enough to move that one God to protect him. Three weeks in Mississippi had been enough to make the drug of his youth wear off. Now he desperately wanted to live—yet he still, and maybe even more than when he'd come, wanted to work for justice, the small daily efforts that made the pickup truck pace back and forth in front of the house, which were also the only things that made his fear recede even a little. The work tired Frank's arms, though it left him buoyant, too, when he built shelves for the community center or cranked the mimeo machine; it wearied him but left him glad when he played teacher's assistant at their local "Freedom School," where he had to remember not to imitate the severity of his own teachers—"That is *not* an *n*"—but instead to follow the movement's pedagogical theory and correct while affirming, saying with fond, necessary foolishness, "*Yes,* this is an *m.*" The work bored him when he helped old men with their Social Security forms, though it left him guiltily pleased with himself that he *could* help; and the work left his hands shaking like an old man's from the emotional strain of tending the phones in the office, waiting for "check-in" calls from traveling organizers, Frank prepared with numbers for the FBI and the Justice Department, who would come if called, Sugar said, "go *tsk-tsk* in their bloody faces, and then do *nothing* officiously," and he imagined his taut nerves could only be smoothed if he ever got to ride the roads himself while someone waited for *his* call.

But the work wearied him *utterly* at the cabins where he tried to convince people to take the long walk to the registrar, and the men standing on the porches of the shotgun shacks nodded and said "yes sir," with a compliance that meant *please leave me now,* an agreement worse than hatred, so that he soon grew tired simply from being white, and refreshment for *that* fatigue could only come, he imagined, from *not being white,* which was seemingly impossible without his also not-being, or so their compliance implied, it saw him as so thoroughly simply *that.* He almost agreed even to that requirement, though, for if *white* had made a fear as deep as these downcast eyes, this mumbled assent, then his own anger against his world must—he dreamt—go just as deep until he despised not only his own color but all that was suddenly bound up with it—the wide lawns of the suburb where he grew up, his huge bedroom, the plush shag carpet, his mother's love that oiled his bones, his wary way of looking at things; *his life.* But he only *almost* agreed, for since he'd come to Mississippi he'd learned how very much he wanted to live. After all, if he lived he could work to make people see that he was one who would really struggle endlessly to stop this hell from continuing, that he was not what Beth called "a good German"; if he lived he could make people see him as he truly was, or as he would *become,* if he continued to struggle for justice. If he lived.

But however tired he was from his work or his whiteness, he did write to Beth when he could, more than to his sister or to his mother, though his letters, he said, were to be read to all of them, and Beth scrupulously followed Frank's dictates, not just sending the letters back from Wellesley, but shuttling down standby to recite them to a group that now seemed a year and a lifetime younger than her. They met twice a month in Laura's bedroom of frilly valances, French Provincial furniture, and Miss Dior bottles, a room very far, she thought, from the seriousness of her own bare dormitory single.

Laura lay on her double bed as Beth rocked and read, surrounded by her doll collection, and with the pile of books by her feet that Beth had helped her choose—*The Souls of Black Folks, Invisible Man, Blues People, The Dutchman,* words that Laura hoped would help her to walk in her imagination beside her older brother. Laura's hand rested on a present Frank had sent her from Mississippi, a little black girl made of wood, with painted cornrow hair and a head with four faces, all on a swivel so you could change her expression to show your mood for the day. Sometimes, when they were drunk, they passed the doll around to show their feelings.

Arkey sat on the floor, his heels tucked under him Japanese-style, feet crossed behind, an Oriental trick, Laura knew, that he thought would make him seem taller; and particularly to her. Superstitious Arkey's gift from Frank had been a *mojo hand,* a red flannel bag smelling of oil and musky perfume, pierced with a needle, seasoned with a root doctor's herbs and incantations, a rolled-up piece of paper inside it that brought luck in your pocket if you never unwound it and looked at its words—though of course Arkey did, accounting, he thought, for his failure at poker.

Jeffrey and Jesse had their backs against the wall, and Billy, Beth's little courtier, lay prone, his body held above his sketch pad by his left elbow, so that with his other hand he could draw a picture of her in the Kennedy rocker, letter in hand, or of a cabin with a fire in the dirt road in front of it, or of a Negro boy reading a book with an encouraging (or at least not *discouraging*) white shadow over him.

"Maybe my coworkers don't hate *me* precisely," Beth read from the rocking chair late that February for her family of lost boys and girls. "It's more a matter of principle—like to become friends with me, to imagine my point of view, would make them inwardly weak, and would show a lack of solidarity with the Negro masses."

Except, that is, for Chuck Taylor, a state rider for SNAP who traveled the dangerous roads between the projects, stopping in Lovette twice a month. A short, round, bald man with a beard that made him look like a topsy-turvy, he had at age fifteen so strongly dreamt that Jews were the bearers of secret gifts that he'd converted to Judaism. After his bar mitz-vah, his Baptist mother said, "They've cheated me all my life at their stores, and now they've stolen my son from me." But Chuck deeply loved the Law and the moment-by-moment instruction it gave him, a *certainty* on how to act to heal the world—just as if, Frank thought, he had *ashe* and a god spoke within him.

"Israel," Chuck told Frank, "has been scattered all over the globe so they can go into the *kelipoths,* the most evil of places, and raise the sparks of divine light trapped there."

Frank looked down at his plate of beans. It almost made him laugh that Rabbi Waxman's teaching helped him understand about zero of what Chuck had just said.

"Well, I'll tell you," Sugar said, "those sparks must be buried in some deep shit in Mississippi. Take strong arms to pull them out."

"Strong stomach, I'd think," Frank said, stirring the pork fat around a little, give the beans some flavor.

"When the process of freeing the sparks is nearly complete, the Mes-siah appears," Chuck promised. "He gathers the last sparks. Then evil won't have an element it can act through. Good and evil will be forever separated."

"Man," Sugar said, "I don't think those Jews been working hard enough!"

Chuck forgave Frank his interest in the blues, while Sugar and David were as angry at Frank as Ruth Brown had been. Chuck even tipped Frank that there was a preacher just outside Lovette who used to be a blues singer before God called him, a man who boasted that he'd been such a star that he'd had six suits made to measure for him by an Italian tailor in Chicago.

"What's his name?" Frank asked, greedily swallowing some beer.

Chuck didn't know, but years ago, well into his ministry, this preacher had fallen into the blues again, come to the very juke where he and Frank and David and Susan were drinking now, on the highway that ran between flat plantation land and a swamp where flamingos stood in silent contemplation, a place sometimes called Snookey's, and some-times The Last Cafe, because it had a sign in the window saying, LAST NEGRO CAFE IN THE DELTA. Anyway, after a month of Snookey-style sex and damnation the preacher had crawled back to his flock to be rocked in their many strong arms. Chuck had himself heard the preacher play on that in his sermon last Sunday, say that, *yes,* the blues were coming on him again and only the love of his flock could save him! People in

Lovette listened to what this preacher said about things, so *they*—meaning the SNAPs—desperately needed his help. People in Lovette were choked with fear. They all knew that the police in Lovette were just the Klan in tailored blue sheets. No one had tried to register to vote in more than a year, and no matter how many times the countrypeople might nod and say *yes sir* to Frank, they were even scared to sign up for the Freedom Democratic Party, let alone go down to the registrar for the real vote. Frank, Chuck said kindly, was trying mighty hard, but SNAP was failing badly in Lovette.

Frank tilted back in his broken-legged chair, stung by Chuck's mournful, sweet plaint. He needed to use the toilet in the back, but it was missing a wall, and he was embarrassed, even though there were only ten or twelve people here, mostly young black men. He and Chuck and David and Susan were very foolish to be here among them drinking beer—excuse enough for the police to arrest them. And it would be dangerous to drive the highway at night even slightly tipsy, not looking out for an ambush. The admonitions taped to the juke's walls warned them: "Be Nice or Leave, Thank You" and "O Lord Please Help. Me. To. Keep. My. Damn. Nose. Out. Of. Other. Peples. Busness." But the SNAPs just couldn't stand being packed as tightly in the lines of Mississippi life as a prisoner in a Parchman sweat box; and maybe the three couples who swayed to music from an old gray phonograph felt the same way (*They may kill me baby,* Jimmy Reed sang, *do me like they used to do / My body might rise and swim to the ocean, and come back home to you*), sharing their desperation and turning it into ephemeral art (*Ain't that loving you, Baby?*), moving with sharp, decided motions that made restriction look almost like a necessity of joy (*Ain't that loving you, Baby? / And you don't even know my name!*). He had to figure a way to use that phrase, Frank thought, in his next letter.

Strong cords ran between the dancers, whose names Frank would never know, though in his dreams he loved both the men and the women. The short woman in the yellow blouse tugged her partner's shoulders about by shifting her weight from hip to hip, his long leg between her shorter ones forming an axis for her, her leg forming an axis for him, as they did the snake, or was it the slow boogie, the bump, the grind, the drag? *Oh, let this,* Frank prayed, more than a little drunk from his few beers, *oh, let this*—meaning Chuck and David and Susan, meaning these dancers and their truly magnificent juke joint, its walls parti-colored with daubs of bright red and blue and yellow paint, all the more beautiful to him for being a poor man's difficult effort at gaiety, so different from Leonard's in Great Neck—oh, let *this* please be my beloved community.

Thinking of a parable from the holy book of Kafka, Frank smiled wryly. He said, "Maybe the preacher could fall into sin and return to the church again and again. Then Snookey's would be part of the ritual." In that way, he explained drunkenly, the fallen world would become a part of the church, the church mixed up with the fierce and beautiful world, and God, well, God would be everywhere.

David Watkins didn't like the boy's smile, his nice, even, stupid teeth. He rubbed his lukewarm glass of beer against his cheek to cool his temper. "You don't understand what a serious business the soul is in Mississippi," he said. "One wrong drunken step, and the Cossacks push us into the river." The Church and the Juke, he explained with feigned weariness, God and the devil, had to be kept absolutely separate. It was a matter of life and death. *Black* life and death.

Chuck, with a kindly smile, nodded. If their much-loved preacher were to fall again, he said, the saints would throw him the hell out of his house and cast him from the church. The man was too old for the fields. Too corny for the juke. He'd be ancient history.

That church of his was a weathered gray wooden building with a huge, thin cross on top, tall windows, decorated with more crosses painted on in thick black bands, and, like they couldn't get enough reminders that He'd bought the farm, yet another frighteningly rugged wooden cross standing over behind the altar. Frank remembered Lenny Bruce's joke: if Christ had been killed in the twentieth century, there'd be pictures of electric chairs everywhere. Well, thank God, he thought, there wasn't also one of those tormented suffering manikins pasted on the cross to make him queasy with fear and embarrassment. The preacher whose help they needed, a gaunt man, sat in a thronelike carved wooden chair directly underneath the biggest cross, greeting his congregation with a glowering, dyspeptic look. Frank's heart sank. He was pretty sure there'd be no help here.

And maybe David Watkins was right, that was because Frank *didn't* understand about the soul, the black soul, his stomach sick in the different churches where the civil rights workers spent every Sunday, and no less anxious, as it turned out, in a church where the minister was supposedly a former blues singer. And was that *him*? Frank didn't know most of the faces of the artists he most admired.

Anyway, the church was the best place to enlist aid for the project, the only place, Joshua (who'd come with David Watkins and Frank this

Sunday) instructed him, that belonged to Negroes in Mississippi. In *their* place, which is out of time and history (which means, you know, oppression), Negroes could become what Frank, in *his* fantasy, had always dreamt they already everywhere were, soul-saving wonder-workers; and filled with that sense of their power, they might, Joshua said, be willing to heed SNAP's call and come vote.

At this church, where they so desperately needed the dour man's help, there were only thirty people in the congregation today, and three of them were civil rights workers (which gave Frank an idea of just how badly he was doing in Lovette), but the crowd worked overtime to fill the building with a big noise, pleading that God might remember them, which was, miraculously, the song that Ruth had given him, turned right side out again, though the longing *still* sounded so intense that you might think this time that not even a Jesus Christ could satisfy it, the feeling building and building till a man in black pants and a white shirt couldn't contain or resist the aching, almost pleasurable yearning anymore and had to move about, beating time, walking down the aisle and back, arms akimbo, knees bent, a waddle that compelled Frank's attention and, though it was also almost sublimely comical, his adoration, it looked at once so antic and so very sad, for even when singing of good news, the music had a deep and mournful moaning, at least to Frank's ears, the very source, he thought, of the rumble he'd heard in Blind Willie Johnson's voice, the arterial spirit-blood that ran through all veins, thick with a gravity that made sin seem just a name for something more inevitably bound up with all that held us to the earth. Frank yearned to feel the sadness they felt, to have the uncanny mixture of freedom and control the choir showed in their precise gestures, as if fierce abandon were given you—as it was to the duckwalking man—once you truly acknowledged gravity, your shoulders and head able to move in a rolling but exact notation of the beat even as faces were upturned, ecstatic, and not seemingly counting earthly time.

A deacon in a brown suit stood up and led a thanksgiving prayer that told of his own passage from darkness to light and song, making the preacher himself, a thin-faced man of about sixty in a black suit with a long, beautifully tailored coat and pockets that sagged open from carrying the Bible, get up from his wooden seat by the podium and shake his long arms in the air alongside the choir. He smiled at them all with glinting teeth, striding back and forth in front of them, and he'd sat so still in the tumult before that Frank found this participation deeply moving, as if their singing had chafed his stiff soul until he could take over playing the portable organ, bringing his hands down on the keys in percussive, stiff-finger style, testifying to how his deacon got over. The preacher began to shout from the organ, stopping the music and letting his paragraphs roll on and on, until, as they built to their conclusion, he let his hand bring down chords of confirmation to mark the point of the lesson, which was, today, a warning against false prophets. For a man shouldn't speak until God *causes* him to speak, orders him to speak, fills him with the spirit to speak so the words *must come,* and he does not choose them but is chosen, does not make fine-sounding sentences, but is sentenced. The true prophet is no stand-alone man, no big-mouthed put-himself-first man. For the false prophets say go into the world, while the Lord says, "Just keep still," and the Lord says, "Wait on your change."

Joshua Battle leaned forward, his face made smooth, his eyes squeezed down to show interest. Frank thought it was part of Joshua's enormous politeness, consideration, thoughtfulness, that he would indeed actually consider this sermon, which was, of course, directed at him, the least puffed-up man Frank had ever met. It was, Frank thought, just cowardice talking in the preacher—understandable, he knew now, after his first month in Mississippi, though that fear might be.

"Vengeance is *mine,* saieth the Lord. Yes, and it don't belong to you. Yes, hmmm, and it don't belong to me. Yes, it belongs to God. Yes, we don't need no one's help but God's. Hmmm, mmm, yes, He *is* God. He always will be God!"

Men and women anxious to show that all was in God's hands shrieked or gave low moans till the whole church was filled with a painful, shimmering, almost ugly sound, like oil on water. The legs of the man next to Frank trembled and pounded the wooden floor, and a fat woman fell down, groaning, her arms held above her, making the preacher take decided long-legged strides down from the pulpit to pray with her. The woman's big legs flailed and her dress almost hiked over the tops of her stockings. The deacons threw a cotton blanket over her; a woman in white fanned her; the preacher pushed down on her forehead; and they all together prayed with God to save her, for men could call on God, plead with God, but only God could really work miracles, even in this house and especially in this house. So maybe Joshua hadn't gotten it, and the saved felt powerful here in how weak they could admit they were, how much suffering they could bear, how much they yearned for God. To defeat the devil this woman had emptied herself utterly, her last best trick, and now she . . . waited . . . able to do no more, as if the *art* of bringing on possession were to empty yourself out until your very helplessness forced God, or an angel, to be the good mother Who filled your mouth with His breast, or the husband Who occupied the house you had made clean and bare for Him. Frank, too, begged his one God to help this poor woman, for there was an awful complete nakedness to what she'd let happen to her, which Frank had *thought* he wanted for himself—until this moment when he saw that it was not so calm, so temperate as playing tapes in his bedroom in Great Neck, that his soul perhaps was truly lost because he would not possibly go through *this* loss, it would just *embarrass* him too much to be so vulnerable, so out of control and downright ugly; and he felt doubly a fool knowing that his fear of embarrassment had turned out to be a lot stronger in him than his yearning for godly possession.

Finally she grew still, and two white-robed women from the choir helped her rise.

Now the preacher strode forward, Frank sure that a god would talk from his mouth, an orisha, one of those African angels, emanations of the one God, Olodumare, but these angels love our bodies enough to put them on like a well-tailored suit, to speak through our mouths. Will it be Obatala, god of purity, or Shango, god of war and justice? The preacher, though, was already shouting from the pulpit of the suffering of the damned when the Son of Man would come—and yes, we don't *know* the day and we don't *know* the hour any more than we know when death will come slipping in *our* room. And the damned will call out then as those they tormented on earth had called out to God so many times before, but God would not hear the damned, yes, hmmm mmm, God would abide their evil no longer, hmmm mmm, and the devil would flay their skin from them, as they had *so many times* whipped men on earth. And when the preacher said *yes,* and hmmm mmm with a growl from deep in his throat, Frank could hear how he meant this to be the holy spirit—the orisha, the *ashe*—breaking through, marking time for a moment and then pronouncing judgment, and he almost wanted to say amen, but when those poor damned souls called out from hell the music went out of the preacher's voice and his soft vowels grew stiffer, so everyone would know the damned were most definitely white, and all the church could be joined together because they fervently believed in *that* judgment, its severity, its necessity, while Frank could not help wanting to be among the saved, and could not help feeling among the damned, and maybe *his* hell (for Frank thought he was *not,* surely, worst among whites) would be no more or less for him to feel then just as he did now, isolated, alone forever and ever, a boy without a date for the prom.

But he felt, too, a deep revulsion for the handsome old preacher. *This* couldn't be the voice of the African angels who love our bodies—or maybe something in the New World had soured them on us? There was too much ingenious cruelty in this man's religion, as if the real joy of being saved might simply be in seeing others damned, the moral equivalent of having the bigger house in Kennilworth, and even your pretend tears of pity for the fallen just dripped down from heaven onto the lost like a basting sauce for those who couldn't join the country club. The preacher botanized torment with a different shade of pleasure for each gradation of pain, in a voice that was high but not feminine; not masculine either, but a being-beyond-human creature who had an implacable quality that Frank now was sure he recognized from his tapes as the sharp falsetto sound of Caleb Carter, who had learned the Bentonia style (an open E-minor tuning, picked with three fingers in a complex pattern) from Skip James (who was a teller in this for Henry Stuckey, who'd learned it from a Bahamian man in France during World War I). Carter, if it was him, had once walked the Delta with Robert Johnson, terrifying his hearers with his direct, piercing cry, a wounded sound that made the listener shiver when Carter told how he was gonna lay his 32-20 on his lying girlfriend or said—today—how God was going to lay something far worse on all those who had so many times 'buked Him and His chosen ones. And so Frank's fantasy was fed once again, and all he'd seen and heard and dreamt in the church was retrospectively shown to him to be the truth, for if this was one of the blues' greatest geniuses, Caleb Carter, then all Negroes Frank met must also potentially be bearers of magnificent gifts, and the woman who had lain on the floor *had been*, likely as not, ridden by a god.

Afterward, standing on the porch in a spring sun made cool by the strands of tall trees with thick, tangled roots that shadowed the back of the church, Frank, as if he were showing what a good student he was— on which kind of goodness he had previously been sure his salvation depended—said, "You are Caleb Carter," thinking that the preacher's smile meant he was not entirely displeased to be recognized.

"Listen to you!" the man said irritably. His white shirt was soaked with sweat. "You are telling *me* who *I* am! Don't you think I know who I am?" He laughed, mirthlessly. "Are you here to learn the blues? You white boys want to play the blues so badly," the preacher said, "and you do. *So* badly. But *I* don't do that no more."

"But I don't," Frank said. "Play, I mean. I just want to record them. Preserve them."

"Sure, and keep the money."

Frank, mighty tired of a sudden of all this hatred-on-principle, decided to *just keep still* while Joshua and David spoke to Caleb Carter about holding a meeting in his church.

"But Caleb," Frank wrote to Beth, "said he knew about the three church burnings in Lechien County and he was not about to risk his people's only refuge. 'Weren't you boys listening?' he said. 'I have to protect my flock.' He turned to me furiously, as if I particularly had affronted him. 'You are here now,' he said to me, 'and so some Treasury men are here, too, traipsing along behind you, Marys following the little white lamb. But *you* don't know how they gonna do us when you go.' He turned to Joshua. 'But you *do* know, Mr. Battle,' he said, 'and *you* should know *better.*' And he walked back into his church."

Jeffrey, listening to Beth read this letter, was sure *he* knew how the fat woman felt pleading for the spirit to enter her. He saw Arkey, his long hair brushed across his forehead à la Veronica Lake, using a pencil to poke at a thigh probably filled with bubbles from the scrunched-up supposedly Japanese way he sat, and Jeffrey grew a little angry, thinking that *really* Arkey knew, too, but he would never admit even to himself that he *wanted* to be lost, that he *wanted* to be filled. Even Jesse, who would, he decided, someday become Laura's lover, because he was surely the handsomest, and the kindest of them, would still probably make himself furious or heavy in his motions with her to deny that he wanted not just to be inside her but to be her, to have something in himself. He saw Billy look adoringly at the amazing Beth, whose portrait he drew now, to offer to her later as a tribute, gazing the way Jeffrey himself once had at Frank, and Jeffrey thought that if maybe the yearning were great enough, and if maybe—because he was weak, slight, and therefore "unmasculine"—Billy didn't or couldn't make himself hard, brutal, falsely commanding enough to deny how helpless and abject he also was before that certain feeling, then Billy might join him, might know the nature of this wanting, too. Until then, though, it was Jeffrey's secret knowledge, and it made him special, older and just a little lonelier—more, he thought, smiling, a man. He was glad, though, that Frank at least knew that he wanted to be filled even if he still apparently feared it. It marked a kinship between them—like he was walking in Mississippi, too.

But when Ellen Jaffe heard the news from this letter (for Beth, worried for Mrs. Jaffe, often passed Frank's letters on to her), her heart beat with furious anxiety. If there were Christian people who would burn a church, what might they do to her son?

. . .

Frank, though he feared he'd be rejected by this revered Christian man, distilled enough courage to face Caleb Carter again. If he could record *him,* Frank would have a precious treasure that would make him famous with every blues collector. "The minister and his wife have a brick house in an open field by the church," Beth read that March,

a rare, solid sight in the Delta. There's a sign by the porch that says *Juicey RaBBits for Sale. 1$,* in neatly painted black letters, and a big crowded hutch with a barbed-wire front.

Mrs. Carter, a woman as tall and thin as Caleb, stood by the hutch watching me lug my heavy reel-to-reel tape recorder out of the car, and the sight of it filled her with such fretful scowling rage that she forgot, thank God, her deference to my damned white skin. Lovette's midwife hates me not because I'm white (or not *only*) and not because of the civil rights stuff, but because I'm interested in the devil's music. There seem to be so many reasons to dislike me in Mississippi, yet my life feels more real to me here; sharp, painful, vivid, and true. Her husband gets salty, she says, when he even thinks about the blues, and what if he starts drinking and plays all night at some juke? The deacons would surely take their house away from them then. *He'll* have to spend eternity in a sealed-up place where he can't ever get out. And *I'll* have been the cause of it. "Do you understand what I'm saying? Do you *know* what hell is?"

Do I, Beth? Rabbi Waxman never said much about it in Sunday school, though *we* are supposedly a vengeful people. I looked up at the cloudless Mississippi sky.

Fortunately, Caleb Carter himself came out then, in black pants, a black jacket, and a crisp white shirt, with a ribbon-tie in a wide bow around his neck, as if he were about to preach. Mostly to defy his wife, I think, he said I could interview him. But he wouldn't let himself be recorded.

We talked on an old sofa on the porch, an aluminum awning shielding us from the sun. I'm sure that Mrs. Carter will never in this life allow me into her brick house, but she brought out big jars of lemonade, her scrunched face more sour than the drink. (I guess her sense of proper hospitality was stronger even than her hatred for me!) Caleb Carter sat perfectly stiffly while she put the drinks down on a small wooden table. He has pouches of fat under his eyes like he hasn't slept much this millennium, and a measured angry manner just this side of hatefulness. He opened and closed the cuff of his jacket, to show me, I suppose, that it had been made to order. Once he gets going he has a boastful, heedless, even an insecure quality—a great artist severed from his audience—telling me first that he didn't know what the Bentonia style was, and then, a few minutes later when I mentioned it again, holding his hand up to stop me, saying that he, and *not* Henry Stuckey, and *not* Skippy James, had invented it. This, I thought, was too good to miss, and I turned on my tape recorder, thinking maybe he wouldn't remember his previous commandment either.

But Caleb put his jar down with a bang and made his face stony. "Did I give you permission?" he asked. Then he saw that the hurt in the boy's eyes meant he had a power over Frank, and wondered if maybe he could use that power for the good, if he could maybe bring the boy to see the majesty of Jesus. He would show him how the blues led to hell, and yes, how Jesus led to glory, and if he could walk this precious treasure forward before all his people to the cross, wouldn't that be something? *Use the line about sour mash,* he thought, and yes, use the boy's love for the music, hmmm mmm, and yes, the blues—the preacher told Frank— is dangerous as bourbon whose sour taste is like a flat note that fools you into thinking the drink is your friend because it knows the truth inside you, because sometimes your soul-balance gets to a brimming point of pain and bitterness—a place (though Caleb didn't say so) that he was pretty near to being at now, with a nearly last hope that bringing this boy to Jesus would help Caleb's reputation and his worn and tired spirit. Frank's keen-faced admiration pleased him like the fervent shouts that buoyed him up on Sundays and let him ride through the Mississippi week whose acid ocean of hatred was never far from destroying him, Caleb's nature as sensitive to each "nigger this" and "nigger that" as Joshua Battle's, so that the joy of his church was, in part, that he didn't work for whites, didn't have to talk to them or even see them most weeks. But if he could lead *this* one on to glory, yes, if he could make him rise up and say amen? Well, then! The colored people of the Delta would notice Caleb Carter again, and once more laud his genius—which, in truth, he believed in just as much as Frank—and renew his spirit.

And Caleb felt powerful, giving this tall, graceful boy the gospel truth, a lesson that was not only in him but was him, his life, his body, yes, so that the telling of how he was lost and then saved was a special comfort to Caleb, though his words about overseers who dogged and cussed a man till he couldn't bottle up anymore and almost crossed that line forever were (he began to feel almost as soon as he started talking) just bedtime stories for the boy. He could carry that big machine of his for eternity, like his ear needed an *extra* ear to work right, but he'd *never* understand what had been in Caleb's finest music, the particular suffering that his particular genius had transformed. And suddenly a demon jumped up, and like Richard Hartman (who would no more have seen his kinship with the great Caleb Carter than William Faulkner, sitting less than fifty miles away, would have recognized either of them as his colleague), Caleb was overcome not with a desire to frighten Frank and then save him but with a sore need to hurt this boy with his history, to raise red welts on his pale soul, to see that his story wounded him more deeply than anything Frank would ever otherwise feel because it was sharper, more painful, more vivid, and more true; then Caleb could be sure that *he* existed in the big open spaces of the Delta. And, after all, why not hurt him some? The boy would just go back to his friends in town, to his family up north, to his big house by Lake Michigan. He would listen to Caleb's stories, then go sailing in a big white boat. What lasting damage could Caleb Carter do to a boy who went sailing? So he'd show the boy how he worked from can't to can't doing halves, his thighs so chafed walking behind the owner's mules that his blood came out in time to his pulse, trying to earn money for mules of his own so he could step up to thirds and fourths, and finally, the promised land of rent farming—a Canaan so far away he could barely dream about it. And the forty acres receded every time he was paid off in plantation scrip and cheated at the robbissary, so that somehow between the furnish and the settle it turned out the white man didn't owe him even one more bean, but presto-chango, I owe U. So he and his wife hungered, and his children grew weak eating mock make-a-day of corn&water, water&corn, week after week, and it seemed like he buried one child each and every winter. It so often got to be too much for him to bear, and he felt *God will not come,* not to the colored of Mississippi, there is no heavenly judgment and no judge, there is only this godforsaken world, and then what he wanted *here* on *earth* he wanted hard—so give me a drink, please, or I'll die, give me a willing woman, please, or I'll die, and *when* I die *please let me die with my hands around one goddamn white man's neck.*

That couldn't be big news to the boy—could it? Yet a small satisfying shock flickered across the boy's eyes, for Caleb had near *sung* that litany of his deepest desire, using the painful falsetto that he knew very well could be like an invisible knife that carved images in his listener's brain, probably making the boy feel the hands around his neck, and the joy he'd feel breaking his windpipe, the pleasure he'd have hearing him gurgle at the end for air. The boy's shock soothed Caleb, and he remembered again that salvation for all was his earthly task. He smiled at Frank then, to welcome him to the church. "Well, now, see, *that's* the blues talking." And he told him not to trust the blues, something that you wanted that bad couldn't *possibly* satisfy. The blues were like whiskey, after you indulged in them, you came down with an aching head, and you craved just one more spoonful, one more spoonful, just one more spoon, to cure you of the world's pain and the headache the cure itself had given you, because the things of the world never satisfied, neither its violence nor its love, for only Jesus truly satisfied. Because there *was* a judgment, and yes, there *was* a Judge, and yes, there was another, better world coming where there would surely be a proper settle, so it wasn't a man's hands that should take vengeance. The living God *would* make justice. He would! So make your faith strong, Caleb said (putting, he thought, some fine pleading into his voice), and then there was no more need for the blues.

Caleb's long fingers curved almost all the way round the jar of lemonade, gripping it as tightly as the longed-for white neck, but his smile—which was crooked, as if his jaws didn't line up quite right—turned almost welcoming, as if an anger so deepened and so endlessly unfulfilled was one that even the white man whose neck might be wrung (by God or by Caleb) could also share in. But only *almost,* thank you, because Frank, in Frank's considered opinion, *didn't* deserve to die, not that Caleb had said *that* in so many words, but Frank—who interrogated Caleb's gestures as he would those of a teacher, a poet, an analyst, or a god—had certainly felt how Caleb had wanted to hurt him, first with his words and then *either* with his own hands *or* with God's stronger ones.

Frank looked out over the field. Empty wooden shotgun shacks lined the plantation across the interstate, their front doors facing toward the highway and its promise. Many of the people had gone north, and the rest had spread out in the field today, chopping cotton with short hoes. Peacocks strutted about in the dirt, artists who looked like they would tip over, as maybe Caleb had, from the difficulty of bearing so much splendor. Frank longed to make justice, but he also, and more strongly still, the more time he spent in Mississippi, simply wanted to live and see for all the ill he saw, and he smiled back at Caleb Carter, as if his wanting to live were a fine achievement on his part, and the wish surely sufficient (though thanks to Lovette, Mississippi, he already knew better) to guarantee its fulfillment.

. . .

Frank's smile, so damn sure (Caleb thought) that a world must be good that had him in it, made Caleb Carter wonder again what in God's name he had *ever* thought this white boy could know about being human in this black body, this Mississippi, this country, where Caleb would be in exile all his life long. If Frank didn't know what *this* hell was, he just as surely couldn't long sufficiently for *either* whiskey or heaven, and so Caleb Carter, from defeat and compassion, surrendered before Frank's innocent smile, gave up on Frank's soul, and instead of telling the boy how much so many wanted his pain in this world that he thought so nice, he told Frank the sorts of things he knew he'd like to hear, about the rambles to Memphis with Robert Johnson (though really those trips felt more like falling down stairs), and the parties (though it was generally at parties that his friends got cut up and that Robert died on his knees, barking like a mad dog). They hung, he said, a coal oil bottle with a wick from a tree—he knew Frank would like hearing that—and some enterpriser would sell fish sandwiches and whiskey. They'd sometimes made a platform for Caleb with a brush arbor over it, a little house in the wilderness of the Delta for him to play in, like the Jews' holiday houses that Chuck Taylor had told him about. And when he played the right notes, or so he remembered it for the boy, it was like an end to their wandering, you see, a promise fulfilled, a moment's paradise. He liked talking about those times in these big biblical words, but the comfort just made him sadder and more bitter, too, for life on the Delta was a remnant now, the machines marched like demons doing a job that never had been fit for humans, scarring your fingers and your soul—but with the worst jobs gone, his people now had no jobs and were left to dream almost lovingly of a past they'd so often and so rightly hated. He remembered the last time he'd fallen into Snookey's, its walls smeared with such sad-looking paint, a few couples stupid-dancing to the little record player. Were these folks *the saving remnant*? Who would come for them? This piddling boy and others like him led by Mr. Joshua Battle whose nonviolence shit was bound to get some more colored people killed, just the way it had done Herbert Lee? The earthly Department of Justice? Oh, hardly! Well, then, Jesus had better come soon if He was coming! Caleb set himself on fire every Sunday, but fewer came to see each time, and the young went to Chicago and the old ones died, though Chicago was so cold you could hardly tell the difference. *I'm a dead man,* he thought, *in a dead land,* and it sounded to him so much like the first line for a bad song that he almost gave up the ghost. "The blues *won't* help the colored," he said again, not to save Frank anymore but to beat back the moan starting up in his head. "Whiskey can't save you, hurting can't save you, women can't save you. Only God can save you," he said, unsure himself anymore, repeating this Bible lesson in a toneless singsong while Frank went on smiling that innocent idiot smile. The spirit went and left Caleb. He had nothing more to say, and no one to say it to. The boy, he said, should pack up his extra ear and go.

Nonethe—and how could it be?—less, this bittersweet talk with Caleb Carter was the inward jewel that Frank contemplated for strength as he took his first group of registrants, two young members of Caleb's own congregation, down to the courthouse, past the men in overalls dreaming of murder who sat on the raised sidewalk in front of the barbershop. Frank dreamt that *his* coming victory would lift this great old man up, show him that *men* could make justice in Mississippi. Caleb would join them then and lead the rest of his flock with him. Joshua would smile, even David would have to approve, and Caleb would grow to trust him more, would play for him, let him record him and send his rediscovered genius out to the world, or to blues collectors, anyway.

When the registrar saw Frank standing in front of his counter smiling at his vision with two serious-looking niggers beside him, his broad, unhappy face went tomato red with rage. He took a pistol from the shelf under the counter, reached over and whacked Frank across the jaw, making it pop from its hinge so it would ache for whatever more of life Frank had left. He slid to the floor, his mouth filling with blood. The registrar ran shouting from behind the counter to hit Frank again on the top of his head, and when the two people he'd brought with him tried to get between the madman and Frank, the registrar used the pistol butt to crack their heads open too.

The cops, called to arrest all three for assaulting the registrar, sprayed Frank with deodorant to get the nigger smell off him before they slammed his hand in the cell door and threw him in alone, while the bleeding men from Caleb's church were put in separate but equal cells, away from any more of Frank's contamination. "Please excuse my handwriting, but I can barely hold a pen," Frank wrote that April, with an intentional pathos not lost on his mother when she finally saw this letter. She remembered heroic Little League wounds (before they realized that nearsightedness led to baseballs falling on his head) that were borne with a false stoicism used to con Pez, comic books, and now, she supposed, bail money. She began to cry with fear. They had made his beautiful smile crooked! What else might they do to him? She would beg him to come home before it was too late.

"When I didn't check in, Joshua, David, and Sugar came from Meridian to ask the sheriff what had happened," he continued in faltering, crooked letters that his young friends passed from unbroken hand to hand, gazing at them not as portents of danger but as signs of how even the weak could be strong in how much pain they could bear.

So they, too, were beaten by the sheriff and his deputies. One deputy ripped Joshua's SNAP button off his overalls and jabbed it into his leg over and over, so he was tossed in with me bleeding from thirty (we counted 'em) deep but tiny wounds. Sugar was thrown in later that evening. As always, he'd mouthed off and gotten the worst beating. Tonight at the sink he pissed a thin stream of urine mixed with blood; or maybe vice versa.

We have a couple of Bad Ears comics and we passed them 'round while we waited for someone in our Jackson office to contact the Justice Department. Joshua says that so many people know where we are, and there are so many of us, that *we don't have to worry that they will kill us.* I looked shocked, I guess, causing David to say that Billy Bad Ears (Issue #12) was less naïve than most whites about how little a human life was presently worth, and he (the comic book character) truly felt how intolerable that was in a way no non-comic white man he'd met ever had. I had finally grown furious with David's continual insults and said, "Auschwitz," thinking of your father, Beth, who I thought knew as much as David about *that,* and truly, maybe more.

"Oh, were *you* in Auschwitz?" Sugar said with a condescending smile.

I think I would have hit him then if Joshua hadn't played the right note, saying, "That's why we're *all* here, to restore the value to a human life." Sugar saw me knocking on a wooden bed slat, my all-purpose prayer and tranquilizer, and he came up with a comic book idea called Kudzu Man, born when a radioactive sludge or something makes a black man (for Sugar wants me to ask Billy why there aren't *any* Negro comic book heroes) meld with the kudzu vine, a creeper that was meant to halt erosion but that now covers everything down here and chokes big trees with its fifty-foot runners, and chokes me with its smell, which is like grape Kool-Aid. Sugar said Kudzu Man was like the way we grow into plants after we're dead, and maybe I knock on wood to get in touch with the spirits of the dead that control the plants. Anyway, K-Man can direct plants to do I don't know what against criminals. David, lounging on the cot, said the plants would probably be like SNAP: they'd weep for the Negroes, but they couldn't protect them. After all, the plants can't protect themselves. I hope I haven't given you all the wrong idea about Sugar. He is a little hard to understand, a lot of edges to him that might cut you. David Watkins is always more polite; he's got such good manners that I'm never really allowed to get close to him. But you feel like you could really be Sugar's friend—in a way because he won't be polite; he'll be absolutely brutal with you when you say something racist.

Anyway, after he plotted out Kudzu Man, we were all silent for a while. Then David declared that we were finished in Lovette. I knew that he meant our failure was somehow especially my fault, and I wanted to cry out to Joshua, *Is he wrong?*

Jesse Kelman, listening to this letter, looked toward the window. In the mild April air the line of dogwoods that marked the border of Mr. Jaffe's land was tipped with pink. Like his red-haired mother, they offered their beauty to anyone, but she couldn't do anything to save herself from his father's endless insults, and they were helpless before the gardener's pruning shears. He longed to protect the righteous men in their cell, maybe gain their release. He looked at Billy sitting on the floor, cross-legged, head down, focused on his drawing, and he felt protective toward his still, small body. Joshua Battle and Frank, he was sure, had had this same desire to protect the weak, and he experienced a kinship with them that (he dreamt) the others couldn't possibly share.

A night. A day. Another night. Joshua wrote his daily letter to his brother Jacob, and read it to the rest of them. It praised the brilliant Sugar Cane (no doubt to make up for his earlier sharp correction, the siding with Frank). "Sugar, though the most committed to nonviolence of all of us, is also the one with the fullest economic analysis of the situation in the South. The Southern plantations must be divided up. Right now a hundred people control more than sixty percent of industry in Mississippi. So just getting the vote won't be enough. The people also have to get land, jobs, power over their schools. Will the vote be enough to break the oligarchy?" Oligarchy? Eleven years old, Jacob couldn't possibly understand a lot of what his brother said, Frank thought. Well, who could? Did he? But Jacob probably liked it that his brother treated him as an adult. *After all,* Frank thought, *I do.*

Then the prisoners read the same Bad Ears comics again, sang to raise their spirits and annoy their jailers, and pitched pennies, for neither

the messages they sent to the ancestors via the wood network nor the
phone calls to the Justice Department had apparently arrived. Then they
just sat in the twilight that leaked in through the small, dirty window
high up in the back wall. Bitter at heart, Frank moaned a little dirge
whose wordless tune said, *There is no Law in Mississippi.* He remembered Caleb Carter's promise that judgment *would* come, and his imagination laved itself now with the sublimity of hell. Frank wanted God to
kill the people who had probably broken his fingers . . . no, he wanted to
keep them alive but far from help, lonely and abandoned, . . . and, *yes,*
the torture *should* go on *forever,* God must make them hurt as he hurt,
his hand and his face throbbing still, so why *only* flay their skin till it
hung down in strips from their backs? Why hadn't Caleb mentioned
how God would surely pepper the wounds by applying fire to them? . . .
But wouldn't that mean—a black man in his dream wearing a string tie
asked—that he, as long as he was white and Jewish, might also have to
take some of God's terrible judgment on himself? And those were things
Frank either couldn't or wouldn't change, so the hellfires burnt low, then
out, and life without that comfort seemed, just as Caleb had said, almost
unbearable. Frank moaned. If he had had Caleb Carter's records to
listen to, or Richard Hartman's not-yet-written books, he could have
perhaps received some small refreshment for his pain in the seemingly
endless task of defining all that had created that suffering, as if delineat-
ing that chain of causation (as the Buddhist Joshua Battle, who sat next
to him quietly counting his own breath, thought) would have led him to
a painful unity with all creation, perhaps the only communion he might
ever have known. But there were no poems then, and no records, no
discourses on breath from Joshua, just the mild distraction of Bad Ears
comics (which were not truly worth meditating on until Billy himself
regularly took over drawing them) and pitching pennies, and listening to
the frightening sirens whose opaque meaning lacked art's terrible clarify-
ing questions. Anyway, Frank, his face a misshapen lump of pain, was
not strong enough then for the consolations of art, or the pleasures of
whiskey or sex that Caleb had assured him could only disappoint; he
barely had the strength to moan his wordless tune again, whose words
could have been: there is no judgment, and there is no judge. Not for
Mississippi, anyway. Well, was he wrong, he wondered, was he wrong?

The night of Frank's deepest despair, Caleb Carter, carrying a high-
chimneyed coal oil lantern, let himself into his church and knelt on the
threshing floor in front of the altar. He even remembered Frank in his
prayers and the members of his church whom Frank had led into jail.

The boy's self-satisfied grin rankled Caleb still, Frank's bright, even teeth implying that Caleb was a coward, his preaching just an act, the soul just an excuse to get a brick house. The boy couldn't see that the church wasn't a lie *because* it was a refuge for Caleb; no, that very protection was the day-by-day proof of his church's truth, for it stood and sheltered him like a brick house. Did the Jewish boy have a soul, Caleb wondered, or had it maybe twinged once, like a bad tooth, and so he'd had the rabbis pull it out? Maybe soullessness was the Jews' get-ahead trick! He didn't trust *any* of these young people, not even his own daughter, Fannie Mae, for their faith was not in God or in their own race, but in their wit and the government—the powers of *this* world. Still, they may be an *opportunity* ... Jesus, could that be? Oh, Jesus, was it a *sign* when Northern whites came to Mississippi, their smiles dripping admiration for things Caleb just knew they couldn't understand? He'd failed to lead the white boy to Jesus, but maybe there was more harvesting to be done, maybe the time had come when he could build up his church to be a refuge for all the colored of the Delta? Those church members in jail, what did they think now? Were they angry with the Freedom Riders, or did they think Caleb was a coward? Were they becoming part of Joshua Battle's flock? Oh, what would Jesus say? What would Jesus say if He came here, to Mississippi, and saw that the young were leaving Caleb's church, and if He heard a sound in their music now that was taking them away to perdition, mixing the church sound with earthly love, but doing it *backward,* using God's music to sanctify the snake's slither? What would Jesus say if he saw Caleb's knees growing stiff on the threshing floor and his soul growing stiff from holding the world of the devil apart from the sanctuary of the gospel all these years? Still on his knees, he let his hands fall and cross before him, and he played with his left cuff, buttoning and unbuttoning it, the way he did when he was nervous, to remind his self of better times. Shadows cast by his hand flickered and jumped on the wall next to the cross. Once he thought of what Jesus would say, Caleb would say it in Jesus' name to his people that Sunday, but *that* wouldn't make it true, it would just be a prideful dream of his *unless* he made them shake with the truth he'd poured into them and *they* said amen. *Then* he would remember always how Jesus had come here this night and spoken with him and said those very things. But what if they sat stony-hearted, saying with their silence that he was a puffed-up man? Would the deacons take away his house then— for there were watchful serpents among them, he knew, who had never forgiven him for Snookey's. It was easy to make shadows dance on the wall in front of a lantern, but his hand wasn't Jesus and a jumping shadow wasn't his flock crying out amen! "Oh, what would Jesus say?" Caleb cried in his high, almost inhuman voice that mixed pleasure and pain so finely that you could not tell which was which in this vital death. But there was no one on the cross, Caleb was Caleb's only listener that night (wasn't he?), and his wail only carved the question into his own brain: what would Jesus say? *what would Jesus say?*

Well, what had Jesus said when Caleb Carter had said to his overseer, Sir, the count ain't right, and the overseer pistol-whipped him across the jaw? Jesus had said a lot of *nothing* then, that's what Jesus had said! And He mumbled more nothing when they had slung Caleb Carter in jail. And when Caleb Carter turned moaning to God, praying to see a vision of the time when these sinners would tremble and be cast down screaming into the fiery pit, what had Jesus shown him? Why, nothing again! So when that cell door swung open, Caleb Carter had walked toward Snookey's to do his business, because there is no judgment on sinners here in Mississippi. God has abandoned Mississippi. Well, Jesus, was he wrong? Will You stop him as he walks the highway to Snookey's, the way You jumped Saul on his way to Jerusalem?

Nope, just more nothing from the Lord Jesus! So Caleb Carter slunk on to Snookey's juke and he played the low-down dirtiest blues that any man ever played, and played them in the low-down dirtiest way any man *ever* played them, because God's not there, yes, hmmm mmm, He won't see and He won't care, so black folks should have a good time, drink their whiskey, dance the snake. And was he wrong? *Was he wrong?*

"Hmmm mmm, oh, yes, he *was* wrong! Caleb Carter was wrong! Oh, yes, I was as *wrong* as a man can be! Because He came to me, that Heavenly Judge, He came to me, *even there,* He came to me. He always has. He always will. And the Lord Jesus told me, 'Caleb Carter, I *was* there in that overseer's shack, and I *was* there in that jail, and *I am* here, and there's no place, not even Hell, not even Mississippi, where I don't reach down My hand. That is why I brought you low, Caleb Carter, and why I brought you here. So you would meet Me *here,* not in your good church, among your good people, and surely they are *good,* and surely I *am* there. But *here I AM,* where *you* thought I could not be! Hmmm mmm, yes, you preachers deceive the people when you tell them that God is *not* here, God is in the *Church,* but He is not *here.* They think they can flee from Me here, hmmm mmm, yes, but the colored man can't hide from Jesus! *For I AM here!*

" 'Now, Caleb Carter, you go back and you tell the saved the Lord Jesus wants them to do something harder than they have ever done before, because *it is time,* yes, it is time.' When a shoot is young and green you hedge it 'round, but when a tree is strong it can stand, yes, and Jesus says your faith is strong and it will stand! It will stand! Hmmm, yes, the Lord Jesus told me you *will* be tried. You *will* be tempted. But *you* will stand!

"So, children, you have to go into Canaan now, you have to go down to teach all people how to make a joyful noise to the Lord God, for the Lord God is *there*, He is listening, He *must* be in their music, and we must teach them how! Teach them how! And we must tell them that God is surely, surely in the courthouse, even in the white man's courthouse, because it doesn't belong to the white man—Lord no, it *already* belongs to God, because *everything* belongs to God! And the vote doesn't belong to the white man! *And we will teach them how God will be in the vote!* Teach them how! Teach them how! Yes, we have done many great wonders here in His house—*but Jesus showed me the whole world is His house!* And hmmmm mmmm, yes, we can mix our mighty blessedness in with their sin until people fall to their knees and praise God *in the very place* where they thought to sin, so they remember God *in the very place* they thought to flee Him and forget Him. We can show them how to vote God's way. Have to show them just like Jesus showed me, *God is alive in Mississippi*! Always was! Always will be! So will you join me now? Will you? I say let us ask Mr. Battle and his friends to come here and tell us how to register and help get us ready for the change! So am I wrong? Am I wrong? Will you say amen?"

And the congregation, to Caleb's exalted eyes, shook with the spirit like shadows on a wall; and they said amen.

So that next week the Klan came and burnt their wooden church to the ground, as if the lantern that had first cast those shadows had been knocked to the threshing floor and spilled out its fire. And when Caleb, beyond calculation again as he had been in that overseer's office, ran outside bare-handed to stop them, they beat him, breaking his broken jaw again, by way of saying, don't speak no more, be a little baby again and cry, *but* Caleb Carter wouldn't cry, *so* they beat him some more. And when his wife came to kneel by him, they knocked her down and kicked her over and over in the stomach, just as they had her daughter, Fannie Mae, to make sure that there would be no more daughters. And as the blows came down and his mouth filled with blood, Caleb dreamt not that God was far from Mississippi—*that* would be beyond his bearing!—but that *He* had sent these blows as punishment for misreading the signs, punishment for being made stupid when a nearly blind white boy thought that Caleb was a prophet possessed by God's holy spirit. He was wrong, oh, he was wrong! And the white men gave him that lesson all over his body, beating him till he passed out.

Though really they beat him for standing upright in the Delta, and more than that to bring Joshua Battle and the Jew scurrying back to Lovette to investigate their friend's calamity, to stand around looking mournful and important, to fill out reports, To. Stick. Their. Damn. Nose. In. Other. Peples. Busness. And when they came, Sheriff Price and Deputy Buford would arrest them, put them in jail till nighttime, and then sling them out (which would make it clear the Sheriff's Department most certainly hadn't been a part of what would follow). Then (while the sheriff was at home watching *Bonanza*), the deputy would help his Klan brothers stop the famous nigger's famous car, making it all legal in Judge Lynch's court. They would accompany them down the road to the dam that their Klug, Martin, was building on his land, and, following the plan their Grand Wizard had seen in his dream, they would kill them and have a Caterpillar cover them with tons of rocks, gravel, and good Mississippi dirt, granting their wish: black and white together. Frank may not have accomplished much in Mississippi, but he'd annoyed the Klan in Lovette six ways to Sunday, his spectacles had offended them, his sharp, self-satisfied smile had even rankled one of them so much he couldn't wait to write the boy's family once he'd killed him, tell them all about how their son's fast words had made them all feel like they were drinking poisonous Jewish vomit. So the Grand Wizard of the Klan (who was also the owner of Big Al's Used Cars in Jackson) dreamt that when the Kleagles dipped their hands in the Jew's annoying blood they would become the Grand Wizard's minions forever, which would make the so-called better class of whites on the Citizens' Council see how devoted his army was, and how necessary that made Big Al to the white man's power. And the Wizard was so sure of his hold on his Klan that he let the Kleagles vote on his dream.

And they all voted yes.

For the Kleagles had their dream, too: that the killings would make them certain, finally, that they were noble men despite what their work in sawmills and gas stations every day told them; certain, finally, that they wore a rich white mantle inseparable from their skin, one beyond any power of a boss to give or to take away, they were the real royalty of Mississippi, the White Knights of the Ku Klux Klan. For within them there was also the awful dream that had to be forever answered, the one that said, *you are nobody,* you are made and unmade and jerked around each and every day by those who are richer than you, who had the luck to get here first, because Luck is all there is, Luck makes you, Luck unmakes you, and if you have a mantle it's a thing of tatters that can easily be whisked from your white shoulders, whose white maybe means *empty,* means, maybe, that you are no-color, void, essence of *nothing,* a blank page for any luckier man to write on. So each man dreamt that when he killed a man the gun would thunder out the irrefutable proposition: that *I* can bring such bad luck to *you* means that *I AM,* beyond chance or change, even in the wide fields of the empty Delta whose harsh, unforgiving sunlight said to them over and over, day by bleaching day, you *are* just barely, and soon you are *not.*

And just as foreseen by the Wizard, Frank and Joshua, though they felt they might be entering a trap, drove fast down 61 under a blue cloudless sky to investigate the church burning. After all, Joshua said, every day seemed like a trap; they couldn't allow *that* to stop them. They would meticulously take statements, call the Justice Department, and then, while the Justice Department did nothing, they would sorrow helplessly and, in Frank's case, especially deeply—for Frank felt he had helped cause this burning, destroyed a great artist's livelihood. He had blown down a brick house.

In a rapid, nervous, guilty voice, he told Joshua about Schlesinger saying that SNAP had been infiltrated by Communists who wanted rich white kids in the most dangerous places, hoping the whites would be beaten, hoping even that one of them would be killed; for his guilt toward Caleb Carter made him worry that he'd have to pay, *should* pay. He wanted reassurance, or just to talk about it—though he knew (David had told him from the start) that SNAP thought people might be killed during Freedom Summer, and if one of the people murdered was a white person, well, *good,* it would focus the country on the horror of Mississippi. Joshua, not looking toward him, said what Frank already knew, that it wasn't the Communists' idea to put powerfully connected whites in the most dangerous places, it was *his.* And awful as it was, *that,* Frank felt, had been what he'd most wanted to hear; he'd wanted Joshua to say that *he* was responsible, he wanted to hate someone *in particular,* someone whom he also loved, as if *that* would help him to accept his situation, or—like the flat note in the blues, the sour taste in the mash—at least make his confused feelings answer to it. "That's why I've stayed with you," Joshua said. "I thought I would draw down danger, and if I did, I wanted you to be there, too." He turned to look at Frank, unsmiling, his face immobile as they rocketed down the highway, the Ford shaking like Frank's own sides as he thought, *He's telling me that he's trying to have me murdered.*

Joshua turned back to look at the road and swerved to avoid a raccoon, making Frank laugh and think, but *he's* gonna kill me pointlessly before *they* get a chance to kill me, using this mythic car where Jimmy Branch had been cradled by Joshua, blood dripping on his lap, the same car Joshua had one night, running from the Klan, simply flipped into reverse while doing a hundred, spinning around, leaving the murderous stooges whizzing past him the wrong way while he headed off back to Jackson. Or so they said. "But now they hate you maybe more than me," Joshua said, and Frank knew that *that* would be a powerful lot of hatred. "It's you they're after in Lovette." And then Frank had the almost comforting fantasy that Joshua spent so much time with Frank *now*—when Frank was himself already sufficiently hated to spring the trap—because whatever happened to Frank, Joshua wanted it to happen to him, too, or he would feel too guilty afterward, because he cared for Frank so much. "So, look," Joshua said, so quietly that Frank had to lean toward the wheel to hear him over the roaring of the wind past the car, the ratchety sound of the metal about to fly apart, "maybe you've done enough. Look, maybe you should leave Mississippi."

But this reprieve was no reprieve because of the man who offered it, for what could Frank say, almost too sick with fear to say anything, when, truly, Joshua had just been flattering him. Joshua was hated far more than Frank. Joshua had risked far more than Frank ever would, and nothing could be clearer than that Joshua Battle was not leaving Mississippi until each man had one vote. They passed a cypress grove festooned with white dotted vines, and Frank saw his corpse rotting there, half in and half out of the water, his body ugly, bloated, out of his control forever. He thought: *Has Herbert Jaffe given his only begotten son so that the people of Mississippi could be free?* and the irony was an ulcerous bile in his throat. He pursed his lips angrily, thinking, *These are not my words and this is not my story. David and Sugar were oh so right: It should be their movement, their nonviolent Christian movement. Dr. Jacobs had been right; our prophets told us that there's a difference between killing and murder, because every living thing should protect its life. Even a white thing. Even me.*

The day was hot, but the car windows were up, like that would at least deflect bullets. Frank sweltered, yet his body began to shake. There wasn't nearly enough air in the car to tell Joshua he'd got it right, that though it was only early June the heat was too much for Frank, he *should* go someplace cooler, or to say that his hand or his jaw wasn't healing right, so he needed to see a specialist and the top man in the field of hand&faceology was at Mount Sinai in New York, or that he needed to get back to his family, particularly his poor worried mother, or that Joshua had no right to ask these things of him by not asking, and it was no good to sing *this* lullaby to him because no song could soothe Frank anyway because the fear was too much, too very very much for him, he couldn't bear it any longer.

But when he saw Caleb Carter lying in his wooden bed in his brick house, his face swollen and misshapen, his leg broken, his concussed head wrapped in white bandages by his skillful angry wife (whose own ribs, Frank knew, were taped and aching), Frank's fear left him, if only for a moment, and he dreamt he might cradle Caleb in his arms and sing a Gullah spiritual to him that would help restore him. "Remember me," he said aloud.

"Oh, yes," Caleb said softly, as if Frank were a doctor administering a mental status test, "you're the Angel of Death," and he didn't blame Frank any more than one would blame an angel. He was a sign that Caleb had read wrongly, that God must have wanted him to read wrongly, to make him a lesson. For there was only God.

Frank cried from that, and from his fear. Did Caleb's wounds mean he wouldn't ever be able to say, *yes, Joshua, I think I should leave now?* How could he leave Mississippi (he dreamt deeply, the billows of his own rhetoric carrying him forward on great gusts of sentiment; the music of his own sentences, like a call in church, re-forming him to become someone who *had* to say amen at the end) until a judgment came, a hell to make the settle for the white people who did this, for all of them who had done this to a good man, this great artist of a great people. But even if it meant a fiery end and all white people were consumed? Even if it meant a judgment on himself? Ruth Brown asked, handing him a precious vinyl record. Yes, even if. And what if only *his* death might bring down that judgment on Mississippi, David Watkins said, what if only his death would bring the federal government, the country's concern, and justice for Caleb Carter? So will you empty yourself out, utterly? asked the fat woman who had been taken by the spirit in Caleb's church, will you let your face become ugly, and put your body in His control, let Him possess you and use you as He will to bring down justice? Hmmm mmm, yes, Frank thought, mad with care and mad with fury, pleasure and pain so finely mixed that you could not tell which was which in this vital death, yes, let us bring it down, yes, let us bring it down, yes, let us bring down judgment. And even *if* . . . ? Yes David, yes Ruth, yes Sugar, yes Joshua, *even if.*

That grand feeling lasted only a moment, of course, and then the breathtaking fear returned and the sense of being trapped by Joshua's courage and decency in a story that really wasn't his. But three months later it was an intuition of the motions of her son's mind, his education in the necessity of sacrifice to bring down judgment, that led Ellen Jaffe, in her best dress, to tell the Credentials Committee of the Democratic Party that she was certain that if her son had it all to do over again, knowing even what they knew now, he would have to have done what he did, it mattered that much to him. Ellen Jaffe had been educated and transformed in her turn by the greatest loss of her life so that she truly did now know the price of values. She was possessed by her son's truth, and she spoke with a fine pleading in her voice, but with great precision—as if an uncanny mixture of freedom and control were given you once you truly acknowledged gravity. This committee, she said, safe in this air-conditioned hotel conference room in Atlantic City, New Jersey, should not betray all that her son had died for and seat the segregated all-white Mississippi delegation to the Democratic National Convention, but should instead vote yes on seating the Freedom Democratic Party slate. There was an awful and complete nakedness to the way she asked, an utter vulnerability as she left the value of her son's life to the Credentials Committee's measurement.

And *so* they voted then.

And they voted no.

Hubert Humphrey, crying at what he had to do, offered a compromise of two seats at large for the Freedom Democratic Party and a future rules change, hoping to spare President Johnson the rebuke of any more moving and embarrassing television appeals on Frank's behalf. The SNAP leadership, Sugar and David Watkins and Fannie, who saw in Joshua's and Frank's deaths that they must hold to justice only, voted no to that, and went out to the boardwalk to sing, among other songs, that Gullah spiritual "Remember Me."

But Caleb Carter, his ribs and jaws aching now and forevermore, said to his daughter, "I've sung enough for a while. Those boys' deaths have offered us a gift. Because Jesus *does* want us to go down into Canaan, hmmm mmm, *yes,* He *does* want to mix our mighty blessedness in with their evil." And Caleb Carter went into the air-conditioned hall to be an at-large delegate at the 1964 Democratic National Convention.

Three months before that day on the boardwalk, and three days after Frank and Joshua had stood by Caleb's bedside, David Watkins felt sure that Joshua was dead—and that his murder meant that all the seer's winter visions were now true, not just like an experiment that had succeeded, but as if he'd provided the black blood that transformed possibilities into certainties. That vision, he thought now—though Joshua had never said so—was no doubt detailed in the extreme, and had been of David in particular—which meant David would live helplessly now inside all that Joshua had *already* seen that winter day in Washington when his face had become as smooth as a mask and his eyes had bulged out because they'd had a god's eyes behind them. Whatever David did the next minute or the next day (and what could he possibly ever again do for himself or for anyone?), Joshua, he was sure, had foreseen it in large and in small. Joshua must have seen David's hands reaching for an envelope to write down the notes that he would need when he called Frank Jaffe's family because his mind, he knew—and Joshua must have known—might stutter with grief.

David considered for a moment that this feeling might be a way of pushing back his grief and his anger toward Joshua for abandoning him here in Mississippi, here on this acrid earth, a way of keeping Joshua with him by feeling himself always within Joshua's vision. Certainly true—but that idea didn't change anything.

And so, just like Joshua knew he would, he wrote a few words on an envelope that had once contained a fund-raising letter from his Howard fraternity, watching his own hand form the words outside his control, as if it were not his hand anymore.

1. The Jaffes' son and Joshua Battle are missing.
2. They were last heard from two days before, when they had gone to investigate a church-burning near Lovette.

3. SNAP had called every sheriff's office in Mississippi, but no one reported having seen them.
4. So SNAP feared the two might be dead.

He rehearsed himself, but as he read into the receiver, his soft voice cracked with desperation, realizing again, again, that he was alone now in this big world.

And Ellen Jaffe didn't (as Frank had once told David she would, if they ever spoke) tell him the sinfully high cost of a long-distance call from Jackson, Mississippi, to Great Neck, New York; instead she responded helplessly to the pain this young man clearly felt, saying, "You sound like you've been up all night," and David, who knew that now he finally spoke to someone whose loss was as great as his, wept fulsomely, released for a moment from his own possession, or Joshua's, or History, whose long arc, as it bent toward justice, had robbed him of the person he needed and loved most, and crushed David, too, beneath it.

Then, as Joshua had foreseen, the television news shows sent camera crews to stand by the burnt timbers of Caleb's church in Lovette, Mississippi, where Sugar acted as SNAP's spokesman, his attention more tightly focused on the task at hand than David's. Sugar didn't see Joshua's complicity in Joshua's own death, just the quotidian brutality of crackers and the horrid impersonal grinding of racist forces that had finally gotten Joshua and that would someday probably get David and Susan, and Fannie Mae, and Sugar himself, or any black person with courage—until, that is, their nonviolent sacrifices forced the federal government or the Messiah to come, either one seeming to Sugar at the moment about equally likely.

And then—as Joshua had dreamt that day in Washington—Frank's father, the well-connected lobbyist Herbert Jaffe, used his considerable network of favors and friends to try to save his son, leading the clamor for the army to be sent to Mississippi along with the federal marshals and FBI agents to investigate the disappearances. Joshua had meant to jujitsu the racism of the nation against the racism of the nation, but could he *ever* have imagined, Sugar Cane wondered, just how racist that country would turn out to be, how very different a white death would be to it—so that the overwhelming lesson the black SNAP workers would draw down from these deaths would be the infinitesimal relative worth their lives had for their countrymen, tipping some of them, Cane could see, into a heedless despair that might lead them into beatings or even gunfire. But when Sugar said this to David, he replied in that new zombie tone of his that yes, Joshua *had* surely known, and that they were surely meant to live with what Joshua had wanted to show them by dying, and he sounded to Sugar as if life were now all some unavoidable, onerous piece of homework back at the Bronx High School of Science. Sugar, looking out at the newsmen's cameras and their avid white faces, couldn't disagree.

The television news cut from Willard "Sugar" Cane outside the charred timbers to the governor of Mississippi, a broad-beamed man with a mean, sour smile, who said that this whole thing was a stunt by these so-called nonviolent so-called students. The colored boy and his friend were no doubt enjoying a vacation up north or in Mr. Fidel Castro's Cuba and laughing all the while at how they'd made Mississippi look bad in the eyes of the nation and chortling, too, probably, at how they'd scared their own poor, dear mothers to death.

While Ellen Jaffe, watching the television in Great Neck, hoped—when she had taken enough of the Miltowns Dr. Jaffe prescribed to be able to hope again—that the sour governor who spoke from the pale video light in her bedroom had got it right, that her son might be a vicious liar instead of a martyr. But no, she knew Frank to be a kind and truthful boy. So she begged God then that her son might have been kidnapped . . . even lying wounded in a swamp, if that were God's will, but please God not yet dead . . . and then she prayed that he hadn't been hurt too much before he died . . . and then she prayed that the anodynes she'd taken might deaden her own suffering just a little while longer while she waited and waited for news of him. And then the whole horrible declension started again, and she prayed, again, anxious with hope that clawed at her heart, please, God, let Frank be lying to everyone; or captured; or wounded but, please, God, still alive, down again into a despair that lay on her chest like a mountain of sand, for he was certainly, certainly dead, her body growing weaker with each new fall, yet rest impossible, though her eyes needed to sleep and the muscles in her chest ached from sobbing.

Herbert held her, but that didn't help; she couldn't stop her whimpering that began to sound like a cat purring to him, and he dozed off. But she couldn't sleep, though sometimes her last prayer was meagerly answered, the drugs muted her feelings, and she lay in her husband's sleeping arms, imagining she was a desperate little girl running away from home in a heavy wool coat the year after her father's death had left her abandoned to her shrewish mother and endless work in their board-inghouse kitchen; and as she ran in her dream, her grief for her son grew more distant behind her, larger and more vaporous, looming outside her and over her, like a cloud above the row houses in Flushing, New York, which was her street, her city, her country, *she'd* been born *here,* not in Austria like her cramped and paralyzing mother, though the buildings were still covered with gloom (why was that? what caused this gloom?) and as strange as Europe to her today in her dream, her neighborhood but not hers anymore, like her feelings, her life, all hers, but made by this drug not pleasant, but somehow not so close anymore, as she ran and ran, and never got away. And her son? Was he hers anymore? Who did he belong to now? To History? To the Angel of Death? Oh, her son!

Three weeks later it shamed Arkey Kaplan, age fifteen, to sneak past the bedroom where Mrs. Jaffe lay crying. Always polite toward those elders who weren't his annoying parents, he felt he should say something com-forting to Frank's mother, but he was burdened with, or gifted with, secrets that she couldn't yet have: her son was dead. And yet *not.* Arkey and his friends having maybe heard from him. He'd been shot, and he was buried beneath tons of earth—yet he was still in frightening pain, they knew, because he'd sent letters to them—or had them sent—in strange, childish handwritings. To say something as ghoulish as *that* to her could only make Mrs. Jaffe hate Arkey for his stupidity, his cruelty.

So he just continued quietly down the carpeted hall to Laura's room, wondering why crazy, slightly sinister secrets should excite him so, make him rush to see Laura and the others as soon as he got up each morning, drinking his breakfast Coca-Cola as he ran the quarter mile to her house, his bowels pleasantly heavy and the molecules of his legs and chest at once fizzing as he passed Dr. Jacobs' dogwoods—the same feel-ings as when he sat in the bathroom, knowing he was going to open the *Sunday Times Magazine* to the lingerie ads at the back and masturbate. He was certain that Ruth, the tall, sad-eyed maid who'd let him into Laura's by the kitchen door, had seen how exhilarated he was and that her fierce look condemned him for his obscene excitement, but he couldn't help himself, he *had* to get to Laura's room as soon as possible to hear what Billy Green would say today, had to discern with them what would happen to *their* lives, too, because of these events, so awful and yet so wonderful.

Wonderful? He knew he had been a bastard to be thrilled yesterday when Laura's mother screamed at the maid because of a stolen prayer shawl, shrieking until Dr. Jacobs came over to make her take her pills and try to sleep, but hearing her shrill voice skitter between registers, he'd felt the way he had standing on the balcony of his room at the Fontainebleau Hotel in Miami Beach as a hurricane wind whipped him with warm rain, smashed a few misplaced beach chairs against the windows of the Bon-Bon Cafe, and devastated South Florida. How could he *not* find it wonderful to be at the center of such titanic forces that now convulsed the country, even if the wind wrecked homes and made women cry; how could he not be thrilled when he and his friends knew what no one else in the country but the murderers could: that Frank Jaffe and Joshua Battle had been dragged from the Lovette jail at night, when no civil rights workers, Frank had already instructed them, would ever willingly leave jail, murdered by Klansmen, including the deputy sheriff of Lovette, and then buried beneath tons of earth.

Knew? Wait, please. They didn't *know* any of that for certain, did they? But Billy *had* already been right once, hadn't he, had foreseen the truth when Beth had gotten an envelope postmarked Mississippi with the address in odd block letters, and inside a fragment ripped from a cheap sheet of paper, with a pencil scrawl of half-formed letters: *I am dyed, I am done, I am dead.*

They'd handed the letter around.

"It looks," Arkey had said, "like a girl's writing."

"Or a child's," Jesse had said.

"Not Frank's," Beth had said.

But when Billy had touched the paper, he'd looked up from where he lay prone on the carpet by Beth's feet and had said quietly, solemnly, "Frank's dead."

"Don't be stupid," Beth had said.

"What do you mean, Billy?" Jeffrey had said. "Like he's actually writing us to say, *Hi, I'm dead?*"

"No, the letter," Beth had said, "it must be like a fragment that Frank had dropped on the cell floor in jail, left behind when he'd been released. One of the jailers mailed it."

"But why would Frank ever have written that crap?" Laura had asked, terrified, like she somehow knew that Billy might be right. "And why would the jailer send us Frank's letter?"

" 'Cause he feels guilty," Arkey had said—his own favorite motivation, after all.

"Frank had been in his jail," Jesse had said. "Frank had started to write something, maybe, a poem or I don't know what, then the man mailed it, that's all."

"Look," Beth had said, "we don't even know who this is from. It's not Frank's handwriting. It's not signed. It doesn't make sense or anything. Why does everybody think this is even from Frank?"

"It is," Billy had said, "and he's already dead." Laura had screamed then, Beth actually kicking Billy not so gently in the chest, but Billy only repeated in his soft voice, "I don't know how I know, I just do. They've murdered him and buried him under tons of earth."

Jeffrey had started to ask something again about how if Frank were dead, he wrote letters, but Billy had already run from the room and down the stairs.

Then the very next day David Watkins had called to say that Frank and Joshua Battle had been thrown out of jail in Lovette, but had never returned home, so it was possible, he had to tell the family, it was possible that they'd been murdered.

So the day after that Arkey had run to keep Laura company—kind of to sit shiva with her—but most of all to see what else Billy would say.

"He just made a lucky guess," Jeffrey had said to Arkey, as if Billy weren't there. Laura had wept on her bed. "I mean about Frank and Joshua Battle being missing. We don't know they're dead."

Dr. Jacobs had doped Laura up, turning her blue eyes to glass, like all but one of the dolls that lined the bed.

Billy had looked at her but mercifully didn't say "he's dead" again.

Jeffrey had said maybe Frank had worried that they were going to kill him and had written that note. Maybe the jailer had mailed it. He wouldn't do that if they were going to kill them, would he?

After that, they didn't know what to do. They didn't want to leave Laura alone, or maybe, like Arkey, they hoped something else cool might happen. So they had made fun of soap operas on TV and played hearts while Laura stared into space. Then, around dinnertime, they had agreed to get together the next morning.

The next day Beth had got another envelope, addressed with block letters again. "*I'm still in pain,*" Beth had read from the rocking chair. "*If anything, the pain is worse. How long how long how long? Oh, God, what if this is hell?*"

She had handed the letter round. More screwy printing. A child? A near illiterate? A man with a broken hand?

"My thinking is," Jeffrey had said, with slow sarcasm, "if this is from Frank, I mean, if we're still getting letters, then he's probably *not* dead." He'd grinned, swiveled his doll's head around the room.

Jesse, in chinos and a button-down shirt, had raked Laura's hair lightly with his maimed paw, which was, Arkey had thought, dirty pool; the woman was doped up, for God's sake. Touching her would be like fucking a drunk woman—something Arkey hadn't yet had the opportunity to do, but would, he hoped, have the chivalry to resist.

Beth had said, "I don't think this is from Frank, either. It doesn't look like his handwriting."

Laura had turned her head to the side, like an animal who stares bewildered at a talking man.

The letter had got to Billy's hand on the floor. He had gripped it between two fingers, sucked his nutty nourishment from it, and closed his eyes. "No," he had said quietly. "He's already dead." The squared-off, badly formed letters in this letter and the last one, they didn't look like they were in Frank's handwriting because they weren't. The dead, if they'd, like, died in monstrous, unjust ways, could sometimes make other people write for them, the people who did it not even knowing what they did, something just taking control of their hands, like, you know, someone sleepwalking. Billy had read about it in a story.

"What a churl," Arkey had said, "what a whirl, what a twirl, what a girl." Meaning, let's not forget that Billy, his best friend from third grade on, was a well-known nutcase.

Billy had just stared at him. "What?"

But Arkey didn't want to hurt Billy's feelings any longer—or not as much as he wanted to hear more. "Nothing," he'd said. "Just an old song."

Jeffrey had said, "Billy, I think you read that in your dad's **Magic of the Kaballah**, Issue #5."

"The way the writing looks," Jesse had said, "that's probably because the sheriff mashed his fingers in the cell door again."

"And the words," Arkey had said, "look, all they say is that he's sick of Mississippi."

"Right, Frank's probably in some rural jail," Jesse had said. "Maybe he's badly beaten up and hating Mississippi like hell. It's agony to him. That's what he meant in that other letter, too. He wonders how long before they'll let him out. You know, how long is this going to go on for? Then he probably gave the letters, you know, to another prisoner, and he mailed them for him."

Jeffrey had said, "Look, maybe Frank's not even in jail anymore. Maybe he and Joshua Battle *are* hiding out, like the governor of Mississippi said. The letters are to tell us, you know, that he's really alive. He disguised his handwriting so the FBI can't figure it out if they intercept one." He'd passed a bottle of Southern Comfort around that he'd wheedled from an older man, the kindness of a not-quite-stranger, further proof, he had thought, of how sophisticated he was about the world, and consequently, how right about these letters.

Arkey had wondered if it would be insulting to Jeffrey if he wiped the bottle neck with his shirt? Like what if Jeffrey, you know, had kissed other men on the lips! And his tongue? Jesus, what about the other guy's tongue? Did guys do that, French-kiss and all? Still, Arkey had taken a drink, it seeming very serious, very melancholy, this bittersweet syrup in the middle of the afternoon, like they were adults, even like Hemingway, say, whose stories he'd been reading at the John Dewey School.

"Billy," Jeffrey had said, "is just having some fun with us. He pretends he has visions. He's a deadpan joker, like Warhol," probably a way of reminding them that Jeffrey had silk-screened with the maestro, had also taken speed and smoked pot. Arkey knew that made him—in Jeffrey's own opinion—at least a thousand years older than his friends, so he should be allowed to break their thralldom to Billy Green, curled cat-like, with such false sweetness, on the floor by the rocking chair and his Beth's legs.

Billy had sat up. "He's dead," he'd said again. Then, as if they might purposely misunderstand, he'd added angrily, "Frank's dead." He'd put the letter on his leg, had stroked it with the tips of his fingers. That seemed to calm him. "Listen," he'd said insistently, softly. "He says it right here. He's dead. He's worried that he'll spend eternity in a sealed-up place, you know, for all time. Like forever."

Arkey had looked over at Beth, in her loose-fitting Wellesley sweat-shirt and tennis shorts, beautiful, but unavailable to his lust because she was Frank's widow and to want her would make him too intimately connected to death—supposing Frank was dead. Then Beth had looked wonderingly down toward Billy, her large hazel-green eyes growing soft, which made Arkey want her, widow or not.

Billy had clasped his knees and rocked back and forth on the floor, his eyes closed, and he said again, quietly, emphatically, "Look, they let him out of jail. They came for him on the highway. They murdered him. I just know it."

"How do you know? How could you know?" Laura had said, her voice a shrill, unmodulated sound knifing uncertainly through Miltown static. Then her mind had lost the station and her eyes had gone blank again.

"I told you, I don't know how I know," Billy had said angrily, resentfully, like a child unjustly accused, "but I *do* know. I'm sorry. I don't want to know. But I do." Then, of course, he'd begun to cry, putting his hand on his lip to wipe the snot away. "God, I'm sorry. This is disgusting." He had run from the room, and they'd heard him clatter down the stairs.

The next day, toward afternoon, Billy had rocked again, this time sitting in the chair President Kennedy had given to Mr. Jaffe, grasping the two letters in his hand, balling them up. "They were taken from the jail." He'd swayed back and forth, his upper body ticking to the chair's tock, his eyes closed—for better reception, no doubt, Arkey had thought, with the same Dewey School contempt for Billy's mumbo jumbo that he had for spooky TV shows. After all, he was as sophisticated as Jeffrey, wasn't he? *He* went to private school. But he had wanted to hear more, too—just like each week he also wanted to watch the spooky TV shows. "And the deputy sheriff," Billy had said, "came for them on the highway," Billy speaking in a high, hesitant voice, as if trying to discern something that was slightly out of focus.

"So it would seem legal," Jesse had said.

"Yes, so it would seem legal," Billy had repeated, not looking at Jesse.

"But why didn't Joshua drive faster?" Jesse had asked, cross-legged on the bed by Laura, trustful as a child.

"I don't know why. But he didn't, he didn't drive faster. He stopped, and they were taken from their car. They were driven to a field and dragged out of the car. 'You must,' Frank said."

"Jesus," Jeffrey had said, "why would he say *that*?"

Billy had stopped. He had pulled some hair on the side of his head, making it stand out like Gyro Gearloose's. "No, that's wrong, Frank didn't say anything."

Beth had said, "He must have said something."

And Billy had repeated, "Yeah, he must have."

Jeffrey, taking a long swig, had watched Billy's face draw inward. "He aims to please." Meaning Billy, probably.

"He must have said, *I know how you feel.* And the man's hand shook, the man saying, *Don't you dare understand me when I feel fear.*"

Laura had whimpered from the bed.

"Then," Billy had said, "the man shot Frank."

"Fade-out," Jeffrey had said, quietly, and then more loudly, like he was the only one with any feeling for what Laura might be going through, "And the lights come up in the theater."

Laura had wept, and Jesse stroked her long black hair. The rest of them sat silently, listening, the sound connecting Arkey to something larger than himself, and *much* larger than Great Neck, though *that* was true only if Frank had died. So Arkey, in his mind's theater, had seen Frank kneel on the ground, surrounded by hooded Klansmen in white silk robes. Frank took a kazoo from his work-shirt pocket and played a song he'd once spun for Arkey, about letters mailed in the wind (Jesus, had that been a *sign* he should tell everyone about?), his face growing smooth in Arkey's imagination, his eyes bulging out, as if from the effort of humming through the tube—though Arkey knew that humming into a kazoo was no effort at all, really. But Arkey, killing Frank in his imagination, had sweetly wanted to give him what he thought Frank wanted—namely, *ashe,* which he'd said meant being possessed by a god, seeing the future, which meant Frank would foresee that in the very next moment the man would shoot him dead. Still, maybe Frank wanted the gift of prophecy more than he wanted life itself—or so Arkey had imagined, because he was so very young and protected, and because it added to the creepy sublimity of the scene. Then, history being history (which meant Arkey was just being realistic), and because to deny it would bleach Arkey's life of both a rich red thread and a magical, perverse feeling, he had murdered Frank.

Two days later another "letter" arrived, this one the torn end of a sheet of paper, with cursive writing: *Agony end time.*

Billy had held the fragment in the palm of his hand and rocked. "Frank still feels pain," he said. "I knew it."

"Which is, let me say again, impossible," Jeffrey had said from the floor. "His being dead and all, according to you."

Billy had shrugged, like he was saying, Arkey thought, that he wasn't responsible for making sense of this nonsense—it had, you know, *come to him* on the special unassigned frequency used for transmission by the dead, picked up by magical fillings in Billy's soul's teeth. But again, Arkey had wanted more, had that *Sunday Times* lingerie feeling, strange, profound, a little dangerous.

Jeffrey had laughed at Billy's shrug. "So the dead feel pain, huh? Well, what'll they think of next!"

Billy, not even giving Jeffrey his borrowed Dr. Jacobs–style tight-lipped smile, had said matter-of-factly that after they shot him, they'd dragged Frank along the ground, and then there'd been earth and more earth, and a grinding sound over him. Frank felt tons of earth crushing him. "I'm sorry, Laura, I'm sorry, but Frank is in agony."

Laura had rubbed her eyes hard, as if she were trying to rub the tranquilizers from her mind, and Beth had reached out to touch Billy's leg, as if, Jeffrey thought, he'd fooled her into thinking he was the one who needed comfort. Jeffrey had made the *Twilight Zone woo woo woo* again. "Good story. I mean, Jesus, Billy, what a load of crap."

Billy had opened his eyes. "Is it just a story? Yeah, maybe it is. I *hope* it is."

"You do not hope so," Jeffrey had said angrily. "You *know* so. It's a story. You made it up. Tell everyone you made it up."

This time Billy had given him a Jacobs special. "Maybe you're right. When I sit here and rock with my eyes closed, talking, it does feel the same way as when I make up a story, a good story. It just comes out, you know, one thing after another."

"Like taking a shit," Jeffrey had said, though Arkey had known Billy meant to signal *inspiration:* God's breath; i.e., truth.

So every morning for three weeks, Arkey threw on a pair of corduroys, slipped into his loafers, and carrying his Coca-Cola breakfast, trotted back to the Jaffes', braved the condemnation in Ruth Brown's eyes, and, almost sick with excitement, tiptoed past Mrs. Jaffe's bedroom, just the way he did this morning. That he and his friends had been given to know these things already trembled for Arkey on the edge of some revelation about *himself,* his fate, his future greatness.

If, that is, the letters had come from Beyond the Grave or someplace like it. *If* they knew that Frank had died, and how he died. *If,* that is, what Billy had told them was true. *Then* surely that Arkey had heard these things meant that he, too, had been *chosen,* a distinction whose meaning would someday be revealed to the whole world in other, grander ways, like admission to Harvard, or the Nobel Prize in . . . in Something Important.

Johnny Ryan would think he was an asshole nut, Arnie Golden would make him feel like an idiot, and Jimmy Benjamin would have everybody laughing at him. So, until the king of Sweden crowned him, or whatever they did, he had to spend every day with his friends, the only people who could reassure him that his life wasn't just going to be the stale work of getting good grades and sucking up to some fat senior so he'd get a position on the John Dewey School literary magazine (*The Dew Drop*) or maybe the current affairs newspaper (*The Dewey Debate*), and not the grand, mysterious matter of discussing God and history's hidden secrets with his friends, all of them, Billy said, linked souls since the beginning of time, which was why, he said, they had long fingers. He'd made them hold up their hands, and bingo, he was right.

That warm June morning, Arkey dared to sit on the double bed with Laura, who stared past him as if maybe he weren't a future Nobel Prize winner, as if, in fact, he weren't there at all. Jesse joined them on the bed, and they all sprawled with their limbs everywhichway, each leg with a teenage mind of its own, so that Arkey could "unconsciously" touch Laura's calf with his, feel her long leg twitch rigid&soft&rigid with the alternating current of terror and hope, Arkey feeling for the first time the imperious nature of his desire, that at such a time, and maybe especially at such a time, he would still want to do that. Which meant that a sufficiently drunk woman, he realized, wouldn't stand a chance around him.

No one spoke. Laura, hugging a four-faced doll in a gingham dress to her chest like she was giving suck, or maybe actually smothering the eerie wooden dream child to death, frightened Arkey with her absent eyes and pointless concentration. He stopped "accidentally" touching her and looked away to the window, to Dr. Jacobs' dogwoods, each blossom standing out distinctly in the sharp sunlight. Between the rows of trees, Beth, wearing dark red Bermuda shorts, walked toward them, an embroidered leather pouch around her neck, her last gift from Frank-Alive, called "a nation sack," an African custom re-told in the New World by black *tannaim*. Arkey had watched her hide Frank's last letter there, like a precious relic, Beth palming it, he thought, to get some extra specialness for herself. But Arkey hadn't said anything, because like all of them, he feared Beth's down-turned lips and flashing anger, and besides, the theft reassured him: Beth was brilliant, Beth saw through things, Beth was in college, and she thought what Billy said was true, which made him even more expectant and excited. He wanted her to arrive. He wanted more confirmation of Billy's powers and his own specialness. He wanted. He *wanted*. He WANTED, until he thought his body would break if he didn't jerk off, which was his current temporary cure for everything in the time of Yearning, the endlessly recurrent theme of his teenage life.

Beth, the ingenue lead in his movie, clattered up the stairs and through the door. Billy sat unmoving in the rocking chair, pasty-faced, mouth-breathing, and blank-eyed, like another of Laura's dolls.

And then nothing happened.

They read magazines and comic books, let Jesse go get hamburgers for everyone on his bicycle, a magical machine handmade in New Jersey by a man named Drysdale from an almost weightless aluminum, which Jesse needed to ride alone as much as thirty miles a day, never so happy perhaps as when he felt free of everyone. With the hamburgers they drank real, disgusting Jeffrey-provided liquor. The air conditioner hummed, but Arkey felt hot, on the edge of vomiting. He hoped Laura couldn't see how he felt.

Then after sunset, Billy shut his eyes and rocked again, till they all looked at him, and Arkey forgot his stomach for a little while.

"And he's terrified, bewildered," he said, "afraid he'll be trapped there, waiting, forever."

"Trapped there?" Jesse actually looked worried. "Where?"

"In the grave. He can't see. He can't move. But he's *aware*. He feels what's happening to him."

Billy turned toward each of them, but he didn't open his eyes. Arkey felt weird when Billy's lids were on him, it had a carnival feel. "We have to help him," Billy said.

"Oh, blind Tiresias," Jeffrey said, making the *woo woo* sound with his hand over his mouth. "Man and woman both."

Arkey couldn't help smiling, which fortunately Billy couldn't see. *Could he?*

Billy ignored Jeffrey. "We have to, like, keep Frank in our hearts and do acts of justice. Or he'll be trapped there forever." He opened his eyes, and, oddly, he smiled sweetly, still rocking. "That's what we have to do."

"Not likely," Jeffrey said, drinking some of the sweet liquor and passing the bottle to Arkey.

Arkey wasn't sure if he meant that Billy's story or the acts of justice were unlikely. Or both. He decided it was *more* manly to drink without wiping the bottle.

Billy planted his feet, leaned his little body forward; the chair went still beneath him. "We have to remember them," he said angrily.

"Them?" Jeffrey said.

"The Jews," he said nonsensically. "The Jews who died." He began rocking his body again, forward and back, back and forward, harder and harder, like a crazy man.

"Okay," Arkey said, wanting to stop Billy before he shook his head loose. "We'll remember them. We will. Count on it." Billy's furioso rocking made him dream of the sorrowful face of his mother, who had, she told him about once a week, gone through two entire days of excruciating agony giving birth to him, and had also, by the way, given up a really great career as an economist to stay home with him, not to mention, "what he had to have noticed," she said, "he wasn't stupid, after all," that she stayed in a very bad marriage with a verbally abusive Isaac for his and June's sake. Now his mom's resentful face was getting nonsensically knitted up for him with these other shadows—all six million—*plus* this one corpse whose suffering he *personally* was supposed to ease. He felt sick.

Laura flung her four-faced wooden child at Billy, but it clattered against the window. Its head fell to the carpet, thin painted smile upward. "You're full of shit, Billy. You get out of here now, little boy. You're totally full of shit! All of you. Get out, get out, get out, get out, get out!" her voice growing weaker and weaker, as if she'd forgotten why she'd begun shouting at them. Jesse, over six feet tall now, stood up beside her and stroked her black hair, nodding gently to the rest of them, and Arkey saw that what they all felt this summer *was* very close to sex (like all intense feelings for him, even hitting his thumb with a hammer), might even tip over into the Real Thing, but that Jesse had already got to Laura, because Arkey hadn't had the courage to try or because he was too short or too ugly, while Jesse was the tallest, the bravest, the curly-haired handsomest; which left Arkey both resentful and embarrassed as he tiptoed sick and unsteady down the back hall past the maid's room, ashamed of his cowardice and his skinny body, and his desire itself, which because he'd never be able to satisfy it, hung useless around him, a protuberance, an outmoded fashion, a vestigial organ. When they got outside, he ran behind a copper beech tree, knelt on the ground, and vomited, two hands suddenly grasping his shoulders as he shook; Jeffrey, concerned for him, thank God, had followed him.

Then he and Jeffrey walked home together, Jeffrey pouring buckets of cold acid all over him. They didn't know that *anything* that Billy had said was true, Jeffrey said. Maybe Frank was missing, but Frank had told them *that* might happen. They didn't know how he had died, in a field or where, they didn't know *if* he'd died, and they didn't know if he had been shot by the Klan or where he was buried, *if* he was buried. They most certainly hadn't been chosen to do anything for him, because if he was a corpse and already buried, he didn't need anything more done.

Billy, Jeffrey said, wasn't any good at baseball, was he? Billy had had a growth *trickle* instead of a spurt. Billy could barely lift a basketball. He couldn't get up the rope at gym class. He couldn't dance. All he had to keep him from being the smallest, most worthless nerd in the school was a knack with a scary story. Then he'd started drawing comic books for his dad's company, the kid superhero who draws himself or some shit. Brilliant marketing, okay? But what could be more obvious now—he used to do Leo Jacobs' stories about Auschwitz; then the scary comics; now he's combining the two in this Mississippi epic.

But if it was just Billy making things up, Arkey said, desperate to hold on to his chosenness, how had he known *before* David Watkins called that Frank would be missing? That was lots more than lucky guess.

"Was it? Well, maybe Frank is in cahoots with Billy. Maybe he *told* him he and Joshua were going to disappear."

"And terrify his parents?" Would Frank have done *that*? No, Arkey concluded (as Ellen Jaffe had before him), Frank was a kind and decent man, believing it all the more fervently because it made Frank a suburban zombie saint who communicated from the grave to Billy, who, in turn, spoke *only to them*. Which made them special.

"Do you remember in the sixth grade," Jeffrey said, "when Billy gave that report? He said he was dead but he was still talking. Well, he wasn't dead, comrade, he was *just* talking. And, trust me, the dead ain't talking to him."

Jeffrey turned and went on alone, down toward the water and his parents' house, while Arkey stopped for a moment at the front of the long, oak-sheltered driveway of 42 Frog Pond Lane, and felt Billy's vision increase him, his soul making him feel he had a soul that might expand into the soft summer air above the treetops, and making the warm suburban darkness a presence of spirits for his new big-style soul to mingle with. But when he breathed in, his diffused self returned, and with it the remembrance of Jeffrey's sour skepticism. Arkey knew that Jeffrey was homosexual, but he didn't often allow himself to think what that might mean, just let it blend with the glamour of Jeffrey's life in New York, his almost unimaginable initiations into the world of famous artists, his general *knowingness*—all of which gave Jeffrey's doubts an added force, even a charismatic glow. Maybe to doubt was a lot cooler than to believe—even more special. He threw some pebbles up toward the stars and thought: *Jeffrey's right. There's no one there. None of it's true.*

Then a few small stones came down stingingly on his head—confirming his doubt or chastising his lack of faith? Well, which was it? Would they find the bodies? Or was Frank like hiding out in Havana? Would they ever know if Billy had *seen,* and they were all special? Or if he'd only dreamt. Or if he'd imagined it all like a good story. Or, most likely, as Jeffrey had said, if he'd lied.

Jeffrey had stopped a little farther away, turned back to say one more thing *au sujet de* Broadway Billy's monte game, and seen his friend scatter pebbles on his own head. He laughed, took the bottle from his pocket, and had another drink of the hot, sticky, disgusting liquor. Arkey, refreshed no doubt by his pebble shower, walked up the driveway, and Jeffrey started for home, lonely and sick to his stomach, outside the circle of their belief, he told himself, outside their hetero-sex—which felt, that warm June evening, outside not only yiddishkeit but life itself. So he could be fond of the others maybe, cynical possibly, carping perhaps, but certainly always an onlooker at *the festivals of their lives*. He *loved* that phrase. The bourgy festivals, he thought, of their tiny lives!

Maybe, he dreamt, Arkey would someday join him Outside. Maybe that's what the pebbles meant—self-hatred. But Jeffrey could show him there was no need for that, a whole world much more interesting than Great Neck waited for him. Sometimes Arkey and Billy, he thought, both had that look, *his* look, too much smiling, too much coquettish eyelash batting—but they wouldn't admit it, even to Jeffrey, no matter how he hinted.

Or maybe the pebbles at least meant Jeffrey had gotten Arkey to doubt their little wonder rabbi. Jesus H. Christ, how could they believe Billy's crap, all of them so stiff-necked, proud, touchy about how smart they were in comparison with each other or Bobby Fischer, so why did they just roll over like credulous puppies and accept Billy's right to make them shiver? Was it because Billy had been a patient of Beth's father, and a child who went to any therapist was different and maybe spookily sensitive, but one who had gone to Dr. Jacobs was weird with Holocaust wisdom? Yeah, that must be it. *Dr. Leo Jacobs had survived Auschwitz,* and Billy, day by day, had told his story on Laura's yacht. So to doubt Billy and his letters dictated by ghouls was almost to doubt Dr. Jacobs, and *that,* even the glorious Beth maybe thought, would be contemptuous of the Jewish people. While there was no place in *those* tents for fags, anyway, Jeffrey knew. You could look it up.

The others all wanted Dr. Jacobs' approval, and that must be what they thought Billy could give them if they believed him, because it must really seem to them like Dr. Jacobs spoke to them from the rocking chair, instructing them all on how to find the Law, even when God had gone AWOL.

A foghorn sounded offscreen. Jeffrey could smell the sweet decay from the shore, which meant he was nearing home—or, anyway, his father's house. No, he thought, Arkey would never join him. "Your little friends are like your parents," the dealer Gaston Weil had said one afternoon. "They can't live without a prophet to make them feel chosen." He played sleepily with Jeffrey's dick, saying, "So they make one out of an undersized boy in a yarmulke. Or out of a pasty-faced zombie with an infuriatingly blank stare."

"I prophesy the dead will rise," Jeffrey said—pointing to his cock and thinking himself *very* bold. Gaston took Jeffrey backstage on the

Jews. Gaston called his parents the "junkyard owner and his wife." Gaston bought him the Southern Comfort. Gaston lectured him in *very* full sentences, as if Jeffrey would understand. Altogether, a strong mixed drink. Jeffrey quickly grew stiff again.

Gaston stared at it, almost appraisingly, with eyes at once intense and sleepy. "They even revere Andy more because he's *so* indifferent to them that he hires doped-up boys to do the fucking work for him. After all, wouldn't a real prophet think they were full of shit?"

Jeffrey didn't understand all Gaston said, but he understood what Gaston's mouth was doing. His back arched and he came.

"So you think he's a fraud?" Jeffrey asked. Gaston was the smartest person he'd ever met; he'd read everything; and he'd seen him win a hundred dollars one afternoon, too, hustling chess games in Washington Square. He'd *know.*

Gaston smiled, Jeffrey's come dribbling from the corners of his mouth. "No. I think he's a genius."

"I mean Billy."

Gaston laughed. "Sure. Him, too. Why not? For fifteen minutes anyway. I don't know if he has legs."

Still, one thing still tugged at Jeffrey: why didn't Billy himself wink to *say* this was a fraud the way Gaston did by sleeping with the buyer's son and revealing his trade secrets? Or just one day blankly declare it was all a show, the way Andy would, so bereft of feeling you couldn't tell if he meant it or not? Why didn't Billy want *credit* for making his friends believe such hooey? Did that mean Billy believed it too?

Jeffrey stopped outside the T-shaped ranch house by the water, a modern reproach to the more stately mansions. "Your father thinks solidarity with the New will wash the junkman's money," Gaston had said one afternoon, the two of them standing in the driveway staring at the winged monstrosity. Gaston smirked. "Artists are the antennae of the race, blah blah blah, and the Junkyard Owner has been spiritually large enough to hear the voice of What Will Be. He's chosen. And one way or another, junkyard owner, or Great Neck princes and princesses, we Jews *must* have that!" Gaston had lit a Gauloises, and coughed. "I hate these shit-fingers," he'd said, looking angrily at his cigarette. He stuck it back in his mouth. "But your mother expects it of me."

Jeffrey had been stunned. "You're Jewish?" It hadn't diminished Gaston for Jeffrey; it had burnished Judaism.

Gaston had kissed Jeffrey on the lips, his mouth—post-Gauloises—tasting like fecal matter.

Gaston had smiled. "Maybe. And maybe I'm not really French," he'd said. But he said it in a French accent. So did he mean, Jeffrey had wondered, that being Jewish made one not really French—like Billy had taught them all in the sixth grade. Or that he was, like, from Queens?

Before he could ask, Gaston had strolled inside the JYO's NEW— and, his son thought, très nouveau—house.

For the last few months Jeffrey somehow hadn't gotten around to asking Gaston if he'd been born in Paris or Flushing, and had also never asked if Gaston had picked Jeffrey because (as he'd once said) he had a good eye—or fucked him because sucking his dick maybe got him even with Mr. and Mrs. Junkman for the indignity of the mandatory shit-fingers? Like his little friends, Jeffrey had to admit he'd wanted his myth too: the Franco-Jewish Mephistopheles who'd chosen *him*. He took another drink to deepen his melancholy—because that *sublime* sadness, that seeing-through-everything, even and especially himself, would be, he decided, *his* great distinction, his guidance, his necessity. He waited for the kitschy foghorns, and when one sounded, he screamed "Stella!" as loudly as he could—because he was sophisticated, he was skeptical, but he was also still a teenager. *Look at me,* he thought with happy sadness. *I even see through my own bullshit.* Then he took the key from under the big rock near the magnolia tree and unlocked the door to his bastard father's house.

The next day in Laura's bedroom Chet Huntley's voice intoned a Western-accented open-voweled dirge as U.S. soldiers walked in a line through a Mississippi swamp. So far, he said, the search for the bodies had turned up five rotting corpses, all Negroes, two buried in shallow graves, one torso found without a head in the Mississippi River, and two dead women simply thrown by the side of the road. Then there were pictures of a whole division of highly trained men pushing poles into a swamp, each soldier probably hoping that someone might get lucky, strike the right white arm or leg so they could all get the fuck away from these mean-ass mosquitoes and out of the hell of Mississippi.

Cut to: two annoying twins repeating and repeating and repeating their obsessive love for Doublemint gum.

"If he's dead the army'll find him in the swamp," Jeffrey said. "That's where I'd dump a body."

"Dumped a lot of bodies, have we, Jeffrey?" Arkey asked, angry that Jeffrey had made him doubt Billy and his own future Nobel.

"No," Billy said emphatically. "He's not *there*. He's under tons of earth. He's in pain." Laura shrank away from him, holding up her four-faced doll for protection, but she couldn't stop staring or close her ears to him.

That July, Billy had begun to wear a white long-sleeved shirt, black pants, and yarmulke, the skullcap frightening his parents. Nathan and Elizabeth had cut a deal with Billy: if he would go to a regular college (like, oh, Harvard, say) they would pay for yeshiva later, the parents praying, Dear Lord, please let our child outgrow his belief in You. For now, Billy studied Talmud three times a week with ill-tempered Rabbi Meltzer. Billy, refusing to eat otherwise, had blackmailed them, too, into obeying the kosher laws.

"You . . . look . . . hot," Laura said to Billy, as if it were worth fighting through the sedative fog to give the boy helpful hints. Billy gave her a tight-lipped smile just like the ones that bloomed nightly on Laura's mother's lips, the expression a contagious disease. Then, jab-jab-jab, she remembered that Dr. Jacobs had been in Auschwitz, and she felt again that she could never turn away from Billy, who looked and acted now more and more like the observant men from the communities her parents had run from but could—in their own dreams, and the ones they had given her—never quite escape, shouldn't even have ever wanted to escape. Laura knew Billy wore the fringed garments underneath his clothes and ate only vegetables to avoid unintentional mixing of meat and milk in his parents' ever-insufficiently-koshered kitchen, because "performing the six hundred and thirteen mitzvahs," he told them, "will help raise Frank," though in her drugged state Laura didn't see how not eating lobster would be an act of justice on her brother's behalf.

Then, for two weeks, Billy didn't say anything more about Frank or justice, and they lay around together in Laura's air-conditioned bedroom, drinking Jeffrey's endless supply of Southern Comfort, which they all said they hated but all wanted lots more of. And day by day, Laura spoke less and less, her eyes growing much too big in her small face, until Arkey was scared for her and hoped to God that they *would* find Frank and Joshua stashed alive in some redneck cabin, or hiding with Fidel, even if that meant that Arkey wasn't connected to any grand event, but was only the dupe of a minor fraud, and that all that was left to him was nothing more special than high scores (God willing!) on the SAT's. Beth played a record, and James Brown screamed in the background, while Arkey wondered what Laura would sound like when she came, what any woman would sound like, actually, and did they each sound different? *That* was what he really wanted to hear, he decided, not more teaching from Billy Green.

Then, a few days later, Jesse read to them from the *New York Times* what Herbert Jaffe had told his family that morning: the FBI's special-case agent, a man named Olson, had walked the top of a new earthwork dam with an oddly long divining rod, until it had mysteriously pointed down just above where *the bodies had been buried under tons of earth.* Which made rednecks say the whole thing was a setup, that the bee-eyes and the SNAPs had done the killing, and which made Arkey believe that Billy *had* seen, Billy *had* known, that Frank *had* written them letters from the grave, because he most certainly *had* been buried under tons of earth, *just the way Billy had said*—and something under all that earth had had the power to know what was going on above him, had taken over the body of Special Agent Olson, made his hands point that pole down in the right place. Frank, though dead, had power to move men's hands, to draw a long pole down—and how different was that from making a man write a letter he didn't even know he'd written? Arkey felt a shiver go through his body, because that also meant that Frank, though dead, was in agony until the end of time, unless, Billy said again—as Laura wept and wept—his pain was eased by the acts of justice his friends did in his name.

"You people are all going mental again," Jeffrey said, all of them, even Jeffrey, ignoring that Laura whimpered uncontrollably, her brother dead now beyond doubt. "Billy just made a lucky guess about the tons of earth. I mean, really, like where are dead people put anyway? Under earth."

"And Olson?" Arkey said. "What drew the pole down?"

"He made a lucky guess, too." Jeffrey saw they weren't buying it and took another swig.

What had Billy just said? Or was it Arkey? Laura tried to remember, but it scampered away from her, her way of bearing her brother's death and Billy's teaching being to bewilder her mind, the syrupy alcohol doubling the effect of the drugs, helping her forget whatever ghoulish thing Billy talked about almost even as he said it, which was *not*, she swore, to doubt him—because that would be to *decide* to lose her brother again, to make him not, utterly not. She took the bottle from Jeffrey, took another drink while Billy said something about justice, the word making her tongue go backward as if she were supposed to swallow it; then it thrust forward as if she should spit it out, her throat locked up tight. Spit and booze sprayed from her mouth. She couldn't remember how to swallow! She couldn't remember how to breathe! She flailed, until Jesse caught her arms, pinned her, rocked her. Thank God for dear Jesse, she thought. Her throat opened again, and she gulped air like a drowning swimmer, while the others looked on from around her room, inured now to her pain—or even, she dreamt, greedy for it, like it made them feel special.

Well, good, she thought, as Jesse made the rest of them leave. She had plenty of shows left to give, because her brother's agony underground had already become her own personal horror story, a body she couldn't stop dreaming of both night and day, flesh coming apart that yet was always and forever sentient, inner tissue oozing and dissolving, black spots of rot on bone spreading while he was still awake, in pain, and the pain, if anything, growing worse, for how long? Worms gnawed at him, but never devoured his mind, never put him to sleep. That awful dream meant she could eat only vegetables that summer, just like Billy, nothing that had flesh, and she could hardly swallow a mouthful of those; her weight went from a hundred and twenty pounds to ninety and she felt faint whenever she stood up. Her mother was afraid that Laura had become anorexic, begged her to see a psychiatrist, but Laura knew that she couldn't tell a doctor what haunted her, that her brother's dead but sentient body was suffering still, skin tearing from stomach, guts leaking into the earth, blood congealing in his veins, all of it, she knew, like a horror movie—to keep it distant, unreal. And it was—or this little boy and his stories were. But it was also horrible. Her brother had been murdered. Each morning when she weighed herself she felt a grim satisfaction that soon she would not be.

That August Billy seemed to be the only one who could help her find her way out of the grave where she lay trapped along with her brother; so she might scream at Billy sometimes, might even claw at him like a drowning woman and drive him and the others from her room, but she also called him on her Princess phone each night to make sure he was coming over the next morning. His high, small voice, his quiet promise that he'd come, was the only thing that allowed her finally to sleep.

His day-by-day homilies gave her mourning a mission. Laura tried to bewilder her mind and forget his words, but really, she knew she couldn't have handled her brother's murder without Billy's teaching that if they did mitzvahs in Frank's name it would be like the healing surgeon's knife, separating his soul-fragments from the pain of his buried body, raising them from beneath the mounds of earth to a special anteroom. There, the souls waited until they were refreshed, ready to return and heal the wounded community. "If we help Frank," Billy had said, "then others will help us when we die and need our sparks raised."

Soon she stopped drinking so much. She took fewer pills. She nodded and listened. And—because this was an American miracle—she could eat hamburgers again that Jesse brought her from Frederick's

Luncheonette. From then on, she knew, the others felt that to doubt what Billy said was to hurt her, and though Jeffrey might carp mildly ("Oh I *believe*," he'd say, actually making her laugh. "Look, I'm clapping, too! Please don't let Tinkerbell die!"), but nobody truly argued with Billy—though Laura also *hated* him sometimes for teaching that they could help Frank, because it meant that by doing nothing they could hurt him more; and nothing was, mostly, what she felt she did.

Even worse than that, they might do the wrong thing. So Billy made them pledge they'd always be faithful to Frank's path, that they'd always be nonviolent warriors.

"Yes," Jesse said solemnly, standing by the side of her bed, like he was pledging allegiance. "We must be neither victims nor executioners."

"Where?" Jeffrey wondered. "Against the hitters at Carvel? Soft Serve Now! Soft Serve Now! But look, guys, the Little Neck ice cream stand's already integrated. And the tough Negro kids are just as likely to beat on you as anyone."

They ignored him, though Laura couldn't help it, she had smiled again.

Impossible job, Arkey thought: Make Justice. Raise Frank. But even if he decided to accept it, Arkey didn't know what to do. Give blood? Join the NAACP? Not grand enough considering the enormity of Frank's suffering. Besides, if he knew what to do, would he have the courage? Even the thought of lying on a cot in the Dewey School gym with a thin, transparent hose snaking from his arm, a bottle filling with his blood, God, the idea made him want to puke.

Not knowing how, not knowing if he'd have the courage if he knew, he found a family member who cared enough to argue with him instead, already sensing that this had become an irritable reflex with him. Don't have the nerve to call a girl? Then fight with your parents about their sick middle-class sexual mores. Can't do anything to change the world? Find an adult who loves you and lambast them for calling the maid colored. Arkey felt how he put too much energy into these arguments, his voice too high, too strong, almost crying. But he couldn't stop.

Specs laughed. " 'Justice? What is justice,' joked doubting Pilate," he said, while they waited for the foursome ahead of them to tee off. "Rational, shrewd, sober, learned, and clever. That's the *lamedvovniks* for us, Arkey. Why?" Specs bent over, still talking, and put the ball on the little red tee. "I'll tell you why." He whacked the ball in a high arc, more loft than needed, it falling just in front of the water. "Because those are the values good for our side."

Our side to Specs meant his family, the Jews, and his business, where he managed money on his own now, for "high-net-worth individuals," some of whom, June admitted, might have gotten that lofty amount from criminal enterprises. Had these *always* been his secret friends? Had he even lied to Arkey's family about it? After all, Arkey had dreamt of it. He'd known. Hell, he'd even *wanted* it.

Their mother thought Ralph was a good Jew. He made gifts to the Temple each year, had seats in front on Yom Kippur. And he was a good husband, too; a good father, who doted on his son; and a *very* good provider, Specs and June now owning the house F. Scott Fitzgerald could only rent, right on the water, at the very tip of Kings Point, a place bigger than Frog Pond Lane, bigger than the Ritz even, like a wedding cake of rectangles one on the other, the place Arkey had actually read about in Fitzgerald's essay "How to Live on $36,000 a Year," which didn't sound like so much, but would actually be like maybe a million 1964 dollars. Also Specs and June had already given his parents a grandson, and June was pregnant with No. 2 already—the last one, June had said, when she'd told them about it at Passover.

If it was a girl, anyway, "the Talmud-mandated number," his Grandpa Abe had said, looking at Arkey, "being one of each sex."

Specs asked Arkey to do the math: how many children per family would most Jews have if they followed that injunction, each pregnancy a fifty-fifty bet, so the series ending where on average?

It had been beyond him. Arkey said he hoped it wouldn't be on the SAT's—or that they wouldn't make him drink Manischewitz before the test.

Arkey's father had betrayed him then, laughing at Specs' question, his son's inability to answer, maybe because Specs had helped make tax liabilities disappear for Arkey's father, made union problems go away, Ralph not a bad man himself, his mother had decided, just one who had fallen in with bad people, the way Kel-Kap had. "They're using him," Arkey's father had said. "What can you do?"

Arkey's drive lay nearly halfway down the fairway, or a third of the way, anyway. Not bad for him. He got up to Specs in two shots.

"Jewish values, they're good for me," Specs said, continuing the lesson, "they're good for my family, they're good for my son. That's enough for me, Arkey. I don't need to be chosen by anyone."

Money—gained by knowledge, used to buy Rolex watches and Cadillacs to be enjoyed without guilt. Was that Specs' Judaism? But June said Specs didn't seem interested in most of the things money could buy, didn't notice the long silk socks June put out for him every morning (as if the kosher laws had said, *Never show a stranger the skin of your calf*), the Louis Quinze sconces, or the chamber pots decorated with pastoral scenes she'd cunningly transformed into lamps for the entryway.

"The only thing he cares about, I mean, besides me and his son, is his paintings," June having seen him rock back and forth on the balls of his feet for half an hour on end staring at a canvas, his face filled with wonder. "And he has taste, too," Gaston Weil had told Jeffrey who told Arkey. "He buys bold, audacious, emotional paintings, really gets them." Like the ones Arkey called Vampire Whores From Outer Space, Arkey rarely having seen any picture of a woman (line drawings, photos, June Cleaver on TV) that didn't give him a hard-on, while these paintings, they scared him limp, like they were giant Aunts going, *I could eat you up,* and meaning it. He had the feeling that that anti-aphrodisiac effect must be what made them art.

"But what about the Law, I mean, God's judgment if we fail to, you know, do justice?" The putting green made Arkey feel solemn. Soft, perfect, smooth, the way the women looked in *Playboy*; and something else, too, like he was looking at an old painting in a high-ceilinged museum. But blank, featureless. Money, that was it—the green looked like money made into grass! The admission price for this club was fifty thousand dollars, his father had told him, admiringly, and you had to pay dues each year on top of that. Someone probably knelt down and trimmed the grass blades with little scissors every morning.

Arkey took a few steps toward his ball. The tender, obedient grass beneath his feet felt illicit, exciting—like he'd taken one of his mother's minks from her closet and spread it out on the floor just for the pleasure of walking on it.

"Every tribe tries to construct a world that lets it triumph using its particular talents," Specs said as he leaned over the ball, the pocked white sphere looking helpless beneath him. "Then we say, That's the way God wants the world to be, so you better do things His way, *or else.*" Specs' putt overshot to the left, his big muscles great for driving, but barely controllable here.

While Arkey's skinny arms turned magically wiry underneath his T-shirt. In in one.

Specs' second putt bounced around once and rimmed out. A sign that maybe Specs didn't know what he was talking about either, had got it wrong about God and justice and judgment, Specs not knowing that we're *all* in pain in the grave, money managers, mobsters, even martyrs like Frank, our soul-sparks trapped there unless people whose soul-sparks are linked to ours think of our suffering in the grave and do justice in our name, bringing the blessed realm's power down to raise us up. *That's* how the system really works, Arkey knew. But he'd promised his friends not to say any of it; that, and he didn't want to seem like a lunatic.

But justice? Specs finally tapped his ball in. Arkey picked up the long handle of his cart, started toward the next tee. He needed to see his friends, think things through with them. What was justice?

"My mom," Laura said, "wants to have Frank cremated." She meant: *does that matter? Is that justice?*

Apparently, it was a bad idea, making Billy rock harder and harder, crying, a viscous globule of yellowish snot under his nose already sliding slowly toward his lips. "He has to be buried. He has to be buried." He carefully put his finger to his face, pushed the mucus into his mouth, even though everyone was looking right at him. "You can't let him be burnt, Laura. You can't!"

Beth, sitting by the chair's runner, reached up and stroked his cheek.

Laura remembered Mr. Hartman's class, when she'd thought the snot-nosed boy was probably crazy. Or vicious. How could Beth stroke his cheek like that? How could she actually make love with him?

"I mean, he's so queer. I mean strange, you know," she said to Beth the next afternoon, just the two of them running together round and round the empty cinder track at GN North, Beth having decided that the exercise, the repeated pointless foolishness of it, would be good for Laura.

"I feel like he's the only person as angry at the way the world is as I am," Beth said.

I'm angry, Laura had wanted to say. For God's sake, it was her brother who had died! "Billy? Angry? He's too little."

Beth turned, stared at her for a second, then pulled away a few strides.

She got the message. Little Billy *knew* what the world was like, and he hated it. Beth *knew*. And Frank most certainly knew. Laura, the one whose brother had actually died, *she* was the innocent one.

Beth stopped, ahead of her, hands on her thighs, looking at the ground, panting for breath. Laura pulled up beside her and looked up at the blue empty sky, taking gulps of air into her burning lungs. Billy and Beth *should* fuck each other, she thought, plenty angry now herself. She hated them both.

. . .

But "You mustn't," she said to her mother. They stood outside the door of the antiseptic basement room where her son's body waited.

"Mustn't what?" Ellen Jaffe said, scared for her daughter, who had lost too much weight and spoke in broken, inexplicable sentences. But Laura wouldn't talk to a therapist, wouldn't even take her tranquilizers anymore, the thought making Ellen suddenly furious. "Laura, this isn't happening just to you. This is the worst time in all our lives. And you are not helping."

Laura began to whimper. "You mustn't let them do an autopsy. And you mustn't let them burn his body."

Ellen pressed herself against the concrete wall. There had to be an autopsy so the murderers could be tried. "Herbert," she said, "why is she doing this to us?" Ellen wished she hadn't brought Laura with them to Mississippi, where Herbert had had to use his influence with Hubert Humphrey so that they might even get to see her son's beautiful body, bullet wounds in his delicate temples, the chest caved in from mounds of earth.

There was no air to breathe in the autopsy room. Ellen, thinking she would suffocate, would go crazy from her daughter's raving, looked around the room like a panicked animal.

Special Agent Olson, a crew-cut man with a square face, flushed skin, looked back at her sympathetically but distantly. It was her son, but she wasn't part of his case. The sharp-nosed deputy sheriff of Lovette, his cowboy hat tilted up, stood beside Frank's body, a smirk on his face, like he was mocking her. He told Olson he had to accompany them "to make sure no one tampers with the corpse," like the family was in league with her son's murderers! The thin, ferret-faced man's parts didn't fit together. He shifted from foot to foot uneasily. He was hiding something; Ellen was sure he knew who the murderers were, was maybe one of them himself.

While her daughter *knew* that the deputy had used his sheriff's car to stop Joshua so that the murder would all be legal, as he had said, in Judge Lynch's court, *knew*, too, that he'd been the man who had put the high cowboy boots that he wore even now, even here, on her brother's chest, crushing Frank's ribs down toward the no-longer-beating but still feeling heart. But she couldn't say anything to her mother without seeming insane, or to her father, or to Agent Olson, or to anyone but the five people in Great Neck.

And to Frank. She stroked her brother's cold cheek. "I remember you, Frank, I remember you, Frank," she murmured, "I remember you, I remember you, I remember . . ." *Can he feel me stroking him? Can this soothe him? Does it make justice?* Her body shook, bewildered by fury and love.

"I told ya', little girl," the deputy sheriff said angrily, looking for an angle that would let him muscle the corpse away from the FBI before they figured out something more from it, supposing they needed to know more, someone clearly having ratted them out, or how could he have found the corpse? Could a dowsing rod really do that? "You can't touch evidence."

Laura thought, *This man's voice will hurt Frank.* She yearned to cut his neck, see the blood gush out, but her lust turned back into her body, making her uterus cramp, and she felt herself trapped in this room, trapped in her soul's divided longings, the smell of formaldehyde like sharp bitter wood in her nostrils, sickening her, making her a helpless girl, standing beside her brother's dead body, facing the man she was sure was his murderer. And so she collapsed; not all at once, but as if her foundations had been destroyed, and her body was coming down story by story, her voice growing weaker and weaker, and she was outside her body, watching the letters that made up her words growing smaller and smaller, like Alice become tiny, as she went on repeating, "I remember, Frank, I remember . . ."

Her father left his wife's side and knelt by the ashen girl, lifting her head onto his thigh, stroking her hair. Once again, Ellen Jaffe thought, her daughter had made herself the center of attention. Ellen dreamt then of a fire that would consume her son's ruined, disfigured corpse, all Mississippi seeing that if they'd done so much harm to such a perfect boy that his mother could no longer bear to look on her most precious treasure, then what hell must wait for their sheriff and his deputy, for their ugly, ferret-faced, murderous bodies, their worthless state, this unjust earth?

Her husband stroked his daughter's thick black hair, and—as always in their predictable father-daughter pas de deux—sadness and concern began to water Herbert's weak brown eyes. Soon, Ellen knew, he would discard his wife's wishes like so much wadded tissue, just to make his daughter smile wanly up at him again.

The next day, Herbert and Ellen accompanied Joshua Battle's mother to see her son's mangled corpse, which was at the FBI's morgue near Jackson, and Althea Battle felt the world rush away from under her as she looked down at her son's body on a metal gurney. Her mind filled with the memory of a sidewalk outside a cigar store in Chicago when she'd once stared at a rack of magazines. Summer had been turning to fall, and right next to *The Defender*, the cover of *Ebony* showed the open casket at Emmet Till's funeral, his face looking like it had been made from wax and held too close to a fire, the bones of Till's nose and her son's nose crushed the same way, and a knife maybe dragged deep across the left eye socket, nearly severing the bone. Or did she remember that wrong? Till's face; her son's face; her confusion, she knew, a mechanism to let her bear this sorrow, let her feel like this had happened before and to another, let it be less her son that lay on the gurney in front of her and more a thing from the past, a piece of history that had happened and would happen again; the present but not the present; same old, same old. A boot had come down on his head, or maybe a rock—a blow that made a gully across the forehead, the upper half sloping down now, backward, the whole world backward, she thought, the son dead before his mother.

Ellen Jaffe put her arm around her, to steady her. She and her powerful husband had gotten the FBI to let her see this dismal sight, and she was grateful, but how could she tell Mrs. Jaffe that she must please not pretend that Ellen's loss was equal to hers, for Joshua Battle had been the hope of a whole people.

"They must have beaten him," Althea said, "beaten him for a long time before they shot him."

"I think," Ellen said, "Frank was spared that."

Althea felt Ellen was making an acknowledgment, recognizing that white was an entitlement even in the killing field, or maybe, of course, especially there. Althea wanted that known, for right now the weight of her suffering, she thought, was her only distinction, the only way the world had to measure the greatness of her son.

For the same reason that Ellen Jaffe had wanted to burn her child's corpse, Mrs. Battle wanted her son's smashed face *seen*—just the way Emmet Till's had been; she wanted the world to compare it to a picture of Joshua when he'd been whole and radiant as few men are ever radiant, maybe use a snapshot from his time in Japan, when he'd built that man a ladder up a mountainside. That's what her son did, she thought: he built ladders—for Japanese monks, for Mississippi voters. She would tape the picture to the lid of the coffin—just the way it had been when he'd died before, when Emmet Till had died.

"Cassius Clay, do you know who Cassius Clay is?" she said to Ellen. She stared at Ellen Jaffe, surprised at how sympathetic she looked, her face not as empty as a child's elbow.

Frank's mother nodded.

"He saw young Emmet Till's face, do you know who that is?"

She nodded again.

Who knew if that were true? Who ever knew? "Well, Cassius Clay," she said, "he saw that picture in a magazine when he was a teenager, just the way I did, and he went and clear lifted up the railroad tracks near his house." She laughed. "Can you imagine that? He wanted to derail a locomotive. He didn't know me. But he did it for me."

Ellen understood, of course, she, too, having wanted just that for her son, wanted someone to make this powerful world go right off its tracks. She hugged Mrs. Battle.

But when David Watkins looked down for the first time at the casket that lay before the altar in the wood-frame church, he felt sick with a fatigue that he worried would maybe never leave him; and *that* foreboding just made him more tired still, that feeling returned that if he spoke to the people now, he would only be saying words that Joshua had known he would say over his corpse, and the thought made him wearier still. So he would say nothing—maybe that would free him from the trap. He started for his seat, and realized that he'd failed; Joshua, he knew, had seen the nothing he'd say. He could barely lift his lead-filled legs, his back even bending over a little from the weight of the corpse he carried everywhere. He thought: *Sweet Jesus, I actually shuffle now. That's what Mississippi has done to me.* He'd had just enough energy in him the night before to gather the others 'round him, urge that Sugar deliver the eulogy instead of him. You *had* to see that Sugar's certainty, his reined-in anger, made him the one they needed now—the leader who could maybe take over from Joshua (and if David said *that,* then Joshua had foreseen that Sugar would be their leader, Joshua wanted it). Everyone knew David hated Sugar for his taking Susan from him, so if David still wanted Sugar to lead, then *it must be.*

They quickly voted Sugar Cane to deliver the eulogy—which scared the national leadership, the Democratic convention coming up, and the Lord knew what Cane might say. But Sugar whispered to them that he understood, said the killing had just reinforced his conviction in his and Joshua's nonviolent way. He'd keep it cool.

And maybe he would have, if Joshua's brother, Jacob, hadn't started wheezing like a piece of rusty farm machinery from the close air in the small church, from the loss of his brother, from seeing—Sugar imagined—a father in Sugar himself. Sugar, standing by the pulpit, stood silent for a moment, so everyone could hear the small boy trying to breathe.

Seduced by that clanking sound, Sugar dreamt that if he said the right words it would take the stone off Jacob's lungs, let him breathe more easily again. He looked directly at the boy, who stared back at him longingly. He had to tell him, first, how often his brother's name was even omitted from the reports in the papers, how Joshua Battle was called "the black youth" who had been killed with Frank Jaffe, the white *man,* had to tell them that blacks raised white children, but their parents didn't even notice our dead. He had to tell Jacob how tired he was now, how very tired, though even as he told him he felt like his legs and arms could move more freely again, like he was waking up from a long sleep, his life returning to him, from where? From the coffin with Joshua Battle! He needed to shout, with a desire so great that it felt painful to him, and Jacob, listening, began to nod, Jacob never having met Sugar but having read lots about him in his brother's letters, and the whole train ride down from New York he'd been longing to see him, somehow knowing that Sugar Cane would understand how he felt. His chest hurt a little less, didn't rattle so much as the air found a way in, Jacob losing himself in wonder of Sugar's strong black body, his shining eyes, his anger, Sugar's arms gesturing like he'd seen far ahead, his words telling them about it without any doubt in his voice, Sugar like a point guard shimmying in the space between two defenders, whose next moves he'd long ago divined.

And Sugar heard the boy's sound change, heard the world grow a little easier for the both of them. So he had to tell Jacob how he wasn't going to cool it anymore, not for the sheriff here, or for the president in Washington, because he knew now that the greatest faithfulness to Joshua was to learn what Joshua *must* have wanted to teach him by his death. "You should know, Jacob," he said quietly, as if the others in the church were just listening in as a man and a boy talked together about what was bothering their hearts, "that your brother was a great black genius when he was alive. So why shouldn't he have been a genius who taught us, who maybe even meant to teach us with the death he surely knew might be coming for him?" Sugar himself now knowing that he had to help Jacob Battle have the life he deserved, which was a warrior's life, free for as long as they fought together as nonviolent warriors for what Joshua Battle believed in.

Jacob heard people murmur, looking over at him.

So, Sugar said, he couldn't lie to Jacob, little Jacob, he had to tell him the truth, didn't he?

The black people in the audience said yes, he did, he had to tell him the truth, and Sugar got that preacher sound. His brother had had that once or twice himself, when he talked about their right to vote. But with his brother it had sounded like if whites didn't give them the vote, they were mean people, taking food from a crying child, and sometimes, Jacob had to tell Sugar soon, when his brother talked like that, it had made Jacob feel weak and womanly—when the last thing on earth Jacob ever wanted now was to be like some crying, wheezing, snotty little girl. Sugar swore he would always be nonviolent like Joshua Battle, but this Sugar-vote sounded different, hard, heavy, dangerous. That could be all right.

And like a preacher, Sugar tried to pick them up in his arms, saying that for centuries black mammies had raised white children, loved white children, wasn't that the truth?

It was.

Those women did what they could to protect and nurture and form those children, didn't they?

Yes.

Helped them to know right from wrong. They even loved those children. They loved them! And wasn't that the biggest job in the world?

The crowd said amen to that.

"Well, now, listen, if our mothers are good enough for that, good enough to raise your children, then *I* am good enough to rule over you as you have ruled over me," Sugar shouted, and Jacob could feel *the vote* that Sugar meant as if it lay in his hand: it was a rock; it was a thousand rocks in a thousand hands. Give us what's ours. Give us what's ours, Sugar was saying. Or we'll use these rocks to take it from you.

Sugar didn't stop talking, but he stepped down from the pulpit and walked right over toward Jacob and his mother, like they were the most important people in the world, Jacob feeling all their eyes on him, waiting to see what he'd do. He got up and ran toward Sugar, and Sugar opened his arms and gathered him in, the two of them crying. He put his head against Sugar's chest and smelled the beautiful odor of Sugar's sweat flowing into him, healing him, Sugar's smell like special black milk that filled him, he dreamt, for as long as he helped Sugar to finish the work his brother had begun.

Afterward, standing on the porch, Herbert spoke to Mrs. Battle about a scholarship for Jacob to the John Dewey School, where her son had once taught algebra. "It's a very good school," Ellen Jaffe said. She put her hand on Laura's shoulder. "I just wish they took girls."

"It's only an IRT ride from 125th Street," Herbert said.

"Is that right, Mr. Jaffe?" Mrs. Battle replied, smiling, not certain yet that she would turn the offer down but wanting them all to know that it wasn't just a simple gift they offered. "I think, really, it's a *lot* farther away than that."

Herbert understood, looked down at his shoes. "You may be right."

"I know you mean well, Mr. Jaffe. But do you know how many Negro students they have there?"

No, Herbert had to admit, he didn't know.

"I have a friend who goes there," Laura said. "He's a really good kid. He'd look out for your son." Arkey, she knew, would be glad to have this way to help Frank.

Jacob looked to Sugar Cane.

"You know what your brother would say, Jacob?" Sugar said. "We have to transform a very hard world. We need to know everything we can about it. If they know it at this school, and if they'll make you work to learn it, then maybe you should go there."

Mrs. Battle looked at her son's big eyes staring up at Sugar. She knew what he found there, having felt a little of it herself when the man was talking—and she knew that she would never hear the end of it from her son if she didn't do like Sugar said. And she had to admit she'd felt something, too, when she and Ellen had looked at her son's ruined body, like these Jaffes were good people, and maybe this was the right thing to do. And maybe, she thought, not meaning much of a muchness by it, it would ease her son in his grave to know his brother was being taken care of.

That August in Great Neck, Laura and Jesse lay most nights in the tax-loss field where Beth and Frank had last made love, and sometimes they talked about the funeral. Laura told him what her brother had looked like in the morgue, and Jesse told her that when Billy talked about Frank's pain he felt like he could see a tightly bound little man, cramped muscles in agony, afraid he would spend eternity in a sealed-up place, a dream that Jesse said made him into a child again. He couldn't even sleep without the lights on because in the dark he felt he became like Frank, trapped, like in that Poe story, unable to move, yet he could see and hear and think. Now the days scared him, too. It was like he felt the earth over him. Laura held him in her lap to comfort him. She stroked his cheek, the curls of his hair, and when he pulled her down toward him, she felt she couldn't pull away from him anymore, and they made love for the first time, her terror at doing this mingled with her fear and sadness about Frank, each feeling distracting her from the other so she could bear the pain of his entering her body, Jesse coming almost at once, and trembling and trembling after he came, so she had to comfort *him* again, after what she'd just felt, which was painful, exciting, and empty.

Fourteen years later, when she saw Jesse at Beth's bail hearing not scared of the judge or the FBI, she wondered if Jesse had *really* meant any of those things, or if he'd just played up his fear to get her to make love to him. Or, more likely, it had started as a way to get someone to fuck him—the real beginning, after all, of most adolescent boys' ideas, poems, science fair projects, and touchdowns—and then, just like with her, the fear for Frank had hooked so deep into his brain he couldn't get rid of it, like he had practiced madness to win her, the way Beth had practiced the violin every day, even though she had hated it at first, until soon, she'd said, days when you can't practice, you feel unclean. So step by step, Jesse had driven himself crazy, until he'd become . . . a defense attorney, which was also, probably, another way to get girls, Jesse having told her one night after a college SDS meeting that he wanted to protect others because he had nothing else to offer them, no vision, no project, no strategy. She could tell by then that he'd been looking for sympathy, comfort—that is: he wanted to get her in bed again; and she, though she had a boyfriend, Michael Healy, wanted him, still. So they did it.

Anyway, even if everything had started as a way to get sex, Jesse's fear that summer soon had seemed even greater than hers. And that had allowed Laura to feel the rightness in comforting him, in gently unraveling and re-raveling the tight curls of his black hair with her fingers, as the cows stirred in their bovine fantasies, allowed her even to take a little pleasure in making love.

Probably she'd have gone mad from Billy's teaching and his impossible-to-fulfill commandments if loving Jesse hadn't distracted her, grateful almost that every day Jesse grew helplessly younger so he had to have a bunny night-light in his bedroom, and he needed her to be a child along with him, he was her bunrab, she was dumpling, kitty, soft foods, soft animals, as if by being children they moved farther and farther from the end of life, which wasn't the grave where they might be trapped, suffering forever.

Yet for children they had certainly been fervid, she thought now, as the lawyers went back to their desks, the face of Bobby Brown, the federal attorney, looking like a smooth mask, while Jesse curled his beautiful lips inward over his teeth with worry. She and Jesse had been always kissing, licking at each other that summer, even entering each other, her fingers in his mouth or his ass, his prick in every part of her, coming in her hair, between her breasts, a polymorphous Eden of knowing kids where she was somehow, she'd dreamt, also like a mother to him, and when he entered her cunt he was going even farther back, past childhood, into her womb, farther and farther from the grave that was no grave, because he'd gone back before he was born, was a baby inside her, and in her dreams she was there too, she was his prick inside herself, safe along with him, along with her, not ever dying because not yet ever born.

But they *had* been born. And soon Jesse and the comfort he gave Laura, and the comfort she could give him, weren't enough for her. She thought of them all sitting in her bedroom—that sacred pink frilly space!—and she was furious not with herself or with Arkey but with Billy, the little boy in his funereal garb who, rocking in her Kennedy chair, had put a fucking curse on her life, Billy having done the deed for Dr. Jacobs, done his live-action suburban Holocaust comic, hadn't he, and smeared the world with sticky guilt, a BillyBook that could be called **Frank Jaffe Suffers in the Grave**, called, in fact, their lives so far.

Her brother *had* died, for God's sake. She should have just accepted it then, not deluded herself for so long that some magic would raise him to heaven or bring him back to earth reborn. And if Billy hadn't convinced her for a while that her brother was still alive, suffering in the grave—the very place whose true name *had* to be *there, where no one can suffer more,* or after all, what was the point of death?—she wouldn't have needed his instructions on how to ease her brother's imaginary suffering, commandments she naturally failed sufficiently to fulfill, so they hadn't really ever comforted her, they'd only added to her anxiety, left her for a long time *always* a little guilty, just as Billy and Dr. J. might have wanted, which *must* have eventually harmed her immune system, allowed the sclerotic spots on her nerves to multiply, the ones that meant she couldn't have children without losing the use of her legs, control of her bladder. It was enough to make a girl cry, wasn't it—another blockbuster in Laura Jaffe Productions' endless schedule of Weepies. In fantasy, she stroked dear Jesse's cheek for comfort again, her desire getting mixed up with her longing to be back in her very own childhood with all its mistakes and fantasies. "I'll always remember you," she whispered as she stroked Jesse's dear face. "Always. You were the first, the very first. I'll always remember you."

Arkey, seeing Laura's lips move, looked at Beth, thinking it was maybe a communication for her. Beth fingered the nation sack around her neck as if it had magical powers, and looked toward the bench. Beth's face had been almost beatific as she'd opened that leather pouch for him a year before that, like it contained the remnants of a saint. She'd carefully placed the little worn piece of paper on his Formica kitchen table with its bent metal legs, uncurled the edge of the paper with one gentle, careful finger. That was meant to remind him that they were linked throughout life and ever after, and from the time when the vessels had broken until the Messiah came he'd have to buy her and Snake Greyhound tickets to Arizona, which was what she supposedly wanted money for that evening.

Or had she just been working *him,* thinking *he* was a hick who'd give gelt for her special mojo? Anyway, it had worked then, and it still worked now. He looked around at Billy, and Jesse, Laura, and even Dr. Jacobs. If he had to sum up his life, then Laura's bedroom in Great Neck, and his friends from there, had been the closest *he'd* ever come to Frank's "beloved community," or to the kabalists in the *klaus* at Safed. He swore he would pay whatever they needed to bail Beth out. He'd dig her out of the box she was in with the checkbook in his jacket pocket, he'd cash his life insurance if necessary (but how much could the bail for mere jumping bail be?), having no one else to leave the money to anyway (and dreaming, too, that being so self-sacrificial about the insurance money meant that he might not have to die). He would *end* her *agony,* so she wouldn't have to do *time,* and by his charity also help to raise Frank, that maybe being the meaning of the fragment Beth had uncurled on his gray kitchen table, glistening for him there like infected blood: *agony end time.*

The crew-cut judge stopped shuffling his papers and banged his gavel.

Then the lawyers stepped back from the bench, Bobby's face a smooth mask of triumph, while Jesse curled his lips inward over his teeth.

"Given the extraordinary circumstances of the case," the judge said loudly, "and because Miss Jacobs has already so often shown her contempt for the law, I am forced to take extraordinary measures, and set her bail at one million dollars."

The spectators, no matter their p.o.v., gasped at the size of that one. *That* sum, Arkey Kaplan thought, was more than his insurance was worth; more, Laura Jaffe thought, than she could borrow from her father; more, probably, Jeffrey thought, than he could get for the paintings he owned; more, Billy figured, than Billy Green Originals might be worth; and more, for sure, Jesse Kelman knew, than he would ever earn as a public defender. Too much money, Arkey decided, even for Jews from Great Neck, Jews With Money. (Possible title this time?)

2

1980: BAD DREAMS

That summer and fall, two years after Beth Jacobs had gone down a rabbit hole for the second time, Arkey Kaplan often had the same bad dream: Beth buried in a wooden box in a Mississippi graveyard—yet still feeling pain. Unless her friends rescued her she would spend eternity trapped in that sealed-up place. Arkey stood above her fresh grave, looking down sadly at his own long, empty fingers. He had nothing to dig with.

All through that Indian summer, he would wake from the dream in the dark of his third-floor Cambridge apartment, sweating, bewildered, feeling guilty and bereft.

The whir of an airplane . . . the heart-lung machine . . . the air conditioner brought him back to where and who he was; and then he'd remember that Beth Jacobs *wasn't* dead. Still confused, though, he'd think that Beth was in jail and that his dream meant that he had failed her, hadn't paid her bail, hadn't gotten her out of the sealed-up place. Then, like a reprieve, Arkey would remember that Jeffrey Schell had hocked the best part of his art collection to Arnie Golden and come up with her bail money. Two days later, it had been bye-bye Beth, adios art, farewell farthings; like the rabbi's permission to eat on Yom Kippur if fasting would endanger your health, the Band's pledge to uplift each other until the Messiah came seemed to have had a codicil that permitted jumping bail, even if it cost a pal a tidy fortune.

So thanks to Jeffrey's long-gone loot, Beth Jacobs *wasn't* sealed up in the Tombs anymore, and she almost certainly *wasn't* in a tomb, either. She'd gone *underground*, not by dying, but by leafing rapidly through the pages of local newspapers in the library of Passing Through, until she'd found the name of a prom queen killed decades before by a drunk driver, had her fake birth certificate sent to a mail drop. She'd have stripped her hair again, dyed it blond with foul-smelling chemicals, and put on contacts to turn her green eyes brown for the postage-stamp–size picture on a driver's license issued in the resurrected girl's name.

Beth was dead and buried to Arkey, though. No more late-night knocks on the door, like the early seventies, Beth/NotBeth saying, "Don't believe the hair. It's me." Then she'd sip a cup of peppermint tea and extend her fingers to show off her nail polish. "It's called Red Metallic Neon Whore. A perk of life underground. You know, like when I'm someone else I can wear this stuff—hell, I have no choice, right?" In those days she'd boast about the Eggplant's superpowers at eluding the police, the FBI, and especially her own Wile E. Coyote, FBI agent Olson, a man, she swore, who'd made it his life's work to nail her.

And maybe he had. Maybe he still did. Arkey sometimes heard a clicking on his home phone, found his letters frighteningly pre-read before delivery. Twice, there'd been break-ins at his apartment where nothing—alas—had been stolen. He knew that FBI agents had talked with senior members of his department at Brandeis, too, men—bless their withered leftist hearts—who were at least as outraged as frightened by Olson, though the interviews would undoubtedly turn out to be one more reason not to give him tenure.

This night, Arkey's fingers rubbed the rough place on his shoulder where the latest patch of skin had been excised. He feared not getting tenure; but he *dreaded* that even thinking of Beth would say *get back to work* not only to the FBI but to the tumor cells that had been sent to punish Arkey for failing to raise Frank's soul-spark, Laura's brother being the "real" corpse buried in a wooden box in Mississippi.

Arkey turned then to look gratefully at his fiancée, her long, graceful arm thrown out to the side as she slept, a gesture that seemed almost intentionally to reveal the sides of her breasts to him, and that he thought of as openhearted, confident, reassuring him that he was now far from radiation therapy, far from wooden boxes and sentient corpses, far from girls who summered at mental hospitals and friends who jumped million-dollar bail bonds. Safe.

Well, *almost*. "No new melanomas this half," the doctor had said that morning at Beth Israel. The guy had a mordant mouth, like he'd just told a joke. "Two more years," he'd said, "and we call it a cure." This time he shared the humor of it all with Kate. "Actually, 'cured' means the patient survived five years. Anything comes back after that, we call it a new case. Better for our stats that way." He turned back to the patient—him. "Anyway, melanomas like yours, we keep finding them early, you'll be fine. We'll go on checking you every six months, okay?"

"For how long?" Kate had asked. *Could she be getting tired of this business already?*

"How long? With his skin? The rest of his life."

As they'd driven home, Arkey, getting a buzz from the warm bathos of it all, had said, "After the two years, maybe we could get married."

"No," she said. "Can't wait." She'd switched the radio off. "I want to inherit." Both of them knew that Arkey had nothing worth a will, that Kate's *mot* (but don't call it that!) had been a pleasantly acidic valentine. He loved her, but his no-doubt-ambivalent heart made him start to say, "Je t'aime" before remembering Kate's inexplicable phobia about French, even a syllable of it making her lips form barely audible spells designed to keep harmful spirits away from those she loved, including, miraculously enough, *him.*

And his prayers? Arkey still draped himself in his tefillin, wound his phylacteries, but he could feel God growing distant. Would he marry a gentile? Dear God, he said, look how Kate smoothes my sexuality down to something less perverse and driven, and observe, most of all, how she lets me share in her continuous Mayflower confidence, get off the manic chosen/worthless yo-yo.

A poor argument. After all, God wouldn't value a gentile woman because she might pull Arkey away from the very Law God had graciously bestowed on him, to make him chosen. And without it, in God's eyes, he was, let's face it, worthless.

Arkey *had* deeply enjoyed the pain of the mitzvahs he'd managed. A little obsessive from one point of view, yet the endless, intricate dietary laws, the kitchen sweep for flour on Passover, the signpost between his eyes, gave a small glow to his life. He felt that the world, or he and his kitchen anyway, had been momentarily wrenched from the mundane; become less tawdry; made worthy of God's attention. *Maybe even of His protection.* Now, as he felt the warmth from his fiancée's long body, he almost heard God whisper angrily, *I can see you're already eyeing the buffet lobster!*

Kate, alone, without God, wasn't enough to soothe him when the cancer fear was on him. Arkey needed the rituals, too, the peace of the sabbath, God's regard, the chance to atone, to feel almost confident, for a moment anyway, that he'd be written once more in the Book of Life.

Well, boychick, you can't have my rituals and Kate, the Russian-accented voice—God's or Grandpa Abe's?—whispered in the middle of the night.

"But God, look at what You want me to give up!" He stroked the light hair on her arm. "*I* finally have a fiancée"—and one who knows she can sleep however she wishes, flinging herself about because the space around her *wherever* she is has (*en effet, il lui a dit—comme un homme un peu méchant*) belonged to her and her family for generations. He smiled. Even factoring in the French, Kate was *not* an *amour fou*, like his lovely sometimes slave, sometimes mistress, Gail Wagman, with her daylong crying jags; and she didn't not-so-secretly disdain him mildly the way Laura Jaffe certainly had. He *should* marry Kate. Which meant, again, that only one wrinkle remained in his comfort blanket: *if he married her, who would Arkey pray to, to keep him in this life?*

And *that* left one eye-of-the-needle path for him: *get Kate to convert.*

Fat chance of that, though, Arkey pretty sure that predestination had guaranteed there'd been no relatives of future converts on the *Mayflower*. An American aristocrat, yet what Kate particularly resisted about Judaism—more than the mikvah and the waiting period after your period—was the chosen people angle. It reminded her of the prep schools she'd attended—the ones where people like his brother-in-law, Specs, had thrown Jews into ponds. Kate, the Smith College sansculotte, hated her own people's, or *anyone's*—even God's—discriminatory ways.

So that night Arkey tried not to think at all, just stare at the speckled plaster ceiling, listen to the delightful whir of the air conditioner—still a close friend in late September. He breathed deeply from his belly, let his mind drift. Maybe his recurrent dream of Beth-in-the-box meant permission from his unconscious: he could raise her by writing about her, explaining his generation (middle-class Jewish division), get people to understand her—once, that is, he did himself. Which could be good for everyone if it pleased his conscience, or his ever more remote and probably unpleasable colleagues, meaning it would be a book less—the department chairman had leaned back in his huge desk chair, searching for the right poison—less, "gemütlich," than *Our Brilliant Careers*; which meant, they both knew, less popular in Great Neck and related venues.

"This next one," the balding chair had said, "needs to—I don't know"—he'd closed his eyes, spread out the stiff fingers of both hands and pushed them forward, a gesture borrowed from a man at a conference who'd known someone who had once studied with someone who had met Wittgenstein at Cambridge—"it needs to . . . sober up." Meaning: sixteen copies sold to libraries, boyo, maximum.

Quietly, so as not to wake his sleeping beauty, Arkey peeled off his moist white pajamas. He felt with his hands along the chipped paint on the walls, turned on the light in the narrow hall, and walked boldly, though naked, to his study.

Titles

1. *Princes and Princesses: Second-Generation Jews in America*
   (Or, *On Long Island.* Or is that too narrow?)
2. *Sentimental Education*
3. *The Promised Land: America's Jews*

Or: *America's Successful Jews?* Or: *Somewhat Successful Jews?* After all, he knew they had more money in Beverly Hills even than in Kings Point, Great Neck.

He stopped, put his pen back across the yellow pad on his new cherrywood desk. Titles, alas, had become his *specialité*. Whoops, *specialty*. In fact, aside from short, mean-spirited reviews of other historians' pathetic efforts, this making up of monikers for never-begun books was now the only writing he did. And what did it have to do with labor history, anyway, the field he'd been hired in? His books should be his noble, moral actions about the workers' noble, moral actions, while this one, the Book of Beth, could only come from a confusion of motives and describe a confusion of motives; a tangle he'd be no better at unraveling between covers than he'd been in his real and only life. He remained too fond of his friends, too understanding, to produce the truthful critique of which his conscience—i.e., the late Grandpa Abe of the ILGWU—would approve. So why should Brandeis deem it tenureworthy, or anyone read it, or God care about it, so he might be permitted to go on living?

No, he couldn't write this story. He hadn't even told Kate yet about Frank/NotFrank's letters, and when he imagined it (where? by William James's grave, or at a candlelight dinner in a dark cellar restaurant like the Peacock, maybe, you know, on the Day of the Dead), *this* variety of religious experience seemed not sublime but embarrassing, like telling her he'd been abducted by aliens and subjected to an anal probe.

He walked slowly back to bed. Maybe tomorrow he'd know what to say. To Kate. To his Talmud study group. To his class on the ILGWU. To God. Or most important of all: to his notebook.

Nope. Which left him three more years, he thought as he drove from the Brandeis library after eight hours, no pages—not even one new title.

Would he go to Talmud class tonight? He followed Trapelo Road from the campus instead of the Pike, past McLean Hospital where Former Girlfriend Gail, poet Robert Lowell, and singer-songwriter James Taylor had all done time. Past Greer's Seafood. *Lobster roll?* No, not on Talmud night, for God's sake! Arkey smiled at himself. Lobsters were disgusting-looking creatures, probably assembled by a committee—like Reform Judaism. But delicious, too. Arkey missed its tang of the forbidden. Like licking Gail. Not something Laura or Kate had liked. They both liked lobster, though.

"Why *not* eat lobster?" Specs had said. "Why shouldn't we pick and choose among the laws?" Arkey, Kate, and his brother-in-law had stood in the immense driveway, near Specs' Rolls.

Inside the house, June put the finishing touches to a Rosh Hashanah outfit she'd been working on since August. "Moses just made it all up, after all." Arkey stared toward Long Island Sound. Hot for September, a sour, briny smell of cooked seaweed and sewage came off the water. Kate, in a blue Irish linen dress, her long blond hair worn straight to her shoulders, smiled at Specs, looking like the lovely senator's wife, comfortable anywhere.

"Maybe Moses made the rigamarole up unconsciously," Specs had said that day, "but it's clear *why* he did it, Arkey. To keep the group together."

So Moses wasn't really saying, *Thou shalt love the Lord thy God,* but *Hey, it's good to have someone to watch your back.* "Is that what we are, Specs? Just another gang?"

"No, we're a people with shared history, and now we have shared values that come from that history. So we don't need the kosher laws anymore."

But Arkey did—because if God gave us the Law, then there must definitely be a God there who could save Arkey from skin cancer.

Maybe he could discuss the conversion thing with his Talmud group tonight. Two college professors, an orthodontist, a real estate speculator, an accountant, and a neurologist—traditionally when a member died the group helped form a minyan with some farm team players and buried the departed member. They would pray for him for seven days, keeping his seat open for that length of time. Just courtesy, though. *They* didn't expect he'd come back—or even that he'd move their living hands from the grave.

Would he be the first to die? He wrapped his scarf more tightly around his neck in case a tardy sun ray tried to sneak into his car. Then he had to turn up the air-conditioning.

Their group's rabbi, a thin, sad man, smiled wanly upon his stumbling students, all of whom lacked the mamaloshen for Talmud—the honorific word for the language nearly exhausting, for example, Arkey's own knowledge of Yiddish. But the rabbi had been talmudically enjoined to do the best he could with this frayed cloth.

"*Kayn az matkhil be-ezrat hashem,*" the rabbi would say tonight. (Subtitles provided by his accountant neighbor, leaning his swarthy face toward Arkey's ear: "*Yes, then we shall begin with the help of God.*") The rabbi would gesture with his hands, as if he were digging a point out of the text, a gesture borrowed from a man at a conference who had once studied with someone who had met . . . Rabbi Akiba.

"You *still* going?" Laura Jaffe had said on the phone that afternoon.

Annoyed, he'd put his legs up on the desk in his concrete office cubicle, Laura's attitude toward his group having always an undertone of professional condescension, as if Talmud study were a low-level therapy session run by an MSW. Still, he thought, she at least understood the need. Arkey had been diagnosed the year after they'd split up, two years after she'd found out *she* had multiple sclerosis; so each of them had problems that attracted celebrity spokespersons, national telethons, and attendant difficulties in telling potential loved ones. Like STD's. Their big-time diseases formed a bond between them that had outlasted love.

He'd told her that he imagined that if he just kept at it, year after year, *Seeds* followed by *Times, Women,* and *Damages, Holy Things* and *Purity,* the Talmud would cure him not of fear of death but at least of his stark, incapacitating terror.

"You still think about little Gail, and your master-slave scenarios?"

"Christ, why do you bring *that* up?"

"I thought that made you less scared, too. Like Talmud."

How had she known? Of course: SheWolf intuits men's deepest desires and hidden fears. It made him think of the one time he'd tried to introduce some kinks to their own bed, Laura a try-anything-once sort of girl. Then in medias fuck, she'd risen, the blue sheet wrapped around her, to make a cup of coffee, smoke a cigarette. "No," she said, as firmly as any mistress. "That's not me." Not a word or a tantrum. Just: *Not me.* In fact, she'd said good-bye to cigarettes and to far-less-addictive him in the same decided way.

"Silence means consent," she'd said this afternoon. "You're still thinking about her."

"Says you." Who should know, after all. He'd snuck off to see Gail a time or two when he'd been with Laura—though she'd found out, of course. A poor sneak. Everyone always found out everything about him eventually. Or soon.

"I'll bet you haven't told little Gail you're getting married."

"Well, it might upset her." Like during graduate school at U.C., when he'd dumped Gail for Laura, who was conveniently finishing medical school at Stanford. Gail took a halfhearted overdose of aspirin, then headed back to McLean for a tune-up. In fact, she was just out of McLean again when he'd run into her this time, working at the Harvard Bookstore, the little shopgirl ever so desirable in a man's white shirt and simple skirt. She'd said she was writing some stories about him and his family.

Why not? Gail had the gift to imagine others, even become them. After his diagnosis, she'd started to develop the very same superstitions as he did, managed to sweat in elevators, an intimate empathy—like a chameleon's, another gifted, strangely cold-blooded animal.

Off the anti-psychotics, she'd lost the drug-induced fat; her huge, beautiful eyes stood out plaintively, darting here and there over his face. He could see her equilibrium was delicate, and *that's* what had kept him quiet. *Wish to die.* That and a surge of jealousy, this very desirable woman wasn't his anymore, never would be again. Intolerable that men would see her here! He had wanted to stroke her breasts again, taste the delicate salt between her legs, hear her "beg" for him—theatrically, yes, as scripted, sure, but still . . .

"Upset her, Arkey? Don't you think if you tell her you're getting married, it might free her from you a little more?"

Whoops, he missed his turn. Well, he could follow Walden to Massachusetts Avenue instead. What would his study group say, he wondered, when he finally told them the Good News, something worse than eating lobster: Arkey and Katherine Morgan Chase announce their winter nuptials, even though he hadn't yet drawn her to bind herself to laws that Arkey didn't actually follow much anymore other than to study them once a week. Rabbi Goldstein was no Meltzer, but in Arkey's fantasy his clean-shaven face grew a long white beard, and his thick lips turned down as disapprovingly as his grandfather's would have if he'd told the old man he was voting Republican.

There had to be *some* wiggle room, right? Sick, you could eat on Yom Kippur. Surely he could marry Kate if he really really loved her?

Nope. Father Abraham, the group had read just a few weeks ago, sat before the gates of paradise, saying of the circumcised, "These are mine." So every cut Jew makes the cut, so to speak—even those who sin a little. But just a minute, buster. *Not* those who had traitorously married gentile women. Father Abraham was like his parents that way. But how could his God and his parents act so coldly toward this magnificent shiksa, simply because she'd had the misfortune to be born among the country's elite? "Specs is a goy, too," he'd said.

"*Was,*" his mother pointed out—hurt, perhaps, that Arkey had chosen someone so totally NotMom to marry.

His father had nodded approvingly; Specs, after all, was the one who helped him in the family business instead of wasting his time on the history of Jewish labor (i.e., Grandpa Abe), his son's career—first book to the contrary—a not-so-veiled disparagement, his father felt, of his own life. Arkey had maybe got some things right in *Our Brilliant Careers,* but—*en garde*—at any family dinner Papa Abe's ridiculous socialist ideas might suddenly spew from his own son's mouth.

So loving Kate barred him from family *and* paradise, and meant he didn't have a powerful Friend to fix his little skin problems. Even with the Toyota's air-conditioning going full blast, sweat bloomed all over his chest, turned its sparse hair into a rain forest.

At least Laura, despite ragging him about Gail, had sounded happy for him that afternoon. So wholehearted, in fact, that he'd actually felt a little hurt.

There'd been a commanding knock just after he'd told her, an entitled "Professor?"

"Just a minute," he'd said.

"What?" Laura said.

"A student." He'd stretched the phone cord out so he could reach the door with his free hand, swing it shut. "Have you heard from Beth?"

"Jesus, on the phone, Arkey!"

"I forgot."

"Anyway, it doesn't matter, because the answer's a resounding *no.*" She sounded a little teary. "I miss her, Arkey. My life's boring without her. She's my Stagolee."

"Which is what?"

"My mad, bad wildness."

"Therapy's working, huh? You see the neurotic connection?"

She had snorted. "When I used to see her, I mean before she jumped bail on us, I always just wanted her to leave before the FBI battered my door down. Now, she's gone and I want her to come back and teach me more words like, you know, *Stagolee.*"

Arkey's car made its way into Davis Square, unchanged since college, since the Civil War probably. He swerved to avoid one of the old people who wandered regularly into the streets around the square, burnt-out brain cells making them as heedless as entitled teenagers. Tonight his group at Tufts Hillel would have a rip-roaring discussion of which spots on calves made them unacceptable as burnt offerings. But he was eager to get there anyway. Their mixed excited voices reminded him of Laura's bedroom and his shrinking band of friends, the Dead Letters. There, too, he'd pretended he'd been chosen—but *that* gag hadn't had legs.

"Have you heard from Jeffrey?" Laura had asked that afternoon. "I leave messages but no one answers."

"He's probably gone off with a new boyfriend."

"He hasn't told me anything."

"It's a boy, I guarantee it. It'll be over soon, and he'll call you. You're still his one and only."

"No, I'm just his friend. Beth's the one he adores."

"Or wants to be."

"If, I don't know, you hear anything or anything, call me."

"Sure." He'd known he was being dismissed. Just as well. The student outside had been pacing, preparing arguments for why her six pages equaled ten, his generous C+ for effort actually should be an A for brilliantly figuring out that Marx was German, and a self-hating Jew, to boot.

His car passed the long Tufts football field, a thick darkness settling slowly.

He pulled into a space near one of the frats, Donna Summer still insisting she was a bad girl from the huge black speakers on its lawn. He locked his car and walked up the road toward the brick Hillel building.

"And Arkey?" Laura had said, just before she hung up that afternoon. "I mean it. Congratulations. You're doing the right thing. Katherine sounds like a swell broad."

Arkey smiled at the thirties-comedy air of that, saw a top-hatted, long-legged chorus, all of them looking like Laura—with Kate in front, the new frail. It seemed a fine way to think of his romance, his marriage. A swell broad. And he took from it, too, that Laura *had* maybe been satisfyingly bowled over by the news, maybe even, perhaps, felt one teeny-weeny twinge of regret.

Laura hadn't meant those congratulations, or anyway not in the big-smile Gidget way she would have *liked* to mean them—though that was *not,* she told her unseen audience, because *she* wanted Arkey Kaplan for herself. No, she just wanted *someone* for herself, didn't want to be for-ever alone, walking nightly through Washington Square, tapping the ground with her cane, on the way to Yet Another Disappointing Blind Date. *Tap tap tap,* each of us blind, she thought, in our own way, not because we don't see anything, but because we see our dreams every-where.

Like tonight's date—Prince Charming? Husband material? Arkey and Kate were as dream-blinded as she was, she'd just bet. Couldn't Kate see the groom was still all knotted up with little Gail, the ties as variegated as the hues of a carny barker's rainbow ("I have to see her because I feel so guilty toward her . . . she might go mad without me . . . no one else cares about me the way she does"). Gail, it galled Laura to admit, had It. Boys had always followed her around, tongues dropping down like Wolfie's in a Tex Avery cartoon. Once, just after the abortion, Jeffrey had said to her, "Around her, men melt inwardly and get hard at the same time."

Didn't do much for her self-esteem. She squeezed her small face into an old lady apple. "You *saw* all that?"

"I felt it myself, believe it or not." *So there.*

"Thanks a lot," Laura said.

So probably the marriage would never happen. And if it did? Well, good luck to him—and to Kate, especially. Poor little WASP, she'd need it. (Now was *that* the kind of thing Gidget would say?) Someday soon—after Kate had spent endless hours listening to Arkey yatter about poor Gail's suffering—she'd get a letter like the one Laura received from McLean. *"Dearest Laura, when you came to Boston for your interview at Mass General Hospital, you may not know that Arkey visited me in this shithole called a mental hospital. But don't be angry with him, please. Can you imagine the first shaft of light that comes into a prisoner's dungeon? That was how it felt to me.*" Gail had been right. She hadn't known about the visit. Or that Arthur Kaplan was *ever* a shaft of sunlight. "*I wonder if you could ever see Arkey as I do, Laura, with love instead of disdain?*" Had he actually told Gail that she was disdainful? Well, she was *now,* goddamn it! Sneaky bastard! "*His beautiful downturned lips . . . the little knots he makes of his hair to keep off evil spirits . . . the Baryshnikov way he moves.*" My God, the woman was *truly* loony! Arthur Kaplan could hardly walk through a room without knocking a lamp over!

After five years on the Smerless couch, Laura knew she'd always been just as blind as Kate was now—and not just about Arkey. Think of all the other fantasies with which she'd peopled this very park, starting at age fourteen when this had seemed the place where non-Disney wishes came true, the magical forest called Not the Suburbs, or Utterly Elsewhere. Then, alas, those little notes from Mississippi had arrived; Billy had looked up from the floor of her room saying quietly, "He's dead," and had told *how* her brother had died, where his body lay alive/not alive under mounds of earth, and that they had to make justice to ease his pain. Billy's voice had turned Great Neck into Caligari-land; out of kilter; eaten by shadows; home, Toto, but not home anymore. *Elsewhere,* uncomfortably enough, might be anywhere.

But Greenwich Village had fortunately mutated into another kind of *not here* for her—a place for adventures that didn't have *anything* to do with making justice, that were adventures because they *weren't*—thank God—holy obligations.

Two gay men passed, hair cut short. Clones, Jeffrey had called them, on the day he became one. A handsome black kid tilted slightly on his skateboard, snaking toward her. She hugged her purse to her chest. He flashed her a smile as he went by, meaning either *you got me this time* or *you racist sow,* she would never know which. A couple of emaciated white kids, earlobes bearing whole gaggles of safety pins, stared at her cane, reading her out of the Land of the Dead, which for them was, *of course,* the Land of the Living. *Good's bad today, black's white today, wrong's right today, I suppose.* And if they knew SheWolf walked among them now? Were BillyBooks savage enough for their tastes? Or what they imagined their tastes *should* be?

When she had first come here, before the letters, the square had been folksingers with ironing-board hair, surrounded by kids in blue jeans and work shirts; her and Beth bobbing, too, in costumes meant to signal purity. Now the kids wore the black of punk nihilism. Had these suburban kids with the lacerated earlobes really decided they were (Johnny) rotten trash, or was their tender, wounded flesh meant to make the Absent God (or parents) weep? Or was it all, more likely, just a charade, with style tips provided not by Satan but by *Life* magazine, roles to be discarded next year for jobs at the mall, or a return to college?

Which was a version of *her* past, she knew, she knew, she knew, all of it equally imaginary—their damnation, or the purity of her in fall 1964. Beth came home weekends from college and they'd take the LIRR train here, Beth impelled, she saw now, an analysand herself, by her endless fury at her father's abandonment and by sadness about Frank. Laura had fled Jesse, she supposed, and all he needed, all she wanted to give him—which was too much. Dear Jesse, his response to losing her had been to become *concerned* for her safety in New York.

And how very unsafe, how *wild* she and Beth had thought themselves on those trips—Laura scorning Jesse's protectiveness because she secretly so very much wanted him (and her father, and her mother's analyst) to care, certain she was hurtling toward sweet perdition. . . . Or romance? She and . . . Jack . . . would meet at a bar . . . no, wait, she was too young for a bar . . . at a coffeehouse. He'd be hairy, bitter, wild—but she took his dare, showed she could be just as wild as ever he was. Jack the Bear would be drawn to her by her sexual openness; she could be even more imaginative in bed than he was! (But *what* tricks she'd imagine for him—for them both!—she couldn't, even now, imagine.) Still, he was led by that sweet, sinful fire in her, led, paradoxically, to a deep, abiding love. And he soon felt that what he really desired most in the world was the healing balm of her sweetness, usual boilerplate goes here, he wanted to care for her, marriage, children, and a book-lined study where she was finally able to write her own poetry. Sometimes, if Beth didn't jabber too much, she'd dream that fairy tale all the way past Flushing Main Street and on to Penn Station, never imagining the sex much, always the particular grain of the bookshelves she and Jack would have later, the little secret garden in back of their mews apartment.

And fortunately she'd never told Beth even one gooey drop of it. Instead, on the train rides to the city, they'd talk about the orgasms they would have—maybe that very night, if they saw swains they deigned to choose. Would they be the real kind this time, the mature womanly, vaginal kind—the Big O!—or just the immature clitoral ones that Laura was pretty sure was all she'd ever had so far? But how would it actually *feel* different? (Yes, of course they'd wanted the old men in the other seats to hear them, to look around.) And she remembered they'd yattered about *The Dutchman,* too, and the genius of LeRoi Jones, and how perfectly understandable black rage was. (Did they say "black," then? Or "Negro"? Which maybe, she thought, smiling at herself, was just the kind of confusion that made them colored folks so damn angry.) And wasn't Gauloises absolutely the best cigarette, the one with the deepest, most sophisticated flavor? Sometimes they'd pretend they were so absolutely desperate for *les magicaux merde-fingers français* that they had to ride between the cars and let the wind blow the smoke back through their long, straight hair. Strangely, she didn't remember their talking much about her brother those evenings—though he was surely always there for Laura, because what she'd sought in her mostly dream lovers wasn't just freedom from Jesse, but someone who would Touch Her Profoundly, returning her nerve endings to the present moment—so she wouldn't be anymore helplessly buried in her imagination with Frank's dead-yet-not-dead flesh.

This evening she walked past the spot that used to be the Cafe Au Go-Go. God, even that name was an embarrassment now! The Blues Project with Danny Kalb! Those had been days when Beth would still sometimes go to hear a white band. They'd been pretty good, too. What had happened to them? Between sets, a stocky black guy with a corny goatee had knelt by their table, and while they sipped horrendously expensive iced mochas he'd crooned to them about his uncut cock.

"Have you ever had one of those?"

Laura pieced it together like a rebus: knife with an x over it (i.e., *uncircumcised*); mentioned because Big Nose (i.e., her) + Dark-Complexion (i.e., Beth) = Star of David (i.e., Jewish); the combo of profanity and stereotyping making her feel flushed, dizzy, disgusted.

Beth, as always, thought fast. "Too sensitive," she said. "The damn things squirt too quickly." Then Beth turned and smiled at her, as if to say, *like is that true?*

Laura had shrugged. Big talk aside, she'd only ever had one dick—Jesse's—which was, she was pretty sure, circumcised.

The man stared at Beth, who gave him her frozen face back, which Laura could see made him want to hit her. He said not to worry about *him,* he always snorted a little H before he balled a choice chick. Then he could keep it up all night long.

"Was ever woman in this humor wooed," Beth said, smiling meanly.

He ignored that, said they could use a room at the Chelsea, "which is where Bob Dylan stayed," a name, Laura knew, that had approximately no magic for Beth, who already shuttled between Wagner's leitmotifs and Bobby Blue Bland's melisma, ignoring the white pop stations in between.

Laura had imagined the guy—well-muscled, handsome, but heavy, maybe two hundred pounds—banging away at her all night long with that ridiculous goatee and his permanently stiff, never-too-excited cock. Oh, joy.

She put her hand on Beth's arm. "We gotta go meet . . . my brother." She meant, Back off, Ever-Hard boy, there's a guy in the picture and we're under his protection. Which, in a way, she thought, they were. They left arm in arm, giggling, the men always less important to either of them than the stories they could tell each other about the men.

And tonight's man? Thank God Beth didn't know *this* story! The meet was set for a bar on Eighth Street. She headed out of the park, strolling slowly, the wolf's pricked-up ears digging pleasantly into the flesh of her palm, reminding her that she wasn't crippled; reminding her, too, that *that* song ended: *not yet you're not.* The wolf head on the cane was the graven image of SheWolf—*herself,* kind of, transformed in the teary ocean of Billy's imagination. A love child who has been raised from the dead by a mad young Irish scientist, she is one day transformed by her anger against Zargon into a Venus en fur de lykos, able to run blindingly fast, until a disease—or was it a magical curse?—fucks up her legs. You could have read about that *in advance of Laura's actual problems* in a story called "SheWolf's Dilemma" (Issue #26, and very hard to find, Wolf Pack members!), where Something makes the amazingly strong muscles of SheWolf's legs twitch and fail just as she is about to capture . . . who was it? Dr. Death maybe? Or Voltage?

Naturally, the comic book problem is that her nervous system gets taken over by dreams. Fortunately, with help from little Dr. Why?, the magus who educated all the Outsiders to control their gifts, she analyzes her dreams—and finds out they're not even her own! With long training at the Scarsdale Center, SheWolf learns how to become conscious of the fantasies of others that make her legs move, can take control of them again, while projecting the fantasies of others outward—as holograms that show evildoers their perverse cravings and repressed terrors, so they flee; or run forward—toward her claws. A psychoanalyst of sorts? Laura had had Billy's drawing cast into silver by a gifted Swarthmore graduate who hadn't wanted to go into his family's used-car business. A shop just at the edge of the rotting tide of the East Village, which had been, for a while, Laura's new improved Elsewhere. And now? The last time she'd passed it, on the way to the clinic, he'd been washed out to sea or back into the family business, his space boarded up.

Where are they now? Danny Kalb, the silversmith, all displacements of the real missing-person question: *where was Jeffrey?* Two weeks now since she'd heard his breathy, slightly British tones in her phone. The longest AWOL before had been three days when he and a true love had gone to the Hamptons to play out what he had called later "the abridged version of *Gone With the Wind.*" Jeffrey did hang out sometimes with the kind of rough trade it made her shiver only semi-pleasurably under the blankets to hear about, phone pressed to her ear, Jeffrey whispering to her with mock horror about his colleague Gaston Weil, who rang up pay phones and propositioned whoever answered.

"Whatever *man* answers," Laura had said.

"Right. He's not an equal opportunity employer. Are you, sweetheart?"

Laura giggled. "Mais non!"

Jeffrey laughed, the tones etched with meanness. "Well, maybe you just haven't met your Gastona Weil yet, darling. Anyway, once he gets them to his loft, he leads them into more and more intense sessions"—he drew in a breath—"with Gaston as the Top."

"He's the Eiffel Tower," Laura hummed.

"He's the purple light of a summer night in Spain."

"He's cellophane!" Laura concluded.

"Is this exciting you?"

Unsure, she giggled. "It seems," she said, "I don't know, like very hot, but lonely at the same time," the link between the torturer and the tormented even more tenuous, she thought, than the marriage vows.

And her life? How hot was that? Her leg ached where the working muscles did overtime for their slacker sisters. She perched herself on a fraying green bench, her psyche, like her body, kerflooey nowadays, depressed and anxious at the same time—stagflated like the economy—scared to get to her blind date and its inevitable disappointment.

Especially now that Arkey—perhaps free of the It Girl and her Weil-like games—had found his dream lover. Laura and Arkey had never been each other's fantasies. They should have divided their books up after the first six months together. But she had applications to do, tests to take. They'd hung on for three years, Laura taking the internship at Physicians and Surgeons to be in the big city, but also to keep Arkey away from Gail—though by then Laura had barely wanted him for herself. Then, the summer of '76, the MS had given her double vision, and had nicely focused her mind, multiple sclerosis making her wonder hard how much life she might have left in her, and did she want to spend it with someone she, well, only *liked*—and *that* only some of the time. And then the pregnancy! An Arklet that could leave her crippled!

She had to admit it, though, the forthcoming Kaplan-Chase bliss *had* sharply underlined the "Will You Ever Be Generative?" chapter in *What Are You Doing with Your Life, Laura Jaffe?* Should she have had Arkey's baby? At least she'd have someone to keep her company! But the stress of pregnancy might have weakened her Maginot Line against the virus. She'd have to ride around in one of those ugly-looking motor-powered carts that she'd only glimpsed in her neurologist's office because she shut her eyes quickly when one whizzed by, as if seeing them might make her unconscious add a chrome tricycle like that to her Christmas list.

But she could have raised Beth's child. When Beth had surfaced in '78, she'd stayed with Laura until Jesse thought he had a deal in place. Then, when the government had its arms around Beth, it decided oh, no, the woman was the spider at the center of a worldwide terror network. It delayed the bail hearing. And in jail Beth had admitted she was pregnant. *That* child would have been two now—supposing Beth wasn't carrying a fantasy fetus fathered by panic.

Or a scam to make sure her friends didn't leave the Madonna to rot in the Tombs, where Laura and Beth sat a few times with a wide table between them and a matron peeking in every few minutes through the smudged glass panel to make sure they weren't necking. Or passing weapons. "It will be your child, too, in a way," Beth had said. "You convinced me to have it."

She meant, amazingly enough, the cockamamie lecture Laura had given her in her studio apartment near Mt. Sinai. She'd been two years with Smerless by then, and had tried to be Ultra-Orthodox Freudian. For a woman to be happy, Laura had told Beth, she must become fully generative. Yes, she must have orgasms and a career, but also, if she could, a child. Thank God, she'd left out the part about the child being the next best thing to the longed-for penis! She remembered that Beth had lifted an earth-toned mug, held the warmth to her cheek, inhaled the vapors from her cup. She had blue contact lenses and blond hair, but she still took comfort from the smell of peppermint tea.

That day Laura hadn't mentioned the real Topic A: her own pregnancy. But as she talked to Beth she realized how much she truly (and not for Smerless) wanted a child—and that she couldn't have one, the strain of pregnancy maybe meaning she might never again be able to draw on her eyeliner, control her bladder, or speak without slurring. If she took *that* risk, it wouldn't be with Arkey Kaplan as the father! All of which probably put a stronger pleading in her voice when she spoke with Beth about childbearing. She had wanted Beth to be pregnant *for* her.

And Beth, she'd suspected a year later in the Tombs, had maybe been lying, too. Laura's Freudian blarney hadn't convinced her. She just wanted Laura to feel implicated, related to the baby.

So Laura had kept Beth's pregnancy *her* secret—a last stop to pull out to make Jeffrey come up with the bail money; a secret that made her link with Beth—and, even more, her link with her child (if there was one)—extra-special.

And the father? Beth said Snake was staying underground no matter what, thought she'd betrayed the world's people by surfacing. He wouldn't want to raise a child.

And Laura? Oh, yes, she had decided that day in the Tombs, if some turn in History's endless irony were to put Beth in jail, then Laura would love to raise the sweet product of mutual incomprehension and fantasy. But what if the baby were colicky, keeping her up all night, making her anxious with its angry, indecipherable crying, rubbing the myelin off her nerves?

Yes, God, *even if,* Laura had promised.

Laura had been furious when Beth jumped bail. Laura would probably never get to see her dream niece now, certainly wouldn't get, she told Jeffrey, actually to take the child to the Metropolitan Museum and Rumplemayer's, the way she would have if Beth had been put in jail for . . .

"It was just a bail hearing, you know," Jeffrey said, "before trial. You're dreaming about actually raising the child—you know, like Beth hadn't jumped bail, then had been, how shall I say this? *Convicted.* Sent up for life." Jeffrey gave her a knowing but not precisely Smerless-quality smile, his being too much tinged with open mockery. "Not that you actually would have *wanted* that, of course."

Tonight, she took an extra turn down Eighth Street, to avoid getting to her rendezvous with the very man who'd tried to put Beth in jail. Well, maybe she could make him more sympathetic to Beth, or, like Mata Hari, find out something useful for her. So dating him was good, then? And it might have been mean of her even for a moment to have wished her friend sent to jail, *but* good that she would want to raise her child—those sorts of tangles part of the problem about the doing-justice racket, or so jesting Pilate and Hans the Fizzyits had both said, the good and the bad often getting too intertwined for Laura to separate. Maybe Arkey went to Talmud study group so he could parse those things properly.

Tonight, she passed a boy who seemed to spin on his knee in precise, articulated segments, while a boom box spit out rhythm for him. His eyes flashed by, catching the light from the shoe store behind her, giving his face the brightness of a shooting star, like Jacob Battle's eyes, she thought, the few times she'd seen him after the burial. Where was *he* now? She remembered him best, age eleven, clutched in Sugar Cane's arms at the funeral. It had seemed *just* to help him go to Arkey's school, the place where his own brother had taught, where Bobby Brown had gone, if it comes to that. She put a dollar in the break-dancer's hat.

Her family, really, had put some extra dollars in his hat, too, paying for most of what they wanted him to think was a scholarship. But the school had been mostly gravel and stone to him.

Or so Arkey had told her, fall weekends in 1964 when Beth couldn't come back from college to play with her. Laura and Arkey would sit cross-legged together in his backyard, a radio playing, drunken teens stumbling around them, and Arkey trying to win her with all the beer he could drink, and all the justice he'd supposedly done for Jacob Battle at the John Dewey School.

"The kid *has* to be lonely," Arkey had said, "like he's one of only two black people in the whole school," the other one being Bobby Brown, a boy with the same last name as Laura's maid.

"A lot of Negroes have the same last name," Laura said. Her brother had taught her that American slaves had been given the last names of their owners.

"This Bobby Brown is on a football scholarship. He used to go here, to GN North."

Could he be related to Ruth? But Ruth must have heard at the dinner table that her family would be paying for Jacob Battle's tuition, so she'd have told them if she had a relative attending the Dewey School.

"Anyway, Jacob Battle, he carries this dirty manila file folder around everywhere he goes, I mean even to lunch. I guess after a while the other kids got curious. I mean, you know, they wanted to know what it was all about, so one of them, this bushy-browed kid, Adam something, like, just grabbed it out of his hand."

Arkey tilted another brown bottle backward proudly, and didn't take it away from his lips until he could turn it over on the lawn, white foam dribbling out, for after all, what girl wouldn't be impressed by that?

"I thought the kid had gone crazy, you know, the way he threw himself at this much bigger kid."

The way Arkey told the story—with such becoming modesty—Laura could tell she wasn't meant to realize that the enemy force was five years younger, a prepubescent Country Day student in a size twelve blazer and Rooster tie. So she said, "What was he, Arkey? I mean, like a seventh grader?" She smiled.

"Yeah. *First Form*," he said, putting her in her public school place. "But I mean, you know, the kid himself, Jacob, I mean, *he* was the danger."

"He bites, huh?"

"No, I mean, I don't know *what* he would have done. But he was really furious. He might have done something crazy, gotten himself thrown out of school."

In fact, Arkey had barely been able to hold the flailing boy, who wanted something more forcefully at that moment, Arkey had felt—the folder back, or to kill the kid who'd taken it—than Arkey had maybe ever wanted anything in *his* life.

"I do not need your help," Jacob had said, staring at him.

"No, I can see that. Y'a wudda mu'dhed the basta'd," using a pitiful mock-Brooklyn accent, to reassure himself—because he dreamt that maybe Jacob actually *would* have murdered him. And the coldness of Jacob's stare then had chilled Arkey's muscles, like now Jacob wanted to kill *him,* too—special penalty for bad Brooklyn accents. He let him go.

Meanwhile, the bushy-browed kid had just stood there gawping, terrified of Jacob's rage, or maybe of the Fifth Form boy. He'd held the folder out to Arkey, and then ran away. Arkey had handed it to Jacob, who'd very precisely tucked it under his arm.

Amazingly, Jacob had wheezed, "Thank you," and clawed at his pants pocket, fishing out a white plastic gizmo.

One of the letters had fallen to the floor, and Arkey had bent over, thinking that while Jacob sucked on his inhaler, he might get to read a little of what this boy thought so precious. But he'd seen Jacob staring down at him, furious still, so he didn't even try.

Jacob had seen Arkey's blue eyes flick toward the paper, then away, but making that part real broad, like Jackie Gleason saying, *See, Alice, I'm not looking.* Fear of the wild black boy? Well, *good.* If Arkey *had* looked, Jacob swore he *would* have killed him, just like he would have destroyed that other moron if Kaplan hadn't held him back.

Jacob's shoulders sagged then. He knew better. When Arkey had had him wrapped up in his arms, the pain had grabbed his lungs from within, squeezing, too, until he could barely stand. So what exactly would he have done if he'd gotten free? Terrified the kid with the way he could make his chest sound like a wrecked engine? He knew Kaplan had rescued him—and *that* had made him furious with Arkey, and furious at himself for being so small, so weak still whenever he got excited, the asthma making him feel like *they'd* made him beg for air in a place where he'd sworn he would never ask for anything. And Arkey's touch had made him feel like an even littler boy, the one who'd spun round and round, shouting, "I'm dancing," when his mother played "One O'Clock Jump" on the record player until he suddenly couldn't breathe, and his mother, terrified by what she'd done, had held him in her arms and carried him to bed.

He rushed out of the cafeteria, across the courtyard, away from her imagined sorrowful eyes. He walked slowly up the stairs, and still he had to stop on a landing to suck on his inhaler again, the other kids moving past him, not even noticing. *Inconsiderable,* that's what he was here, *beneath notice*—or a black eyesore that everyone just looked away from, an embarrassment, a mistake. Like, *who let* him *in?* He started to sweat, and the suit cloth felt way too heavy.

His mom had bought him the suit for the Democratic convention. The blue wool pants had been much too hot for Atlantic City, too, his legs itching as soon as he put them on. But "Nice threads," Sugar had said like he meant it. He'd put his big arm around Jacob's shoulder, and they'd walked into the committee room together, the bright lights on poles for the TV cameras making it even hotter than outside.

"What do you think of *my* bar mitzvah suit?" Sugar asked him, smiling, opening his arms to show it off. Jacob knew that meant a Jewish thing, but not what. "Great, man. You look great." He smiled back, not so much to fool Sugar into thinking he knew something when he didn't, but because he liked the way Sugar talked to him, like he was an adult, in on the joke, even when, like now in this long, low-ceilinged room, he could already feel that the joke would probably be on them.

His mom had sat near the back. But he and Sugar took folding seats in the front row. The six men behind the table didn't look at them. The big television cameras turned toward them, though, then back to Fannie Mae. She rolled up her sleeve to show huge, raised bruises, a tattoo from the Klan. A fat man with a blank, impassive face swiveled a big light on a stick toward her arms, making the bruises shine a sickly blue, like a shimmer on oil. The lights made Jacob sweat, too, but the men behind the table didn't fidget or scratch. "They gotta be burning up," Jacob said.

"That skin, man, it's tougher," Sugar whispered, smiling. "Like rhino hide."

Kidding probably. The gray-haired man banged his gavel, and soon as it started the session was over for the day, lights out, cameras off, Fannie Mae's bruises blending with her dark skin then, almost invisible. Sugar looked furious, so Jacob knew that whatever had happened had been bad. Reporters rushed toward them, but Sugar stepped in front of him, then swiveled, nearly picking him up as he turned him around and pushed him away and out of there, back through the lobby, and all the way to a raised sidewalk made of wood that ran along the hotels and past the shore. Old women in wicker chairs had floated by on soft wheels pushed by white men on bicycles. The way the men pushed from behind, the pedals making them scrunch over, it made ferrying the fat women around look like a demeaning thing to do, like cleaning toilets. Jacob had turned back toward the convention hall, wanting to shout at the reporters. Sugar'd put one hand on his shoulder, near his neck now, like he was gentling a horse, patting him. Jacob stopped. No one, he knew, would hear him if he shouted. He was too small; Sugar and Fannie Mae were too small; his brother's death was too small. Maimed, wounded things, they'd been weighed up and found wanting. *Inconsiderable,* Sugar had said. He and Susan Lems argued with some old man in a black suit and a string bow tie.

"They're offering us a compromise," the minister had said.

"No," Susan had said, "they're offering us one half of one percent of nothin'."

"Plus all the shit we can eat on national television!"

"Children, I'm thinking I'll go back in. You have got to let time do its work. They'll give us what they promised."

"Black folks," Sugar had said, "are always holding our hats in our hands, saying 'See how we suffer, sir. Look at all the sacrifices we made.' Then the liberals say, 'Just wait here boy' and go into their smoke-filled clubs and sell us out every time. We have to get our own power," Sugar had said. "Our own votes."

But by then he was saying it to the old man's back.

Then the first week of school, he hadn't heard from Sugar anymore, even though Sugar had promised he'd write or call every day until Jacob got settled in, and that promise was what he had to keep him going, thinking *this* had been Sugar's idea, he'd sent him here, a mission behind enemy lines. But now it turned out he didn't matter to Sugar either. Inconsiderable. So by Friday of that first week, Jacob decided Sugar was *like that,* sweet like his name, but not a man of his word like Jacob's own brother.

Then, Thursday evening, two weeks later, when he'd given up hope, he'd gotten the first letter. Sugar's big news had been that Harry Belafonte, the guy who did those corny banana songs his mama liked, was going to send Sugar and Fannie, Chuck Taylor, David, and Susan Lems to tour Africa, 'cause, Sugar had said, they were all burned up in Mississippi, in fact by the time he read this, they were gone, they were *there.* It terrified Jacob to have Sugar so far away, in a place his mother said was filled with dangerous animals and incredible diseases. He lay in bed at night worrying what he'd do if something happened to Sugar; then the next day, in first period English, he'd been so damned tired he kept splitting infinitives, seeming like a fool, disappointing Mr. Hartman, who was maybe the only one in that school who expected better from him.

Finally, a week after that, a letter arrived—and then one came every day or two. But he still felt sick to his stomach on the days between, even though he knew he couldn't *actually* get a letter every minute, or a letter saying a letter was coming, and anyway, then he'd need another letter saying that a letter was coming soon to say that a letter was coming soon, 'cause he needed it to be like there was never a time when he wasn't receiving a letter from Sugar, a tortoise-and-hare thing. He laughed at himself, but his stomach still felt tight, and he needed to leave a light on at night again, the way he had after Joshua died, so he wouldn't see his brother's smashed-up face staring up at him out of that box, the bone of his forehead tilting off to the side, crushed by tons of earth.

Now he had exactly one dozen letters from Sugar Cane. He stuffed his inhaler back in his breast pocket and pulled one of them a little way out of the folder, letting it poke over the edge, just so he'd know it was there. Prepared, he entered his geometry class. The tall, big-nosed teacher with the funny German name had his back to them, drawing a diagram on the board, an easy one. The teacher had a tracery of broken blood vessels on his schnozz, like a juicehead—which was also maybe something the other kids didn't know. Before he finished drawing the diagram, Jacob had it solved, the square of—what had that bushy moron said yesterday? "The square of the hippopotamus." The whole class laughed, and the dope smiled, trying to be cool, pretend like he'd meant it.

Do you remember when Fannie Mae was speaking to the Rules Committee, and everyone on the committee wept? Suddenly all the newsmen began to jabber, and the bright TV lights went out. That was because President Johnson had decided he just had to address the nation about soybean policy! Really, he didn't want the country to hear what Fanny had gone through to get justice from his convention.

Well, the President of the United States wouldn't let Fannie talk on television, and he wouldn't meet with Fannie Mae any more than he would sit down to dinner with the family maid. But the President of Guinea asked to have dinner with her! He knows who she is, and honors her.

The other students bent over their notebooks, calculating. Jacob stared right at the teacher, daring him to think that he wasn't paying attention and call on him, when really he'd already done the numbers in his head. But Hansel wasn't dazey like most juicers. He remembered Jacob had fooled him before. He knew he knew.

So Jacob looked at the other students—tiny businessman dolls in blue or gray blazers. If he hadn't had Sugar's letters he couldn't have put on his jacket and tie every morning—which was still an ordeal for him, his fingers fumbling with the cloth not because it was hard to do, but because he didn't want to go where he had to wear this thing.

"It *is* hard," his mother had said, standing behind him the first few mornings, guiding his hands over and under, while he watched in the mirror. "Your father had the same problem. Couldn't get the lengths right." A lie, he knew. His father had worn a suit and tie every working day. He'd gone to the same Transit Union office as his mom. But it was nice to hear her saying something about his dad, like his death hadn't just been wiped off the boards by his brother's.

Now he could see the bushy-browed kid, Adam, stumbling with *this* over and under, looking like he was about to cry. Sugar had said that they had to speak to the whites castle to castle—which made Jacob think of hamburger stands. "The Jews at the John Dewey School already know *that*, know not to trust gentiles. So they got a country of their own, with its own army." Actually, Jacob doubted it. He wanted to tell Sugar that these kids didn't know shit. Meanwhile, in the back row he saw Adam slyly working a Life Saver out of the package with his stubby fingers, like he thought he was invisible. These kids aren't Israeli commandos, Sugar. They're New York hymies. No big deal. Jacob was smaller than most of them, but he was a lot older, really, and more grown up even than Arthur Kaplan, the boy who thought he'd played bwana in the cafeteria. Kaplan was the kind of jerk who became a big deal here, worked on the newspaper where these kids published their prattle about politics—but he'd bet Arkey Kaplan didn't know as much as Jacob did about the nitty-gritty of the world, like the kinds of deals liberals made. "You're growing wise in ways of the serpent," his mother had said almost fearfully when he told her some things from Sugar's letters—which meant, Jacob thought, the ways of his fellow students in their blue blazers and tweed jackets. But how, he wondered, did these *inconsiderable* little kids become serpents? Was this somehow their school for that, too?

Maybe during lunch periods he should read through all of Sugar's letters instead of eating, and that would *make* a new letter come. He should do that every day, read them all over again from the beginning, get the strength to go on here the way his brother and Sugar had gone on in Mississippi. He felt like when he read the letters he could hear Sugar's high voice in his head, he could feel his arms wrapping him 'round, even smell him. He wanted everyone to know about the way Sugar talked to him, wanted them to know the deep things he'd told him. Maybe, he thought, he could tell Bobby Brown—but he was a senior, the star of the football team, always rushing past him somewhere, like he didn't want to see him. Or maybe he could tell Mr. Hartman. No, *that* was a stupid idea. Hartman was a teacher; Jacob couldn't talk to him about anything but grammar or Shakespeare. Anyway, they'd maybe none of them see how important the letters were. So maybe it was best if *no one* knew about them anymore, he thought, especially his mother.

"What's he writing you all the time?" she'd said the night before, as she handed him that day's letter. "You boys making secret plans?"

"You know. It's the usual big-brother stuff."

"He's not your brother."

He *knew* that, was ashamed for having said it. "He's telling me I got to study hard."

"Let me read them, then."

"It's, look, it's to me." He scrunched his face like he was going to cry. "They're my letters."

She thought for a minute, probably studying his face, to see if the tears were real; then she smiled fondly, said, "Okay," and let it go.

He ran down the hill as soon as the bell sounded, almost alone. Most of the kids stayed after school, like they couldn't get enough of the place, playing tennis, or begging to work on *The Dewey Debate,* or *The*

Dewey Record, or *The Dew Drop,* which was the faggoty name of their literary magazine, the school spilled more ink than a small city. They were all extra-credit scams for the colleges. He'd heard a couple of kids talking about the *Dew Drop* editor and Yale as he walked across the big football field to gym class.

They'd looked over at him.

"You don't have to worry about college," a pimply-faced kid had said, probably thinking that Jacob would never go to college, he wasn't even there like Bobby Brown, who would maybe beat someone out for Harvard because he knew the great nigger get-ahead trick: *running fast.*

Today a few other boys ran onto the train before the doors shut, grabbing at each other's Mars Bars. That meant he couldn't read the letters here. The subway was almost all white people eyeing him suspiciously for a few stops, like they knew what he thought about: namely, the long-legged woman who sat opposite, Jacob hoping that she would maybe just put her legs apart a little. It was amazing: while he was *in* the school he didn't think about girls much, which was probably good; he could concentrate on his work. He knew they all thought he came to their school to be with a better class of people—a better *species* was probably what they really thought. *They* had the money, *they* had the teachers, they had a whole green football field that belonged just to them. Not that they knew what to do with it. But he was there for one reason only: to study. To get an education so he could better serve *his* people.

Not that his people would mostly speak to him anymore. He'd stood one whole evening right at the edge of the court on 126th, watching his friends play, loving the sound of their complicated curses, home again, watching Baby trying to dunk, getting his fat ass maybe halfway up before the ball just rolled from his fingertips and plopped on the ground with a *sorry chump* sound. Weary, the kid from the projects with sleepy eyes, looked over at Jacob and laughed. But no one said a word to him, and the sound of their voices shouting to each other became a wall. He wished he'd brought Sugar's letters to read, decided he'd take them everywhere from then on.

He got off at 125th Street, and he could see the few other kids from Dewey thought poor Jacob was getting off in the jungle, and if he showed up in school the next day, that could only be 'cause these animals at least didn't eat their own young. He rushed down the steps from the platform, nearly falling. He *had* to get home before his mother, make sure that he snatched Sugar's letter before she did.

And there it was! Through the grillwork he saw a blue edge among the white and brown envelopes. Some bastard had already bent the lock to their mailbox, then maybe'd heard someone coming and run away. Jacob pried the chipped silver door open the rest of the way, hoping she'd think the junkie had come back and finished the job. He fished out the aero-letter, where the envelope was also the thing you wrote on and then folded up to make the envelope, so you had to be really careful not to tear it when you unfolded it or you lost some of the words.

He heard the super coming from the basement, and ran up the stairs to his bedroom. He took his tie off carefully, not disturbing the knot, so he could just slip it over his head tomorrow, then sat down on his bed to undo the letter.

The President of Guinea is Sekou Touré, and when he led his country to independence, the French made all their technical people go back home, thinking they'd starve Guinea to its knees. But Sekou Toure made an alliance with the Communists—and then the Western countries were the ones crawling back to him, begging to give him things!

If our African cultures can maintain themselves, can even throw off the vultures, then aren't our cultures as strong and valuable as any on earth?

Jacob had to point his lamp right at the page. Sugar wrote in the teeniest handwriting he'd ever seen, maybe because it cost so much to send even one page from Africa.

Africa, with all its flaws, makes me know that we were formed by, respond to, the demands of a valuable and different world. They thought they had stripped us of everything that makes us human in the Middle Passage, but despite all that was maimed and is now half-remembered, I can see we did smuggle our memory of Mother Africa to America in our music, our way of storytelling, the rhythm of our drums—as complex as the harmonies of Europe—and in the song that is our slang. Maybe in our religion, too. My friend Chuck Taylor used to be a Jew, like so many of your schoolmates. But he tells me that what he had always hungered for was the gods of Africa.

The whites won't hear us, Jacob, can't see us, not because we're inconsiderable, but because we scare them, our lives are too strong, too beautiful, too ecstatic for their ears, the colors of our clothes too bright for their blue eyes. And when we dance together, the community we make shakes the foundations of their banks, their offices, their governments.

At your brother's funeral I said, "We can rule over you." But in my heart I wondered if we really could. Now I see for certain not only that we can, but that we have much to teach the whites about what it means to be truly human. Toure and Nkrumah and Jomo Kenyatta are the brave geniuses of Africa, Jacob, forging new political communities not guided by greed and hatred, ones fit for human beings to live in.

Jacob read a little more before he heard the front door lock turn, the door creak open, his mama coming home. Quickly he refolded the letter, hid it in the manila folder, and stuffed the folder under the very bottom part of his mattress. He had to sleep with his legs bent, trying not to let his feet go down where they might wrinkle the thin blue paper.

Now he grabbed a shoebox filled with baseball cards from under the bed, so she'd think that was why he was on his knees. Those little cardboard pictures of mostly white people made him sad now, they seemed so young—not meant for people like him, he thought, wise in the ways of the serpent.

He wished he could have told his mother his big news, that tomorrow in Ghana, Sugar was going to meet Malcolm X! Now he could never tell her.

"Oooh," his mama would have said, followed by proud tears in her eyes for Malcolm, the hero who'd gotten all of Africa to condemn the government for her son's murder. Jacob wished he could someday do something like that for his mother.

"Malcolm X," she had said, "is a black prince." Jacob had run to hug her. "Like your brother was." She had patted him, like *he* was the one needed comforting. "Don't you ever forget that. Your brother was a prince." Now Sugar would have tea with Malcolm—who had asked for the meeting alone, with just him, Jacob's friend, Sugar Cane; and he couldn't tell his mother any of that, or she'd for sure figure out that he'd snuck the letter out of the mailbox so she wouldn't read it.

He opened *Macbeth* to the part they had to memorize, about sleeping, but he couldn't stop thinking about Malcolm. Sugar had said Malcolm wanted the meeting in a small tea shop in Accra, by the port, and Jacob imagined himself there with them, looking up at the ceiling's wooden beams. Or would it be one of those Quonset hut things? The ceiling would have a fan with big blades going round and round and round, knitting up the raveled sleave of care. It made him so sleepy to think about that turning blade that he lay back against the pillows. He wanted to give himself to his dream of Africa.

The night after the meeting with Malcolm, Sugar stayed awake, trying to make the new world fit in the small space of an aerogram to Jacob. "Such teeny-tiny writing," Susan had said one night in Mississippi, flirting, "kind of like a girl's." David Watkins had been the rider that week, traveling the highways from office to office.

They'd done it on the floor. She'd bit his shoulder, drawn blood. Afterward she looked at him, sunk in himself, naked still. Guilty toward David, he said.

She pulled her flannel shirt on. "Don't you think you're entitled to some pleasure?" Carefully, she put a bandage on his bite. "Or to anything, comes to that. Sugar Cane, he's not a *comfortable* man, is he? He is a live wire!" But Africa had changed him. He felt gratful to be alive. David was bitter at the breakup, but smiled, and Sugar felt pleased to have Susan in his bed. They had a honeymoon, and Sugar, for the first time in his life, felt like he could let go, go out of himself, be in her, and part of her. Maybe the gods of Africa had done him a favor, the way Chuck said. "These gods, Sugar, they love our bodies. They possess us, even speak out of our mouths." Sugar, he'd had enough gods for his lifetime, but he was glad to see how Africa had met Chuck's needs for guidance. The priest casts palm nuts—like dice, probably—and they tell the believer what to do, make him certain in his actions.

"Thought that's what the Talmud and the rabbis did for you?"

"Thought so, too." But no more. It was Ifa for him now.

Well, maybe the gods, Shango, Yemoja, or Whoknowsa, would guide his hand writing this letter to Jacob.

The tea shop, he wrote, *turned out to be a bar*—though Malcolm only drank tea. Sugar had felt near hypnotized listening to him, Malcolm pouring his thoughts right into his brain, the same way he'd felt sometimes with Jacob's brother, even when he was furious with him. Maybe he should write that to Jacob? Would that please him?

Africa had changed Sugar, and meeting Malcolm here—Sugar Cane sitting across from the Prophet in the port of Accra, in the free country of Ghana—had affected him mightily. He talked and talked to Susan, David, Chuck, and Fannie, thinking they almost got it, too, but not *all* of it. So Jacob became the test for him: could he make the young man feel about Africa the way he did? If he could bring Jacob along, put the continent in sentences a twelve-year-old could understand, he'd know he could use Africa in his organizing. Maybe first he should make Jacob feel the moment when *he,* Jacob Battle, had actually been someone Malcolm X had been thinking of, as Malcolm sat by the port in Ghana, Africa.

"Tell your friend Jacob that he has to make his mind very subtle. Generations of workers," Malcolm said, "have accumulated the secrets of physics and chemistry, literature and biology, and these are things our people need to know. But the white serpents have stolen the books, and they sit with their tails coiled round them, spewing racist poison on every page. This poison may make you feel you're not worthy to know what's in these books—unless you make yourself like the serpents and hate your own people. You must wash the apple, Jacob, before you eat it!"

Which was, Sugar thought—pausing for a moment to look out at the different shades of black the ocean made—pretty much just the way Malcolm had run it down. The man had homilies for every occasion, the man a minister after all. But he knew he mocked Malcolm because he feared him now as much as he loved him: *Malcolm had plans for poor Sugar.* Still, it was a nice paragraph, Sugar having censored it a little, like leaving out about what a stupid, dangerous idea Malcolm thought it was to go to a white school in the first place, be surrounded all day by that hatred and condescension. How could a man, he said, *not* learn to hate himself?

"I went to the Bronx High School of Science," Sugar had said. And Malcolm had just smiled. Like to say, Prove me wrong, Mr. Cane: *join me.*

Sugar had also added the last bit about the apple, just to join himself to Malcolm—though adding words felt like it made him an extension of Malcolm's body, which they both knew had a bull's-eye drawn on it.

Sugar turned to the side, away from the page, and his hair brushed the mosquito netting. He'd let it grow out the last few weeks—"a bushy halo," Susan called it. Chuck added, "Now Sugar's an African man."

Sugar laughed, liking the sound of that. This place, it enticed him, *flirted* with him, he loved its smell, its bright colors, and proud poverty, but it scared him, too—like Africa had plans for him also.

He brushed a big, obstreperous biter from his arm. These damn African mosquitoes weren't like the teeny Delta kind, more like the ones from his island childhood but worse, like the African mosquitoes were maybe *their* fierce and frightening mothers. He looked out at the ocean, shushing him in the near-dark now, and thought that he wanted to be buried here, in the bosom of mother Africa. He smiled at that, adding,

But not yet, please Jesus, not yet, Malcolm's plans for him to the contrary, Malcolm clearly wanting to bring SNAP and Malcolm's new organization together. But the way the Nation of Islam felt about Malcolm, that would be a world of trouble.

The waiter, his pants ripped down the leg, his white jacket spotless, had brought Malcolm mint-flavored tea in a ceramic pot that looked like barely shaped earth. A wiry old man, with long fingers, he'd carefully put down a beer in a green bottle for Sugar. Malcolm gave it a sideways look, but before the minister could jump down his throat about alcohol or pork or women, Sugar slipped the yoke, said that someday he wanted to have the boldness of that waiter.

Malcolm had nodded, almost delicately, raising his eyebrows slightly, knowing immediately what Sugar had meant. "Not obsequious," he said, "but gentle, helpful." He poured his tea through a small woven basket, filtering out the leaves.

Sugar took a big swallow of his beer. "When I speak to a bus driver, or a waiter, or even a porter, I wonder, until I live in a country of my own, can I ever have his dignity and self-assurance?"

"It's not just a country of their own that changed them," Malcolm said, "it's how they got it. Have you read Fanon?"

Sugar smiled, remembering Joshua saying to him, "You know what I learned at college? I can say, *I haven't re-read that recently* with a straight face." He'd been talking to a sour-faced, goggly-eyed Jew at a fund-raiser in Great Neck, then, a camp survivor. Modern art and liberal condescension all over the walls. "Have you read Primo Levi?" the man had asked, and Joshua had lied, though Sugar, losing his edge in Mississippi, where there was no one to hustle and not much that wasn't as sharp and clear as a knife's edge, hadn't even known Joshua was lying. Which had been like seeing a pimple sprout on the football captain's face: Joshua, who never cared what anyone thought, wanted *that* old Jew to think well of him.

But Sugar knew it wouldn't be a good idea to hustle Malcolm. Besides, he hadn't had the college courses in lying. "No," he said. "I don't know Fanon."

"You should, Mr. Cane," Malcolm said, admonitory, precise, so much the teacher always that it was hard to take offense, nothing personal about it. "It will help you to understand what changed the slouching hustlers of Lenox Avenue into the free men of Ghana." He drank some tea. "They're not looking over their shoulders," Malcolm said. Then he smiled at Sugar warmly—and looked over his own shoulder. "I'm sure my CIA observers are here somewhere."

But they were the only people in the place besides the waiter and the owner, a smiling fat man who stood by the bar, polishing glasses. "Him?" Sugar asked.

Malcolm shrugged. "Who knows?" He sipped some tea. "Perhaps you." He stared at Sugar, making his face cold. Sugar must have looked shocked, because Malcolm laughed out loud at poor Sugar—*the sucker.*

The government, Malcolm said, had taken *special* notice when Malcolm had gotten the Organization of African Unity to condemn Joshua Battle's murder. Men with cameras sat in sedans outside his house, every phone clicked, his own car was always followed by an obvious convoy. His statement made the U.S. look bad with non-aligned countries, and that changed the game: Malcolm became an enemy of the State in the Cold War. *So* they targeted him, the CIA doubling the FBI, dogging his steps.

But this year Malcolm would ask the UN Commission on Human Rights to examine the situation of the Negro in the United States. He would drag the U.S. government before the World Court.

"Johnson's gonna wig out." Sugar took a pull on his Dutch beer.

Malcolm shrugged and sipped his tea. "If a state decides it wants to kill you, Mr. Cane, there's nothing you can do about it."

Sugar smoothed his face, hooded his eyes, tried to hide his shock. He'd been thinking that they would make life hard for Malcolm, follow him around, check his taxes, or whisper "nigger" into his phone, not murder him, like they were the fucking Klan.

Then Sugar looked at Malcolm's smile and wondered if maybe Malcolm had *practiced* that casual shrug. He could feel anxiety pouring off Malcolm's seemingly calm body like heat waves—just the way a force field had come off Jacob's brother; and the waves flowed not just into Sugar's brain but into his chest, his stomach, made him want to say he would join Malcolm, promise him that if he died, Sugar would pick up the burden, leverage Africa against America. He controlled himself, though, poured the rest of the beer down his throat without stopping.

Malcolm had been quiet for a moment, with that Joshua-style silence that steals all the sound from the room. It made Sugar jumpy. He wanted Malcolm to talk before he found himself saying something he'd regret. But he couldn't take his eyes from Malcolm's smooth face, thinking, he used to be a thief, a pimp, a drug dealer, the kind of man Sugar's family had disdained, the trash of the cold continent, while Sugar had been a star at the Bronx High School of Science. But it was Malcolm who would be the leader of their movement soon, now that Martin's time was coming to an end. And Sugar could tell it was right that the

torch pass to Malcolm, because even after all the beatings Sugar had suffered that Malcolm had been spared, he didn't resent taking instruction
from him. He smiled at himself. *I took the wrong courses,* he thought.
Not college, like Joshua. Not street, like Malcolm. *Maybe I'm not good
enough to pick up the flag from him if he falls.*

And maybe that sentimental regret made him give himself a few
extra lashes that night when he wrote Jacob *When you see someone on
the street doing wrong to our people you should stop him, but you
shouldn't put him down.*

And a week later, Jacob smiled as he re-read that. He got off the subway
at the end of the line, thinking: Yeah, I shouldn't put him *down,* Sugar,
'cause I sure don't want to get beat *up* by him. But like should I really
say, Now you stop, brother, and give that nice woman her purse back?

What would his mother say? Hate the sin, but love the sinner. Isn't
that what Sugar was saying too? With the Lord's grace, every sinner can
change himself. *The men white society has sent down the sewers to the
prisons will someday transform themselves through our struggle, will
become our leaders,* Sugar had written him.

*Then why am I walking up this cold motherfucking hill to a place I
hate, that hates me?* Jacob wondered. *I thought this purgatory was how
I became a leader, Sugar.* But he knew that last-shall-be-first churchy
tone of Sugar's, had heard it times his brother spoke about the folks in
Mississippi, saying, *They may be slow but they aren't stupid.* Yeah, but
they aren't especially smart, either, are they? That's why they needed
Joshua Battle, and Sugar Cane. That's why they would need Jacob
Battle.

The kids around the White Castle had on their "loden coats," shapeless things with little leather buttons. They drank cardboard cups of
coffee and stuffed their mouths with burgers before school. Only the end
of October, but their mamas had wrapped their precious necks with
mufflers. Jacob walked past them, coat buttons open, the winter air feeling like it wanted to toughen him up, like prison, or a gym. *The man in
the street knows how to fight,* Sugar had written, *but he doesn't know
who to fight. He needs to learn who his real enemy is.*

There ya go, Jacob thought, wise in the ways of the serpent. Jacob
and Sugar: *they'd* be the teachers, which meant they'd still be in charge,
like Mr. Hartman, who had them make up a scene like in *Macbeth,* little
boys plotting to kill the king, and suddenly they all forgot how to talk.
Then the teacher stepped in, showed them how much better Shakespeare
had done it.

Mr. Hartman was a stern man, with a funny accent himself. Isn't that something, Sugar, he would maybe write that night, you come to a fancy school so a foreigner can teach you how to speak your own motherfucking language?

And for a while at the school, Jacob had felt like he didn't know how to talk English anymore, embarrassed even by the way he sounded. Then, after all the drills and grammar and pronunciation exercises, he'd realized that maybe the hymies at the Dewey School didn't like the way *they* sounded either—like this school was meant to make them into someone else, too. He could tell some of the teachers thought, not unkindly even, why shouldn't their patented method work the same for the colored boy? They just didn't get it, not even Mr. Hartman: white folks hated him so much *more* than they hated the Jews, they weren't ever going to care how he *sounded*.

Jacob was pretty sure Mr. Hartman was a fag, but he liked him anyway—he treated Jacob fairly. So maybe it was like the jazz musicians who went to Europe and said it wasn't so racist there. Mr. Hartman's corrections felt like they were good for him—like the winter air. He thought about *later,* when he would be teaching his people. He would try to remember to be like Mr. Hartman.

"Oh, no," he could hear his brother say, "we're not petty dictators like the man you describe. We make it possible for the real leaders to emerge." He had loved listening to his brother, but he hadn't always understood what he meant; he understood, though, that everyone still talked about Joshua Battle, so he was still maybe more than just another "wave in the ocean of the people." Sugar said even Malcolm X admired him.

But Sugar also said Malcolm called Joshua and Sugar's nonviolence folly. "One has to admire Martin," he'd said, "for portraying the fantasy of us as nonviolent and even getting blacks to go along with it. But we are not a pacific people, Mr. Cane. I think Joshua Battle would have learned this about us, if he'd lived."

Jacob didn't think so, didn't think Sugar thought so either. The only thing he'd ever seen his brother hit hard was a baseball. He began to feel a pull coming from Sugar, though, like first they were all family, burying Joshua, mourning Joshua, living inside Joshua together, but then it was like maybe Sugar was telling him "I'm leaving home," and he wanted Jacob to say it was all right or he even wanted Jacob to come with him. As he thought about it, he heard Mr. Hartman in the background, crying:

All my pretty ones?
Did you say all? O hell-kite! All?
What, all my pretty chickens and their dam
At one fell swoop?

Jacob didn't like this part in the play, felt just the way the other Malcolm did: "Dispute it like a man," he thought, the way that Macbeth does at the end. He'd even memorized some of *those* speeches, though no one asked him to do it. He snuck Sugar's last letter out, and put it on the desk, under his book, just let it lie there, you know, not like he was reading it.

I don't know why, but in my whole treasury of Southern beatings, it was one of the first, at Parchman Farm, that I remembered when Malcolm said that. I had been dragged down a corridor, holding on to a mattress, and the guards had a huge black trusty named Pee Wee wallop me hard while they dragged me to the isolation shed, a place where you had to sit hunched over in your own shit until your spine or your spirit broke. As I slid down the hall, this intolerable drumming tattooing my chest with bruises, I'd sung spirituals. Sitting with Malcolm in Africa, the memory of those songs made me sick.

Right, Jacob thought, instead you should have said, "I will not yield . . . And be baited with the rabble's curse."

"Allah is the God for warriors," Malcolm said, like he was reading my mind. "And the blue-eyed Christ is a lie meant for slaves."

There was nothing new in what Malcolm said, so it must have been hearing him say it, by the port in the country that Nkrumah rules so brilliantly, that made it rush into my heart this time. Or maybe it was that I'd been so long *ready* to hear this, and it was like the right note that finishes a chord, resolves it. I saw a body wrapped in linen. The men carried it into the cave and rolled the stone into the opening, then returned to Jerusalem—to lives of defeat and bitterness, comforted by lies they told each other about what was, they said, no longer in that cave.

Christ fell away from my spirit then, Jacob. I felt a cringe leave my soul, like I could breathe freely for the first time. I will never willingly strike a man down, Jacob, but I will no more turn the other cheek. I will defend myself!

Jacob felt like when Sugar said *Jesus*, he also meant *Joshua Battle*, and he couldn't help himself, he laughed out loud in the middle of class, 'cause he knew just how Sugar felt not wanting to carry his brother around for the rest of his life. Besides, there had to be a lesson in his brother's death, and maybe the lesson was: *turn the other cheek and they'll kill you dead*. Then his chest tightened. He fished out his inhaler. Jacob didn't believe Sugar had meant it about Jesus. The man had nearly been a minister. There was too much gospel in him to just drop Christ by the roadside like that.

Hartman looked at him, to say something about the laughing probably, but the bell rang, and Jacob ran from the room, sucking on the plastic.

Sugar had said that that was the last letter he'd get from Africa, though he hoped Africa would always be with them both now. *When you're back in Mississippi,* Malcolm had told Sugar, *remember your brothers in Africa are with you. If you think you're alone, you think you got to beg, or you got to be a martyr. That kind of stand will never enable you to win a battle.*

Jacob tried to walk proudly, like an African man, down the hall toward his geometry class, free, independent, uncaring about the opinion of others, his destiny linked to his powerful black brothers, all of them in one struggle, in Mississippi, Angola, Mozambique, Southwest Africa, Ghana, Georgia, Harlem, Guinea, Johannesburg, and even maybe the John Dewey School; "one blood runs through our veins," Malcolm had said, "one sun has colored our skins."

Why should I play the Roman fool, he thought, *and die / On mine own sword? whiles I see lives, the gashes / Do better upon them.* He bumped hard then into his bushy-browed enemy, spinning him to the side, making him drop his notebook, papers scattering on the floor, and fuck you if he was gonna say he was sorry, because *it was his hall, too,* he had as much right to be here as anyone. He watched the kid picking up his blue binder, stuffing the papers in, and he waited till the kid could see him watching, see him laughing at him.

His enemy saw, dropped his books again, and came charging down the hall at Jacob, running head down right into his chest, knocking him backward, Jacob's head banging hard against the linoleum, his inhaler skittering out of his pocket. The kid saw it go. He'd grab it. Start a game of keepaway.

Adam picked it up, handed it back to him on the ground. "I'm sorry," Adam said. "I just lost it. I'm sorry."

"Yeah, me too," Jacob said from the ground. He couldn't get up yet, his chest closing, the heavy air pushing him down like a hand. Adam reached down for him, pulled him up off the linoleum. While Jacob wheezed helplessly, Adam picked up the rest of Sugar's letters and handed them back to him. "I hate this fucking class," Adam said, looking like a condemned prisoner as they walked through the door. But Jacob was actually glad to see the long-nosed teacher, drawing clear, plain lines on the board. He set to work. You wanted it demonstrated, he thought, *and that I did.* Case closed. So leave me the fuck alone.

And that night he didn't look at the letters again the way he usually did, just put them under his bed and took out his baseball cards. But the pictures didn't work. He wasn't little, and Sugar had said they were counting on him, not saying who was doing the counting, which just made it worse. Did he mean him and Fannie Mae Carter, Chuck Taylor, David Watkins, and Susan Lems? Did he mean his brother in the grave? Malcolm X? The whole Negro race?

His mother came in, and she smiled, pleased probably to see him playing with those cardboard pictures again. He bet she was glad those letters from Sugar Cane had stopped coming.

"I got you something." She held up a blue blazer with silver buttons. He smiled, and jumped off the bed to take it out of her hands, really liking it—the buttons especially, with their heraldic crests, geeky but somehow dignified, as much his, he thought, as the Jews' he went to school with. Or maybe they belonged to anyone who earned them.

But that made him think about *earning* and *honor* again. It was going to be heavy to wear that jacket. His mother must have noticed that he looked different from the other kids at the school, not just his skin, naturally, but his clothes, and thought it bothered him. Which it did. That's what she'd been doing on the weekends, he decided, working some second job.

"Thanks, Mom," he said, embracing her, burrowing into her head-down, the way he had when he was little, like if he could get back inside, then he'd be safe from the bad air, the bad people.

Then a month later, Sugar called on the phone from Alabama, a place that he'd written him was far more dangerous than Africa, worse snakes, more vicious alligators—and crackers, too. Malcolm X, he said, he'd been shot by three black men. But Jacob, wise in the ways of the serpent, already knew that was a lie, the men surely white on the inside, agents of the State that had shadowed Malcolm and Sugar all over Africa, taking pictures, taping their conversation, the State that if it wanted to kill you, would. Had to be so. In a choked voice, Sugar swore that *he* would die for what Malcolm had believed in—what Jacob believed in, too, right?

"Yes," Jacob said, seeing his brother's face, the way it had looked lying in his coffin, bent and smashed, the most fascinating sight in the world, and he felt terrified, certain that if he dreamt of that face too long, he'd have to join his brother, crawl into the coffin with him.

It was Joshua, Jacob thought, who'd gotten Malcolm killed, made Sugar cry. If Joshua hadn't been murdered, then Malcolm wouldn't have asked Africa to condemn the U.S. and the CIA wouldn't have had to kill him. His brother had used Malcolm, had grappled him down into the grave with him. The State would want to kill Sugar soon, too. And then Jacob, when he took Sugar's place. And if a state wants to kill you, if a brother wants to kill you, if a race wants to kill you, Jesus God, he thought, there's nothing you can do.

The next day at school, he walked upstairs next to Arkey Kaplan, who hung around him now, not like he was his protector, though, but like Jacob had something Arkey wanted, even though he was younger than him. Anyway, most times Jacob was glad for the company.

But not today. Jacob, sweating under the heavy wool blazer, though the hall was freezing, wanted to be alone, maybe figure out how he was going to avoid his dead brother's gaze. Then his English teacher came down the stairs, looking at the floor the way he always did, as if he were scared to see one of the students outside of class. Jacob still carried Sugar's letters with him, but he'd also stuck something else in with them, the list of geniuses this fag had handed out in class last week, each one graded first-level geniuses, B-minus geniuses, shit like that. He pulled it out of the folder and said, "Mr. Hartman, why is every one of these god-damn men white?"

Hartman looked at him blankly, like he didn't know who he was, like he was suddenly invisible to him, too.

"Where's Duke Ellington? Where's Malcolm X? Where's my brother?" Hartman was no different than the rest: black men were *inconsiderable* to him.

"It takes many, many years for the world to weigh a man, to see if he has genius."

"Where's Frederick Douglass, then? Where's W. E. B. Du Bois? This is a racist list. There are no black people on it, alive or dead."

. . .

Hartman knew he could have told the boy that Augustine of Hippo was black. Or Pushkin. But the words mangled up in his mouth, defensive, empty; wrong somehow; and he grew angry with the boy. Jacob might be right, but he was also being disrespectful, arrogant. "I am a victim of my education," Hartman said quietly.

"Yeah," Jacob said. "And I'm gonna be a victim of *mine*."

He threw the folder at Hartman, the list and Sugar's letters floating around and down the stairwell, where boots, Jesus God, might walk on them!

Hartman held his hand up as if to protect himself, and then furious, let his hand dart forward, like he wanted to hit the boy. Jacob must have seen the way his arm had gone back, then started toward him. A squint closed the teacher's eyes for a moment.

"You're right," Hartman said, sick with himself, letting his arm fall to his side. This boy's brother, he knew, had been the school's own martyr to ending the racism that had killed Hartman's parents. And their son, Richard, such was history's good humor, was no better than a Nazi in the martyr's brother's eyes, simply by loving what he loved, forsaking all others.

Worst of all, Arthur Kaplan, who knew him from his humiliation in Great Neck, stood next to the boy now, ready to pour poison in his ear. The two of them walked away, Kaplan's deadly arm around the boy's shoulder, where Hartman himself wanted to put his, knowing that it's a precarious thing to survive martyrs, you live the rest of your life perched on the edge of their graves, and the stream of your tears is like a rope that leads into the abyss and lets the dead, at any moment, whimsically tug you down to join them.

A brilliant boy. Hartman should keep his eye on Jacob, help him make a wooden tag for himself perhaps, so he wouldn't forget his name, here in this hard, cold place. *Jacob would?* No, *that* was sentimentality. The John Dewey School, Hartman reminded himself, wasn't a transit camp. And Hartman didn't know how to help this boy, didn't know his world. Isn't that what Jacob Battle had just told him?

Beneath him, he saw fragments of Jacob and Arkey through the banister posts, bending over, picking up the fallen papers. Impossible for Richard to transform himself so he could understand what the boy went through here, just as the boy couldn't transform himself to understand Hartman. And why would he even want to know an old man, head filled with straw? Each suffering is different; every unhappy individual, Hartman thought, unhappy in his own way.

Still, if he *could* help Jacob, it would be an act of justice, wouldn't it? Recompense for the damage he'd done without meaning it with his white lists, meaning something else surely by them, but what did that matter? Perhaps he should go down and help them retrieve what they'd lost? No, he couldn't squat with them in the cold hallway where all his students might see. He turned back to his classroom, eager to jot some notes down. *Tears . . . rope . . . abyss.* Turning the line over in his mind, trying compounds to overcome the inappropriate softness. *Abyss-world? Rope-tears?* No, in this language the joinings looked ad hoc, lacked the obdurate before-the-beginning-of-time solidity of Celan's German. Lucky Celan, he thought, forced by fate to write in the murderers' own language!

Jacob and Arkey hunted under the radiators for the last of the letters, Arkey making a broad point still of not looking at them, all the while telling Jacob some confused story about Hartman and Great Neck, the place on Long Island where Kaplan lived; but Jacob didn't follow, more bewildered about what he'd done to his most precious treasures even than he'd been over the smashed mailbox. *Jesus, who am I?* he thought. The wild black boy? No, it was more like when he'd been three years old, in the throes of a tantrum that Father and Mother couldn't reach, and he'd scraped some Mother Goose stickers he'd truly loved off his bedroom walls with his fingernails. Kaplan was saying something about how he'd once admired Hartman, too—like maybe he was telling him he was a homo. Well, *you* can suck his dick, Jacob thought, but I ain't gonna. He ran toward the cafeteria then, Arkey chasing after him, saying he really wanted Jacob to write something for *The Dewey Debate.*

"About Malcolm?" Jacob said, drawing his sleeve across his eyes.

"Who's that?" Arkey asked, not caring about the answer, or not caring nearly enough.

It made Jacob feel so old that he laughed. Kaplan wanted him to write about the John Dewey School, "from, you know, your perspective," meaning call them down for their racism, dig his grave here. "Don't bring out the forces against you till you're ready to fight them," Malcolm had said to Sugar—like that mattered. Like Sugar had said yesterday: as soon as you stood upright, said *treat me like a man,* Hoover put dogs on you specially trained to kill *the black messiah.* But maybe Jacob would write some little thing for their paper, maybe tell them the real story of what happened at the Democratic convention, educate these kids about their democracy. Would Arkey's newspaper print that?

Or was Arkey, Jacob asked, a *liberal?* He left the question hanging, turned and went in to lunch.

Bobby Brown saw Arkey chasing after a crying Jacob the day after Malcolm's death, Kaplan doing, he thought, just what *he* should have done long ago, if he hadn't been so focused on college applications, advanced placement tests, so caught up in *showing them*—or maybe just adding *that* as an extra impulsion that would help him get what *he* wanted. Well, which was it? Did *he* want it? He didn't know.

Or maybe he just didn't want to be seen with Jacob, because then he wouldn't be the football star; the class president; then they'd make a set: the colored kids; the pickaninnies.

But today was different, today was the day after Malcolm had died. So he waited till Arkey left Jacob at the cafeteria door, and after a few minutes he followed Jacob in, surprised to see that he wasn't eating alone, the way Bobby had his first year here, but with some kid with thick eyebrows, the two of them bent over the kid's notebook, Jacob laying out the steps to solve a geometry problem.

Jacob pushed the notebook toward the other kid. "Here, Adam. The trick is just to know which kind of triangle it is. Then you'll know what formula to use."

The kid nodded, but there was no light in his face, Bobby thought. Not like Jacob, who was all light, all energy—a live wire. Dangerous to touch. "So what's a bar mitzvah suit?" he heard Jacob ask.

"Don't know," the kid said. "Maybe it's something the rabbi hasn't explained yet. Or maybe it's an Orthodox thing, you know, that we don't do. We're Reformed."

Suddenly Jacob said, "Jesus, I'm so thirsty," and took a drink from the kid's cup. It made Bobby laugh to see it, remembering when he'd done that experiment himself.

Adam pushed the cup aside oh so casually. "I don't want any more," he said and picked up his tray to leave. Jacob twisted his lips upward, confirmed in his pain.

Bobby sat down with him. "I found some of these," he said, handing him the blue sheets. "I didn't look at them. I know they're private."

"That's okay. You can read them," Jacob said. "They're pretty interesting. They're letters from Sugar Cane. One of them's even about meeting Malcolm." He wanted him to see them, Bobby realized. He actually *pushed* the folder at him.

Bobby reached over greedily. *Malcolm!*

. . .

"I can see why he hid them," Bobby Brown said to Laura Jaffe fourteen years later. "They were his mojo, you know, the stuff that made him special. And I can see why he wanted me to read them, too, share the burden—before the letters killed him dead. The drum beat in them. *Join us.* Implacable rhythm. No kid could resist it, unless he had some strong help. I couldn't resist it myself, turned out, so I was the wrong man to draw him back from the brink." Bobby buttoned his shirt, hiding the tight black curls she wanted to feel spring under her hand again.

He put on his pants slowly, but threw his suspenders casually over his shirt. *Not* running *out, though, right?*

He read her mind. "I have court in the morning."

"Oh. I mean, court, huh?"

Again, he got her drift. "No more Weathermen, Laura. I'm part of the Civil Rights Division. Always was. Corruption in police departments, that's what I'm about. So I'm not on a vendetta to get your friend."

"Of course not," she said, but feeling *Oh, thank you, Lord.*

"Olson put me on Beth's case. He's a very powerful guy, he could do that. He saw I came from Great Neck, probably thought that would give me a little extra motivation. The maid's nephew wreaking vengeance on the white bourgeoisie."

"Right." *The maid's nephew. Her maid, actually.*

"The FBI thought Beth had done the Defense Department, which really pissed them off. And Olson told me she had other things planned. Worse things, he said. Anti-personnel weapons. Murders, Laura."

He stared at her, his large eyes unmoving, like she would know if it were true. Once upon a time, she'd pieced together what they'd been doing in that town house: *a pipe bomb filled with nails, for an officers' dance.*

"*But we hadn't decided to deploy it yet,*" Beth had said the same night they'd talked about pregnancy.

But you could *have decided to do it, right?*

America wasn't ready for the heavy stuff yet. We would have seen that.

Did see it. But not until everyone had run in horror from the nails sticking out of Beth's boyfriend's head. So it was killing that made them see the country would be horrified by killing. It *might* have been murdering the soldiers that would have convinced them . . . of what? Not to murder the soldiers? Too late.

Which meant Laura *could* tell Bobby that Beth wasn't going to murder anyone. But she'd have to add, *not yet*. She never knew fully what was in Beth's heart. Better not to say anything.

"Anyway, Beth Jacobs is ancient history now. Olson told me there'd be bombs. But she fled and none went off." Bobby moved her cane a little—the first time he'd even seemed to notice it—and bent over to tie his shoes. But he didn't ask about it, and she didn't want to talk about it yet—scared her MS might terrify him. After all, she thought, it frightened *her*. Later, maybe, if it mattered, she could talk about it—and she realized that yes, she wanted there to be a *later* between them, or at least a second date. He looked at her wolf head, but he knew part of what that was about, the wolf *outside*. He'd even made the usual jokes about whether it was safe to have drinks with SheWolf, to kiss her, to make love to her. Not the first to make the jokes, not the first to fuck her. Not her first black man, either. But this one in sync with her. Very sweet and very passionate, too, stroking her legs slowly, clearly taking pleasure, and she knew how much she wanted more of him, because she had the fantasy that his touch was healing, was driving the wolf inside away.

"Do you know what happened to Jacob Battle?" Beth might be ancient history, but Laura still wanted to change the subject.

"To Jacob Battle?" A measuring squint narrowed his eyes—did he trust her enough to tell her what he knew? "No," he said. "Last I actually spoke to him he was maybe only seventeen, getting into all kinds of trouble because of Sugar Cane." He looked sad. "Him and me both."

"Maybe he's fine now," she said. "You are." She thought about telling how her family had paid for Jacob's scholarship. But, no, she had the feeling he might not like that.

"The kid had really been crushed when the Democrats sold out the MFDP. Sugar Cane's stories about Africa had been like balm for the wound, you know. The way the Jews feel about Israel, maybe, after the Holocaust."

"A wounded people," she said, "need to wound others to feel strong again."

He laughed. "I was thinking, need their own country, their own army, their own power."

"Anyway, the beat goes on." And the beatings.

"Yeah, I guess. Anyway, that's what was in that file folder, the dream of Africa—no poverty, no tribal warfare, just *kente* cloth and wise leaders. That's what Arkey Kaplan saved for him." He buttoned his suspenders. "What happened to Arkey, by the way? He wasn't a bad guy."

"Arkey? He teaches labor history at Brandeis."

"Labor history?" He chuckled, like he thought he had Arkey's number.

"Arkey used to talk about you, when we were at Harvard," Laura said, wanting to defend Arkey—and maybe herself—against that chuckle. "He noticed how many people thought you were there because you were black. But Arkey knew better, he knew you had been the valedictorian in high school. No, I mean at THE JOHN DEWEY SCHOOL. Anyway, even in college he was still looking over his shoulder to see if you were gaining. Arkey thinks blacks are like Jews, you know."

"Sure. Give us a chance, put us in good schools, and we'll come out of the ghetto superpowered."

"Which *you* did, didn't you?"

"Yeah, I suppose so." Proud of it; and embarrassed, too—*his* endless American dilemma, probably.

"Look, just about the only black people he'd met, you and Jacob, they were just like he'd imagined. Then he saw how other people treated you. It was a little lesson in racism for Arkey."

"That right? Does sound little, you know. And he never talked to me about it."

Laura knew Arkey *had* tried to talk to Bobby at Harvard, but Bobby had been ShadeMan then—hidden behind the sunglasses. Or maybe he should have been IceGuy—Bobby Brown in those days doing what Laura knew now was a piss-poor imitation of the Stare—the one her vet drug-dealer/addicts used to immobilize a honky therapist at fifty paces. Maybe, she thought, Bobby felt Arkey had valued his attention too much, or in the wrong way; a trophy black friend. Which was perhaps a lesson to her in How to Keep a Black Man: don't want him too much. But she couldn't do that one anymore. "You intimidated him," she said, which was true, in addition to being flattering. "Great student, athlete, head of the Organization for Black Unity."

Bobby smiled, very pleased indeed. Ah, the Dewey School, Laura thought—something extra sweet for Bobby about his having been admired by someone from *there*—from high school, for God's sake!

"You and Arkey," he said, "you used to run together at Harvard, didn't you?"

"Run? Yeah, sometimes, from the tear gas. And we used to live together, too. Not at Harvard, though. After."

"That right?" he said, disappointingly without interest, thinking of something else. "Jacob," he said, "that boy didn't have a chance." He snapped the last button on his suspenders, readjusted them in front. He dressed awfully well for a government lawyer.

"The school?" She was glad now that she hadn't said anything about the tuition money.

"Well, the school certainly didn't understand him, a confused, brilliant black kid. I made more sense. I was a football player." He bared his teeth. *Beware*, they said to her. *See how well we can do false amiability.* "Yeah, the Dewey School sure as shit didn't know what to do with Jacob Battle. Not the faculty, not the other kids. They shouldn't have taken him."

They *hadn't* wanted to, really. "But his brother—"

"Right. Joshua Battle had handed out algebra tests at the John Dewey School. Their precious martyr. Jacob was the martyr's brother, endless mourning and reflected righteousness combined. A sad saint in training. But who was he, really—to himself, I mean? I'll tell you, you couldn't survive in that school if you didn't know who *you* were, what *you* felt. If you didn't, it was a killer."

Could Bobby not realize that self-knowledge like that was as rare as it was difficult? After all, to find out who *she* was she talked to Smerless four times a week; and that's why people came to see her, too, making *her*—of all people!—into the One Who Knows. And maybe that's what she was doing here, with Bobby Brown, namely, *making too much of him,* Arkey getting married, so her unconscious had made Bobby Brown into the Last Train Leaving Lonely Town.

No, this man would be attractive at any hour to her, decisive, moving surely from his center. He seemed so confident, so self-contained; it made her want to be the one thing he *needed.* So what that he was their maid's nephew!

So what? Well, *that* was gonna be a whole other load of bricks!

"Carrying his brother's corpse around," he said, "Jacob couldn't ever find out who *he* was."

It was sweet how sad he sounded for this kid who she thought he'd hardly known. But it was funny talking like this about Joshua, yet never mentioning her own brother, *her* martyr. Endless mourning and reflected righteousness combined—yeah, she maybe knew a little something about that herself.

"And then Sugar Cane made Jacob feel he had a big role in the whole Black Power thing, Joshua Battle's brother, Sugar Cane's protégé. Jacob wasn't just hearing the jive on the radio, either. He was *there.* Hell, it's 'cause of him I saw some history made myself. And that Black

Power thing, it made sense. The truth is, you know, *I* was deep in it for a time."

"For a New York minute, right?" But she was teasing him. Yeah, she *knew* he'd led the OBU.

"More than a minute, truth is. But I was older. Jacob was way too young for that game. It drove him crazy." For some reason he took her hand then. "He was a *really* brilliant kid, you know? Not like me. I mean *really* smart. He could do calculus equations in his head, he could run down a situation, analyze it, the way they say his brother could. And all that Black Power noise, it made him think that maybe everything he was good at, everything in books, was white. It made him think he had to play double dare all the time, show he wasn't one of you, show he was street. Most of all, it made him think he had a mighty army behind him. So he did stupid things."

"He wasn't alone in that," she said, thinking again of her friend, the vanguard of the Third World Revolution, hidden *here,* among the rest of us . . . whites.

"No, that's the truth. He was *not.*" He let go of her hand and adjusted his lovely silk tie. It was a design so subtle it seemed it had been woven into the silk, blue on blue. A prosecutor, she thought, but a dandy and a hedonist, too. He likes the look and feel of expensive fabrics, enough even to scrimp probably somewhere else in his life.

"I met you then," he said quietly.

"I know," Laura said. "I wondered if you remembered. Sugar Cane's speech in Roxbury. My friends thought we were courageous just being there."

"You were. And I thought you were beautiful."

Strange how delighted that made her feel; after all, they'd just made love in the present. "Really? I thought it was . . . my friend you liked."

"Don't want to say Beth's name, huh? Ancient history or not, the man's a fed, so let's not awaken the sleeping giant? Really, Laura, Beth's not on my playlist." He put on his watch. "It was you I liked. That smile of yours, like you had the sweetest sexiest secrets. I had a lot of fantasies about you."

"Jesus, you did? Why didn't you say anything?"

"Because *then* if people, I mean black people, saw us together, it would have meant one of two things to them: I was getting revenge by fucking you or I was betraying them."

"And now?"

"Yeah, some might still see it that way. But *I* don't care anymore. I know who I am now, what *I* feel." He grew quiet, maybe considering if that was true? Did *he* care what others said? Her heart fluttered, like her own life balanced on that question.

"Are we going to see each other again?" he asked. "Or was this just an experiment?"

She smiled, as sleepy-sexily as she knew how, delighted beyond measure by that sweet vulnerable question. "You mean, like My First Black Man?"

He nodded, already knowing better (not the first, not the issue here), while Laura turned her grin into the Mona Lisa version of the Smerless special.

"Or the nephew of the family maid," he said. "You know, Miss Ann Visits the Slave House." Bobby smiling too, but both of them knowing this was going someplace *very* dangerous.

"The *big* black buck, you mean?" She sat up, pulling the sheets over her breasts. "What about you? Are you getting even for the way my family treated your aunt? Fucking the boss's daughter?"

Jesus, *that* actually made him think, sitting on the edge of the bed they'd just made love in, but *this* more intimate than they'd been before. "You know, my aunt really liked your family. It was a little rough at first—you know, like she had to use her own plates. But you people changed, she said. And you introduced her to Martin Luther King. She forgave you."

Laura bowed her head, meaning it, too.

"Ruth was pretty important to me, more like a mother than an aunt, and, let me tell you, she loved your brother, Frank, enough to make me jealous. What she didn't love was being a maid. She was a great singer, you know."

"I know." But she didn't want to lie to him. Then she reviewed her track record. Okay, she didn't want to lie to him *yet*. "I mean, I didn't know that then, but we found one of your aunt's forty-fives with my brother's things in Mississippi. He really treasured it. 'Remember Me.' "

He smiled again. "I will." He put on his suit coat, and stood up. He bent back down, kissed her on the cheek, and she didn't get up to let him out, which felt more intimate to her, like they already had a relationship, like he knew his way around.

The slamming door shouted, *Will he really call?* That question made her shiver. To calm herself, she walked naked through her apartment. She set the long iron bar of the police lock back in place.

What was she doing with this man? Well, she knew *part* of the answer, of course. One night and she was hooked, had to cop and blow again (or blow the cop again?), making her like all the haunted desperadoes on her client list, in the grip of something imperious that transformed and commanded her the way drugs did them. Namely, *sex,* yes, but also what this sex *meant,* she'd swear, which turned out to be something she had no words for except *again,* and all of it annihilating what she *should* feel. Her friend's prosecutor! Ruth Brown's surrogate son! She stopped and took a piece of hard lemon candy from her silver canister. *You have to know what you feel,* he'd said, *who you are.* Well, she knew *what* she felt—she wanted him to knock on that door again, right now—but still she'd become something strange to herself.

So would he call her *soon,* and not just wait till the next time he wanted to fuck? She got back into bed, sucking on the drop. *That* was the kind of question she worried about now, she thought, almost reassuringly, *not* about making justice for her brother in the grave. But tonight that word turned into an unordered wake-up call. *Justice?* Like crushing a physicist's auditory nerve—her current grand achievement in that line?

She rolled away from the damp spot, pulled the duvet cover over her mouth. The rebus: wiggly little guys + ovoid shape = well, thanks to the Pill it equaled o. Which reminded her of a finding in the *New England Journal*: estrogen might be bad for recurring/remitting MS. She had to consult with her neurologist. Perhaps condoms in her future?

Would that be all right with him?

And more: would he be willing not to have children?

And why did she keep thinking about *that* tonight? Arkey Kaplan of G.N., L.I., announces his engagement to Katherine Chase, of Gentileville, Conn.? And *if* he can shake the Gail virus, the happyish couple will soon tell the world about a blessed event. That news, yes, but mostly Bobby Brown. *This* was someone focused, reliable, smart; she could all too easily imagine him as the father of her child.

But respecting the man who impregnated you was *not* a cure for multiple sclerosis. Still, the disease was a mystery, a series of spotty statistics inscribed on her body; no one really knew if a pregnancy *would* endanger her or not. Sometimes she thought she'd given up on having children as an offering to God. *I won't have this which I so much want if you'll spare me another attack.*

But wouldn't God *want* her to have children? Jewish ones, though, right? How would Bobby Brown feel about that? Which made her chortle. How would a man she'd just met feel about the religious education of their biracial imaginary children! Sex had made her insane.

She crunched the last of the lemony bits. Anyway, psychoanalysis had shown her she maybe put too much worry into the MS so she wouldn't have to confront some other fears. Like would she be a good mother? Would she have enough to give her child? Her own mother always held herself apart, even when they embraced, afraid Laura would muss her makeup. Her own mother always ended the embrace long before Laura had drunk in enough of her powdery smell, her roses-and-lemon perfume. Where would Laura have learned to give more than that? Most of all, *was she destructive?* Like, would she get angry with her child one day, or every day, and somehow destroy it? Her eardrum, anyway. She sensed that Smerless—not that he'd actually said anything—thought she feared her own anger too much, like it would hurt people.

He thought, or anyway she thought he thought, that she was drawn to people like Beth—her wild, bad Stagolee—who acted out her repressed feelings. And once anyway, had drawn her into her backdraft, carried her out the door to the phone booth to make a warning call. For a bomb. That *had* truly hurt someone.

But when they'd become friends—she started to tell Smerless, tell Bobby Brown—Beth hadn't wanted to hurt anyone. She had wanted to . . . make the world a better place, just like Miss America, say. It hadn't been Oedipal feelings that made Beth—made any of them—want to raise Frank's soul-sparks. Or not just that.

She thought of Beth, a lifetime ago, organizing a teach-in at Wellesley on "Joshua Battle's Legacy." "Harrison Baker, a man who worked in

Mississippi just after Frank's murder, spoke about the path of the non-violent warrior. He went slowly, but everything he said was worth hearing," Beth had written Laura. "Still, not one of Wellesley's bow ties could find time to attend. They were all home, reading 'Dover Beach' to their families or dressing for Evensong."

Laura pulled the covers over her lips. Was the Book of Beth the story of all of them somehow, like Arkey said? And if Beth had gone astray, did that mean she had?

That November, her sophomore year, right, Beth had published a four-page peace supplement to the student newspaper, "We Owe Our Children an End to the Arms Race"—"but," Laura had read, as she'd rocked contentedly in her Kennedy chair, "the sweater-sets and circle-pins had been too busy painting Jackie K's face on Easter eggs even to argue with it." Laura had smiled: Beth sounding bitter and isolated at Wellesley meant she was still Beth's bestest friend.

For a while, anyway. Around January '65, Beth had joined Harrison Baker at an SDS picket line around Pine Street Elementary, a rotting pile of separate-but-unequal wood in Roxbury, "where snow fell on us," she'd written, "as we circled the overcrowded, rat-infested firetrap, and I felt for the first time since his death as if your brother walked beside me again." Laura had wrapped her shoulders in a lacy Portuguese shawl, to keep off the large wet flakes falling on the SDS marchers, though the scene made Laura feel flushed, too, stuck in the hot tar pits of jealousy. Beth had actually *felt* her brother's presence, Beth had the good fortune already to walk in the Big World, where there were run-down segregated schools, rats, and so many greater opportunities to make justice.

And in February that same year it got worse. Beth used her nearly supernatural powers of persuasion to move her reluctant Chinese roommate's living hand, made it forge Beth's signature nightly on the dorm's sign-in sheets. That meant Beth could actually live with the other members of the Roxbury picket line in a Somerville commune, "a mangy house," Beth had written, "of flaking plaster walls, furnished with a rotting gray sofa and high ideals"—a mild irony meant to hide, Laura had known, Beth's attachment to her new "beloved community" in Somerville, far from Laura's bedroom, and her little friends.

In Somerville, the letters they'd studied at the SDS house didn't come from a dead man, but from his living comrade, Sugar Cane, Harrison Baker's mentor from Freedom Summer. Sugar had sent Harrison north to work with students from SDS and bring poor whites into the Movement. Sugar still wrote and called Harrison often, revealed to him the *real* meaning of events Laura had maybe *thought* she'd understood when the NBC Movie of the Week, *Judgment at Nuremberg,* had been interrupted to show demonstrators kneeling and praying in nonviolent witness on the Edmund Pettus Bridge, waiting meekly for Sheriff Clark's men to descend and beat them right back down the streets of Selma. Her own father had said he wanted to fall to his knees to thank He Who Made the Universe that Reverend King hadn't been there that day, for these madmen would surely have murdered him. Then Laura heard with her own ears as her father talked on the phone with King about plans for the next march. King having been spared this time meant he would have to be in harm's way the next, and their voices on the phone meant that her family's wood-paneled library in Great Neck sat at the very center of America's moral universe. Now Beth said that all the secret things that Laura *thought* she knew didn't matter somehow, because there'd been an inner meaning—a Negro meaning—to those events in Selma that she probably couldn't spell for herself until Beth told her what Sugar Cane had said and what Beth's comrades had figured out from their discussions of Sugar's letters.

And *they'd* concluded that the message from Alabama was that Negro lives, Negro sacrifice, just didn't matter in America, and maybe they never would. "Did Laura know," Beth asked, "that a young Negro man named Jimmy Lee Jackson had been beaten senseless by cops in Selma, then shoved against a wall and shot to death *before* the march Laura'd probably watched on television? No, *she* probably *hadn't* known that—"because no white newsmen," Beth had said, "gave a damn about *that* story!" But when the crackers murdered Violet Liuzzo, a white woman from Boston, thousands marched in New York, and Lyndon Johnson finally got around to proposing the Voting Rights Act. "So you tell me, Laura, will white people *ever* really open their hearts to *Negro* suffering? Will even supposedly well-intentioned liberals ever truly care about a Negro's death?"

Laura had been one of those sad, bundled people walking dolefully past St. Patrick's Cathedral and Saks Fifth Avenue, black and white together—and now Beth was saying she'd just showed how racist she was by weeping for brave Mrs. Liuzzo! Her throat tightened with fury.

"I feel Frank understands what Sugar Cane's talking about. You know how injustice must hurt him, the world remembering his name, but not Addie Mae Collins or Claude Hays or even Joshua Battle," Laura hearing Beth say that her own brother would condemn her as a racist because she pressed *his* memory into her heart more than the little girls murdered in Birmingham or a man in Selma she'd never heard of before this moment! How *dare* Beth say that to her!

Yet so much did Laura already dream Beth her superior in courage and insight that she couldn't help wondering if Beth was right that no white person ever truly felt a colored man's suffering? "That's why they let Johnson rain bombs down on the yellow people of Vietnam, and why they've let Watts decay until a maddened people finally burnt it to the ground." To make justice for her brother, did Laura need to love him less—so she could care more for these other people she didn't even know? How could she *ever* do that?

Then Beth had written, "I wish you could join me here," and Laura couldn't help it, the idea filled her with a soft, delicious expectation. "In Somerville you could talk with people who understand the hell we've made in our cities, and you could work with us as we try to figure out how to help put a stop to it."

That meant helping welfare mothers get more money so they could buy toys for their children. When the women went down to the welfare office, Beth took care of their kids, read them *The Cat in the Hat* over and over, as often as they wanted. "I don't know, but I think it's driving me mad! / This Cat and his Hat, he DOES NOT make me Glad! / Oh no, I want to garrote the bazoo / Or feed his fat ass to Thing One or Thing Two! Anyway, the mothers have taught me a lot. Like how to cook, and iron my clothes—the basics of being an independent person, things left off the Great Neck curriculum." Laura couldn't wait to go to the SDS house, to join Beth in working for justice and for Frank, to learn what she needed, finally, to be a whole and independent person.

In September of 1965 Laura visited the peach-colored SDS house in Somerville, on her way to an interview for the promised land of Radcliffe. She arrived in the middle of a meeting because (she learned quickly) NOTHING EVER HAPPENS IN SDS UNTIL THERE IS A MEETING ABOUT IT; which turned out to mean NOTHING HAPPENS *BUT* MEETINGS.

She plopped herself down on the living room floor and flipped through what Beth called the Welfare Haggadah, a mimeoed how-to manual for mothers on the dole. "Ways," Beth whispered to her, "to give the women a place at the table."

Baruch Cramer, known as B.C., stuttered, "They g-g-got. To. F-f-fuck-fuck-fucking d-de-de mand wha-wha-wha-wha-t's already. Theirs by Law!"

How, though? Ah, to decide *that,* everyone in the SDS house had to "democratically participate"—i.e., talk and talk and talk—until "consensus" was reached, which would feel, Beth said mockingly, lovingly, "like everybody has got all curled up inside everybody else."

Laura had had a long trip . . . their pursed, insistent voices rarely changed tone . . . her eyelids drooped . . . and shut. Passover . . . welfare mothers . . . Jews in housing projects . . . no rent for Pharaoh . . .

"Sh-sh-sh-sh . . ." B.C. stuttered angrily, waking her. He stopped, looked plaintively toward Beth. Laura disliked B.C. almost from the first, but his terrified, pleading eyes reminded her of her brother as she'd dreamt him on the edge of that dam, telling his killer *I understand how you feel.* Did her thinking of Frank mean that B.C. was about to say something Laura needed to do for him—Laura given to that kind of madness then, hearing her dead brother talking to her from a living mouth, or through knocking heat pipes that meant Frank seconded what someone had just said. Not that the pipes here provided much guidance—or much heat. Laura had left her coat on, and she wore black tights, but her hands felt like heavy ice.

Anyway, whatever her brother wanted to tell her, B.C. couldn't get the words out.

"Shouldn't we," Beth said, looking through narrowed eyes at B.C. in his plaid flannel shirt, like the boy was a living glyph and she its interpreter/telepath, "say something about Vietnam in our leaflet too?" Palms up, her fingers in the air. Beth, wearing two sweatshirts, beat her wrists up and down on the floor.

"R-ro-ro-rolling f-f-f-fuc-c-c-king thunder!" B.C. finally shouted, scattering spit-bombs. He stared, bug-eyed, around the room.

That must be the message from Frank, Laura thought. She had to do something about Vietnam! *She?* And: *Like what?*

"Vietnam's important," Harrison Baker said, "but we need to stay focused on getting the ladies' heat turned up before the winter comes."

Everyone but Beth, B.C., and Laura nodded amen—like, Harrison had talked to Sugar Cane, so Harrison *knew.*

But he doesn't, Laura wanted to say. *Frank does, my dead brother who I just saw staring from Baruch Cramer's square and pimply face—* though B.C. had an abrupt way about him—lips bitten, fingernails bitten, his arms pushed into his sides to hold his chest together, and his torso trying to twist angrily on itself—altogether the opposite of her brother's easy, if wary, grace. And B.C., she saw, disliked her right back, had pegged her as *fluff.*

Two months later, when Laura visited Beth again, B.C.'s skin had gone clown white—Laura heard her mother's voice saying, *You know, these people definitely need more sun.* But winter didn't dull their determined, serious manner when they talked to each other. And talked to each other.

Laura listened, switching from couch to floor and back again, picking long gray strings from the sofa rips, all through the *endless* cold November afternoon. The SDS students tried to reach agreement now on how to respond to the mayor's having actually cut off the tenants' relief money as punishment for the women's having participated in the SDS-led rent strike to demand more heat for the winter. By five o'clock, the windows dark, Laura was sure she wouldn't feel her brother's presence here today—equally relieved and cheated by that. In fact, all she would ever feel that day was *hungry,* maybe like in a fairy tale actually never getting to *leave* this house to get food for herself, condemned instead to listen for the rest of her starving life to these serious, impassioned, insane voices, Beth's new, annoying family. At the same time, she wondered how to get them to accept her. Then, maybe, like Beth, she would find that this talk fed her.

Finally, they all *agreed*—not *voting,* mind you, which would have meant they were still separate people, hadn't all merged into one big family, one big *organism* even, with twenty arms and legs—that tomorrow they would sit in at the mayor's office.

The SDS house then had been mostly innocent, scrubbed graduate students, even the non-Div ones seeming like the kind of people who joined the clergy because they were scared of sex—and Laura feeling a little less scared of *that* herself when she mocked them. Still, Beth seemed to love arguing with her friends about "cybernation and the new economy," a world where we would probably all work less, all talk more—while, no doubt, eating disgusting Crisco sandwiches, each person in the house having to live on no more than sixty-seven cents per day, so they'd be, Harrison said, "organically like the poor."

Could this *really* be what the poor ate? Laura had wondered that afternoon as she'd bent over the shit-stained toilet throwing up her lunch of lard mixed with peanut butter. In which case, *why do the poor want to go on living?* But Harrison Baker had taught everyone that these daily small sacrifices—no butter, no movies, no television—gave them a moral authority that the welfare mothers would respect, a righteousness that he'd once seen shine from Sugar Cane's glowering face, a man Laura remembered then as punishing her family at Joshua Battle's funeral, her brother just having died and still his high voice beating and beating against them. Harrison Baker, a thin man in his twenties who'd dropped out of Harvard Law School, had legs as long as Honest Abe and huge front teeth stained Chesterfield-yellow by the cigarettes that he used his soft Southern voice, his beseeching manner, and his "moral authority" to bum from everyone, even the welfare mothers who—thanks to him—had no heat or relief money anymore. The students bent toward Harrison when he spoke, because he almost whispered and because he'd walked with Sugar Cane in deadly Lovette, Mississippi, even still got weekly calls and letters from Mr. Cane about his current and most audacious organizing project, in bloody Lowndes County, Alabama, a nearly all-black county with not one Negro voter, a place where even when it rained, a Negro made sure to duck into the weeds until the sheriff's car cruised past. But the Voting Rights Act meant Negroes would get federal protection when they left the tall weeds to walk to the registrar, could maybe even get a Negro sheriff elected. So

Sugar and his people had started a new political party to take advantage of this great moment—a party not just for blacks, though, but for organizing all the county's poor.

Which was, Harrison said, precisely what *they* were trying to do in Somerville, getting the welfare mothers to organize a sit-in at the mayor's office. Beth listening, sitting upright on the floor now, her large green eyes wide with glee, probably imagining the cops struggling to pick up her limp body. Her hand stroked B.C.'s long Frye boot with a rapid fretfulness, and her right foot shook furiously back and forth in a scuffed sneaker, like a tennis-playing prisoner trying to worry herself free from binding ropes, restless probably for the same reason Laura was herself: at nearly eighteen years of age they'd done so little for justice.

But the next day Laura didn't do anything either, just stood to the side of the dirty city hall corridor as two guards dragged Beth down the floor, Laura having to catch the Eastern shuttle home that afternoon, take an advanced placement test in calculus the next morning instead of going to a much more glamorous bail hearing; which made Laura feel like a child, unworthy of the wink Beth gave her as she slid by.

Laura shuttled back to Somerville as soon as she could, to make sure Beth still liked her, and bursting to tell her, too, about her magnificent series of test scores—a five on the AP to add to her amazing double eight hundreds on the SAT's, not a thousand of those in the country!—though she was clever enough (check out those scores) to know as soon as she arrived that she shouldn't embarrass herself by seeming to care about *that* instead of Vietnam, which was the only thing the house talked about now. Sugar Cane, Harrison said, had asked SNAP's leadership to speak out against the war at the national meeting.

"But is that the right thing to do?" Harrison wondered aloud, Fannie Mae having said to him once, "It's bad enough being black in America, Harrison, without being Red, too."

The students once again sat scattered about the living room. Beth and B.C. perched cross-legged on the floor, Beth hugging the popcorn bowl and throwing stale kernels into her mouth. "Vietnam's draining resources from the poor. It's killing innocent men and women. It's just plain *wrong.*"

"Well," a pale Div student said, looking hungrily at the bowl, "I don't *know* the Vietcong. I mean, that's not *our* movement." He stroked his thick red beard. "We can't vote on what *they* do."

Fuzzy, his long-faced wife, added, "Won't the people here, you know, feel that we, in effect, are supporting Communist violence in Vietnam?" Thoughtful tones edged with anguish and uncertainty. "And this is still a nonviolent movement, isn't it?"

She must be right, Laura thought; Frank had been nonviolent, and she and Beth, in her bedroom in Great Neck, had pledged to follow his path.

But Beth stopped eating popcorn, looked grave and disappointed. "Look, I'm not saying it will be easy, eh? But I think we should support people who stand up for their rights when the ruling class tries to massacre them. Here or in Vietnam." She put her hand on B.C.'s fist, which rested on the floor. "People may call that violence, but Sugar says that's self-defense."

The students looked over to Harrison for instruction, but he just sat like a Buddha on the couch, contemplating the ceiling, wondering what *he* really knew anymore. Beth, after all, had just run it down pretty much the same way Sugar had on the phone to him last night.

"Oh, I've learned a lot in bloody Lowndes, Harry Boy," Sugar had said.

"Tha' right?" Harrison had said, truly looking forward to being put in the picture, learning from Sugar again.

"Yeah," he'd said, like they were still sharing a joke at the juke. "I learned that all the black farmers in Lowndes got rifles already."

"Oh," Harrison said. "Well, that hasn't done them a whole lot of good, has it, if they still have to hide in the weeds when the sheriff's car goes by?" He'd leaned against the wall then, accidentally dragged the phone off the radiator.

"What's that?" Sugar said sharply. "Is your phone tapped?"

"Maybe. But I just knocked it over." He stooped to put the base back on the flaking silver pipes.

"I'll tell you, Harry, one has to admire Martin for portraying the fantasy of the Negro as nonviolent, and even getting blacks to go along with it. But we are not a pacific people."

One had to admire. In Mississippi, Sugar's talk had been fierce, sometimes, but warm, too, not a professor's even tones. Now his talk about violence felt distant, disembodied.

"Have you read Fanon?" Sugar asked.

"No, sir, I have not."

"Well, Fanon shows that it's fighting for our freedom that squeezes the slave out of us. Destroying our opponent makes us into men."

"That," Harrison had said to Sugar on the phone the night before, "sounds to me like a Marine recruiting poster. War makes a man out of you. That kinda thing."

"We're not looking for a war, Harrison, we're looking for justice. You know what Malcolm said to me once?"

Harrison did. Everyone who knew Sugar did.

"He said, if America won't give us our freedom we must be ready to destroy America." Sugar's fury rushed all the way north through the phone line, striking any opposition dead. "By ourselves if necessary."

"Or with the help of Allah." That caused a sharp intake of breath on the other end, like Sugar thought Harrison had maybe insulted Malcolm. Sugar the Christian become Sugar the guerrilla, equally fervent, though, both times.

"You don't believe we can do it, Harrison?" Sugar giving him a jab or two of *full first name*; meaning: *nickname intimacy canceled.* "We're well placed, Harrison, in the cities, by the subways, in the capital."

Sabotaging subways, for Jesus' sweet sake! Harrison's mouth near fell open. Sugar, SNAP, Freedom Summer, Harrison had felt it all slipping away from him. But Fannie, David, Chuck, the rest of the SNAP National Committee—for the first time Harrison found himself hoping they would tone Sugar down, get him to bottle up.

"We *will* have our freedom, Mr. Baker, by any means necessary. You watch, Harrison, see if the national office doesn't agree with me." And then the receiver clicked down: end of the conversation, end of the affair. End of the nonviolent black movement, too, unless the National Office stood up to Sugar.

Then Beth and B.C.'s laughter dissolved his vision, and he looked over at them again. Beautiful animals, he thought; implacable, ferocious as Willard Cane, filled with good appetites, plus (in B.C.'s case) a very desirable pack of cigarettes rolled into his T, near his no-doubt-manly, enemy-destroying muscles. He glanced at the other sprawled bodies around the room, seven serious good young people that he'd led into this movement and Beth's attractive, plump-cheeked friend, all now staring back at him in confusion, like astronomers watching something as rare as a supernova going dwarf, namely Harrison Baker having nothing to say.

And goddamn the world then, if just before the national meeting some cracker gas station attendant hadn't shot a Navy veteran, Sammy Younge—the dumbshow signaling that blacks fought for the U.S. in Vietnam but got murdered at home for wanting to take a piss in a Whites Only bathroom. So the SNAP National Meeting stood up with Sugar Cane, spoke out for Vietnamese self-defense abroad, black self-defense at home, tossing nonviolence into the ashcan of history. Which also meant, Harrison bet, that Johnson's federal marshals would stop protecting Sugar and his people in Lowndes County. Then, with the marshals gone, they had better start protecting themselves—the whole thing knotting together nicely, Harrison saw, like a black hand around a gun.

And less than a week after that, Harrison heard from friends that Sugar would pull out a picture he said the USIA distributed all over Africa, namely Harrison Baker in jeans, Sugar in overalls, arms around each other in Mississippi, black and white together. "Look at this *fool*," Sugar would say, pointing to himself. "They made me the motherfucking smile on the face of the American hyena!" Well, Sugar wasn't gonna let himself be used like that anymore. He'd stopped talking to whites. No reason to, anyway. "People like Harrison Baker," he said, "the boy in that photograph, they *never* truly understood our struggle."

So by the time Laura visited in April, Harrison didn't speak much during meetings, and most of the sallow men and earnest women had left, replaced by students in jeans and denim shirts who wanted to work against the War, these new recruits faster-talking, more agitated. Sure, too, that the government hated them for their antiwar work, so they and the welfare mothers were all in it together, Outcast Enemies of the State, which meant, fortunately, that they didn't have to imitate the poor any-more, could at least have big aluminum pots of spaghetti for dinner, with plenty of meat in the red sauce.

"Sugar Cane says that local governments in the Black Belt are illegit-imate powers," Beth told Laura, as the house sat down at a long table made from a board over sawhorses. "Just like the U.S. in Vietnam." She looked over at B.C., his hair in a short ponytail, something Laura had never seen before. He nodded, not like someone confirming her opinion, Laura saw now, but more like obedience. White strands disappeared into his mouth, sauce dripped down his chin. "The government in Viet-nam," Beth said, "and the ones in Alabama, they all have to be changed, so that they work for everyone."

"Fine," Harrison said, nervously making a few too many cuts in his spaghetti. "That's what ballots are for, Beth. That's how we'll get the U.S. out of Vietnam and get black people into the government in the South."

"Well," Beth said, "isn't that what Sugar is trying to do, Harrison? Get people to vote, like you say? And if the vote succeeds, well, great. If it doesn't, then we'll have to find another way. By any means nec-essary."

"By any means necessary!" Harrison cried. "Jesus God, what does anyone mean by that?"

"Fu-fu-fuck you," B.C. said. "Th-th-tha-tha-that's wh-wh-wh-what he means." B.C. pounded the table in frustration. "F-f-fu-fuck you!"

"B.C., darling, Sugar's making you fat with air." Harrison showing his long yellow teeth in a false smile. "You'll give birth to wind."

If *he* was going to listen to talk all day, Harrison drawled, it had better be some that really could be used to help the poor. So he wanted everyone to know tonight that he'd be going back for his last year at Harvard Law.

"Yu-Yu-Yuh, You are the one fu-fu-full of hot air," B.C. (Columbia, '65) said. "Harvard!" he shouted. "Ya, Yhh, You, You'll work fu-fu-fur-for Standard Oil!" His face twisted from hatred of Harrison; big business; the language; his own recalcitrant tongue.

"Face it, Harrison, you're already crawling back to your class." Beth smiled broadly. As long as she pronounced anathemas on her class *she* clearly couldn't be crawling back to it.

Laura looked down at her long legs in their plaid tights. Tomorrow she would take the Eastern shuttle back to Great Neck. Her father, she thought, had probably done legal work for Standard Oil. And her most cherished dream was to attend Harvard.

And on April 15, 1966, Harvard, like Zeus, had come to Laura and Arkey and Jesse and Billy in a shower of thick acceptance letters, making them pregnant, surely, not with air but with a sublime and satisfying future. She turned her doll's head to Smile.

But did admission to Harvard mean they were all ruling-class lackeys, too, and therefore damned, the way Beth implied—even though Beth had gone to Wellesley, for Christ's sake? She twiddled her doll's head uncertainly, Happy, Sad, Happy, Sad.

Meanwhile Jesse held his admission letter aloft and danced about her room, kicking his long legs high. Empty New York adventures over, they'd been sleeping together again.

That they'd all gotten in must mean, Jesse said, that Billy Green had been right: they were linked, both here and *there*, throughout eternity—chosen to make justice and to rise together.

And Jeffrey? Well, if Jeffrey Schell hadn't gotten in, long fingers or not, maybe that was because he'd always been skeptical of Billy's vision, a spot on his soul no doubt discerned by the Harvard Admissions Committee. So he would have to attend Columbia.

Frank came rushing back to her then. For if this really meant they were linked, then it also meant Frank suffered, that she had to help him. That made her right leg ache all along the side, from the bone outward. Did that mean Frank was feeling pain there now? Jesse said something about the Playhouse on Saturday and his all-time favorite movie, *A Man for All Seasons*. Why, she wondered irritably, couldn't he wear some new non-blue colors?

"I saw it again with my dad already," she lied. She had bought some brightly striped shirts for his birthday once, but he left them in his drawer. "And I ought to, you know, spend some time with my family on the weekend," an excuse so obviously lame that maybe Jesse would get the point: they just had to put an end to this affair before their new wonderful, burdensome lives started in the fall.

Before *his* new life started at Harvard that fall, Bobby Brown knew he'd better make some big change, too, or he would jump right out of his skin. For three years at the John Dewey School, he'd felt like he was being directed by this cold, joyless hand that pushed him to get A's, get into Harvard, get ahead of the others, Bobby going round and round and round, like on the indoor track today as Jacob Battle told him about this Mississippi march, running because everyone else was running, then running to run faster than the others because that's what runners did, not thinking much about what he might want or where he was going—which was *around*.

Bobby Brown had gotten A's, had gotten into Harvard, which meant he'd gotten ahead of everyone here, but he still didn't know what *he* wanted out of this big life they all said was about to start for him. *He* didn't know what it was he didn't know, either. But he'd always felt it about himself too: that he'd do something big, more important even than going to Harvard. This Mississippi march Jacob was telling him about, it could be a way to find out something about what was in him, what was making Bobby Brown so damn nervous all the time that even in his head he talked about himself in the third person. Anyway, at least the march would get him out of town for a while.

"They're gonna protest James Meredith's getting himself shot," Jacob had said as they circled the track, Jacob following a "regimen" that Sugar Cane himself had sent him, one that Cane said had worked fine for another asthmatic boy, Che Guevara. Jacob had sounded reverent, but Bobby didn't want to ask Jacob exactly who that was, his head filled right then with the AP in modern European history and the execution of Charles I. "Meredith, huh?" he said, legs churning, mind elsewhere . . . in 1648? 9?

Jacob probably heard the empty sound. "He's the guy from Ole

Miss. Sugar says he's a little nuts now." Meredith had marched down the highways of Mississippi with a pith helmet and a walking stick, a one-man freedom band, singing, *We can walk anywhere we want; into your universities; down to your registrars,* a few reporters following after. *So* on the second day, an out-of-work hardware salesman darted out of the scrub, pumped three shotgun shells into Meredith to show everyone he'd gotten it wrong. He could *not* walk just anywhere.

Bobby had seen the photo: a Negro man facedown in thick, inky shadow, a pool of his own blood. He'd put it out of his mind, though, even half forgotten the name; which was yet another reason why he had to go on this march, not remembering Meredith's name maybe meaning that Bobby Brown didn't remember who he himself was anymore, or maybe had never known. Or so, he bet, Sugar Cane would have said.

Jacob had started wheezing like an unoiled metal bellows. He threw himself against the railing, pretending to be James Brown panting, "I can't do no more! I can't do no more!" They leaned over together, watched the third form kids below play basketball—*nothing but net* here meaning that the guy had hit only the pristine net, missed the basket and backboard entirely. Jacob told him that Martin Luther King and Sugar Cane had cut a deal standing right over Meredith's hospital bed. They would lead a march together, all the way through Mississippi, make speeches in a dozen towns, "like a face-off between Nonviolence and Self-Defense."

The Deacons for Defense from Louisiana would protect the marchers from snipers—SNAP's idea. "But you have to understand, if you go," Jacob said, his voice sounding a little higher than usual, "the Deacons can protect the march against the Klan, but they can't throw down on the cops. And cops in Mississippi are just Klansmen without sheets."

"That right?" Bobby said, not entirely liking being lectured to by a younger boy, even Joshua Battle's brother.

"Yeah, it *is* right. And when the police and the crackers attack you, the marchers have to remain nonviolent—King's way."

"Got it."

"Do you? You better think now, can you do that, Bobby? Sit still while a cracker goes upside your head?"

"Could you?"

"I don't really know." He smiled. "On the other hand, what else *could* I do?"

Bobby laughed then, remembering the hours at his desk studying for the AP test in modern European history. *Yeah, that's one thing I can do.*

I can sit still. Wait now, boy, a voice said. Sit still for a beating? Like football with your hands tied, getting tackled and pummeled, no rules, no relief? He turned away from the players in the gym below and smiled at Jacob, not so sure anymore that he *could* do that.

Jacob must have seen his uncertainty. "Still, I wish my mama would let *me* go, 'cause something else is gonna happen on the march, too," Jacob whispered hoarsely now, raising his eyebrows a little. Then he turned and walked back downstairs to the locker room.

Bobby got undressed for the shower. "Yeah? So tell me, Cub, what's gonna happen?"

Jacob toweled his sweat off, started to put on his shirt. "*You'll* see," he said, teasing Bobby. "I mean, you'll see *if* you go." Bobby hearing how he wanted him to do it, wanted him to be his eyes and ears, probably wanted him most of all to get to love Sugar Cane the way he did.

Well, he *had,* and he *had.*

And now Jacob wanted Bobby to tell Baby and Weary and the others on the 126th Street basketball court all about what he'd seen in Mississippi, but everyone listening to him, Bobby knew, more because he was supposed to be a star football player who lived on Lenox than because he'd been to Mississippi and had marched past thick mangroves, trees like in stories his grandma used to read him, with branches a witch's spell might make into long, thin fingers to grab you 'round the chest from behind, slit your throat, leave you to bleed to death while photographers took your picture for UPI.

They'd marched through little towns, and Bobby wondered which of the white people on the raised sidewalks, spitting at them, or baring their teeth, would try to kill him or one of the hundred or so other demonstrators and reporters.

Reverend King had taken off his suit jacket, thrown it over his shoulder. He was more muscular than Bobby had imagined, and Bobby's hero still, and his grandma's hero, too, though marching behind him was not quite working to tell Bobby what he should do with his life, who he was—maybe because the sound of the countrypeople's talk had something Bobby Brown didn't take to, something too soft, slow, and, Bobby thought, kind of apologetic. And though there were only a few whites on the march, still, one of them was a professor from Harvard. He stuck close to Bobby, and Bobby, calculating that it was bound to be a good thing to know a professor, had chatted mostly with *him,* about the world to come, the world that had made him feel different in the first place

from the countrypeople, and from these kids today, too, in their basketball shorts and too tight T's and cut-off sweatshirts, Weary and Baby the
only faces Bobby even recognized, 'cause their people had places near his
in the project.

The kids looked at him blankly, as bored with the story so far as
Bobby had been living it, except that Bobby had been scared too.

Bobby told them how the marchers had been near eaten alive by
mosquitoes as they went—and not the teeny-weeny Harlem kind but
their giant mothers. And they'd been tear-gassed for setting up tents in
the Greenville schoolyard. The slower or more obstinate marchers had
gotten their heads broken, too.

"The stu-pid ones," Baby said, bouncing a basketball to entertain
himself.

Sugar had been dragged off to jail by four cops under the clouds of
pearly tear gas. At the torchlight rally that night maybe fifteen hundred
people, farmers mostly, had held their children up to see Martin Luther
King standing alone in his suit, moaning, "I know I'm gonna stay nonviolent no matter what happens. But a lot of people are getting hurt and
bitter and they can't see it that way anymore. It's getting too hard, Lord,
too hard," but the keening church sound his hero made denied the threat
his words contained, made it seem too much like he was saying, *Please,
sir, don't hit us anymore.*

Then Sugar Cane, bailed out at the last minute, had marched from
the jailhouse, and across the grass to the rally, the coal tar flames jumping and everyone cheering like God—and not a hundred dollars of
SNAP's money—had opened Sugar Cane's cell door. Cane took slow
steps up to the platform. "This is the twenty-seventh time *I* have been
arrested," he told the crowd in a high-pitched, tired voice, "and I ain't
going to jail no more!"

David Watkins, one of the march leaders, had smiled at Bobby at
that—probably because he knew it wasn't true. The soft-spoken man, a
Howard graduate, had taken an interest in Bobby.

Maybe, Bobby had thought, *this* is the big showdown Jacob had
promised, Sugar saying, *I ain't going to jail,* and King saying, *Please
don't take us;* which wasn't much of a difference: they would take King,
for sure, and Sugar would always end up in jail, anyway, 'cause what
were they going to do to stop it?

"Just wait," David Watkins had said to him. "He's priming them.
He's gonna drop it on them soon as they're ready."

"See how they do me?" Sugar had shouted. "See how they do me?
When are we ever gonna learn, people? There's just no point in pleading

with the white man! Blacks can't ever count on cooperation or support from the white man!"

"Got that right," one of the kids on the basketball court said, probably thinking of a teacher; or a cop; or a social worker; or a clerk; or a landlord. And so on.

"Unh huh!" the others said here—and in Lovette, too.

"The white man," Sugar had shouted, "he sends blacks to die in Vietnam, to die for the white man, to kill the colored men."

"We fight *for* the white man in Vietnam. We fight *against* the colored man," Jacob shouted back from near the foul line, high-pitched and out of breath too, which made him sound even more like Sugar. "We got to have the courage to fight for ourselves!" Jacob saying word for word what Sugar had said next. Maybe it was all those letters from Africa, maybe Jacob knew Sugar so well now he could imagine where this was all going, what Sugar would say. Maybe, Bobby saw, Jacob was even making himself ready *to become* Sugar if anything ever happened to him, just the way Sugar had followed Malcolm.

That thought scared Bobby, like the boy had a mortal disease, and he looked away from the thin, asthmatic body with its concave chest to the metal nets on the baskets. He remembered the shadows that walked at the edge of the Lovette woods where Jacob's brother had been murdered. "Yeah, we have to have the courage to fight for ourselves!"

"We gotta do it on our own!" Jacob responded.

"*You* gotta do it?" one of the kids said to Jacob, getting annoyed now.

"Yeah, what the fuck *you* gonna do, little peewee boy like you?" Baby said, fat belly rolling out from under his T-shirt; grown now but still with the smoothest, youngest-looking face, eerie when you saw how empty the eyes were, and you knew he'd splashed gasoline on a guy's clothes, near burned him to death. And maybe done that to more than one guy. He put the basketball under his foot for a moment and sucked beer from a giant baby bottle—his way of saying he, yeah, he was *definitely* in on the joke.

Bobby walked over to Jacob, put his hand on his bony shoulder. "Nah, you got it wrong, Baby. This boy may be little, but he's got *the knowledge.*" Bobby smiled at Baby—uneasy still, but proud of himself too. After all, these kids knew he was a football player *somewhere,* and they could see he had muscles. But they also knew where he'd be going come fall. They might just throw down on him. "You may not know it," he said, "but Sugar Cane thinks the world of this boy." *Thinks the world of me, too,* Bobby wanted to say.

"All right, then," Baby had said, stepping closer to Jacob, but in a friendly way now.

In Lovette, though, Bobby had wondered what Jacob *actually* knew. Was *this* the big thing Jacob had promised him: blacks got to scuffle for themselves? Whites won't help? That wasn't exactly news in this neighborhood, he'd thought.

But by the time they got to Jackson, fifteen thousand people waited to hear King and Sugar, so maybe it *was* news in Mississippi. And once again, by the time of the rally, Sugar had just been bonded out of jail, Bobby having figured out by then that that was part of the act. Sugar Cane had come by as Bobby talked with the Harvard professor, put an arm around him, pulling at him. "'Scuse me, but I need this man right now. Jacob Battle tells me *this man* will be a leader!" He'd taken him right up on the podium with him, giving him a place in the world—a big, Bobby Brown–size place—not five feet from Reverend King, Bobby standing next to Susan Lems, her eyes bright too as they looked out at the jumping crowd.

Sugar had shouted, "Are *you* people gonna let them arrest me anymore? Are *you* people gonna let them do that to your black brother?"

"No, sir," one of the kids said quietly to Bobby. "We won't let them do you like that." It had worked in Jackson, too, Bobby thought, everyone abashed, like it had been their fault Sugar had had to go to jail.

"We have been asking for freedom for six years now," Sugar shouted, "and what have we gotten?"

Baby, eyes bright as new pennies now, smiled at his new friend, Jacob Battle, and said, "One half of one percent of nothing." Beer-filled baby bottle in his left hand, he bounced the basketball higher and higher with the right, making a festival of the words.

In Jackson, Bobby had heard David Watkins lean toward Sugar, saying, "Drop it now, brother. They're primed. They're ready. Drop it now!"

"The white man ain't never gonna change," Sugar had shouted then. "*We* got to be the ones to change! *We* got to say: *We* want the power to protect our own! *We want Black Power!*"

The faces in the Jackson crowd had looked bewildered then, and the word *black* had even sounded new to Bobby coming out of Sugar's mouth that day, had made him look down at his own arm—covered with welts from mosquito bites he'd rubbed raw—and he'd thought, *Yeah, that's what I am, not colored, not Negro,* almost surprised by it, like it was a discovery, though he'd really heard the word a thousand times a day.

Sugar had stopped then, seeing the confusion in the crowd. But Susan had nodded, "Go on, baby. Tell it now, tell it!" something about that b-a-b-y making Sugar start up again, revived, telling about the power the black man had shown in Africa, how he'd made the white man flee. And in Vietnam, too, look at the fight the colored man put up there! Africa and Vietnam had both been colonized by the white man, "until the colored people said no more! They said, we want the power to rule over ourselves! We want the power to protect our own!" He paused, stared right down at everyone. "So what do *we* want? Tell me now. What do we want?"

The crowd, trained for years by Joshua Battle and David Watkins and Sugar Cane himself, thought they surely knew the answer to that one. "Freedom!" they shouted, black and white together. "We want Freedom Now!" And Bobby probably would have goofed himself, except he was pretty good in schoolrooms, knew when a teacher was teasing you, leading you to screw up so he could make a point.

Sugar bent forward, like a chiding mother. "No, no, no," he said. "We *don't* say that no more! *Now* we say we want power! We want Black Power!" He leaned back, smiled. "So tell me: What do we want?"

Some people—black and white together—still said "Freedom Now." But the ten or eleven kids here in this Harlem playground, *they* got it right away. "Black Power!" they shouted. "Black Power!" They danced around, screaming it, Baby bouncing the ball off Weary's head, then on the ground, shouting, "We gonna rescue our black brothers in Vietnam," getting the idea right, even if the hue, Bobby thought, might be slightly off.

"That's right! Black Power!" Bobby smiled, maybe having had some doubts when he'd been listening to Sugar in Mississippi, but his confidence soaring here, the kids responding like that basketball under Baby's fat hand, souls bouncing higher and higher.

In Jackson, though, Sugar hadn't got the mojo working right yet. He'd tried again. "What do we want?"

The chant had grown stronger, falling into a rhythm and the words coming clear. "Black Power!" "Freedom Now" dying out. One of the few whites in the Jackson crowd looked pleadingly at Bobby up on the courthouse steps, a sick expression on his pale face, probably thinking of their good talks about college, hadn't he sounded like he couldn't wait for Bobby to come? Still, Bobby had felt himself fed by the way the man's cocky expression fell away, leaving his face slack, beaten, 'cause welcome was nice, he'd thought, but the man had always sounded like

Bobby was going to be a guest, and lucky to be invited, which had made him feel, *Where's my home, then, where you're the guest?*

The crowd sang with him now, and Sugar's voice sounded not so shrill anymore. He waved his arms up and down in the air, like flapping wings, pumped more volume from the crowd, got more and more of them to shout louder and louder, "Black Power! Black Power! Black Power!" the whites in the crowd growing quiet, looking around with worried expressions, *Freedom Now* and *Black and White Together* quickly forgotten as the crowd in Jackson or the ten kids on a sunny day here on the playground screamed, "Black Power! Black Power! Black Power!" and Bobby, here or in Mississippi, not thinking anymore about the white faces, but only the black ones, beautiful old head wisdom in the soft vowels of *my* people, *black people,* all of it musical, like a slow, deep river he couldn't bathe in enough now. The shadows in Mississippi, the Deacons for Defense, rifles slung across their backs, walked along the edge of the parking lot in Jackson, peered through the park trees for snipers. A beautiful sight: blacks protecting blacks. "Black Power!" Bobby shouted back into the roar of the crowd, he and David Watkins and Susan Lems with arms around each other, laughing at the beauty of it, shouting themselves hoarse.

Bobby Brown looked at the kids on the playground, laughing and shouting at *his* words. Well, Bobby Brown had always thought of himself in the third person, seen himself from without, because he believed history would see him someday, too. *A leader.*

Today in Harlem, Bobby Brown put his arm around Jacob Battle, weak, asthmatic Jacob, and promised History and his people: We *will* protect our own.

Bobby and Jacob marched off to Al's barbershop then, leaving the kids to their little boy games.

As they came in, an older man on the sofa said, "Aren't you a friend of Sugar Cane?" The man's two pals sat next to him, like always when they didn't have a run.

"Yes, sir. I am," Jacob said.

Bill, that was the man's name. He'd been around Jacob's house after his father had died, till his mom had sent him on his way.

"The Black Power man," one of them said.

"That boy may be a friend of Sugar Cane, Al," Bill said, as Jacob took a seat in the chair, "but Sugar Cane is no friend of yours."

"I don't know the man," Al said sourly. Al booked numbers, he said, and cut heads; he didn't march. "So how could he be a friend of mine?" He whisked a white apron around Jacob and clinked his shears in the air near Jacob's ear.

"Have you seen that Sugar Cane's *hair,* Al? I don't think he likes barbers!"

"Well, I don't care what Sugar Cane likes or *dis*-likes. I'm going to cut his boy's hair," Al said, setting to work on Jacob's head, and setting him up, Jacob knew, with the "his boy," Al cackling a little to make everyone ready for the takedown: "And I'm gonna cut it just the way I know his *mama* likes it."

Al would stop laughing, Jacob knew, when Sugar's party won in Lowndes, when Sugar Cane showed them all the way to power, *Black Power.* He let Bobby run it down for them now, about the election coming up in Alabama, the candidates all black in a mostly black county, so they were sure to win this time, and for their *own* party, too, not Republican or Democrat but *Black,* the Black Panther Party of Lowndes County.

Jacob liked the smell of the place today, the lye and the fresh scent from the jar of blue disinfectant where the combs lived.

One of the men laughed. "Man, you gotta be stupid to actually *say* you want power. Now you look at the Jews. They got all the power in the world, don't they?"

His friends nodded.

"But you ask the man about it, he shrugs his shoulders, says, 'Me, sir? I'm a poor little Jew-boy. *I* ain't got no power.' "

"I don't get it," Bobby said. He stood next to the edge of the couch, his legs spread, his tone respectful, but angry too.

"No. And looks like you never will. What I'm saying is, those who *have* power, they *deny* they have it, they don't *boast* about it and make everybody angry at them. So you know what your friend Sugar Cane is?"

"No, sir," Bobby said. "You tell me."

"I *will* tell you. He's a *fool,* that's what he is," giving the word a lot of extra *o*'s, and like saying it was the same as spitting.

"No, sir," Jacob said, matter-of-factly, turning toward Bill.

"Watch it, man," Al warned, "I nearly nicked you."

"He is *not* a fool," Jacob said. "Sugar Cane is a prince. A black prince."

Bobby, gravely, nodded amen.

By the middle of November, Jacob dreaded going to Al's. Sheriff, assessor, even coroner, every single Lowndes County candidate had been defeated. One half of one percent of nothing. But he felt like he had to tell Bill and Al personally. Besides, the headmaster at his school said he had to get a haircut or he'd suspend him.

"I'll tell you what happened to Mr. Sugar Cane," Al said as he whisked the bib round Jacob's neck. "The plantation owners told their tenants, 'Sugar Cane's boys win, you don't have to come back to work tomorrow. And git your family right out of yur house.' "

"Your *shack*," a colleague on the couch corrected.

"Yeah, that's right, your *shack*. He said, '*If* you're still alive, that is. You know what happened to Rastas.' "

"Who's Rastas?" his friend said.

Bill giggled. "*Ex-actly*. He's that spot on the road, who used to be working for the Lowndes County Freedom Democratic Party. I mean you would have to be a *fool* to think getting candidates on a ballot's gonna be enough to down those white people."

"And Mr. Sugar Cane," Al said, "is no fool."

"He knows we have to love ourselves more," Bill added.

"That's right. There has to be more black pride, just like Sugar Cane says."

"We need black jobs, in black-owned places of business."

"Up South, too," Al says.

"Right. Did you see what happened in Cicero?"

"You know what they say," Al said, letting the electric razor buzz next to Jacob's ear. "Down South, you can get as close as you want, long as you don't get too big."

"And Up South you can get as big as you want, long as you don't get too close."

"Reverend King led his little lambs into that nice suburb, and these nice white women with their nice pocketbooks came out to shout, 'Nigger, git!' and slam the little kids on the head with those pocketbooks."

"*Big* white mob."

"Not just peckerheads."

"No, sir. Up here, it's *every* fucking white person. I saw where mothers brought their little children to the march, had 'em throw rocks at the marchers."

"We need *black* guns," Bill said.

The idea of fighting back made the man grin, and that was nice to see.

"That Sugar Cane," Bill said again. "he understands things the way I do. Now, Jacob," he said, "you remember and tell Mr. Cane I said so."

. . .

The last day of school, Jacob showed Mr. Hartman the photo in the SNAP newspaper, let him learn that Sugar Cane was nobody's fool, too. It showed some scared men in kaffiyehs up against a brick wall, an Israeli soldier pointing a rifle at them, the caption saying: *This is the Gaza Strip, Palestine, 1967, not Dachau, Germany,* and the photo *also* showed, Sugar had told him, that SNAP didn't take orders from anyone anymore. They would take a principled black stand, no matter what the cost in Jewish donations. Well, it was the same for him, Jacob thought. Mr. Hartman had seemed to like him, but he had to know where Jacob stood or that liking didn't mean anything.

Mr. Hartman glanced at the picture Jacob had thrown down on his desk, and then started to rub his eyes. "I see," he said, though his lids were shut, and his hands worked at his eyeballs like he wanted to crush them. Jacob squirmed. He wished Mr. Hartman would stop. "I can't talk about this now." Finally, Mr. Hartman opened his eyes. "I think you can come to my house on Saturday if you want to talk." Jacob had run out the classroom door, ashamed suddenly of what he'd done. "I'll give you a cup of tea," Mr. Hartman said behind him.

But when he told his mom that a teacher had invited him to his home, she said, "What does he want with you?"

"He just wants to talk to me."

"To you? About what?"

"Israel."

"Really?" She laughed. "Now don't let them talk you into joining one of their armies," she said. "Well, they *should* take an interest in you. Their prize debater! You're a special, special boy." She sounded a little uncertain, though, or maybe just a little frightened for him. After all, she'd had another special, special boy—maybe that was a dangerous thing to be. "You're a little Adam Powell!" Then she frowned, even *that* not looking so safe nowadays, the new rules being, you can't get too close *or* too big.

Still, he'd decided to go, had even looked Mr. Hartman's number up in the phone book himself and called him to seal the deal. He'd wanted Hartman to know who he was, wanted to get him ready to add another name—*a black name*—to that genius list of his.

He'd prepared for the day all week, studying Israel, putting his points on five-by-eight cards, reading them over again as he walked to Hartman's apartment, only twenty blocks and a world away, down across the magic divide where the faces, with each year that he grew,

grew a little less friendly. In his back pocket he carried a pick for his Afro. A lot of whites glanced at the handle, and their eyes flickered with fear, sure it was a razor.

Now, on his way home—back in friendly territory—he stopped at the bodega at 120th Street, the one that had the picture of a bare-chested monster, chains across his chest, a big-assed machete in his hand. Some kind of badass god, he knew, Sugar having told him some things. Africa, he'd said, had its own gods. Powerful ones, too. "They just might jump into your body, too—look out of your eyes, shout from your mouth." But Sugar had laughed, too, said he didn't have much use for gods anymore. Señor Wences, as always, eyed him suspiciously. Jacob bought a bottle of Coke.

Hartman's apartment didn't have any pictures on the wall, just shelves and shelves of records and books, running all the way up to the high ceilings, piled everywhere on the floor. Thick blue curtains had blocked the sun from outside, like maybe Mr. Hartman was recovering from an illness and the light still hurt his eyes. Or the place was like a hideout—so if Mr. Hartman got everything he ever wanted into his apartment, he wouldn't have to see anyone again; he'd be safe.

Mr. Hartman made tea for them in a tiny kitchen. "Sugar says SNAP isn't anti-Semitic," Jacob had shouted through the kitchen door, wanting to get the fight about Israel started. "It's anti-Zionist."

Mr. Hartman, returning, had laughed and waved a thin hand in the air. "I'm sure. After all, *no one* is anti-Semitic anymore, are they?" He'd smiled. and handed Jacob a cup, then sat opposite him, his own small portion balanced on his knee.

That casually waving hand of his had knocked all the words out of Jacob's mind. He had sat silently, scared to take a drink, like Mr. Hartman had maybe put something in the tea.

"You know why American Jews love Israel so much, Jacob? It's because they're sick of feeling weak. Once, perhaps, they had thought that was a distinction. We were scholars, not soldiers, moral men, students of the Law. Like your nonviolent preachers, say. Now we want to be hard men. Dangerous, powerful men."

"Jews do?" Was he kidding him? Still, the way Mr. Hartman talked to him made him feel at ease, like he belonged in this library, like they were equals. Jacob tried the tea; it was smoky and, weirdly, made his throat feel drier.

Hartman had shrugged. "I understand them. I'd like to be a hard man myself. But I'm *not*," he said, like maybe Jacob might be confused on *that* subject! "But I think that's why your Sugar Cane loves the PLO. They're his dream body—carrying guns, killing coldly. Or so he dreams."

Dream body? Jacob didn't get it; and he wasn't buying it, either. He wasn't going to betray Sugar for a cup of tea. "We *are* fighters, Mr. Hartman," he had said, his voice becoming a little higher in pitch. "We're part of a powerful, worldwide revolutionary movement."

"Really? Well, I think *you* are a scholar, Jacob. Like me. A yeshiva bocher."

Fag? No, *student*, probably.

Mr. Hartman had drunk some more Jewish tea. "We have a ceremony when a boy turns thirteen," Hartman said, like he was revealing a secret.

"I know, Mr. Hartman. I went to Adam's bar mitzvah."

"Well, did you know that was a test of his manhood? Like killing a lion?"

"That right?" Jacob had laughed. "I didn't see any lions on Park Avenue." The Temple had been a huge place, like a theater, with no one too close up to what might happen, very quiet, cold and sad, too, like a funeral for someone whose body had washed out to sea long ago who'd finally been declared dead.

"No man-eaters on Park Avenue? I'm not so sure, Jacob." Hartman had laughed—but not *at* Jacob, so that was all right. "But anyway, our test of manhood is to read the congregation something from a foreign language and give a little speech. And I hear you're the school's best debater already."

Walking home, he wondered if Hartman had been trying to convert him—foolish, but flattering in a way. Did he think you had to be Jewish to be a genius? Jacob passed the barbershop. School over, he let his hair grow out. *That* had once been his pulpit, where he gave some speeches, like the hand holding out the bag with the bottle in it had been saying, *Today you are a man.* Al waved to him anyway as he went by, and he waved back, not smiling, though, distracted still by what he'd gotten himself into with Mr. Hartman, as if Mr. Hartman were pulling at him still, all the way back downtown, asking him to become more . . . what? scholarly? Something like that, maybe—but it felt grander, too, more important than that. Well, next week at the Metropolitan Museum he and Mr. Hartman could sort that all out.

He walked past the still-broken mailbox. He thought how jealous the other Dewey kids would be when they knew that Jacob, Sugar Cane's friend, was also Mr. Hartman's favorite, and that Mr. Hartman probably had picked him for a genius—which made the little mailbox thing almost fade into insignificance.

But only almost. He went up to get some tools, see if he could fix it finally.

The next week, Hartman walked through Central Park on his way to his therapist—his now famous therapist—Dr. Leo Jacobs. Fame hadn't changed the way Leo Jacobs did analysis, though. What had done *that* was that boy, Billy Green. Richard had run into him sometimes in the little alcove in Dr. Jacobs' house, the two nearly knocking each other over in their rush to get in/out and avoid the other. His report over, Richard's job gone, Green had seemed a very small, very ordinary boy—shorts and shirts with an alligator over the pocket instead of his paper Star of David. But after Billy started seeing *Richard*'s doctor, Dr. Jacobs didn't talk to him as much; and Dr. Jacobs' having become a more ordinary therapist had made him into a more ordinary patient.

Before Green, when they'd talked, it had been about how they couldn't talk about the camps, not in this kind of ordinary sentence. This world and *that* one didn't fit together. Celan had shown them the only way to say the unsayable; words stolen from silence, falling back inside themselves into silence. Then they would sit in pious silence. A comfort of sorts, the only kind Richard could accept, bitter, isolating, and so no comfort at all. Hartman smiled with closed lips, in his doctor's style.

Then Dr. Jacobs had published his essay in *Commentary*: the wonders of guilt. Jacobs said he *knew* that chance saved him at Auschwitz. No reason to feel guilty; no judgment and no judge. But he had passed sentence on himself anyway, and only his wife and daughter had kept him afloat until he realized he must respond to his guilt.

And those of us, Richard had wondered, *who have no wives or daughters? Well, we have our analysts—for as many hours as we can afford.*

The guilty man, Dr. Jacobs wrote, must heal the wounded world—wounded, Richard Hartman had to agree, by bearing us. No extraordinary language there; Auschwitz became a lesson a cat or dog could read.

Long ago, Dr. Jacobs had joined with him in loathing those who'd made *their* lives into a lesson, turned Auschwitz into *now we can go on sadder but wiser than before.* Now almost every week Richard saw his doctor on some pious Sunday morning religious TV show like *Unto This Light* doing just that, telling stories with beginnings, middles, and ends, decorated with prosaic pieties that Leo Jacobs knew were *not* the truth. But the interviewer, ah, *he didn't* know. He looked at Dr. Jacobs with an overfull heart and tear-filled eyes. How could his doctor's ego not grow fatter by the day?

Until last Sunday, when Dr. Jacobs' friend Herbert Marcuse had "joined the discussion," the man most Herr Doktor Professor—as if he'd heard the truth from *his* professor who'd heard it from Hegel. Now he kindly passed that message on to the dummkopfs of today, including, amazingly enough, Dr. Leo Jacobs. "You say our guilt means we've wounded 'an order that every day creates and re-creates us.' That *sounds* very grand. But really, Leo, it means the order of the bourgeois world!" Richard had to confess—had to confess, too, that he looked forward soon to confessing—that it pleased him to hear his analyst treated like the foolish child in the Four Questions. "You used to criticize Freud, the burgher," Marcuse said. "But, Leo, you've actually outdone him. You're crawling back to the shtetl, and you, you go the rabbis one better. They said, follow the Law left us by a God we can't even get a smell of anymore. *You*, Leo, you *admit* God never existed, but Rav Leo says we should follow the Law *anyway* because we feel guilty if we don't! But it's not God's law, and it doesn't belong to the *whole that creates us*. It's the law of the bourgeoisie and *the world as it is*."

Marcuse's example gave Richard courage today. He began the fight innocently enough, telling Dr. Jacobs about his conversation with Jacob Battle—knowing from the first, though, that he'd done *that* as a way to criticize his doctor, Hartman hearing from acquaintances in Great Neck the stir that Dr. Jacobs and his wife had made when they started going to Temple again—and specifically to hear Rabbi Waxman glory in Israel's victory. Dr. Jacobs, Hartman had implied, was just like Mr. Sugar Cane, in love with tough men—victory in the Six Day War perhaps scrubbing off a little of the stain of the camps for him?

"Had he perhaps seen," Hartman wondered aloud from the couch, "Rabbi Meltzer of the Great Neck Synagogue's perceptive piece in *The Forward*? He warned Jews not to make a messiah of the State of Israel. The victory of a worldly state—mired in compromise and power politics—could never indicate the coming of Justice."

"Hmmm," the old cat behind him purred.

Hartman wanted to ask, "Why do you want to be with Jews again? Don't you still believe *at all* in a larger identity for humanity?" But he was certain he'd get the usual reply from his doctor: *Why do you ask?* And if the Israeli Army made Dr. Jacobs feel less of a victim, was that bad? A pity it hadn't worked for Richard!

Still, if there are only *tribes,* he wanted to cry to Dr. Jacobs, and no civilization—no beautiful, neutral ground where we're dumbstruck with wonder at each other's magnificent creations—then wasn't there only the narcissism of small differences, pointlessly precise rituals, and endless warfare across the world's many Jordan Rivers? "I know you tell me these things about Meltzer's article to criticize me," Dr. Jacobs said slowly. "Now that you're feeling better. You need to show you're growing independent of me."

"Of course," Hartman said. *That* sort of insight was small beer. "The Israelis and I," he told the indifferent white ceiling, "fight for our independence at the same time." A joke, he thought, which was as close as *he* would come to joining with *his* tribe, the People of the Witz.

"Or perhaps you're a little confused by your feelings for Jacob Battle. Really, perhaps, you need to talk about *him,* and his attitude toward Israel?"

"Do I?" Hartman said, glad and embarrassed to be discovered.

"Perhaps the strength of your feeling for him frightens you a little?"

Hartman laughed, thinking that's why he still kept the man on his payroll—he was even better at hide-and-seek than Hartman.

"After all, what if you lose him, too?"

"*Should* I feel this way, I wonder? I mean, he's only a boy."

"As *you* were, once," Dr. Jacobs said, and Hartman thought he actually *heard* the corners of Dr. Jacobs' lips rise in a smile. "Perhaps it's a way of protecting and caring for the boy you once were, who had no one to care for him?"

But *had* Jacobs understood? He had meant: he's a *boy,* nearly grown, quick-witted, lithe in movement, and Hartman was a homosexual.

"The little warmth you've known in your life has been directly sexual," the doctor had said, all too immediately. "So you distrust your feeling for Jacob. If you had children . . ."

"Wait," Hartman said, both frightened and pleased. "Do you think that's a possibility?"

"Do you?" Dr. Jacobs said.

No, Hartman thought, not unless they've invented a way to do that without any other human beings involved. But Dr. Jacobs' question, he could tell, had been merely a reflexive pause to gather himself. "I meant," Dr. Jacobs said, "if you had children, you'd be more familiar with these kinds of feelings. By the way, the Met's a good place to go with them. Children like it."

. . .

The child in question waited for him now at the top of the Metropolitan Museum's steps, wearing a red shirt that was much too large, like a bright flag wrapped around his body. A hand-me-down perhaps? Could a martyr, Hartman wondered, have owned such a bright shirt? He laughed at himself. Of course, when he was a teenager, Joshua Battle probably hadn't known he'd be a martyr.

Hartman rushed up the huge stone steps. Dr. Jacobs was right, he thought. His feeling for Jacob was protective only; all desire transformed into a platonic wish to educate, *that beauty might be born in the beloved*. He bought tickets for the two of them.

They walked quickly down the halls of Renaissance paintings—the pace at which Hartman liked to look at things, "as if you're on roller skates," one acquaintance had said, with mild disapproval. "Or like you're cruising the paintings." Yes, Hartman thought, as he stared at one and asked, *Are you the longed-for friend? Are you my transformative angel?* No? Then onward to the next possibility—the next disappointment.

As they strolled, Jacob unfolded more of his unhappiness with the John Dewey School, all that was oh so valuable that he felt he had to give up to fit into *their* world—as if, like so many before him, he thought he bore another magical way of being inside himself: poetic, cooperative, community building, with the new wrinkle that Jacob would have added to the list: *and black*.

"There's only one civilization," Hartman said, hoping he could believe that, even for as long as he was teaching someone else to believe, "one that we can all contribute to." He faintly remembered when he'd dreamt that the *one civilization* might change utterly—become, in fact, more poetic, cooperative, community building; all, no doubt, because he longed for some relief from his own ferocious analytic mind. He still did, perhaps; but he knew it was not to be. If history had a goal, he thought, it would already have reached it. There was only this: the slow accretion of masterpieces, brief rest for the spirit.

And Jacob's dissatisfaction with this civilization, Hartman thought, *that* was mostly adolescence—as his own probably had been. Adolescents don't want to give up the exuberance of youth for the work world. *That's* what Jacob would really be sacrificing, not Africa. He looked at the thin, graceful, darting kid. Too bad, really. But inevitable.

"I've learned all this . . . stuff," Jacob said, pausing for breath, Hartman in his rush having forgotten the boy was asthmatic. "But what does it matter," Jacob said, in a high, whiny voice, "to the Harlem wino or the cotton picker?"

Hartman smiled. *Those* must be words from his friend, the leader with the comical nickname. "Mr. Cane agrees with Sartre, hey? What use is a book to a man who has no bread?" He laughed. "I don't think, you know, there's *ever* been a moment when Sartre actually hasn't had enough bread. Still, there's something to that. *Erst komme der fressen.*" He looked down, hoping the boy might be impressed by the German; then paused, surprised, still, by his own need to impress him. "First grub," he translated, "then ethics." But the boy, no doubt, had something else on his mind. "Do they call you names?" Richard asked.

"Like *kike?*" Jacob smiled at him, a little too slyly. "Yeah, some of them. Sometimes. And some of them are scared to get in the swimming pool with me, like I'm greasy and it might rub off. And all of them stare at me in the shower so much that I sneak off after gym without cleaning up. So I bet now they think I'm dirty, too." He tried to laugh at the whole thing.

Too large, Hartman thought, too small; smelled funny—a teenager's nightmare! Thank God Jacob's not homosexual, too, or he'd be suicidal by now. *Or was he?*

"And they *all* condescend to me," he said. "If I screw up, they think it's 'cause I'm inferior."

Hartman smiled. "You don't 'screw up' much, though, do you?"

Jacob smiled back. "You bet not. But when I win, like I beat them in a debate, I can see they think, no, that couldn't have happened. The judges must have taken pity on him. Because they just *know* they're smarter than me. That's why I like math tests best."

"Not a matter of opinion?"

"Yeah, right. But as long as some white kid does better than me they can think, *Gee, he's really good for a black kid,* like I'm in this special category. King of the monkeys. Like it doesn't matter then that I did better than almost all of them. What they really hate is when I'm the best in the class. *Then* they gotta think I must have cheated." He stopped. "Look," he said, "I don't want this. I just don't want it." He spun around on his heel in the middle of the roomful of women in bright, wide dresses, under lanterns, watching horse races and ballets. "I don't want this, I don't, I just don't," and Hartman thought he knew what that meant. All the colors here blended for Jacob to the one ghastly all-consuming hue: white.

"It doesn't have to be a white world," Hartman said, "if you enter it and change it."

"Well, it sure 'nuff won't be a black world either," Jacob said, not spinning anymore, smiling, and reminding Hartman of nothing so much as his own Zionist uncle. How can we have a fully Jewish life in a Christian world? his uncle would ask, over flanken at Squire's. Shouldn't we go to Israel? But Hartman, in truth, had *never* simply wanted a Jewish world. He stopped to look at a ballet dancer, the paint somehow all magically *en pointe* as she was, yet reminding him also, as always, of Degas' anti-Semitism. Did it matter, though? Was it hidden in the brushstrokes? *Don't be silly,* he told himself—but he could never feel sure, not about Degas, not about anything. After all, the woods, a neighbor's face, a brushstroke—well, who knew where murder might hide?

He looked down at Jacob, who enjoyed the painting, perhaps, despite himself, Hartman suspecting that Jacob felt something like he did in his dark, his *black* moods: that to connect with this *civilization* was to join with those who had murdered his family, that the same world that had made the paintings and written the books had made the killers too—all of it just the endless nihilating negativity of will to power, no respite anywhere. *Hmmm,* Hartman thought, smiling at himself. *It seems like my "early insecurity" means I can't be the advocate for civilization, color-blind or otherwise, that this boy needs.*

Still, he must try. "You're not just African anymore." Hartman felt his legs grow heavy and slow as they moved on to Renoir. "For example, you're also American."

"Yeah? American, huh?" Jacob said, smiling. "What's that?"

Hartman nodded. "It's a difficult problem, isn't it? How not to lie about *any* of our family tree? Especially when the different parts all want to murder each other. Murder each other right inside us!"

A pretty young woman looked over when Jacob laughed at that, and said, "Shush." Hartman smiled at her. This place, no doubt, was her church, too—and their laughter, maybe Jacob's in particular, had desecrated it.

Jacob had laughed, yeah, but he hadn't understood entirely. Still, it had seemed funny. Like he didn't understand, but he was *understood*. He felt sure Mr. Hartman saw something in him, and valued him for it. By Friday, Jacob wanted to talk to him some more—even though going to the zoo, which was Mr. Hartman's idea, sounded like a thing a much younger kid would do, and there were lots of boys who wanted to play some hoops with him now, or just hang out. After all, Jacob Battle was Sugar Cane's friend—which was also part of why he didn't want to spend Saturday in Harlem, hearing that drum beat in people's voices when they talked to him. He wanted to tell Mr. Hartman what *he* prob-

ably *didn't* know: that there were *two wars* going on now, here and in
Vietnam—and *both* of them shooting wars. Black men had cut and shot
black men before, over nothing, Jacob knew that, even had heard of
boys who had died 'cause they'd body-checked the wrong someone on
the basketball court. But this was different. *This time, Mr. Hartman,
they shot a white person;* and even Jacob knew that payback would be a
bitch; no end, really, to what the white people would do. Like the cops at
a college in Texas, Jacob might tell him (knowing the name of it, but
even in his imagination pretending he didn't—to keep the danger a little
farther away from him). They'd arrested a black man. "Which happens
all the damn time," he would say to Mr. Hartman. "You dig? But *this*
time, like Sugar says, we protected our own." Students flung Molotov
cocktails; a cop had died; and more black kids had been arrested that
night, he wanted to tell Mr. Hartman, than all the white ones that went
to the John Dewey School.

Then at Jackson State the cracker cops had chased a car back to the
campus and tried to arrest a black man. "For what? What the fuck you
mean, for what? For nothing, man!" Jacob would shout, growing
annoyed at how bone-wearying Mr. Hartman and uneducated people
like him turned out to be. Hundreds of students at Jackson agreed with
Jacob, throwing rocks at the ignorant cops who hid behind metal barricades. The cops fired thousands of rounds into dorms.

"A round?" Hartman would probably say.

"That means a bullet. They killed one of ours this time."

"One of theirs, one of ours?" he could hear Mr. Hartman say with
mild disgust.

"Once the shooting starts," Jacob would say, "that's how it is. How
it has to be." Did it? *Or did Mr. Hartman know some other way*—the
whole thing feeling not fair or unfair to Jacob but making him glad
Sugar didn't have much time to call or write him anymore—'cause each
time now it seemed to him like he was really telling Jacob *make yourself
ready,* Jacob seeing it unfold like in an old movie on television, the boy
bearing the regimental flag always the one who got shot, falling slowly,
and the hero struggling over corpses, shells zinging around him, to pick
the banner up again, Jacob wanting to shout to him, "Don't do that,
chump, it'll just make you a target!" Well, maybe it didn't matter *what*
you did, he thought, you were a target anyway, *if a state wants to kill
you*—and they sure wanted to kill Sugar now. Atlanta, the night after the
last call, Sugar, hot with rage, had made a speech: "We will make Vietnam look like a holiday!" and the feds arrested him pronto: *inciting to*

riot. No free speech for Sugar Cane, Mr. Hartman, only real *costly* speech.

He would tell Mr. Hartman that he really wished it was *ever* going to be as simple for him as standing up in front of some people—hell, you could make it all of Harlem, if that's what it took—and translating something from the French.

Still, he wondered if Mr. Hartman might just say something that would make it all right not to pick up the flag? Or something that, even for as long as they were talking together, might make Jacob feel safe?

At the Central Park Zoo they ate hot dogs slathered with redemptive condiments while they strolled, Jacob giving a theatrical "Pee-yew!" to the monkey house smell, and Richard, in response, taking a huge, theatrical whiff. "I think I could turn and live with animals," he said. "They are so placid and self-contained. They do not sweat and whine about their condition."

Jacob stared at him like he'd *already* joined those creatures.

"It's a poem of the American, Walt Whitman," Richard said, laughing at himself, thinking, *This boy says he won't join the white world, but listen to me, I won't even join the human world*—like he was competing in suffering with Jacob.

In truth, this Independence Day, walking with Jacob past the monkey cage, eating this mediocre steamed sausage in its soggy, tasteless bread, he actually wasn't suffering much at all. The chimps smiled at him and groomed each other's heads carefully.

He and the boy, he thought, had a bond, too—a *therapeutic* bond, perhaps, or at least something that could be used for Jacob's own good, Hartman certain today that it might make Jacob feel better to know that Hartman knew what Jacob felt, knew about the *almost* wanting to die. Who knew, if he could free Jacob from that, perhaps he could also free himself a little?

Even if it meant denying himself restful sleep for weeks as punishment for lying no matter how hard he tried to tell the truth about *his* rescue from Drancy, his sister's and his parents' death? *Yes,* he thought before he began, *even so.* "I was spared, you know. My sister wasn't, my parents weren't. So I'm left with this impossible question: what right do I have to be alive?"

Jacob shrugged, pretending, Hartman thought, that it wasn't his question.

They walked back into the sunlight, and stopped by the panther's cage. Step, step, step, and step again, the paws so much wider, softer, more enticing than one expected. *It seems to him there are a thousand bars; and behind the bars, no world.* But perhaps, he decided, Jacob might be spared more poetry for a while? Hartman tried again: "Sometimes I think perhaps you feel a little bit the way I did."

He could hear Jacob's difficulty breathing. Was he weeping, too? He watched the cat pace more, not looking down toward the boy, so he wouldn't embarrass him. "So maybe sometimes, you may feel you have to continue your brother's and Mr. Cane's work—whether you want to or not. As if you owe your brother your life?"

"It's not his fault," Jacob said.

"No. It's not."

"I miss him," he said.

"Yes. Of course."

They strolled for a while in silence, until Hartman suggested that they go back to Jacob's home together today. "Maybe I could say hello to your mother?"

They took a bus to Hartman's apartment, so he could pick up a present he'd gotten Mrs. Battle, then they decided to walk uptown, to prolong their conversation, Jacob putting his arm around him, then, like a much younger boy, the one he'd perhaps never gotten to be. They walked along companionably for a wonderfully long while, Jacob wheezing a little sometimes, but not wanting to rest, until above 115th Street, where the faces, like traffic lights, turned from white to black. He read suspicion in the faces on the street. Probably they wondered what he did with this boy. As if *they* were the protective ones! *And if people on the street thought* that, *what would the boy's own mother think he was doing with her son?*

And what *was* he doing? After all, he wasn't Jacob's therapist. He wasn't his father, or his brother. And there was something to his feeling for Jacob that his doctor, he suspected, had been too quick to exonerate. That beauty might be borne in the beloved, Plato's definition—that should have been a warning to him. Or did Richard suspect himself like this because he was scared not of what he felt but of what others would say, of what they would do to him out of their confusion and misunderstanding? His body stiffened. By 120th, each step grew harder; then, midway down the block, impossible. He shouldn't have told Jacob about Drancy, his sister, his parents. Did he think that helping this boy, even if he could, would entitle *him* to live? He looked about. Some well-muscled protective black man would soon deliver the answer to that question! He stopped. "You know, Jacob, I'm tired. Maybe we should do this another day."

Jacob took his arm away. "Yeah, okay," he said, his voice choked with bewildered disappointment, a sound that Richard knew might drag *him* right down to hell that night for his cowardice. "Right. Another day."

Nineteen sixty-seven, his first year at college over, Bobby Brown kept the faith with Sugar Cane, working at a SNAP office—which meant Delon—in Roxbury. He and Delon, a tall, good-natured guy from the state college, leafleted to drum up support for black-owned businesses. They did the Maximum Feasible dance. And they came up with some actions their people could take with the white anti-draft movement on the campuses, stop the hemorrhage of young black men to Vietnam.

"But where exactly," Delon said again, "are our *people?*" They never got more than twenty to a meeting, usually the same twenty, too.

Then, after a few days of handing out leaflets with Sugar Cane's name on them, they filled a whole damn theater. Sugar himself, in a black leather jacket, white shirt, and dark shades, stood on the sidewalk outside, letting the crowd wait a little, talking to the men from the SNAP office like he had nothing else on his mind, no federal and state indictments, no jail doors somewhere longing to swing open to include him in, no speech to make that would get him busted again for sure. Bobby shepherded his white SDS people over, one of them the daughter of the family that had employed his aunt. They'd even played together a couple of times as kids—dolls, unbelievably enough, Bobby on his best behavior. *No*, he thought, *let's forget that Dewey School circumlocution, and say where the aunt who helped raise me worked as* the maid. *Still does, goddamn it*. Then he thought, Jesus God, forget *circumlocution*, and say, *crap*. Laura Jaffe had lovely long legs in a short blue skirt, and he worried that she would look at him in his black leather jacket, white shirt, and shades and think he looked like Sugar *Junior*, when really, baby, Bobby Brown was so much more than that.

Yeah, right.

"I'll tell you, in the past, young black leaders, even before they started to move," Sugar said, like he was reading Bobby's mind, "they were apologizing to the white man, reassuring *him*." He made his high voice higher still. "'Oh, no, master, we don't want to sleep with your woman! We just want the vote!'" Sugar looked over everyone's head directly at Beth Jacobs and Laura Jaffe. "But I tell you, I'm *tired* of reassuring white men. *Massa,* I tell them now, *your mother, your daughter, your sister is not the queen of the world.*" Laura Jaffe stepped back closer to Beth Jacobs, who stared impassively at Sugar. "She is *not* the Virgin Mary."

Beth Jacobs hooted at that, and Sugar, like he couldn't help himself, smiled back at her.

"She can be made. Oh, she can be *made.*" The black men laughed, almost willfully. Laura Jaffe's face glowed red from the spectral slap. Beth turned to her, said loudly, mockingly, "What does he mean, *made,* Laura? We like a good time as much as the next guy, eh?"

Laura Jaffe tried to smile, but she still looked like she wanted to weep.

"But, Laura," Beth said, making her voice carry, "do you see any men here who look like a good time to you?"

At that Sugar pivoted and marched into the theater, turning the men who scrambled to follow him into his entourage.

And then he high-stepped in front of the blank movie screen, shouting at everyone, sparks nearly flying from the heels of his nervous boots as they stomped the stage. Black folks, he said, had *got* to own some of the stores in Roxbury—and he didn't care if they had to burn the white man down and run him out to get them. "Detroit exploded!"

"*Yes, it did!*" the First Church of Christ the Firebomber murmured.

"Newark exploded! Harlem exploded!"

That right? Bobby thought. Shoulda, maybe. But hadn't yet, feeling himself hanging back just for a moment—then he got caught up by the roar when Sugar yelled, "It's time for Roxbury to explode!"

"Right on!" he heard himself say.

"Black folks built America!"

"We *did*!" Bobby said emphatically.

"If America don't come 'round, we're going to burn America down, brother. We're going to burn it down if we can't get our share of it!" Sugar stopped, looked up at the stucco ceiling. He moved his legs apart, then stepped slowly from side to side.

"I'm ashamed of you people!" he said, fake quiet, still gazing at the moldings, like he was communing with the chubby cherubim. "I *heard* about all those demonstrations in front of Pine Street Elementary all these years. Well, how long, oh, Lord, how long, are you gonna put up with that place? I saw it, and it's a death trap for our children." He stared at the audience, basilisk eyes filled with disdain. "What are you people thinking? You gonna march and talk and march until one day that school catches fire and burns our children up inside it? And then what are we gonna do but just mourn some more!"

Then he turned his face upward toward the moldings. "Do you think you maybe should have stopped talking and torched that raggedy-ass school a long time ago?" He sounded almost thoughtful.

"Unh huh!" Bobby heard himself say, along with the rest of the crowd, though he also noted how Sugar had framed it as a question in the past tense, Sugar maybe thinking of the charges to come: *inciting to riot.*

"*Then* you could go take over a nice elementary school on the other side of this town. It should be ours! It should be ours!" Sugar's shadow danced on the white screen. He tilted his head back down. "What do we want?" he screamed.

"Black Power!" a mostly male chorus shouted back.

"Black Power!" Sugar shouted.

Bobby snuck another look at Laura Jaffe. She watched Beth, who stared at Sugar with glazed eyes and whispered "Black Power" to herself over and over. Two men in the row behind them looked over at her. One of them hissed to Bobby: "Tell that silly bitch of yours to shut the fuck up!"

Bobby leaned over to his white charges. "You got to get the fuck out of here, *right now,*" he whispered harshly. He'd tried to form it like an order.

They obeyed, scurried for the exit just before the crowd surged into the street. He hurried them to their car, ran back up the hill toward the school, already smelling the bitter, harsh smoke, redolent of chemicals. My first taste of combat, he thought. The Battle of Pine Street Elementary School.

By the look of it, though, the school hadn't put up much resistance. The roof of the two-story building fell inward as he watched, the melting tar paper and timber crashing down a full floor. His eyes filled with tears from acrid asphalt, wood, and confusion at what he'd just been part of, all certainty departing from him as the last of the crowd disappeared right back down the hill, all but Delon rushing back toward the theater and the business district. He looked down the dark street. "Why are there no motherfucking firemen?"

Delon, giddy with what he'd done, laughed. "Ain't that just like us! First we set the school on fire, then we complain that the firemen didn't come soon enough to stomp out the fire."

"Yeah," Bobby said, "it all makes as much sense as . . . four hundred years of slavery."

Still, burning a decrepit firetrap school *could* make a kind of military sense in tomorrow's paper—a preemptive strike, call it. When Newark had burnt and Detroit had gone to war, the ignorant papers had acted like it had been *nothing* that started it, a cab driver roughed up a little by police, a blind pig smashed, when suddenly, by black alchemy, blocks and blocks of downtown had burst into flames, tanks rolled down the avenues, machine-gun fire sliced up the fronts of housing projects like Vietcong villages, and helicopter after helicopter whirred above the urban rice paddies. Bobby had stood up in the middle of Burr B, at a lecture on "urban policy," told them all that only white people asked what caused a riot. The right question was, What miracle had ever held things in check so long? Some of the white kids gave him shy smiles of support, while the professor condescended back with sentences that signified: *Listen, son, you don't poll the animals to find out about the zoo.* Well, burning this shitty school, it made sense. Even a Harvard professor could figure it out.

He and Delon strolled around to the back, to the parking lot, D. taking those long, graceful dancer strides, clutching his dented red kerosene tin to his chest like a partner.

"Jesus, man, you got to get rid of that."

Delon hurled it into the building and the fire flared, black smoke curling through a window, asking how Bobby was going to return in the fall to that university that offered maybe two or three meaningless courses about his people, his moment? At first he'd thought the brothers on campus could organize to change that, but after Texas, Jackson, he hadn't been so sure it was worth the risk, not sure he could ever go back to college now that the shooting had begun, even if his aunt would weep and his grandma would moan.

He could hear the sirens behind him now, back by the theater.

"Look, man," Delon said, "I think we had better get out of here."

"I just got to watch a while more."

"Roast some Wienie Man weenies?" But D. didn't wait for the answer, took off down the hill. After all, he'd set the fire.

Alone, Bobby's heart pounded like it was going to break through his chest wall, but he couldn't tear himself away. Maybe if *he* had a crowd around him again, him shouting and the crowd shouting right back, he'd feel all right, like on Lenox, with Baby bouncing that basketball higher and higher as he spoke, like flames leapt up under it in response to Bobby's voice. But *this* playground would soon be charred tar where nobody was gonna play much ball anymore, and he could feel his own eyes bulging out from the smell of it all, like he had other eyes behind them. *We just burnt down our school. We're saying, You better rebuild it! Or what? We're gonna hurt ourselves some more, burn some more of our things down?* He *saw* for sure that the white fire department would never come to put this fire out, they'd just let the school burn till there was no future left in it, and *they'd* never rebuild it; plywood boards would go up on the stores next to the theater, and they'd never lend black people the money to open their own stores, which meant that the plywood would never come down. And then where would everyone go?

Hell, where would *he* go? More glass was sucked inward then by the vacuum the fire made, like shooting stars, and bile rose in Bobby's throat, disgust with himself that nearly choked him. *He* couldn't be part of many more fires. That wasn't who he was.

But how could he go back to school, either? Maybe if he helped fight for a Black Studies Department, forced Harvard to put up some resources to tell his people's history? He remembered this thing that Jacob had told him Mr. Hartman had said: "It doesn't have to be a white world if you enter it, and change it," which had certainly sounded like Dewey horseshit when Jacob told him about it. Hell, it *still* sounded like horseshit. After all, tell their history to whom—the dozen black students at Harvard? Besides, what would a Black Studies Department matter to the people trapped in the Columbia Point Projects?

But where else could *he* go, this fire having burned him out of *all* his homes. He didn't fit anymore with Sugar Cane, so maybe he should try to change Harvard, where he *also* most certainly didn't fit—even if they threw him out for trying. And *that* made him laugh at his own empty bravado until he near choked. Twenty-five dead in Newark, fifty more in Detroit, and he could hear the high-pitched sound of rifle fire behind him now. Near genocide everywhere in *his* nation, he thought—while, UPI take note, Mr. Bobby Brown states he'll risk being thrown out of Harvard and making his aunt Ruth cry!

Well, 'scuse me, Sugar, but wouldn't I be drafted then, too, and become part of the only *truly well-armed and -trained black fighting force in this world: the motherfucking U.S. Army?*

A police car screamed past him, scattering red light on the trees. The cops stopped, looked at the burning building for a moment, then over to where Bobby stood by the edge of the playground, having his little moment, laughing at himself. Bobby saw a white arm reach for a rifle then, and he turned and ran like hell.

All the way back to his grandma's house in the Bronx. He needed to get some laundry done. He needed some home cooking. He needed to see his aunt and figure out who the hell he was. And he needed to warn Jacob, get him off the path to this school in Roxbury that was no longer a school.

But warn him of what? That when Sugar said, "Burn, baby, burn!" sometimes things actually did? He could tell this story was just making Jacob think a whole lot more of his Sugar.

They walked to what had once been the barbershop again. "No, man," Bobby said, "you don't understand, we *need* schools."

"We don't need death traps, Bobby. We don't need places where they tear us down and fill our heads with lies." Jacob had turned into a string bean already, a few inches taller even than Bobby, but gawky still, different parts of his body going off on their own.

A man in a dashiki, colors of New Africa, made a fist, said, "Hello, brother," to Jacob as they walked by. Jacob, altogether the fifteen-year-old community leader, smiled back. "Those riots," he said, "they burned some poison out of our hearts."

Thing was, Bobby couldn't disagree. Not to be trusted, sure, all this brother / sister stuff, but it was *something,* the Afros, the *kente* cloth, something for our eyes, beauty by *our* standards. (Though *that* had never been a problem for *him,* he reminded himself. Women of all races loved *him.*) "But, Jacob, you *got* to admit Sugar's crazy to shout that political power grows out of the barrel of a gun, when all the motherfucking guns are on the other side. These riots, they're not battles, they're massacres."

"You don't get it, do you?" Jacob said, like he was the older one. "Our guns are out there already, Bobby. Our guns are in the Third World, and they're pointed right at the heart of the beast."

"Well, Sugar's sure as shit still calling down the heat before we're ready *here,* naming Johnson a wild mad dog like that." Bobby couldn't help himself, though, he smiled saying it, had to admit it had a lovely sound. Ah, Sugar of the nervous feet—despite himself he loved him still.

"Johnson's a cracker," Jacob quoted. Laughing, he imitated Sugar's high-pitched voice. " 'An outlaw from Texas. You got to arm yourself, brother. If America chooses to play Nazis, black folks ain't going to play Jews.' "

"Violence is necessary," Bobby finished off, making his voice as squeaky as Minnie Mouse's to mock Sugar, to hide how sweet the words sounded to him. "It's as American as cherry pie!"

"Maybe," Jacob added, "if Sugar talks too wild sometimes, it's because they're driving him crazy with all those subpoenas, indictments, jive trumped-up charges."

"If a state wants to drive you crazy . . ." Bobby said, reminding Jacob, he hoped, of the bond between them, that he'd been allowed to read the sacred text, the letters from Africa, the meeting with Malcolm. *Sugar Cane's* meeting. *You mean to draw Jacob from Sugar, but all you say ends up adding to his glory!*

"Yeah. They say Sugar was the one burned that school."

Bobby shook his head. "They lie," he said. Not sure what answer might dim the glow Sugar Cane gave to Jacob's eyes.

"Yeah, well, they charged Sugar with arson, anyway."

"And inciting." *Ad majorem . . .*

"Yeah, there. And Atlanta, and Washington. And Dayton. He wasn't even *in* motherfucking Dayton. It was Rap Brown."

"You *know* we all look alike."

They stopped to get sodas, then turned down 125th, where Al's used to be. "You and Mr. Hartman still go to museums?" Bobby asked, meaning, really, maybe that old man will have better luck with you, Bobby feeling too divided to argue right. He shouldn't have laughed at Sugar's hijinks, but he couldn't help himself, that shit still made him giddy.

"Hell, no. I mean, I miss him sometimes. We had good talks, I could show him how this world really works. But I don't got time for that anymore." Sugar had Jacob busy leading a SNAP study group, "to inculcate a new black consciousness, which will be the foundation for all future - struggles." And when Al's had gone under, the old man had even given Jacob's group the rest of the time on the lease, contributing to the very cause, Al said, that had helped do him in.

Now kids Bobby half remembered from the playground sat on the sofa, drinking sodas, listening to fifteen-year-old Jacob teach them about Fanon, Douglass, Du Bois.

Jacob had put pictures up on the walls over the mirrors, one of them his own brother, a portrait standing by an open coffin so the young face of Joshua Battle stood over a crushed misshapen thing that asked: *Will you protect each other now?* By way of response, someone had taped up Bobby Seale and some badass Panthers, carrying their rifles into the California Legislature.

Which was all anyone wanted to talk about today. So like a good organizer, Jacob worked with the people where they were, ran down the Ten Point Program, the Panther street patrols to monitor police conduct. When the pigs tried to arrest people, Panthers would be there, he said, armed with shotguns and lawbooks. "*We* got to go out there and talk to the street, too. Brothers who have been out there robbing banks, brothers who have been pimping, brothers who have been peddling dope, brothers who ain't gonna take no shit, you organize those brothers, Huey says we'll get revolutionaries who are too much."

Bobby laughed at Jacob, talking 'bout the "lumpen" to kids who ain't. Except for Baby, maybe, who'd done some time in Rikers already. *That* had most certainly made a new man out of him. No fat now, all muscle; plus the requisite frozen, hooded eyes, jail having taught him the trick of keeping them always half shut—like he was behind fortress walls, peeking out.

"You better get yourself a gun, you want to survive the white man's wrath," Baby said.

Even the playground kids, who were goddamn children themselves, nodded at that, all and each of them having heard the shouts one time or another: *Up against the wall!* and *Kneel down! Hands behind your head!*

"Hey, Baby," Bobby said, wanting to force some recognition from those cold, cold eyes.

Cold? Mr. Baby's eyes suddenly turned sub-Arctic. "Look at me, motherfucker. Do I look like a *baby* to you?"

"No, you look like a proud black man," Jacob said. No irony. Soothing praise. Meant to mollify.

He smiled. "And my name's Shakur now."

"Right, man. *Shakur.* I got it."

Baby turned and grinned at Jacob, dismissing Bobby, who was just not part of their world. "*We* should set up those motherfucking street patrols. You carry the lawbooks," he said to Jacob, "I'll carry the rifle."

The other kids looked at Jacob now, interested in what he'd say back, like they were measuring him.

Jacob said he'd talk to Sugar when he came to town to give a speech at Columbia—a mistake, Bobby knew, like *I'm not the man. I got to ask my daddy.*

"Co-lu-um-bia!" Shakur said, giving it a whole lot of extra syllables to signify *that white place.*

The other kids nodded amen to that.

Baby/Shakur becoming the leader, Bobby thought, taking the group away from Jacob. He wondered if Jacob knew that yet, and wondered, too, what Shakur would do with Jacob, after. The fat become muscled, and the last shall be first. Nothing meek about this new Baby, though; not *the downtrodden* that Jesus had in mind, praise the Lord. But Bobby was beginning to suspect that Malcolm had got that right—Jesus the linchpin of the white man's plot against them, and meekness not all it had been cracked up to be.

Jacob shrugged. "Sugar says the white students pay for him, and the money he earns pays for our meeting places. Black people talk big, but they don't put up diddly for their own organizations."

Shakur thought about that. "Maybe we ought to make them," he said.

Jacob laughed, but Baby wasn't smiling.

At Columbia that August, Jacob laughed as Sugar did a medley of his greatest hits, *Tit for tat, Mad Dog Johnson. More shooting than looting. Loot yourself a gun. Cherry pie,* the place looking like white rows and black ones, more like a fancy layer cake, but some of the whipped cream yelping amen right along with the chocolate, like *they* couldn't wait for the fire next time either. Most whites squirmed, though, making Jacob wonder why they came back time after time to get their faces slapped. Still, it *was* always sweet to see.

Sugar called out his name, had him stand up, as the head of SNAP in New York, "and it's 'cause we have men like this," he said, pointing down at him from the stage, "that I don't have to worry about what the crackers might do to me. When my time comes, this man and his brothers will be there to take over."

People applauded, making Jacob proud and scared in equal measure, and mostly eager just to sit the fuck down. Afterward, he gathered around Sugar with Susan Lems, David Watkins, and some young white lawyer named Harrison with a Southern voice and big yellow teeth, like a dying horse. David Watkins shouted at Sugar with real fury, "You son of a bitch!" He pointed to Jacob. "You've painted a target on this boy."

Sugar ignored him, folded Jacob in both arms and kissed him on the cheek. Before Jacob could tell David, "I don't need your help, I can take care of myself," four uniformed cops came up to Sugar, handed him a piece of paper. One of the cops tried to grab Sugar's briefcase off the table, but Sugar wrestled it away.

Jacob rushed to bear-hug the cop from behind, but David pulled him backward, nearly bringing him to the floor. "Leave it to the lawyers now, Jacob." He had a soft, even, precise voice, like a Dewey School teacher.

Sugar had opened the briefcase slowly, held a pistol up by the barrel, wanting everyone to see it before he handed it over. "I got a permit," he said. "Not that you pigs give a shit."

While Sugar and Harrison spoke to the cops, David and Susan hustled Jacob to the side of the stage, then out a door and down a fire escape. Around the front of the building an armed squad of cops stood squared up: rifles, Plexiglas face masks, and big blue shields. They looked like bugs.

"They do this in every city," David said, as they hurried across the campus. "Hoover's gonna bust him and bust him till we can't make bail anymore."

"J. Edgar thinks Sugar's the black messiah," Susan Lems said to Jacob.

They hopped a bus. "I'll tell you, I think Sugar's beginning to think he's our messiah, too," David said. He grabbed a handful of coins from his pants pocket, and the machine chewed them up.

"They spread the most god-awful lies about him," Susan said as they walked unsteadily to the back. "Watch out they don't start doing it 'bout you, now, Jacob."

The very next day Jacob sat on his bed in his jammies, reading about the speech in the *Times,* seeing how Susan had got *that* right:

> NY police report that Sugar Cane left one of his top aides, Mr. Jacob Battle, to set up a New York operation. Mr. Battle gave the membership assignments to lead study sessions that, according to police, would "teach the Negro children hatred for the whites, telling them the white man had done nothing for them."

Jacob felt like he should maybe reach around his pajama back, see if he could feel the target.

> One tall Negro boy at the speech said, "The white man has never offered us anything but one half of one percent of nothing."

One tall Negro boy? That having been *him*—like he was the extra in the scene, running around playing every part, so you wouldn't notice how small the crowd actually was. Which made him laugh. Then he read that the cops had raided the SNAP office, "and found dynamite, and the material for Molotov cocktails."

So he tore down to the headquarters, sneakers unlaced, knowing the cops must have planted stuff there that would turn his life into a big pile of shit. He barely even wondered why there was no yellow police tape on "the crime scene," no cops on guard this morning, even as he threw the door open and found Shakur already inside, sitting on the couch, reading the newspaper and laughing.

"Hello, *Mister* Battle."

Jacob must have looked like a poleaxed mule. "Hello, Mister Baby," he said, without thinking.

Shakur measured him; then smiled, nodded.

Turned out, Shakur already heard from a friend, it had been the Young Lords' office that had been raided. "But it's bad niggers sell papers, Mr. Battle. So they put it on us."

Then the next day the new school year started, with Jacob immediately called down to the head of guidance, Mr. Appleton, a broad-faced, stuttering man. He had a bad heart and a mean temper. You whispered in his class, you had to write *the quality of mercy is not strained* until you couldn't clench your fingers. Everyone knew Appleton was a mad dog—which must be why, Arkey Kaplan had said, they'd made him the guidance counselor.

He offered Jacob a seat, then just stared at him sadly—every rookie cop's interrogation trick.

Jacob stared back. Mercy combed his six strands of white hair over his ocean of scalp, like that fooled anyone.

"I want to help you with your problems."

"What problems?" Jacob said, thinking, *I don't have a problem, except for crazy white people like you.*

"You know, we've received this picture . . ." Then he slid a photo across his desk, Sugar and him hugging each other, probably at the rally, but everyone else blocked out of the photo, erased—*and Jesus, they'd done that to make it look romantic!*

"If you want to talk about *this*?" Mercy said to the tune of *please-please, oh I would so like to hear.*

"About what? How did you get this shit?"

He ignored the *profanity*. "The authorities are concerned about your welfare. They alerted us that an older man might be taking advantage of you. You know, in that way. I mean—"

But Jacob laughed. He heard the stumbling eagerness in Mercy's voice. Jacob reminded himself to do what Malcolm said, keep his mind subtle, keep his balance. He took a deep breath, like before a foul shot. This was just more FBI bullshit, he told himself, and *he* had to handle it the way Sugar would, giving the gun ever so slowly to the stupid redneck cop.

"Don't you know *who* that is?" Jacob said. Shit, there'd been pictures in the *Times* that very day of Sugar Cane with the man Hartman had talked about, Sartre, the bread eater. "Jesus, how could you not know him?" You stupid flushed-face peckerwood!

"Boys your age are sometimes confused, and older men can get them to do things that, well . . ."

Bet you know all *about that,* Jacob thought, but he said, calmly, coldly, "He's a friend of my family. You can ask my mother."

He went back to algebra, wondering if Hartman thought he was a queer, too, if that was why he used to take him to museums, waiting for his chance to come on to him? *Son of a bitch.* Put him on the list, too. But then he couldn't shut off this voice in his head, that said, *Well, boy, why is it* you *don't have any girlfriends?* He tried to say, *It's 'cause there are no girls in this crappy school,* and 'cause he had so much goddamn work that he didn't even have time to think about them, he had to watch himself every minute of the day, or these people would get at him, send him back to his mother with a note pinned to his jacket, *We tried to make something out of this sorry nigger, but it's beyond us.* But the voice already knew all that, and it was like it was smiling at him anyway. *Fuck you,* he said to himself about himself. Jesus, what had the Dewey School done to him? He *had* to get some pussy before it was too late!

How could Mercy *not* have known the man in the photo was none other than Sugar Cane? He'd been all over the papers that month, hugging Sékou Touré, Nkrumah, and Ho Chi Minh, who was the man who was kicking Uncle Sam's ass in Vietnam. And then Fidel Castro had given him an *embrazzo,* and Fidel was no faggot, was he? Sugar had given a big speech at a meeting in Havana: "American blacks look to Cuba and to Che for inspiration in rooting out corrupt, individualistic, anti-communitarian Western values."

"Marxism is more Heeb shit," one of Shakur's friends said at the barbershop when Jacob read it out. Monroe lay sprawled in a barber chair, a stocking on his head to protect his wave. "Stokely runs it down, man. We don't need *that.* We need an African way of thinking."

"Sugar," Jacob said, "he shows how Che and Castro are Hispanics. They *are* part of the colored world."

"Fucking spics," Monroe replied, chewing a big wad of gum as usual. "They better not try to be part of *my* world."

Jacob wanted to get them focused back on the speech Sugar had sent him, a letter from Che Guevara. They had to be ready to make another Vietnam in *this* jungle, prepare to be urban guerrilla fighters.

Weary looked like he didn't know what that meant—or knew and didn't like it.

Jacob couldn't blame him. Every time Sugar spoke anywhere, more rifles pointed at the target on his own back—always a police car right outside the headquarters now, or somebody in white socks taking pictures of them from across the street. Bobby *couldn't* be right and Sugar wrong, but *for the moment* all the guns sure seemed like they were on the other side.

Still, he could hardly believe that Sugar had actually gotten this letter from Che Guevara, had passed it on to him, to tell people about here in this barbershop in Harlem, Che probably writing it by lantern light in some jungle where it was hard for him to breathe the thick, humid air, just the way it was for Jacob here, Che maybe gathering the peasants just like Jacob did in this barbershop, each one teach one, telling them about the world race war that was about to start: "We must become violent, cold, selective killing machines," Jacob read, feeling as he said it that he was way past ready. Live like a man, he thought, or die like one, but no more crawling around like a fucking cocksucker!

Weary looked sicker and sicker, but Monroe smiled. "Something to *that* spic," he said, passing a j to Shakur.

"*We* should hunt down some pigs." Shakur gestured toward the window.

Eyes turned, everyone thinking, Jacob knew, *Look at them in their uniforms. They're trained. They got nice guns.* And soon the talk changed, imperceptibly, but no one saying why, and they were talking about some *black man* who had overcharged, who had too much, who had disrespected Monroe, and they planned going off on him instead, not even noticing what had happened: they were scared of the Man still, they were going after their own, Jacob finally telling them, "We got to stop killing blacks," not saying it's 'cause you're scared, just, "We have to stop burning our own buildings down." Monroe's dope-tired, red eyes looked emptily at him while he sucked on Jacob's words, sensing there might be some ground-glass criticism in them; then he swallowed them anyway. "You got that right," he said slowly, almost dreamily. "We ought to go *downtown,* do our looting there."

But that started the whole cycle over again, all they ought to do to

the Man coming back by steps no one wanted to trace to the black gro-
cer who ought to know better, who had to learn a lesson.

Not ready yet, Jacob thought. But *soon.*

Well, with all that secret knowledge, was it any wonder Jacob saw
just how corny the Dewey School was? He should be back in Harlem,
teaching Shakur, Monroe, and Sack Eyes who the real enemy was, them
and the others Shakur brought to the center now, even two Bloods back
from Nam, guys tight only with each other. Proud, self-confident men,
and they said Sugar spoke the truth: a revolution was coming, a race
war. Not everyone ready for it yet. Most of the playground crowd had
scattered since the cop cars had started showing outside the glass every
motherfucking day. No matter. Malcolm had got it right: the guys who
had done some time, prison or Nam, they just needed leadership and
they'd be ready to rise.

Huey Newton knew *that* for sure—that's why he'd invented the
Oakland Blank Panthers. Lumpen soldiers. Monroe had put up a new
picture of Huey, in a beautiful leather jacket, on an African wicker
throne, spear and rifle in front of him. "He's the man," Monroe said.
But then he started to take down the photo of Joshua's coffin.

"Leave that," Jacob said.

"Fuck you, man. I *know* we die. Brother Huey says it's time to be
about fightin'. If you gonna die," he said, pointing toward the cop car
out front, "Huey says take some pigs with you." He went on prying at
the tape on Joshua's picture until Jacob put his hand on his arm, pulled it
away. Monroe rapped him in the face with his fist, had been about to do
it again when Shakur grabbed his arm, held him back.

"Don't be doing that," Shakur said. "And leave the motherfucking
picture alone. *This* is *Jacob* Battle you're hitting. This is Sugar Cane's
man."

Jacob wiped the blood that spouted from his nose with his shirttail.
Man, that had stung like a motherfucker. He could already feel the
swelling. What the fuck was he going to tell his mama?

"And this is *his* place," Shakur said. "So just leave it the fuck alone
and sit the fuck down."

"Newton's the man," Monroe said lamely, as Shakur pushed him
into a barber chair.

"The Panther," Jacob said, "that's Sugar's idea. He made it up in
Lowndes," but then his nose started to bleed again, dripping red down
his chin, ruining his brother's old shirt. "You know, the Lowndes Party's
symbol. A panther," he said. But Jesus, that sounded lame.

"Who motherfucking cares about that?" Monroe said, but he had his head down, busy lighting a joint, scared of Shakur.

Jacob said that everywhere Sugar talks, there were riots.

"Yeah. Where we *get* shot."

"Sugar gets busted for guns."

"He don't *use* them, though, do he?" Monroe said. "He just fucking carries them in his briefcase. Supreme Commander Huey P. Newton, he offed a pig yesterday, did you even motherfucking know *that*?"

"That's right, Officer Mother Fucker Fry," one of the vets said with lip-smacking satisfaction. "He belly-shot him, man, with his own revolver! Whatcha think of that?"

"How many pigs has Sugar Cane killed?" Monroe asked.

They like the toys, Jacob realized. Not the Ten Point Program, but the uniforms, the patrols, the slogans, the jive-army-titles. Before, he'd been telling playground kids about "the lumpen prol"; now Sack Eyes, fresh from federal time, smoked a reefer in the barber chair and told *him* that he was the longed-for friend he'd been mouthing off about, the brother who was too much, the stone-cold revolutionary. "Look at you, man," he said to Jacob. "You don't get it, do you? Your skin's too light."

"Too white," Monroe said.

"Not right," concluded a vet, laughing.

Shakur stepped in then, said Jacob had to forgive these sorry-assed fools who couldn't see that Sugar Cane was a far-seeing man and that Jacob Battle had been there with him from the beginning, had shown more courage than any of them. "We got to leave you boys now," he said, putting his arm around Jacob. "We have some women to meet." Which had been a knockout surprise to Jacob.

They walked slowly through the soft fall night then, to this after-hours place Shakur knew about, Jacob thinking like a little boy that he couldn't stay long, had to get home so his mama wouldn't worry.

"Where's that white dude you used to dance with?" Shakur said, gibing him.

Jacob shrugged. He meant Hartman, and Jacob half wished he was sitting in that man's book-lined tomb, talking about justice or Thomas Hardy. For a second, he felt like there had been this contest for his soul, Sugar and Hartman. But Sugar knew his black soul a way Hartman never would, didn't want to.

"Yeah, the guy comes on to you," Shakur said, "but you say, I don't play that way, and he runs off. I know *that* tune."

"Yeah. Something like that."

Why was everybody picking at that bone? Jacob wondered. Sure, he'd liked Hartman once upon a time. Yeah—but in *that* way, he thought—like a kid listening to his mom tell a foolish story. But not a *fairy* tale.

Meanwhile, Shakur was saying maybe they got to do something, get some money before the lease on the shop ran out, the center had to close.

"Yeah," Jacob said, still thinking about his mother, "like a fund-raiser, a rent party or something." His mom had really liked the book of Thomas Hardy that Hartman gave her. She sat, the television off for a while, read to him, " 'Crass Casulty obstructs the sun and rain / And dic-ing Time for gladness casts a moan.' " It cheered her up to think the world was like *that,* strangely enough—or maybe just that someone else had felt the way she did.

"I think it's time," Shakur said, "for us to make the street pay us some dues."

Jacob's mind had gone blank.

"Time to take down one of the dealers," Shakur added. "Tithe him. Get us some rent money." He pointed to Jacob's hand-me-down high-waters. "And a little something for ourselves. You'll see, you'll clean up *good.*"

Jacob felt his guts churn with fear, and maybe *that's* why he'd con-sidered it, Shakur always helping him to take the dares, grow from them, so he could go on running with him, with Monroe and the others, and lead them, teach them, Jacob hearing the contradiction—*so who's the teacher then, fool?*—but not wanting to think about it yet.

Besides, Jacob mostly liked the ways he'd been changing. His mom didn't say anything, but he could see she was proud of his body filling out, his Ali-arm muscles nearly busting out of his brother's old T-shirts, his asthma never stopping him from doing things anymore. He didn't back down from fights, and when he walked by the playground he could see the little punks starting to fear him a little. Girls had got interested in him, too, flirting with him at the grocery store, the luncheonette, one of them passing him a note that said, *Do you think my friend is cute? She thinks you are.* He had. She had nice titties already, gave him a hard-on. But he hadn't known what to do next, had fled, not finishing his Coke. Those women *deserved* to see him in some better clothes, he decided. Then maybe he could get them to go that little extra distance.

Maybe that could happen tonight, even, if Shakur really meant it that they were going to see some women. That was when he decided to blow off the test for sure, fuck all night if he got the chance, stop when he ran out of jism, which would be never—a scientific fact he knew from his long, hard solo experiments. Why would he *ever* want to go to the cold white place up that motherfucking hill again, he thought, where there were *no* women, no way to show that he was *not* a boy anymore. Where the faggots thought *he* was gonna be a fag, too! He didn't think translating from a foreign language was gonna do the manhood thing for him. He needed pussy!

He and Shakur strolled past a cop car then. Were there more than usual out, maybe even shadowing them? Shakur handed him a joint. *Fuck it,* he thought. Fuck Bobby Brown and all his phone calls, quoting Malcolm back at him, *the secrets of physics and chemistry, literature and biology are the things our people need to know.* Yeah, but there were other things *he* needed to know, too, he wanted to say, so he could run with the people he had to lead, things Bobby didn't understand because Harvard had made him too white, not right.

Jacob took a hit then, sucked the harsh smoke deep into his lungs.

The next day, he walked down the corridor at school smiling grimly, about to fail a test on God knew what, and who cared? He might disappoint Hartman, though. He felt tugged at by what everyone *outside* wanted from him—speeches, leaflets, wild acts, too, to hold their attention. Hartman, though, he'd talked about letting something grow *inside* him, like a poem, say, words he would have for himself, great works made by Jacob Battle. As a . . .

Yeah, *as a what?*

Besides, Hartman must have decided he didn't have it in him. He didn't even call on him much in class anymore. *Inconsiderable.*

So fuck him.

But that made him damn near cry—like *he'd* failed Hartman!

And now he would fail Mercy's test on European history. BFD. He wouldn't have minded if the Dewey children had known where he'd been the night before, hanging with some friends, drinking, smoking weed, making love to a real woman.

He didn't need to be a student anymore, didn't want it either. What he *wanted* was to see if that woman that Shakur had introduced him to last night would give him another chance, Jacob knowing he'd come too fast, just a look at her beautiful nipples, the smell of her pussy, and he'd been long gone. She'd been nice about it, though, stroked his face; then she'd passed out on him before he'd had a second chance to show her what he could do.

And *that's* what he was thinking about still when the old queer came up to him in the hall, said he'd like to talk about why his grades were falling off this term. Mr. Hartman put his bony hand on Jacob's shoulder for everyone to see, which was *not* all right with Jacob, this man who couldn't see that Fidel Castro talked man to man with Sugar Cane, no *fantasy* connection there, but a new world coming, and he and his people bound to be in the vanguard—which meant no time for playing anymore. Then he remembered when this bastard had almost hit *him*, probably stopped only because he thought Jacob too little to take it. Fuck that! He pushed Hartman away—no big deal, but with the muscle he had now it knocked the old man on his ass and halfway down the stairs—which should give him a pretty good idea that Jacob was not a boy anymore. Not a butt boy *ever*.

The boozer geometry teacher started to help Hartman up. "No, no, no," Mr. Hartman screeched. "I'm fine, perfectly fine," he said, but like he was scared for Jacob rather than himself, maybe saw what was coming. "It's nothing, absolutely nothing. Slippery floor."

Jacob floated like Ali on the stairwell. *You liar,* he thought furiously. *It wasn't a slippery floor, it was my mighty right arm that did that to you.* Jacob wanted everyone to know that, the students, the faggot head of guidance, even the smug headmaster, they should all know what was in store for them someday. Of course, when they realized he wasn't their puppet they wouldn't want him around anymore. He could already see the headmaster at Monday assembly, flicking a dark speck off his thumb. "Oh, I've thrown that little black fly right out of our buttermilk," he would tell the assembly, his nearly locked jaw barely opening, then snapping shut again. "Praise God and skip to my Lou, my darlings. Our beloved Dewey community is lily white again!"

That same week, B.C. handed Beth a newsprint-wrapped package adorned with his self-taught Osmiroid italics: *For the Magnificat of All Hallows' Eve!,* the bleeding black ink giving the letters' edges anxious angel wings.

"Mm—mm—mmm-im-agine," B.C. stuttered, eyes agleam behind gold-rimmed glasses, "my little wi-wi-witch has a Hal-lo-lo-" He looked like he was choking. "Birthday!" he shouted, in a voice rich with triumph and self-loathing.

She opened the wrapping, found a pamphlet with smudged pages. Well, at least it had come all the way from China.

So that night, mostly to be polite, she'd begun Lin Piao's analysis of the world situation, B.C. lying awake beside her, looking over her shoulder sometimes, or watching her face; then jealously stroking her thigh to distract her from a gift he hadn't wanted her to find so much more interesting than him. But his hand and his presence faded to nothing as Lin Piao's words went directly into her blood, telling her what she needed to do to ease Frank's pain in the grave, what arduous, courageous feats would help justify her life and also something beyond her life, greater than her life, that still needed her help, still needed to be justified and made whole.

Everything Sugar Cane had said about self-defense in Vietnam and Georgia came clear to her now, its necessity, its ultimate, hidden, *black* meaning. Imperialism—the seizure of the fruits of this world from those with darker skins—was racism, like the death camps that had nearly killed her father.

But the countryside, Lin Piao showed, surrounds the city; and the countryside is the black, brown, and yellow people of the world; the U.S. bourgeoisie is the city. Besieged, the ruling class would inevitably turn fascist. Like a body undergoing rigor mortis, it would try to strangle

American blacks, and then all the poor and working class, in its death grip. Only a fighting force like the Vietcong—along with their allies here in the mother country—could pry fascism's stiffening fingers from the neck of the world.

She tore the title page off the pamphlet, put it in her nation sack to mingle with a precious fragment from Frank. She put the sack on again under her nightie, felt its almost supernatural warmth next to her breasts. Beth swore she would do her small part to help overthrow this racist, imperialist government; to free the black masses, the American working class, and all humanity. What was between her breasts would feed the world! Racist capitalism would fall! It would die! Long Live Justice for the World's People! Long Live the Victory of the People's War!

B.C., too, recognized in Lin Piao's dicta his own life's task. So he and Beth worked together every night that winter to prepare themselves for the struggle, reading *Black Skin, White Masks,* also *On Contradiction, The Eighteenth Brumaire,* Regis Debray's great *Revolution in the Revolution* (July/August *Monthly Review*), and even Che Guevara's *Guerrilla Warfare*—which B.C., squinting to see by the radiance of a Coleman lantern, sight-translated—not stuttering when he read aloud, or at least not when the words had been written by Saint Che.

Laura, joining them sometimes, tried to dream along with Beth and B.C. that they sat under mosquito netting in an amalgamated East Asian–African–Latin American–Somerville jungle. But she mostly felt like they were camping in someone's backyard in Great Neck. Like why a lantern, for God's sake! Beth—maybe feeling a slight corrosive haze drifting in from Laura—looked up frequently from the blinding light of Che's word and the soft radiance of the Coleman to instruct her how those wounded here and those fighting there—the welfare mothers, the Vietcong, even Laura, Beth, and B.C.—had all of them been oppressed and distorted by the same imperialism. And the guerrillas *there* would be like their own hands—*if* they struggled mightily for them *here,* leafleting, organizing, sitting in. *Then* one vein would connect them, the sempiternal upsurge that would make the new world. And Laura felt the pull of this bitter yet exalted concentration of self—*she, too, was oppressed!* and she felt extended at the same time: *heroic people would be her hands!*

Then B.C. babbled "Long live the victory of the Pe-Pe-pe—" and Laura's vision tattered. Mercifully, Beth interrupted him, shouting "People's War!"

Restored to her ordinary, small, scattered personhood, Laura stared at the burning mantle in the lamp, alight yet seemingly never consumed. Could this be what Frank really wanted? Had the means people needed to make justice changed so much? War? Even *a people's* war?

And how the hell would *she* ever know?

Confused, she walked the next day with Beth and Billy door-to-door among the asbestos-sided triple-deckers of Somerville, looking for supporters for a state referendum on the Vietnam War, votes that Beth promised no one would care about or probably even count. The agony in Vietnam would go on and on. She stamped the pavement with her black low-heeled shoes.

"So why are we doing this?" If Beth was right, she might as well be home studying.

"We do it because Che says you have to exhaust all legal, electoral means, show them up for the farce they are. That makes people ready for the next step."

That would include things like the cops shot dead at Texas Southern, black kids killed in Jackson, tanks rolling through Detroit. The students at the SDS house the night before had leaned toward Beth as she told them of these signs and wonders and begged them not to be so damn blind anymore: the war had *already* started in the ghettos. Soon whites would *have* to join.

Billy walked beside her in black pants, a white dress shirt, and a black yarmulke, his face moist with September sweat as he strained to hear the world-healing wisdom Beth dispensed. She floated ahead of them past the Bruised Fruit Stand and down a side street, deeper into the world revolution that would stop the killing of the Asian peasants who in Billy's dreams, Laura knew, had become semi-Israelis, both being peoples who defended themselves (in the Billy-view) against a hostile, racist world.

"Why can't Beth see that?" he'd wondered to Laura once as they walked to class. "Why does she think the Arabs are the victims?" Beth's fury about Israel bewildered him, but her audacity, Laura saw, hypnotized him, made Beth forever Billy's irreplaceable, unpossessable older woman.

Maybe Beth's full-lipped mouth did still occasionally give Billy a kiss when B.C. wasn't looking, but those same lips, Laura knew, usually offered him an angry rebuke for his Zionism, and an invitation to an SDS meeting; all of which meant that the teen world's ever growing geek-boy tribe could read Billy's response to Beth's abandonment every month in Green Co. comics, where the heroine—called "Athena X" or "Deborah, AKA the Prophet," or "Ninja B.," depending on what series she appeared in—was always dark-haired and buxom, with large eyes and a long nose that had a slight downward turn that mirrored the disapproving curve of her mouth, that most dangerous of organs, able to emit a brutal scream that would make a boy's blood run from his already wounded ears, or—if turned to a secret seductive frequency—make him follow her helplessly to his death.

Or maybe just into a brown Somerville three-decker to collect votes-that-didn't-matter against a war that did. The entryway door had a busted lock. They pushed inside, and Billy and Laura knocked for the downstairs tenants, while Beth disappeared upstairs.

A few minutes later Laura heard a man shouting, "He's our president! Just maybe he knows things you don't know!" Beth reappeared then, along with a full-bellied man who had his hands on her shoulders, pushed her backward down the short hall to the top of the stairs. Beth grabbed the chipped wooden banisters with both hands and planted herself. The man put both his big hands on her chest, "though it was really strange," Beth told Laura, Billy, and B.C. at the Hayes Bickford later, where students, rummies, and working-class women in frayed coats ate griddle-fried muffins, drank grainy coffee. "There was *nothing* sexual about it, eh? My tits were like, you know, just protuberances to him. Handles."

Billy had run up the stairs. A pasty-faced teenager had flown out of the open door from the apartment, started beating at the man's broad back. The man had let Beth go, and bear-hugged the boy, lifting his feet off the ground so they flailed about. "You're hurting me!" the boy screamed. "You stupid bastard, you're really fucking hurting me!" The older man had carried him backward toward the apartment, his face not angry anymore, Laura thought, but resolved, concerned—like Jesse's when he'd saved Billy from the Sound.

A few days later, Michael Healy came toward Beth as she waited for a bus. "Look, I'm sorry, you know, for my father's like nearly murdering you."

"Not as bad as all that," Beth said, smiling at Healy's long-sleeved white dress shirt and black pants. He must have glimpsed Billy's outfit and imitated him, thinking it might be what she liked.

Soon she had him helping her hand out JOIN leaflets at the Somerville welfare office. And within a few days she'd convinced him that if his scientific gifts were as big as he said, then he could get away from his family the way she had, by applying early to college. And he had something about him, she told Laura later, that made her believe he might have real talent. "There's this autism almost, a way of looking at me, sometimes, like I was a stone." He could maybe even jujitsu the ruling class into scholarship money at a top school, where he'd get the best training to help the anti-imperialist struggle. Beth told him she knew a famous old Fizzyits at MIT who might help them.

"Jesus, you *know* the man? It would be an honor to meet him."

"He came to our house when I was little. He was this total klutz who broke *everything* he touched." Healy's darting eyes went still for a moment, bored into her face, like she'd insulted Hans. "He laughed at himself," she added defensively, "said theoretical physicists shouldn't be allowed to touch *any* equipment, even wineglasses."

"Yeah?" he said, like he was filing that away, would make a point now of becoming clumsy.

The next week, in Hans's dusty office, Michael listened to the Fizzyit gabble some numbers. Hans wore a white, short-sleeved, wash-and-wear shirt in a slick and repellent poly-fabric. Michael stood in front of his desk, still wearing black pants and a dress shirt, which made him look just like what he was now: a schoolboy being tested.

A smart one? He gabbled numbers right back at Hans.

"We're petting Schrödinger's cat," the old man said to Beth, who perched between piles of journals on a moldy urine-smelling couch—cat piss, she hoped, though Hans looked ancient now, white-haired, rheumy-eyed, maybe weak-bladdered, too. Then Hans smiled at her like he knew she wouldn't understand what he'd said.

Condescending prick, she thought. *Fuck him. Fuck the cat, too, whoever he was.*

"He's everything you promised, Beth." He laughed, mildly, like the effort took more breath than he could spare anymore. "The poor boy has some very medieval ideas, though." Hans smiled at Beth, or some-where near her face, anyway. "I'll have to disabuse him of his faulty metaphysics." He turned back to Michael. "You'll have to disguise yourself as an ordinary freshmen, of course. Don't worry, though, that's how all of the freshmen feel."

Meaning, Beth wondered, that Michael was the same as them, they all think they're geniuses? Or that *he* really was one?

Anyway, Hans would arrange for Healy to start the next semester at the place Michael called "the Church on Massachusetts Avenue," mock-ery meant to hide his real awe for what he believed went on under the school's imposing dome, the decoding of the hidden message from God that is our universe.

As they walked down the high stone steps, Beth watched men playing Frisbee on the grass by a flying saucer. She tried to laugh at Michael in a teasing way she figured he'd like. He maybe half meant that stuff about God's code; but she knew boys; he mostly wanted something gaudy and mystical-sounding to make her think he was cool.

Well, Hans did. So she did. She put her arm in his. Giddy, they didn't bother about a bus, marched all the way back to Somerville.

This late in the year, though, the school would give him only a partial scholarship; Michael could afford this church's lessons in scientific gematria only if he lived at home. So despite Beth's promise, he remained still *here*, and *not* cool, sharing a bathroom with his beer-bellied Da. But Michael said he could bear his dad's sullenness now, because he'd also really be *there*, which meant not just MIT but the hidden realm of the universe where Bohr's impossible contradictions offered their revelations; "no certainties, you know, but the probabilities always match what the data eventually produce. Which is like free will and predestination reconciled."

"If you say so," Beth said, feeling that she'd done a little something here for the worker's child, and so for the people of the Third World, and so for the revolution, repaying Michael for his gift to her when he'd walked toward her a month ago at that bus stop: a vision of the children of the proletariat, "the ones," she'd told Michael, "whose blood gets spilled in every racist imperialist war," marching forward in their white shirts and woolen pants to follow their black and brown brothers toward the Revolution.

"Oh, don't be ridiculous," Laura's exasperated father said to her when she told him about it that Chanukah. "You people talk about the working class, but you don't even know anybody *from* the working class."

"Sure we do, Dad," she said mildly, thinking of Michael, ungainly, uncoordinated, uncomfortable in his body, but definitely working class. "And thanks for the fuzzy sweater. It's just what I wanted."

"Your problem is, darling," he said, "there's no outside to your world. You and your friends leave one room with a worn sofa and a knocking radiator, and you walk into *another* room, with *another* ratty sofa."

He'd got that right. Life now was SDS houses, Progressive Labor and Spartacist houses, Situationist communes and Young Socialist

Alliance klatches, each one with a different flavor of Marxism "and another empty Coke bottle lying on the floor."

"And more people just like yourselves, saying the very same things."

And also, thank God, always another joint, fuel for yet another discussion of the working-class role in the Revolution that everyone in every ratty room she entered seemed sure was bound to come any day now.

"Metropolitan workers are bought off with crumbs from imperialist superprofits," Beth instructed. "When the People's War makes the empire start to crumble, the workers' comforts will disappear." She stroked B.C.'s leg. "Only then will they be ready to follow their children into the fight led by the black and brown people of the world."

Laura dragged on a joint in fond farewell before starting it on its journey to Michael Healy, who was prized, petted, and condescended to by all sides at the SDS house as a future "organic intellectual of the working class," an oracle—or was he more like an idiot savant?—of what the workers felt. Twenty students waited now to hear what Michael would say.

He puffed. "B.C. and Beth got it right." He opened his arms. "Until they're ready to join the world revolution, fuck the fucking workers." Michael turned to stare directly at Laura then, his eyes shining with feverish pleasure. Stoned, Laura found them frighteningly bright—glowing lamps that measured her, and probably found her too bourgeois.

Laura Jaffe, Michael thought, had the widest, most beautiful blue eyes. For him, the right answer to what the workers' role would be in the world revolution was whatever the fuck she wanted it to be. Sure, Laura wasn't as built as Beth, but *everyone* wanted Beth, and part of *his* genius, after all, was calculating transition probabilities between two states (initial preparation, final detection), including a girl in this room, and a girl in bed with him. Better odds for Laura than Beth. Besides, she had lovely legs, which made Michael decide *he* must be what his friends called "a leg man." That sounded sophisticated to him—though the imagined other women-parts, which he'd never seen naked either, *all* meant an instant hard-on.

Pretty women gummed up his works. He couldn't go inside himself to think when he was around them, but he didn't know what to say to them either; which left him trapped helplessly on the surface of his skin, exposed to every disapproving flicker of Laura's eyes. Maybe if he could get her to take acid with him he could reveal *his* vision to her and she'd see why she should want to talk to him, touch him, let him touch her—

because right now, he could tell she didn't find him as exotic as the other students did for simply being part of "a class" that his father had never mentioned to him, certain that they were "middle," if they were anything, and thinking, probably, that "worker" was another Anglo-Saxon curse word meaning *mick*. Thinking of his old man made him sorry he'd said that *fuck the workers* thing, but Beth would have said that, and Laura was clearly crazy about Beth. Besides, B.C. and Beth also thought they would eventually *need* the workers—key part of "the great mass of humanity"—to make their revolutionary gizmo work.

Well, could be, he thought—at least when he'd smoked enough dope to forget his own quick-to-weep, protective Da. Tears? Impossible for a worker! The proletariat, he'd learned at this peach-colored house, didn't cry, they got angry. They also had nothing to lose, so they would run faster to the barricades than the middle class. Also workers were really direct about fucking—which was maybe the *biggest* news for Michael. Did that mean Laura would like it if he grabbed her?

Look, he'd be happy to do and be whatever Laura wanted, if only he could figure out what that was. So after the meeting, he sat in the SDS kitchen working on that insoluble problem.

Laura watched people with pots of water scurry around Michael Healy, who sat stock-still in a red chair, Michael a magician of concentration who could disappear within himself even with all that noise, the only glimmer he was alive the intense light from his blue eyes. Probably he was doing "thought experiments" in a blank white room.

Then he emerged, and sped about with the rest of them, bringing heavy white bowls to the table, finishing people's sentences and poking his index finger at them—the same gesture, the same impatience as Beth. Laura couldn't help herself, she wanted the approval of someone *that* certain of his own intelligence. She wanted him to put up a picture of her in his amazing inner room.

But a few days later, when he came on to her at the Brattle, he just seemed like a high school kid who moved his arm in a gawky way and stroked her hair too hard. She reached up, took his hand off her. Then she regretted it, decided that maybe "the world's first actual *prodigy* at quantum mechanics" paraded to a different drummer, and his frightening, flaring anger and bright gaze must be the outer glints from a world-important inner life. She agreed to go to another movie the next night.

There, blind Audrey Hepburn's terror reminded her how very weak and frightened *she* was all the time, too, besieged by something much worse than Alan Arkin, a demon-saint she couldn't ever placate. Maybe someone as smart and special as Michael could help her. She bent toward him, and he stroked her hair again. This time she murmured, "Hey, slow down . . . I like that."

He slowed down.

And she did like it. Liked him, too, truly. Also, Michael was two entire years younger than she was, but considerate always; and he even gave her moments when she felt *knowing*. Or *almost*.

In return, he taught her physics—a place where he was most definitely the knowing one. After making love, they walked along the Charles watching a sculler make waves. Or particles? "So which is it?" She squinted, trying to see the light in the water as packets thrown down on the river, golden atomic coins.

"Depends on who's asking." He laughed—a mechanical sound, like an assembly line dropping the *ha*'s into a big metal bucket. "Really, it depends on *how* you measure them. Photons are two in one, particle and wave."

"Like Certs."

"Or the Father and the Son." He cupped a joint behind his hand, puffed away as they walked, making her nervous about cops. But she reached out for it anyway.

"Look, you just have to believe that there's a part of the world that doesn't work like the one you know," he said. "Like the Kingdom of Heaven that is among you, the truths of quantum physics are not to be apprehended by common sense." Father Healy put his arms wide for his flock of one. His school jacket with its big felt *S* fell open, showing a bulge taped to the lining, more dope and rolling papers, probably, hidden in an idiot place where any cop could find them. He made the sign of the cross in the spring air, smiling.

"You're kidding me," but she knew from his smile that the cross was dead serious to him—X marks the spot.

"Not me. God's kidding you. Tricking you into surrender. The mind's crucified by the paradox. It has to die and be reborn with a new understanding."

She couldn't stop herself. "Michael, for God's sake. You're only sixteen."

He smiled. "Until next month."

"Right. Then you'll be seventeen."

She took his smallish hand. Blond, a stocky build, with strong legs, but shorter than her, about Arkey's size, altogether an aerodynamically good shape for gliding through water, the felt *S* having been awarded by the Somerville varsity swim team. "What does Hans think about the Kingdom of Heaven?"

"Hans smiles. He offers me a cup of tea. He says he's heard it all before."

Well, that was diminishing, but reassuring, too—at least Michael wasn't insane.

"But he also said he'd never heard it from someone who was so good with the numbers. That makes me piquant. That's what he calls it. Like Tabasco, I think." He stopped. "You know, Hans is, like, really old, I can tell his brain doesn't work as quickly as mine anymore." They strolled on. "I'm like his chance to be part of things again."

She smiled fondly. Michael wanted to think Hans needed *him,* when really, Laura knew, the dependence ran the other way. Michael resented being treated like just another freshman with required courses, tests to take; the only thing that made him certain he was special, different, *chosen,* was that Hans met with him a few times a month to disabuse him of his religion.

"So you're the only son," she said, continuing the Christ thing to flatter him.

"Well, not *only,*" Michael admitted reluctantly. "There's another guy, too. A graduate student." Turning thoughtful. "Gifted," he murmured. But she could hear the undertone: *but not as gifted as me.*

Ah, the river sparkled, and the trees had just pricked out a leaf or two. She walked along in a Danskin leotard, a wraparound skirt, Capezios on her feet—a Radcliffe coed dancing her way into med school. Today, she thought, Cambridge would do for her nicely just the way it was; no Revolution necessary, *this* could be her Kingdom of Heaven.

A few weeks later, Michael promised her another kingdom, too—an attic on the corner of Green and Bow Streets, part of a house his cousin wanted left empty until he came back from his tour in Vietnam, the G.I. paying the mortgage for a good-luck charm, like the Cong wouldn't kill a man who had a place he could go home to.

There, Michael revealed that marijuana only worked for beginning-level courses. For advanced quantum illumination you needed LSD—her first hit already waiting for her in the center of his small palm.

"This won't make me crazy?"

"No crazier than me."

"Not reassuring." But the Beatles gulped whole jelly jars full, right? Michael placed the small orange pill on her outstretched tongue, in nomine Domini RingoPaulJohnand me. Besides, acid was something Beth didn't have the courage for; in addition to showing Laura God's face, taking it would put her ahead of Beth for once.

And by that afternoon she and Michael sat on his cousin's unmade double bed, naked, studying their *souls' investiture,* AKA their bodies, not even trying to fuck—any touch lasting too long and sending unpleasant sparks along Laura's legs in unpredictable directions. Which was probably, if she'd understood Michael correctly, Heisenberg's fault. All of it shone brave and new to her, Michael's almost hairless body, lysergic acid, probability amplitudes, Schrödinger equations for quantum linear superposition—meaning that electrons are smears that are everywhere at once, the cat both alive and dead, until a Nosey Parker's measurement causes a "collapse of the wave functions," and a time of decision for the poor feline. Laura loved all of it, the just looking at each other's amazing bodies getting mixed up for her with his gibble-gabble about quirky particles and the way the light from the window picked out dust motes that moved in grave morris measure—making, she'd just bet, a three-dimensional representation of the underlying order of the universe, if only she had eyes to see. But that meant each mote had to move right and left at the same time? Up and down? "They do!" she said, pointing. "Look!"

They both watched the dust for a while, slowly spinning its way back to being . . . just grains that made her eyes red, her nose stuffy. She needed him to talk more, so the world would be amazing again, and also so she wouldn't fall into herself, grow anxious, start to worry about the saliva pooling in her mouth. Could she swallow?

Say something! Then you'll be able to swallow again! "Tell me. More. Photons. Two places. At once?"

He started in again.

They dropped drugs together every Sunday afternoon that spring—her mass, she said once, her wafer.

"All praise to LSD," he replied, all too seriously.

She moved her gray KLH to the attic so they could play a song by Paul Butterfield she liked, called "Driving Wheel," over and over, or "Sad-Eyed Lady of the Lowlands," or the Goldberg Variations, sound to cling to in the few moments when Michael was silent.

Once, when his lessons got to be too much for her, they talked about their childhoods, with the exception of that one little thing on her part that she'd promised never to speak about—though when the acid hit and their souls stood so perfectly naked to each other, she hated having a secret from him, felt an awful sneak.

They'd swallowed several disgusting peyote buttons for that session. Michael said Coyote had put the bitterness and nausea in to keep the uncommitted away. And soon Laura couldn't talk about her childhood, or Great Neck, or anything but the unbearable stomach-wrenching pain. She put her arms around herself to keep her molecules from flying apart.

"Are you cold?"

"I'm discrete." Particles, she meant.

"I trust you completely," he said.

"Bach got it wrong," she said. Or maybe Bach had understood, and all those busy notes, all that fugal order, was just a frenzied game of *let's pretend* because he *knew* the nonexistent God *did* play dice with the universe! Michael smiled at her, his long teeth dripping terror. *That* must be why Michael wants so desperately to reconcile quantum physics with Jesus and Mary Watching Over Us; he knows it's all really chance, that there's no meaning anywhere, and Nobody watches over Nothing. He thinks if he can get the drugs just right he can have ten seconds where he believes the Universe has an order when really he knows it's random all the way up to where Heaven *used* to be, but now collapsed stars fall inward on themselves forever, black holes with gravity so incredibly dense that they swallow up even the poor light that happens to traipse by.

Then the drug hit, leaving her stomach still roiling, but distantly. She spread her legs, grasped her toe muscles with her hands, feeling the magnificent pain from the stretch in her groin. Michael stared between her legs.

"In the beginning all matter in the universe was at one point," he said.

"Dense with nerve endings," she said.

"That's the universe before the Big Bang, the explosion that started everything."

Her clit was the universe? Her orgasm started everything? "Yeah, I saw something about it in the *Times*." A man with a wasting disease, on his way to being a black hole himself, he'd proved it. "But just because there's a Big Bang, that doesn't mean there was a Big Banger." She laughed. He didn't. Blank blue eyes that scared her again.

"Look, everything we see, it comes from this one point. And at the beginning there would have been an exact balance of matter and anti-matter. They should have annihilated each other. So why is there any matter left?"

"Is there?" she said, looking at his dick—big enough banger actually. He ignored her; waited.

"Ok. Chancre?" she said. "I mean chance? Is that why?" the word making her stomach turn, which sent peyote fumes to her brain, coyote-farts to increase her terror.

"No," Michael said solemnly. "I don't think it could have been chance. The equations always come out right. So like why was this time different?" He looked over at his jacket, like his junior high letter would confirm his wisdom.

"Okay, then, how about, God said, 'Let there be light, and there was light.' How's that?"

Great, apparently. Joyful awe suffused his round face like maybe *she'd* made the universe. Had she? She couldn't remember. "Exactly," he said. "Yes. Now. I mean, look, there's something I have to show you, okay?" He went to the chair where he'd hung his blue cotton and leather jacket, and squatted next to it, naked, working at the lining.

He handed her a folded piece of notebook paper with dirty Scotch tape around the edges. "Here. Read this."

The paper looked like it had been refolded a thousand times, the magic marker writing smudged, hard to read:

LSD lets me see **THE SINGULARITY.** No space. No time. *Without form and void.* My mind was sucked inward by the emptiness.

All law annulled?

I HEARD A VOICE SAY: "NO! LAW not yet created! God in-scribed the laws of space and time in a vacuum. Before 10 to the -43rd $\times 56.4 \times 10$ to the -44th ABB *YOU* cannot see! He made Law that you might see!

Then the Quantum Fluctuations began!—and I was permitted to view them! Perturbations of His Holy Spirit as He brooded over the darkness! Photons appeared!

A voice said: "LOOK! Light is wave and particle at once! This is impossible and yet it IS! LIGHT IS THE IMAGE OF GOD WHO IS FATHER AND SON AT ONCE!"

Angel? she thought. Was this like a poem for the Somerville High lit magazine? Or did Michael really maybe think a heavenly being had shouted in his ears? She looked over at him, staring back at her. Her naked boyfriend was mad—or a prophet. Or was that like wave and particle? Could he be both at once? After all, this was *her* Michael, whose inwardness astounded her, Quanta's only prodigy, the genius whose vision could protect her and Audrey Hepburn both.

> The Angel shouted: "LISTEN: The collision of photons at the Beginning of Time IS the CRUCIFIXION! God crucifies God so that men might live and see—HIM!
>
> "HIS AGONY gives birth to Matter and Anti-matter!"

Michael—the same name as an Angel! The Angel spoke to Michael so he might speak to others, like her, a girl who would be deafened if she'd heard that voice directly. He'd listened to the voice of God's messenger—and now she'd been chosen by him to hear it, too! Magnificat of Peyote Coyote!

> I asked the Angel, "Why wasn't all destroyed when matter and anti-matter collided?"
>
> The Angel shouted: THE BLIND SEE CHANCE. THE SAVED SEE HOW HIS HAND CHOSE MORE TO LIVE THAN TO DIE—SO THAT YOU MIGHT SEE!

She felt the capital letters inside her skull now, like someone hammering at her temples. She definitely wasn't strong enough for this, could barely contain this much magnificence, her head and bladder competing to see which would be the first to break.

> I heard the light scream on Winter Hill! Photons collide still! God crucifies God! New particles flash in and out of existence! Christ is in agony until the end of time! Thank God for that sustaining agony!

The bed rushed away from Laura. She put her hands out to keep from falling, then brought them together and looked toward the heavens, or the cobwebbed beams of the ceiling from which the Madonna awaits the Parakeet. "Oh, God," she prayed, pointlessly, the effulgence now really too much for her Hepburnish body. Why *that*? she thought. Why *agony*? Why *end time,* the same words as on that torn paper from Mississippi! "Why?" she said, meaning *why me;* and why had her

brother died, why had he written to her, blighting her life with the tearing of his dead muscles? Had Frank written to prepare her for Michael,
so she might know the truth of this crumpled, folded paper? For the
risen Christ! Jesus, what would her parents say about that?

"Read on," Michael said, smiling, as if the question had been to
him. Well, maybe it was. Michael would know why Frank had written,
what his letters meant and how to comfort her. Blood rushed to her
head, almost singing in her ears: Her Michael knew the nature of light,
the path of the electrons that is everywhere at once, he would see the
truth of her brother's letters, the way to make justice, all of it one thing
somehow, a pattern that thanks to his genius she would now see, too.
She looked down. Only one line left:

"Must it be?" the Angel asked. "It must be!"

She laughed. *That* was a tag from Beethoven, one Beth sometimes
used. Borrowed words? *Why would an angel use borrowed words?* Like
maybe her Michael spoke to Angels *when he was on acid*; and maybe
that wasn't so uncommon, maybe it was like having a lizard in your
room, or a great collection of old Coke bottles—things that made you
feel special, made you think you weren't so pathetic that the oh so opposite sex would never be interested in you. So what Michael had seen
wasn't the pattern that connects us all but just a gaudier kind of varsity
letter—while the world danced spastically on, random, discrete, and
meaningless. Then she remembered, too, where she'd read about a
vision sewn into a jacket. "Pascal," she said wryly. "Right?"

Michael looked crestfallen—like he wouldn't have minded if she'd
said, *I think you're nuts,* but wasn't ready for her to decide he was a
pretentious phony, that this whole charade, hearing God, listening to
the light, had been his way of saying, *See, I'm a genius, like Pascal.* He
tugged the edge of the paper. "No, wait," she said, sorry she'd taken
the piss out of him. "I mean, like you should *sew* it into the lining
of your jacket, the way Pascal did, okay? Not just use Scotch tape.
Look." She walked slowly across the room, to get her purse. "I'll do it
for you."

He brightened. "It was like my very first trip," he said. "I took the
stuff alone on Winter Hill. You ever been there? It's Nowhere carpeted
with dog turds. But when that Voice started to talk to me, you better
believe I just hugged that ground like it was the Holy Land, pushed my
lips right into the dirt."

"Good place to be, the ground. No farther to fall." A Puritan had said that in an English course. Now that she'd stood up, she could see Mr. Puritan's point. She nearly dove back to the bed.

"So you don't think I'm like crazy?"

She managed to pull the rich man through the eye of the needle, which was definitely a miracle, she thought, and must mean this attic was a Singularity. All laws annulled, or not yet created; including maybe her vow of silence. "You know, I had, I mean, my friends and me had this thing that happened to us, that's a little like what happened to you." She said it because she wanted to reassure him that she didn't think he was a phony, even if she did. And because, maybe, she was also tired of his doing all the talking. "I promised I'd never tell anyone, so you like can't tell them I told you."

"I won't."

"Swear. Swear on the Angel you spoke to at Winter Hill."

"I do," he vowed, and then, once she got started, she realized how much she needed to tell someone about the letters, about Billy's *seeing* from her rocking chair, someone who might believe. And then, *at the same time,* listening to her voice say, "So we have to do acts of justice to help ease his pain," she heard the something else she wanted from Michael: that he would be the one who would say, *No,* dear, I spoke to an honest angel, while yours is a Long Island grifter, contrary to the laws of physics, outside even the infinite unpredictable possibilities of Singularities. *Oh, I believe,* she thought, *dear God, help me to unbelieve—so I don't have to spend the rest of my life with my mind wrapped in my brother's decaying body, hearing him talk from a steam pipe.* And if that meant the universe was just chance, dear? *Well, fine.* That would be better than her ghostly burden.

But no such luck. Michael's face looked as utterly credulous as they'd all been in her room in Great Neck. "I feel honored," he said, "that you would tell me about this." He pulled on his faded white boxer shorts and his blue jeans, to show respect, she supposed. "It really all makes sense."

"How *could* it?"

"There's a linkage in the universe, Laura. As your brother changed in the grave, particles in Billy's mind changed, too."

"You think?" This wasn't what she wanted to hear, or not altogether; and she hated herself for not entirely wanting it.

She handed him his newly sewn jacket, his vision secure; and hers now, she thought, hung forever around her neck, too. Agony end time. Always and forever.

Oh, fuck.

Which was how the next week she ended up standing with a hundred other students, waiting in an alley as Secretary McNamara's limo pulled into view. They sat down in the street, Laura's roommate, Helen, on one side, Beth on the other in a heavy red coat, a bright spot among all the blue pea jackets—though actually sitting in front of a car, Laura thought, had to be the world's stupidest idea. Infectious, though. Billy sat next to her. Arkey and his girlfriend, Gail Wagman, sat next to him, Gail's big eyes moving frantically, like a trapped little animal's. Laura watched the car's bumper approach . . . and slow, thank God . . . and . . . yes, stop.

Then the Secretary of Defense of the United States stepped out, climbed on the roof of his car,

> growing in size, revealing his true dimensions . . .
>
> larger than the students . . . the two-story build-
> ings . . . the trees,
>
> "*Ungrateful children,*" he shouts—scattering the
> few remaining leaves from the trees, bringing the
> weak branches down on the students' heads, "*you,
> too, must kneel to THAT WHICH IS!*"
>
> Not this time! Athena X—trained by Dr. Why?
> to see through disguises—detects the verdigris
> hidden underneath the giant's slicked-back hair,
> smooth face, and thick glasses.
>
> Athena emits a sharp, eerie, coruscating scream

—sounding remarkably like the one the shawled women give in *The Battle of Algiers,* and practiced each night in the SDS house until the neighbors began to wonder if Beth's boyfriend's dick had barbs on it or the shrieking dead had finally risen. Beth didn't want to arouse the secretary's tiny conscience, she wanted to hurt him on behalf of the Vietnamese, wanted to stop soldiers from lining up body bags on an airport tarmac—

> every plastic sack stuffed with a man unable to
> move or speak, but whose eyes—

in a panel famous for its evocation of claustrophobia and terror (Ish. #36 of *Women Warriors*—"Zargon Revealed!")

> snap open in the dark!

A long-legged woman in the crowd seconds Beth's scream—

> and a dense black cloud forms in front of her face!!

> Fur grows on her arms!!!

> Her face lengthens and grows forward . . .
> Her jaws are immense . . .
> but her teeth are surprisingly still small—useless
> and all-too-human—

Well, this is her first scream after all. She'll need plenty of practice to become SheWolf, Athena's companion and rival in the fight against injustice!

> The giant beams his horrid eyes directly at her!
> He smiles!

> "NOW YOU KNOW YOURSELF, LUPINE
> ONE! COME AND JOIN US! WE WILL
> TEACH YOU TO USE ALL YOU NOW
> POSSESS!"

> SheWolf, confused—perhaps even tempted for a
> moment—looks toward Athena X.

In her wisdom, Athena only smiles. SheWolf must choose for herself. . . .

The two boon companions fall into each other's arms laughing. Their arms will soon bear many scars from shared battles!

The giant's face fills with slathering fury! His immense hand reaches down from above and seizes SheWolf's locket from the hair on her chest!

Laughing, he dangles it from fingers as enormous as saplings! "Without the Knowledge in the Stone that you wore so unknowingly you will never learn how to bear the dead that a Wolf must make to live!"

Did the giant mean the very grandmother whose dying gift that locket had been? SheWolf had been wolfishly out at a ball when Bubbie had most needed the doctor's help!

But before she can ask, more and more student speech bubbles join the Women Warriors! They fill the air with "Aaauulllaaaahs!" The force of their righteous screams makes the secretary's disguise peel from his face . . .

Revealing the scaly skin, the rodent nose, and thousand-faceted eyes of Zargon, Engineer of Death! The DEATH ORG.'s most faithful servant!

Athena's cry has ruptured Zargon's capillaries! Tears of blood drip from each plane of his insect eyes, making a hideous chandelier!!

He's blind now forever, outwardly as inwardly!!!

But Athena X's own greyhounds foolishly taste a drop or two of Zargon's eye-blood! The blood transforms her dogs into human hellhounds!

Will they someday turn on their former mistress?
(To find out the answer Fellow Warriors mustn't
miss issue #37: *The Haunted Desperado!*)

Meanwhile, Arkey led Gail Wagman, weeping terrified but bloodless tears, back to his narrow dorm room in Kirkland House. Her crying turned him into a contestant on *Teen Beat the Clock*. His challenge: get Gail to stop bawling before parietal hours ended. The prize: they'd make love. And for boobies? The Green Line to the airport so she could hop her plane back to the University of Wisconsin.

Gail was as brilliant as anyone Arkey had met at Harvard, but she'd spent her years at Dana Hall Prep taking acid every other day, writing poetry she wouldn't let anyone see, and probably fucking a lot too, though Arkey couldn't think about *that* without feeling both desperately scared and very excited.

Gail's parents, though, had been more frightened than aroused; they'd stuck her in McLean Hospital—which turned out not to be as good a college application thing as the Model UN (where Arkey had represented *la belle* and murderous France).

Arkey boiled some water on his hot plate, Constant Comment to calm her. "But no fucking," she said, sitting down on his bed crosslegged in a short skirt and black tights. "Not today. That giant on the car freaked me out."

"Giant?"

"He felt so *entitled* to be angry, like it was just the machine humming through him—the world system, right? So it didn't matter that *he* actually knew he was lying."

"Of course." Important not to upset her more and get a scathing, rapid, and insightful analysis of his flaws, almost flattering in its discerning attention to his cowardice, a boy who couldn't commit himself to his grandfather's socialism or to a woman, every moment of his inconsiderateness or inattention measured, the nasty shadow around every loving act revealed, turning it and him to dross. Her critiques made Arkey feel at the same time crushed *and* strangely *warmed*—the way, say, radiation therapy might be said to warm a person—by her meticulous, piercing attention.

That afternoon though, she transformed herself into a kid whining for one more story before bedtime, something about Arkey's family, please, and those big rooms in the Garment District where broadshouldered Grandpa Abe had helped organize the ILGWU. Arkey felt pleased actually that she could possibly care about him or his family, certain, too, that Gail, so perceptive about his own flaws, would also see, by contrast, Abe's massive righteousness.

So the hour passed. They took the Loser Line to the airport, holding hands, Arkey wondering why **OurKey**'s girlfriend had become the **Story Teller** in *Tales of the Outsiders*, #33, the Band's bard, when all Gail ever did was listen to *his* stories?

"Is that her? The one in the comics?" Laura heard a blond freshman girl ask an even blonder boy, a month later. In the well in front, **Beth J. / Ninja B. / Athena X / Deborah, AKA the Prophet** unfolded her vision of the holy and redemptive People's War to the hundreds of students who filled the round bowl of Burr B lecture hall. Not just *her* vision anymore, Tet having convinced people that maybe Lin Piao had got it right: the country surrounds the city.

Laura's roommate, Helen, leaned forward toward the preppies. "Yeah," she said. "That's Athena X. Her scream made ZarNamara cry blood in *WW*, Issue #36."

Helen had translucent pink-tinged skin, which positively glowed from inside now for Billy Green, his thin, small body not weak but *gentle*—like, to avoid blinding them, he must be constantly tamping down those magus-like powers that could turn ink and paper into art, and art into money.

"A lot of people in New York think he's like a genius," Helen said. She was Lionel Trilling's niece, so she could give "a lot of people" the special Claremont Avenue emphasis that means ones *you* don't know, *ones who matter,* her condescending smile making clear that to Manhattan, Great Neck was Sioux City, Iowa—though it was Helen who had the smooth skin, the round, corn-fed–looking face.

Naturally, Helen said, Billy stayed up all night drinking tea and drawing, "which was probably more or less what Van Gogh had done at Arles, after all," Billy's membranes equally as permeable as the mad artist's, open, Helen said, to everyone's emotions—this fleshly woman confusing Green the artist with Bad Ears the character, and his yarmulke probably seeming to her a magic beanie for muse-transmission; though now that he was catnip for girls Laura had the feeling Billy wore the cap less and less, sex maybe everywhere and always the universal solvent for faith. Billy even had *several* girlfriends—which had made him, Laura thought, more confident, and far more ordinary. He seemed shrunken, less vivid, quieter. No more class reports to terrify them; no more stories of Leo Jacobs' life; no more prophecies, just special double issues without end, as if the colors had been leached from him to feed his bright pages.

"Athena X," the preppy-looking kid drawled, "like, she's Malcolm's sister, right," an irony meant to mask giddy pleasure. Laura could see how Billy's month-by-month transformation of his heartbreak over Beth *there,* in comics, had not only helped his love life with Helen *here,* it also had added to Beth Jacobs' power to lead them all into non–comic book dangers, whispering harsh seductions that slowly walked SDS toward *her* vision, one that delighted these undergraduates for the same reason it hypnotized Beth, because just by sharing her ideas you became an extension of the brave, implacable Vietcong *there,* in history, even though what you did *here* might look to the uninitiated like stepping lightly through the morning dew of Harvard Yard to put leaflets under freshman doors for a rally against ROTC. Laura sleepily trailed after Beth, supportive but hesitant, because no matter how long Laura listened to Beth, the Vietnamese, to her, were still bent-backed women who worked in rice paddies; they were *those who suffered,* not those who fought. To kill, even *there,* even with that provocation, was to contravene, if not God's law, then her brother's and Martin Luther King's.

Then in April, Martin Luther King was murdered on a motel balcony in Memphis, and all the world seemed to shriek, like Beth, in ululating pain. On the tiny screen a thinned-down Sugar Cane in a black leather jacket shouted, "We're going to stand up on our feet and die like men! If that's the only act of manhood possible, then goddamn it, we're going to die!" Behind him the ghetto in Washington celebrated a drunken funeral.

"A wake, that's called, darling," Michael said. The little TV with its bent coat hanger antennae showed another burning city. Laura, Beth, Arkey, and Gail smoked dope and watched from a ratty green brocade couch someone had left out for garbage. Nearby, six silver-backed bales of pink fiberglass insulation lay against the walls, waiting to be tacked to the rotting wood beams.

"The colonies are rising!" Beth shouted.

"Right on!" Michael amened.

Beth gazed at the organic teenager of the working class, his eyes alight with televised flames. "They're the Third World within the U.S.," she instructed. "Forty dead already, twenty thousand arrested. Black Power is Tet come home to America." She stared at Michael, testingly.

Michael, confused, drew his lips tightly up and back, showing his chipped front teeth. His cousin, his mother had just told him, had lost an arm in Tet, so he would be coming home to America. "Black Power?" he said quietly.

"Black Power!" Beth repeated, louder.

"Black Power!" Michael echoed.

Again, Beth shouted back.

And Laura looked on, unable to join in, unable to look away as Beth and her Irish lover, two loony backup singers, chanted "Black Power!" to Sugar Cane on a tiny TV in a nearly empty attic owned by a now one-armed Vietnam vet.

The next week, Laura flew home to her family, people who knew that a great and good man had left the world. Her father, just back from the funeral, lay in bed, eyes half shut from weeping. Laura sat on the edge of the bed, the way she had as a little girl, while her mother pretended to leaf through *Life* magazine.

"Beth says that the profits made by black slaves are what built America." Why had Laura repeated that now, she wondered. Did she think it would comfort her father?

Her father smiled weakly, his lips curling in unconscious imitation of Dr. Jacobs. "I suppose that may be true."

"And now, she says, it's the exploitation of black labor that maintains this rotten system. When they rebel, the whole system will fall."

Her father's own fantasies ran more to how very superfluous the Negro could become after the War—which might mean, he feared, a casual, almost unmeant genocide. He patted his daughter's hand, trying to find within this story some kind intention on her part, as if telling him of the importance of Martin's race would comfort him for his loss.

His wife, listening beside him, said nothing, but moved her lips in silent prayer, reminded by her daughter of her lost son's fond, nonsensical belief that every Negro person was an artistic genius, or a prophet, or an emissary of an African god—a sweet story, she'd thought, until those imaginary black angels had carried Frank to his very real grave. *Dear God,* she whispered, *dear Lord God, please spare my little girl.*

But why would He? After all, He hadn't spared Martin!

Alive, Martin Luther King had made a chasm between Herbert Jaffe and the Kennedy brothers. Herbert knew they had agreed to Hoover's wire-taps of Martin, and, in fact, of the Jaffes themselves. The Kennedys had walked a too careful line on civil rights, not usually willing to risk too much of their political capital. "Remember, Herbert, nothing can be done without power," Bobby had told him.

"And apparently," Herbert had said, lifting the last drink he would have with Bobby while he was at Justice, "nothing can be done with it either."

Tonight, waiting for Bobby to come back from putting his kids to bed, he walked over to pour himself another scotch. *While you're up*, he could hear Bobby saying, *get me a presidential nomination*.

Perhaps he should do his part. Bobby, as the junior senator from New York, had been reborn. Again. "That crude buffoon," he would say, filled with bile for the way Johnson had ridden the martyr's coat-tails—and Herbert's own son's murder—to get his civil rights bills through the Congress, forgetting how hesitant he and Jack had been even to try for something that big, uncertain that it would be worth gambling the South, the whole election, and all they *might* do.

Herbert knew that a long analysis of Lyndon's or Bobby's motives might be fun on a doctor's couch but was pointless as hell in politics, so he'd simply agreed with Bobby. However large-souled LBJ was on civil rights, Vietnam would drive the children crazy and turn the working class against everything Martin had tried to do for America. Bobby stood on the brink of repudiating the War—not saying that he and his brother had once thought it a gallant, twilight crusade. A hard step for Bobby to take—not just risking his chance at the White House, or criticizing himself (Bobby wouldn't even notice that; from Joe McCarthy till now he shed identities like a molting sea lion sheds his skin), but condemning Jack, too, his own heart's lodestone.

Herbert looked down at the traffic from Bobby's apartment at the UN Towers, listened to Michael and Joe wrestling in another room, Bobby trying to get them off to bed. One family for Bobby, one wife, while everything else changed utterly, ambition and righteousness confused so thoroughly that he played each new role he took on as if it weren't even a role for him, but till death do us part. But it never had been, had it? Herbert sipped his scotch. Hard to trust Bobby. But what choice did he have? Politics was life's blood for him, he knew that now, a connection to power—a new president who would take his call. And maybe also another chance to do something that felt like it mattered. Eugene McCarthy had shown Johnson could be defeated. All honor to him. But McCarthy didn't have the inner strength—maybe even that ability to forget his past convictions—that a man needs to win. Bobby was his only possible horse.

While he waited for bedtime to end, he picked up Bobby's cream-colored phone to make some calls.

And he'd known that working for Bobby was the right choice from the way his well-meaning, foolish daughter dreamt that Bobby might unite the working class, the farmworkers, the sharecroppers, the Mississippi

Negroes. All those hands reaching toward RFK, like his touch would heal the scrofula, stopped Laura's puerile talk about revolution. She'd been content with her job answering phones.

It had been one of the happiest times of his life, he and his daughter celebrating Bobby's California victory together, Herbert on the phone to Laura in Great Neck when the returns came in. Meanwhile, down below him, in the hotel kitchen, Bobby Kennedy had been murdered.

From then on, Herbert's dream and his daughter's diverged. All Laura saw now, Herbert knew, was a man desperate to hold on to his connection to power, "or how could you actually even think about helping a war criminal like Humphrey?"

"He's the one the unions will back." He and Ellen shuffled along in the airport line, waiting to put Laura on the shuttle back to Boston. "The only one with a ghost's chance to beat Nixon." He begged her not to go to the ridiculous demonstrations in Chicago. Daley, he told her, thought the middle-class antiwar kids ungrateful brats. *His* constituents might cheer if he told his cops to beat the crap out of them. Even in America, when hatred and expediency coincided, blood might pool. "And a disturbance there," he said, "it just makes us look like part of the problem. Like we can't run the country."

"Maybe you can't. Maybe you shouldn't. I mean, maybe the people should finally run their own country." Beth, she said, had shown her that she'd been a fool to think politicians could stop the War. For that, the country had to change radically, masses had to take to the streets, live up finally to Martin's dream. Why couldn't her father see that?

"If you mean a revolution, then let me tell you, dear," Laura's father said, "that's something no one wants."

He had bags under his eyes now that had come to stay, Laura thought, black-tinged fat pouches that slipped farther down daily from age and worry. But somehow she couldn't stop worrying him. "Tell it to the Vietnamese," she said.

"Well, no one in America wants it, darling."

"When imperialism crumbles," Laura said, "Beth says the workers' comforts will disappear. They'll be forced to confront the world's enemy face-to-face."

"Beth is a . . . she's a comic book character, for God's sake!" He opened his tired eyes wide, plaintively. "Am I the world's enemy, darling?"

Her father's broad face looked so hangdog. "Of course not, Daddy," she said. "A few wealthy corporate boards rule."

But if she didn't think her father was consciously working for evil—
and how could she?—then she had to believe that the man she'd once
thought stood at the center of all things was actually kind of naïve. Still,
the rush of love she felt reminded her again that she wasn't Beth, nor
would she ever be. She *didn't* long for the final confrontation. She just
wanted the War to stop so she could go back to the country club and go
swimming with her father. Thing was, she didn't want to want that
anymore, because unless America changed radically—which meant, she
suspected, no more country clubs—the War would never end.

Ellen watched her daughter cross the asphalt tarmac, climb the
metal steps to her prop plane, amazed by how quickly the young could
change their visions, each one—like Bobby's, after all—till death do us
part. Then sweat formed under Ellen's arms, because she'd thought the
word *death,* and she took off her linen jacket.

"Death to the DEATH ORG.!" Laura chanted in September, with two
hundred students at a faculty meeting that would vote on whether the college should continue to train officers who would order the destruction of
Vietnamese villages. Then, in October, a hundred students sat blocking
the door to a tiny office where a Dow recruiter waited, unable to interview
people for careers making the psych-drugs that make you the DEATH
ORG.'s zombie puppet; or maybe just burn some children's skins off.

And in November, Jesse Kelman—*everyone* feeling how he only
wanted what was best for them—helped convince Harvard and MIT
SDS to try to shut down the Instrumentation Laboratory at MIT—long,
low, sinister buildings, where they would go on designing guidance systems for missiles to destroy the dreams of the world's peoples . . . unless
Laura and a hundred and eighteen others (she counted them over and
over) marched in a big circle in the I-Lab's asphalt parking lot.

Six o'clock now. In the next two hours the police would come and
beat her. Worse, they might *arrest* her—which would destroy her
chances of going to medical school. A sodden sunrise. The dark sky driz-
zled cold rain. Each time she passed a puddle Laura reached down to dip
her bandana in the muddy water. B.C. had said they should breathe
through the damp cloth when the cops gassed them, "which," Beth had
said, "would be the nicest thing you can hope for from the *pigs,* eh?"
Laura realizing then that she'd never heard Beth use *that* word before.
Beth had fought—well, suffered, anyway—in the Battle of Chicago,
where Daley's cops, as her dad had predicted, had beaten even "the fools
who lay down nonviolently." Beth had smiled radiantly. One cop had
even broken the skin by her hairline so she'd needed five stitches.

A tall, one-eyed man danced from leg to leg on the flat roof of the building, like a drunken sailor. A rifle in his left hand, he shouted through a shorting bullhorn that he'd "fuck . . . step . . . livelihood."

Michael looked terrified. "That's Draper. He started the lab. It's his baby. We move toward it, he might really fucking shoot us."

Arkey bent over and picked up a penny. If it was tails, Laura knew, he had to put it in his shirt, jiggle, and make it drop through his underwear and out his pants leg. If it came up tails three times in a row he had to swallow it.

She kind of hoped that would happen this time. Then she slowed by a puddle again, dipped the magical bandana that she'd bought the night before, when B.C. and Beth had led them on a field trip through the overflowing wooden shelves of the Army and Navy Surplus Store in Central Square. *We're pretending to be in a battle,* Laura thought, *wearing castoffs from a real war.*

Billy had transformed B.C. into A.D. (for All Deliberate) *Speed,* made him into an Outsider, even. And Speed wanted them to get steel-tipped boots to kick the cops with, work gloves, to throw back tear gas canisters. But Jesse, in army surplus khakis now, had convinced them to remain true to Frank's legacy and be nonviolent warriors.

Or, in B.C./A.D.'s and Beth's opinion, "Great Neck Pussies."

Laura saw that Michael yearned now to run with Beth, Speed, and Paulie, a fat guy with a crooked smile, their arms padded with newspapers to stop the clubs, the boys' balls protected with plastic cups—soon to be Speed's molybdenum codpiece in Ish. #58 of *Ninja B.*—their metal-shod toes ready to kick Kops. Still, Michael would stay with Laura—his girlfriend, after all, a sacred position to him, she knew, mortared tight by the sticky goo of Top Forty hits, Mary Solidarity, and Catholic guilt, his particular resolution of that quantum state by which a woman could be two-in-one, both Madonna & whore.

They made another circle. Laura's stomach turned. B.C. took too many black beauties. Puddle water couldn't really be a revolutionary anti-gas Visine. And waiting for cops to come and beat you had to be the world's stupidest idea. She couldn't go through with this. *Dear Frank,* she prayed, *do I have to do this to ease your pain?*

Then an older guy in a tattered green jacket with CGC TRAVIS stenciled on it said, "We have to stay. The I-Lab *has* to be fucking smashed by whatever means necessary," and it was like he'd answered for Frank. She couldn't leave.

Not *yet,* anyway.

Two yellow school buses pulled up a hundred yards away, on

Massachusetts Avenue. In one, tactical police sat stiffly by the windows with long riot batons in their hands. The cops' visored helmets *here* making them look like the giant Bugs they'd already become *there* (get to the store now for another helping of "Zargon's Revenge," in *Ninja B.* #58!).

"They make the infrared detection equipment for the Bolivian Army. The fucking I-Lab," Travis said, running his hand through his long, dirty hair, "they fucking murdered Che."

"Yeah," another kid said. "They also manufacture the Shrinking Ray that the DEATH ORG. used against the Defender." He had his bandana wrapped around his head and wore molded leather padding on his arm, like MyKill's outfit in Issue #17 of *Deborah, AKA the Prophet* ("Which Side Is He On?"). "Do you think this is like the Fortress where Zargon hides SheWolf's Knowledge Stone?"

CGC Travis stopped, dipped his bandana in the water. " 'Course SheWolf's making good progress with Dr. Why? learning how to use her powers. Maybe she doesn't need the damn stone anymore."

One bus had only a driver.

"To take all the bad children *somewhere*," Arkey said, "for an extra-long detention period."

Then forty cops marched off the first bus and formed themselves into eight neat rows. The police raised their long black riot batons over their shoulders and quick-stepped toward the demonstrators. Army surplus, Laura thought, pretend battles, but real cops and actual wounds. Minor, by war standards, but real; or close enough for government work. Laura wanted to scream.

And, naturally, Beth *did,* giving the ululating cry that challenged the heavens; or her father; or a comic book opponent. Anyway, the cops took it for a signal and trotted forward. Half the students—*the smarter half,* in Laura's opinion—ran away.

Laura would have run, too, but Billy sat down in a puddle. He had his yarmulke on, like it would make the Lord—or, equally likely, some Jewish cop—spare his head. Laura, surprised that she was more worried about disappointing Helen's little Romeo than she was about well-armed riot police, sat too, although balanced on her haunches, in case she changed her mind.

Michael plopped down next to her, his lovely muscled legs probably aching to leap forward at the cops. A hissing silver canister landed near his Keds. Beth, an angry kitten who'd forgotten to put on her mittens, ran over and grabbed it with her bare paw. *Don't do that,* Laura wanted to cry, *you'll burn your hand!*

"Don't do that," CGC Travis shouted behind her, "they'll shoot us!"

> But Ninja B., shrieking from the scalding heat, hurls
> the Nervous Gas bomb back toward the Bugs!

> Will they shoot?

> No! Before they can, the Gas goes off, making
> the cops despair—

And the long-legged woman next to B. sees that the arcing motion of Beth's hand was heroic, beautiful. A psychic cop—probably trained by Zargon's wizard PsyOps—read Laura's criminal thought bubble, picked her up by the collar of her pea jacket, and ran her legs out from under her, launching her high into the air. She came down by a gray bicycle rack,

> the air pushed from her chest, so she can't scream
> and transform herself into SheWolf!

Laura rose and spun around, crying from the gas, cradling her broken right arm with her left.

> MyKill the FizzyMan, master of the Photon
> Beam, a bandana over his mouth, grabs her
> around the waist!

> Should he make the Band disappear with his
> Beam? But he can only do it Uncertainly! They
> might show up in Paris or a Hoboken sewer, or
> head down in a block of cement!

"No," Laura screamed, "we can't go yet. We have to find

> the Defender!"

> "To hell with him!" MyKill screams. "I must
> unleash the Uncertainty Beam before more Bugs
> are hatched!!"

"There!" Laura shouted.

They run to where the Defender and CGC Travis
bend over writhing from the Nervous Gas that
makes a man so anxious—

that his mind stutters, *is my wife cheating on me? is my boss plotting*
against me? is that a mole or a melanoma? are we a form of weevil
crawling in God's shit? or worse: is the universe random all the way up
to where heaven used to be?—

and they want to kill themselves just to get some
peace. CGC Travis,

the Outsiders' new Michael J. Pollard tagalong, begins to vomit by the
door of a Quonset classroom building. Miraculously, a jealous Michael
Healy put his arm around her former lover

the Defender!

Panic everywhere! Bugs use their long metal legs
to club justice workers to the ground!

"You bastards!" SheWolf shouts. Zargon's Nervous Gas fills her chest!

Laura gasped for air, taking big gulps of poison—

And dies!!

Only to be dug up in the next issue ("All Hallows' Eve") and revived
by a photon ray built by the FizzyMan. The Nervous Gas makes her forever prone to anxiety, but her time in the Underground Realm has also
hooked SheWolf's tracery of nerves to the realm of tangled roots, the
deep wisdom of the vegetative. Now wherever she is, the low whispering
of trees and plants vegivises her of doings half a planet away, tells her
secrets that make her weir-woman wise (with a tip of the Hatlo Hat for
Sugar Cane and his screaming good idea—Kudzu Man—in that Mississippi jail!).
    Meanwhile, two cops came toward Jesse, Laura, and Michael. They
abandoned the others to their beatings and ran.

Soon after, Beth signed Laura's cast "Hasta Siempre, SheWolf" and abandoned her to go to Chicago and her real comrades, the SDS leadership (self-named "the Foremost Five") to work on a manifesto called "You Don't Need a Weatherman to Know Which Way the Wind Blows."

"It's from someone's song," Beth said. Laura held the phone to her shoulder so she and Helen could go on cranking the SDS house mimeo machine, turning out fliers for the next day's rally against the DEATH ORG.—or, in this case, ROTC. Laura, up all night, had a stomach awash with caffeinated acid.

The paper feed jammed. Helen made a why-do-we-always-make-the-lasagna face at her and quit working for a moment, stopped to sniff a page, the blue ink smell probably reminding her of every schoolkid's first brain-cell–deadening high. Then her finger lovingly traced Billy's drawings, young students in caps and gowns marching along the margin, turning into Orphan-eyed zombie soldiers.

"Bob Dylan," Laura said into the phone, smiling at Helen's finger. She glanced at a sign taped to the wall: DON'T SAY ANYTHING ON THIS PHONE YOU WOULDN'T WANT ON THE FRONT PAGE OF THE *NEW YORK TIMES*. Well, the *Times* could have this news flash. "Dylan's very popular with the young people." Beth had the Marx down cold, Laura thought, but she sometimes lacked the American fizz.

"Yeah, popular with *white* young people, eh?" Beth putting Miss Ann in her homogenized, suburban place. Beth only listened to soul singers, a tribute to Frank and her own version of a Leo-style contempt for American culture, here transformed into disdain for honky pop; Beth maybe even dreaming that the melisma would put some melanin back in her skin—give her the chameleon power of Ninja B., who could change her skin color so the DEATH ORG. couldn't find her when she hid in the Baby Colonies.

For though infertile motherland customers can have infants test-tube grown, there's still, discerning families feel, a superiority to the handmade product and a frisson to saving a child from the poverty of the Farms, even if it's the overcrowding on the Farms—for the customers like to have a large selection of breeders to choose from—that produces the poverty.

"We think the time is right," Athena X/Ninja B./Beth Jacobs said tonight—meaning the time for students to dance in the streets, smash windows, occupy college buildings, do whatever small things they could to help the Third World revolution.

Laura heard the meaningful elongation in Beth's *we*, signifying that *she'd* been elevated to the Weather Bureau, the new SDS Central Committee that had just made the Foremost Five into the Sexy Sextet by adding famous Beth, the comic book star, a coronation due to her own efforts—and those of her father, Leo Jacobs, the prophet of guilt. Clothed in the grave prestige of his torment in Auschwitz and his short, exact, harrowing books, he'd published an essay in *Commentary* about their whole destructive generation, whose sense of itself as "useless, powerless children expresses itself," Dr. Jacobs wrote, "in a hatred of the advanced world and its machine-like hum of necessary complications" (thus their actions against their own universities) "and in fantasies of escape to a simpler time" (thus their poster boy: Third World Robin Hood, Che Guevara). "The protesters' hyperbolic, violent actions make them feel powerful by joining them in fantasy to armed movements; and even more fantastically, to that Nietzschean chimera, 'the sempiternal violent upsurge of the world.' " But there was the danger, Dr. J. warned, that under the misguidance of dreams they are barely aware of, the protesters might be co-opted by unscrupulous, even fascist, leaders.

"I mean, really," Laura had said, "he just wants to keep you from doing something that might get you beat up." Laura had smiled then to calm Beth's fury, and to mask that she, too, was terrified that Beth would march over a cliff, probably dragging Laura right along in her charismatic wake.

Maybe Beth would have forgiven her father his good advice if a reporter from *Life* magazine hadn't used Dr. Jacobs' essay to transform the antiwar movement into a family drama ("Does Father Know Best?"), complete with photos of little Beth in giraffe-covered rompers holding a beach pail (how had they gotten that?) and toddling toward the ocean. Then, Beth at twelve, near the *Freedom,* her breasts already budding. And an even older, buxom Beth, her secondhand Coast Guard jacket open, wearing steel-toed work boots—her work gloves forgotten in her back pocket—her arm extended over her head as if she had just flung something toward a line of tactical police, their clubs raised high above their riot shields, ready to crash down like a wave on the protesters. The whole sequence ended with Beth's BBook apotheosis as Deborah, AKA the Prophet, alias Athena X, alias Ninja Beth.

Well, you can't trust anyone over thirty to get a comic book character's name right. And all of Dr. Jacobs' efforts to protect Beth resulted in making her ever more famous, more powerful, elected now to the Sexy Six, and all the more able to lead students toward . . . would it be fascism or the revolution?

So the next day, when someone shouted from the top steps of Widener Library that the time had come to occupy the Harvard administration building, Laura felt necessity pound in her ears. She *had* to show Dr. Jacobs and her own father that she didn't want to escape to some prelapsarian Sherwood Forest, she wanted to prevent any more Vietnamese and Americans from being fed to that humming machine of Zargon's called Necessary Complications. She followed three hundred other students toward Zargon's Ice Tank (see their furious twisted faces already drawn for you in the famous red and green, Delacroix-become-expressionist cover to *Athena X,* Issue #62, "The Whole World Is Watching").

But are the others, the without-fur fools, going to follow SheWolf and the Defender all the way into the Ice, where Zargon's lieutenants make their world-controlling plans? Is it an ambush? Get ready for the surprising answer in Issue #63!

When Beth got back from Chicago, she felt on her skin how right the bureau had been about the change in the weather. Billy had probably shit his pants when the cops ran over him on the way into the administration building. Jesse had actually blacked out when the cops dragged him down the stairs and out of it, finally emptying his kurly kopf, she hoped, of all that nonviolent krap. Arkey Kaplan had even spent one night in jail, which might be enough to revive his moldy-Oldy Lefty heart. And Laura had been pinned by a Bug's leg as bystanders had chanted—with becoming Harvard modesty—"The whole world's watching! The whole world's watching!"

"Yeah?" the Bug had droned. "Fuckin' A! I hope they see this!" He brought his riot baton down across her chest.

Her friends had been what the newspapers called *radicalized—*

which meant mostly, Beth knew, *affronted*. Now she had to broaden their compassion until they felt how Third World people were degraded every day of their lives. Beth had to move them toward the next, the necessary, the violent and irrevocable step that would bind them forever to their black and brown comrades, one bloodline running through them all.

Beth dipped her brush into the bucket of red, and carefully daubed the walls of the SDS house. Holes in the crumbling plaster soaked up paint, made the letters implode inward: OOM YOOOSOLF OO HOOM OOOOSELF. Next to her a square-faced kid with big hands wrote POWEO TO THE PEOOLE! and THE OOOOLOTION IS NOT A OINNOR OOOTY! red paint crossing yellow, making a pleasant mess. That guy, Paulie, overweight, and pasty-faced, he was on her Fuck Schedule that night—the Weatherman Way to Smash Monogamy, AKA bourgeois possessiveness, meaning that she spent too many hours contentedly brushing B.C.'s beautiful long hair, felt too excited when his thick mane spread over her like a protective tent, and his sharp, speeding eyes scanned her face from above as they fucked. Well, in actions, you didn't want lovers who just looked out for each other, so scheduled intercourse made sense, but she didn't take much pleasure in it, she'd admitted to the Weather Fry last night. She felt guilty toward B.C., even though he'd be on the very next mattress in the fuck chamber balling Priss. All of which just proved once more that guilt wasn't a message from the absent God or the order that created us, it was just a rotten red and yellow pus that she still had to squeeze out of herself.

"Acid will help," B.C. said now, his hair held back in a ponytail.

She felt terrified that the drug might push her off the knife's edge she walked each day, drop her right into the bin. But she couldn't go forward either, couldn't face fucking Paulie. Now was the time. She put the acid on her tongue.

B.C. shook his head. "Not enough," daring her because she was afraid of acid, and fear was a bourgeois brain implant that kept them back from fresh pleasure and vivid violence. "More."

A long reasoned derangement, she thought, then hated herself—all that European crap! Well, maybe swallowing another pill would be the antidote, like what Frank had found in the blues. Maybe it would give her *ashe,* make an orisha possess her, look out from her eyes.

Paulie handed her a beer to wash it down with. B.C. tacked up a poster of Huey Newton, leather jacket, black beret, sitting on a wicker throne, surrounded by spears and rifles, a kitschy piece of Afro-oiserie.

Until the acid kicked in and she saw the genius shining from New-

ton's beautiful eyes. He must have an *African* god's eyes behind his—
that's why the throne and spears! He had seen that lumpen blacks are
not bound head and foot by bourgeois morality. Hustlers, pimps,
dealers, street kids, *they* didn't want to belong to anyone, like she did
with B.C. *They* would act with guidance from the African gods—surely,
precisely, and by whatever means necessary. *They* were the rightful
vanguard, and Newton their leader!

"Look," Newton said to Beth from the picture, "the Panthers really
fucked up SF State!"

"Right on!" she shouted.

"Look how me and Sugar inspired the cats at Cornell in their lace-
up boots and black berets. They scared the shit out of the pigs who
wouldn't let them study their own beautiful African gods!"

"You inspired them! You and Sugar Cane!" She felt her heart beat
faster.

"And who do you think put steel in Bobby Brown's heart? It was me
and Sugar!"

"They better not touch you!"

She'd seen Sugar Cane on TV shouting, "Brother Newton is flesh of
our flesh, blood of our blood! If Brother Huey's killed, take it to their
offices! Take it to their suburbs! The sky's the limit! The sky's the limit!"

Well, if the Bugs harmed Huey she would do those things. She would
be blood of his blood, too, one vein running through them all. "The
sky's the limit!" she screamed. "The sky's the limit!"

Behind her, Unpleasant Priss, long-haired, taut—and fellow Wellesley grad—chimed in too. "The sky's the limit! The sky's the limit." In a
minute, Priss would scare herself, run upstairs to tell Dear Diary, Priss
being the kind of white girl who didn't know what she'd done till she
wrote it in that little book—carefully locked each night so she could pretend the cops or anyone on the planet would want to read what she'd
written there.

"He has paid his dues," Speed shouted, the acid having given him
the superpower to read Ninja B.'s mind. "He has paid his dues!"

Paulie screamed, "How many white folks did you k-k-k-ill today?"
He pressed his big lips to Newton's pictured feet.

Laughing, Beth and B.C. fell into each other's arms, tried to do it
on the floor. Paulie watched, hoping to pick up some pointers. Priss
giggled hysterically, and B.C. sat up in medias res. "I can't remember
where to put it," he said, underwear around his legs, limp cock in his
hand.

· · ·

The next day, Paulie and B.C. followed Beth's orders and picked a fight with a cop at a mostly empty Carvel in Revere, probably so that she would see that their *two* limp dicks didn't mean they weren't soldiers to be counted on, and so the World's Grease could see that they had to come to Chicago for the coolest fight of all: *the Days of Rage.* They would rampage through the Loop, and show the world what some stone-cold revolutionaries thought about the ORG.'s fucking conspiracy trial!

Another Bug came up behind Paulie, clubbed him on his head and shoulders till he fell to all fours. The Grease in the donut shop had liberated hair, a couple of them even dressed like the Haunted Desperado—one of Athena's greyhounds who'd been shape-shifted when he'd licked Zargon's eye-blood—in hooded sweatshirts with surgical masks. But the Desperado had always been an equivocal ally for Athena X; and these dogs just looked on and laughed when the pigs cuffed Paulie's hands behind his back and dragged him out of the store and across the gravel parking lot, Paulie bravely screaming "Power to the People!" all the way to the black&white.

"We'll do Paulie's bail later," Beth ordered. "Time for a walk on the beach, eh?"

A light, cold drizzle, but a few dozen kids still played in the metal-gray ocean. Three guys in leather jackets and jeans leaned inward in a circle, smoking a joint. B.C. planted the National Liberation Front flag they'd sewn themselves, and a few swimmers came to have a look. The Weathermen handed out leaflets, until the dopers came over and pushed the NLF flag down, just the way B.C. had said they would. Now the Weathermen would show the Grease they were serious; they *liked* a fight. A fat guy goobered on B.C., and B.C. punched him in the face, splitting the kid's lip with his ring. Then the other greasers jumped B.C., and they all fell to the sand, the whole thing making Beth laugh, it looked so much like their own flailing across mattresses, the spazzy group gropes that they called wargasms.

She bent over, feet wide apart, and whispered in the dirty ear of a fat guy with a snake tattoo on his right cheek, "Hey, ya wanna meet Ninja B.?" The kid stopped pounding B.C. and turned his face toward her with a charmingly crooked grin. She swung her full weight from one side to the other—just the way Michael's one-armed cousin had taught her—bringing the edge of her palm hard against the bridge of Snake Boy's nose while imagining her hand going right through his skull. A cherry bomb went off in her sinews, but the blob of Grease fell off B.C. like a snot ball shimmying slowly from a runny nose. The kid's blood joined

Beth to her Third World comrades, made her their hands on this beach in Revere. Blood poured down his face, his dark eyes rolled back toward his skull, and Beth's heart leapt.

Then she felt a little sick, like what if she'd actually killed him?

No, the Snake Boy put his shirt to his nose to sop up the blood. He smiled at her, like she'd said something awfully witty!

The rest of the Grease ran away, and her troops marched off the beach, left arms raised, chanting, "Madam Binh, Madam Binh, NLF is gonna win!" Now the wind would carry the news to the teens of Revere: the Weathermen are fucking serious! And *you* have to make a choice: are you gonna be cogs in the war machine or fight alongside your black and brown brothers to smash it? Join us for the Days of Rage!

A week later, Laura waved to Beth and Snake, back from the Days of Rage, just as the last speaker dribbled to a close at the October 15th Mobe, where fifty thousand people stood on the darkling plain of Boston Common, saying, Laura thought, nothing more than *Look, God, we are here.*

Beth didn't wave back. She and the other Weathermen caucused near the fence, getting set to reinforce the lesson of the Days of Rage, when they'd run through the Loop trashing windows, tipping over cars, blowing up statues, and maybe beating cops unconscious.

Or then again, maybe they hadn't. She'd just heard rumors. The newspapers hadn't said all that much about it, maybe so as not to encourage others, or maybe because there hadn't been much to say in the first place.

Beth raised the bullhorn to her mouth, shouted, "The Mobe's a picnic for cowards!"

"Isn't that the girl from *Life*?" CGC Travis asked.

"Yeah," Michael said, all too admiringly, "that's Deborah, AKA the Prophet."

"Ninja B.," Helen said.

Laura couldn't help herself, "And Athena X. SheWolf's friend."

"I heard she led the Weatherwomen's action," Travis said, "the one against the Chi draft board."

"Yeah, seventy women. Lead pipes in their sleeves, bricks in their hands," Michael said. "Three hundred cops there to stop them. But they didn't turn back."

"The cops, they said, 'Drop your fucking weapons!' " Travis jumped from foot to foot like he needed to pee.

"SheWolf gave the cry and they fucking charged the Bugs, claws out, ready for blood! Can you believe it?"

No, Laura thought, *I can't. She Wolf means* me, *and* I *wasn't in Chicago, birdbrain, I was in bed, making love to you.*

Michael threw his chest out and strutted a step or two like Mick Jagger, that bold street-fighting billionaire. God, her genius looked stupid!

"And then they were all taken to jail, right?" Laura said, having read *that* in the *Times*, not in BillyBooks. "Did you hear that part? Every fucking one of them." Michael stared, surprised, she knew, not by her bitterness but by her saying "fucking." Telegraph the Vatican: Mary Mother of God curses like a stevedore!

Beth's beautiful nose, Laura noticed then, still had dirty tape over it, like it had been broken, and she noted that she felt more worried for *that* precious proboscis than for her own *nez ordinaire*. "She's out on bail now for—"

"Using the Death Palm on a cop," Travis said. "Making his kidney shake apart."

"No," Laura said quietly. "For conspiracy or some shit like that."

"Nope," the kid they called Snake said, coming up behind them. He'd put his long hair back in a ponytail like B.C.'s, which nicely showed off his dark eyes. "Mob action. Assault. Resisting arrest." He put his helmet on, threaded a lead pipe up the sleeve of his leather jacket.

Helen stood hand in hand with Billy, listening to Snake. "Wow," she said, cheeks aglow with excitement, thus her name Glow Girl, and her puny superpower—she could light the Outsiders' way when they used the sewers as their secret highway under the city.

B.C. came over and stared. Beth had told Laura that B.C. nearly shook apart with jealousy, couldn't stop stuttering around Snake, even with his methicine. B.C. found the way Beth and Snake had hooked up the ultimate Hollywood meet-cute—girl k.o.'s boy; and Beth had made it worse when she told B.C. the real reason the guy got called Snake.

Snake not exactly a working-class hero, though. His dad turned out to be a contractor, his chums the kids of people who worked for his father. Snake felt guilty about the way his dad pissed on their poppas; he wanted them to forgive him, like him, let him run with them. So he bought them Gansetts. But Beth had made him see that he'd lots more to feel guilty for than those Revere workers, that Amerikans were the enemy of *all* the world's people—unless and until they ran with the Weathermen.

Now Beth put her white motorcycle helmet on her head, and screamed "All Power to the People!" Then she pierced the chill air with the Athena X war cry and ran down Beacon Hill, Billy and Helen and a few dozen other kids streaming behind her, a lot of them wearing spiked metal headbands like Ninja B.'s and trying to give the Death Shriek, but sounding a whole lot more like kids in gym class when the shower's too cold.

Michael tugged at Laura's hand, a little kid who wanted desperately to go on this e-ticket ride, but the cops, Laura thought, would use clubs to break this gym class's bones. The cops would use tear gas to tone up their lungs. She loved Michael now—loved the magical way he could go inside himself for hours to worry a problem; loved his clarity, his knife-like certainty when he emerged from talking with J. Christ or N. Bohr. She held hard to his hand to protect him. B.C. strapped on the KrazyKeds MyKill had made for him and ran off, careful not to go faster than the speed of light or he might crash into himself from behind. His long black hair flew in the wind, and Laura had to admit he did look cool, full-maned, with piercing eyes, and muscular, too, Beth forcing him to finish his growing foods before he got a meth dessert. The two of them made a commanding, royal-looking couple. Amazingly, the Defender followed after them—and not, Laura could tell, to preserve and protect. He wanted in on the action.

Which turned out to be rocking a police cruiser over, "while the two cops," Beth said later, when they all met for a spaghetti dinner at the SDS house, "just stood by and watched, scared shitless. Travis set the thing on fire, and Jesse and me, Travis and the others, we danced around it for a minute. Then we ran like hell. It was out of sight."

"Now is the hour of the furnaces," B.C. said, laughing, speed-dilated pupils set at F2.

"Now is the time," CGC Travis said.

"A choice has to be made," Jesse shouted, still high from not quite being himself. Would he become addicted to that ecstasy? Laura wondered. Would he come back to them?

"Are you for or against the world's peoples?" Snake demanded.

The next week "the John Brown Collective"—which was probably, Laura just bet, like five kids in a Dorchester apartment—decided the time was now and made the choice to pour gasoline through a window of the ROTC classroom at MIT and throw a lit rag in after. By the time Michael and Laura arrived, the fire trucks had packed up, but maybe a hundred kids still milled around, a couple of girls wearing long fake fur leggings, so they'd look like SheWolf, and some breathing the wood smoke like incense at a festival. And the week after that some Rads in New York figured out the way to Beth's heart: break into the Columbia bio labs and sweep the beakers and stuff off the counters. They left a lovely bread-and-butter note: "Fuck you. Sincerely yours, The Up Against the Wall Motherfuckers." A few days later "Friends of the Outsiders" smashed the desks and chairs at an Army recruitment center in Buffalo, New York, jimmied the file cabinets, and burnt the records; and in Berkeley, a hundred students torched the Center for International Affairs. The next day Gail called crying to tell Arkey how "the Northern Tupamaros" poured gasoline through the windows of a building in Madison, Wisconsin—but too much speed and too much fear distorted the Guidance of History, and instead of burning the ROTC classroom, the Keystone Kommies had hit the temporary primate lab.

At the Bick, the day after, Beth spread out pages of the *Boston Globe* with photos of the wounded but still living monkeys, skulls half-caved, fur burnt from their chests. Beth put her coffee mug down on a man in a white coat giving a chimp a lethal injection. "Well, pilgrims," she said in a fair John Wayne drawl, "looks like those folks in Madison have gone and burnt the wrong monkeys." Beth gave Billy the Stare, wanting him to know she would despise him if he wept for some chimps while the Vietnamese were being slaughtered.

A short street dealer in an OurKey wizard hat of blue silk, decorated with hand-sewn yellow *aleph*s and *bet*s, made the rounds from table to table, even to the defeated women snuffling crackers into soup, their heat probably never turned back on after the SDS rent strike. "Acid? Speed? Gumbo? . . . Acid? Speed? Mescaline? Gumbo?" He wore fur leggings, too, this Wizard being of the party that thought you could mix and match totems—an offense to the purist camp, where the fan adored one Outsider only.

A boy at a table of high school kids said, "Gumbo, like from Dr. Why??" The kid had long unwashed hair, a concave chest.

"You know it," the Wizard said, "the best." Everyone knew that Dr. Why?, trainer of the Band, was a real but *hidden guru*. He'd been the man who'd actually *taught* Billy Green to tap into the Collective Unconscious, helped Lennon write "I Am the Walrus"; and then gone on tour with the Dead. (*By the way, Jerry,* Laura wanted to say, *you should know that the Dead are* not *really very Grateful. They're in agony until their sparks are raised.*) Anyway, Why? made better acid than Owsley, and mixed up special recipes, too. BillyBooks—for those who had eyes to see—often gave coded recipes for these "gumbos."

"Like did you see the last number of *Girl Guerrillas*," the Wiz was saying now, "where SheWolf hears plants? Well, you get that by mixing mescaline and acid with just a little dollop of speed. That's what the mushroom-looking thing near her foot meant. And I got some tabs that Why? himself made for Pigpen."

"From the Dead? No shit?"

"No shit for sure. And I could like sell a couple to you."

"Yeah?"

The Wizard smiled, showing discolored stumps. "But you must promise to use your powers only for good."

"Speed? I don't know. I got kind of fucked up last year with speed." There already being barely enough room in his sunken chest, Laura thought, for an extra-thin set of heart and lungs.

"Yeah, well, the Outsiders think Speed is okay, right?" the Wizard said. "A.D., I mean, he's called Speed, don't you think that *means* something?"

"I thought it meant he was like fast."

The Wiz gave the naif a you're-so-cute smile. "Besides, it's just a dab of meth to make the whole thing work right."

The Wizard came to Laura's table next, stopped, looked into her eyes for a moment. She hoped he hadn't figured out that *she* was—sort of—the one who could vegivise. She wasn't strong enough for Disappointed Psycho Meets Real-Life Original today.

"I know how you feel, sad-eyed lady of the Bickford," the Wizard said.

The words Frank had spoken to his murderers. That painted bile on Laura's throat.

"And I got what you need to feel better."

Goddamn it, she had to study for a chem exam tomorrow, but she *had* to take a tab now, Frank having said he had something he wanted her to see.

"Two-for-one sale," Michael said, eager to join her—MyKill, as always, a magnificently brave consort for SheWolf, his sublime alchemical powers complementing her own magic; and the whole thing giving luster to their union in Laura's own eyes, and in many other pupils on campus as well, making them prom royalty almost.

She ate one more bite of her flat griddle-fried English muffin, then she and Michael started to make their way back through the Uncertainties to their home. And by the time they got to the Harvard Bookstore the acid had kicked in, making the War&The War Against the War wash Cambridge with an extra coat of black, hiding plots that could at any moment fill the world with flames and burn them all up.

"Spare change?" some street kids said, lethargic hands reaching toward her, today's version of *to each according to their need*. They passed some bald Krishna chanters in ugly orange dresses, their skinny bodies shaking with the pallid, ungainly tremors they called dancing. She heard that spastic beat everywhere, now, like at the dorm's last invite-a-beau Strawberry Breakfast, when Helen had shown the table a picture of a handsome dark man dressed in a similar frock, said they *had* to make a pilgrimage to India to sit at his lotus feet.

"Do people think he's a genius? You know, the people who matter?" Laura had asked meanly. Maybe Manhattan was as credulous as Calcutta. Or as Great Neck. Should she tell Helen about the revelations of Rav Billy? Or had that already been pillow talk between them?

Helen had just smiled. "They're not like Krishna-chanters. Si Baba can make ballpoint pens appear from nowhere." She'd spooned up some berries.

"Ballpoint pens?" a girl had said, giggling. "Like with his name and address on them?"

Helen had gone on smiling with annoying serenity. Laura had preferred her when she'd been a warrior against male chauvinism. Now Laura felt like at any moment Helen might shave her head, get a wig, go sit behind the screen in the Hindu version of the women's section.

Meanwhile another girl said she'd heard about a round-faced Sikh who taught you how to make your Kundalini rush up your chakras, turn your brain to neon; and somebody else told about a ten-year-old who could teach you to taste Brahma's nectar at the back of your throat.

"Get you seriously fucked up, huh?" one of the visiting men had said—the real prayer being always, with Krishna's name or the Wizard's LSD: *I'm so scared, so small, so guilty. Please, please, God/Brahma/ Mother Acid take me away from here!*

She pulled Michael back from the traffic at Putnam Square, then led him from the cheap, repetitive, fundamentalist faux ecstasy and back home. Or the attic where they stayed—no direction, like Mr. Dylan had said, seeming exactly like home to her anymore.

But bed turned out to be no better, her legs aching now with a spectral pain—not bone, not muscle, not here, not there, so everywhere—the acid telling her that meant she must be feeling Frank's legs, the ones she had never helped much, didn't know how to help anymore. Should she pick up a gun? And do what? To whom? How? She begged Michael to hold her, and for a moment the heat from his body seeped into hers.

"It doesn't matter if I die in a demo or something," Michael whispered. "Because if I can't help stop them killing Vietnamese, I feel like I'll have to kill myself."

FOR CHRIST'S SAKE, she wanted to shout, I'M ONLY TWENTY YEARS OLD! AND YOU'RE NOT EVEN EIGHTEEN! "Oh, God, darling," she said, covering his cheek with kisses. "Please don't feel that way." Could he *mean* such a stupid, grandiose thing? But even as she stroked his cheeks with her lips, she felt how far away he was now; or probably always had been, in his inner white room. Laura felt tethered to everyone she cared about by a thousand invisible strands that, when anybody moved, tugged at her arms, legs, her *heart*. She was the whole world's puppet! But lucky Michael—most of his cords had been severed at birth; and now the War had severed the rest. He would float in a dark space forever if she couldn't hook him onto her body right now. Or so she dreamed.

So she kissed his milky cheek over and over, his small ears, his soft hair, her smooches accompanied by his cousin's heavy boots hitting the wood floors downstairs, patrolling his dream jungle. Maybe if she held Michael's wiry body against her chest, he'd be bound to her, knitted up into her, flesh of her flesh.

No. Pre-med, Laura knew a biological impossibility when she fantasized it. And she couldn't do it, most of all, because she understood too well why Michael talked so self-importantly. Beth had been right: five hundred thousand people standing in a field just gave *them* a self-congratulatory melancholy glow, while clashing, ignorant armies went on sending one-armed men back to pace beneath her bedroom. Something more had to be done to stop this dreadful, unjust war.

The next day, they all met in the Attic—aka the Singularity, the Band of Outsiders' Fortress, protected by a MyKill beam that placed it outside the Continuum. Michael knelt on the bed next to her, pasting two Zig Zags together for a thick white turd of a joint. Michael loved to get super messed up, bombed with his counterculture boilermakers (meth laced with acid, followed by a dope chaser); and maybe, she suspected now, he didn't do it just to number God's quanta and know His secrets, but to get out of Space and Time altogether, some no place before God had inscribed His laws, far away from *here*. One piece of the cartoon mural Billy had done for the walls and phony columns at Tommy's Lunch showed a goofy elongated Michael hitting himself on the head with a mallet. "It *doesn't* feel so good when I stop," the words in the balloon said. "So I never stop." Someday soon, she worried, he really won't care if he lives or dies, and he'll bang too hard, wreck the finely calibrated mechanism of his amazing mind. He'll finally get *wasted*. Wasn't that army slang for killing? "Is that what it means to bring the War home?" she said, following her own sequence.

Jesse, his palette now always shades of surplus brown, lay on his back against one of the rolls of fiberglass, poisonous cotton candy that she and Michael had never found time to tack up, looked wonderingly at her. "You're right," Jesse said.

Right about what, exactly? Laura wondered. For instruction, she took another drag on the joint.

"We have to do something more to the I-Lab."

"Yeah, I can relate to that," Billy said.

Relate to what? Laura wondered. To figure that out, she took another toke, then passed the joint to Billy, who wore cream-colored bell-bottom cords from Krackerjacks today, pants so ridiculously tight that when he leaned forward from Michael's desk stool to snag the joint she could see the outline of his genitals.

"We'll only harm property," Jesse said. In his imagination, he stood in open court and told everyone what he'd done, rocking the cruiser, blowing up Zargon's lab. A judge joins the whole watching world in seeing the justice of his action. Reluctantly, sadly, he gives Jesse Kelman six months of jail time. "I can do that," Jesse Kelman said.

Do what? Laura wondered. The joint had burnt down to a charcoal-tinged speck.

Michael remembered the giddy crowd outside the burning ROTC building, property become light to illuminate even the dimmest conscience. "Yeah. People will understand."

Understand what? Laura wondered. "I have totally lost the threat." She laughed. "I mean the thrall. The thread, that is." She needed more dope to get it back. Michael rolled another joint. "Faster," Laura said.

"No, we shouldn't go too fast," Michael said. "We've got to plan this carefully." But he was thrilled Laura was with him. He lit the joint, took a record-setting toke.

"Jesus, what are you guys talking about?" Arkey said. He lay on the grimy green couch, spoke to the ceiling. Arkey wore National Health glasses and Brooks shirts, like a prep school John Lennon, Laura thought—if Lennon had lost thirty pounds to get out of the draft. Arkey's eyes, his sharp nose, his lips, all seemed too large now, swam on what was left of his face.

"We're gonna blow up the I-Lab, Arkey," Michael said.

So that's *what we're talking about!* Laura thought. But it's *just* talk, surely, and "Thank God!" for that. She put a hand on Michael's thigh.

"Yeah," Michael said, "thank God we're finally going to do something!" He clipped a roach holder made from cow bone to the joint and passed it to Arkey, who his vet cousin had nicknamed the Little Jew with the Nickname. He got to be **OurKey** in BillyBooks, though his power to see the future was accompanied by untreatable B.O. (*Tales from the Kabbalah,* #16, "Origins of OurKey"). Michael sniffed the air to check if that was just poetic incense.

"You guys are nuts," Arkey told the ceiling. "We're only students." He took a long hit, held the harsh smoke down as long as he could.

"I wish," Jesse said seriously, "it didn't have to be us."

Arkey sputtered smoke. Jesse's orotund vowels reminded him of a fat *N.Y. Times* reporter who'd come by the *Crimson* office that morning, asking obsequiously, "So, look, what are you kids reading?" Tomorrow it would probably be on page one, and someone from *Life* would come by to find out what they were wearing. Then *Playboy* to ask how often they fucked. How many different partners per week? How many at a time? And in what never-before-seen positions? *High Times* would wonder what new drugs they took, and what God had revealed to them lately. The world had conspired to drive everyone in his generation mad with their own importance—and BillyBooks meant he and his friends had got a fatal double dose. "Jesus, Jesse," he said, "it doesn't *have* to be us. It's *not* us. We can't blow up buildings." He inhaled the dream-smoke of prophecy. "We do that, they're gonna start shooting us. Remember, guys, I can see the future."

"Yeah?" Michael said. "Well, I think maybe that's like right now. They're already shooting people, Arkey. Like Rector. Yeah, I think they like *definitely* already shot him." He pointed the silver staple gun at Arkey, the one they'd been supposed to use to tack up the insulation between the beams in the house that cousin Jack rented.

"They shoot black people every fucking day," Beth said. She sounded really angry, Laura thought, so they'd all know that she took it really personally. After all, she could change her skin color, was black a lot of the time in the Baby Colonies. Or someone like her was.

"Right. Look at Orangeburg," Jesse said. His long curly hair made him into Harpo Marx—but a really hot, desirable Harpo. "The kids actually held up their hands, to ward off the bullets. Can you believe it?"

"Bet it didn't work," Michael said from the bed. He took another turn on the joint.

"Look how they did Li'l Bobby Hutton," Beth said. B.C. had got it right: the street stuff was going nowhere. In the best of all possible worlds ten thousand angry kids would have fought for the world's people in Chicago. In this world, though, only a couple of hundred had showed, all from Weathermen collectives. She'd looked at them, milling around the headless police statue in Haymarket in their steel-tipped shoes and army surplus jackets, and thought bitterly, *We fucking few, we happy happy fucking few.* Then B.C. had jammed his helmet on and led them screaming downtown and she took off after him. Sweet now, the way the little monkeys in this attic thought she was Tania the Guerrilla—or Ninja B., natch. But B.C. had told the truth: the Days of Rage had been BFD, the state's bail haul equal to the cost of windows broken, so the whole thing just meant extra profits for Corning Glass Co. Vietnam writhed in agony. They had to do more here right now, and street actions meant no real harm done, except to a few kids' heads—which only scared most other kids away.

In the Singularity, though, she could see a different future: underground urban guerrillas like the Tupes, cells too small to be infiltrated, large enough to carry out secret actions. Even if the Band got busted, crowds would stand outside the police station, shouting "Free the Outsiders!" before they went home to make their own bombs and blow up a bank. "Now is the time," she said.

"TM," Laura said, meaning, that's Beth's mantra.

"Yeah." Michael smiled. "That's Athena's trademark."

Beth smiled, looking so smug in her tight blue jeans that Laura hated her—while she wondered, too, what she could possibly do that would make Beth love her again.

The next night Laura was lying on the bed in her flannel nightgown studying organic chemistry when Michael ran up the stairs and threw down two red sticks that looked like the flares her family kept in the locker on the *Freedom*.

"My father told me they're incredibly careless with the stuff," he said. "And, boy, is that ever true!"

"What stuff?" Laura said, but she already felt her stomach muscles weaving themselves into tight restraints—prison garb, she thought, or a shroud.

MyKill laughed "Ha! Ha! Ha!" (hear it in the amazing Special Double Issue of *The Legends of Athena X,* #28–29, "Assault on a Black Hole").

"They're atom dissolvers! It will make the Hole's
electrons resolve themselves into light spectra!!"

That made Laura furious. "It's not an Atom Dissolver, you asshole, it's dynamite! It's fucking dynamite!" She leapt out of bed and gave him a SheWolf-worthy smack across his face.

"Jesus, Laura!" Blood poured from his snub nose, dripped down his top lip. "That hurts, you know? That really, really hurts."

She packed his nostrils with ice wrapped in a paper towel. Then she put an overcoat on over her nightgown and ran all the way back to her dorm room to lie alone, rigid with panic, until eight, and her chem exam.

The next week, B.C. sat cross-legged on the attic's uneven wooden floor surrounded by coiled green wire, batteries, and tiny metallic gizmos that looked like the Heathkit Arkey had built at fourteen. Well, tried to build. His radio never got any stations. "And if we're really lucky," he told Gail, "this one won't either." Gail didn't smile, just stared at B.C. bent over a board with a soldering iron. Liberated from his impediment by speed and melody, he sang, "Daddy's in the alley / He's lookin' for the fuse / I'm in the streets / With the Tombstone blues." A plume of rancid smoke curled near his bent fingers.

"Shut up, Speed," Jesse said. "Michael's trying to concentrate," **Speed** and the **Defender** having already reached a truce so they could work on "The Assault on Zargon's Palace" (Issue #36 of *Athena X*).

Michael, at a distance, heard his name; ignored it; went back to penciling the numbers in his small black notebook. Simple math, but crucial.

"You people," Arkey said, "don't have enough merit badges for this." Really, he meant the message for Gail. *Please God, don't let her think this is a good idea.* "Someone could get hurt."

"Yeah, well, some people *should* get hurt," B.C. said.

Jesus. The Singularities space/time warp bent him back to Specs in Great Neck one afternoon saying, "Those Outsiders, they're your gang, huh?"

"And Nixon, his people, they're yours?" Specs ate a salad on the country club patio. He and Specs were like friendly adversaries now.

"You think the Vietcong are different, Arkey? They're just a gang in black pajamas." He squeezed some lemon into his iced tea. "That's an idea, huh? Maybe we should make black pajamas for our spring line." He smiled, showing large, even teeth.

Our people, now *our* line; Specs had become a Kel-Kap principal, the surrogate son. "This way," his father had said, "we won't have to pay protection anymore, won't have to worry about some putz wanting to become a 'partner,' stealing dresses, making us borrow money from banks, then forcing us to declare bankruptcy."

"The Mafia's like Cutberg," his mother had said, "but stupid."

Anyway, Arkey had no vote; he'd made it clear that he would never join the business.

"The spring line," Specs had said to him, sipping his tea. "That's the line you should care about, Arkey, not the party line, the spring line."

Whose line? His dad's and Specs' and Jesse's father's, whose son peered now at a diagram in *The Anarchist's Cookbook*. Jesse pointed something out to B.C., who aimed his gun at another wire.

. . .

A few days later, Jesse carefully nestled the timer and blasting cap in the stained second-floor bathtub.

Arkey stood in the doorway, feeling the world ready to spin him off. "We're not going to do it till we vote again, right?" he said into the whirlwind.

"Sure," Beth said. *Like once you have a bomb in your hands,* she thought, anyone *could resist using it!*

"Don't worry, Arkey," Jesse said, coming back to put an arm around him. "*If* we do it, no one will be there. Or we won't do it." Beth and Michael's daring had made Jesse sick with himself, led him to a rancid part of himself where he wanted his father's tuition money so much that he hadn't ever sufficiently protected the Vietnamese. *This,* he'd told everyone one night, would help cast that self-serving piece out of all of them.

They all took a step back from the door then, and listened to the ticking.

"And Michael," Jesse added, "is making sure there'll be plenty of time to get everyone far away from outside the building, too."

Laura heard the singsong rabbi's tone in Jesse's voice that meant *please God help my unbelief.* She remembered the primate lab in Madison. "The monkeys think it's all in fun," she said. "But it's not."

Michael looked at his watch. *Who were the monkeys?* he wondered. The criminals who worked at the I-Lab? Them? Like so often, he had absolutely no idea what Laura was talking about—her mind was so quick, her experience so much wider than his. But he *never* wanted her to suspect that. "One monkey won't stop this show," he said.

What monkeys? Arkey wondered.

No one knows what monkeys these fools are talking about, his grandfather Abraham replied, *because this whole thing is meshugah! This is* not *a revolutionary situation!* "This is wrong," Arkey said. "It's sneaky. We have to fight in the open, so, you know, we can build a mass movement. Like Madison."

"Madison has got to take it to the next stage," Beth said, "or they're gonna be wiped out."

Maybe so. This last week, Gail said, the National Guard had occupied the campus, had used grenade launchers to lob so many tear gas canisters into Miffland that the cockroaches all died. The next demo, cops circulated in the crowds and just whaled kids to the ground with saps; and now the National Guard had set up machine-gun emplacements. Maybe Beth had it right, and they shouldn't line up like ducks in a bowling alley. Maybe they *should* stop throwing rocks and getting Maced and clubbed, and just blow the I-Lab the fuck up.

Or not. The alarm clock had gone off, but the cap only made a tiny metallic sound. No smoke radio. Maybe the timer had agreed with his granddad: its services weren't necessary yet. This was *not* a revolutionary situation.

For two weeks Michael checked and rechecked his calculations; B.C. fiddled with wires till the timer worked; and Billy did midnight reconnaissance to make sure the building would be empty when—or if—the dynamite exploded. That night, they would take the final vote on whether they'd actually leave the package.

"But who would I be?" Laura whispered into the phone that evening, "where would I be going, if I did something like *that*?"

"Where will you be going?" Jeffrey Schell mused, sounding more and more breathy and queer by the day. "Jail, probably?"

"Shouldn't you be here with us tonight to vote on this?" A silly thing to say; she just wanted to pad the vote on her side. "I mean, aren't we supposed to all rise together when we make justice?"

"Oh, no, dear. *Stonewall* for us."

He'd elongated the word, as if it should mean something special to Laura. "What's Stonewall?" And who was *us*?

Jeffrey laughed. "I mean bombings are like having children," he said. "Not for me."

"Me neither," Laura said, giggling. "Babies and bombs, both too messy. I'm gonna vote against it, I guess." She felt guilty for laughing, though. The Vietnamese died every day. Didn't she owe it to them and her brother to be pressed against the facts, without the distance for irony?

Then Jeffrey said, "Laura, darling, I've been thinking. Should we, you know, be talking about *this* on the phone?"

Jeffrey put the receiver down. "Don't say anything on that thing," he said to the empty room, "that you wouldn't want on the front page of the *New York Times*." He gazed at the polished wood Nouveau Factory floor, thinking, But Andy wants *everything* about himself on the front

page of the *Times*—with a picture of himself if possible, half smiling, in
one of his hundreds of white wigs (better to look already old than have
everyone watch as your hair turns gray and disappears), a leather
bomber jacket, tight jeans with panty hose underneath, the Andy Costume . . . Trademark . . . Golem . . . this Thing that Andy had created.
Then curled up inside, Homunculus Andy, forever desperate to get the
Andy Façade in the papers, so L'il Andy peeking out from inside could
feel reassured that he *existed*; fame meaning that others see you, therefore you *are*—for fifteen minutes anyway. Was that what his G.N.
friends wanted? Still, what good was it, to either Andy or them, coming
that way? His friends couldn't sign their bombing, and Li'l Andy never
got photoed—it was always Outside Andy, the Golem Andy, in the
papers the next morning. He remembered Li'l Andy's voice, years ago,
talking from his bed, the phone probably pressed to his ear like a lifeline.
"I get so tired," he'd said to Jeffrey—thrilled in his Columbia dorm
room that Andy had chosen *him* as the one worthy to wake at three that
night. "Sometimes, I just want to come home and take my Andy Suit
off." But the rare times he even tried, the blackness poured in too fast,
nonexistence washed over the little man's feet. Andy was terrified of
death. *We all are, right?* Yeah, but Andy more so—which is maybe what
made him the artist. "So could you like meet me at the Factory, and we
could, you know, work some tonight?"

"It's awfully late."

"Aw, c'mon, Jeffrey," Andy breathy, desperate, probably lying there
afraid of the dark, worried his heart would stop between beats. It had
been Jeffrey's freshman year at Columbia and he had a test the next
morning on Aristotle; but he'd found a cab, helped Andy screen Coke
bottles—that unchanging, immortal undying sphinx of a thing, the
industrial sublime. Or were they screens of a world transfixed with rigor
mortis—death come back to bite Andy on the ass, turn him and the
bottles into skulls?

Well, whatever; he'd been honored to work till dawn, sure that each
pull of the squeegee *for Andy* would help make *him* into an artist, too,
one of the people his father sucked up to even if he didn't suck them off;
as opposed to Jeffrey's being merely a fag failure, one of the people his
father apparently *hated*.

Could Harry Hennessy help him become an artist? Maybe tonight
he'd take Harry up on his offer, his dare—his *command*—to fuck him
and Suki together, and "seal their marriage," as if they'd be doing *him*
an honor if they moved into his apartment at the Chelsea!

Jeffrey did feel High School about it, though, sure that Harry would be a great artist someday, even if his recent stuff—famous newsphotos redone out of focus—only confused Jeffrey. The times are out of focus? We never really know the famous? Or we only see through a glass darkly? Or Harry needed a motif to cover up the fact that he couldn't draw? Harry had the looks and style of an Artist, anyway, a long, chiseled, *classical* face, and a commanding manner—a little like Beth's. Like Beth, Harry would find a vision to follow, too, something to batter the world with till it conformed to his view.

"Is a vision like a theme or something, I mean, a motif, you know?" Bill the bass player had stuttered once at Max's Kansas City, as they drank Jeffrey-paid-for rum and Coke, Cuba Libre renamed a Trust Fund.

"Something like that." Harry had this way of looking up at the fluorescent lights, like the Angel Moroni perched there to feed him lines. "A vision is a world elsewhere. A heaven or hell by which this world can be judged."

"And very like a whale," Jeffrey had said—for a little learning, a few Great Books courses, can go a long way if one had a nearly photographic memory. Actually, he knew what Harry meant; it had to be what his Great Neck friends had found in those letters, in Billy's tale of Frank trapped in pain in the grave. Something that made them feel superior, gave them a mission. If Jeffrey had a thingamabob like that he would have something to paint, something he had to accomplish with his paintings beside his becoming famous.

But he had seen through Billy's nonsense, so the letters wouldn't work for him. And Billy had stolen Beth from him, who should have been *his* subject—*he'd* loved her first. So where was *his* vision? Or his career, even? Two years of cramming for Andy meant he'd had to drop out of Columbia, nicely confirming his father's prediction: twenty years old, he was already a failure. He didn't make art himself; he just helped Andy. He couldn't even cry to his lovers, because, until Harry anyway, he only fucked so he could tell Andy about it. (Well, not *only*, but *mostly*.) So far his one accomplishment in life was that Andy Warhol liked him.

"You?" his father said. "Or the buyer's son?"

"You can't stand it, can you? The great Warhol's interested in *me*."

"You," his father had said, "or your cock?"

Jeffrey had hung up the phone. Andy had never come on to him. Or not that way.

So he'd had Andy and the amphetamine-heads (which was how he'd learned the etiquette of dirty business on the phone), and the openings, and the frantic late nights helping Andy make silver balloons that were supposed to be clouds, or wallpaper cows that were supposed to be . . . cows. He envied his little G.N. pals' concern with stopping the War —that being a hell, certainly, by which this world could be judged. Tonight, after Laura's call, that seemed more important even than silk-screened cows to him. No one even mentioned Vietnam at the Factory. Instead they talked about . . . Andy . . . helping Andy . . . finding ways to make other people talk about Andy all the time, the way they did. Obsessed with Andy, you had to find new members for the Andy cult. Like Krishna-chanters.

Jeffrey slid across the pristine polished wood, past the bowl ever replenished with rose petals—something new since the shooting. Locks, too, were new, After Valerie, and intercoms for the door. Jeffrey flicked off the light switch near the desk, closing up for the night.

Once upon a time, Andy had been a lifesaver for him. To Jeffrey, Lost in Great Neck, Andy had made queer seem all right; glamorous even. Andy had liberated Jeffrey from a father who hated him, not just for being gay, he swore, but for being . . . Jeffrey—whatever that was. Andy had been the accepting Father, the appreciative Father, the one who thought Jeffrey's ideas great, his taste swell. Never indifferent, he wanted to know all about Jeffrey's life—Andy wanting him to live *for* him, Jeffrey saw now, so Andy wouldn't have to; and never having lived, he would never die. "Oh, wow, Jeffrey. You and Gaston did *that*? What's Gaston's cock like? Is it big? Does it bend? I'll bet it bends." Andy had been permission, too. "You want to be an artist, that's so great. Why don't you come help me?"

"Warhol's an amiable listener," Jeffrey's therapist had said. "You must have yearned for that after all the coldness from your real father at home."

"Coldness, Doc? You still don't get it, do you? The junkman wants to kill me!"

He laughed now, and the sound echoed off the bare white walls, this place empty, dead at an hour when the old Factory would still have had boys in their Jockeys—Andy having perhaps whispered once that he pre-ferred briefs over boxers—sacked out on the stuffing-deprived couch or jerking themselves off; amphetamine-heads shooting up in the bath-room; he and Edgar working the screens.

He sat down now on the new black leather couch. He could hear his mother's voice. "Is leather a good idea, boys? For jism, I mean. It's very hard to get animal fats off leather." But the young men who'd come to, and at, the old Factory had gotten thinner and thinner with the years, and disappeared finally, melting away, the hustlers d'antan. Still, Jeffrey had stayed. And stayed. Waiting for what? A vision?

Or Valerie Solanis with a gun? They'd filmed her once, reading from her SCUM Manifesto. "All the evils of the world emanate from the male incapacity to love." Okay, that was probably as good as the ideas in the Communist Manifesto. But SCUM turned out to be fairy dust—probably just like Beth's meteorologists; a story that let crazy Valerie believe she had an Army of Women pulling the trigger with her.

When Andy returned from the dead—*how can you kill him,* Gaston had said, *when he's already dead*—he'd stopped working much, *choosing* much. He'd moved the Factory to this fancy mausoleum, the tomb of the mummy TutAndykhammen, clean floors, locked doors, blue vases of flowers mixed with perfume, a parade of society clients to be conned into commissioning their own silk-screen portraits. No more late-night phone calls from Andy. No more *Oh wow*s. No more "That's so smart, Jeffrey." He missed that. It had been a Gardol shield against his father's hatred that came at him from inside and outside.

He needed something else now to jazz him, protect him, give him a purpose. He needed, finally, to be an artist himself. He needed to feel the same commitment, the same willingness to risk himself that Beth had. What Beth was about to lead them all to do was most probably wrong, but they were doing *something,* believed something, worked for something bigger than the careers they were probably about to blow up along with that building. Or were they just wanna-be superstars playing for someone else's camera? Like Mao's—the Director Deluxe, a living god. Possible silk-screen subject? Yeah, *for Andy.*

He'd have to leave here to find his vision, his subject. Maybe Harry and Suki really could spark something in him. He would drift by Max's back room tonight, casual as a high school kid. *Oh, you guys here?* Did Harry, he wondered, just see him as a way into the art world? If he broke with Andy, would Harry still be interested in him?

But how could you break with Andy? Jeffrey stepped onto the big elevator. All you could do was stop coming to the Factory. His stomach dropped a little as the gears and pulleys moved him downward. Andy was like the Catholic Church. You couldn't quit; you could only *lapse.* There might be a buzzer on the door now, but it would always open to Jeffrey. After all, the one big thing Jeffrey didn't tell Andy was that his father loathed his son. He'd kept that a secret all these years so Andy would always think, *Be nice to the boy; his father might buy something.*

He shut the street door and heard the automatic lock click. October 31 had turned chill. Jeffrey wished he'd worn a coat. It would be a cold night for the kids out trick-or-treating.

In Cambridge, midnight of All Hallows' Eve, Billy Green sat like a little tailor on their Indian bedspread, stitching a statement for the newspapers on his drawing pad. "WHO WILL SPEAK FOR THE DEAD?" He began to ornament the edges with Asian corpses rising from the rice paddies and moving up the page, ravaged arms extended, their paper hands rotting as they rose.

"You can't do that," Arkey said, squatting on the floor on his heels, to look taller. "We haven't voted to go ahead on this yet."

"No, you can't do that," Beth said sharply, "because it's like a goddamn fingerprint."

Gail, in town for the Big Event, smiled fondly at Billy. "Everyone knows your style. Very distinctive." Gail had ringed her eyes with kohl tonight—Death, if the specter was a busty size six.

Billy looked to Jesse, who sat leaning forward toward them on the green couch. Even Billy, Laura thought, knows that Jesse sees what's best for them.

"Yeah," Jesse said, "Beth's right."

So Billy tore off the decorated border, leaving, he thought, the pith: *We've listened to our guilt and it has instructed us: Hard acts are necessary to save Vietnam and to heal America. We do this bombing like a surgeon cutting into a patient—for as Che says, the revolutionary is guided by great feelings of love.*

Beth took a bite of her Turkey Deluxe, her mouth puckering pleasurably from Elsie's vinegary version of Russian dressing, and from the memory that Che had *also* said that we need to become cold, violent, selective, killing machines. Little Billy Green wasn't ready to hear *that*—not yet, anyway. But tonight at the I-Lab he would help blow up a building and along with it some of the bourgeois crap her father had fed him about guilt. He'd be one step closer to joining the struggle of the world's people.

And the Second Act for her? Maybe she would join the leadership collective in New York. Or maybe she'd stay with the Band—and they could all rise together. Suburban pussies, Speed called them; but she couldn't help herself, they had a past; she was unreasonably fond of them. Except for Arkey, who thought *he* could read the Agenda of History to *her*.

"Look, I don't know," Arkey went on, "I think we should just be sure this is the right next step."

Arkey put his hand over his heart, like he could calm it that way. *Your friends dream they stand outside the Winter Palace,* his grandpa Abe said. *See the big flakes falling on their Zhivago hats! But this ain't St. Petersburg, boychick, and this is* not *a revolutionary situation.* "This is too soon," Arkey said. "This will just alienate people."

"I've checked all the calculations," Michael said, hunched over on a high stool. He stared down at his sawhorse desk and the puddle of light from a gray Tensor lamp. "No one will be hurt." He swiveled toward them and held up his yellow pad. Rows and rows of tiny blue numbers.

But who but her beloved, Laura wondered, could even guess what those numbers added up to?

"This will actually energize people," Jesse said, and Laura felt her chest tighten. What if the flames from the cop cruiser had transformed Jesse, what if he was, finally, *for* doing this, Jesse, the one who had less neurotic static than the rest of them and really wanted to do what was right? Fear rocketed into her chest.

Billy closed his eyes, began to sway back and forth, humming one note over and over until everyone grew quiet.

Michael looked to Laura. "Is this, like, it?" Michael's small eyes alert, eager. "Is this the thing, you know, that you told me about?"

She nodded quickly, meaning, *Yes, this is it, I think.* These last years, Laura had come to think of Billy as barely *here,* a quiet ghostly presence, mostly outside the frame, drawing them. Could he really prophesy again?

Jesse looked over at her, his lips pursed disapprovingly—he knew she'd blabbed. But his eyes were as expectant as Michael's. Or her own.

Gail turned her head to the side, about to hear a bedtime story, a child in a white peasant blouse, cheap stuff from Truc, and black tights—the elfin terrorist. She put her hand in Arkey's.

Meanwhile, Billy rocked and hummed.

"Now," Beth whispered harshly, "tell them now."

Didn't Beth know, Laura wondered, that her brother would tell them *not* to do it? Even if no one was hurt, a bombing couldn't *ever* be the nonviolent way. Could it?

"This *will* help," Billy said slowly, his eyes still closed, his voice raspier, deeper than usual, less like a cicada's with sinus congestion. "*This* will make justice. If we do this, people will see there are things, there are things, they will see, there are things they can do to stop the war. We should do this. *It must be.*"

Arkey looked up toward Billy's tender eyelids, his bladelike face, felt acrid sweat dart all over his chest and under his arms, overwhelm his cologne, like he was being smothered by the weight of the little boy on the bed—though really Billy's skinny body would have been more like two-hundred-and-forty-four damp washcloths. "Jesus," Arkey whispered. "Oh, Jesus, *no.*"

"Yeah, come on, Arkey," Beth said. "Even *you* have to listen now." OurKey would have to admit it was Ninja B. who could read the Agenda of History!

"We'll do it," Jesse said, quietly.

And I have to help, Laura thought. Frank had said it didn't matter that she'd probably never get to medical school. Frank had said that if she wanted to make justice in *this* world, she'd better be as wily, as violent, as lawless as their enemies. Well, fine! Maybe they'd all learned what Frank sure as shit must have already understood in the grave: you need a strong faith in the holiness of your enemy's soul if you're going to believe that seeing *your* suffering is going to change *him.* Frank's murderers hadn't changed. Soulless creatures, they'd danced from the Mississippi courtroom to murder some more.

Now Frank had told them the explosion would wake people up. He'd said that no one would be hurt. So why should they sit in, or march in a circle, waiting for cops to take batting practice on their heads? They shouldn't, they fucking *should not.* She should join Beth and Jesse, be the one to deliver the blow this time. "Fuckin' A," Laura said, her jaw lengthening, her teeth growing, lovely fur thickening all over her body and her legs shaking restlessly, as if a long winter's hibernation was ending. "Fuckin' A!" she screamed. She didn't have to be Laura Jaffe anymore. She could rip a man's face off with her claws. "Fuckin' A!" she shouted, her legs strong now, without any spectral aches, ready to leap and break someone's neck. This must be what Billy had seen in her, what the Knowledge Stone would have told her, she *is* a wolf—and her brother's weight would be made bearable when the justice she did for him was courageous, difficult, and bloody enough. "Fuckin' A!" The people who had murdered her brother, the Bugs whose souls she was supposed to save, maybe she'd do that by feasting on their fat. "Fuckin' A! Fuckin' A! Fuckin' A!" That felt so *good,* the blood throbbing in her ears, her throat opening. She smiled at Athena, showing her big sharp teeth.

Then she realized Jesse was staring at her, sick-faced, like he'd awakened from a dream to find himself in a bad place.

"No," Jesse said. "There's something wrong."

"There's nothing wrong," Michael said. "I fucking told you already, asshole. *I* checked all the calculations." He'd turned to them, his letter jacket on his lap, the fingers of his right hand stroking the lining. "My numbers are right. No one will suffer." *No one but MyKill,* he thought. All BillyBooks ever showed was a Gyro Gearloose, but when he placed this package Billy would see that Michael had a spiritual depth greater than the Defender's or even Billy Bad Ears' own.

"That's not what I mean," Jesse said, his eyes moving over Laura's reddening face. "This isn't, I don't know, Laura, whatever it is, it isn't, you know, Fuckin' A." Is *that* what they would become if they planted a bomb, he wondered. Shrieking, cold-blooded, hysterical? "I think Arkey is right. We haven't built the base. Even if no one's hurt, this will just frighten people," *the way Laura had just frightened him.*

Laura put her hands over her face. Jesse'd shamed her and made her absolutely furious. It had been *his* words that had led her to this leap. Now, even as saliva frothed around her lupine jaw, he was saying she was just another young girl brought up on the comics. "But, Billy," she said angrily, then she didn't know what to say after that. Billy Bad Ears told the Outsiders to make justice, but it was the Defender who knew what justice was, who told them what they should do to make it. She had seen herself reflected in Jesse's eyes—a misshapen thing, no wolf, for sure, not even the komic kind—because if she *was* why would she care what Jesse thought about her and her anger? She *wouldn't*. That was the whole point of being **SheWolf**! Which she would never fucking be. *She* was anger brought up short by guilt, love marred by envy; an unhappy neurotic mess, with no Knowledge Stone anywhere to help her.

"I mean, we've done illegal things before," Jesse said, "I know that. But we always said, take us to court, right? We *want* to stand up for our actions. This, I think, we're not ready to stand up for."

"*I* am," Michael said angrily. "I fucking *am*."

Jesse held up his palm, like a crossing guard.

"Oh, fuck you and your missing finger," Beth said, standing. "Jesus, it isn't even a whole fucking finger, and it doesn't make you God." She slammed her Coke down on the top of the TV. "In fact, what you are, Jesse, is a coward, just like Arkey. You're a fucking liberal coward."

"Fuck you," Arkey said, his eyes bulging.

Who are we, Laura thought, *if we don't help each other to rise together?* "We shouldn't fight." She wiped her sleeve across her eyes to clear them.

"We *should* fight!" Beth shouted at her. "Don't you get it? That's the whole fucking point! Now is the time to decide, Laura. Are you for or against the world's peoples?" But she already stared past Laura. "Come on, Billy. Let's do it."

Billy stood up on the bed, like a little boy about to bounce, then stopped, and just sat down again. Laura smelled a rotting, swampy odor. "Wait. Please," he said.

Beth walked over to the bed and put both her hands on Billy's cheeks, turned his dazed eyes toward hers. "You're not like these pussies, Billy. You're like me and Michael. You can do your job."

Billy's face went slack. "What is my job?"

"Jesus, Billy, your job is to go check the fucking I-Lab parking lot." Beth paused and took a breath. "Your job, Billy, is to think of Frank as you do acts of justice and raise him." A piece of blatant manipulation, Laura thought, that at the same time Beth also truly believed in *and* imagined *and* thought and dreamt, everything all in alignment for her, an inner unity that gave her words a fascinating, gleaming certainty. *She's not like me,* Laura thought. *She's flat, without edges, like an agit-prop poster. Or like my father said, she's a comic book character. Like in ads for movies: Beth Jacobs is Ninja B.!*

"You're right," Billy said to Beth, nearly toppling off the bed and into her arms. She stood him upright, gave him a little push in the back toward the door.

"Wait, Billy," Arkey said. "Don't." They had rolled on the grass in the playground; they were joined still in his dreams. "Stop, Billy. This is just too fucking dangerous."

But Billy couldn't hear him or didn't care; he staggered out the door like a child who's had too much Passover wine.

Beth zipped up her black motorcycle jacket, turned to leave. "Come on, Michael," she said commandingly, as she passed his stool. "Let's go."

"No!" Laura shouted. In *her* dream, a policeman sees Michael walk up the steps with her flowered carpetbag. He shouts at him to stop, but

Michael goes on up the steps, because he isn't really *there,* he's sitting in a white empty room inside himself, forming the equations that reconcile the ways of God to Man.

The cop unholsters his revolver and shoots the light of the world. Her world, anyway.

She grabbed the end of Michael's shirt, pulled the tail out of his jeans. "Don't go, darling. We need . . ." What did they need? To take acid? To see God? To fuck? Laura felt the slender clear ropes that tied her to everyone in this room pulling her forward and back, immobilizing her. "We need to talk more."

Michael brushed weakly at her hand. "No more fucking talk," he said. "All those words you people use, they're like sand you blow this way and that to blind yourselves 'cause you don't really want to see what has to be done. Because then you'd have to fucking do it! Beth's got it right. Now is the time. Now is the fucking time!"

Well, maybe it was. Maybe she stayed here with Jesse and Arkey because they were all too bourgeois. Maybe she didn't really care about the Vietnamese, and maybe, from the moment she'd been born, she'd known that Frank was her parents' favorite because he was a boy, and so she'd just never loved her brother enough truly to help him. She opened her palm.

Michael looked down at her hand, surprised at how easy she'd made it for him. As he followed Beth out the door, he heard Gail say, "I gotta go on this one, Arkey," her steps following after Michael's.

Laura heard them clatter down the stairs. But then Beth came back in, pulling Gail back through the door after her. She yanked her toward the bed. "Not this one," she said.

Gail, naturally, began to cry, black icicles dripping down her cheeks.

"By the way," Beth added, with a sharp smile for Laura, "don't think you're out of this now. Remember, you and Jesse are supposed to make the warning calls." She cackled. "Or look, anyone's inside, you could just let them blow the fuck up. It's your decision."

She closed the door, laughing still, and ran off.

At twelve-forty-five A.M., Billy Green, misted by a light rain, pedaled his weaving bicycle back up an almost empty Massachusetts Avenue to where Michael and Beth waited in the dust-covered panel van. "It's clear," Billy whispered, just as he had in their rehearsals every night for the last two weeks. The van rolled slowly past him down the street and into the parking lot.

Then Beth saw a ten-speed in the silver rack out front, and a light glowing dimly from the second floor of the target. Blinded by that mild glow, she and Michael sat, confused.

Beth stared at the bicycle; she looked at the lighted window. She felt like she was in gym class and the coach had tossed a softball right at her head, saying, *Think fast*. What if the cops came while they sat here, dynamite and detonators cuddled by her leg? Think fast, think fast, think fast. "Billy *must* have checked it out. Someone left a light on before they went home, that's all."

"And the bicycle?"

Billy had rocked, she thought. Billy had spoken with Frank, and Frank told him to set the charge. Besides, Michael and Billy and those two Warning Call Cowards, they only had one try in them; they had to complete this step or they'd never move on to the next. Maybe, she feared, that might even be true for her. So now is the time, the one and only time. "Go!" she said.

"Yeah." He opened the door, walked casually toward the long, low building, the way they'd practiced, jacket unbuttoned. Something bulged in the lining. Jesus, was he holding tonight?

Michael felt the rain drip on his forehead. As planned, he walked casually toward the building. Right foot: *His suffering makes light*.

Left foot: *His light ends suffering*.

Right foot: His suffering makes light. Left foot: If we're found out, then let it be *my* suffering, Lord. They'll never know about Beth and Laura and Billy and Jesse. *I alone will suffer*.

Right foot: The bombing makes light. . . . Left: The bombing will make me suffer. . . . Right: My suffering will make light in people's minds. . . . Then the whole thing became a jumble, a sonorous mass of weighty, indistinct, glorious words, like a Magnificat heard at the back of a cloister, where dusty sunlight streamed through columns of alabaster. Still listening, he opened the door, dropped the flowered carpetbag in the entry to Zargon's Workshop, and ran back to the van—*I alone, I alone, I alone will suffer,* resounded inside him—the words making him feel a lovely mixture of righteous power and pleasant, deep woundedness.

Forty-five minutes later, Arkey sat across the street in the MIT student center, this huge upside-down flying saucer. The shape made him uneasy; he imagined that the hundreds of other students could tell *he* didn't understand the structural principles that held this building up, which meant he wasn't entitled to be inside it, out of the rain, drinking the twice-boiled engineer's coffee from their open-all-night snack stand.

Then he heard a loud bang, like the backfire from a truck, and was surprised that the bent glass didn't shimmer inward and smash to the floor. A minute later fire trucks screamed by, and he and a hundred other students ran across a broad, empty Massachusetts Avenue toward the red lights at the Instrumentation Laboratory.

Its entrance—wood and tin and tarpaper—had crumpled, a few two-by-fours hanging down. The explosion had started a fire that would suck all the oxygen from Cambridge and probably the rest of Arkey's career into it because he'd even sat in a room where this bombing had been discussed. This broken wood and melted black paper was *the fact,* and he'd been an accessory before it. Or something like that. After all, Mitchell's grand juries put people away for lots less than this. He began to cough, more from nerves than from smoke. He really shouldn't be here. After all, no one had asked him to observe, to write the history.

Then firemen came out of the building with their hats off—so maybe, Arkey thought, the warning *had* done its job, the building had been cleared.

Another student said, "Jesus, they're after us now, huh?" Scared, but angry too.

"Not me," his friend replied. He had on a conical OurKey hat, but with π, and ~, and >0 on it. "I'm a geologist."

"Yeah, right, and at Madison they were just professional monkeys. Like what if they make a mistake? These people are not rocket scientists, so maybe they can't tell a rocket scientist from a geologist." He wore a clear plastic bubble-helmet over his head, like MyKill's, a Chinese demon face painted on each side with a different expression, happy, sad, angry, Arkey seeing now that it was a version of Laura's doll, the one Frank had sent her. "And what if they blow up, like, you know, me? I *am* a rocket scientist."

"Yeah?" his friend said, giggling, clearly stoned. "Well, that'd be no big loss to rockets or science. You're not Martin."

Then one of the boys asked how much explosive he thought would do this much damage—the kind of SAT question Arkey couldn't possibly answer. What if the engineers asked him to do the equation, then told the police about the long-haired kid in blue jeans and work shirt, the alien, they'd caught loitering in the parking lot, unable to do simple sine, cosine stuff?

He looked around. Just about all the people in the parking lot were long-haired guys, most dressed in blue jeans and work shirts.

A man with a beard said, "Man, what's that odor?" He looked over at him.

"Yeah, it smells like flowers," Billy having made Arkey so self-conscious that he sometimes dabbed himself with a little of Gail's Jiki. Someone might recognize him soon. Two men in business suits took pictures of the crowd with a flash camera. Reporters? FBI agents? Another man, in blue jeans and a red flannel shirt, walked down Mass. Ave., writing the license numbers of the cars in a spiral notepad, a cop for sure. He should get the fuck out of here.

Just then four firemen brought a body out, and laid it on a wheeled stretcher. "It's probably Martin Kopfman," the boy next to him said with the hushed voice of someone in the presence of the great prestige of death.

He turned away, ran top speed down Mass. Ave. The man in the flannel shirt looked up as he went by, sniffing the air.

His friends waited for his news in a booth at a nearly empty Tommy's Lunch, drinking Cokes and eating burgers, Michael playing *Aladdin*. Like in the poem, Arkey thought: Kopfman falls from the sky and the indifferent crowd skates; or plays pinball. But he had a foreboding that Michael, their working-class quantum genius, might be as much of an Icarus as the man he'd laid out on the stretcher. Arkey stopped to watch him, momentarily hypnotized by the silver ball rolling toward extinction. Michael paused, then slammed a hip into the machine, but he banged too hard, tilted his game.

Arkey slid into the booth, next to Gail, and Michael pressed in next to him, his thigh touching Arkey's, and so, Arkey dreamt, implicating him. He moved away. Michael felt it, and looked at him sympathetically. "You know, like the perfume's not so bad, Arkey. I kind of like it. You and Gail smell alike. It's nice."

"Yeah, I know," Arkey thinking, *I'm not the one with cooties tonight.* He told them about the body the firemen had carried from the building.

"Oh, God," Michael said, his mouth dummkopfing open.

"Will he be all right?" Laura said, imagining herself kneeling by the stretcher in the parking lot, leaning over the stricken face. She turned his head to the side, so he wouldn't choke. But even in her dream she didn't know what else to do to save him.

Arkey remembered Laura's face on the day Billy had looked up from her bedroom floor and wowed everyone with his prophetic gifts, and said matter-of-factly, "I don't know. I think he may be dead." That was more than Arkey knew about Kopfman, for sure, but he was furious with all of them, wanted to hurt them.

Gail screamed and knocked her plate to the floor. Billy slumped over the table, crying and panting for breath. Beth reached out to draw him toward her, stop him, shut him up. Like a drowning man, he scratched at her face, but harmlessly, with bitten nails.

"You saw the lights in the building, you saw the bicycle, you told us it was clear," Michael said to Billy, sounding almost peevish, Laura thought. She had never felt farther from him, from all of them. She wanted to slap him across the face. She wanted to run and never see any of them again.

Billy looked like Michael had hit him. "What lights?" he said. "What bicycle?"

Beth let go of him.

"Keep the volume down," Jesse said to Billy in a clipped, commanding tone.

Billy pulled his denim sleeve across his face and stopped crying, put his hand on Jesse's arm imploringly. "You knew what would happen," he said. "You and Arkey and Laura, you tried to stop us." He sucked up the mucus, looking and sounding, Arkey thought, like a helpless snot-nosed kid again. "What should we do now?"

Jesse stared at them; their faces so *ordinary*, how could they have done something so wrong? He tried to remember the War's litany of horrors. They *had* had to do something to stop that killing, hadn't they? But that didn't help him. If you focus on the man killed, then the killing looks like the action of small people driven forward by petty motives, no matter what they say, because no people, no motives, are equal to all the life the man on the stretcher, the man in the body bag, wouldn't have. No idea, he thought, is equal to one moment of a man seeing whatever it was a man might see. And despite what Billy had said, he was in it, too, all the way. He'd watched as they tested fuses, he'd helped make plans for warning calls. In the end, he'd changed his mind and said no, but that, he knew, didn't tip the balance in his favor. He hadn't done nearly enough to stop them, and he could never push the beam down now, could never again be what in his heart he swore he truly wanted to be, a defender of the weak. They had killed a man, Arkey said. And that meant his own life, one way or another, was over.

But what was it Billy had asked him? He shook off Billy's touch, pressed his hands to his temples. *What should they do now?*—that was it.

Billy, desolated by Jesse's silence, sobbed more loudly. Sweat ran down his face. His body began to give off a swampy odor.

Tommy, a broad-faced Armenian man, looked over from the cash register, brows drawn.

"We better get him out of here," Laura said, looking around the booth. MyKill is Michael, she thought, a smart kid who makes stupid mistakes. Billy is no magus. Jesse doesn't have a clue what to do to protect us. There was nothing special about her or her friends, she thought, except that their sense of being special had made them more confused, more dangerous than most. In her fantasy she already prayed for an ordinary redemption, working perhaps for those wounded in this savage, pointless, unnecessary war.

And doctor she'd become, walking in her long black Anne Klein coat through the derelict life of Avenue B. *See how I've tried to heal the damage I've done,* she told . . . who? Dr. Jacobs? Smerless? Her conscience? Or Bobby Brown? *And telling* him *what*? That she was caring enough to be a mother?

Halfway up the block to her clinic, a thin boy pushed a thinner girl toward her—like an offering. A clear message: *negotiate the price with me, then do what you will with her.* Two skeletons locked together in hell. This world, she thought, needs a lot of tending!

The boy reminded her of Jeffrey in high school, thin, talking fast, absent for days on end. How could she *not* have known he was an amphetamine addict? And now? No, he was clean&sober, rich&successful. But *where*? She would try his office again. Maybe they'd heard from him. Or when she saw Bobby tonight, maybe she could tell him about her worries, and he could get the government to help?

She walked quickly past the Hell diorama, lassitude filling her limbs, the guilt an old friend who'd taken up residence in the sixties with the promise that he would never give notice. And that made her think of a picture of another skinny little girl running down a road, naked, her flesh on fire—as if that was why they'd planted a bomb. But the picture couldn't explain anything, justify anything, mandate anything. "Everyone pleads the wounds," a patient of hers who dressed like the Haunted Desperado had told her once. "If you were for us, you said, 'Look at the sacrifice, look at the body bags. Look at the way the VC makes little kids fight.' " Like a voodoo doll, he wore four silver needles in each ear, meant to stop his craving for the one thing that let him be elsewhere, away from the war inside him. "If you were against us—and yes, me and my friends thought it was *us* you hated, Doctor, not the U.S. government, and not M. Perialism—well, then you said, 'Look at the sacrifice, look at the body bags, look at the way the bastards are burning children.' Lady, I tell you, sometimes the wounds just don't tell you what to do."

No, they don't, though thanks to Bobby Brown she had been feeling a little lighter recently for all she had—and hadn't—done. Pillow talk—better than therapy, it turned out.

"And off the record, okay?"

"Something illegal, dear? You?"

She'd nodded. "And I won't help you investigate it or anything. I want you to know that in advance."

"Won't help me investigate what?"

"I mean you can prosecute me if you want, but that's where it stops. I won't talk about anyone else." Exciting, in a shivery kid's way. Like putting your foot over the edge. *Catch me. Or don't push me, anyway.*

"What are we talking about here, Laura? The MIT bombing?"

She was halfway through the sentence before that had registered: *He knew.* "I voted against it. But they went ahead, so I phoned in the warning call."

"Yeah, I listened to the tapes. Good for you, I think. You tried to keep anyone from being hurt."

"I failed, though." She'd sat up, satiny sheet over her chest. "Sometimes, afterward, I thought maybe the police hadn't followed up on that warning call. It was weird. At the trial they said the call came in much later than I'm absolutely sure it was made. And they said Jesse's call never came in, when I was standing right next to him when he made it."

"Well, some of the people I've met, yeah, they have a very realpolitik attitude. Like Beth Jacobs that way, huh? They could sacrifice a few people to prove a point."

"I know that if we'd never started the thing we wouldn't have needed to make the calls, you know." He hadn't criticized her, yet she was scared to look at his face. "Look, I can't tell you anything about who else was involved."

He'd laughed. "Yeah, you said that. Anyway, did I ask?"

"No."

"It's ancient history now, Laura. A little guy on a bicycle, right. A black-haired woman. Arthur Kaplan."

"Arkey had nothing to do with it." Give him his due—or his blame. "He was always against it. Not a revolutionary situation, he said."

"Yeah? Could have fooled me. I mean, we all did things, those days, we regret now. Like I helped burn down a rat-trap school the night I first saw you." He sat up next to her. "You ask me, Yeats got it wrong. The best were full of passionate intensity. *And* the worst, of course. I guess there's always plenty of intensity to go around." He had reached over to the night table, where they'd left a bottle of vodka, two shot glasses. "Look, I'm not God, Laura. I'm not in a position to forgive you for that man's ear. But you ask me, you're not one of the bad guys."

Perhaps. Or, in time. Bobby Brown wasn't God, but he was a moral person, she felt that strongly. And at least *he* didn't think she was destructive. The weight slipped from her arms, legs, chest—for a moment anyway. She opened the solid metal door to the clinic and put on her doctor face.

And an answered prayer, a miracle really, that she had ever gotten to wear a doctor face. After the explosion, she'd been sure medical school had gone up in flames right along with the entryway to the I-Lab, seen her No Future like a black hole at the center of Special Agent Olson's eyes. Had the FBI chosen her family's hero to question her, to intimidate her, make her feel guilty? Well, nice touch. She *did*.

"Where did your boyfriend get his dynamite?" Olson asked.

"What boyfriend?" Laura said because she couldn't think of anything else to say, except: *I'm an infant. I don't know what words mean.* She felt like she was going to vomit on the long mahogany table in the administration building, which in her dream became an operating table, with her as the patient.

The physicist, a man named Kopfman, had *lived,* she reminded herself, Arkey Kaplan having gotten it wrong as always. Kopfman's hearing might be impaired, but he was alive, thank God, he was alive. She repeated *alive, alive, alive* to herself, a mantra to settle her stomach.

Olson, a close-cropped man with a rectangular face, pursed his thin lips around something sour. "Michael Healy. Your boyfriend. Where did he get his dynamite?"

"What dynamite?" Laura looked toward the high ceilings, the walls of the Faculty Room they'd piled into when they'd occupied this building, huddling together for warmth, breathing each other's smell and Gauloises smoke, while they talked nervously about what they should do when the cops broke the chains they'd put on the doors, and then dragged them away for taking over the Faculty Meeting Room to hold their discussion about what to do when, etc.

The carpet had been cleaned of Gauloises ashes and coffee stains. Plaster busts of famous Puritans again rested on pedestals lining the dark wood walls, their long hooked noses and their sense that God had chosen them making them competitors, Laura thought, with the Jews—so many of whom had usurped places at their Harvard, the college that had once seemed like a very heaven to her and her parents, rejoicing at Le Voisin at how far they'd all come, how high they'd risen. Too far? Too high? The plaster busts looked angry; heaven's chosen, pissed off, would cast her down. She would never get to medical school; she'd never get to redeem herself for what had happened to Kopfman. *Who lived,* she reminded herself. *Who lived.*

Yes, but she should have done more to stop her friends. Okay, what? Should she have turned them in to people like Hoover and Mitchell, who perjured and murdered so the War could grind on? This morning the *Times* told how soldiers from Charlie Company had chosen a whole Vietnamese village for special treatment, then buried the bodies in a mass grave. So maybe Beth had been right. You either help the Vietnamese *right now,* or you slink back to your dorm room and hide, the way Billy had done these last months, wailing like a baby whenever she tried to talk to him. Maybe dynamite had been the wrong way. But what was *right,* and who could tell her? Not Billy anymore. And not this man.

Special Agent Olson stared at her for a long moment with cold blue eyes, reciprocally totaling her soul. Hoover's in a tilting swivet again, he thought, but maybe not so crazy this time, the nauseous Red tide did spread by the day. Last week, ten thousand hooligans had fought the Reserves outside an embassy in Washington, *in sight of the director's office!* Yesterday bombs had shattered plate glass on New York's Sixth Avenue: Chase, Standard Oil, and General Motors, the pillars of the world. "You're making me sick," he told the girl. "You're no different from the people in Mississippi who protected your brother's murderer."

Thank God, she thought, *he doesn't know yet that the person I'm protecting is me*—his other questions having made it clear he was mostly interested in Beth, seemed to know that she'd been the woman in the van. He must think that Beth had phoned in the warning call, too. *Please God, let him think that,* Laura prayed, willingly sacrificing her friend. After all, it's what Beth wants, isn't it? Not medical school but a life of struggle? Olson just went on staring, anger radiating from him. Who would he become in *The Book of Deborah, AKA the Prophet*? F. Bee Eye? A hypnotist for Zargon, injecting truth serum with his stinger till she longed to tell him all? But there'd be no transformation for Olson. Billy, locked away in his room since the bombing, whined that he couldn't draw anymore.

Laura didn't want Olson to have another taste of her voice, maybe discover his mistake, but she had to ask something, with a need greater even than her fear. "How did you know where my brother was buried?"

Olson stared at her again, then decided that he'd give her something, maybe make a bond that he could use to walk her forward toward the stand, the only place where she could truly make things right for herself and her wretched band of friends. "An informer," he said. "A scared little man." He smiled, remembering the Chicago thug they'd imported to stick a gun in the man's mouth, making it all legal in Judge Lynch's court. "Of course, he was right to be scared of us."

"I mean, did he tell you where to dig in that dam? Why did you use a dowsing rod?"

"I can't remember what the snitch said. It was a lifetime ago, Miss Jaffe."

Laura had lost her last drops of courage. So she didn't ask, *Did you feel a force drawing the dowsing rod down?* Maybe she was afraid to find out more, afraid to lose her last tattered remnants of chosenness and become just another unguided citizen of the empire who, like General Westmoreland, had maimed people with no better sanction than her own oh-so-fallible ego. Mostly, though, she just didn't want Olson to match her whine with the one that had made the warning call.

Olson felt he'd gratified her enough; now it was her turn. "Well, what did Michael tell you about the other bombers?" he asked.

"Michael who?" she said.

He slapped her hard across her smug little face.

Anyway, the FBI already knew about Michael Who. He'd boasted to his maimed cousin, who had quickly traded him in for a walk on a drug charge.

So Michael Healy would be the lone defendant in the concrete-and-wood courtroom, specially outfitted for this trial with an emergency button under the judge's bench, closed-circuit TV cameras, and new steel doors to stop automatic weapons fire. Rock-throwing students had rampaged through Buffalo and Champaign-Urbana, through downtown Berkeley, and Madison. Other kids had just firebombed a Bank of America in Santa Barbara. And the Northern Tupes had sworn they'd rescue their hero, Michael Healy.

So Wile E. Coyote (Peyote's stupid brother-in-law) had trailed a huge ACME net from the courtroom's roof and staked it into the street ten feet from the building. Each morning, when the judge drove to work, a crowd of shouting kids screamed at his car, and TAC Squad men stood like confused fishermen, waiting for the day's catch to rush into their traps. No one in fur leggings anymore, Billy's father having let the Knowledge Stone story peter out, leaving SheWolf forever bewildered.

Laura could feel the absence in herself; her face ordinary now, a little cat at best, with a somewhat too large nose, not a fierce wolf—*that* reality being, she thought, the wisdom the Knowledge Stone must have contained: that she had no power, this particular Dumbo's feather saying, *You don't need me, Dumbo, because you really can't fly.*

No leather arm pads today either, or spiked headbands, the Billy-provided patina of pseudo magic having washed away from everyone's life, not just hers—like, *dear fellow Dumbos, let me introduce you to . . . gravity.* From time to time, plainclothes cops sauntered at the edge of the crowd, bagged SDS members on John Doe warrants that said they—or someone—had run with Beth after the Mobe, turned over a police car. They hadn't nabbed Jesse or Travis yet, but she'd seen a grind from her chem class, innocent of everything but a higher grade point average than Laura's, who got sapped that way, dragged off to six months on Deer Island.

Snake had gone down, too, got bailed, and come right back, filing into the courtroom behind Laura now to cheer with the other long-haired laughing boys and lithesome girls, all potential conspirators who oinked to mock the judge in his own courtroom. To mock, Billy feared, even the law itself.

"So?" Beth said, stepping closer to the sitting boy, trying to get him to bend toward her. "So fucking what?"

"*Any* law," Billy said quietly. "Even after the Revolution, even, you know," he said slowly, "even God's Law." He looked sickly, his long, fleshy nose enormous on his crescent moon of a face, dark bags under his eyes. He had, Laura knew, an ear infection from all his crying. But he wouldn't take antibiotics. A hair shirt for his ear? Or a nice finishing touch on his x-rays, a few new scars to convince the Great Neck draft board that he was at least 5- or 6-F.

"No," Beth said, stepping closer still, so Billy might gaze at all he'd be surrendering: her large eyes, her lavish black hair, her breasts set off by her TM unzipped leather jacket. "Some now must take it upon themselves to act outside the law and make a world where the Law will finally, truly, apply."

Like she thinks she's God, Laura thought, inscribing the laws of space and time in a capitalist vacuum so we and the workers might see! But Billy swayed toward her. Beth, Laura thought sadly, always knew the witchy talk to lure Billy—maybe because she really believed in her spells herself.

. . .

Could Beth help him know what comes next, Billy wondered, so he could draw not just single images but a whole story, following the ribbon the way he'd always been able to—until he'd followed *her* out of the attic room and down Massachusetts Avenue.

Followed her? No, Jesse had gotten it right at Tommy's when his anger had felt like a blow to Billy's heart. *He* had been the one who told them it would be all right. When he'd rocked on the bed before the bombing, Billy had *seen* Michael walk up the steps with that flowered bag and he could *feel,* like a lightening, a joy, each step made Frank easier in his grave, sending him closer to the source of all things, so he might be reborn to make justice on earth. Billy had felt that night in the attic just the way he had in Great Neck, in Laura's bedroom, hadn't he? And he'd been right, then, Frank *had* been murdered. Olson *had* found the body under tons of earth. Could that have been a lucky guess, and his other feelings just an unconscious thing, *a symptom,* the way Jeffrey said, knowing him better than he did himself—which meant that he was probably queer, too, the way Jeffrey implied.

Queer? Straight? Vision? Neurosis? He didn't fucking know anything anymore! So when he tried to draw a story, he saw Zargon, teeth extended, sitting behind a desk in a huge eight-sided building, about to put his fangs into . . . his secretary? A telephone? A Mallomar? Maybe Zargon wasn't evil, just hungry, misunderstood, underanalyzed? Billy didn't know *what came next.* Everything might, so nothing did. He'd already missed more than two months of issues, his father, Matt, and the others covering for him, but the fans recognized the change, complained to "The Ear Hears," calling the stories "too simple . . . too mild, lacking magic," hurting his dad's feelings, and, most of all, hurting sales.

He'd tried to work, God knows. He'd stayed in his dorm room night after night, fasting, praying, reading the order on *Damages* over and over for instruction. But he still didn't know what Zargon bit down on, or how to lead his own life. Well, with God so distant, how could a woman in a motorcycle jacket do anything for him? He leaned back on the bench, and Beth walked across the aisle from them, raising her fist in the air.

The others in the courtroom followed Athena X's lead, fists up, shouting "Power to the People!" The judge shouted he'd clear the court if they didn't all sit down and shut up.

They sat down. They shut up. Laura wanted to whack Billy on his little back for his quasi-rabbinical pomposity, and to remind him that the law—and maybe the Law, too, for all she knew—could certainly put Billy and Beth, and maybe, who knows, even Jesse and her, away for many long years. She didn't bother saying that, though, because Billy would probably nod back, uncertain if he *should* go to jail, uncertain who was entitled to send him there. Well, who was certain? Only Olson anymore, and people like him.

But Beth was certain, wasn't she? Was Beth like Olson?

Michael, mouth shut, blond hair shorn, sat stiffly upright at the defense table, a red knit Rooster tie of Arkey's knotted tightly around his neck. He'd agreed to play the exaggerated American and let Harrison Baker put on an ordinary criminal defense that said he hadn't done it, and *if* he had, well, then, *people intending to commit murder don't make warning calls.*

Or have them made, a police dispatcher having already testified that the caller sounded like a nervous woman. She scanned the jury; their opaque middle-aged male faces had the blood fleeing her brain. She grabbed Billy's arm but didn't cry out, not even a whisper, because a police spy might recognize the anxious voice that had squeaked the warning that wasn't heeded, to clear the building, to save the physicist who wasn't quite saved, from the bomb she and her friends had set.

That morning after court, Harrison Baker stood smoking by the coffee stand in the courthouse's cold, dark lobby, giving Michael's family a smile of horse-size discolored teeth. Sugar Cane trusted Harrison for legal work, and that, Laura knew, was good enough for Beth. "Looks like we need your ruling-class bullshit now, Harry boy," she said, amiably.

Harrison ignored her, put an arm around his client and the boy's worried father, promising them that he would plead this down eventually to aggravated assault, or maybe even reckless endangerment. Cheap lawyers walked quickly by in gray overcoats and galoshes with their buckles open. Harrison kept his soft eyes focused on Michael's stocky, sad father. "I will nevah, nevah, nevah," Harrison said, "let them convict your son for attempted murder." Harrison sometimes represented Sugar Cane, but could he be as sure now as his toothy smile and soft tone implied? This morning he'd found his office file cabinets jimmied, manila folders scattered on the linoleum office floor, and Styrofoam cups of coffee placed prominently on his desk—the burglars' way of saying they were sure no cops would come for them, because, hey, dude, they *were* cops, so they even had time for a mid-robbery coffee break.

. . .

That afternoon after the coffee break, Martin Kopfman, a thin, bearded, diffident man of thirty, took the stand, wearing a pirate's patch over his left eye.

If it wasn't covered, he told the jury, he saw double.

The prosecutor said how damn awful that was.

Harrison objected, and the judge sustained.

Kopfman seemed bewildered. "But that isn't the worst thing," he told the judge. "There's also a ringing in my ears." He turned his single eye to the wall above the jury's heads. "So I can't, you know, go away anymore."

"You mean," the prosecutor said, "you have to stay in Boston for your medical treatment?"

"There's no treatment," Kopfman said furiously. "The nerves have been shattered. I mean I can't *think*. Not the way someone like me needs to. My work isn't like yours, it's . . . it *was* very intricate, very difficult. I have to be able to concentrate fully."

He's calling the prosecutor stupid, Laura thought. All of them, really. Probably Kopfman had never been a very likable guy. But did that mean it was all right to have damaged his auditory nerve?

Of course not. Michael, at the defense table, rocked backward, probably getting what it would be like if this had happened to him, if *he* couldn't paint a picture of God's smiling face with sines and paradoxes. Billy, sketching, stopped and looked up at Kopfman too, his own eye, *naturellement,* squinted shut with a tear or two, Billy no doubt crying to think what it would be like for him if his pencil couldn't stroke the paper until he was lost in the process, no longer *here* in his sickly body.

She remembered that body rocking on the Singularity's bed, davening over Coca-Cola. He'd received no message then; he'd seen *nothing*, or Kopfman wouldn't be staring at them like that. And before, in her bedroom in Great Neck? Was that nothing, too? *You bet it was!* She could see it all now. Beth had gotten it half right that day they'd gone round and round the high school track. Billy *was* angry at everyone, but for no better reason she'd bet than that he was smaller than them. Those games of keepaway in the Cherry Lane skunk cabbage had driven him nuts. His whole story hidden in plain sight: weak and scared of others, he can only show that fury in lurid pictures of men in kilts and codpieces, superpowered avengers. Or in the roar of that huge Evinrude on his tiny Boston Whaler. *Or in bombs*—the little man finally getting to make a big bang.

And that anger at the ordinary—those of average height!—was that why he'd hung Frank around their necks? To make them feel as queer as

he did? It was altogether way past time to throw her last rags of specialness down on this courtroom's linoleum floor and just finally admit
what she had really always known: she was connected to no one, and
her brother's insensate corpse only moldered in the grave. She was
trapped *here* now, too, *not* a wolf, and *not* connected to some nonexistent suffering, dead-but-sentient justice-thirsting saint. What she did
here on earth might matter to her, or to someone else, but it sure as hell
wouldn't ever matter to her brother. Nothing would anymore. He was
dead.

She looked at the court, and it seemed brighter to her, but more ordinary, too, even and empty under a wash of fluorescent light. It's like leaving home, she thought; you feel free—but lonely and scared too. *That*
was something to laugh at—to be actually scared that she didn't have to
deal daily with a rotting ghost anymore.

Then the prosecutor said, "A moment, Your Honor," and riffled
through some yellow pages. She looked at Kopfman's big black eye.
Sorry, Martin, she thought. *We listen to you, but we all just mourn for
ourselves.*

Yeah, the poem of his absent eye replied. And your weeping doesn't
change anything, either. Your tears just let you feel superior because you
feel so sad and guilty. But I'm still trapped *here*. And now I also have to
watch a bunch of little ignorant shits like you pity me!

Except for Beth, of course. She didn't cry, not for Kopfman, not for
herself. She just looked back at him with a fury matching his. So Kopfman probably thought only the beautiful buxom woman in the front
row understood him, stared at him directly, unflinchingly, with a grim
unweeping look that accurately measured the horror his life had
become.

That's Athena X, of course! Confronting her newest enemy, HeadMan,
the brainiac savant who builds weapons for the government because
only the government can give him the tools he needs to do the really
complicated mental labor that is the only way to metabolize the special
goop in his brain. Otherwise the sticky stuff turns to a bile-green poison
that will first make him unbearably sad, then stupid, and then (drooling
and stumbling) kill him. Okay, and then? And then . . . Athena X is . . .
maybe she's caught even as her ice pick punctures HeadMan's massive
external brain lobe!

Could that be what came next?

They'd gag Athena X's mouth—of course, they'd do that—so she
can't give the Death Scream, or . . . and then . . . and then what?

Billy looked around the courtroom. The judge? He could be what? A psycho? An obstetrician? An electrician? A dietitian? *That's nonsense, my brain drowning in its own goop!* He had to think of something bad to happen next, something worse, not simple, not mild, but much, much more horrible, more ingeniously awful, the world made worser and worser until the reader could grow dazed with the comic's special delight, ingenious horror to be savored by the young reader who feels oh so sure he lives in the House of the Good . . . Which was where? In Great Neck? In puberty? In the world the Talmud could make—if only we followed its laws! Which Billy couldn't.

He stopped drawing then, not even remotely knowing anymore what came next in the HeadMan story, all of it becoming single panels to him again, severed bleeding body parts, like those things stuck on the Schells' walls. Nervously, he shaded and re-shaded the huge wound on HeadMan's noggin that would now never get worse, never get better, while in the Cambridge courtroom, Harrison Baker asked Kopfman to tell the court exactly what research he'd been doing at the Instrumentation Laboratory the night of the bombing.

But the DA shouted, "Irrelevant," and the judge, unpersuaded by the chorus that shouted, "Shame! Shame!," agreed with the prosecutor. He recessed for the day.

On her way out, Beth stopped by Billy's seat. "Zargon doesn't hesitate to use *his* weapons, Billy. Zargon has killed a million Vietnamese already." She glanced at his sketch pad, where curls of HM's brain stood exposed to the air. "How will you fight him, Billy? With drawings? With comic books?"

Christ, Billy thought, *don't you get it? I can't fucking draw comic books anymore!* But Beth, his greatest creation, probably couldn't tell the difference between his work and the stuff drawn by his father or hacks like Matt.

By the elevators, Beth waited for Michael and Harrison, jumping from tile to tile, playing I-Ching Hopscotch. On white: *I'll stay with the support cadre.* On black: *No, I'll do it. I'll get Michael to jump bail and I'll join B.C. Underground.*

After all, it had been an honor that the whole leadership had voted to take her under in the Consolidation, the only one of them there'd been no dissent about, her militancy clearer to all than Diana's or Ted's or even B.C.'s—plus the dozens of also-rans all over the country who'd have to stay visible as support cadre, like Paulie, Priss, and Snake. She had to admit she'd miss *him* if she went under. Maybe she could get them to vote again on Snake.

But (white again) underground scared Beth. It meant not seeing her friends anymore. Or arguing with her father—*if* she ever spoke to him again. So back to black, and I'm ready, Teddy, to become part of "a mobile, decentralized, self-actualizing force of guerrilla fighters." Except that when B.C. stuttered that—jumping to white again—it took him about a week.

Ah, well, she'd make up her mind later. Right now, here comes Harrison. They had to ready her Kopfman Kounter-measure, cheer Michael up with testimony from Hans the Fizzyits, a man who really knew more about guilt than her father because he himself had actually fucking done something to feel guilty about, he'd helped build Big Boy. Kopfman's doctoral advisor, Hans had told *Life* magazine that Martin was a brilliant student, but also very naïve. "He thinks his work will guide airplanes so they'll use less fuel and never fall down. But really, you know, maybe the Army is not so very interested in that? Maybe they think his work will keep satellites locked on target?"

Hans still lived in a hobbit's heap, journals and books piled so high that only a narrow one-person trail led between them to his desk or couch, which smelled noticeably of piss. Beth pushed a stack of papers aside, the top pages stained with food, tea, and something that she would swear was blood, the mess making her remember what Michael had told Laura: *you know, Hans is like really old, I can tell his brain doesn't work as quickly as mine anymore.* She hoped to God Hans still saw Michael as his chance to be part of physics in the future and would do what he could to save him.

"No," he said softly, and "I was badly misquoted in that magazine. You see, one *never* knows how such fundamental research as ours will be used. It *could* be used for weapons, certainly, or it could mean there'd be no more pilot error, no airplanes would fall from the sky ever, ever, ever again," speaking this last bit in a singsong, a wink probably, so they'd know it was a fairy tale the government had made him tell—like irony made him less compromised, less helpless, saved the pathetic shreds of his dignity. Hans avoided Michael's darting eyes, his nearly blind gaze staying locked on Beth, who squatted on a pile of books.

"These trials, they just terrify you." She smiled dangerously, stage-whispered "Oppenheimer."

"What?"

"You're still scared of McCarthy," Beth said, "the dummy."

"You're right. I'm scared," the Fizzyits said, removing his thick lenses. His eyes, exposed to the air, looked like defenseless sea animals.

He rubbed the rheumy jellies for a moment. "But you're what terrifies me, Beth. The good and the bad in the world are more mixed together than you realize. It's only a very delicate balance that lets people like me and Michael work." He still didn't look at Michael, though, who stared at the ground now. "Can't you see how you anger people? You and your foolish friends are making things so much worse!"

"What could be worse?" Michael said. "Worse, I mean, for the Vietnamese?" But he said it to the floor.

The old mole, thick glasses in hand, finally looked toward his student—now that he couldn't see him. "Oh, there's always worse." He laughed. "Worse people, worse weapons." He put on his telescopes, turned to Beth. "Just ask your father. He knows."

She laughed. "My father," she said. "My father," she repeated pointlessly.

Then she turned, and marched out of the office.

The same afternoon SAC Olson in New York had an inspiration about Beth Jacobs' dear old Da. He'd been dialing right past the snotty wastes of Channel 13 on his way to WPIX and wrestling when he found himself hooked by a shouting match between two Teutonic Titans. In one corner, a Little Man in a Blue Suit—Beth Jacobs' father, as it turned out—battling the Pink Professor, Herbert Marcuse. Jacobs called Marcuse an irresponsible pied piper, "whose silly fantasies of free sex might lead foolish children into a mountain, never to be seen again." It had made a lightbulb go off over Olson's head.

Don't wait on inspiration, Hoover would say. So the very next day Olson stood in the snow with a colleague on the front steps of the doctor's Great Neck house, Agent Olson telling Dr. Jacobs how a boy on a bicycle had seen a buxom black-haired girl in the parking lot of the MIT Instrumentation Lab the night it went bang, someone who looked just like his own big-breasted, raven-tressed daughter, with her murderous fantasies of overthrowing our legally elected government. Could he and his friend come inside out of the cold and discuss that with him?

The Little Man, wearing the pinstripes from TV, shut the door in their faces. A gutsy gesture, Olson thought, his own shoulders slumping until, turning to leave, he'd heard loud, uncontrolled weeping behind him, and imagined the little Jew hunched over inside.

Olson smiled, the whole play coming to him in one miraculous moment. He would make a couple of casebook threats to get the scared old man to testify against his daughter's pal. In the second act, the Jewish family's betrayal would so anger Healy that he would give Jacobs' daughter up. By act three, Olson would have worked the old man into such soft rubber, he might have him testifying against his own daughter, sure that it would be best for both of them. Hoover and Tolson might even come to the courtroom to savor that one.

So Olson's men interviewed Leo's neighbors about his odd habits, Leo hearing about the interviews from Ellen Jaffe, while the Schells' party swirled round them. The agents, she said, used their questions to start rumors that Leo had slept with patients. Ellen coquettishly added, "Did I sound a little jealous just then?"

Leo was unable to speak.

"It's the same kind of garbage they tried with Martin," she said—with, he'd swear, wholehearted concern for him. Her son's death had done what in Leo's experience suffering never did—it had made her more generous, less self-centered, opened her heart to the importance of something besides Ellen's own mother's quite ordinary selfishness and let them successfully conclude her analysis. "Do you want Herbert to help you?"

"Let me think about that," he said, even now having to consider if his help might hurt their therapeutic results. On the other hand, would her former doctor's going to jail help her any? He smiled at that—not meanly, he hoped.

Olson called him the next day to tell him he ought to know that some patients were thinking about suing him for malpractice.

"Who was that?" Ann asked.

"The FBI."

"We need a lawyer." Scared, precise, commanding—he the infant again, the refugee, and Ann the American.

He had no choice. He dialed his former patient's husband. Herbert Jaffe was the most powerful man he knew, even distantly.

But Olson *ordered* Jaffe and Leo to the FBI's offices, said he cared fuck-all anymore what he'd done with his patients. "You lied to get into the country. You fraudulently signed a loyalty oath. And I'll bet you had help from your CP pals to get the visa in the first place. Look, Leo, you want, we can follow the trail, see who moved things along for you." Jaffe had looked sick. Leo, nauseous, his chest covered in sweat, spun downward, thinking strangely of his foolish essays about guilt, when really he had only ever talked to ghosts about what *he* truly felt guilty for, the death of David Weiss, his own survival, the Party's role in saving him.

"Mr. Jacobs," Olson was saying, "we know that woman outside the lab might be someone who only looked like your daughter. But if we're going to help her clear herself, you're gonna have to help us convict the terrorist we've already caught. You don't, then there's gonna be a shit-storm for you *and* her."

Jaffe made it clear to him as they rode down in the elevator that he should think about it. "They're obviously willing to go very far on this."

Terrified, Leo looked blankly at him.

"I watched them harass Martin, Leo, maybe even wink at his mur-der. Now they're doing the same thing to Sugar Cane. They've already shredded the Constitution for their conspiracy indictments. *Maybe* I can protect you, but I'm not sure anyone can protect Beth."

And Leo wasn't sure Herbert *wanted* to protect her—thinking Beth a pied piper, perhaps, in his own daughter's life. The elevator doors opened; cold wind blew in from the entry. Jews help Jews, he thought. Communists help Communists. Fathers help daughters. The world is tribes and families, small, parochial loves. If that.

"Isn't that enough for you?" his wife asked that night.

It *was* now, he thought—now that it was too late. Beth, he knew, never returning to him so he might take her to the opera, or to see the picture she called *The Lady in Red,* a girl far less attractive than his own beautiful, lost daughter.

The next day he phoned her at someplace called the SDS house, in some-where called Somerville. He heard a man shout, "There's someone on the phone who says he's your dad," then Beth's voice whispering to him that he shouldn't say anything that he wouldn't want the government to know about. "And I'm not being paranoid."

"I know." Leo had heard clicks himself on their home phone, furi-ous that she'd done this to him and her mother, but also feeling a deeper kinship with her. Her warning now brought back memories of clandes-tine meetings, safe houses, the comradeship of men not like himself, even a few workers—as if Beth had gone to live in a country he no longer believed in, his own past. Had he given *her* a coded message, he won-dered, one he hadn't been aware of, his voice saying *guilt, restraint, order* but his hands chattering that she must go make the world revolu-tion for him, now that he was *hors de combat?*

"But what am I saying, Dad? What have you ever done that you wouldn't want the government to know about, eh?" His daughter, he thought, didn't know as much about him as the FBI, but to tell her about that past now would seem like boasting, could only lead her to more excesses, greater danger.

She spoke then more gently than usual, saying he shouldn't worry, she hadn't done anything. "Or nothing they can prove." Her laugh brittle, distancing, conspiratorial. "Look, I have to go now," she concluded in a voice filled with teenage self-importance. "We have, you know, this thing we have to do."

The next day Olson laughed too, saying he'd read the transcript of their call, and who knows, his daughter might be right, but if they couldn't get enough real evidence on her, they had whole factories just to inlay fingerprints where they wanted them. "You understand me, Leo. We'll frame her. You know what that means? It's an idiom. It means we paint a very convincing picture, paste your daughter in it, then put a nice border around it for the jury." They'd met in Leo's Great Neck office—his ground, he would have thought. But Olson had insisted; for purposes of reminding him, no doubt, that he had no ground, nothing that couldn't be taken from him, like the house where he lived or his family.

"She didn't do anything," Leo said, not believing it, not expecting Olson would.

"Well, sure. That could be. But we don't need a conviction at trial, right? Just a cooperative judge and an astronomical bail. Then we can put her in a nice box. And in prison, well, who knows?" He shrugged. "A shiv? You know what that means?"

Leo felt the tremor in his arms. *The government wanted to murder his daughter.* And when a government wants to kill you, he knew, there is nothing you can do.

No, he thought, *you can do whatever they ask, for one more minute of life for her.*

Olson stood up. "You don't have to show me out. I already know my way around your house."

He picked up the *Ba* from his desk, Freud's soul, and put it in his pocket. "A souvenir, okay? I meant to get it last time."

"Put it back."

Olson dropped it back down, chipped the edge of an ear that had survived four thousand years. "Look, you say she's innocent, I'm prepared to believe you. I don't really give a fuck about her. You do this work for us, we get Healy for a good long time, all her troubles, your troubles, they disappear. Think about it, okay? Don't reply in anger."

Leo flew to Boston the next day, met Beth for lunch at a place that had cartoons by his former patient decorating fake columns down the center. It made him remember that regrettable time when he'd mistrusted his own attachment to her; too strong, he'd thought, vaguely sexualized, when it had probably been no more than normal. He had been precipitous with her, but stepping away had to have been the right thing to do for her, his sadness surely getting to be a burden, and his daughter deserving the joy of her own youth. But he could see now that Beth might have felt it as an abandonment. Could it have helped lead to this recklessness? A plea for attention?

But she hadn't wanted his attention for years, hadn't even wanted to talk to him, only exchange letters. He wrote carping, desperate ones, and received replies from Marat. This was the first time they'd been face-to-face since a year ago when he'd heard noises at four in the morning that had nearly given him a heart attack. A robber or a policeman? No, his daughter wearing a yellow rain slicker and carrying her fiddle outside its case.

Clumsily, he'd used that occasion to apologize for what had happened with the *Commentary* article, the way it had been used—when he'd meant it only to say that she and her friends might all be getting into dangerous waters. "You probably hated me for it, eh?"

Her face had been blank in reply.

"Well, how could you not? And then that *Life* magazine piece!" He'd smiled, reminding himself to open his lips, show his hideous teeth. How had the magazine gotten those pictures of Beth as an infant? he wondered. The break-ins—his office in New York and their home in Great Neck robbed the same week. That must have already been the FBI.

"Yeah, well," she'd said then, "you made me famous, Dad. Got me elected to the Sexy Six. I should thank you, actually." Her words carefully chosen, no doubt, to let him know that he'd helped put her in even greater danger.

"Can I get your mother?"

"No," she'd said that night. "I gotta go, Dad, B.C.'s waiting," and she'd walked down the hall, the violin perched incongruously over her shoulder like a gun.

Then at this "lunch" place, she said, "If you help them get Healy, you'll never see me again. I mean it. Besides, what do they need you for anyway? They must have dozens of shrinks on the payroll. Are you that fucking famous?" Her voice screeched a little. Making herself hard didn't come naturally to her, he thought. Not with him, anyway, and maybe, he hoped, not with anyone. Though it could be done, of course; it was a trick even a fool could learn.

"No," Leo said. "They want me because I'm your father and you're

Healy's friend. They think it will break his spirit. They hope probably it will turn him against you. Do you think it will?"

"No way." Her face softened. "You should order something, Dad. You look thin."

"But look, darling, if I don't do this, he made it clear they'll frame you. He implied . . ." Leo started to cry, then. "No. He didn't imply. The agent said that if I didn't cooperate they would have you locked up—maybe just because you couldn't make bail. And then they'd have you killed."

"Bullshit." She smiled, lovely, straight, stupid teeth.

"Dear God, do you understand what I'm saying?"

"Yeah, well, I'll take my chances." She bit into a greasy hamburger sandwich, mostly cheap bread. "They're paper tigers, Dad."

Like saying makes it so, he thought, but he didn't smile, meanly or otherwise. These young Americans like his daughter, they were the real paper tigers, he knew, dreaming that the Eighth Route Army waited at their beck and call. She had on one of those blue work shirts they all wore these days—everyone but the workers, probably. They'd only had a few women in his cell in Vienna, attractive in their way, as all women were to him then, but they'd been more dour than his daughter, far less charmingly slangy and whimsical. Would his comrades have listened to a woman then, in any case—made her one of the leadership? The Sexy Six! God, that name! He admired her green eyes, her round cheeks and even teeth. Listen? They would have followed her anywhere.

"You know, darling, I once hoped you'd become a doctor."

"Tend the whole, eh?"

"I think you're very gifted psychologically."

"You mean I know how to hurt you, Dad."

He laughed. "Which analysis of why I called you gifted just proves my point. You *are* gifted."

Beth ate the last bite of her hamburger. "All done," she said, almost proudly, reminding him of herself at three. She had wanted to stand up on the swing at the playground in those days, and he had to tell her no, making her cry furiously, scream that she "really really really didn't like him anymore." She'd always had a big personality, he thought. Operatic—*if* she had been on stage, singing. *Hysterical,* otherwise.

She left him at the booth without saying good-bye, walked out past the pinball machines, up the steps to the street. Still, Leo knew he had to do this thing for Olson to try to save her life—what choice did he have?—even if it meant she really really really wouldn't like him anymore.

"Michael Healy," Dr. Leo Jacobs said from the witness stand, "may have thought he did this bombing because he opposed the war. But many people oppose this terrible war and don't blow up buildings. For that you must have some additional, some additional . . ." He couldn't remember the word, made a squared-off motion with his hand, pushing toward the prosecutor's chest.

Dr. Jacobs, too, Laura noticed, had long, skinny fingers like her own. Would his nonexistent soul join with hers in the nonexistent blessed space, chatting until the Messiah came?

Dr. Jacobs saw his daughter's friend, his patient's daughter, laugh at his ludicrous accent, his weak body, his broken spirit. He lost his way.

"You said some additional . . ."

He tried to concentrate. He had to get through this for his daughter's sake, and do it in a style that pleased his impresario, his Svengali, Special Agent Olson. "Some additional? . . . some additional? . . . impulsion, yes. That is to say, to do such a thing you must also have the additional energy of a neurotic motive."

"And do you know what that motive was, Dr. Jacobs?"

"I don't know his motive. I have an interpretation. A construction."

"Yes?" The prosecutor turned his broad, unhappy face up to heaven for strength. "Could you give us your interpretation, sir?"

Behind her, Laura heard one student whisper to another that Healy had probably blown the place up from envy—sibling rivalry, you know? That would have been the additional impulsion. "Yeah, like who's Hans' true son, him or Kopfman? Why wait till you're old enough to publish papers when you can just blow Martin the fuck up?"

But Laura knew that was crap. Wasn't it? *There's another guy, too,* he had murmured that day by the golden river. *Gifted.*

"Your construction?" the DA said, sounding angry with someone. "Sir?"

"Yes. Michael had been beaten by his father with a long pole until his back bled. Naturally, this both humiliated and terrified him. A person who has gone through experiences like these, he wants to take the power into his own hands, he wants to be the one with the stick."

"The stick?"

"Yes. In this case the dynamite."

"So are you saying that Michael Healy wouldn't have cared whether he hurt people? Or that he would *want* to hurt them?"

"Yes, he would want to hurt them."

"Could you repeat that for the jury, Doctor? You speak so quietly, I don't think they heard you. Would Michael have *wanted* to hurt people?"

"Asked and answered," Harrison barked.

"Overruled."

"Yes, I think he would have wanted to hurt them."

"So you're saying that Michael Healy didn't do this horrible thing to stop the war he says he hated so much? Michael Healy actually did this in order to hurt people?"

"Politics is . . ." He looked over at his daughter, who stared at him, her lovely face distorted with fury. "I don't know," he said. "I mean, what are political motives, really? There's no beginning and no end to the world's violence, is there?" He looked at his hands; his long fingers, most twice broken, infiltrated by arthritis, all aching in unison now. "Maybe Michael's father and the war and its violence are made of the same cloth."

Michael's father—wearing a broad red tie whose large, unruly knot looked like it was attacking his throat—leaned forward, hands on his thighs, to hear better, to drink in all of this man's putrid lies. He had only once in his life struck his son in anger, and that had been to protect the boy from this very man's demon daughter—his seeing the evil in her dark eyes from the first moment she'd stood at his door. Then he'd taken his son's wrists, tied them together with his belt, and for the first and *only* time in Michael's life, got the broom handle from its place in the back of the coat closet, beat his son with it across his back and shoulders, praying that just maybe if he whacked him hard enough now, Michael might yet grow up to be a sensible man, and not follow those rich bastards and their murderous seditious dreams that could only lead him to the black-iron gates of prison, while his lordly comrades would go strolling back up the circular drives to their grand white homes.

And now the father was as bad as the daughter. Government agents had threatened John Healy, too, told tales to his boss, insinuated things about the dynamite, so he'd lost his job. And yesterday the bank had called to say they wanted to speak to him about his loan. All because he wouldn't turn against his son! How could a man live with himself, talking like that and after swearing to God to tell the truth? Did this bastard understand that his lies would send a brilliant boy—so much more worthwhile than himself or his daughter—to jail for twenty years?

"Perhaps the men who order the killing in Vietnam," the doctor said now, "on both sides, I mean, are people whose parents have scarred them, and their parents before them . . ."

The prosecutor wondered if he could object that his own witness's answers were irrelevant. Too late. Jacobs was still going, almost whispering to himself now. "You know I sometimes think that to be a parent, even to educate . . ." He turned toward the jury, thinking not of Vietnam or beaten children but of his own much-loved daughter, who stared at him with such anger, slamming her foot down on the wooden floor over and over.

The judge shouted, "Young lady, stop banging your foot," but Beth was already up and walking out of the courtroom.

On the way, she looked at Billy's sketch of her dad. "Maybe you should call it," she said, "*the good German,*" her lips going awry in a grim parody of a smile, though, because that was unfair, she knew. Still, his weep-for-all-woundedness wouldn't do, either, she thought, because weeping for all but *doing* nothing was no different than being a murderer in times like these, when silence means consent, when choices have to be made. Why couldn't he see that?

A journalist from the *Herald* stood in front of the door. "Miss," he shouted, "how does it feel to have your father—"

She knocked him over a standing ashtray. That would be another assault charge, she thought, as she ran off down the five flights of stairs, each step teaching her how foolish she'd been, how much she still loved him, had long ago swallowed him whole, and even the withering disdain she wanted to direct at him would be done, she knew, with *his* tight-lipped, disdainful smile, and a sentence ending with an *eh?* To hate him was to hate herself, leaving her with a wearying bitterness that ate at every part of her.

She ran down First Street for the bus. Worst of all, he'd lied like that for her own good, to save her from government goons with shivs. She dropped her fare in. How could she hate him for that? No, the worst was, she didn't *want* to go to jail, she feared the goon with the shiv, and despite all her threats at Tommy's Lunch she wanted him to make her sit down on the swing, wanted him to save her. How could she ever make up for that cowardice?

The next day, Beth walked around the empty SDS house getting her things—the temperature rising, she felt, even as she moved from room to room, boiling to a certainty. Two weeks ago she'd been indicted in Cook County for the Days of Rage, but not charged with conspiracy—only because, you know, how could a *girl* have actually *planned* something? And she'd been indicted in Suffolk for burning that fucking police cruiser, some pig having taken pictures of all of them, hands in the air, dancing 'round the flames. And then the Middlesex pigs added the demos at University Hall—when she'd actually been in Chicago! But they didn't give a damn, figured they'd get her on one thing or another, or just run her around like they did Sugar Cane, so many busts on him now that the liberals had abandoned him and SNAP couldn't make bail anymore. He had to spend months in jail on every cooked-up firearms charge—till, oh, my, what a surprise—they found that his permit checked out.

That morning a cop had arrested everyone in the collective for shooting out the windows at the Cambridge pig station. "Oh, how I wish I had done that," Beth told the guy who'd cuffed her, but it had been a totally bogus beef, and all Paulie's fault. He'd gotten caught shoplifting a couple of bottles of Southern Comfort and had crumbled when the cops beat his kidneys, signed this lie about the windows and her as the ringleader. The charge had been "conspiracy to commit murder and promote anarchy." She'd barely made bail.

Still *that* had heft, made her almost proud that the pigs had finally started doing a white woman the way they did Sugar Cane, but she just didn't have the inner strength to do time the way Sugar did. She piled her Al Green, James Brown, O. V. Wright, and Bobby Bland records into a suitcase, and put her books, her poetry, her letters, her journals, and her violin into the bathtub. She splashed the pages with kerosene they kept for cocktails.

Must it be?

Oh, for God's sake, she thought, *I'm quoting Beethoven.*

Well, roll over, Beethoven. She dropped a match in the tub. *And give my father the news.*

Flames singed the ceiling, smoke stunk up the place and made the audience's eyes sting. She backed away. Her father might cry to see her burning Rilke's poetry, but why couldn't he see that Rilke had got it

right—she must change her life. This was the funeral pyre of the old
Beth. Still, remembering him made her reach in, grab the violin by the
strings. The rest of her resolve didn't weaken, though. By next week, she
swore, she would have a new name, a new hometown, a new driver's
license, a new hair color, a new past, and a future that would be written
by the necessities of the People's War. She would join B.C., who even
then had the great honor to be training under Sugar Cane at a farm in
Kansas. Her Weathermen comrades would be her sisters and brothers,
and the Third World's freedom fighters would be her father and mother.

That same night, lying in bed in the attic, Laura felt how Michael's spirit
hid from her, though she stroked his legs to woo him. Maybe she'd
begun to cling to him too hard, now that he held Beth's life, and maybe
hers, in his hand, become too much the courtesan, like the housewife
who does it for the Bloomingdale's charge card . . . or not to be beaten.
Not that Michael would beat her, or anyone. Dr. Jacobs was awfully
wrong about that. What he *could* do was cut a deal for himself, probably get years off for turning Beth in. Olson longed to have her in his production. Because she was the camp survivor's daughter? Rebecca, the
buxom Jewess? Athena X, the comic book heroine? The subject of the
Commentary essayist? The *Life* magazine star? The Weatherman leader?

Well, maybe Michael *should* trade Beth. She traced his thigh sinews
with a finger. For a long time now, she had deeply loved Michael, his
brilliance, his forthrightness and honesty, and, alas, his daring. *Ah, love,*
she thought without mockery, *let us be true / To one another! for the
world, which seems / To lie before us like a land of dreams . . . Hath
really neither joy, nor love, nor light.*

She stroked his stiff dick lightly, until he suddenly came into her,
holding her arms down—not one of the games they usually played—and
pounded at her furiously.

When *he* came, her usually considerate lover just rolled off. "That
man today," he said disgustedly, "he's wrong about me. Totally wrong."

"Jesus Christ, of course he is," she said, running her fingers softly
over the ridges on his back. She looked up at the silver segments of insulation that she and Michael had finally stapled in between the beams of
his cousin's attic. "And Harrison will just take him apart tomorrow."
Was Michael really angry that the doctor had called him neurotic?
Didn't he know that for Dr. Jacobs that was just another word for
human—which was really what Dr. Jacobs himself had blubbered on the
stand: the Vietnamese guerrillas, the U.S. presidents, all make history
from neurotic motives. Which meant, she supposed, that only the ana-

lyzed are well adjusted—like Dr. Jacobs—and prove their health by having no motives, making no history, doing nothing but weeping for the world.

Michael got up and sat alone, naked, his thinning frame hunched on his stool, staring out the window at the Yellow Cab sign. Laura watched him but couldn't think of anything more to say, any more history to make. So she cried for him, for herself, and for the world until she fell asleep.

"I want to plead guilty," Michael told Harrison. "I want to use this trial to make a statement." Michael didn't care if the jury, or Hans, found him innocent of attempted murder. He wanted to be found to be *justified*. Michael was what her father called an *allrightnick*—though her father had been talking about the family ghost then, her mother's therapist, his client, Dr. Jacobs, the one who had helped drive Michael to this extremity. Whatever Michael's fantasy had been the night of the bombing, now he didn't want to take the long pole from his father's hands and beat somebody else. No, he wanted the whole world to watch while the government beat him. "My suffering," he said, "could bring light."

Should she tell Harrison his client was insane, thought he heard crucified photons screaming in agony?

"No," Harrison Baker hissed. "Don't be a fool. You let me do my work now, Michael." He would show it couldn't have been attempted murder or there wouldn't have been a warning call. The DA had overreached. He could win this.

"No," Michael said. "I have to use this trial to talk about the War."

"No, you *don't*," Harrison said. He grabbed Michael's skinny arm and twisted it behind his back. "You do *not* have to."

Even thinned down, Laura thought, Michael could have sent his lawyer into next week. But that wasn't his style. He looked up at Harrison with docile eyes. "You're really, really hurting me, Mr. Baker."

"Damn right I'm hurting you." Harrison pushed his arm still higher until the veins became visible in Michael's temples. "But this isn't half so bad as what the cops are going to do to you today in jail."

"Today? I'm not ready to go to jail today!"

Harrison laughed and let go of his arm. "My dear boy," he said, "it's like death. No one's *ever* ready to go to jail. Hey, you're really surprised, aren't you? You didn't know that they'd cancel your bail as soon as you plead guilty."

"Harrison's right, darling," Laura said softly. "Please come home with me tonight."

"Mr. Baker, I need to talk to Laura alone."

He took her arm, and they walked up and down the dirty corridor. She heard a gavel bang, another trial starting.

"I have to do this."

She didn't know what to say, except "Please don't."

"You remember that day I showed you what I . . . learned on Winter Hill. I told you that there's a linkage in the universe. Your brother changed, there, you know, in the grave, and Billy's mind changed, too. Faster than the speed of light."

"Yeah, I forgot that there's nothing faster than the speed of light." Thus leading to Billy's mistake about the I-Lab.

"Right. That's what Einstein thought. A two-proton particle is split," he said, "and each proton follows its own path. And remember, before you look, the proton's quantum states are superpositions, so it spins in both directions at once."

"Right. Overcome with ambivalence."

"Okay. But then you measure it and the proton has to choose. Which means that at the exact same moment, its twin, over in France, or on the other side of Saturn, for that matter, it has to change, too, no time to think about it—so the equations will still balance the way they should."

"How does the twin know?" And why does he care? But it was probably like her and Beth, her and Frank: the poor twin cares; she can't help herself.

He shrugged. "Exactly. It would have to know faster than the speed of light. Which is impossible, Einstein said."

"So they must have got it wrong." I.e., her brother didn't suffer in the grave, or if he did, Billy sure as hell didn't know about it.

"Yeah. But they can't do the experiment yet. And *I* think the protons *will* turn out to be linked forever, and by something faster than light."

"What's that?" she asked, happy to be his straight man. All of this too awful, what had happened to Kopfman, what would happen to Michael.

"Love," Michael said. He leaned forward and kissed her on the lips. "It's faster than light. I think we're linked particles, Laura. You and me. Whatever happens to you, I'll know wherever I am, even in jail, and faster than the speed of light."

It was sweet, it was wonderful, but it was too grand—like a comic book. Jail, she thought, would probably turn out to be the one place even photons couldn't go.

. . .

Still Michael made *his* deal with the DA, which the DA accepted even though he knew it wasn't what Olson wanted. He wanted the dame, famous daughter of the famous asshole. Well, too bad. This, the DA thought, is close enough for government work. Healy would plead guilty to the maximum charge, attempted murder, the charge that had been Agent Olson's vindictive idea, and one that they'd never had a fucking chance of winning. In return Healy could present mitigating witnesses who would apply the most precious balm to his wounded heart: they would say he had done the right thing.

Fuckin' A, the prosecutor thought; *You can condemn this moronic war till the bars close, for all I care.*

The next morning the defense presented Vietnam vets who cried as they described strafing school busses and assassinating village leaders and torturing Vietcong suspects in airless wooden boxes. They told stories of napalming, Zippoing, and phosphorus-bombing villages, and murdering mothers holding babies, tossing their bodies into a ditch and then, and then . . . and then Laura drank a big cup of green bile for hanging back with Jesse and Arkey in their attic room and not helping Michael and Beth and Billy to end the War; no longer knowing if she'd hesitated because the idea had been a bad one and she somehow really foresaw the wounded man, or like Beth had said, the State hadn't said it was all right to oppose their daily murders, and she was a cowardly, obedient, good German.

That afternoon a white-haired former senator said the government's lies had already made too many wounded. And a priest said that if Michael hadn't been beaten by his father, he surely *had* been by the class system, and so he'd perhaps come to feel the pain of the world more inwardly and deeply than others did—for who but somebody who had felt the nails of this world in his own flesh could speak for the children who were beaten down by the bombs of this war, who else could speak for the suffering, the maimed, or the vast unnumbered dead?

A Berrigan meant a lot, to the former St. Al's choirboy, a special sweetness suffusing his face, while Laura herself thought, *Silly priest, don't you know it's an endless task to help the dead, they need so very much good done for them.*

Then, before the priest had finished, mimes dressed in army fatigues zombie-walked down the aisles of the courtroom, their faces painted white, their clothes daubed with stage blood, their "hands" falling off into people's laps as pieces of juicy liver or delicious beef heart. The

judge, enraged, rose from his bench and banged his gavel, while spectators screamed and jumped in fear of . . . cow parts. Laura looked around
for Beth, to share the joke with her, but Beth must have been off planning some Weatherman action to follow the trial. Laughing, Laura
threw the meat back at a mime's painted head, while the judge banged
and banged and finally shouted to the bailiffs to clear the court.

The next day Michael testified, wearing a knit tie, a green corduroy
jacket, and brown chinos. Jail had already faded his dear pale skin to
mime-white, and he spoke slowly, like a man who hadn't had enough
sleep or vegetables. He turned his bewildered eyes to the judge and
sometimes toward Laura, as if his older woman—how long ago that
seemed now!—could show him the way forward here, too. Laura
wanted to cry, knowing that Michael's white face was the outer rind of a
great mind, one being turned to moldy cheese by jail. Laura inclined her
head, gestured toward the jury.

Michael turned to them, said that he hadn't grown up in terror of his
father, like Dr. Jacobs had said, but of the powers of this world and *their*
big sticks, nuclear missiles that could make his family suck water from
stones, eat their friends, and live in holes. He escaped from that childhood terror, he said, into the numbers that underlie nature—a secret language God had hidden there for us, so we could discover His presence
and what He wanted from us.

He'd imagined that MIT was a cathedral where men worked to
understand that intricate code. Then he found out that they mostly did
science to make even more of the very same missiles! "Look," he said,
"I'm just a physicist. I know numbers. I don't know the words to justify
what I did. But I do know in my heart that it was the right thing to do.
Despite what that man said, I didn't do it to hurt anyone."

He paused and looked at Laura again. "I did see a light in the building," he said quietly. "But I knew that even if there was someone in
there, he would have had plenty of time to leave once the police
responded to the warning call. I mean, I wonder if the cops are maybe
the ones with a little extra impulsion, you know, maybe *they* wanted
people to be hurt." He took a tiny black notebook from his shirt pocket,
looked down at it sadly. "Because I've been over and over my calculations, and I still can't find a flaw."

Michael read some numbers, that might be, SA Olson knew, right
as rain, local police counterintelligence having been told by its FBI
advisors—such was Hoover's inspiring audacity—that a few small dis-

asters could be staged to wake the country up. Maybe they'd followed his lead. Olson raised his brows and nodded to the judge.

"That's enough for today," the judge said.

That afternoon, Olson and the prosecutor offered Michael a last chance to redeem himself before judgment: give up Beth, do a smidgen of soft time, and spend Christmas 1972 with his family. Refuse again and he would spend an eternity in a swimming pool filled with donkey piss.

"Who's Beth?" Michael said.

The next day the judge said confidently that he didn't believe Michael had acted alone. Michael lied still, and in the judge's opinion his plea was no plea. He gave Michael Aloysius Healy the maximum sentence for attempted murder: twenty years.

People rose from their seats shouting, "Pig! Bastard pig! You're the liar! You're the murderer!" Laura, forgetting the danger of her telltale voice, screamed along with the others, while TAC Squad cops waded in from the front, holding their long clubs with both hands, and pushed the spectators toward the door. Jesse sat down on the cement floor and cops handcuffed him, then lifted him up off his feet by his arms and dragged him out backward.

In jail, though, Michael Healy certainly had to act alone. He sat with his legs crossed on the cold cement floor of the dark cell, terrified. Each moment in hell, he remembered a priest saying in sixth grade, becomes infinite. Eternity is an eternity of infinite moments. Twenty years! He hoped he'd done the right thing when he'd tried to do something small to stop the War, and when he'd said no to the crew-cut Satans who came to him with Judas deals. But now he found he couldn't even hope to bear the consequences for what he'd done unless there was a secret way to lose himself for a while and not be *here,* when he was, the judge had promised, going to be in this damp, cold, concentrated, unkind darkness forever.

He tried to do some equations in his head, but, like Kopfman, he couldn't use the numbers anymore. Too scared, or maybe he'd never learned enough, or he'd made too big a mistake with them, because even if he was right about the time and the warning call, all that meant was that the police had collaborated with him in hurting Martin, a cat smeared out, neither alive nor dead, till Michael had opened the box.

Jesus, *why* had he ever opened the fucking box?

Well, *most* people think the cat's alternative fates are murdered along with the cat, Hans had said once. But maybe the other universes go on living, too. "Perhaps every time we make a measurement, we create an alternate universe that has the other quantum state in it. Some universes where Schrödinger's cat lives; some where he dies." Universes as numerous as bunnies, and each with an alternate Michael, another Kopfman in it, too! A zillion universes where he hadn't walked up the steps with that idiot singsong, *Light, me, suffer* shit jingling in his head. And some universe maybe where the police responded to warning calls and cleared the building in time.

Or maybe not. "I'm dubious," Hans said. They had paused for a moment, breathed in the well-aged dust of his office, saying farewell to the other worlds.

Another time, they'd been talking about Hawking's new paper, sipping Lapsang souchong, which, for as long as they talked, was the most delicious beverage Michael had ever tasted. Hans took him seriously, played the game the old man called *Why is there anything rather than nothing?* "But that might be the wrong question. Ask why not just anything," the old man said, "but *this* anything. *This* universe, with its physical laws, is the only universe God could have made if He wanted to make sentient moral agents. *If* there is a God. And if we are sentient moral agents. Two very dubious premises."

And *this* universe *had* to have both order and entropy—"which perhaps for a physicist means good and evil"—had to have them all mixed together, just the way they are. Otherwise, there couldn't be life-forms like Hans and Michael—two people sitting here in a dusty office, drinking smoky tea, thinking about how intertwined are good and evil.

Was that comforting? Evil accounted for as necessary to life, just like oxygen—and no oxygen either, if you didn't have evil too. Michael had repeated to Hans something a priest had said to him once: "Sin has been ordained by God, in relation to redemption; for otherwise redemption itself could not have been ordained."

Hans had smiled wanly at that, showing teeth stained by millenniums of tea and cigars, the mischief in his eyes suddenly burned out, turning him into an old woman wearing a tight dress too young for her years, this whole God-thing, after all, Michael saw, just a game with words to him, Christ, evil; that stuff meaning . . . nothing. Nice of him to play it with a child, he thought; angry, though, that he was suddenly a little boy in the old man's rheumy eyes.

The cell walls pressed in on him, and the fact that this universe had to have evil in it didn't comfort him much if *he* was the evil. He wasn't entropy, he swore; he wasn't evil. "I made a fucking mistake!" he shouted.

"You and me both," someone yelled back.

And what had Kopfman worked on in that building? Wasn't *that* the real mistake? Hadn't Father Berrigan said so? Which meant Michael *wasn't* the evil one. But Beth's father had been right in a way, too; Michael knew he wasn't an angel either. What he was, actually, was a man in jail, with no mythological tatters, no alternate universes or smeared cats left to wrap around himself. He felt the cell, the whole fucking universe, getting smaller and smaller, denser and denser, his heart beating harder and harder, as they all moved toward the end of time, a region of infinite density, like the one where God had once cast Satan. That was the foreordained inevitable end of the universe and of Michael. And unless God decided to pull a new creation in the next county, all the supposedly resurrected bodies would have to occupy a few cubic centimeters where time and space had come to an end, with Mr. Lin's entrails tucked nicely inside Mr. Yin's eyeballs. Well, could be. Maybe God *had* left everything to run down just like that. Good idea, Michael thought. God cancels a project gone bad. He'd never felt comfortable in this universe, this body. Oh, maybe once or twice gliding through the water at the end of a long race; but he always touched the wall. Or maybe after his indictment, when he'd asked Laura to ride him— but that had only filled him with shame in the end. Anyway, he knew he *shouldn't* feel comfortable with this pissing, shitting garment. God had taken off his Suit of Light one time and put on a human body; and it had repelled him so much he couldn't wait to get crucified to get it off.

Fine. Best of all, then, would be if Christ was right *here* in the crap with humanity, but no trapdoor this time, no Judgment and no Judge, Him suffering like Michael *here* in this piss-smelling cell, this shit-smelling body, shrinking along with the universe, disappearing like that dot on their old television set.

Or maybe, since that was perhaps beyond his powers to bring about, what he needed was just to make his own mind disappear like the shrinking universe. No more mind-*expanding* shit for him—he wanted heroin, the black hole medicine, the one that let you fall inward on yourself forever. He'd snorted some once with his cousin, just back in the world after Tet, the two of them sitting openly on the porch of his own family's three-decker in Somerville, his cousin slowly, teasingly stroking a pimple on his nose, then finally handing the plate to him, not as if he thought they were so golden that no one would come for them, but as if his cousin just didn't care who came, because someone bad, his cousin knew now, surely someday would, and he wanted to be good and stoned when that happened.

Michael had put a thin straw into his nostril and snuffled up the bitter powder, then closed his eyes and felt his grief grow slowly more distant, the War and his bulky father both become a dark cloud behind him, a thin black dispersal over their house, over the whole street, where the triple-deckers and their porches seemed in his mind's eye to lean into each other like drunks at a bar, the gloomy father-cloud now spreading behind them, as if *here* wasn't quite *here* anymore but a new world covered over by a darkness that wasn't kindly but that was at least spread widely, thinly, distantly.

He got down on his knees in his cell and actually heard himself praying to the Christ he'd just told to kill Himself, asking that God let his clever cousin get smack to him in jail so he wouldn't have to be here with the other prisoners who shouted, banged on the bars, played little sour pipes and harmonicas, wouldn't have to be *here*, most of all, with himself, with his rage, his guilt, and his heart's long-meditated desire to make its very own jailbreak from his body.

Ten years later, Laura felt like she was on the way to meet someone a little like Michael, a man so morally certain of himself that she couldn't help longing for his approval—though *this* guy had tried to slam her best friend in jail. And tonight was All Hallows' Eve, Beth's birthday!

So Bobby was a prosecutor, and that meant she was . . . who? . . . the prosecutor's moll? But this was the same guy, she told Beth-in-her-mind, who had led a protest at Seale's trial. There had to be a lot of good in him.

In fact, she'd gone to New Haven herself that time, seen Bobby in action, rallying his troops. "The president of Yale," she'd written Michael in jail, "scared of a rampage, turned the place into every Rad's alma mater. We listened to speeches, shouted 'Free Huey,' and 'Power to the People,' while the Bugs stood on the sidelines, helplessly beating their legs—or their billy clubs—on their shields." Laura sent Michael updates like that almost every day of his first year inside, toting up each slogan chanted, every rock or bomb thrown after Nixon waltzed into Cambodia—as if each missile carried the message "Michael Healy Did the Right Thing." A hundred colleges had gone on strike that June. Kids ransacked armories, rioted for two nights at San Jose State and Hobart, drove the cops right back off the campuses. "Some students in Ohio fire-bombed their ROTC building; then they launched so many rocks at the firemen that the governor had to call in the National Guard. On TV, I heard Rhodes say he'd *eradicate* the rioters. Jesse turned to me and said, 'Like Orangeburg.'

" 'Or Newark,' I said, to stay in the game.

"So maybe Rhodes means it, Michael, maybe we should all watch out."

But then and now, she thought, blacks and whites lived in separate houses—and the white kids figured they didn't need to know what happened in Newark or at Orangeburg. "The students at Kent State didn't back down," she wrote Michael the next day. "Maybe they should have, though. Maybe the white has kind of worn off our skins, at least for a while. The vice president says we're Nazis, and true Americans should 'act accordingly,' that is: kill us."

Every time she'd gone to a demo after that she'd nearly vomited. And she wasn't the only one who'd sucked down too much Nervous Gas; the crowds got smaller and smaller, soon the same faces over and over, and those faces more bewildered with anxiety each time, or twisted with fury. Then "the New Year's Gang" (a couple of kids? a mighty army?) made more light from ANFO at the Army Math Building in Madison, and bagged another mathematician—struck him dead this time. "But *we're* life," she wrote Michael, "*they're* death. Right?*"

"Remember, Laura," Michael had written back, "*the War hasn't stopped. And the War is death in a very concentrated form.*"

Helen—renamed Sat Siri by her guru—offered to help Laura with her anxiety; but Laura had just enough Kundalini left in the tank to run terrified and despairing past the soldiers at Dupont Circle, or in Berkeley after the Chicago verdict, or in Cambridge to protest Michael's sentence, her and a few hundred of his (or were they MyKill's?) admirers streaming down Massachusetts Avenue shouting "All Power to the People!" Jesse and street kids he'd organized in Worcester had set off toward the Center for International Affairs, while Arkey and a few men Laura knew from her Social Relations class tore up bricks from the sidewalk near Adams House. Then they charged down the street, tossed their red missiles through the huge windows of Design Research, and the Holyoke Center and Cambridge Trust and Krackerjacks, which was a store that sold "unisex" bell-bottom pants and shirts with floppy collars, *a store that sold us,* Laura thought as her cab moved uptown now among the big banks whose plate glass the Weather Underground had once actually bombed, *not the things we could never get, but the things we could so easily have, that we wanted, that we paid for, and then were so disappointed by, raging at the ORG. because the magic hadn't worked, we remained trapped in our singular bodies, our singular gender.* No more famous than before, no more beautiful, no more desirable. No less guilty. Still *here.*

That day in Cambridge, Billy had shouted "Stop!" at the kid from Revere, the greaser seduced by Beth's fierce bravado, not yet underground with Beth. But Snake had gone on drawing his arm back, set to hurl a brick through the lead-mullioned windows of Adams house, when CGC Travis, everyone's pal, revealed himself as an agent provocateur,

long-hidden minion of Zargon, rank with the B.O. of hell. He grabbed
Billy by the neck instead of Snake, threw him to the ground and kicked
him in the head a few times, furious probably that CGC was always the
sidekick with the idiot grin, giving his artist the beating that Laura
dreamt *she* deserved for what she'd done to Kopfman and to Michael;
and for all she hadn't done to end this fucking war. Clouds of tear gas
swirled up around them, and Laura began to turn in a circle, doing her
familiar bewilderment step, stumbling and spinning down Bow Street,
abandoning Billy to his beating.

But as the taxi turned up Sixth, she could hear Jeffrey Schell warning
her not to let LJ Productions make a three-hanky story out of *that* one.
Billy Green could still breathe despite his slightly flattened nose, he could
still run a successful comic book company, become the ever-more-
famous Billy Bad Ears, still dig secret tunnels so he could leave *here*.
Kopfman, and most of the vets she saw each day, they couldn't ever
manage that.

Though after Kopfman had testified, Michael's one-armed cousin, the
Vietnam vet, had approached him in the hallway to the courtroom,
promising to help with that very problem. "You know you're not the
only person who wants to escape this shithole. I know how you feel."

"Yeah. Well, I doubt it," Kopfman said. Not nearly so naïve as
Hans thought him, Kopfman had known just what he'd been working on at the I-Lab: ways for the Army to use heat-seeking systems
to target missiles. He'd felt a tiny twinge about it at first, but forgot
the whole mess when he lost himself in the math, the problems keeping
him up happily late at night. Besides, he'd decided that the president
knew something he didn't know, so he was actually doing the right
thing. Then those fucking vets at Healy's trial had confirmed what he'd
felt all along: the president and the secretary of defense maybe did
know many things, but they never spoke the truth about any of them.
Now he felt furious, guilty, and, worst of all, implicated in his own
maiming. How could this one-armed man know about feelings as confused as that?

Michael's acne-scarred cousin laughed. In his family, he said, his
father had taught them that those rare times that someone offers to help,
you should say, *thank you*. But the cousin—who also took the best job
the government had offered, and also rested himself in the dream that
the president knew something he didn't—understood exactly how Martin Kopfman felt. So he forgave Kopfman his rudeness, and in a com-
radely way showed Kopfman how even a one-armed or one-eyed man

with ringing in his ears could cook the magic powder in a bent spoon and tie off the vein. Kopfman had grown to thank him, to depend on him for help, and to thank him some more, to thank him and thank him, sir, as much as Michael's cousin demanded, and whatever way he demanded, Kopfman's abject obedience reassuring Michael's cousin that the stick was in his hand now, he was the being-beyond-human one, alive, still, in all the world's sniper-hiding emptiness.

Then one night when Martin had just found a new syringe for himself, the young former physicist remembered the newspaper picture of the wounded monkeys in the primate lab at Madison. The white-coated arm had held a syringe like the one in Kopfman's hand that evening, the needle in the photo just about to enter the monkey's chest, and put "Sigmund" to sleep. *Be careful now,* he told himself, *if you don't want to end up like poor little Siggy.* He tied off, made a vein nearly overflow its bed, swabbed it down with a little cooling alcohol, and darted the needle in. "Pop goes the weasel!" He pushed the plunger.

"Bring the War Home!" B.C. nearly shouted when he read Kopfman's obituary to Beth in New York that March, his tongue steady but his hands crinkling the newspaper like an epileptic's accordion, B.C. already well pumped with his morning blend, crystal meth laced with the dream of making bombs they could use to do the courthouse where Murtaugh railroaded the Panther 21 the way they'd already done his house, or maybe the Centre Street Police Headquarters. "Bring the War home!" he shouted. "Bring the fucking war home!"

Six in the morning, almost everyone in bathrobes or boxers, fuzzed out from last night's dope and Weather Fry, Diana drinking coffee, Ted looking at the sports page, an ordinary American family of professional revolutionaries. They all ignored B.C.

All but Beth, eyes unfocused, who listened carefully to the little fizzyits' obit. She felt she'd been the fatal link in Kopfman's life—along with the War, yes, along with the class system, yes, but she, too, she kind of *personally.* And despite the self-criticism sessions, the trashings, the fights with the Grease meant to overcome her bourgeois fear of violence, still, this newspaper report filled her with lassitude. She remembered John Healy's hands on her breasts, trying to push her downstairs, like that touch had been the beginning of the end for Kopfman. *Resist!* she'd thought then. *Hell, No, We Won't Go Downstairs!* Michael's dad had screamed, "Bloody cunt!" and actually spit a great gob of poisonous phlegm at her. She'd probably have gone falling ass over teakettle if Michael hadn't come flying out of the apartment to her rescue. His father had let her go then, so he could bear-hug the flailing boy and drag him back into the apartment.

It had been Michael's pride, Beth knew, that had made him chase after her to the bus stop to ask, "Are you all right?" when really *he* was the one who wasn't all right, who couldn't protect himself. Could she? Because the question wasn't would they come for you with something a damn sight worse than a broom handle, but would you fight back when they did. And guilt? That wasn't the yattering of an absent fucking God; it was just the police inside you, saying *go along quietly now.* She'd made one last try to get Michael to jump bail, join her here, but he'd felt too guilty, wanted priests and judges to say he'd really been a good boy.

"Yeah," she said to B.C. "Bring the war home!" That helped beat the darkness back down inside her. Diana, the earliest riser, already in jeans and a man's white shirt, looked up from her coffee mug. Ted rubbed his hand across his stubbly cheeks, smiled weakly.

Cleaver and Stokely had been driven into exile, Beth reminded herself, and Sugar Cane had been nailed for the Roxbury school, of all things, sent away for ten years. "You're an accomplice to murder, Your Honor!" Harry had shouted as they dragged him off, too, for contempt. "You know the government will have this man assassinated in that prison! Just the way the FBI shot Fred Hampton in his bed!" The War at home had most certainly already begun, while Beth Jacobs and her friends went on drawing breath and doing nothing. Would she be one of those cowards who needed God's or the State's permission to do what needed to be done to help the world's black, brown, and yellow peoples? Most white kids weren't going to join that rainbow yet. Hell, even most blacks, Beth saw now, wouldn't join the struggle till the land was finally in flames. Well, good. She was honored that until then the Weathermen and Panthers would be the Vietcong's hands within the U.S.! "Bring the War home!" she shouted. "Bring the War home! Bring the fucking War home!" Alone; underground; but the Weathermen were ready, *so* fucking ready!

B.C. looked around the table bright-eyed, eager. Maybe, he said, they should fucking go ahead and put a bomb at the Fort Dix officers' dance—or anyplace, B.C. said, where there were white pigs who deserved to die, like the war criminal Martin Kopfman, like everyone who wasn't a Black Panther, a Young Lord, a Weatherman. "Bring the War home!" he shouted. "Bring the War home!" B.C. whooped, hand in front of mouth like a movie Indian, rallying the collective to vote for the bombing campaign. Che got it right, he shouted. Saint Che always got it right: now was the hour of the furnaces and only light should be seen!

. . .

Who knew what these little shits would burn next, Special Agent Olson thought, looking at the *Times* and eating breakfast at a lunch counter on St. Mark's Place. The smug students might think that because Kopfman was dead this show was over. *But it wasn't.* Because Kopfman, in Olson's considered opinion, wasn't dead by his own hand. He had been murdered, and there was a link, Olson was ever more sure, between Kopfman's death and the brilliant career of Beth Jacobs, the busty girl from *Life* magazine and all those comic books; and bloodlines, too, between her and all the other little shits who had so innocently said, "Who's Michael?" to him at Harvard, and "What dynamite?" as if they had thought they were so rich and powerful, such *chosen people,* that the law couldn't touch them. Probably some of them had placed the bomb at Judge Murtaugh's house. But the law would reach out to them, he swore—for he, like Dr. Jacobs, thought that he served not law, but Law, though he had, he would have said, a more realistic idea of what that meant than the good doctor, Hoover and hard experience both having taught him that both law and Law sometimes required intimidation, bribery, threats, even lawlessness if it were to have any presence at all on this fallen earth.

An anti-personnel bomb, though? Jesus, Beth thought, is that what she'd meant? They'd talked about things like that, sure, but was now the time for it? Beth's stomach knotted. Wasn't that still a job for their brothers overseas—soldier versus soldier?

Thank God Cathy said, "Shit, B.C., we're not prepared for the heat that would bring down."

That, too, Beth thought; not enough lawyers, bail money, or safe houses in their world for that. Weathermen had some tepid support now, but it would disappear when they actually killed anyone. If they even wasted somebody by accident, the whole country would turn right around and cheer the fascists when they crushed them.

B.C., embarrassed, pretended he was looking at the crossword in the *Times* while Diana said, "Maybe we should go after the court building next?"

"Yeah," Beth said again, sorry to see B.C. look so defeated. "We can still have lots of good fun that is funny." Someday, though, she promised, when the time was right, when the country surrounded the city, they *would* bring that fascist plague down on the whole fucking country and finally make white Americans decide: will you join the pigs or the world's peoples? Will you be targeted by our guns or theirs?

She would do that? Or wouldn't she always be one of those cow-

ardly Jews who needed God or the State's permission to defend themselves? No, she'd be ready, she swore. Like a promise to the future, she
gave the Athena X war cry then, the ululating, coruscating scream that
could lead men to their death, make the five people in the kitchen want
to leap from their skins into another braver dimension, and make B.C.
want to live up to all he imagined that scream contained. He didn't have
to wait for a vote! Beth had said *no* with her words, but Ninja B.'s
scream had said, *Do it, Speed! Do it now!* Make that fucking pipe bomb
and I'll love only you, not Snake, not Paulie! Only you!

So high on meth, History, and his secret identity, B.C./A.D. **Speed**,
early adapter of ponytails, sight-translator from the Spanish, indefatiga-
ble driver of the FolksWagon, lover of Beth, comic book star, and enemy
of imperialism, followed by drowsy Diana and Ted G., went down to the
basement to mix up the medicine. This time the KrazyKeds MyKill had
made for him went too fast; he ran right into himself from behind, the
collision making his hand shake so he accidentally touched the red wire
to the yellow instead of the blue.

Ten years later, Laura's cab went by the street where the house had been.
An apartment building had gone up there, replacing a town house that
had been built on the ruins of the one that B.C.'s bomb had destroyed.
Every March still, people came to the site and held candles—mourning
their lives probably, all they hadn't done for the War or because of it,
more than weeping for Diana Oughton or Ted Gold or B.C.

She had never gotten to know Speed, really, put off by his stutter and
his anger. Or maybe she'd never really tried, wanted him to be completely unknown and unknowable—utterly *not like her,* when really he
was all too knowable, and a lot like the rest of them, B.C. just not having
had Jesse's eyes there, at the last minute, to mirror his slathering jaws for
him, show him what he'd become and so stop him.

Jealousy made it hard for her to be fair to B.C., though he was in
many ways the *least* male chauvinist radical she'd ever met. B.C. always
helped do the dishes, the only man in the SDS house, and perhaps in the
known universe, who did. And days and nights, straight no chaser, he
would chauffeur Beth, asleep in the backseat, to Ann Arbor to win campus militants to the Weatherman line, then back to Great Neck to get her
violin from her father's house. B.C. liked strong women, argued with
them like they were his equals; and when they were the leaders he followed their orders, too, kept the bullshit to a minimum. But he knew
Laura wasn't you-bet-your-life serious about her politics, and he had no
time for that.

They'd maybe talked together precisely once. He'd been on speed, of course, but he'd had nowhere to drive the FolksWagon that day. "You think I'm too angry, right?" He'd pushed the long, dirty fingernails of his right hand into his left arm then, the pain probably meant to make him sit still, wait for her to reply.

But he couldn't. "Well, like how angry *should* I be at racism?" Hand shaking, he drank some coffee from a thick white Bickford cup, sloshed it down his chin.

She'd shrugged, agreeably, she hoped, feeling like a girl in a cage with Leo the Lion—and the cat shooting meth for days.

"Or like I'll bet you're one of those people who think it's really my stuttering makes me so angry?" The words all in a rush, like in an A.D. Speed speech bubble, tiny letters pressed tightly together—sometimes so much that they became unreadable black lines. "But you think I just put that anger somewhere else, pile all of mankind's grievances since Adam's Fall on the White Whale's humped back, huh?"

That being his favorite book. He = Ahab. Whale = the Leviathan States of America. Laura had nodded, wishing she had a whip and a chair.

"Well, look, if I'm like bullshit about the way my mouth gets twisted up when I just want to say some simple thing like *give me a donut,* so fucking what? I *use* that anger. It gives me more energy, you know—a little extra speed." He smiled—tensely, but he smiled. Or showed his teeth anyway. "I know what's important. And it's Vietnam, not the fucking donut."

She seized the opportunity to hear her own voice. "But it maybe means you can't see the situation clearly, B.C., you know, like you might choose the wrong target, blow up monkeys by mistake."

"Yeah, but I *know* that, Laura. That's why I leave it to Beth to choose the targets. Then I like use my extra energy to drive another thousand miles in whatever fucking direction she tells me to."

She hadn't looked for another chance to chat with him. Maybe she didn't want to know B.C. because she was just plain jealous of him; he'd replaced Frank in Beth's heart. No, he'd replaced *her,* that's why she'd hated him, had hated her own brother a little, for that matter.

She told the taxi to stop in the middle of Twentieth, leave the meter running a moment. She dabbed her eyes with a Kleenex, tried to put on a little more liner, smear on some lipstick. Remember, she told herself, Bobby Brown isn't the last train leaving town. Besides, she wasn't sure she wanted to leave Single Town. Think of Helen Gilman, her former roommate, **Glow Girl** become Sat Siri become Mrs. Billy Green. Did

Billy the seer know that Helen, no doubt pissed off about her puny superpower, cheated on him—the way Laura's mother had cheated on her father, she thought, with a man she'd never slept with. Is that what Modern Marriage meant? Then it was like bombs and babies—not for her.

She gave the Haitian cab driver an extra-large tip, went in to join her beloved for dinner.

Where Bobby and the waiter had seemed to enjoy themselves choosing the wine, vintages and vineyards and berries, the talk sounding convivial, though, not too much one-upsmanship. Now he held the stem of the glass in his hand, swirled the liquid, "nosed" it. Bobby seemed to know what he was doing, Laura thought with surprise—surprised immediately then by her own racism. The Dewey School. Harvard College and Yale Law—why wouldn't he know about wine? Once, she thought—to comfort herself—her own father must have confronted just that attitude, like that made her attitude here all right: her family had paid its dues, should get one pass. She remembered the sommelier at Le Voisin, a tall, pompous man with a hugely ridiculous silver medal around his chest and a tiny silver goblet for tasting. What had the expression on his face been when her father had chosen their bottle? The difference being that her father *hadn't* known jack shit about wine, clearly found the whole exchange a bewildering humiliation, while Bobby pronounced the wine good, and he and the waiter seemed well satisfied with the whole exchange.

"Did you know Beth was pregnant?" she asked Bobby out of nowhere. "Then, I mean. At the hearing?" The waiter poured some wine for her. It smelled deliciously of exotic spices.

"Why? Do you think that would have made a difference in what bail I asked for?"

She could see Bobby might get angry here very easily. "No. I don't know. That's not what I'm trying to tell you." Well, what *was* she trying to tell him? That she'd been *sorry* Beth had made bail? That she'd actually wished he had put her friend in jail for a couple of decades, so she could have raised Beth's child? *Or that she wanted a child,* his *child.*

She could feel a tremor in her leg. *Was it starting again?* Or was that her body offering a brief reminder that a child was not for her. She looked at his broad nose, the lovely, very marked planes of his face, and hated him for bringing this up in her when *she could not do it.* She took a sip of wine, trying to taste berries in it, and "tar and tobacco notes," which sounded ghastly. The bitter taste of the alcohol just made her feel worse. Tears massed behind her eyes. Any second now he'd be talking about her time of the month.

Fortunately he changed the subject. "You remember Michael Healy?"

"Don't be stupid," she said.

His face froze. Actually, what time of the month was it? she wondered. But she could never remember when her last period had been without consulting her date book, each one marked with a little red heart, to celebrate what Helen / Sat Siri called the miracle of menses, the power of women. "Yes," she said. "I'm sorry. Yes, I remember him."

"I was just going to say that you've really helped him make an adjustment, get some therapy. He's doing much better."

"If this is all ancient history, though, why are you reading his letters?"

"Letters?" Repeating the last word, a sure tell, she knew from her patients, that he was covering something up. "I'm not reading his letters. They know we're dating, and the guy in charge of his case, he told me."

Liar. He'd read her letters. She tried to remember what had been in them. Michael's had mostly been an unstable combination of children's book sentimentality and honorable anathema-pronouncing fury. She'd urged him to accept the therapy sessions the jail offered. Maybe shrunk he would lose the strong rush of his beautiful, righteous anger, but co-operation might, finally, also earn him the get-out-of-jail-but-not-quite-free card that the parole board would endlessly withhold until Michael saw himself not as a moral prophet but as an unstable case given a little "extra impulsion" by neurotic motives.

Michael took her advice. Maybe he'd thought that therapy would be a way back to her, too. But the times she'd visited him, they'd sat together silently with a barrier between and a sign overhead that said: DO NOT GIVE THE PRISONERS ANYTHING. She'd wondered, *can the photons communicate through scratched plastic and steel, over telephones?* No, or only, umm, you know, like, I mean, in broken halfhearted sentences. Had she returned to her class, and he to his, cheated by her and her friends (*and* the War, and the State) of his one chance to move upward the way her family had, through education? Or was it just that MCI Norfolk didn't give you a lot of small talk?

Anyway, his ferocious energy *had* been dulled by prison—and probably by group therapy, too. Sallow, wary, hidden, all that was left of her Michael was the mild autism of mathematical genius; the disconnect that let him go inside himself, not hear the buzz of others' emotions. He'd said some things about computer programming, which was nice, but not like the First Church of Christ Quanta with its yummy sacrament of sex and peyote.

She couldn't imagine sleeping with him anymore, even for old times' sake. Laura knew more physics now: when the state of one linked photon changed, Bohr thought its chum's condition would change, too, wherever in the big universe it was; but Michael had forgotten to add one thing: *it always changed in the opposite direction.*

1975 that had been. Implacable teenage guerrillas, boys and girls with guns, had gone house to house in Phnom Penh, their eyes as cold probably as the drug dealers on Avenue A, emptying the hated city, destroying all its irony and disdain. The country surrounds the city, Beth had used to say, but the nursery rhyme had turned murderous, a forced march to the countryside, a patient with IV tubes still in her arms, the bed pushed by another patient, the lame leading the blind out to die. *Her* patients? *No*—meaning *not* that she was innocent, but implicated all the more, an unindicted powerless co-conspirator. She remembered a bearded divinity student, long ago, saying, "Look, I don't *know* the Vietcong. I mean, it's not *our* movement. We can't vote on what *they* do." He meant, We should work for ourselves, here, not for others who are less controllable than our bodies in dreams. And he'd been right, hadn't he? But Beth had laughed at him, and so Laura had, too.

"Laura?"

"Sorry." She smiled. "Acid flashback." She looked down at her ceviche. Then she remembered what she and Bobby had been talking about before she'd fugued out. *That* had been weird. "You read my letters?" she said. "You read my goddamn letters? Did you think I'd find that flattering or something?" She imagined Bobby behind a desk piled with neat government files, her and Michael's letters sorted by years, the files getting thinner as his sentence dragged on. Other evidence, too, probably. Wiretaps. Photos of her and Michael lighting up a joint on the Cambridge Common. Her and Michael in bed under the silver insulation. Her on top, comforting him just after he'd been busted. "Fuck me, fuck me hard," he'd said, but desperately so it sounded almost sweet. Did they get that on tape? It was Bobby's job, sure—but she still felt violated. The man she loved was a cop at heart.

"It didn't bother you," he said, "that I'd listened to the tapes of that warning call."

She ignored that crap. He might think Beth ancient history now, but he'd gone after her, hadn't he, like an attack dog, because they'd told him to do it. *Just following orders!* Now he wanted to make her feel like she could be a good mother; then he could knock her up, cripple her bringing a child into the world she was bound to damage. She could barely contain her anger at him.

Clearly, *this* whole thing was impossible. Maybe she shouldn't see Bobby for a while? She didn't trust him anymore. But she couldn't stop herself from that nameless, bottomless wanting—and even as she thought she shouldn't see him for a while, she began to imagine taking him to Le Périgord to meet her parents. He could teach her father about wine. Then maybe he'd take Laura to meet his aunt—the woman who'd shown her how to stuff her bra with Kleenex, how to use a Tampax, for God's sake. And she didn't even know where she lived anymore—because *that* woman wasn't her grandma or her sister, but her family's maid.

Well, if Ruth's nephew was going to spy on her, Laura thought, maybe he could help her, too. "Look, I don't know where to turn. There's this friend of mine missing." She sipped some wine. "But I forgot. You know who all my friends are, don't you?"

He didn't smile, or look away, just gave her a level stare.

He *knew,* she could tell. "Jeffrey Schell," she said. "He was an art dealer, now he runs his family's carting business. Or he did. He had sold the business to the city and just disappeared. I used to hear from him every day." She waited for his questions: How long since you heard from him last? He didn't ask. "I get these cards from him, saying he's all right. But they come from like Phoenix and Newark on the same day, like someone mailed them for him."

No response, no Why are you worried? Why should you care? Instead he went on staring at her, then swirled his wine. "The situation is a little delicate," he said.

"The situation? What are you talking about?"

"I can't tell you, Laura. Not until I clear it, anyway. But he's all right, I'm sure."

"Clear it?" Jesus, the good German was just following orders again. "What the fuck do you know about Jeffrey?"

He tried to deflect her anger. "Mouth like a sailor," he said, smiling.

"Fuck you."

"I know how it seems, Laura, but *you* should know by now that you can trust me." He sounded furious. "And I'm telling you that it would be safer for both of you if you left this alone for a little while." Concerned tone, but his prosecutor's face said: *No Appeal.*

Condescending, protective lying prick! This was too much. He read her love letters, and he knew where the Uncertainty Beam had taken her best friend. She stood, gathered up her handbag, her coat.

So strange, like an eerie silence all around her. She *knew* this terror about being crippled wasn't his fault. She knew her accusations were miles unfair. But the bad feelings just welled up, like poisonous oil, or like a dream that commanded her, made her flee, a power to it as imperious as her desire for him had once been. She put on her coat.

"I will leave it alone," she said. "And maybe us, too," she said.

Wasn't he going to stop her? Or did he think sometimes about that meeting between her and Ruth? Was he embarrassed to bring this white woman home? Fuck him! "*Alone,*" she said, savoring a word that made her instantly once again the star in a Laura Jaffe Production, yet another Weepie called "Yes, darling, I'll certainly leave us alone."

3

1981: DEAD LETTERS

"Team Death's strategy," Jesse told Jeffrey the Sophist, AKA (in this case) Jeffrey the Ingenue, "is to make as many pre-trial objections as ever we can—"

"The jury's not racially mixed," David Watkins interrupted, "the judge is biased—"

"And the pollen count's too high," Jesse said.

Jeffrey had rolled his rented red Cadillac straight from the airport in Jackson to this office in a converted Victorian, its warrens filled mostly with ambulance chasers and tax attorneys, men hardly worthy to share the house with Messrs. Kelman and Watkins, Les Deux Musketeers of Team Death, dedicated to saving killers from the gas chamber—the utter worthlessness of the lives surely making this enterprise as holy as any a man could hope for.

And thus making it worthy of the stranger who stood by the bookshelves, a demigod in a blue cotton tennis shirt with curly black hair and strong forearms, a D'Artagnan of Death. The man languidly brushed the side of his large, well-modeled head with his fingertips, and a stab of lust gave Jeffrey a moment's relief from his new troll companion, fear of death. *Oh dear God,* he whined, *please let the mob—or that tacky part of it that's after me—lack the stick-to-itiveness to have followed me to Mississippi!*

"We organize community groups for the accused," white-haired David Watkins said. Short, and very trim and dignified, Watkins sat incongruously on his desk in a spotless white cotton suit.

"We say, *This forgotten boy, this beaten woman, this retarded man,*" the beautiful hero in the tennis shirt intoned with a disappointingly churchly air, "*is still one of ours. You cannot take him from us to die.*"

Jeffrey tried to compose his face in response: attentive, respectful.

But what if D'Artagnan had been ironic, and Jeffrey looked too credulous, not Jeffrey the Sophist but Jeffrey the Hick?

"Demonstration; confrontation; annoyance in the extreme!" Watkins had a clipped, precise manner, seemed an elegant, self-contained man. "But Mr. Schell, you're probably thinking, Why all this talk about demonstrations? The courts, the judges and juries, shouldn't they be immune to pressure?"

Sure, he thought, *if I'd never been schooled by Beth Jacobs I might think that.* But he nodded politely.

"But if the body on trial is a black one, then justice is always far from blind. Criminal *justice* is always only criminal *politics.*"

Before Jeffrey could say *amen,* Watkins was in full flow. "People think politics is only a clash of economic interests, when really it's much more than that. Sugar Cane used to say that politics is angels wrestling, a struggle between people's most deeply held intuitions about how a community should be. And *those* always come down to a body: will you help feed it, care for it, house it? Or having failed at all that, will you send it to the gas chamber? In which case, we are usually talking about a black body."

That reminded Jeffrey of Harry Hennessy telling a rapt wanna-be leather boy—Jeffrey Schell, in fact—that "nothing in life is serious unless a body is marked." Harry had been talking about a black body, too; one to whip—or to whip him. Suddenly Jeffrey felt filled with expectation, like that night on the way to his first SM session. Maybe lust for D'Artagnan was the engine, but there was something else for him here, too: a vision for his art. *It all comes down to a body*—the murdered, and the murderers murdered in their turn—could that be his vision, a hell by which this world could be judged? Could he have found his vision at the very moment when he thought his life had come to a squalid dead end?

"If there's no justice," Watkins intoned, "then we have to let love speak through our community's anger and concern."

"But you work for white people, too, right?" Jeffrey asked, as if he might be planning a murder, need counsel. *More likely,* his new troll pal reminded him, *you'll be the one murdered.*

"We defend whites to defend the principle that all life is holy," Watkins said. "But it's my people who most need that principle honored." A secret acid coated David's words, making a white person wonder if his soul's garments had taints of racism. Jeffrey might see through Watkins' sleight of hand, but he *still* wanted David Watkins to approve of him, forgive him for something or other he'd done, now or in the past, or just hidden deep inside him. *That* talent, Jeffrey could see, might well save a black body or two.

"We demonstrate," D'Artagnan said, doing the catechism, "to remind people that this man is cared for, that his life, too, matters."

"You make enough trouble," David Watkins said, "the DA positively longs for us and the case to go away."

"Then," D'Artagnan (the paralegal?) said, "we offer a cut-rate deal: absolution and an end of the annoyance if they give us a plea."

"David's the King of the Plea Bargain," Jesse said, smiling fondly, proudly at his mentor.

"You try the case, you've lost the case," Watkins said to Jeffrey—but looking at Jesse, like he needed to repeat a lesson there. "And if we do have to go to trial, and we do lose, then Jesse finds some reversible error and we start all over again." A chuckle of appreciation for the Defender's analytical skills. "Basically, though, courts aren't for the black man. We need Theater, we need the Church, we need the Street to save us." Jeffrey had been only half listening anyway, openly gazing at his new hero's strong legs, his long lashes. *Go on,* Jeffrey prayed, *let your fingers brush the side of your head one more time.*

After Rev. Watkins' service, Jesse, and Johannus—AKA D'Artagnan—retired to a nearby plastic-looking bar, Jeffrey nearly in a fugue state now from the strong mixed drink of sexual attraction and this fugitive, wonderful new motif, this theme—this Vision!—*death everywhere,* men killing and trying to stop the killing, Johannus's tanned arms all the more beautiful against that dark background. He hardly noticed the C&W on the jukebox. A lawyers' bar. *Lots* of seersucker—think Peck in *Mockingbird*—and even the occasional leisure suit come to Mississippi to die of shame.

Arkey waited for them there, tallboys already on the table, his shirt buttoned to the top and a white scarf around his neck to keep off any sun that might sneak in here; his skin so pale by now, you'd think he slept in a coffin.

"He's a truly repellent person," Jesse said as he sat down—meaning the accused who'd given them the tip on the True Origins of the Spooky Letters, which was Jeffrey's ostensible reason for being here, his friends not knowing that he mainly needed a hideout.

"The condemned man, Barkely's his name, we've just come in to handle the penalty phase for him. Our first meeting he says to me, 'Your wife was raped, right?' " Jesse paused, uncertain perhaps if he'd betrayed Carol by mentioning that.

"A stink came off him like you wouldn't believe," Johannus added. "The man apologized, but he wasn't fool enough, he said, to shower with niggers."

"Anyway," Jesse said, "something like that rape business has happened once or twice before. Their idea of establishing a bond, like, 'I think I went to Choate with your wife's third cousin.' " He gestured to the skinny black waitress for another round of Lone Stars.

"I deadpanned him. He said, 'Yeah, she's a birdy little woman, right?' That meant nothing, though. Time to time, Carol's picture's in the paper with me. So I just opened my briefcase, took out the manila file, the yellow pad. He said, 'You believe I did her?' Like *will you defend me anyway?* But I swear, some pride in there, too. Then, 'Yeah, I'm pretty sure I did her. I didn't always kill them then, you know.' The man, he cocked one fucking eyebrow and twisted the corner of his lip in a vicious little smirk." For a moment Jesse looked stiff, furious even. "Barkely's already confessed to one rape-murder, so it's difficult to know what to do with him. No group's gonna march for this guy, whatever David thinks. No prosecutor's gonna plead it."

"The only thing that might save Barkely," Johannus said, "would be Jesse's finding reversible errors each time a jury sends him to die."

"Until someday," Jesse said, "we all grow weary of it, just let him rot to death. Not likely, though. As long as people still take any joy in killing, they will find pleasure in killing someone like Mr. Barkely." It looked like Jesse himself might like to do it. He tilted a bottle back, and the drink sobered him. "Anyway, that's the guy. And he said to me then 'Where you from, counselor?'

" 'New York,' I said. Give him that, I thought, see if I could stop the bullshit.

"He said, '*From Long Island, right?*'

"Which made me smile. So he'd read where I came from, had just been fucking around.

" 'Don't give me that shit-eating grin,' he said. 'It's Great Neck, right? The Lovette murders.'

"That made me snap to. After all, it had been a lot of deaths ago. For everyone.

" 'My uncle,' he said, 'he helped do those people.' Then he added, 'Unc sent creepy letters to someone in Great Neck after he killed the bastards. He thought that was a riot. That's why I remember the name of the place.' Without thinking I said, 'Yeah, how'd he get the address?'

"Barkely said, 'Fuck if I know. Maybe he saw something about the family in a newspaper?' "

"Jesse went white," Johannus said, sounding concerned for him. "Paler than the jailbird. Paler even than you," he said to Arkey.

"Because the letters went to Beth, and her name wasn't in the papers." Jeffrey paused. Maybe he should keep *something* secret. After all, he didn't want to start a trail that might lead back to his darling. He still adored her above all, liked to think even that knowing he would forgive her had been what allowed her to steal from him in particular; though in sober moments he knew he loved Beth because, unlike him, she wanted no man's forgiveness. No white man, anyway. Only Mao or the Black Masses could possibly absolve her. "She was Frank Jaffe's girlfriend," Jeffrey said to Johannus, "the murdered man." Ancient history to Johannus, after all.

Arkey gazed up at the ceiling. "I always imagined the guys, like it was Death itself took them over, moved their hands. Their eyes all rolled up into their foreheads, they couldn't even see what their hands did. Then I thought they walked like zombies to the mailbox."

"Anyway," Jesse said, not listening to this precious reminiscence, "he gave me a way to get in touch with the uncle."

"Wanted to be ingratiating," Jeffrey said, "after those charming remarks about your wife."

"But the uncle, when we found him, he's not so sure he wants to relive old times, even for his nephew's sake."

"He keeps setting up meetings, then canceling them."

"But don't worry," Johannus said—*with a smile for Jeffrey.* "We'll close the deal for you guys."

Take your time, Jeffrey thought, hoping the delay would give him more chances to tease out his vision—and close *his* deal with D'Artagnan.

And the next morning had good news on both fronts: Jesse and Johannus let him tag along to the prison with them to meet Houston Ferris, a white body just inches from the green chamber door. A slug-pale, dead-eyed boy wearing a silly-looking leather cowboy hat, he wasn't *playing* at emptiness, like in some SM game, but truly seemed a *creature,* a *thing* waiting for Death to animate him, make *his* hands move. In the first place it had been Ferris's partner who'd led him to torment, rape, then murder an old woman so they could steal some twenty-eight sock-hidden Krugerrands the lady had boasted about to a clerk at a 7-Eleven. Yet listening to Jesse talk softly with him, fold him in his concern, made

Jeffrey feel—for a moment anyway—that it was the world that made Houston that should be judged.

Could he do a painting, Jeffrey wondered, that would show the images that played behind Ferris's washed-out eyes? Would they be memories rotted out by anxiety, shimmering apart? Or more precious because soon to be snatched away, death turning each moment for Houston into a piece of Houston's own sluglike sublime?

"We have one more chance," Jesse told the client, but that didn't put much gleam in Houston's hooded orbs, the boy probably not even understanding much of what his lawyer told him, his IQ, Jesse had said, maybe eighty-five at best. And when Jesse's soft, quiet voice stopped, Houston's murky eyes began to look both empty and dangerous to Jeffrey again; easily deflected toward murder.

After, Jeffrey shamelessly squeezed into the front seat next to Johannus—the equivalent of a lunging kiss.

And Johannus turned and smiled at him!

So for a few blocks, Jeffrey hardly heard a word of what Johannus was saying . . . a retarded mother . . . drinking all through the pregnancy.

"Which is very bad for the embryo," Jesse said. The proto-Houston, that must be.

"And the pesticides in the fields where she worked probably stultified the fetus a bit more."

"So Houston got sent to a home for the retarded."

"Where discipline meant the teachers stuck his head underwater, raped his ass, dragged an emery board across his cock."

"That kind of thing," Jesse said, only one hand on the wheel, the man a great lawyer, probably, but a terrible driver. "You know."

"Well, no, I'm not familiar with *that* kind of thing," Jeffrey said, thinking Jesse might have been hinting about his SM past, and Jeffrey not wanting Johannus to get the wrong impression. Or the right one. Not yet anyway.

"Right," Jesse said distractedly. "In our line of work, Johannus and I hear a lot about the far reaches of human ingenuity." He slammed on the brakes at a red light and snapped Jeffrey's body forward. "Anyway, the trial judge told the jury not to let pity for Houston's regrettable childhood count as mitigation."

"So they voted to give him the gas?"

"Well, our client and his comrade, they *had* taken the cops back to the stairwell, acted out the murder for the police video." Jesse turned again, gave Jeffrey a warmly condescending smile. "*This step, I hit her* on the back of the head. Then I got down here, pulled her panties down." He looked back at the road finally and just avoided piling into a beige Toyota.

"Geez, Louise," Jeffrey said, a phrase he'd heard Johannus use, and so a way to signal *gosh, I really like you.* Liked the awful story too, for that matter. Outcasts at the margins—where nowadays all the best subjects are mined. Billy had Beth, but he would have this instead—*At Last the Distinguished Thing,* or *The Mississippi Death Trip.* Gallery installation? Viewers in cells. They can only see fragments of the action as it passes their bars, hear screams, but not know from where or why?

"Jesse, though," Johannus said proudly, "he's the Cat in the Hat, right? He's got lots of good tricks."

"We got it overturned on appeal. Repeated state-sponsored rape as a kid, maybe that does count as mitigation."

"But someone else handled the next trial, and Ferris lost again."

"Then we took over in the penalty phase again. I usually call on the guards from death row to testify, and they say my guy's making a good adjustment to prison life. Which he probably is, by the way. Most of these boys were born on the penitentiary track, after all, the way we were on the college track. And the prosecutors, they object, say what fucking difference does it make if he's a good prisoner? So far the judge usually upholds the prosecutor, disallows the question."

"So what good does that do?" Though it must, or why were they telling him.

"Well, there's a case headed to the Supreme Court next term," Johannus said. "Same question: will he make a good adjustment? Meaning, he won't shiv any other inmates, so maybe you don't have to kill him. Same deal in that case, too, it hadn't been allowed. But Jesse thinks the Supreme Court may overturn. If they do, that'll start the whole thing over in every damn case that had that question in it."

Jesse spun the wheel a little—and pointlessly—making the car jiggle. "So I petitioned that Houston's trial lawyers hadn't done a competent job, because they hadn't tried to ask that question. Yesterday, the prosecutor didn't want to fight over the competency thing, so he lied, said it *had* been offered in chambers, and the judge disallowed it. Bullshit, yes, but good for our side, so I just agreed. Now it's part of the record."

Then, getting off the highway into Jackson he nearly sideswiped another car.

"Jesus," Jeffrey shouted, fear for his life having been added to fear for his life.

But Jesse misunderstood. "It's insane, isn't it? Ten murders, nine of them the prosecutor pleads, but one of them, an election's coming, he decides he better show how tough he can be. Then all the resources of mighty Mississippi are bent to killing this pathetic bastard. And we have to work like the devil to save him."

Jeffrey would bet it wasn't the arbitrariness of things that galled Jesse, though, but the way it *forced* him to care, Laura having told him once that Jesse couldn't be touched when he slept. He'd wake up instantly, saying, *Are you all right?* Now he had all these killers to watch over who were most certainly not all right, and never had been. And tomorrow Jesse had to go back to the prison, watch one of them gassed to death, his first irrevocable loss.

They drove down the street to the Holiday Inn, past unbuilt lots filled with broken masonry and thick shadows, Frank Jaffe's fate mixing there with Jesse's condemned men and Jeffrey's own fear. That and the rest of this place's peculiar history spread some impacted paste of guilt and vengeance wonderfully thick on the ground here.

They pulled into the nearly empty motel parking lot, and Jeffrey hopped out. Then he leaned down toward the window. "Do you think I could come with you tomorrow?"

"What?" Jesse stared across Johannus, brows tightened.

"The execution."

Jesse peered up at the car roof, more than sadness in his eyes this time. Something, actually, more like disgust. "I'm afraid that won't be possible." He pulled away so fast, Jeffrey couldn't see the look on Johannus's face. Did he despise him now, too?

But as he stopped at the soda machine on his hall for an ice bucket and a Coke, he couldn't stop dreaming. *Gallery installation: Actually fill the gallery with a harmless gas,* he thought. *Or one that stings the eyes?* Jeffrey had felt something powerful in the prison, the courts, the small Team Death offices; the condemned and their confrontation with the void had something more profound than the amusement park lies where crowds try to distract themselves from the truth, or the churches where they try to fool themselves into thinking they'll live forever. Jeffrey's Mississippi Death Project could have more incitement, profoundity, and terror frissons than Hennessy's magnificent portraits of SM, his leather-clad gods and demons.

Grinning, Jeffrey nearly pranced back to his room. He had come to Mississippi to hide from death; but deeper comfort would come from making art out of it. Like Isak Dinesen had said, *Any sorrow can be borne, if you can put it into a story.* Or if it has a hero like Johannus you can run back to your room and jerk off over.

. . .

And despite Jeffrey's seemingly outré appetite for the Gas Chamber, Jesse invited him to dinner with Johannus the next night. Afterward, at the door, as Johannus bent down and kissed Carol good night, Jesse pointed back to the living room to say, *please stay.* Surely if Jesse wasn't *desperate* to talk to him he wouldn't have asked Jeffrey not to follow Johannus out that door and to the ends of the earth. So Jeffrey waved a wan good-bye as the door closed on Love.

Carol threw her arms around her husband and, standing on tiptoe, gave him a fulsome good-night kiss. All through dinner her eyes had darted over Jesse's face. Jesse had a rapid tic in his left eyelid that called out for care. If he grew quiet, she chivvied him with questions about the past with Jeffrey in Great Neck, about the carrots with brown sugar she'd made for dinner, about anything that might keep him from sinking downward toward the morning, the dead man, his defeat. Now she stood for a moment just stroking his cheek slowly, as if Jeffrey weren't there. Her fingers magically made the tic go away. "You take care of him now," she said finally, her work done.

The Sophist should tend the Defender? Impossible. "I will," he said.

"Then good night, y'all." A Southern sound overlaid on Scarsdale. Jeffrey had seen her only once before, at her wedding. A brilliance about her then, witty about Harry Hennessy and art galleries, all of it seemingly part of her world. No art here, though. Hardly any world, either; the place was so wonderfully eaten away by death.

Carol walked up the stairs, into the dark hall, and Jesse and Jeffrey wandered back to the living room. No world there, either: They had two skinny floor lamps wearing ruffled white cloth shades encased in crinkly plastic at either end of the convertible sofa; a brown knotted throw rug; a square low table of cheap blond wood.

Jesse, from the kitchen, read his mind. "It's a modest living. But steady. Not much competition for these jobs. And the world never seems to lack for murderers."

Though what Jeffrey felt then was the crazy glamour of Jesse's life, his cheap, always gray suit, his luftmensch indifference to gain, his interposing his cleverness and his caring between the condemned and the pendulum that slowly descended into the man's pit. Jesse's goodness was the guarantee that Jeffrey's art would have a moral dimension that Harry had never got in his SM canvases. *Possible gallery installation? The pendulum descends and a murderer faces his own murder. The man learns what he'd done in the image of what was being done to him, and so knows himself, like a gift given by death.*

"Who?" Jesse said. "*What?* You're kidding me, right?" With slow steps, he brought jelly glasses filled with bourbon. "I saw my client today," he said, "just before they took him to the chamber. Doped to the gills. So, sorry, Jeffrey, no possibility of his seeing the face of Justice. Too retarded anyway."

"Jesus," Jeffrey said. But he felt sure Jesse had lied. A condemned man's life is a relentless conversation with death. There *had* to be invaluable knowledge in that for the man—and for his lawyer.

"My client who died today, he never in his life had any real idea what was happening to him. I was with the family when they said good-bye, and he cried, asked them to take him home with them. Like he'd been bad, had to stay after school."

"Jesus," Jesse repeated, pointlessly.

"Yeah, weeping suffering Jesus." Jesse looked at him almost cruelly, widening his eyes. "My client, he'd been the trigger man in the robbery/ murder of another seventeen-year-old boy for his jackknife, right? Then they'd raped and murdered the boy's fourteen-year-old girlfriend."

"So first you make me cry," Jeffrey said, "then you say don't be sentimental, huh? Very postmodern."

"I'm sorry. I can't ever get it right myself."

Jesse's first loss; it had painted a shadow in eyes that had previously always been able to promise *I've seen the worst, taken its measure, and will deal with it for you.*

"So tell me why you do it," Jeffrey said. "Defend them, I mean?" *And tell me the truth this time. Tell me how they make your life more profound.*

"Don't know exactly why I do it, Jeffers. The death penalty always revolted me, even when I was a kid, reading Camus. Didn't I used to natter on about it on Laura's boat? *Be neither victim or executioner.* And I suppose Billy had something to do with it, too."

"Do justice? Raise Frank's soul-sparks?"

"Yeah, that. Make up for that physicist's ear, too. His *life,* actually, that's what we took from him. But mostly it was Billy's boat ride seminars, Doctor Jacobs telling Billy, Billy telling us how Auschwitz was racism writ large. That got mixed up in my mind with Mississippi, Joshua Battle and Frank and all. Well, this death penalty business is mostly racism, too. David Watkins showed me that."

"And the white guys?"

"Them, too, in a way." He took a swallow of his drink. "For a jury to vote to kill someone, they have to feel he's not like them, that he's not even human anymore. Mostly that means he's a nigger. But could be he's retarded. An animal. A monster. Garbage. Which is probably just what Houston had been told about himself his whole life long."

No wonder Houston had wanted to enlist in King Death's army, feel powerful himself for one moment. Jeffrey imagined telling blubbery Sam that Jeffrey's failures were his fault, then he'd turn the junkman to junk, blam! blam! blam!

"My job," Jesse said, "is to tell the man's story so he climbs back up the food chain, has a human body again like yours. Then the jury can't pull the lever." Jesse closed his eyes. "And this time, Jeffrey, I surely failed to tell that man's story right."

Jeffrey went over and put his arm around Jesse. But, hey, a touch equals a demand to this guy, so Jesse rose, went to the kitchen, came back holding the whole bottle of Jack Daniel's this time.

"So why do I do it?" he said, giving it another try, for Jeffrey. For Carol, too, probably. "I guess I think, All the suffering in the world, why add one more drop?"

On the other hand, he heard Harry Hennessy say, *why not, if it spices things up?* In fact, lanky Jeffrey himself had asked to have his own back whipped a time or two—to make his coming stronger.

Jesse sipped his bourbon then, made a face—Jesse most certainly a *good,* but *not* an old, boy. "Truth is, this work, I get to be histrionic and clever." His lips made a wan effort to smile. "In a good cause, of course." His face had sunk into a loose drunken mask, the Defender blotto—another sight Jeffrey had never seen before, even on those Southern Comfort afternoons in GN. "That guy, Barkely, we're at the penalty phase with him. The question is, should I ask the guards if he'll make a good adjustment, get it disallowed, maybe get the case turned back?"

"Is this like really the guy who . . ."

"I doubt it. But I can't ask Carol and *then* defend him, even if he's not the guy. It would drive her nuts." Jesse wiped his fingers slowly across his brow. "So there's only this skimpy police report for me to go on. He's the right age, that's all you could say."

Jeffrey, drunk himself now, couldn't figure how to arrange his face for this.

"Barkely has this way of raising one eyebrow, like *fuck you, little man, what are you gonna do about it?* Reminds me of my brother after he'd smack me."

"*You* have a brother?" His tone arch: *any more like you at home*— to dilute the melancholy stain descending on this cheap furniture. Any moment, he felt, his own particular fear might flood back over him.

"Had. My brother died in an accident. A car ran into him. Or he ran into a car. I was only five when it happened."

And Barkely cocked his brow like him. Well, true for love, Jeffrey thought. A handsome man brushed his forehead with his hand or slowly stroked the side of his temple with long fingers, Jeffrey felt like he *had* to have him. Why not the same mechanism with hate?

"Thing is, I can't even remember for sure if my brother really raised his eyebrow like that." He drank deeply, like the bourbon would help him remember, or not care if he didn't. "Anyway, I'm just playing with the idea. I'll put the guards on the stand. I'll ask." He paused, smiled almost slyly at Jeffrey. "*Probably.*"

Jeffrey pushed his eyebrows up. *Both of them.* "But you're the Defender!"

"Right. Like I said, I'll do it. But the next time I see the guy, I'd like to say, 'I'll take care of you. *Probably.*' See if he cocks his brow then, huh?"

Probably—that had been the bon mot of the FBI agent who'd murdered sleep. *Probably no one's after you.*

Probably? panicked Jeffrey had gasped.

Yeah, well, nothing's certain in this life, right?

"Sick of protecting them, huh?" he said to Jesse now, trying to stop hyperventilating. "Ungrateful lot, I imagine."

"No, most of them couldn't be more grateful. It's just, I don't know, that man's death this morning, I'm tired tonight. And Lord, I can see how my work is wearing away at Carol." With overfastidious drunken precision, he put the glass on a thin metal coaster. "The thing is, when we got together at the coffeehouse, Carol and me, it was before I was a lawyer."

He knew: organizers together, they'd set up a stand near a Marine base. Hot Joe for Jar Heads, laced with radical solace and agitprop, commie-coffee to get the recruits to do the right thing, disobey orders.

"She had so much curiosity then, she loved to talk to people at the coffeehouse, at the DMV, bus stops, anywhere, get their whole life story. Like Studs Terkel, but better. She knew so many things I didn't, she opened a lot of worlds for me."

Sex?

Jesse sat soddenly, looking like a drunk about to cry. "We knew I'd do defense work when I went to law school, but we didn't think about what kind of people I'd be defending. Draft dodgers, we thought. Soldiers who refused to fight in Vietnam."

"Honorable men."

"Precisely. Not . . ."

"Scumbags."

Jesse pursed his lips and made Jeffrey despise himself. These doomed men were an art project to him. Lumpen proles to Beth. Case histories for Laura. But something else altogether to Jesse: human beings. Clients, anyway.

"It's like now she sees each of the men I defend as the one who nearly killed her. And here's this guy, he actually *boasts* he's the guy who did it."

"Jesus."

"Right. Million to one, but I'm telling you that if Carol even heard that a guy I worked for even talked like that . . ." Jesse put his glass down too hard, sloshed bourbon on his hand and the broadly knotted rug. His Out of Service eyes filled the barely furnished room with something worse than Nervous Gas, some mixture of sadness and terror. Johannus suddenly seemed a distant, very momentary comfort for Jeffrey; and marriage a pointless burden for Jesse and Carol, bound to end in melancholy defeat.

Which feeling most certainly called for another swallow, the bourbon adding to the pain of the world—or of Jeffrey's stomach, anyway. But he wanted it. Like Harry had said once about a nipple piercing, sometimes pain is better than lying candy-ass harmonies; truer, anyway.

"She says she wants children, but after we make love I can hear her in the bathroom, douching."

"I don't think that works."

"It has so far. And there's been a lot of abstinence, too. Like we have to save it up, only do it when we might conceive. Then she has to make sure we don't." Not a complaint, precisely. Or not just that. "I have to think, you know, is Barkely, or my own self-image really, worth scaring her like this?" He sipped again, and his body shuddered, the man just not used to this imperfect, bitter, guilt solvent. He stared emptily at Jeffrey, the corner of his eye beating like a metronome again.

That beat made Jeffrey totter to the spotless bathroom to get away from the murderers murdered and the defeat in his friend's shoulders, bent toward the floor in their off-the-rack suit.

But when he splashed cold water on his face in the bathroom his avidity for those touched by death returned, for the ones on their way over, and his friend who tried, not always sucessfully, to hold them back. Jeffrey's work would show death at work everywhere, forming the world. Even Jesse's sadness, that pull of his shoulders, that was death; like Jesse felt *gravity* more than the rest of them, a constant effort probably to hold himself upright. *That* should be in Jeffrey's art, too. *A statue with a sports jacket, tie loosened. A metronome mechanism to make the eye twitch. And have the shoulder and head pulled slowly downward by clockwork springs?*

A week later, morning in the Delta, and Jeffrey, still warmed by his first-ever *genuine* art idea—*and* his green love for Johannus, of course—sat upright behind the wheel of a rented Samillac, though the car, unlike his dad's hyperbolic fifties Cads, had stubby, uncertain-looking fins. Like America, at the moment.

But not Jeffrey. He roared along the empty road, one hand on the wheel, one in the bag of biscuits he'd snatched from a *very* picturesque black woman's shack, its hand-written *carte de jour* tacked to the wooden wall: *Sweet Pie, Boiled Peanuts, Bag Biscuits: Big for $1 and Biggest for $2*. He bit down on his first. Yeasty, but very good.

Got to get 'em home while they—and Johannus—are still hot. He did eighty past truly *endless* fields of cotton. He could swear he had never felt so good about himself in his life, though if Johannus, age twenty-five—eight enormous years younger—hadn't already had a bald spot forming, Jeffrey wouldn't have the courage to do what he was just maybe about to do: ask him to come back with him to New York. Oh, yes, once he was absolutely, positively, beyond a shadow of a doubt *certain* there was no one gunning for him up there—Jeffrey's own tawdry encounter with the void. And if it weren't for the memory of Johannus's warm body, anxiety about that would shake *him* apart right now.

So, first order of business today: ask Arkey to wheedle Specs to get him out of this jam so he could go back to New York *with Johannus*. But what could he offer Johannus in trade for an enterprise as sublime as saving the despised? How about: *Choose art over life, Johannus. Come to New York with me and work on the Mississippi Death Project, instead of Team Death*. Jeffrey planned to get his hidden paintings out of storage, too, maybe stock a new gallery. He just couldn't call any possible backers yet, wouldn't let himself even phone someone to find out how his mother was doing; or Laura—she must be frantic about him by now—to tell her where he was and the good news about Johannus.

A miracle he'd even *answered* the phone that night he'd snuck back into his apartment, obsessed suddenly with getting his old underwear. He'd felt like a fool. After all, wouldn't the bad guys watch this place? And wouldn't it be stupid, he had thought, even as he reached for the receiver, to reveal where he was if the mob was calling.

But the voice on the other end, thank God, had been Jesse Kelman's. "I have this lead," he'd said, "on those crazy letters we once talked so much about. You remember?"

"Nope." He'd laughed, overcome with a relief Jesse couldn't possibly understand.

"You've got to help me check this out, Jesse. Arkey's here, and he wants to talk to you, too. He's working on a book about us."

"About what fools we were? Over my dead body, he does."

"Or someone's, huh? Anyway, *you* weren't ever a fool."

"Is Billy coming?"

"No. He says he's got these business things to do, but really I think he's scared to get close to this again. Anyway, it's you we need, Jeffrey. You didn't believe any of it before. If it turns out to be crap, you'll tell us. It won't make you feel like a jerk."

Dear, Doubting Jeffrey, the one who stuck his fingers in the guy's wounds to prove that the new candidate was *not* the risen Christ. And Mississippi had sounded like an answered prayer to him—a Deep South hidey-hole. Besides, believer or not, hadn't Jeffrey's digits been right there with the others in Laura's bedroom when they held up their long fingers, pledged to raise each other's soul-sparks from wherever they might be trapped; and hadn't it been *his* hand that had actually written the check to raise Beth's sparks, her piece of the Shekinah from out of the Tombs? He deserved to be the detective who broke the case of the Dead Letters.

Those letters, he thought now—slowing down so he wouldn't blow right past the motel—ought to have a role in his Mississippi Death Trip Project. Suburban kids, desperate for the profundity of death, imagine that Mr. D. moves living hands to write to them personally. Which maybe sets Jesse in motion to stop his clients from suffering endlessly in the grave.

Jeffrey turned on the car radio, heard the parabolic twang of pedal steel that always made his soul's sinuses hurt. He quickly switched it off, opened his car window so he could Rex-Harrison *I don't like you but I love you* to the asphalt. The wind brushed his cheek. He pressed the silver button to roll the window back up. Besides, he did *like* Johannus very much. Johannus was funny without being cynical, had a pleasing downward turn to his lips that wasn't quite sardonic, and a knowing but not dismissive smile.

Plus he asked for more and more stories of Jeffrey's childhood. Jeffrey reminded himself to ask some questions about the quarter-back's life—second string, maybe, but still—get him to talk more about himself.

Or not.

"Why did you leave Warhol?" Johannus asked again.

"A hard one. No room for advancement, maybe? The inner circle were all lapsed Catholics." Post-coitus in their Delta motel outpost, Jeffrey felt happy as a just-fucked clam, glad to ramble on about himself. "I thought it would take too long to join the Church and then lapse."

"I'm lapsed myself, you know."

"Nope. Poor joke, then."

"Don't worry." He lightly stroked Jeffrey's balls. "Very lapsed. No place for me in that church."

"And one night, I met Harry Hennessy at Max's Kansas City. And we . . . we liked each other."

"You loved him?" Johannus said, a glint of jealousy—Jeffrey prayed—in his big browns.

"Well, I loved his energy, his ambition, his *certainty.*" And actually, yes, he had loved him, too. But no need to say that now. "He had this charisma, like Beth Jacobs did. I wanted to steal some of that for myself. Now I want some of your Bible-thumping righteousness and intimacy with death."

"And he's *very* good-looking, no?"

"Not as good-looking as you," Jeffrey lied.

"He's got a square face, right, but with something intriguingly depraved around the mouth? The handsome farmer, who sucks off the sheep?"

"Or has them whip him." Johannus rolled from back to side, reached across Jeffrey's chest, foraging past the K-Y. Buying that in Jackson, Jeffrey had felt like he'd broken a sodomy law—might become the Strange Fruit Fruit. Johannus's big hand firmed around the water glass. Jeffrey wondered just how dangerous this place might be for them. Like what if the maid walked in—supposing this place had maids, this being the sort of motel where the hygienic wrapping paper on the water glass looked reused.

Johannus poured himself some Coke, though it should have been Jeffrey's throat that had dried out, all the stories he'd told, all he still wanted to tell, pour his life into Johannus's ear. It hadn't (he would say) just been Harry's looks (though, right, it wasn't *not* those looks either) but that moving in with Suki and Hennessy gave Jeffrey a collective like Beth's; a family, really, he the paterfamilias with the large suite at the Chelsea and the large trust fund, a little something, thank God, his mom's father had insisted on setting up when he'd given Sam the company to run.

And Suki and Harry had been the kids . . . the . . . consorts . . . parasites . . . the gods, for him to chase after, tall, bony Sukila loping along Alphabet City in tights and a skirt, trying to keep up with her wayward big brother, Hennessy in jeans, the three of them mad for . . . what? visions? pleasure, fame? No, it had to be all three wrapped together, the prophecy-art-sex that *must* wait for them at the end of that rainbow called the long reasoned derangement of one's *sensation,* Suki's version this evening being "Long Raisin! Re-Ranger me! Oh, Sensational!" Hennessy shouted, "Lawn Ranger! Your Range Mint is Sin Nation!" Then they looked toward Jeffrey to see what he might add; which turned out to be, as usual, applause for the two of them. That night Harry had got his nipple pierced while Jeffrey took the Polaroids for him; and Suki—former captain of the Bloomington Indiana High cheerleaders— had danced around the filthy shop chanting, "Pin it! Pierce it! Run it through! Harry Hennessy has the tit for you!"

"That was like my bris," Harry said. "The pain must be like that intense when the rabbi slices your dick, huh, Jeffrey?"

"I don't know," Jeffrey said. "I don't think it's a rabbi exactly. And when you have your bris, you're pretty little. Anyway, you would know, Harry. You have one yourself." A trimmed dick, he meant.

"The pain I felt, it was like a piece of dissonance, instead of all these fake candy-ass harmonies. It was like a rip in the world that let something fresh in."

"Yeah, gangrene, probably," Suki said cheerfully.

Jeffrey had cackled, to hide his nausea at the sight of Harry's poor mangled flesh. Now, after his time with the Mississippi lawyers and the condemned, he could see what Harry had longed for in New York, piercing by piercing, lash by lash. *Death on the installment plan, and all the visionary gifts it brings.*

And then one morning Beth Jacobs had shown up at the Chelsea trailing even more of the grand glamour of the Almost Dead. Suki stood in the center of the living room, giggling wildly, flapping her long arms. "Is she such good roommate material, Jeffers? I mean, the *Daily News* says she blew up her last house." But when Beth began to cry, Suki put her arm around her, led her to the couch.

That week, nipple piercing had been replaced at the Chelsea by that new/old re-ranging drug, the Revolution, as embodied by Beth, out of her mind then with loss for the long-haired, handsome B.C., gone forever now, Beth saying in a weak, broken voice that *she'd* done it, sounding almost contrite—until she added that she'd set the bomb off with a scream.

"Probably," Suki said, "she's rehearsing her insanity defense."

With her trapped green eyes, her perfect bones, and grimly set jaw, Beth made a wonderful widow-undone-by-grief, in the wildly disordered style of the stage-Irish countryside, a banshee woman wailing for her speed-freak lover. You could almost see her lank, unwashed hair blowing in an imaginary wind from the moors or the peat bog, or whatever. Beth would forget to eat for a day at a time, until Jeffrey finally fulfilled his dream by becoming her loving attendant, wrapping her in blankets, stroking her oily hair, levering spoonfuls of soup into her mouth between moments of her endless, repetitive newscrawl, "now is the time . . . now is the hour of the furnaces . . . a choice must be made . . . part of the problem or part of the solution," etc. Sometimes, before Jeffrey could grab them, Beth's fingernails would furrow her pale cheeks, septic self-hatred always the eventual destination of her river of slogans.

"There are too many fucking white people in the world," Beth would shout—meaning mostly herself.

"You got that right," Hennessy agreed, having a preference for black men himself. But Harry and Suki felt this white girl's charisma, coaxed her to live the explosion over and over for them, like *that* rip in the fabric of things was what they longed for now. Beth said she'd always had a roar inside her, and "then suddenly it had gone outside for a moment, my mind silent for the first time in my life. I thought I had died. Or the world had."

No, Jeffrey had wanted to say. *It was B.C. who bought the farm.* To Jeffrey's surprise, Beth's usually sublime theatricality—her way of both playing a role and believing it utterly—didn't convince him today. Maybe the bomb had dissolved her certainties, so the parts didn't work together properly anymore. Jeffrey had never agreed with her quite, but he still wanted the old Beth back—so confident about what should be that she was nearly blind to the world that is; like an artist that way.

Meantime, Suki pretended to listen to Beth, head turned to the side, seemingly so caring, though Jeffrey knew she probably hadn't heard more than a few words Beth had said. Suki's eyes darted around Beth's face, her clothes; imitated the way Beth bit her plump lower lip. Soon she would clip the gestures into a Suki sound collage, riff on a fragment or two, make Beth part of the rhythmic, ferocious Suki-flow.

Though now all Suki did was oooh and aaah—which actually seemed to piss Beth off. "If we were real revolutionaries," Beth said, "we'd kill our parents. We'd kill white babies." Her head turned to the side, eyes narrowed, daring them to be shocked.

Wrong crowd. "Yes!" Suki screamed, meaning nothing by it, this clearly performance art to her—maybe to Beth, too. After all, in Laura's bedroom she'd pledged to be a nonviolent warrior. So this talk must just be temporary fucking insanity on top of the temporary fucking insanity of the bomb they'd been building . . . to do what, actually? Smash more glass, probably.

By then Beth had been hissing, "Are you cowards willing to pick up the gun?" She stared at Jeffrey in his overstuffed chair with a large red-and-green floral pattern, his tasseled lamp beside him.

"Fuck no, darling," Jeffrey muttered.

"I will," Harry said. "I would look great with a gun. One with a curved clip to set off my square features. One that meant Death in my hands!" He went over to his pile of cardboard and paste on the dining room table, collage materials. "Harry Hennessy become one with the mighty destructive river that makes and mars the world."

"I'm nonviolent," Suki told Beth. "I could only hurt someone in self-defense. Or to make them come."

"The cops are an occupying army in the ghetto," Beth instructed her. "You kill them, that *is* self-defense," her mind on autopilot still able to do the catechism.

"Right," Harry screamed, raising his left fist in the air. "Fuckin' A!"

"The NLF has shown the way!" Beth shouted, a cheerleader at heart herself. "Now mother-country radicals have to show they're willing to make the sacrifice too."

Jeffrey wanted to pull her back from this edge; Beth, he knew, only posturing—trying to prove to herself or Saint Che that she really was a revolutionary killing machine, when the worst thing she'd be capable of destroying would be Jeffrey's furniture. On the other hand, he also wanted to peek over the edge of her abyss, gaze into the depth of her desperation.

But by then, Beth had fallen asleep on the couch, Suki cradling her, stroking her hair, herself asleep soon, too.

Jeffrey tucked a blanket around them both, though he felt furious with Suki for horning in on his action. Now that Billy Green couldn't draw anymore, Beth belonged to him. *He* was the one who *really* loved her.

The next day Suki dressed up in a beret and Beth's leather jacket, played Tania the Bisexual Guerrilla. And Che/nnessy the SM Revolutionary carried a machine gun he'd made for himself out of papier-mâché and wood. Jeffrey, as instructed, took the Polaroids of Harry and a nearly catatonic Beth, as Suki shouted, "Spunky Reds, grab a knife! / Tie up Dad, and take a slice! / Show your mom your fork-power move! / Let's get in the Manson groove!"

Virgil Thomson knocked on the ceiling then, to tell them they were talking nonsense and doing it too loudly to boot, a Red by any other name being mighty annoying. But Suki and Harry had ignored him, the natives chorusing, "Kill your parents!" over and over while dancing in front of their dead-eyed SHE and the photos coming out one after another, falling on the floor, waiting for pink fixative.

"Kill yourself, too, why don't cha?" Jeffrey said to Hennessy, meaning it like the movie slap that snaps someone out of hysteria.

That only works in movies, though. Beth stared at him, then started to weep with Isabel Archer delicacy, her beautiful green eyes leaking just a few drops of water. For a moment Jeffrey wondered how such sparing tears had managed to soak his couch, then realized that Beth had wet herself.

Screaming, she ran to the bathroom. Jeffrey got a rag from the kitchen, wondering the while what the third act of this psycho-drama would be? Harry maybe doing something stupid to a draft board instead of his nipple?

But his beloved and her comrades had found a safe house the next day—*Don't ask where*, the carefully printed note on his kitchen table had said, *not* that Jeffrey would have dreamt of it then, an article having appeared that same day in the *Daily News* claiming that the corpses in the town house had been studded with nails. The Weathermen had been making an anti-personnel bomb. True? The DEATH ORG. could have planted that story with a stooge reporter. "Or maybe," he said to Laura in Cambridge, "Beth and her pals aren't just killer groupies." Jeffrey had grown up with her, adored her from afar on the *Freedom*—while longing to get so close that he would become her—but now he didn't fully know who she was, where the War had taken her.

"Or maybe," Laura said, "we need to figure out where we all are if Beth can act that way?"

The news story sobered Harry, too, reminded him that *that* wasn't the pain he wanted to give or receive. So instead of taking target practice, Harry scouted out the hidden places that existed before the Ramrod, the Mineshaft, the Anvil, bars whose backroom had a backroom.

Usually Jeffrey went along, and Suki joined them sometimes, too, her small breasts taped against her chest, hair cut shortish and slicked back with Brylcreem, her a him and the Master, Harry, eyes downcast, the Slave; and Jeffrey in his dress pants and loafers the Jeffrey as always. Hennessy, flat out about his role, had Suki lend him out to other men, like he was a thing so essentially slavish he couldn't even speak for himself.

"No more tattoos or piercings," she'd specify to the borrower. "This body is to be returned to me as delivered. Otherwise you can do whatever you want with him."

The nipple piercing had taught Harry that he longed for pain, degradation—

"What the world calls degradation," Jeffrey had said, trying to make it more hygienic, like his mother had misunderstood what it meant to stick a whip handle in your ass.

"No, Jeffrey," Harry said patiently, "what *I* call degradation. That's the fucking point." He'd drunk more beer, the two of them in a bar's front room one night, waiting for Suki to find a suitable consort for Harry, and listening to "These Boots Are Made for Walking" for the umpteenth fucking time as someone tied a hairy guy up to the jungle gym in the center of the room. Harry had been describing his last big night out, "the pain this guy gave me, it was so intense, it destroyed my ego. My master—"

"Who is the master?" Suki said, coming up to the table empty-handed.

"He wouldn't tell me his name. Very commanding eyes, though. Very precisely trimmed black beard, and this accent I couldn't place, my mind going into a haze by then. He said, 'Feel it? God has left you!' Then my master whipped me more, and I felt just what he told me to—the big, empty universe, and only him left for me to cling to, writing *his* law on my body."

Meaning what? *The Queer Talmud? The Little Mauve Book?* Still, though Hennessy had been there first, Jeffrey hoped that the lash and the tit clamp might give him a touch of the numinous too, be his substitute for dead letters, for pipe bombs and world revolution, a vision equal to Beth's by which this bourgeois, capitalist, imperialist, hetero planet— AKA Sam's world—could be judged and found very, very wanting.

"You bet," Handsome Hennessy said amiably. "SM, Jeffrey, it's everything your friend Beth has, and more. It has the true seriousness of Christ's flesh and blood."

"Oh, not Christ, for Christ's sake."

"Dear child, you must learn what your friend Beth Jacobs already knows. Nothing in life is serious unless a body is marked."

"Do you want me to find your master for you?" Suki asked the next night as they strolled down Houston for Jeffrey's coming-out party. She was dressed as a man again—a cute one, in Jeffrey's opinion, wiry, her loping walk looking smart somehow without the dress.

"No," Jeffrey said, opening the door to the bar, "thanks, I'll do it myself." Suki being the spirit of whimsy—Puck, Loki, or a seven-year-old with a loaded gun.

But "don't forget to tell your Top about your tennis elbow," Suki warned—showing her motherly side even in this locale where naked men in blindfolds lay suspended belly down from the ceiling, and other men were shackled to the walls in leather harnesses, smiling through the pain like a Miss SM America being whipped for world peace. On the plywood stage a sixty-year-old man with a sunken chest displayed a cock he could keep stiff for hours without touching it. It was a place, in short, where you could find someone for a man with a small chin and beaky nose in a leather jacket that had belonged to a mad bomber, the sleeves way too short for his scarecrow arms. After all, he still had that most precious commodity, *youth.*

"Don't expect too much in the looks department from the Tops," Suki said. "Mostly, they're the uglier, older guys. Portly. Guys whose piles mean they can't be fucked in the ass anymore."

"Yeah, it's the Bottom who gets the workout," Harry said. "And the really obscene come."

"*If,*" Suki added, "your master lets you come at all."

He had—and the man had instantly become not a master but a failed lithographer with pocked skin, and the dungeon a screened-off nook in an unenchanted, if large, Westbeth studio.

Still, Jeffrey had enslaved himself a few dozen times, dreaming always of the exaltation Hennessy found in servitude. But he never felt the glory much, and the Tops who commented on his being *cut*—meaning *circumcised,* as opposed to Mr. Top's prime meat—made him shrivel, in memory of the covenant and his grandfather who'd given him his trust fund. A few too many times, too, he'd hooked up with some (bottle) blond who wanted to play SS and Jew. That felt immoral; which was probably why he couldn't enjoy the scene, or make art out of it; though he always gave "Hans"—circumcised himself, usually, this being America—a polite good-bye suck before he slunk back home.

"They're singing songs of pain," Jeffrey crooned over cocoa late one night in the kitchen with Suki and Harry, "but not for me."

Suki smiled, she not exactly true slave or master material either, her line of inquiry being *Am I a man or woman?* Her special talent, she said, being that she could actually live the question.

"Don't we all?"

"Yeah, but I don't get my boxers in a bunch about the answer."

So for her research, Suki picked up gay guys and straight girls in her Brylcreem, boob-taped custom—not that a lot of tape was needed—and brought the demi-johns back to the Chelsea, never letting on that Sam's a Suki, dispensing blow jobs only—or, if her partner was a slave, forbidding them to turn around while she did him or her in the ass with an impressive—*Oh, Master, you're so big!*—dildo.

Che and Mao, Jeffrey thought as he watched her scribbling down a song about her adventures, they cobbled together their so-called New Communist Man, but he and *his* pals knew our identities were lots more malleable than anything dreamt of in Commandante Guevara's heterophilosophy. "Which makes us better revolutionaries than the Weathermen, right?"

"Yeah," Suki said, looking up from her notebook. "And that makes you a better Beth than Beth, right?"

Then one night Suki/Sam took You're-So-Big to Central Park, smeared with sweat from Hennessy's and Jeffrey's privates. A guy started to suck it, then realized what was (or wasn't) up and stuck a switchblade in her latex. Suki ran screaming from the park, the blade still sticking from her cock, but the girl-artist not too stunned to study people's faces as—cock out, knife in—she rode the IRT home, the trip providing choice bits for her song cycle (and later, platinum record), *Blade.*

A week after The Night of Knife-in-Cock, Billy Green knocked on the door, a large flowered Felix the Cat carpetbag in his tiny hand. Broken Billy, lots more than his ears gone bad by then, had made the rounds those years from one Band member to another, a month with Jesse, a week with Laura, time enough for him to display his pathetic inability to draw anything more than comic book covers, stills from someone else's story, and the misery that not doing narrative caused him; caused the Green Co. bottom line, too, the country's teens less than mad for Billy's father's cartoons, and the covers that Billy sometimes drew just making people feel cheated that his work wasn't inside—so thousands of the books got sent back to New York, covers ripped off; and a few even with bomb threats stapled on, *Hard acts are necessary! We do this for love of all Billy Green has made.*

And all of that an important lesson for Jeffrey in his own career as an artist, his piecing together of his vision, namely that he didn't have a vision and would probably never be an artist if it didn't matter to him so much that not working would send him into a terrifying, bewildered depression the way it did Billy.

Mornings that had news of a Bureau of Corrections office or a court building turned to garbage—or mildy damaged, usually—were the worst for Billy. Nearly catatonic, he stared at the newspaper like it had been his hands that had done the deed. The stories shocked Jeffrey, too, but at the same time they reassured him: Beth had put herself back together, had regained her terrifying, fascinating certainty.

But the bombings now did nothing one way or the other for Harry and Suki, thrilled to have a new doll—the Broken Magus to dress up—once again using Beth's leather jacket, the sleeves way too long for this new initiate in the fluidity of gender. They took him out to bars, like—what a nice surprise!—a Band of Outsiders–themed bistro, with a few customers in MyKill's bubble-helmets, OurKey hats, Haunted Desperado's codpieces, and even a few good men in Defender kilts, the place with its long empty tables (just like the ones in the Fortress, kids!) looking as dispirited and uncertain as the Uncertainty Beam's creator's creator. Jeffrey worried that Billy would be horrified to see these caballeros using his flotsam and jetsam in their sex games, but no, the Marlboro Midget's eyes had lit a little; he even struck up a conversation with the owner/bartender, a moustached guy with a protruding lip, Billy maybe expecting he'd get to do an incognito prince thing, reveal that, yes, *he*—the little fellow before you!—was none other than BBE himself, auteur of the Outsiders!

But the bartender, it turned out, really regretted the theme now. "The whole Outsider world," the owner told the Hidden Billy, "it's become the same old superhero crap. I'm going to change this place, I think. More of a hellfire motif or something."

The four of them slumped into seats at the long table then, sipping consoling Cokes and rum, when an SM wind had blown in none other than Gaston Weil, Jeffrey's former lover, a dealer's assistant still, but stockier since he'd sucked him last, with a carefully shaved black beard now and a closely cropped head.

"Hello, Master," Harry said.

"Eyes down," Gaston ordered.

Instantly, Harry obeyed. So *Gaston,* Jeffrey's own Franco-Jewish Mephistopheles, had been the man with the odd accent, the one who'd been, for the length of a whipping, the sub for God Himself!

Gaston placed himself in front of the table, arms akimbo, scanned the scene. "We *must* all go elsewhere *immediately* before we, too, are infected."

He ordered them to rise, and they trailed him into the night, Gaston dangling various amusements over his shoulder, including "a new club for people who want to have sex with corpses."

"You're joking," Billy choked out.

Gaston had been, Jeffrey was pretty sure, but he said, "If the dead can feel pain, why can't they come, too?"

"Oh, *can* the dead feel pain?" Gaston asked. "Lucky them!" He led them into the Demon Pit, a place both homo and hetero, he said, "to ease your friend into the scene."

That night's "demons" included a naked man lying curled up in a big bathtub, waiting to be urinated on. Harry took some Polaroids, for "a piss collage" that would be made all the more real and redolent when he soaked it in his pee and taped it, dripping still, to Jeffrey's Chelsea walls.

On a small plywood stage behind the urinal a black woman dressed in a leather bikini paddled a naked alter koker, and a kneeling man blew a hairy guy.

"Look at the penis on that man," Billy said, trying to be a good sport, or pretending to be a good sport because he was embarrassed that he'd been, truly, so impressed by another man's penis.

"Say *dick,*" Suki said.

"No, say *cock,*" Gaston instructed, giving Billy the Stare that had caused hundreds to kneel, and hundreds more to buy paintings. Jeffrey prayed that Billy wouldn't melt, too, become our millionth customer to decide that disco music revealed that gosh, darn, he'd really been gay all along—thus making Jeffrey's whole scene fodder for Billy's art, supposing he ever drew again.

But before Billy could say—or do—*cock,* Gaston was off on another flight of fancy about the advantages of the Master/Slave relationship, in terms Hegel would probably have understood, if Georg Friedrich wasn't distracted by the men walking around wearing nothing but leather chaps. Some of the guys tuned in to Gaston for a while, everyone liking a little theory with their masochism. Gaston had a reputation already; the Man, slaves gossiped, able to work two at once, take you places you'd never been, where he just watched as you obeyed him and savagely whipped another man senseless, Gaston making you this unstable combination of slave and master.

"You know, Jeffrey," Gaston concluded, "you're a shapeless lump of a thing. You desperately need a guide." He stared at Jeffrey with super-Sam disdain, like he was daring Jeffrey to look away. Jeffrey felt drawn forward, sure this man was *his* longed-for master—after all, Jeffrey had belonged to Gaston *first,* long before Hennessy. Maybe Gaston could shape Jeffrey, teach him what he needed to become an artist, give him permission to terrify and instruct others through his paintings. He swooned tenderly, disappearing into Gaston's great controlling power, and the hubba-hubba around him disappeared but for the words that came from Gaston's mouth, that beautiful, dangerous Black Hole.

Then Gaston turned toward Suki, and Jeffrey felt the power pulling away, abandoning him. *No!* Jeffrey wanted to shout. He'd be honored to spend his life in Gaston's service, to give his life utterly, have Gaston's sublime weight pulverize him—a death that his master would have chosen for him, making it so much more sublime than the chance suburban fate that awaited him otherwise!

"No, I think I won't take Jeffrey for my slave," Gaston said.

Jeffrey felt his shoulders twitch like a wet dog's.

Gaston smiled at the shimmy, no doubt read a tribute to his power. His thick hand clamped Jeffrey's neck. "I have other plans for him." Gaston had heard how Jeffrey had been introducing Hennessy to collectors, friends of his parents. "So why not do that with me," Gaston said, "at the gallery, turn a profit? You'll feel powerful for the first time in your life." He turned toward Harry, like Jeffrey was in Hennessy's giving. "Jeffrey could be a great salesman if he had me to teach him. I've become a master at *that,* too, you know. I make the client so ashamed of himself, he longs to be nearly bankrupted by what I charge him for a *masterly* painting."

Gaston took a sip of beer, popped a cap of amyl under his nose. "Grrrrrrr!" he shouted, his eyes nearly rolling up under dark brows. He rose majestically, pointed to two nearly naked young men who stood at the bar in chaps—had one of them been slug-pale, worn a silly, ill-fitting leather cowboy hat?—and made a rapid but lordly gesture to the back room. The cowboys-become-cattle sashayed off, ready for branding with the coveted G. *How Jeffrey envied them!*

"Wait," he barked, and the two boys turned to puppets, their legs jerking the way Jeffrey's shoulder had. Gaston got in front and led them. A different night, who knows, it could have been up a stairs to an old pawnbroker and her Krugerrands.

Jeffrey got his Krugerrands his first week at the gallery—and from Menachem Cutberg's new wife, the famous "Chi-Chi" girl from Las Vegas and the *Tonight Show*—Menachem having turned Ellen Jaffe's idea of buying undervalued companies and selling off their assets to pay for the money he'd borrowed to buy the undervalued company in the first place into Chi-Chi's incessant squeals of faux delight—*chi-chi-chi-chi!*—and his workers' screams of "Where the fuck have our jobs gone?" Which made Jeffrey feel more than all right about overcharging his wife. That, and that her main criterion for her purchase had been that the painting fit, or be made to fit, into Menachem's private jet. Jeffrey had to steer her away from a Kline that "I'd only have to trim a *little*," she'd said, in strangely unaccented English, "some of the white space"; and on to a Warhol Electric Chair. "Don't you think people might find the Kline petit bourgeois and vulgar someday?" he said. "While Mr. Warhol already laughs at himself?" Implied in his smile: *Like* you, *Chi-Chi.*

Selling someone else's art *had* given Jeffrey the surge of power Gaston had promised, but it would be meaningless, he knew, unless he could alchemize that force into energy for his own paintings. So nights Jeffrey went back to de-raising with the gang, the new items in Harry's pharmacopoeia being cocaine and LSD combined, a combo that either sent them to each other's throats or turned them into supine lumps with blank stares, even the chatty Suki-doll barely able to dribble a few words out.

Then, on the third day of a marathon Vision-or-Die trip—or was it the second? Or the ninth?—Billy carefully unpeeled the taped edges and took down a Polaroid collage of *Suki's Knifed Cock.* He laid it next to him on the floor, and gazed. Suki, in an old cheerleading skirt, rose and slid down again in an impressive long-legged split. Jeffrey, sprawled on the couch, looked at her crotch, wondering what lay inside her panties today.

Then Suki crawled over to Billy, cooed and whispered into his ear. Back in Bloomington she'd told Jeffrey once, she'd turned a football team's intended gang rape of her into a circle jerk with her leading the strokes. Billy—because what difference did it make, or because he thought Suki intriguingly cute—opened his mouth, let Suki put another killer dose of acid on his tongue.

Time went by. It does, right? But how much? Starting when? The dirty light from the high windows turned to evening. Billy sat tailor-style drawing a big panel of Knife in Cock, the side of his pencil making sheets of shadow fall over and over like ominous jism from the penis tip, probably because he had lost interest, the image just a penis going nowhere, not a story with a beginning, a middle, and a moral come shot.

Suki sat next to Billy, watching. "Whose cock is it?"

"What?"

"That's always the question, Billy. Whose is it and where do you want it put?"

"Nowhere. On the page, I mean. Why? Do you think I'm a homosexual?" Billy just inquiring, like he'd be happy to have his problems so neatly solved, say that repressed desire had fucked up his spook phone line, made him think Frank had said, *Blow up the I-Lab,* when really he'd whispered, *You want to blow me.*

"So, think, whose cock is it?"

"I thought it was yours."

She pulled up her skirt, pulled down her underwear. "Nope," she said. "I don't have one."

"So, whose, then?"

"Traditionally, it's your father's."

"Nathan's penis?" Billy looked sick at the idea.

"Or like it's Dr. Jacobs' penis, then," Jeffrey said, not having anything special in mind but blasphemy—like it would be even more remarkable that sainted Holocaust survivors fucked than that your parents once had.

"Who is the doctor?" Suki asked, her legs straight up in the air. "He your analyst, Billy? He fucked you? Fucked you up, I mean?"

Billy drew another cock going in a man's ear and out the other, bits of gore on the end, and the speech bubble saying, "This feels so . . . shit, I can't remember the word without my brain!" He tore the page out, crumpled it up, and threw it toward Jeffrey's chair, giving everyone his empty-eyed look, worst for Jeffrey, who remembered how Rasputin-bright his eyes had once been. "It's not about cocks!"

"Wrong," Suki said. "No matter who or what you're fucking, for you boys it's *always* about cocks." She rolled over, put her head on Billy's thin thigh, pulled her skirt over her stomach, showed her white panties again.

Jeffrey, meanwhile, retrieved the first drawing, uncrumpled it, and stared at the penis with darkness dripping from its tip. Billy ran his fingers through the cheerleader's short black curls, the two of them looking sweetly companionable, some weird married couple who liked to play dress-up games.

"You're thinking about HeadMan, huh?" Senorita Blade said.

Billy nodded.

"You know whose dick that is, then?" Suki grinned, a long-legged malicious elf. "Your conscience's."

"My conscience has a penis?" Billy smiled wanly.

"Of course your conscience has a dick," said Suki. "And you want your conscience to tie you down, beat you up, fuck you hard. That's what guilt is, you know, a good hard SM-style fucking from your conscience. But you don't know how to do it right. You make it endless. And you never come."

All that being background noise to Jeffrey as he stared at Billy's drawing, which was, Jeffrey was sure, really *his* own cock, made grand, doomed, stabbed by Sam, and with deathly shadows dripping from the tip. "He hates me for having one." But the dope-tinged insight receded from him as his marijuana-enhanced—which was also his pot-weakened—mind chased after it, wondering why oh why *he* should feel guilty for having a cock; or a body; or a life?

"No, wait, Suki," Billy had protested that night. "I *should* feel bad about what I did."

"Yeah, well, it's not like you set out to hurt HeadMan's ears, is it?"

"No. I don't know. No. I didn't."

"It was collateral damage. Like Superman flying through the city on his way to stop Lex Luthor. Bound to create a whirlwind, right? Probably teenagers necking in cars get swirled into the air and smashed down, crushed to death by tons of hot metal."

"I don't draw Superman," Billy said, but he stared down at Sukikins like she was or had the burning bush.

"Yeah, well, whoever. I mean, no one's innocent. Not even Soup, if you ever got to see the whole scene."

Meanwhile Billy had already begun to draw, leaning the pad against Suki's magical head, she having offered him the first glimpse that day of the nectar of life: how he might work again, make narratives.

"You mean he has to destroy the village to save it?" Jeffrey said. Too easy a resolution, in his opinion, like that Superman might have accidentally—*and in a comic book*—killed someone meant it was all right that Billy had helped maim a non-paper ear in real life. Jeffrey hadn't taken enough acid to see the justice in *that* one. Also, he didn't *want* Billy to draw again. The newspapers spoke of a bomb going off in a Pentagon bathroom; i.e., Beth had *definitely* pieced herself back together, enough, anyway, to blow a bathroom to pieces. If Billy couldn't work anymore, who knows, maybe Jeffrey could now make something out of her himself.

"Wait," Billy said. "The superheroes don't *set* out to destroy innocent things, right, Suki? It's collateral damage. You know." But his hand wavered.

Jeffrey shrugged. "Yeah, I know. And I tell you, boy, I think Henry Kissinger would agree."

Billy's hand poised above the page. Then he must have decided he could draw again *if* his stories could show how the hero was implicated in the disasters, Ninja B. wrecking whole cities and a few eardrums as she set out to make justice. Billy even laced his creations with enough dry, bitter threads to make the reader feel like a co-conspirator in the destruction, as if the ashes of the reader's father's corpse had been used to make the ink of the pictures he looked at, so if you enjoyed the story, you were also savoring your father's death, an artistry that gave seventies BillyBooks their trademark sweet&sour flavor, joy brought up short by regret.

"So what else do you want to do till four?" Johannus asked, as they strolled out of Heaven. "Drive more? I can show you some fine cotton fields in this area, identical to the ones we've already seen."

"Sounds great." What he wanted to do, actually, was tell him everything that had ever happened to him until the moment he'd walked into the Team Death offices.

"See, what I had in New York, that was inferior goods. This is the real deal."

"I love you, too."

"Yeah, that also. But I meant you and your righteous executioners and your dead men walking."

"Your project again, right? *The Mississippi Deathnyland?*"

"Right. What you do is *real*. Real guilt. Real justice. Real death."

"*That* part's as real as it gets."

"It's why I'll be able to do something better than Billy or Hennessy has done."

Sure, Sam said, *as long as it stays a totally imaginary filmogriff/ drawingosaurus with big wings and fins.*

"Death in Hennessy's images," he told Johannus, told Sam, "it's all pretend. The men in chaps, the guys curled up in those bathtub urinals, they were *playing* at death and resurrection, guilt and redemption. Harry can only make copies of pale, distant copies. What you and Jesse do, it's for real, so my work about you can confront death and what we do with it head-on."

"Mississippi," Johannus said, smiling, "land of bountiful gifts."

Jeffrey glanced over. Johannus had taken some sunglasses out of his pocket, leaned his head back against the cushion. Black eyes. Black curly hair. Dark skin. Full lips. *Indeed,* Jeffrey thought, *land of bountiful gifts.*

Like acid that way. For Hennessy, anyhow. The day of the epic trip, Jeffrey had stared and stared at the charcoal cock, sheets of darkness dripping from the tip. But Hennessy sat cross-legged next to him, copying Billy's picture.

Jeffrey looked over at Hennessy's pad. A simple cylinder deformed under his pencil and became a misshapen toilet paper roll. "Shit," Harry said, ripping the page off, smashing it in his huge hand. "Two fucking years of art school and I can't even draw a decent cock!" He laughed for a moment, then began to cry. Suki crawled over to stroke his hair, coo in his ear, but Harry's acid-laced sobs just got stronger. Then he put the side of his arm against Suki's body, hurled her against the wall.

She slid to the floor, screaming, from pain; and shock at what Hennessy did next, tearing down each and every one of his Polaroid collages, crumpling them in his paws. He threw the *Piss Pixs* at Jeffrey. "They're nothing, they're shit, they're tawdry ugly mug shots. This midget's fucking comic book cock has more dignity than anything I've ever done in my whole wasted life!"

"I'll teach you to draw," Billy whispered.

But he'd regained his magus power. Harry stopped immediately, gave him a sweet, almost begging expression. "You will?"

So Billy made big grids on drawing paper, took a heavy faceted red glass from the kitchen, turned it upside down and showed Harry how to copy it segment by segment. Not Rensselaer Poly, perhaps, more like those art lessons advertised on matchbooks, but Jeffrey felt jealous until he'd been added to the class, the three of them drinking pots of the smoky tea Billy made each evening, and he and Harry sitting on the living room floor beside Billy, two little cross-legged monkey-sees working dutifully on their lessons.

And let history record that Jeffrey Schell of Great Neck was a far, far better draftsman than Harry Hennessy. He could do a Ninja B. wielding a ninchuck, or numchook, or whatever, from his first week on. Harry noticed that superiority, too, but instead of throwing a reversed glass or Jeffrey against a wall, he borrowed a wad of cash from him and came home the next night with a used Hasselblad and a tripod. From then on, Harry took carefully staged photos of whatever he wanted to "draw"— first off being Jeffrey as the Nasty Master, and Billy, restored but still agreeable—who knows, maybe even turned on a little—as the boot-licking, leather-leashed slave-dog. Then he blew up the photos, put a transparent grid over the clarified blowup, and Billy showed him how to turn the photo into a tracing he could paint over.

All this swirling energy made Jeffrey sick with jealousy, Harry having truly found *his* way now, his vision: A *Noble Pornography* of heroic, massive, rock-like black slaves, the SM world plus Grecian Formula; his work showing the porno idealization always possible in the classical style, maybe even—as millenniums of teen museumgoers knew— inherent in its kick.

But for those classic lines, Harry had to get the leather straps on the cock rings just so, get the glisten on the arm muscles where it would tickle your eye. So he ordered his models around Jeffrey's apartment like they were idiot children or recalcitrant parts of his own body, savage even with Ellis Moore, his killingly handsome bald model and (more or less) true love. Soon the hot lights took over Jeffrey's living room, the darkroom chemicals, rank with the civet of hell, appropriated the former bathroom, and the artist's carping, hectoring voice invaded Jeffrey's sleep, the shouting worse because Ellis, the slave, was black and Harry, the master, was a control-freak lunatic white artist.

Harry put a perfect grid on the perfect photo, painted over it, adding a few touches along the way to give Ellis's bald head the perfect classical modeling. Then he took a knife to Ellis's image and slowly, methodically, shaved the paint smooth. Then he added layers of shellac, and, as silently as a diamond cutter, or the guy who does the bris, he shaved the shellac with a razor's edge—making it look like age had worn the surface away. More shellac; more shaving; and more; the technique Arshile Gorky had once used to make his murdered mother into an Orthodox Icon now giving a hieratic quality to an airbrushed black man pissing on a short, slightly deaf white man curled in an old bathtub. Jeffrey, pretending to balance his checkbook, was actually dumbstruck with admiration for what Harry's love had made of whips and chains, leather and bar boys. Jeffrey had been *there* himself, or so he'd thought, had spent fond foolish moments taking it in the ass in Westbeth dungeons, but when he looked at Harry's paintings he saw something grand that had been hidden from eyes blinded by morality, something only adoration could see: priests in leather vestments performing obscure ancient rites, and layers of shellac that covered numinous meanings—and fabulous sex—from which he was forever excluded.

Meanwhile, next to him, Suki snorted cocaine and cheered Harry on. Ellis, the subject and audience, read a novel. *Lost Illusions,* probably. And Billy showered the urine off, repacked his carpetbag, and went back uptown to restore his father's comic book company.

Most nights, his roommates' bedroom talk got so loud Jeffrey could make out Harry shouting a lot of *nigger this*es and *nigger that*s at Ellis, and *lick my ass or get the whipping of your nigger life,* the whole thing shocking to the poor Great Neck boy even if Ellis put up with it—or even enjoyed it—Jeffrey thinking, well, Ellis *shouldn't* enjoy it, 'cause where could that lead but ever deeper into a near suicidal self-loathing? He heard: *Take that, nigger,* followed by a whistling, slithering sound. A whip? Ellis screamed—and not playfully either. Alone in his narrow bed, Jeffrey tossed in fear of his own masterly anger, his own slavish masochism, and where it might take him. *To the grave,* namely. But he was, he swore, held back by something more than fear, some last vestige of the Ethics of the Fathers. No matter how much whiskey or pills he swallowed—and did the Fathers say downers were jake with them, by the way?—he still couldn't abide the SS regalia, the racist playlets. Or Beth's Red Guard & Running Dog scenarios, for that matter—supposing anyone in Gay Old New York had agreed to put on those hideous boxy blue playtogs.

So each night at the Chelsea, Jeffrey lay hung out between disapproval and envy. In the mornings, Jeffrey could barely face Harry and Ellis over the spilled but never cleaned-up o.j.—one more thing to add to the list of why—along with the rugs in the living room ruined by shellac and paint scraping—it was time for Harry and Ellis to go.

Besides, Harry had *his* Vision—and a profitable one, too, thanks to visionless Jeffrey, the sophist supersalesman. Harry and Ellis could afford a loft of their own. And Suki had already packed up her notebooks and pom-poms, more successful than any of them with *her* vision-macallit, a tasty spew of her gender exploration done to a strong backbeat. Soon she married her bass player, moved to a comfortable ranch house in New Jersey, probably for an SM game that had the force of sympathy, law, and custom behind it; all her experiments having ended up like a Shakespeare comedy; love, kisses, marriage. Same Old Same Old Toujours.

And that had been the season Laura discovered she wanted to play house, too. But with Jesse, alas, who she'd tardily decided had always been her true love, and the only one of them who truly lived up to his Outsider name. "I mean, I'm not much of a Wolf."

"And I'm not much of a Sophist."

A wan smile on her cattish face with its somewhat quivering cheeks. "Well, yes," she said. "Your name fits too, I guess. Prophetic, even."

"Thanks, I think." He swallowed a shot of vodka. "Beth, too. She's all that Billy says."

"Ah, love." She looked at him wickedly, but groggy, her almond-shaped eyes puffy. Fortunately she had a bottle of Smirnoff always chilling in the freezer. They deserved a drink after their day at Mt. Sinai.

But Laura reached for the bottle again and again.

"Should you drink so much, after the anesthesia and all?"

"Remind me, Jeffers," Laura said, pouring another shot in her glass. "What medical school did you go to?"

"Fuck U," he said. But he smiled sympathetically. The girl had a lot on her mind, her breakup with Arkey, Jesse's marriage, the abortion.

"I almost couldn't do it. But Jeffrey—" she looked to him pleadingly, "under the circumstances, you know, I just couldn't risk it. Being crippled to have a child with Arkey. I mean, the father of my child—"

"Your glorious child. Buddha of the Iron Age."

"My *happy* child. That's all I want for her. Or him."

"You say that now. But soon you'll realize. Harvard Summa. Nobel Prize. Those are the things that really guarantee a child's happiness."

"Anyway, I want that child's father to be someone I respect. Who I admire even."

Jeffrey laughed. "Like Jesse, huh? But your kids would be color-blind, and they'd have atrocious taste in clothes."

"I'm just saying that when and if my baby comes into the world, I want to think it's remotely possible the father and I will stay together. Not happily ever after, but *together*. And with Arkey I couldn't even dream that."

"So let's see if I've got it. From now on you'll only ever sleep with men you respect and can imagine spending your life with?"

"Far-fetched, huh? But look, I'm *never* going through this again. Whoever the father is, it happens, I'm having the child, even if it leaves me in a wheelchair. I just pray he'll be someone I respect as much as I do Jesse." Laura reached for a box of Kleenex. "Carol's a really lovely-looking person, by the way," Laura said. "Delicate features. Shining eyes."

"You met her?"

"No, he actually sent me a fucking picture. She's been raped, by the way. The guy would have killed her, someone hadn't scared him away."

"Wow."

"What I mean is, she's really beautiful. Ethereal. A Pre-Raphaelite miniature. But that wouldn't have done it for Jesse, you know? He needs a broken wing to heal."

Laura unfolded the pages that probably bore the happy news about how he hoped marriage would lift Carol from her occasional gloom, Jesse having written to Laura more as a psychiatrist, you see, not a former lover—like of course Laura could just put their past aside to help another human being, "so fucking noble," she said. "I could easily kill him."

"Could I see the letter?"

"This? This is something else." She'd handed it to him. Cream-colored stationery, black ink, large, squared-off, yet gothic-looking letters.

Dear Ms. Jaffe:

If my daughter were ever to say something to you meant for my wife and myself, you have my word that it would go no farther. I hope you know I wouldn't have testified against Mr. Healy if I hadn't been forced to in order to save my own daughter's life. I would never cooperate with any attempt to hurt her.

In any case, if you can ever find a way, could you give her this, along with her parents' steadfast love? We miss her terribly.

Thank you for your help.

Sincerely
Leo Jacobs

When Jeffrey looked up, Laura was holding out a fan of greenbacks. "Ten hundred-dollar bills." She let the money fall to the throw rug, reached over for another tissue. "The whole thing's so fucking sad. It's like the millionth time he's written me with something to give her. I mentioned it to her just once in California, and she shot a tree."

"Do you see her now?"

"Yeah, sometimes she shows up here, very late at night. You see her, too, Jeffrey, I know that. I always give her what I can."

"Me too." It was a bond between them, he and Laura the charter members of the Beth Fan Club (though *he* saw how tragic bearing charisma like Beth's could be—which made him President of the Club). In honesty, though, he added, "I know Billy has a way to send her something, too."

"I think she sees *that* as a royalty payment on her life rights."

"So she's probably getting rich, tithing from all of us."

"Yeah, well, she'll need the money soon. I have the feeling she thinks the revolution may not be on the agenda right now. She's thinking of surfacing."

Well, maybe it had been a time for everyone to readjust their dreams. No revolution for Beth; no Defender for Laura; and no making art for Jeffrey. But plenty of selling other people's, mostly Harry Hennessy's, Jeffrey's success giving Gaston and him the courage to start Weil and Schell.

They rented a large, attractive space on Fiftieth, Gaston insisting that Weil and Schell get something finer than they (or Jeffrey's trust fund) could really afford, but the bet paying off almost from the beginning, Gaston a genius at orchestrating shows and serving up the right curatorial razzmatazz for the catalogues. Even during the terrible Ford/Carter stagflation, when *nothing* was selling, he got buyers to submit to Weil's wiles.

Like Jimmy Benjamin, standing in the middle of the parquet looking like a hypnotized chicken when Gaston—brows raised, mellow chuckle to the voice—said, "Why not show your friend that Kline that came in today?" He walked Jeffrey to the back of the room, arm around his shoulder, mouth to his ear. "Upstairs," he whispered. "Borrow a painting."

On the way down in the freight elevator, Jeffrey doing as Master Gaston ordered, knifed off the small card affixed to the back of the frame. A thousand eyes on him in the empty elevator, he put on a new card that made it seem the piece had always been owned by Weil and

Schell, so the buyer wouldn't call the gallery the piece had originally come from, see how much W&S had marked it up. Which was the next thing Jeffrey had done—as per Gaston's instructions—adding fifty thousand as the charge for bringing it down in the elevator.

And Jimmy Benjamin had bought the whole fantasy, been photographed with it, full page, in *Rolling Stone* that month.

"You know Jimmy Benjamin!" Johannus yelped—that being the operative part of the story for him. *See,* he heard his dead father mutter, *he's like everyone else. He doesn't love you for yourself, but for who you know.*

"Yeah, Jimmy Benjamin and me, we went to Sunday school together," though he'd thought Benjamin an unpleasant, self-promoting little loon. Not crazy, though, as it turned out. *Or was he?* That being his art; creating flickering fantasies you could believe in, if you wanted, but never had to stake your life on. Just laugh, that was all—giggling at his willingness to play the schmuck, at your uncertainty if he actually was one—and at whether you were being a coward in watching said schmuck humiliate some woman or himself while you did nothing to stop it.

"I love the thing he'd do on Carson, where he starts out plugging a movie, and it turns into baby talk, including his adding whatever his eye lights on, you know the way a kid would . . ."

"Yeah?" Jeffrey said, trying to hide his growing envy.

"And he insists on a night-light as he talks to Johnny."

"Right."

"Or he like repeats Johnny's words, not like he's mocking him, but like he's a three-year-old, you know, doing it proudly."

"You bet." *Jesus, stop him!*

"He gets like younger as you watch, till he just babbles, then goes goo-goo. And then he wets himself."

"Sheer genius," Jeffrey said. But yes, Jeffrey thought, there's no act Jimmy wouldn't do for his act. And how is that different from a baby?

Jeffrey looked over at Johannus, staring out the Cad window at the Nothing that is, and he'd felt sick from jealousy. Why didn't Johannus think Jeffrey was as cool as a boy who wet himself on national TV? Had that been why Jeffrey was willing to lie about the provenance, because it would cheat someone from Great Neck who (God this hurt!) had actually become something more even than a comedian. An artist, namely. That little self-regarding prick!

"Jimmy was like his mother's favorite," Jeffrey said. "She totally ignored his sister," the real message being *not* that Mrs. B. had been a bad, sexist mother but that Jeffrey hadn't had a mother who'd bought him circus tights, beatnik outfits, even a ballet tutu to wear to school, a woman pleased by whatever he did, a Jimmy-joke told badly as wonderful and funny to her as something Alan King did on *Ed Sullivan*, extra cute even *because* it was told badly. Which was, indeed, something Jimmy had carried over into his act, his mom having given him the gift to designate what *he* did as interesting because he did it, like Duchamp and Warhol. That's what Beth had too; her father's fascination. *But not for you,* Jeffrey thought, Sam and Eloise's lesson having been: *nothing you do is interesting. Everything you do is annoying.*

If only Jeffrey had had a dad like Beth's or a mother like Jimmy Benjamin's, then he might be the one hosting *Saturday Night Live.* Or blowing up the Pentagon. Instead he slipped the bomber money, and sold art to the host, with a false provenance and an inflated price, the deal bringing much more Hollywood business, that being perhaps the one pocket of the world that still had money to spend on art. Still, the name/price change had made Jeffrey sick of himself and wary of his partner.

Soon enough Gaston rewarded his lack of faith, spending less and less time arranging for curators and more and more soliciting slaves, his particular "research" involving calling a pay phone downtown, seeing if he could get whoever answered to get in the limo he'd stationed outside the booth with one of his current slaves as the driver and a split of champagne and poppers in the back, a magic chariot to whisk Cinderella to the secret loft, "where the Master awaits you."

Gaston got his slaves to beg for guilt-cleansing beatings that made them pass out, or shoplift shirts for him at Saks, or once even rob a convenience store with a water pistol for a Baby Ruth. Playing the SM God—along with liberal doses of cocaine—unhinged Gaston, made him think he could create a law for himself at the gallery, too. The profits from Weil and Schell flew up his nose, though Jeffrey hadn't gotten the joke until Hennessy had twigged to Gaston's cheating *him,* putting things out at much higher prices than he'd let Harry know about, snorting the difference. Then, when Harry wanted to quit the gallery, Gaston refused to give his unsold pieces back. Jeffrey and Harry confronted him, and Gaston danced nervously from foot to foot, shouting that now was the hour of the furnaces, now a choice had to be made. Meaning, "Is it going to be me or Harry, Jeffrey?"

Jeffrey got Harry a lawyer so he could sue Gaston, his former partner's last words to Jeffrey being, "I should have made you a slave. Would have been better for both of us."

A few days after that, Beth had her bail hearing, and the Band gathered in the heat outside the courtroom. Olson had had a few words whispered into the bondsmen's ears; no one would handle Beth's outrageous bail. This whole thing, Jesse admitted, had become lots bigger than anything he'd ever dealt with before.

The Defender not knowing how to care for them! No one knew what to say to that. They'd looked then to Billy, who seemed most nervous of all.

"Aren't we the Mouseketeers who pledged to raise each other's soul-sparks?" Jeffrey said. After all, this was Beth they were talking about!

"Does that include bail?" Arkey asked with mock astonishment.

On the steps, Billy smiled wanly, distantly, his face sicklied with sweat. To raise a million dollars, he said, he'd have to sell his company.

So, Mr. Bad Ears, Jeffrey thought, *how much do you really care about Beth?* Then the spirit of competition, or something about the memory of that room in Great Neck, must have unhinged Jeffrey, the way cocaine and SM had done in his ex-partner's sanity. Or maybe, having no more Harry, Suki, Andy, or Gaston made Jeffrey want to be part of the Outsiders again, even if his role had been, and would always be, skeptical fag.

Besides, Beth, now and forever, was *his* beloved, his dream body. So he offered to put up most of his collection as surety for Arnie Golden's loan. Besides, Beth was History's own SM slave, the Woman Willing to Suffer for What She Believed; so one way or another, he'd get his paintings back soon enough, right?

Wrong. Beth had skipped, Arnie got Jeffrey's demi and full Johns. Then Jeffrey's father had gone coma-toes-up in a hospital bed from downers and fat, this wreck with the tubes in his nose the improbable bogeyman who had blighted Jeffrey's life with his hatred—and in fact, no less awesome and terrifying to him now that he had stubbled checks, closed eyes, and needed a creaky machine to breathe for him. Jeffrey and his sister stared down at his near-corpse, along with his former wife *and* his current mistress, who was maybe six years away from looking exactly like his mom—Sam's taste in women like his taste in cars, the Cadillac traded in every year for an almost identical fucking Cadillac.

All of them, though, but for Jeffrey, had been ready to pull the plug, turn the junkman to junk. Maybe Jeffrey was the only one who still wanted something from the near corpse, and he was certainly the only one who even half-believed in communication that didn't use the sense organs. Anyway, he felt that his dad's evil mind lived on still inside that occasionally twitching mound of fat. So he asked his father to blink twice if he wanted to go on living.

"Oh, fuck you, Jeffrey," his mother shouted, as his father winked the affirmative reply.

"Best conversation me and my Da ever had," Jeffrey told Johannus as they pulled past a sign that said, LAST NEGRO CAFE IN THE DELTA—TWO MILES.

"Yeah, so then you said to your father, 'You were always a jerk to me, right?' Go ahead, Dad. Just blink your eyes if the answer's *yes*. And keep them open forever if you don't agree."

"Something like that," Jeffrey said. "Anyway, after a while Sam did keep his eyes open forever."

"Meaning he didn't agree he was a jerk anymore?"

"But he'd been one, all right. He probably looked down laughing when Mom and me found out how he'd fucked up the carting business." His mom had to sell the GN house and most of her collection—which made her feel the whole art thing had been a hoax. She'd never been translated to a higher—a picture—plane, had really always been just the same as the other suburban cows, tied to their husbands' whims in mistresses, downers, and stock option plays.

Jeffrey took over the family business, spent restful mornings watching the remaining trucks going in and out of one of the Jersey dumps, afternoons on the phone arranging for barge rentals, landfill deals with the Carolinas. But Gaston bird-dogged him with some thugs he owed for coke. *Big Sam's gone. The Weak Link's in charge.* So they muscled in on the old outfit, the *good* mob guys who sold off-the-truck cartons of cigarettes to the men, or had loan sharks work the crews—you know, kind of like the helping hand. Jeffrey had been far too terrified to go to the cops. "Turned out, though, these new guys were real go-getters. They told me what contracts to bid on and how ridiculously much to ask. Then they made it clear to the competitors that they'd have union troubles if they undercut Weschler Co."

"Your life of crime."

"Right. Most of the boodle went to my new partners, but there was lots left over to pay for Mom's co-op. So I drifted, didn't even think about it. Then one day, Goombah Inc. decided to rationalize operations, take over the company directly. They made this ridiculous lowball offer, less than one the city had already made me. The guys said, 'Well, think of this as your give-back for all that extra money we helped you suck from the city's tit.' And my lawyer said that left me with one choice."

"Your life in law enforcement."

"Exactly. The city would put money in trust for my mom and seize the stuff I sold, if I'd wear a wire instead of a cock ring."

"Wow."

"Yeah, a movie, right. That's how I felt about it. Not *really* dangerous or anything, but exciting. It made me feel important. Gave a spring to my step. Except the real deal got done wordlessly, me and a young lawyer on Park Avenue. And soon as the ink dried, the FBI—my brothers in arms—dumped me. 'We'll be in touch when we need you to testify,' this fat, fifty-year agent says. Like, *Jesus, but I've always hated you, with your limp handshake, your British suits.* I said, 'Aren't you going to stash me somewhere?' The fat man said, 'I'll bet you can hide yourself lots better than we could.' Man, I was trembling by then. The guy must have seen. 'Look,' he said, 'don't blow this out of proportion. The guys you tattled on—' "

"Tattled?"

"Right, that's what he said. He said they were a small, inept group. Not that connected. Couldn't shoot straight. He said the feds would definitely have them all soon, so I should just stay out of touch with friends for a little while, take a vacation till they needed me. I thought he meant lie low. Don't be where they expect." His shoulders slumped, fatigue caused by foolishness. "But maybe he just thought I looked tired."

"So *is* someone looking for you?"

"Fuck if I know anymore. I started out imagining it because it made me more interesting, part of a story as good as Beth's. We were both underground. We both lived with danger. She feared cops, I feared robbers. It made my life feel weightier."

"Geez, Louise."

"Right," Jeffrey said, though at the moment that dear little phrase definitely got on his fucking nerves. "I was supposed to give the feds a few months, then call. But then he added I should use pay phones when I did."

"Geez—"

Stop him! "Yeah, and I must have looked sick again, because he said, 'Just kidding, okay?' Like he was playing me one way then the other for the fun of it. So now I don't know what to think. I wanted to feel like I was in a story. Not a sad one, though. Opera buffa. Then, it's like the story took over, took me into it." He had begun to cry. "Johannus, I'll tell you, flirting with death, I think it has this secret urgent knowledge for everyone else. But me, I am totally in over my head. And I am terrified out of my fucking mind."

"And the agent also said, 'Don't use the same phone twice in a row, okay?' " Jeffrey had started the story over for wider release at Snookey's, all of them now killing time together till Uncle Bastard would walk in the juke—a beer-bellied guy, Jesse had said, with thick brows, and a tremor in his hands.

"I've called the Special Agent in Charge a couple of times," Jeffrey added. "He says *probably* it would be all right to come home. But he's not sure. Oh, Lord, I cry, how long?" trying to keep it light, when inwardly he wanted to scream. And he worried that maybe he shouldn't have shown how eager he was to go home before he'd popped the question to Johannus—so the boy would know he meant *home with you.*

Jeffrey heard the juke door open. At another table, two young black men in T-shirts saw him jump, and smiled. A muscular black man in blue jeans walked in, making Jeffrey wonder why Barkely's uncle had chosen this juke to meet in. More piquant? *I go where I want,* combining with *we get along fine down here*?

The juke was holy ground to most of the people at the table, and even Jeffrey had to admit that he got a buzz from it; like some Latin American peasant crawling to see the statue of St. Someone or Che Guevara's emaciated corpse, he felt closer to a numinous Someone or Something in this juke, like the walls, with their expressionist smears of green and red paint, were about to reveal more of his vision to him, something for his Mississippi Death Extravaganza. *Joy and tragedy mixed?* Which means what, exactly? The most lamentable comedy, and most cruel death of Frank Jaffe?

David said Frank had sat at this very chipped wooden table, watching the dancers, talking kabala with Chuck Taylor. "Frank listened mostly," David said. "Chuck told him that Israel had to enter into evil, raise the sparks of holiness hidden there. To me that sounds an awful lot like your letters." David smiled, pretended to find it odd that anyone needed more than the world's horror and his own skin to know he had to make justice. (Yes, he got all that into a smile.) "I remember Sugar said the sparks here must be buried in some three hundred years of shit." He stared sadly at his beer bottle. "Chuck Taylor, he's an African priest now. And that Sugar, I hear he's raising the sparks in Roxbury, Mass. Harder work, I'll bet, even than Mississippi." He glanced over at Jeffrey—as representative of Up North.

Jeffrey looked away from David's basilisk eyes. He admired David's courage, seemingly so collected while he waited to meet the man who'd murdered his closest friend. After all, it could have been David that day, too.

Jeffrey's bladder hurt, but the bathroom, David said, had a wall down, been like that so long that David thought somebody must want it that way. Strange that Jeffrey could put his dick in a glory hole, but not pee in a black man's juke in Mississippi. He tipped backward in his creaky chair, one leg of it held together by tape and spit. BE NICE OR LEAVE, THANK YOU, a fading sign on the wall said. And "O Lord Please Help. Me. To. Keep. My. Damn. Nose. Out. Of. Other. Peples. Busness."

Too late for that. "Anyway," Jeffrey said, taking things back to Topic A, "I don't have damn all idea how much danger I'm in. Still, don't tell anyone I'm here. Not anyone. My life is in your hands," delivering that line to Johannus with a fond smile. Arkey and Jesse exchanged Meaningful Looks—which reminded him of something. "Did you boys know I was gay, I mean then, when we were growing up?"

"Gay?" Jesse laughed. "Well, that would have been a stretch."

"A faggot, right? That's what you would have called me then," what you probably secretly call me now, he added to himself, glancing over at Johannus.

Jesse shrugged. "No. I knew you were different, though. More sophisticated. Like you'd been to Europe."

Jeffrey laughed. "Yeah, you could call it Europe. But did you know I wanted you, Jess? Then, I mean. You're not my type anymore." Though, on a different day, Johannus absent . . .

"Damn," Jesse said, his face deadpan; always more wit to the Defender than Jeffrey expected. Always a worse suit, too; some shade of gray, and maybe not off the rack but actually mail-order, like being color-blind had affected his ability to judge the cut of clothing, too.

"You would have screamed like a stuck pig if you'd known I'd wanted you, wouldn't you?"

"No. Actually, I knew. Didn't I? Anyway, I think I knew in a way. And I guess, yeah, it made me nervous. But I'll tell you the truth, Jeffrey, mostly it did wonders for my self-esteem. I felt terrible about how I looked after I lost a finger because Billy wouldn't go to swim class."

Hard to believe. Jesse, despite the clothes, had always looked so damn handsome. But nice of him to say it.

"Me," Arkey said, "I just never thought about it. Never thought about anything but myself. My grades, my glorious future. My Intended. My ivory."

"Your brother-in-law. I mean, I need your help, Arkey," Jeffrey said, not able to wait anymore, though it might be a mistake asking in front of everyone—this being Kaplan dirty laundry. "If I'm still, you know, in trouble, I thought maybe Specs could help settle things for me?"

David Watkins meticulously arched one brow. Something most definitely aristocratic to David's manner, more self-confident, less parvenu than Jeffrey or his friends. On the other hand, the eyebrow might unintentionally drive Jesse to throw his drink in his friend's face.

"You know, he could say I was already working with those other guys, so the guys I told on shouldn't have been milking me anyway, right? Or something."

Arkey shrugged. "Mob etiquette's beyond me. And Specs, he always says he's not connected." Which wasn't true anymore, Arkey thought, *in the family*. He and Jeffrey had a zany childhood in common, but they *weren't* family. "But look, I'll ask him."

"And I know I don't have to tell you, Arkey, but don't say where I am. I mean, he's your brother-in-law, and all . . ."

"Right, but he's not your family."

He was Arkey's family, though, for sure—the Cardinal Richelieu of Kel-Kap, the sage counselor, the fixer. Used to be, anyway. Now Specs might not have the juice to help. "He's not himself," June had said, a month ago at that diner she liked, the Sea something, on Northern Boulevard, where Great Neck washed into Little Neck, a favorite of hers since she was a kid, when it had had a wild-side air to it, juvies in leather jackets on Harleys. Now it was insurance agents in brown suits. Probably the same guys. "He's been losing weight," she had said. "He's distracted all the time."

"Yeah, it's been a down market, right?"

"Yeah." She'd turned to the waitress. "Rare, bloody even," meaning her hamburger. "But très complique, pour lui, naturellement," she said, dropping phrases from her afternoon French class; a habit that would probably one day set off Kate's odd phobia, start her on a marathon prayer session. "Exxon's selling dollars against yen. His forward positions are unraveling."

"Hnnn," Arkey said, slurping his chocolate shake, not wanting to seem like he didn't know the intricate machinery of the world as well as Specs. Or his sister.

"And there's the constant FBI harassment. They send these ridiculous doctored photos to Ralph, like I'm seeing Guido or Gino or some disgusting prick on the sly. Can you believe it?"

"Sure," Arkey said. "About the FBI, I mean." Hey, he'd been through the sixties, right? That made it an article of faith to believe any bad thing about the FBI.

"Like they think Specs'll believe their dirty fantasies and take revenge on Gino—you know, cheat him or something. And the guys he works for, *they* get letters that Specs is making piles of money for some other family and stiffing them." She took a little yellow pill with a sip of water. "Still, it's a constant headache—especially with profits off like this."

"I can imagine," Arkey said, not really able to imagine it, and wondering how often June took those mother's little helpers.

"And that jerk you went to Sunday school with, Jimmy Benjamin, he's making trouble, too. He wants to audit the books on a movie."

This was news. "A movie?"

"Yeah, one of Ralph's companies actually funded a film. Look, I don't know why I'm telling you this. But I think Ralph, he often has his companies pay for movies that I bet are never made. I met one of the guys he hired as a scriptwriter once, and he like barely spoke English, unless 'you fucking fuck I'm gonna fuck your fuck' is English. "

Arkey imagined *that* sentence in Mr. Hartman's class at the Dewey School and started to spit malted milk from his nose. Plus, it still gave him a kick when June said *fuck*.

"Anyway, these companies he sets up, they pay big bucks for the supposed scripts. Sometimes they even rent trucks and sets and stuff, and then decide not to make the film. Get it?"

"Yeah, it launders money."

"Still the Harvard grad, huh?" She smiled meanly.

"Jealous?"

"Oh, yes, hurts like a son of a bitch. You'd been the Dewey School valedictorian, I'd have killed myself." A fakey smile. "But you weren't, huh?"

No. *That* had been Bobby Brown. Bobby Brown had gotten Laura, too. For a while, anyway.

She had sipped her Tab. They served it here in a fluted glass. "But then this once, he actually funded a damn film for Jimmy Benjamin. It goes way over budget, of course. The caterers deliver stolen bologna sandwiches and charge for lobster, that kind of thing. Your friend Benjamin—"

"He wasn't my friend."

"Whatever. I shouldn't do this," she said—then put the big hamburger on a seeded bun between her lips, chomped happily, blood dripping down. Always a girl of good appetites. She still had her figure, though, thanks to nearly ceaseless swimming, golf, and gossiping. "Anyway, Benjamin thinks he has points in the film. That means a percentage of the profits. He's been told by Ralph, he's been told by his manager—"

"Arnie Golden—"

"That's the one. Charming man."

Man? Why was Arnie a *man*, he had wondered, and he forever a boy to his sister?

"That there are no profits. None. Nada. Zilch. *Bupkis*. But he acts like that's impossible. *Of course* there are profits, the film was a big hit." She looked down regretfully at the last of her burger.

"Yeah. I saw him on *Letterman*, talking about what a smash it was. I thought it was like a gag. I didn't even know there'd been a movie."

"Probably there isn't," June said, wiping her lips daintily with a paper napkin. "Probably the film stock was never developed."

"They showed a documentary on *Letterman*, Jimmy pretending he's a huge movie star, right? He acted like paparazzi are following him, like some nebbish who doesn't have any idea what's going on is hounding him, ruining his life, or a gaggle of Japanese tourists are really fans asking for autographs." Jimmy's gift, Arkey thought, to live in a world of his own devising, infantile but compelling, like, say, believing the dead wrote you. The Revolution's coming. The Mafia's chasing you.

"I don't get it, myself," June said. "And he just keeps going and going about those profits, no matter what his manager says. Now he's got an investigation started. Why aren't his nonexistent points in this nonexistent film being paid him? And *that* isn't funny, Arkey. Golden, is he still a friend of yours?"

"Yeah, in a way." Insofar, that is, as you can be friends with someone you grew up with who has his name on the big screen and earns astronomically more money than you do.

"Anyway, Arnie Golden's fed up with Benjamin, too." The hamburger gone, she lifted a tomato slice off her plate with her long, blood-red fingernails. "And he's like not the only problem, either. Some plastic surgeon from Lake Success, who Specs let into a co-op deal, he wants an audit."

"Is this the same guy who wanted help getting his wife's lover beat up?"

June smiled. "Can you believe it? Specs tells these people he doesn't have those kinds of connections, but they don't listen. The doctors line up to be part of any business deal he's doing, positive it can't go wrong. Like if he takes a rent-controlled building co-op, who's going to protest? I think it's good for him, sometimes, to have these orthodontists in the partnership. Window dressing."

"But now he's being pursued by a pack of braying doctors? Like in a Wally Wood drawing."

"A cartoon? Yeah, but not so funny. *Now*, I guess, they believe Ralph's *not* mob-connected, so they don't have to be scared of him. After all, if he *was* connected, they'd have made money, right? So they want the DA to investigate."

Once, Specs had liked the docs' tough-guy poses. He'd been attracted to Judaism because it had respect for education, and what he was best at, using knowledge and shrewdness. And not, that is to say, because they were all a bunch of peace-loving rabbis, Specs' opinion being that it would be good if Jews had more fight in them, "better for our survival," he'd said the last time they'd played golf, the *our* nearly stopping Arkey's backswing. "And most Jews agree with me, Arkey. Look at how proud they are of the Israeli Army. You know, 'Hey, we can be tough, too. Our army has kicked the shit out of these people.' "

"Not just that," Arkey had insisted. "We're proud of Israel if it's moral even in the way it uses power, the way *our* Talmud restrains it."

"A guilty army, huh? What would the Palestinians say about that, you think? Leave morality out of it, Arkey."

"Then what stands between the world and another Holocaust?"

"You mean, between the Jews' and another Holocaust? Why, Israel, Arkey. That's the whole point, isn't it?"

Was it? No, that had to be wrong, or anyway not the *whole* point. He remembered Grandpa Abe at a Passover dinner. Torah ethics, the morality of the Internationale, the Jews' gift to world socialism; each part of that fragment now a Messianic hope. Still, to be Jewish had to mean *not* leaving morality out of *anything*—sex, the dinner table, borscht belt routines, whatever. Arkey had neared the green, looked at his big-armed brother-in-law squatting, measuring his putt. *Well, now,* he thought, *I can tell the difference between a Roman and a Jewish nose.*

But he would ask Specs about helping Jeffrey. Maybe pack him off to Israel—for safety!—along with Billy, who Jeffrey said still talked about making aliyah, though he wasn't observant anymore, and thanks to Helen Green—Sat Siri Who Was—spent more time at Esalen than at shul.

So what *did* Billy believe now? Not in *this,* Arkey thought—meaning Snookey's, meaning their past, his prophecy—or he'd be here, right?

But what he believed had grown equally murky to the artist—along with everything else about the scene, though the optometrist said these moments when the frame swam out of focus had no physical basis. Billy tilted the dented spring-style light closer to the page, the architect's lamp having gone from Great Neck to college and back here with him, but not helping him see the future of this story. *If in doubt,* his dad used to say, *black it out.*

OurKey threw down a fireball, and swirling smoke covered the carnage!!

Ah, if only Billy could go to divorce court with smoke bombs, obliterate his marriage.

Matt, the last of the inkers to have known his dad, got up to go home, and Billy hunched lower over his drawing board, not wanting to talk. Writers, inkers, pencilers, any staff who wanted to, work-for-hires included, labored in the same big room that had once belonged to J-Line Dresses, the famous Bullpen, beloved of BABY readers, even Billy-BossEars; and not just to seem democratic, either. No, he did it for *safety in numbers,* though tonight the high chair pulled up to the drawing table made him feel grotesquely small, vulnerable.

"Gonna work late again?" Matt said.

"You know, deadline on *Girls with Guns,*" he lied to Matt, swirling more smoke, *pour ecrasez l'infame.*

"That's why you're the boss."

"Nope," Billy said. "It's 'cause I inherited the business from my father."

Matt had loved Billy's Da, no question. While Billy's family had been home sitting shiva, Matt had decorated the walls here with Nathan's characters, Rubber Man and Ace Detective, huge, in vivid colors. A few days after Billy took over, Matt, worried Billy might feel slighted, had stayed up all night again, adding a Defender, Athena X, etc. Lumpy-looking, muddy figures, though. From loyalty or distaste, Matt couldn't bring himself to draw a decent Outsider.

Anyway, both of them knew he didn't go home because that would now be the Harvard Club, Helen having gotten a restraining order to keep him out of their co-op.

Matt sighed, shuffled out.

And what next? Billy could keep the lassitude off by working, but it would brim up as soon as inspiration faltered, leave him staring at the misshapen wall decorations, wishing his parents had never met.

So kill someone, obviously. *How* was the hard part.

> **A piece of thin copper wire with small black weights on each end, specially balanced by MyKill, flies across the frame! Whizzzzz!**

Or had he used that one a few weeks ago, in "Prophet Deborah's Desperate Gamble"? Hard to sleep on the Aardvark Club's rough sheets, which affected his memory.

> **Hurled with an art passed down to Ninjas over the ages, it takes the false former Greyhound's head neatly off!!! Blood spurts from his neck!!!**

Which made him wonder what Beth herself was up to now. Did she still think her bombs had made justice for Frank? Thank God there hadn't been any of those for a while, each one, he felt, credited to his account. Probably partly paid for by him, too. Well, maybe she'd settled down, changed her name, and lived in a suburb, raised her child, with a . . . doctor. No, he had never felt that in her; had never drawn it and made it so. But he wished her well; she hadn't known about the affair. She'd never betrayed him.

His mind drifted to the Warner's offer to buy his company. Could he trust Arnie to handle the negotiations? Could he trust anyone? Himself, for example?

Ninja B. could use **the Vibrating Palm** on this traitor, shake his kidneys to pieces, make the victim piss himself to death, evaporate from panel to panel. That one hadn't come 'round for a while. But he wanted to work with blood tonight, sprays of it, gouts even, and expressionist drops as an overlay, as if the readers' eyes had been spattered.

Maybe Dr. Why? could have taught N.B. a new palm move—a finger flex that changes the quantum position of the quarks—and makes a dandy hole open in the banker's—whoops!—the bad guy's chest.

Blood fountains over the Outsiders' heads. BBE sticks out his tongue, samples a few drops.

He could already see the crooked smiles, the not-yet-formed faces and avid yet vacant eyes of his unfailingly masculine interlocutors at the next COMCON (in the Windy City! Outsiders, be there or be square!).

"Is Billy becoming like a vampire or something?"

"Me?" he'd say. "Or Bad Ears?" A sure laugh for everyone's favorite shtick—him the little guy in front of them, him the magus in the comic books. That and "How do I get published?"

Some kids would hand him drawings to look at—Bad Ears alone, at night, usually, drinking strong tea, listening to the world's pain. Mr. Intuitive hadn't known his wife was cheating on him, though—what about that bonehead play, fellow Outsiders?

"Good," he'd say, though the panel usually looked like a tracing. "But you've got to develop your own style, otherwise you'll always be only almost as good as someone else. And try to get more excitement in the drawing. Let the steam from the tea go crazy, okay?"

He would turn to all of them, arms open, eyes wild, shout, "Audace, audace, et encore d'audace!" You'd be surprised how many got that, these kids reading a lot, loners whose intense admiration made him feel more lonely. They couldn't keep him company, couldn't even *see* him at his interstellar distance. "Don't try to make it real, okay?" he told them. "If people want that, they can read novels. Don't study life, like they tell you in creative writing classes. Read comics." Which was what they all wanted to hear, Billy and the rest of them having grown upside down, like potatoes, life—mostly meaning the opposite sex—too terrifying for them. "Then make even *that* more so. Off center. Kinked, you know? These are comics, they don't have to be polite."

Often near five hundred kids in line, clutching their own smudged 10-by-15 drawings, Helen not believing it the once she'd come, these eager kids with their testosterone injected backward, not the future Columbia profs she'd expected, preparing papers for the MLA like "Billy Green: Hyperbole and Postmodernism."

But the aging maestro's own next panel? "Once more against the ACRONYMS!" N.B. shouts—modeling from Delacroix's *Liberty on the Barricades,* plus a soupçon of implied nipple. He could feel his body getting heavy, it being Helen's breasts he drew today, from memory from now on; and Billy punishing himself—or the Helen within—because she'd left him. He wanted her—*and* he wanted to give her the vibrating palm. Prophetic bar mitzvah homily: *God will hear the plea for justice of a wronged woman. Restraining our anger by the Law is the work of a lifetime.* Well, he still had the anger, but he didn't have the Law anymore; and his fury made him feel a singular monster who wanted to pay zero alimony.

He'd better do some filler here till he felt better. A new Outsider, maybe—based on the guy Jesse worked with—Watkins, the one who'd known Frank. The first black Outsider!

In 1981—Jesus, he should be ashamed of himself!

And . . . *the ArIstocrat?* The *ArIsto* will be able to move in an upper-class world that the other O.'s don't even know about. A near-British, shaken-not-stirred, insouciance about him. But can the Band trust him? He could be a double agent—or are they suspicious because he's black? That would make for some nice inward-gnawing self-doubt.

> "The ACRONYMS are what Outsiders call
> the agencies the government deploys to beat
> the Commies," OurKey explains at the
> Fortress as smoke swirls up from ArIsto's
> cigarette holder.

> "Ah, the ACROS do the covert Ops, right?"
> the ArIsto says. "The black bag jobs. The dirty
> war requires horrors American voters would
> never allow done in their names."

Cut to:

> Zargon at his WorldBank HQ, shouting,
> "Americans act like spoiled children! They
> want the cheap sugar from empire, but they
> act outraged when they learn who we have to
> kill to keep candy prices down!"

> The Desperado pulls a large yellow switch on
> the control panel. "Americans ask for truth with
> their mouths, but their eyes plead with us to lie
> to them!"

But what the hell is the switch connected to? And has Zargon spent too many frames recently railing at everyone, Billy's own disdain leaking out, like slather, from Zargon's scaly jaws? Oh, he was weary! He needed that Warner's sale. But could Arnie delay the closing without blowing the deal, so the money wouldn't show up in the divorce settlement? Well, he had to trust *someone*.

Which made him wonder if his dear SheWolf had known about Helen's affair? After all, the women spilled everything in their West Side Speak Bitterness group. Maybe he should give SheWolf a few little muscle problems that Dr. Why? *can't* fix. Put her in a wheelchair. He knew they all still secretly suspected he had witchy predictive powers— so the imagined paralysis would freak Laura out, make her nervous; the stress would bring the disease back; and so the prophecy would come true. Which he *probably* couldn't do to Laura, even if she hadn't tipped him that Helen had been cheating on him for the last two years at least.

Add more betrayers? The Band, in its ceaseless quest to restore democracy, is sold out by that seeming ally, network news anchor Spending Paul, redrawn tonight to look exactly like a certain banker, tall, square-jawed as Fearless Fosdick, and . . .

> on the air, the cord from his earpiece sneaks
> through the frame, down past bewildered sewer
> rats, and directly to Zargon's headquarters—
> where a troll minion feeds him viral lies to
> transmit about Ninja B., "the terrorist
> assassin."

Maybe SheWolf should make the WASP newsreader's veneer melt away on air, revealing his poxed face, the fumes of his foul breath, his herpes buboes, which were now, alas, also Billy's. But if sugar prices stay low will anyone care who exactly reads the news to them?

> "A wrestling match or something, that's all we
> are," MyKill shouts as they watch television
> together in the Fortress. (Is that a coat hanger
> used as an antenna—or one of the Fizzyits'

Fantastic gadgets to see alternate quantum
worlds?)

"Yeah, the cowards just want to watch us," Ninja
B. says, her voice a little shrill recently

at least in Billy's imagination.

"No," OurKey says, shaking his sage gray head.
"Americans aren't cowards. They just worry we'll
be as power-hungry as the ORG."

Maybe sometime he'd have the Outsiders end up in charge of the
government—and using their own ACRONYMS to secure *their* power?
Then, **Ninja B.** would purge the group—give the new improved **Death
Palm** to that traitor: **Glow Girl.** Maybe kill most of them. After all, Laura
would have blabbed it everywhere, they'd probably *all* known about
Helen's affair. The BB Universe could be filled with pro- and anti-
democracy superheroes, one turning into the other, over and over; over
and over.

Which repetitive pointlessness reminded him that really he hadn't
done a story tonight, because really he didn't have any point of view
anymore, or anything to draw about. *I mean, these colorful, profitable
images had done exactly what to prevent another Holocaust?*

QED: *he* shouldn't draw. Ah, but the depressive goo in his own
skull? So he'd have to sketch till he dropped. Besides, the people who
worked for Green Co. depended on him—until that Warner's deal
closed, anyway. If that worked out, it would give them all a safety net.
Then if he didn't want to work for a while, he could go to Israel, lead a
Jewish life. Maybe that would be as good a goop-processor as drawing
comics, Israel giving him a life less pointless by letting him build the
Jewish State—or at least *argue* over the Jewish State, which seemed to
count as building, provided you were living there, sharing its hardships;
which for him would mostly mean the shekel's staggering rate of infla-
tion, Billy too old and too short for the IDF and a romantic death. Still,
there'd be the *possibility* of the danger to make his life more profound.

Maybe he could find a Jewish wife in Israel, too; the farthest thing
from one having turned out to be not a Muslim Fundamentalist but a
third-generation Reformed from the Upper West Side, raised in Ethical
Culture at Fieldston, Sat Siri Gilman. Could a marriage to a Jew—a *real*
Jew, an *Israeli* Jew—rejoin him to his people, make them *his* again?

How cute and slightly possessive that sounded! And why did he care if they'd be *his*? Did he think the Jews would protect him—be his *gang,* as Arkey's brother-in-law would say? No, for him, to be *chosen* would mean to have an ordinary life, a child, a Jewish family, be part of a community that maybe couldn't protect him but would sorrow with him throughout his life. That should be enough. All you could expect, anyway.

So, *should* he make aliyah? *That* question, he knew, wouldn't be answered by anything his friends had found out in Mississippi, but the idea of calling Jesse strangely lightened his body a little, helped him make it down from his perch, over to the wall phone to hear about the meeting.

Mostly, Jesse told Billy that night, the guy had wanted to whine—not uncommon with murderers. "The FBI," Barkely's uncle had said, "they brought some thug down, a greaseball from Chicago. He put a gun in this asshole's mouth, made him give everybody over." He'd turned to David Watkins, his dog eyes plaintive as he stared at the black man. "That's not right, is it?" Then back to Jesse. "What can you do, though?"

Anyway, a jury of his peers had found the evidence—the body, the gun, a confession, the risen Christ pointing his finger directly at the accused—insufficient, had let him off so he could kill a couple more niggers, he said, before the Justice Department finally put him in jail for six years on federal charges. "Which means they tried me twice for the same crime, you know, first in state, then in federal court. That's not right, is it?" he'd said again, looking just at Jesse this time, part grievance, part free consult with a lawyer.

Jesse had to agree, that was not the way it should be. And how was the uncle's so different from his nephew's case? If Jesse had been this man's lawyer, he'd have gotten the FBI evidence thrown out, probably gotten him off. He was the Defender, after all. But would that have been justice? That kind of question getting more heart-numbingly frequent recently.

The men at the bar had stared at the table with slit eyes, something coming off this old Klan guy in waves, the air humid now with menace. The man had put his arms wide, like he knew everyone in the place would want to kill him, even thrived on it.

"I'll tell you, I don't know why we did it. Wrote those letters, I mean. I know why we killed the little bastard." He turned to David. "I wanted to kill you, too, if you're who I think you are. You had that same snotty smile then, like you thought you were as good as us."

David had given him the very grin. "Better, actually."

The man had tried cold eyes, but no one was buying; so he smiled, raised his glass. "Well, to old times, right? We're like veterans of a war these kids can't ever understand the way we do."

David had curled his lips in, looked away.

"One of you is like the dead guy's brother, right?"

No one had said anything.

"Yeah, we wanted to do something a little creepy, make you people crazy, way you made us. Submitted for your consideration, huh?" He'd chuckled at his own fabulous mimicry. "Like on *The Twilight Zone*, right? Tell them that their son was rotting in hell, or under like a ton of dirt." His eyes traveled to the sign on the wall. "Make you think twice about sticking your big noses in everybody's business. Didn't work, though, did it?" He'd picked up his shot glass, downed it. "You buying?"

Jesse had nodded.

"You're family of his, though, right?" he'd said again, like that mattered.

"No. And why didn't you write the family?" Jesse had asked.

"Didn't we? Sure we did."

"No, you wrote Frank's girlfriend."

"Tha' right?"

"How did you get the address?" Jeffrey had asked, his voice squeaky, probably from fear, the letters maybe, or maybe just being around a murderer, Jesse remembering his own first frisson at that—the connection to the Absolute Void, Jeffrey would have said; or some such.

The man had shrugged. "The girlfriend, huh? Well, like, maybe your friend told me, wanted me to get in touch with her, tell her what happened. You know, like that could be it. But I couldn't write, *Hey, we shot your boyfriend,* could I? I mean I was drunk, but I know about fingerprints and all. So I wrote some other shit, like you said, about dirt. Meaning, you know, he's under it. Or something. You tell me." His voice wondering, like maybe he'd realized this was the exact opposite of what he'd said before, that he'd intended horror.

"Did you write *that,* about dirt, I mean?" Arkey had asked.

"No," Jeffrey had said, strangely precise, even brutal. "Billy said that when he touched the page. It wasn't in a letter."

"You bet," the man had said, meaninglessly, face going slack, like Jeffrey had slapped him.

Jeffrey had sounded sure as shit, but Jesse couldn't remember. Had the earth come from Billy, been in a letter, or in the newspaper story even? Besides, what did it matter? No spirit had moved *this* man's hand—except the spirit of Jack Daniel's. A dead man's will had turned into a drunk's sodden spitefulness.

But Jeffrey the Sophist hadn't looked disappointed. "So you maybe thought you were doing him a favor," Jeffrey had said, but not acidic—more wonderingly, like a kid listening to a bedtime story.

"Well, could be, right? But, like I said, who knows anymore? I mean we did a lot of drinking in those days." He finished another drink. "Some of the others, they wrote things, too. You should ask them why they did it."

"The *others?*" Jeffrey had said. *But why,* Jesse had wondered, *would anyone want more of this crap?* Acid lapped at the back of his throat, and he'd popped another Maalox. They'd gotten letters from a bastard, so what? How could he have believed otherwise, any more than when he'd put on a cape at Halloween he should really have imagined he was Superman?

The man had seen Jeffrey's surprise, and calculation crossed his pocked and veined face, him thinking, *Do I have to give this up for free? How much do I owe that shit-brained nephew?* Jesse had just stared back until the man scribbled something on a napkin. One name, Rev. something—probably holding more back, in case he decided he could fuck his nephew over, trade it later for his own payoff.

"We left him, just sitting there," Jesse told Billy, "the two guys in T-shirts eyeing him, but probably not daring to do anything either, or wise and decent enough not to bother."

Jesse hung up then, feeling angry with Billy for no reason. He hadn't sent Jesse's life off track, the way he had Beth's. He had at least finally said no to the I-Lab, for what that was worth, and despite Billy's final performance. And he'd have become a defender anyway without the guilt he felt for that explosion. Or for the little he'd done to help Frank. His ever-unmentioned, barely remembered brother Morris was probably a bigger piece of it than anything Billy had said, like save a killer, feel less guilty for wanting Morris to die.

No, he got annoyed with Billy because he hated the way he made his life into a comic book now, and the way he got it wrong, making electrocuted men into Electric Powers when really what they became was sacks of pus and shit. So he'd held out on Billy this time, left Jeffrey out, staring, reaching out like E.T. at one point to touch the bad man's hand, like something would flow through it to him. A comic book moment, for sure.

Worse than that, though, Jesse had to admit he'd actually wanted something from this encounter himself—like a reason why he should go on with his work. David Watkins, long ago, had come to his law school, his eyes filled with an air of kindly, sad disappointment in white people. He said, There's this job you can do, and so Jesse had started doing it, put one foot in front of the other, knowing they shouldn't kill these men. *But why?* Somewhere there *had* to be a Law that said people shouldn't take vengeance. But now he needed to know where that fucking law was written. On our hearts only? Well, that wasn't enough. The world, lately, it seemed a torrent of pain and suffering to Jesse, so why *did* it matter if we added one more drop, killed one more guy or a thousand more guys. Or women. Or children. Just like Arkey had said in the lawyers' bar, Jesse, too, had dreamed he'd find out that Barkely's uncle had written with blind eyes; and he dreamt that would let him feel again like he had in Laura's bedroom, that we suffer in the grave until our soul-sparks are returned to God. That life is holy. That God *is,* comes to that.

Instead he'd got a drunken thug who amused himself making up nonsense to fuck with Jewish heads.

Jesse walked through the house, turning off the lights that Carol, like a toddler, left on each night. He flicked them off because he wanted her to know there was nothing to worry about. But he didn't want to come off as the punitive father, *do you kids think I'm made of money?,* so he left the kitchen light burning.

Looking back on the living room from the stairs, he wondered again why Carol didn't buy more furniture. They weren't *that* poor. Was she planning to escape from him and his retinue of murderous bastards? Is that why she didn't want to have children?

But she didn't simply *not* want a child. Carol, more assiduous and careful than he was, took her temperature every day, heat-guiding the sperm to target. The proper position, too, legs backward, thinking about the Empire of Motherhood. And she wept every month when they didn't succeed, despite her douching sabotage. What had become of his laughing, brilliant wife? The house she'd made was more nondescript than unfurnished, like a motel room, thin standing lamps with vapid shades, and the art on the walls simple geometric patterns, of no interest to anyone, though Carol loved painting, had even once loved teaching color-blind him about it.

Tonight, on the top step, he finally got it. *Nondescript.* Carol didn't want to be noticed. That's what his work, their lives, had done to the extraordinary person he'd married.

Who hid even now, naked in their bed, covers pulled up almost to her eyes. Jesse took off his clothes, got under the blankets, and the heat from Carol's body was like a magic potion, making him stiff, but not quite stopping the horrid memories from last week. In BillyBooks, when they fried a man in the electric chair, he *always* turned out to have worked at a faulty nuclear reactor, so he emerged transformed into Mr. Voltage, or Sparky, a youthful offender who becomes Voltage's sidekick—more powerful than a hand buzzer!

In Jesse's real life, the condemned's drugs wore off, his eyes bugged out, and he looked frantically through the Plexiglas at Jesse, the two of them moaning together, like cows waiting for the hammer. And the gas worked just fine.

Jesse's life was like that now; he ate his burgers, fucked his wife, but he always carried this charnel house inside him where the kid had looked like man become animal become a heavy sack of shit and pus and drying blood, incapable of grabbing a phone and flying across the telephone lines—man become electricity!—and frying the governor's brains on the other end—or his aide's, more likely.

Jesse gazed down at Carol now, her face tilted up toward him, her eyes closed, her legs drawn carefully back so no precious drop would be lost, Carol not outside it, he'd swear, like Jesse tonight, not thinking about a comic book, anyway—in fact this the time of the month she seemed to enjoy most. He tried to keep himself from coming, give her longer, intentionally tried not to think how thrilling Carol's pleasure was for him, her face reddening, twisting up to meet her electrical charge, Jesse become a little like Mr. Voltage—Reddy Kilowatt dipped in the waters of hell, Voltage, who appears as images on the TV whenever he wants to scare the shit out of the citizenry; manifesting himself wherever electricity flows, the electricity building in Jesse's thighs now, the kundaloo or whatever it was called rising toward his brain, about to take the top of his head off. He peeked again at Carol's thin, delicate face, most exciting to him when *he* was there as a force only, an adjunct to her fun. Her mouth rose toward her pleasure like a runner trying to meet the finish line.

Wait, hold back a stroke. He had to remember to draw the divine light down from the buckets in heaven, this kabala thing that Arkey had told him about—white milky light to fill the soul of the child to come.

Or not. Like every month, Carol ran to the bathroom. He heard her fill the bag, water slopping into the sink, Carol soon douching all that swell light away. But this time, when she lay down beside him, he didn't say anything about it, not thinking the douching would work anyway and definitely not wanting to make her cry.

"Jesus," she said, "it's your silence that's the worst." They both stared up at the ceiling, Carol whimpering already.

He rolled on his side, stroked her hair, her cheek, her tears far worse for him than his own disappointment that she didn't want a child.

"I know something will happen to him," she said. "That's why I douche, Jesse. I just know it will and it will be my fault. I didn't leave the lid on the cleaning fluid. I turned away when he was showing off on the jungle gym. Someone in a department store took his hand while my back was turned. I see myself telling you about it and you don't say anything, you hug me and gaze with those sad brown eyes. But you blame me, how could you not, and I can't bear that, I—" by then, little hiccups of tears built into body-shaking sobs.

"Stop, now," he said, hugging her hard, feeling how light her body was, how in need of protection. "Blame you? Of course not, darling, we haven't lost anything," but the implication there, too, *because we don't have anything.*

Fortunately, she wasn't listening to him anymore, had cried herself to sleep. Jesse tasted the bile at the back of his throat, slowly drew his hand from under Carol's head.

He chewed another chalky piece of crap, the taste reminding him of the half roll he'd swallowed listening to that empty, pocked-face fuck at Snookey's talking about the effect killing Frank had had on him. Namely, he said, it hadn't mattered much to him at all. If it hadn't been for the fucking government, he said, he'd just have gone back to logging.

But there are three *letters,* Jeffrey had said when David had wisely opined, "So much for this shit."

"That means," Jeffrey said, "two more stories to track down. I think we oughta hear them."

Did Jesse still have a glimmer of hope that the letters would tell him what he should do with the bastard's bastard nephew? Or how to help his own beautiful wife, lit by the dismal phosphorescence of the TV, her brow edged with worry, Carol on the lookout for danger even in sleep. Was *he* the danger—like she already suspected about the business with Barkely?

David said he respected Jesse because he always put the client first, made him the center of attention. But now maybe Jesse wanted to be the hero of a story—like Jeffrey and his Mafia movie. *Would* he save Barkely? *Would* he still be the Defender? Like, see Ish. #56: "The D's Greatest Crisis"—or some such shit. Maybe, in this story, he even *wanted* Carol to find out about Barkely's meaningless boast, be furious beyond bearing. Then, in the last frame, to save his marriage, the kilted one can drop his big sack of murderers down a well. *No choice, guys, it was my wife made me do it.*

That thought curdled instantly into another magical Maalox moment. Jesse's right hand rummaged on the night table for the new roll of antacids, and something caught his ear from the TV still playing softly in front of the bed. A low murmurous sound, a friend's name? A picture of Jimmy Benjamin in that ridiculous beret he'd worn even at Sunday school. 1948–1981. *A set of dates.*

Jesus, Jimmy Benjamin must be dead!

"Facedown in a toilet," Arkey said, at Jesse's office the next day. He threw a newspaper among the scattered briefs on his desk.

"Yeah," Johannus said. "Seconal and whiskey. Maybe he was trying to make himself throw up, he passed out, and his lungs filled with bowl water. He drowned in a toilet, can you believe it?" Johannus's voice filled with a combination of wonder and pity, like he'd known the guy.

But they actually had, Arkey thought. "Very Benjamin," he said. So could Jimmy be scamming his death, show up next week on *SNL*. Or . . . no, all that a way to avoid the obvious, the death not very Benjamin—Jimmy had never used drugs. It was very mob, Arkey remembering a *Herald* story from college, a Winter Hill hard guy given a choice of deaths—his head axed off, or put under with downers and whiskey, then thrown into Boston Harbor, making him look like an unfortunate boozer who took a long walk off a short pier. Thing was, the guys Benjamin had pissed off were Arkey's brother-in-law and his clients—the nonexistent points in the never-developed, never-released film—Arkey the link between Jimmy, Arnie Golden, and Specs' money. Making him also the one who had greased his friend's way into the toilet bowl.

"And what about that time he pretended he spoke with Howdy Doody?" Johannus said to Jeffrey, the two of them in the Cad's front seat, Arkey and Jesse in the back, David Watkins having said he'd had enough of their letters. And a KKK-murderer-become-Pentecostal-minister was just too sick for him.

"Howdy saying he was in agony, all folded up in a box," Johannus said. "I mean, that's like the letters, isn't it?"

"Yeah," Jesse said from the backseat, "I thought that, too, once. Like maybe Jimmy had sent them."

"Sure," Jeffrey said, meaning, *whatever,* meaning please stop talking about Jimmy Benjamin. He switched on the windshield wipers, like their *whoosh, whoosh, whoosh* could drown out their voices, his envy, Sam's hatred. The houses and stores thinned out quickly now, the outskirts of Jackson not suburbs but scrub. *Here be monsters.* Funny how thinking about this death project made his envy and his own fear of death easier, which made him sure, too, that the *Mississippi Death Trip* would be his entrance to another world by which this one could be judged. *Mixed media for sure*—drawings wouldn't be enough to contain all the connected worlds he'd have to show. Maybe build a Rube Goldberg contraption showing all that had gone into making the murderer—emery boards or what all. Show the ingenuity needed to get Ferris or whoever into the gas chamber. Fragments of legal briefs pasted to the wall? And a row of statues, too, Segal-like mute judges. And the dead letters had to be part of it, too. *They* bore the ethics, right, had set Jesse in motion, they guaranteed that *MDT* would get by his moral watchdog the way SM never could.

"Johannus," he heard Jesse saying, "you have a fresh perspective. What do you think about all this?"

Meaning what? More about *The Benjamin Tribute*!

"The letters? I don't know. Nothing much. Probably like the guy said, they were jazzed by the murder. They got drunk, wanted to pull your chain. Then your friend made a couple of good guesses." He turned to Arkey, like *he* was the believer here. "No offense."

"None taken," Arkey said.

"Don't you get it?" Jeffrey said before he had time to think, his voice carrying a *you rube* undertone. Well, Jeffrey had been around artists, great artists, and though the world talked about inspiration, it really mostly looked like a stupor punctuated by electric shock, spastic jerking muscles. So a divine force that moved a drunken scumbag to write profound words could definitely have also looked like a drunk bastard who thought he was just saying fuck you to the Jews. Why couldn't his friends see that?

"See what?" Arkey said.

"Oh, nothing." Fine, the letters would be his and Beth's secret stash, *their* way to feel the profundity that death gives to life. He looked in the rearview mirror, where both of them smiled at him. He couldn't help it; their grins looked . . . sacrilegious.

"It was a moment when the will of God flowed into me," the minister said. "I think I wrote that letter because I *wanted* what I did to be known. I was sick to death and I wanted to be punished," the minister a thickset man, too, like intercourse with the dead, Arkey thought, led you to eat too many fatty foods. Still, he seemed solid in a leisure suit of metallic-looking threads, sitting in his brick church. A surprise then, when he began to cry, though Arkey suspected that a Southern preacher could turn those waterworks on as needed. "You can't imagine that night. We had blood on our faces, drunk, howling at the moon."

The minister had insisted on their meeting in the pews, the first time, Arkey realized, he'd ever been in a church in his life, the whole place looking plainer than he'd expected, except for a huge, intimidating wooden cross over the altar. He rubbed the patch on his neck, the edges where the lost skin graft had never smoothed out.

"Do you remember what you wrote?" Jeffrey asked.

"No. Something about damnation probably. That's what was surely on my mind that night."

"Where were you?"

He smiled softly at Jeffrey. "Already in hell. You know, some guy's living room. I remember the TV was on, a rerun of *I Love Lucy* in the background, can you believe it? Dear Jesus, if only I'd had the courage to confess everything then! But I wrote that foolish letter instead." Then the man looked to them for instruction. "What did it say?"

"It might have said, *I am dyed, I am done, I am dead,*" Jeffrey offered.

"I don't understand that," the minister said, shaking his long head. "I don't think I would have written that."

"Or," Jeffrey went on doggedly, "it might have been, *I'm still in pain. If anything, the pain is worse. How long, how long, how long? Oh God, what if this is hell?*"

The man had an inward look. "Maybe I wrote that. It sounds like it's about hell, anyway. But I don't remember."

"Or *Agony end time,*" Jeffrey said immediately.

The minister shrugged. "I can't say I understand that, either. Don, that other man I told you about, maybe he knows."

"How did you get the address?" Jeffrey asked, hoping probably the man would say, *My hand just moved.*

"Maybe he had a letter in his pocket, could that be?"

Jeffrey shrugged, looked disappointed.

"I can't tell you how much I wept for writing that letter, whatever it was I wrote," the man said, "knowing that I'd added to the family's pain."

"Displacement?" Arkey said, then regretted it, not wanting to mock the man, or to value him either. Had he really thought this business would have a clue about who he should love, Kate or Gail? Now, he just wanted to go back to the motel.

Anyway, the minister had had some therapy. Who hasn't, nowadays? "Yes, I think you're right. I think it was displacement. I had burnt a good man's church, and helped beat him to the ground. I had watched men killed, and I hadn't done anything to stop it. That's what I should have felt most guilty about."

He turned his broad face to the peaked ceiling. "Wait. Please. Dear Lord, forgive me. I'm not telling you the truth. I shot him, too. The black man, I mean. We all did. Yes, I couldn't confront the enormity of that, so I stayed up every night drinking and crying over those letters instead. Soon I had problems with my memory, blackouts. I went on drinking anyway, and my wife left me. Then I touched bottom, and joined AA. I guess you could say that murder, those letters, led me to a higher power, to my work."

"Work that lets you make up for murdering a man and writing those letters?" Jeffrey said, not the slightest mockery to his voice, Jeffrey not the Sophist anymore, Arkcy thought. More like the Maid of Orleans.

"Yes." The man nodded, like he thought he had a friend in Jeffrey. "We have sinned, and we can, if we're lucky, get a chance to atone for that sin, know that we're atoning for it, even just a little, every day of our lives. Then, if we're really fortunate, we'll be almost ready for God when we die. We won't have done enough, of course, any of us." His voice became kinder. Arkey could see that this man might be a good minister. "I don't mean you all killed someone. But people do things, everyone does. It's original sin, it leads us astray. And we do things. Not as awful as what I did, most of us. But we do things. And if we're lucky we work at making up for them. We show some good faith, you know, like a deposit, a layaway plan. I like to use that kind of example when I'm preaching, but really, it does kind of make sense. It's like at the Kmart. And then when we die, Christ will pay the difference for us."

Pays off the balance on our karmic Visa bill, Arkey thought, the whole thing surely turning to nonsense now even for Jeffrey once Kmart had come up. Attention Kmart shoppers: Christ crucified, a paradox for the Greeks, a stumbling block for the Jews, but a blue light special for you.

The man turned his face up to Jeffrey full of concern. "I can tell you're heavy-laden, son. That perversion is wearing your soul out."

"What?"

"You don't need to hide from me. I'm here to help you get straight with God."

"I don't want help. Never less so, in fact."

"Well, when you do."

Arkey thought Jeffrey would be enraged by that. But when they got outside in the rain, he said, "Man, how did he know?"

He had a point. When he wanted it, Jeffrey's closet had a closet inside; impenetrable except to a Seeing Eye.

Back in his Motel 6, Arkey dried off with a napless towel, let his naked legs dangle over the side of the bed. Gauze curtains on an empty street, stale air; little claws of anxiety skittering on his left side. He could make a call, have some company. But Kate or Gail? Who was his life to come? Gail had called him at Brandeis, when she heard he was getting married. She'd sounded very upset.

"I felt I had to meet with her," he'd told his friends at the lawyers' bar, meaning *please agree that I was just being a nice guy.* "She's a little loony, but there's something reassuring to me about Gail."

"She tells you what a bastard you are?" Jesse had said. "Cries for hours, and goes for tune-ups to McLean? That's reassuring?"

"I understand," Jeffrey had said. "That's the point of those extra drops of suffering. God might play hide-and-seek, but your tormentor's certainly present and accounted for."

Tormentor? Did that mean *mistress?* Had Laura blabbed? *Of course* Laura had blabbed.

So what should he do? Not much instruction from two alkies writing nonsense. No Voice of God quality instruction there—except that he couldn't write a book that showed he had been a fool's fool. And instead?

Well, years ago, his grandfather, voice roughened by a thousand cheap cigars—painful to listen to, even if not God quality either— had suggested, well, ordered was more like it, that he write about the Triangle Fire and the strike. "That," he said, "is a subject worthy of an epic poem. We were like a many-limbed body, all our arms and legs moved by one strong will. *That's* what solidarity means, Arkey. That's how you make justice. Someday you should tell that tale in one of your books. Keep the idea of comradeship alive."

Gail might like that, the story of real outsiders, Jews mostly, chosen by history, and given amazing, if not super, powers by their solidarity.

And Kate, he saw now, would never convert, the Chosen People angle a deal breaker—blueblood Kate the one who turned out to be a democrat through and through, no special groups for her except *Americans,* which group she loved because anyone could join it. While Arkey needed a special dispensation, a God to protect him *in particular.*

Meanwhile, his fingers already pushed the buttons on the cream-colored motel phone. "Hello."

"Obey, slave," Gail said by way of reply—that being her whim today. "Are you wearing what I gave you?"

"Yes," he lied.

"I know what you want to do now. There's no point in lying to me."

"I won't lie to you, mistress." Except, of course, that he already had.

"If I tell you that you want to touch yourself, then you do."

"Yes." On the other hand, not exactly the Amazing Kreskin. Like, otherwise, why would he have called her for phone sex? Still, the dreamy lethargy entered his limbs, his mind cloudy like Pernod with water, the feeling bitter but satisfying. Gail had chosen *him* to be her slave, and the more demands she made, the more she humbled him, the more *special* he might feel, infinitely small *and* infinitely large at once as she critiqued his failures or bit his nipples, the center of her attention; chosen because he was tested, harrowed, humbled; and so exalted. *But add some saliva, too, and keep the hand moving! This isn't a class on Kierkegaard!*

. . . Then Arkey, as always, got plopped back down in a waste of sticky Kleenex. *This* little play hadn't helped make a moral world.

So naturally all his love for Kate poured back in. He wanted to hang up.

But Gail wanted some conversation—the phone sex equivalent of cuddling. Arkey edited as he went, having lied to Gail before, saying he'd come to Mississippi for a book about Jesse and the death penalty. He might share sexual fantasies and bodily fluids with Gail the Mistress, but he wouldn't give Gail the Writer Frank's letters—even though they'd turned out to be worthless. "I had these amazing biscuits," he said lamely.

And it turned out Gail would get to see the biscuits and everything else that had happened in Mississippi, anyway, in the printed version of the mocked-up pages Billy had a courier bring to Jesse's office the next day. Jesse laid the pages out for them at lunch, a redneck undone by the strength of feeling he'd had when his hand had been moved to write a letter from the grave, Billy making it seem strangely sexual—like the killer felt he'd been possessed *that* way, too, that part grabbing Arkey, though the rest seemed comic book *ordinaire*.

"It's like you can see now how Billy's been turning out crap for the last decade," Jeffrey said, "running on autopilot." Apparently, to Jeffrey's eyes anyway, Billy's powers had returned in *The New Origin of the Band of Outsiders,* the true story of the First Hero—the One Who Had

Died yet had made his murderers' living hands write his instructions to the Outsiders, the missives that had first taught Dr. Why? the holy ways to use their superpowers!

"I thought," Arkey said, "we all promised to keep this stuff secret. Not that it matters, mind you." After all, he suddenly remembered, he'd come down here to research a book about these things they'd all promised not to talk about.

> The Sophist rises from the juke's scarred table,
> eyes alight—

for the first time in BillyBook history.

> "These evildoers, these Transmitters, have been
> touched by God's mighty Hand. To harrow them!
> To raise them! To show God's mysterious ways!!!"

"Geez, Louise, what the hell has happened to the Sophist?" Johannus asked—while the real Jeffrey, Jeffrey the Talentless, Jeffrey the Jealous, pushed himself back from the table with tears in his eyes.

"They're amazing," Jeffrey said. "Really amazing. They're all in these ridiculous costumes, but the play of the shadows lets you feel something mysterious is going on in the background, in the corners. A hovering force, a spirit both deadly and gracious, moving across their lives. Ninja B. will be reborn."

"Yeah, it's great," Johannus said, putting an arm around Jeffrey's back and totally misunderstanding him for the first time in their brief and probably soon-to-end relationship, Jeffrey not so much moved by the comic book as desolated, certain he'd been the only one to have seen the truth even as the others had leapt from the train, the story of the letters the rock he could have built *his* work, the Mississippi Project, on. Now that had been taken from him by another artist.

Another? dear Sam murmured. *No, son, by an* artist. *Head-on? Unironic? Your Dead in Mississippi Project would have been pretentious rubbish, if it had ever been anything at all. Thinking about the end—it's just something you play at to make yourself feel* considerable— *like you're the CEO of Death, Inc.*

Sam had it right. Comics, moral when they wish, immoral when they wanted—that was the only way to do anything head-on nowadays. Jeffrey ran from the restaurant, not caring if Johannus thought him a nellie, Johannus sure to leave him when he found out he was a fraud.

Oh, yes, dear Sam had it right. Jeffrey would never have known what to make of the condemned, their lawyers, or the letters. He would have endlessly debated mixed media over easel in his own mind, given endless imaginary interviews to fantasy *Artforum* critics, until his empty days had become years of self-pitying, sodden failure.

And, Sam added, *if you look back you'll see that handsome boy isn't coming after you.*

And no Johannus on the next day's trip to Don's house—the name the Pentecostal had given them. Johannus had been so *callous* that Jeffrey had used his passive-aggressive semaphore (long, hurt face accompanied by a short "nothing's wrong") to convey *your presence is unbearable to me.*

They pulled into Don's asphalt driveway. A fat man in a white undershirt was putting square plugs of grass in the brown patches of the meager lawn, tamping them down with his foot. Probably he wanted to seem casual.

Or maybe, like he said, he just didn't remember that whole part of his life. "Man, that was a lot of drinks ago." He looked round at them, Jeffrey unable to keep the avidity out of his eyes, though his world of dead letters, condemned men, executioners, and lawyers had all been snatched from him forever by the midget's greater powers.

The man looked down at his mud-covered hiking boot, his face coming back up transformed by a crooked smile made the more corrupt-looking by a thin, straight moustache. "Well, now you mention it, maybe there was something like that." And then, "Are you all movie men?" meaning: *Is this worth money?*

"How did you know the address?" Jeffrey asked.

He shrugged. "Maybe someone stuck a gun in the white fella's mouth, made him tell?" He rubbed his hands together, like he was getting dirt off them. "I didn't do any of the shooting, mind you. I only helped after. They took them to a little shack of mine, then burnt it to the ground, I remember that. That would make a good scene, wouldn't it?"

Jeffrey rubbed the sweat from his face with his shirtsleeve. "They found the bodies under an earthen dam."

"That right? Well, I might be getting the details wrong."

"Did Frank—" Jeffrey started to say.

"Who's Frank?"

"He was . . . the white man you shot."

"I told you now, I didn't shoot anyone."

"All right, did the white man say *I know how you feel?*"

"Why the hell would he say that?"

This man's red-haired young son, wearing an Atlanta Braves baseball cap, came to the living room window. He waved at all of them.

The man waved back, a nice straight smile for the kid. "Look, Frank? Frank probably just wailed like a baby. I mean, Jesus, what would you do?"

"Did he play a kazoo?" Arkey asked, with a tight-lipped, laughing-at-himself smile.

"Christ, he'd done that, *I* would have shot him."

"Did you write, *agony end time*," Jeffrey said.

Jesse had already turned back for the car.

"Don't remember, rightly." Then he looked up at the hot sun. "What would that mean?"

Absolutely nothing, Jesse thought, turning on the car engine to get the air-conditioning going. The last rags of his ersatz chosenness had gotten eaten by the humidity, leaving once more a sour uncertainty: why *did* Jesse save men not so different from these—and even if it might drive his wife mad?

"Amazing," Jeffrey said, pushing the seat forward so he could clamber in back. His eyes looked filled with tears. Disappointment probably; or the end of his romance with their paralegal.

Arkey slid in beside him. "Yeah, they'll all end up on *Donahue.*"

"Sure." Jesse started the engine. "Each one accompanied by his therapist."

"The ones who helped them recover the memories," Arkey said. "*Oh, I felt a spirit enter through my ears. My hands moved, forming the words: No tickee, no laundry.*"

Jeffrey's head, brows narrowed, loomed over the backseat. "Jesus, Jeffrey, don't look at me like that," Arkey said. "I don't mean anything by it."

Jeffrey settled back.

"They feel the world has ignored them, probably," Jesse said.

"Yeah. People abducted by aliens get all the press," Arkey said. "What about guys fucked in the head by the dead?"

Jesse would drive Arkey straight to the airport now, send him quickly on his way to get his brother-in-law's help for Jeffrey's probably nonexistent problem—so his friend could go home before he had to come sleep on the couch at Jesse's house.

"On *Donahue* the Transmitters say there must have been a fourth guy, that they don't even know about," Arkey said. "The one who wrote *agony end time.*"

"The Hidden Transmitter," Jesse said. "I mean, don't people always make up a loophole, so they can go on believing?"

"No," Jeffrey said. "God leaves an anomaly that we can't ignore. Otherwise, no matter what people are confronted with, no matter how irrefutable the evidence, they'll find a way not to believe." He sounded angry.

"Jeffrey the Sophist," Jesse said, "become Jeffrey the Credulous." And for once Jesse laughed outright at someone else.

Two months later, Arkey laughed, too, remembering Jeffrey's long, mournful face on his last day in Mississippi, his balding head and dog eyes, Jeffrey now the only worshiper left in the First Church of Grave-Directed Letters. Well, good for him—though he'd be better off throwing the I Ching every minute, for all the instruction he'd ever get there—*that* having been the equally useless way Arkey had dealt with his indecision about Kate and Gail, until his fiancée had found a letter Gail had written him that he'd stupidly saved, filled with . . . instructions.

Had he ever really thought the dead letters would tell him how to live? Or even give him material for a book? Anyway, Billy had ruined his chance for that—those comics would make any possible tenure committee think the letters were material for adolescent fantasies only.

As opposed to what? Sublime?

Still, Billy had actually done Arkey a favor, set him to work on *The Fire This Time: The Triangle Inferno and the Birth of the ILGWU,* easy to title and a better subject for his needs, the book going quickly, too, probably because it had Grandfather Abe's grave-directed blessing. Now *there* was a dead man making a living and untenured hand write!

A book, yes, but no more Kate. Arkey slept alone most nights, in a hell of his own devising. Writing. Sleeping. Seeing Gail when he couldn't take the loneliness and cancer fear anymore, but hating himself for it, half blaming her for the end of his engagement.

Still, Gail *was* company, no doubt about that, their playacting reassuring him (and making his cock stiff even now), the pain, the commands, being bound up in his own neckties making him feel marginally more secure, more certain she was there—*for as long as their one acter lasted anyway.* Still, he couldn't imagine Gail with a family—a baby's crying might take her away from her own work; or her own crying, for that matter. So no future for them.

And not much future left for the Outsiders, he felt pretty sure. He turned on his Tensor light, picked up one of the pile of comic books from his night table, the Transmitters in this one having turned out to be part of a government conspiracy, a CIA program. . . . Or had they? . . . Maybe the conspiracy was just to cover up that the Transmissions had been real? . . .

Jeffrey had got it right. The Transmitters had briefly given Billy a renewed sense of justice. But then that material had petered out, and his work became insipid, pointless, unmoored again, everything obscure enough to lead to another episode, another conspiracy for the **Outcasts** to battle, that being Ninja B.'s new purged-and-purged-again group of Bolshies—no OurKey, no BBE, no Outsiders, all of whom were thoroughly compromised in N.B.'s eyes.

And Beth, the real Beth, he wondered if she had heard that the letters from Frank in the grave had really come from drunks, their faces painted with blood, howling at the moon. Billy probably realized that now, and so his work had become inconclusive, with endless, myriad, conspiracies turning N.B.'s followers mad, their neurons and their guns firing randomly, sometimes for world revolution, sometimes for money; or power; or just to hear the sound of the guns, all of it part of an impossible, never-to-be-resolved stew whose only issue would be the next issue of *Girls with Guns,* each page filled with blood spilled mostly for its own red-eyed engorging beauty, its vivid excitement, with everyone a potential enemy of democracy, a betrayer of the cause, and the cause ever less clear except for Beth's survival, for Beth must not die; she was Billy's Barbie doll, Billy's archetype; and also, of course, Billy's franchise, renewed and amplified the longer he could put her smack in the consumerzen's eye, doing the same again, not as part of anyone's vision of politics but so Billy could find delight, or relief anyway, while his pen moved across the page, his mind lost in its own inventions, his ways of slicing and dicing, it not mattering anymore what provoked the knife, incitement itself clearly all that Billy prized now, anything to keep him drawing.

But worst of all, Arkey thought, was how Billy's readers responded to that emptiness—Ninja B./Athena X/Deborah AKA the Prophet having become bigger even than in the sixties, her fans just wanting to see her kill and kill in furious neo-expressionist drawings, the whole thing beyond good and evil; the more fertile, more profligate, when it hardly made sense and was *utterly pointless and puerile,* Beth Jacobs tried to mind-scream to Billy—psy-sending the Silent Shout that could pulp a rotten cortex in New Jersey even as Ninja B. sipped burnt coffee in a Tompkins Square diner—or in Central Square, Cambridge, where she read the same issue of *GWG* as Arkey did, two miles away, namely #642, where ORG. scientists fabricate replicant Transmitters, part of an amazingly special three-issue series that would no doubt draw Ninja B. into a Walpurgisnacht of cockamamie splatter stuff, killing and kavorting in a metal-spiked black leather breast-harness, some little midget's wet dream SM mistress—partnered by new heroes with lovingly delineated and gleaming muscles. Does Billy still wear his yarmulke, Beth wondered, while he draws these freakish things? And had he actually added an extra-large bulge to BBE's pants, Beth barely able to make out the pictures in the seep that reached her and Snake's bedroom from Zing's Ready Steady night-light.

She fished her pink bathrobe off the bedpost. An anniversary present. Flannel; warm, homey, hideous; the fabric representing the one thing she hated more than spiked leather harnesses, namely being treated like Mother Milk Cow. Another thing she hated, though: when Snake forgot she was Zing's mother and all that meant.

She smiled down at Snake, mouth open, breathing calmly thanks to Shakur's needles, his strong forehead, his plump, smooth cheeks more innocent-looking than Zing's. Snake was much handsomer than B.C., even without the long black locks that Shakur had butchered for the Wienie Man job. After all, his white getaway driver couldn't look like a hippie. He'd left uneven sideburns still on her *faux* hubby—meaning no less commitment for her, by the way, but that state certification wasn't possible for people like Clark Kent, Beth Jacobs, or Snake, i.e., those with hidden identities. They had jumped the broom and then repaired to a filthy parlor in D.C. where he got a nipple ring and she got a snake tattoo like his.

In the kitchen, she put out a dish of Disgusto-Meat for "Mau-Mau." Just whispering his name made her miss his sublime predecessor, the ginger-furred leader of the Catural Revolution, her long companion underground, last seen boarding a bus in Arizona on his way to being assassinated in Cambridgeport by a counterrevolutionary Buick. *This* cat mostly annoyed her, being yet another body who depended on her utterly. She flared a safety match, lit the ancient pilotless burner. And when Zing could reach the cracked ceramic knob?

She put the blue pot on to boil, leaned with her back against the stove, turning the BBook pages again, this time catching the blood motif: drops dripping from the murdered soldier in frame one down each panel after, onto OurKey and Jeffrey the Sophist, as they ate dinner with the president, the compromised bastards not realizing they had stains on their faces; until, at the end, a few drops polluted a priest's white vestments as he performed mass for the Imperial Dogs (named for the greyhounds-become-demons, and all but the Desperado killed by Ninja B. herself in the Walla-Hi War). Billy's once amazing comics, she thought, had become a candy factory—but the blood trail showed that the proprietor *was* still a real Willy Wonka—a clever, clever lad.

She felt fonder of Billy then, remembered their first night—and his very first time—in Tax Loss field, it not seeming a sacrilege to her to use the same mooey place with Billy that she'd gone to with Frank, the two boys now having a spooky subterranean connection. Billy seemed to like being with her, wanted to prolong their time together, talk with her after, which was something she *never* took for granted, knowing she was an odd one, overeducated and strangely old for her age from long contact with her father, implacable, too; boys would be intrigued by the challenge, then soon find her harrowing—or maybe annoying, actually. Not Billy, though, the two of them scabbed by the same Leo Jacobs cooties. They'd sat on the rough green blanket he'd sweetly remembered to bring, and she'd tried to get him to disparage his doctor, her father having told Billy about the camps, and then suddenly not talked to him anymore, abandoning him like he'd become unworthy—the same thing he'd done with her. She'd wanted to make their little *sur herbe* scene into the one in Proust—a proto Weatherman anti-bourgeois exercise, eh?—the lovers spitting on Dad's picture.

But Billy wouldn't join her in mocking Leo. Just as well. Love always made her curses against her dad curl back into her own skin. And for a few weeks she'd almost been able to see her dad as Billy did, flawed, yes, but sometimes saying worthwhile things, too. After all, they did have to find a way to make human life valuable again. She'd even sometimes imagined her and Billy setting up together, near the ocean, of course, in a yellow frame house with a wide porch. Billy would study and work (on oil paintings, definitely *not* comic books), and she would . . . rob Brinks trucks?

For a few months in Great Neck she'd teen-loved Billy Green, though the talking together had been the best part of it with him—which was not his fault, a small boy but with a big enough bulge; she just hadn't gotten the hang of sex yet, this the one domain where she didn't know what she *could* ask for, what she even *wanted* to ask for. And love him or not, Billy was only five foot two on his longest day; they must have looked goofy bopping along beside each other to the Playhouse. She'd already known that his body and face, even the crew cut, might make a kind of sense when he was a teen, but he would soon decline from boyish to miniature, become a funny-looking little man whose size would make his gestures seem fussy, overly precise. Also, or maybe most of all, he sometimes had this half smile that looked too much like her father's, eh?

She hadn't liked *that,* but she'd never imagined he would forget even the few sensible things her father had showed him, his work now a chef's manual of slice&dice techniques, Billy having utter amnesia for the mission he'd sounded so moved and pious about once upon a green blanket, the two of them then the *never again* warriors. And her? Could she explain to him how restoring worth to human life required her to knock over a Brinks truck?

"That's top o' the line," Snake had said when she got the assignment.

"Yeah?" she'd drawled, both of them knowing she'd received this big honor 'cause for a getaway driver nothing could be less suspicious than a cutie-pie white woman. "Very macho, eh?"

"You bet. The Roach Motel where I grew up, we didden wanna be cowboys, no, we wanted to be the guys who knocked over armored trucks."

"And your friends, where are they now?" *Friends* was a little strong, actually.

"I dunno," Snake said, lifting Zing onto the potty just a moment too late. "Jail, probably."

"Then I can't risk it. Zing's too young." Really, she meant: *I lack the cojones. I'll fuck it up.* She couldn't fucking do it, and that was that. Or would have been, if three weeks ago, like he'd been sent by her orisha, Baba hadn't arrived with a lot of good tricks, she was sure, in his Ifa bag.

She'd been on her way to get some paper towels when Snake said pleadingly, "It'll be different for you, Beth. It's the armor on the truck makes it tougher than a Wienie Man, and first of all, Shakur's plan is, we take down the guys as they pick up the money, so we don't have to get into the truck. And then by the time our guys get back to you, if there was any shooting, it's long over."

Shooting? Well, she thought, sloshing boiling water through her faux Chemex filter of paper towel, *that* was precisely what *she* understood, and that her father and Billy couldn't see: *never again* is just sentimental horseshit if you didn't help do the hard things needed to save the black and brown people massacred all around the globe every business day.

Beth sat now right where she longed to be, at the center of the black revolution, surrounded by soldiers, men threatened by death; each vivid moment of their lives filled with danger and wonder. They didn't have a scrim of guilt between them and their lives; they weren't scared of their own violence. People like Jeffrey Schell looked at Beth like that was *her*, too, like she was Ninja B., never hesitating to give the Death Palm. Thing was, though, that wasn't her. Not yet, anyway. But maybe, if Baba and Ifa would help her, it could be.

She poured herself some coffee, took a seat as usual at the wooden table, cold creeping up her legs. Don't turn your death instinct against yourself as guilt, she wanted to tell him and tell him and tell him. Direct it outward, make yourself into a knife that can do the necessary things. But *him* now meant her father, not Billy Green, and that made her spirit sag, the curse snaking round her own body, reminding her: *can* you *do the necessary thing or not?*

After all, Billy had gotten it for a moment in that dusty attic of Laura's; and even after he'd been terrified by Olson and the War of the Fizzyits' Ear, he'd still made himself her secret sharer, sending money to a P.O. box in her name-of-the-month, helping fund their bombings. "He's got a guilty conscience," Snake had said one fine day, as they'd sashayed into squat glass B of A in S.B. to set up a household account for Mr. And Mrs. Phone Eee. She'd straightened hubby's tie in a wifey way, the two of them strolling across the suddenly vast lobby to the clerk. Snake had steady nerves, a relief after B.C.'s endless rattle. "That money," he said, "that's him paying you royalties for using your life." No, she'd said, Billy contributed so he and her other GN friends could feel part of the world revolution they all knew was coming, and she the only one willing to make the sacrifices to feed it.

She turned then to "The Ear Hears," urgent letters this week from kids certain they'd like, you know, transmitted messages from Jim Morrison, RFK, Jimi Hendrix. And Elvis, of course. Plus one who seemed to think Dylan had already died. A few correspondents said they'd died themselves, no kidding, and had commanded a living hand to write this letter. She fingered the nation sack, twisting it around her own throat till it hurt. How dare Billy mock them all like this? Or was she the last one who still believed that Frank *had* written—had maybe done it, in fact, for Beth especially, to set her in motion?

She went to get her underwear from the wicker basket in the coat closet where she kept her dresses, part of the System to keep from waking Nzinga early mornings like this—though *this* would be her first five A.M. getaway, a secret training session for the Big Dance. The words made her feel charged, solemn almost, like dressing for her bas mitzvah, or to bomb the Pentagon. She carefully took down a flower print, savored how she could wear something that didn't open easily in front now, Nzinga weaned and Beth that much untethered—or there could be no Brinks robbery for her. If she did the Brinks job, maybe she'd get more of her life back, like a Cheshire cat who reappeared around her nipples. She could matter again in the world as something beside the Ama-Zing's mother.

And, as if on cue, Nzinga turned in the alcove, her breathing labored from a little cold, a baby snore, her child a restless sleeper always, waking her once a night at least: *Mama, I need you.* Maybe she could ask Baba to cast the pine nuts for Zing, find out why she was so restless? She knew he would shake his central-casting sage's head *no* politely, the almost impolite unsaid being, *how can one invoke the ancestors for a woman whose forebears might have helped slave traders?* Would he change his mind if she helped rob the Brinks truck, showed real solidarity with the black masses? Thing was, she needed Baba's help, the orisha's help, *right now*, if she was going to do the job. Because, thing was, the horseradish her father had left in her brain still fucked her up. *People might be killed on this job.* Necessary killing—but guilt, like a sticky syrup, would slow her reflexes. She would make the wrong choices, throw the van in reverse, break the side mirrors off, get everyone on the job busted.

She'd scanned her past for anything that might fix her up, give her that little extra impulsion so she could rocket herself past her dad's voice. She paged through Che and Lin Piao and Mao. *It is right to rebel* had set the Chinese masses in motion, but it didn't do much for her anymore in Cambridgeport. *I've read all the books,* she thought, *and my flesh is tired.* And the Weathermen exercises? Fuck sessions? Cooking a cat? Christ, even B.C. wouldn't touch the hacked-up pieces, fur still sticking to them. And if he had, they would have been his last dinner. Cat feasts and fuck sessions might be okay when you're talking about the lumpen to bourgy kids who ain't, but they didn't cut it when you found yourself working with kill-you-soon-as-look-at-you guys. *I mean, I'd have to eat an awful lot of pussies before I'd rise to their level.*

Oh, shit, she wanted to shout, *why is an armored car bigger than setting a bomb?* Because someone will die, and blood is powerful magic? *Fine,* then she needed gods who want blood! And Baba had come, opened the Temple of the Mystic Path on Tremont, come to teach about the gods of Africa at the school, and she'd found the angels she'd prayed for—the orishas of Ifa. *They* could transform her, put steel in her, help her do this job with *ashe*; forcefully, decisively—*by any means necessary.* But Baba kept her away from his classes. Alone, how could she find the way to life?

Could Baba be the same Chuck Taylor, the topsy-turvy—bald on top, long beard below—that Frank had met in Mississippi, the black Jew become priest of Ifa? Chuck must have realized like she had that the Talmud was just guilt codified and made endless, the book that told you what *not* to do; while Ifa was a whole different story that told you how *to do.* Ifa would link her to the source of vitality, give her the certainty that guides the improviser's hands on the valves—or the fighter's on the knife. With Ifa, Beth would learn how to do this thing. Baba could cast the pine nuts, give her the god's instruction. Better still, he could show her how to invite the god to possess her, like Frank had dreamt; then she'd have the god *inside* her, acting *through* her.

She fished out some black underwear from the basket in the closet, Beth on her period today. She remembered her first, coming home bewildered, proud, scared, to tell . . . her father. He'd been matter-of-fact, of course, but in the worst way; lips pursed; distaste clear. She felt unclean. But the orishas of Ifa, the gods, *they* understood blood's magic. She hadn't been allowed in Baba's storefront when the sacrifice had been offered before the odu orisa—the sacred vessel—but she knew from Susan that a lot of poultry had already died there. Warm blood had spattered Susan's arms, wrecked her dress, "and the Health Department, it's about to knock at the door any day." Rich with *ashe* and iron, blood fed those thirsty angels.

Right? So far she'd only listened by the classroom door three or four times, begged Susan for tidbits, and pieced things together from what she heard the kids boasting about on the playground. But those orishas, she thought, those angels, had to be what made those kids swing so easily, leap so decidedly; made their games like dances. Beth wanted to have what those kids had, wanted to learn the orisha of *her* head and get his guidance.

Like Shango, he must be Sugar's orisha. Shango of black cats, ram's heads, and drums, Shango who solves legal problems, gets stoplights, protects from enemies on the racist school board. Strength, she bet, streamed from that god right into Sugar's squat, muscular body. Just look at the world his courage and cunning had built on Dudley Street— proof of what a cooperative African community could do to take care of its own. Ambulances, screening clinics, an amazing school.

So how about Shango for her orisha, too? *He* could show her how to get free of all this yattering guilt that hemmed her life, Shango, a god who put on our bodies like dresses, who spoke from human mouths, who accepted our appetites. Yeah, Shango could certainly possess her, *ride* her—so Beth could feel again the way she had when she'd first read Frank's letters from the grave, or giving birth to Zing; or that magic time she'd crawled out that ledge at the Pentagon, set that bomb. Shango would be her own loving angel—each angel, naturally, terrible in its own way.

Beth smiled—closed-lipped, of course—remembering when a line from Rilke popping into her head twisted her all out of shape. Now they mostly reminded her of the home where she'd grown up, its familiar agony, like buoyancy sometimes, like death others, the gravitational pull of love. Since Zing's arrival, she missed her mother for the first time in her adult life, that thin, busy presence who'd been eclipsed for her by her father's vast dark light. She had a thousand questions for her mom more important than the meaning of Rilke's angels, like *How did you get me to sleep through the night?* or *How did you bear the utter effacement of yourself,* and, *By the way,* Ma, *could you sit next Friday while I rob an armored truck?*

But yeah, most of all she wished that Zing could somehow know *him.* "He's an extraordinary man," she'd told Zing, pushing the rubber basket swing in the park across from the convent just a little too hard, too high, Zing all bundled up in a tiny green parka, smiling up at the leaden sky, the world, no matter its worn costumes, still new to her. "They tried to turn him into an animal," she'd said, surprised by her own words, knowing Nzinga couldn't possibly understand them, not even wanting her to. "But he built himself back up. And he's helped many people to feel better about themselves." And some, she had thought, to feel much, much worse. *My father,* she thought, *he's the orisha of my damn head now—and I have to get him replaced.*

His two-year-old granddaughter, she wrote her father, "*can talk about her emotions already. Zing shows no fear saying she's scared; or that she's 'furry o's' with me that I won't give her the breast anymore.*" Beth said, too, that she felt sure Zing was smarter than other kids her age—wanting him to love her. But she was unsure, really, comparing her to distant memories of toddlers she'd baby-sat for Somerville welfare mothers, or read to at the Rez. She couldn't spend any time with kids nowadays, having always, for safety, to keep to herself. Anyway, she *hoped* Zing was smarter—*for his sake.* At the mailbox, she'd slipped some snapshots into the envelope.

Then she tore it all up and went to case the job. Shakur had chosen a shopping mall bank branch. Last pickup of the day, two sacks so heavy the Brinks drivers could hardly lift them—money for weapons when the time came to arm the community, and plenty extra to save the school, which would soon go under without it, thanks to Beth. With an assist from Shakur and the Downstairs, who were scaring the parents away.

Shakur's joke, that. The *Roxbury Action Project* being *the Upstairs,* the aboveground group that ran the school, told the true story of the black man in America, while "a super-select, tight-knit cell"—the Downstairs—shook down drug dealers and pimps to get money for the school. But even pimps, it turned out, had brothers and sisters. "Word's getting round," Jacob said, last time he came to play with Zing, the two of them on the floor for hours, building spaceships out of blocks and milk cartons, long, flat structures, Zing more interested in comfy rooms for her tiny stuffed bears than good aerodynamics. "People, they're hookin' up Shakur and Sugar."

Oh, she *knew.* Parents scared, enrollment had fallen. The hell of it was, Beth should have sent refunds back to the state as soon as that happened. But, look, if she *had* they'd have already had to board the place up. Now the state wanted its money, or they'd put them under.

"Dinner, sweetheart," she'd said to Zing that night, as the girl added some hard wooden beds for the bears. Which meant negotiations, and more negotiations, and then—the Peace Conference having broken down—just sweeping Zing up, putting her in the high chair.

The adults had talked about Baba, then, the orishas, Buster on the jungle gym shouting, "Baba says Shango eats more chicken than you ever seen!"

Snake had brought a plate of beans to the table, and Beth had blown on a few to cool them for Zing.

"I don't figure that Ifa shit the way you do, Bethie," Jacob said.

Beth had had to piece together her Ifa from hints, playground talk, things heard in the hall. There wasn't even an encyclopedia entry—because it's always been a *whites-only encyclopedia.* But she felt sure she'd gotten it mostly right. What other kind of religion *could* have come out of Africa? What other kind of religion than one full of incitement and daring would the white world try so desperately to hide from the black man?

Jacob had smiled at her, his earring gleaming like a pirate's. "You think there's some kind of special black rocket fuel in all that African shit, huh?"

"I think there are more things on heaven and earth," she said back, "than are dreamt of in your philosophy, Horatio."

"Horatio," Snake had said. "A friend of yours?"

"A friend of Hamlet's," Jacob had said instantly; then, naturally, he apologized for knowing. "I had this teacher, he liked *Hamlet.* Good yarn, you know? A dead man makes his son work for him from beyond."

"Dead man, dead brother, eh?" Beth had said. Dead letters, she thought but didn't say, adding "Or a living-but-dead father, my case." She'd said the same thing the time Jacob had shown her one of his sonnets: a rope of tears grabbed by a corpse, who pulled the mourner down into the grave. Pretty good, too, she'd thought. "I had help," he'd said, but wouldn't say another word about it. "You have any more poems?" she'd asked him that last week.

"No time. You know"—he had smiled—"the struggle and all. Poems aren't something I can do on subways. A room of one's own, right?"

"Tell me about it."

"Solitude. Books to the ceiling, no need to leave, no need to see others and let them tug at you all the time."

"Just some quiet, that would do for me."

Jacob had communed with his spaghetti for a moment, cutting strands carefully, making sure no sauce got on his beautiful shirt, red, green, and blue threads all melded together, so one seemed to turn into the other. Jacob, he was like her friend Laura, he *always* dressed well. Looked like a stringbean, though, even his head a little squashed on top near where the stem would be. He shoveled in the food now—one of those people, you think, *Jesus, where does it go?*

Beth had turned pages for Zing, trying to keep her amused, herself distracted. Well-meaning bears, little moral lessons, this one where the cubs learned that people who get hit at home become bullies at school. *But,* Brother Bear said, *you still have to protect yourself.*

Right. Arm your bear or harm your bear! Fight for the right to arm bears! Beth had held up another cooled bean for Zing, pretending it was an airplane, but Zing slammed her teeth shut, the airport snowed in or something.

Not a good idea for Snake to have shown the chocolate cake. It leached the glamour from the beans.

"Sugar," Jacob had said, finally, "when I was a kid at that fucking school, he wrote me this letter about meeting Malcolm." He'd spun more spaghetti 'round his fork. "He said how Jesus let go of him then. Or maybe he let go Jesus, I can't remember. But you know, that was him *wishing* for it. There's still a lot of coulda-been-a-minister in our man Sugar. I think he sees Ifa like you do, Beth. Like the orishas they're gonna gang up on Christ, K.O. him finally, so Sugar won't have to feel guilty all the time, the way things are going now, the school in trouble."

Yeah, everyone knew they'd put off paying the bills. But only Beth knew how deep the shit had gotten. *Because it was her fault.* But she'd said, "Sugar, guilty?" Could there be this *deep* kinship between her and her boss, Sugar and her battling the same demon disguised as God, offering them His leather harness, His breast-confining laws?

Before she could ask more, Zing had finally sucked a bean halfway into her tiny mouth, then cast it into outer darkness on the worn yellow linoleum. So Beth had held up a sippy cup of juice, changed the subject. Naturally Queen Zing had said "wata." Beth, trudging to the refrigerator, had thought, *Another dinner nearly over. To be followed by another dinner. And another. Have a kid, you want to learn the real meaning of* Same Old. But whose fault was that? Zing, twenty-five pounds, she'd become the bigger planet, pulled Beth helplessly into her orbit, endlessly revolving around her in potty visits, bottom wipes, and a swipe of the toothbrush before bed on her keep-them-perfect teeth, then getting her up again in the morning, making veg-wables airplanes, carrying her to day care and getting her safely home in the evening for a perfect tooth of the teeth swipe, sweep tight, Beth's mind so fogged by the end of the day she didn't know what she was saying, and goddamn it *why* was *she* always so tired? The *attention,* that was it; if her mind wandered, her child might die. So put the potty on her—or vice versa—and then off to bed again, all of it ordained by love, Beth giving her life to Zing in that place where *you want to* is the same as *you have to,* those long-lashed eyes, deep-set like Beth's father's, and those smart remarks about her feelings—the kind of thing he'd like to hear about—all *venerandam:* compelling adoration, beyond her choice. Which meant that Beth, where was *she* anymore?

"Shakur's guys," Jacob had said, "they're pretty coked up all the time now. They dipping in the school till? That the problem?" Asking her 'cause she kept the books.

"Nah, they wanted any, they'd skim it off the top, before they gave the tithes to the school, right?" *The problem is,* she wanted to confess, *I didn't give the state back its fucking money. We don't do that soon, I've fucked everything totally.* Another reason she *in particular* should go on the Brinks job, Sugar having promised her the Brinks money would be used to make the state whole, bring the school back into the black, endow it, even. Like Wellesley.

The Big Dance, that was the ticket. A smooth thing for everyone—if she wasn't on it, fucked up by guilt. She would endanger everyone—herself included, *Zing's mother.* Which meant weeks now, rocking like a bell's tongue. *Do it* and *Don't—you're not good enough.*

"I think that Sugar, he's done some coke, too," Jacob said quietly.

"Some coke?" Snake had said, shoveling in cake.

"I like Coke," Zing had said, having tasted Snake's time to time at McDonald's.

"Yeah, well," Beth had said, "who hasn't done some?"

"Right," Snake had said. "Not like Sugar can't handle a taste, if anyone can."

"Right," Jacob had said, scared, Beth thought, but not saying everything, "if anyone can."

The fear she heard in him made her say, "What do you think we should do?"

"About what? About Sugar? I think the way shit's going now, money's short, he's depressed, that's all. Snake's got it right. He won't go too far. And the Dance, it'll make things okay again."

Time to get Zing to bed, then. And time to get to the bus now. She pulled on some laddered black tights. Baba insisted women have their legs covered, and she swore no more hanging back, listening by the door today, she would sneak *into* his class. She slipped on her Bean boots, get ready for the outdoor exercises, her part in the Dance.

The way Shakur had planned the Dance, Snake had said, her steps would be safe as milk. Black men in green jumpsuits wearing surgical gloves, "look like phobic janitors, they overpower the guards before the money gets into the truck." Then, bango, job done, the men hide in the trunks of the getaway cars. "Sure the cars are seen, the license gets taken down by the Brinks driver. But the beauty part is, Shakur figures on that. The getaway cars go to another switch point, and there's a van waiting there. The guys hop out of the trunks, tear the jumpsuits off, turn into black bourgies in business suits, and take a nap in the back of the van. Which has a white driver, that's the thing no one's *ever* looking for—black and white together. So you'll be long gone in the tall corn before the Bugs ever figure out what's up."

Still, so many cars—and all of them had to be legit rides, so even if they're stopped, they don't come back stolen on the radio check. Taking care of that business had been the first heavy thing she'd done, really, since she'd come back from New York—well, that and giving birth. She'd gone to a Catholic store on College Avenue, all creepy bleeding hearts and Marys in Bathtubs, bought a baptismal certificate, filled it in herself, and used it to get a job at Kmart.

A woman in a black lambskin coat had paid by check, used her license for I.D., Beth psy-shouting, *Sister, if you don't ask why I'm taking down your whole life history when you just want to buy a pair of stretch pants, then I can quit this shitty job.*

The next day Beth had gone to the Boston DMV, reported her old license lost, supplied Lambskin's date of birth, weight, height, SS number, whatever the fuck they wanted, and become Mary Daley. Then off to U-Haul with Snake, for "one without windows, please."

"Without windows?" the squashed-face clerk had said sullenly. "I'm gonna have to check about that." Then he hadn't moved, waiting for her to give him a reason.

Beth froze, but Snake, cool as ice, had saved her ass with "We're shooting a TV commercial. You know the one about substituting instant coffee for that awful restaurant piss?"

"No kidding?" the guy had said, happy again, touched by greatness. "I've seen that."

"Right. And we don't want people to know what we're up to, get all self-conscious that they're on TV."

After, she'd shouted at Snake, "What if he checks that out?" her hands going the wrong way round as she tried to get the hang of steering a van—and furious with herself, really, the having gone dumb at the rental counter making her see she would fuck up for sure at the Big Dance, probably bring everybody down with her.

After a while she'd calmed down. "We got to get the brake light fixed," Snake had said, his way with her flares being to ignore them. "Shakur'll kill us, he sees that."

And she'd done perfectly when Shakur checked her out later in the school parking lot, the big man leaving nothing to chance.

"Good job." Shakur had smiled at her. He had the tightest skin on his face, like with such a big space, there hadn't been enough to go round. A smile made you worry he might split like a melon. Truth was, though, she'd been all too pleased at melonhead's praise.

She tiptoed into the alcove, bent down to give Zing a kiss, then thought, *No, it might wake her.* She looked at her face, broad like Snake's. Would she have Snake's blunt nose, or her downturn—or her father's shepherd's crook? God, she loved Zing when she was asleep, she could just stare at her, wonder how this wonder had happened. She couldn't help herself, she kissed the air right over Zing's cheek, then nearly ran from the room like a thief.

Snake would take good care of Zing today, probably do a better job than she did. She lost patience a lot recently; feeling her life slipping away and no compass to guide her.

If she could do this thing, maybe she would get the feeling back that she was on the right track, helping the masses; that she was someone her daughter could be proud of.

But *if* she couldn't get Baba to straighten her out, put some steel in her, then she would choke up, get everyone busted, herself included. *Ding-dong. Ding-dong. Let's ring the Beth gong.* Except the one ringing that was her.

Whatever she would do, first she had to get to Roxbury, and the whole trip ahead felt as heavy as doing time. *Yeah,* she could hear Shakur croak, *of which Miss Ann's done two weeks.* Maybe jail, she thought, was a guilt solvent. Like, *you call me garbage, but you do me like this, then your morality's a joke, you're the garbage.*

She walked up freezing-cold Prospect to the bus stop, the chill wind tearing right through her. Thank God for goose down—though the jacket over her dress and green tights must have made her look like an upside-down Christmas tree to the medicated minds waiting to get their sugar fix at the corner Dunkin' Donuts.

Then her daily Central Square choice: Down into the Red Line to Ashmont, and maybe more white faces, making her a little less conspicuous till she headed into Roxbury. Or the No. 1 bus, the world getting darker all the way to Tremont and beyond.

Okay, it's here, so take it. She dropped the coins in, wondering what god gave them goose down? Olodumare probably. And who's the joker gave us cocaine, she wondered, haunted still by Jacob's hinting, worried face. She slid into a seat by the window. *Elegba?* No, coke would be the *ajoguns'* doing—*witches' powder.* Like what had happened to Shango, Baba said—Beth hiding in the halls to hear—the man a great king whose *ashe* was strong, much loved in Yorubaland, until the witches' powder made him lose control of his appetites. "There came a moment," Baba had said, "when he knew his human side might fall in with evil, ruin himself and his kingdom. What can he do to fight the witches and his own craving? He has only a little strength of his own—"

"To bring the house down, right?" Sugar had shouted. "And he *is* the fucking house!" A dozen eleven-year-old kids listening. "Sugar!" Jacob shouted. Sugar let him do that, while even Baba, he would not correct the man; Jacob like the little brother who could chide Sugar—

and Sugar listening to him because he didn't want to disappoint him, wanted Jacob to go on looking up to him, admiring him.

"Sorry," Sugar had said, letting himself be the lesson. "Like Shango the King, huh? I lost control of my tongue."

She'd heard the kids laughing at that, like it had all been planned for their education.

The bus screeched and fumed to a stop, and a woman in a cloth coat got on, actually sat next to her. That coat, Beth thought, it must feel like paper today. Beth pulled her hood over her face, wrapping her muffler higher to hide herself, thinking, *I'm nobody, who are you?*

Yeah, but once upon a time, she could have told the woman, she had been somebody. She'd led the Weathermen!

You mean like on BZ? Some guy in a bad hairpiece says about the high-pressure zones?

No, I mean the secret force of the Third World, hiding here in the U.S.

Oh, didn't they like blow themselves up in New York?

Well, yes, now you mention it, we very nearly did, she'd say, remembering the cone of noise that had surrounded her even as she ran into the street in her bathrobe. Her head had rung with pain for days after, so fortunately she couldn't really hear all the idiot things said at Jeffrey's apartment. That skinny girl, Suki, who'd become so famous, nice of her to have cuddled Beth, fed her like a baby. Christ, Beth had even wet herself! But Suki and her boyfriend, that racist painter, Hennessy, the more she'd challenged them to pick up the gun, the more they'd made a sick joke out of it, a cheerleader's song, Beth's whole life become like a theater piece to them—with them playing dress-up Tania and Che.

She'd learned from it, though. At the drafty cabin by Lake George— kind of a theatrical choice, too, actually, why not just meet at an apartment on Riverside?—she'd told the leadership that they'd gotten too far ahead, made themselves into geeks. "Stuff we're thinking of, it'll be like a show to everyone."

"Yeah," Bernadine had said, twigging her. "Like a comic book, huh?"

Fuck you, Beth had thought, but she had said, "Everyone's just gonna watch us, like a wrestling match or something, not join with us. We should just damage property now, that's it." Her fingers had ached from the cold then—more than today even—and only three sleeping bags for a three-dog night, which would probably turn into a grope she was definitely *not* in the mood for. Ah, well, she'd thought, mother-country radicals have to show they're willing to sacrifice their own bodies. Meanwhile, she'd repeated, "The country's not ready for nail bombs yet."

"Right," someone out of the dark had said. "Not *yet*."

Then Nixon had invaded Cambodia, and it was like the country rushed to meet them. *Not yet* seemed like *Soon*. College kids ransacked armories, firebombed ROTC buildings and stoned the Bugs, drove them off their campuses. Some kind soul even bombed the I-Lab again, took out a whole floor this time. In the thrall of it, she'd called Arkey up to find out more, his voice trembling when he heard her on the other end. She had stared at her scarred palm, smiled, and said, "Hey, what's the news about the bombing?"—mostly done to make him pull more of his hair out, maybe swallow a few coins.

The black kids got killed at Jackson State, and she could hear the scream get louder, *Pick up the gun! Arm yourself or harm yourself!* Jonathan Jackson was gunned down trying to free his beautiful brother by kidnapping that judge in Marin. Weather had fought back, bombing the courthouse. The cops took the jails back from the NY 21, and Weather had been there, too, with bombs for a courthouse in Long Island City. Then they'd blown out a few windows at the Capitol building, to cheer on the fifty thousand kids coming to West Potomac Park for May Day. When the pigs gunned down beautiful George Jackson, the West Coast crew had blown up the California Prison Bureau offices in San Francisco, Sacramento, and San Mateo—a string of firecrackers, straight from Mao. And after Attica, *she'd* placed the package in the Commissioner of Corrections' Office in Albany. "We did not choose to live in a time of war," she'd phoned in for her comrades. "But we chose to become guerrillas rather than become accomplices in genocide."

The bus pulled up near Bob the Chef's, her transfer stop, Beth the single spot of whiteness; no one even looked at her, though, tired people on their way home from the night shift, maids at the hotels mostly.

The next bus, the white driver gave her a share-my-bitterness look. Beth passed by, face of stone, and slid into a seat, looked down at her hand. A faint puckering still from when she'd thrown a tear gas canister back. A few ridges on her arm from the cop's buckshot at the Days of Rage. Tiny wounds from a war that never happened. She could hear Arkey saying, "It's *nothing*, Beth, what you did with those bombs, it's nothing," Beth having called him again for the pleasure of scaring the shit out of him.

"Which is like a little more than you're doing, boyo." Their bombs might only be bee stings, but at least they showed the world's freedom fighters that even in the Belly of the Beast some white youth were ready to use force against imperialism. And as she went about the country in disguise, she'd heard war drums everywhere, people passing the pipe and dreaming about blowing up military equipment, even wasting pigs, the masses already a blur in the streets, moving toward Weathermen faster and faster. Soon. Snake had got it right. *Soon.*

May again, and Vietnam vets stormed the UN. Thousands had been arrested all over Babylon, protesters had been shot in Albuquerque. *Soon* white kids would be ready to pick up the gun. *Soon* they'd learn what their black and brown brothers already understood: how to take life as well as give it up.

For Ho's birthday, she, Beth Jacobs, had crawled out on a ledge near a women's bathroom in the Air Force wing of the motherfucking Pentagon.

Bango! The next day, thousands of German students marched under the Red flag toward a U.S. Army base, screaming, "Beth Jacobs! Live like her!" like they'd known *that* much daring must mean *her.* Her name from German mouths! *Oh, Father,* she had thought, *can't you see the twist in the dialectic snake, the no become yes, death turning into life?* Soon it would be time for B.C.'s plan: rain destruction down on the imperialists, bringing humanity's bright dawn. *Soon.*

Or not.

Some of the others—had it been Rudd?—they'd had better antennae than she did, had seen that the pietà of Ohio would be a slow-acting virus, turning once-militant kids into timid Arkeys, terrified to hear her voice on the other end of the line. Then the draft had ended. Then the Paris farce cranked up, a fraud to buy time so Nixon and Kissinger could carpet-bomb Vietnam, finish the genocide. Still, the charade let people pretend imperialism had nearly croaked—so no reason for *them* not to finish grad school, take their rightful places in the ORG.'s machinery.

"Nothing's more important than our staying tight now," Snake had said, the leadership meeting on some actor's Marin houseboat. "Our time will come soon." Beth had maybe loved him most at that moment, the two of them separating sometimes for weeks to do jobs, and her looking forward most not to the Bang, but to seeing Snake again, getting high together, comparing notes.

Still, she couldn't feel the Future coming toward them anymore.

Maybe with more dope, she'd thought, walking in Boulder Creek with Laura to find her patch of Maui-Powie, Laura, a med student now, actually living with Nervous Arkey by then, dear Gail having been sent back to McLean.

"I saw Gail, coupla years back," Beth had said.

"Yeah?" Laura had on hiking boots, jeans, a flannel shirt, the canopy of trees in Boulder Creek making it cool in July.

They drifted for a while in placid dope reveries, Wisconsin for Beth, she and Snake having materialized themselves at a demo in Wisconsin, trying to lead the kids finally to blow up Army Math. Dopers&runaways&crazies, rads&working-class kids—the Weather Nation!—had started trashing store windows. Glass had been breaking everywhere and plainclothes cops poured into the crowd, sapping kids, snapping on cuffs, while other kids smashed the cops with two-by-fours. Beth had whomped one undercover pig on the snout with the pipe up her sleeve— a dumb thing to do; if she got busted, she'd be discovered, do some heavy time. Gail Wagman had recognized her then, the pixie in black tights out that night with a new friend who didn't swallow coins when he saw his own shadow. She'd thrown her tiny arms around Beth, kissed her. Beth had put a finger lightly against Gail's lips, meaning *speak no evil*.

Soft lips. The woman had It, a strong sexual penumbra. Men turned their heads sideways around Gail, the feeling flooding their bodies, the warmth in their crotch making them give her dreamy smiles. Like Snake's eyes, then. She'd felt it bend her own body even.

"Yeah," Beth had told Laura. "Madison. A demo. Gail gave me a kiss." Beth felt like the city mouse in skirt and wig and flats, carrying a small black handbag. What had her name been then? Donna something. "With tongue."

Laura had laughed, stoned already, as always. "Cute girl. So small. So crazy. Such large breasts. Like you. The breasts, I mean."

"It was a great day," Beth had said. "The Army had set up a machine-gun emplacement. I saw a couple of guys squatting by this parking lot, dropping flashlight batteries and cherry bombs in a pipe. You know," she'd said, knowing that Laura wouldn't, that being the point. "A homemade mortar. I think they may have fragged the National Guard, eh?"

Laura had looked up at the trees, not so excited. "Probably they just blew their own hands off."

"Fuck you, defeatist queen." But she'd put her arm around Laura.

"Look, Madison, you know, Army Math, that other physicist, it didn't make *me* feel so fucking wonderful," Laura had said. "Like, you know, that's what we did to Kopfman, really."

"*We?*" Beth had said. "Anyway, *we* didn't blow him up. Much as he might have deserved it."

"Yeah, maybe." Laura had stopped, kicked a rock with the toe of her boot. "And I don't know, those pictures of Phnom Penh, the people with IV's still in their arms dragged to the countryside. I mean, I don't know what's going to happen to them."

"Re-education." She had wondered if Laura had any idea where they might be heading in this forest, the two having fueled themselves with a joint before they took off.

"Yeah, maybe. But it's like I have no control over what the Khmer Rouge are going to do."

"Control? Who made you the God of the Future?" She had stopped, heard branches breaking. Someone following them? "*You* can't control the masses, Laura. You join them, you become part of this great living, breathing, many-headed creature that's just starting to stir, to shake its limbs and wake up from its millenniums-long slumber."

"What rough beast, huh?"

"Right. That's how an Aristo/fascist poet might see it. But me, I felt part of an absolute giant the day I left that bomb in the Pentagon."

"*You* did *that?*"

That was more like it. "Me, myself, crawling out on a ledge, praying no one would look up, see me in my red coat, Weathermen's present for Uncle Sam in my paw."

"Jesus."

That had been the response she'd wanted. "And when it went off, I felt how my hands had become part of this great many-limbed organism. I could hear the beast shout my name." *In German,* though she hadn't added that.

Laura had looked at her, but not admiringly. Scared—of the government, probably, like even knowing about the Pentagon bombing might get her arrested. Weird, though—after all, they'd been on their way to Laura's very own marijuana patch then, high in the Santa Cruz mountains, and *that* scared Beth. Like how could Laura know the cops wouldn't be staking it out?

But Laura, she loved her high more than the revolution, more than medical school, apparently.

And Beth? Well, she had to live up to her role in Laura Jaffe Productions and come along—not for the high, though, just to spend some time with her friend. She'd been glad she had, too, even when she'd been saying *fuck you* to her. She always felt at home with Laura, gemütlich; and from her first lover—Laura's own brother—on, until now, she liked having Laura to shock.

Laura had handed her an envelope, the address in her father's long, thin handwriting. "He sent me money for you, too, separately."

The blue airmail envelope had flooded her with longing—to sit with him, yes, but at age eleven, in a gray jumper she'd put on specially for the occasion, the two of them translating Goethe together. Was she like Faust now? No, probably he'd say she was just some petty demon, her father never able to hide his disappointment in who she'd become, but Beth feeling, too, that in a crazy way he would also be like all GN parents: if she made it to the top, it would make all the difference. Meaning what, though? Head of the Central Committee? Saint George putting the stake in imperialism's heart? Her name from German mouths?

But that shout had been a few years in the past by then, anyway, so just holding that letter, radioactive with his love, had made her doubt herself. If she looked inside and he'd said, *How is my darling faring*, she would be undone. How could Laura even have given it to her? She'd opened her purse then, got out her gun, and fired it at a tree, making the birds scatter, screaming.

Laura had screamed, too, which had made Beth feel better for a moment. Then the blackness had sat down inside her again, and she'd fallen to the ground, crying. This time Laura had put her arm around her.

Anyway, they'd never been able to find the marijuana patch. Laura had brought some seeds and stems with her, so they'd just sat under the trees, the air growing chill and dark. Passing the little copper pipe, Beth had felt easier, able to savor the look that lingered still on Laura's puss from her brave tree shooting.

"How are they?"

"He doesn't say. But my mom says they're fine. She says your mother's hair's gone gray, though."

"Does your mom still see him?"

"As a patient? Nope. She's cured."

Beth chortled at that.

"No. Really, she *is* better."

"Guiltier? Ready to tend the whole that makes us?"

"Yeah, he might write that, but that's not what he did for her. She's less driven. Working with your dad has made her like herself better."

"And it made me like myself less." She'd taken a long drag, but it had started her heart to aching again. "Does he say anything else?"

"He said he had to testify against Michael, to save you."

"Didn't work, then, did it?" Laughing made harsh chokesmoke-throat. "Anyway, I never asked him to do that."

"I know," Laura had said. "Mostly he just says he misses you."

"Und Er Felht Mir." Laura hadn't asked; must have known it meant *regret*.

"And he sent you some money."

"Yeah, you said. Maybe he wants to feel connected to the world revolution, eh?"

"Maybe. What should I do with it?"

"Put it in the bank."

"OK. Like a college fund, huh?" Meaning she would come back to them sometime. Have children.

And that had started Beth dreaming about having a child—though her father, strange man, he might approve of Zing only slightly more than of her blowing up a Pentagon bathroom, neither being the grand fate he'd had in mind for his daughter. Or maybe that had been a fantasy of hers. Perhaps he would be glad she'd made a good Oedipal transition, become a wife, mother, bank robber.

She stepped off the bus at Dudley then, heavy with longing and regret. A dirty dawn. By the corner a white man in a blue overcoat handed some money to a tall guy in a parka, something leaning off his head, the white man copping for sure. Did the dealer tithe to the Roxbury Action Project? she wondered. For all the problems it caused, that had still been one of Shakur's good ideas, Sugar jumping on it right away.

Susan, though, she'd found out what was going on—everyone on the corner talking about it—and she'd been furious, actually gone up in Sugar's face when he'd sauntered into the office where Beth hid away, Shakur with him, the big guy laughing then, like *you gonna take this bitch's shit?* Sugar had been calm about it, though. "Sweetheart," he'd said, "there's gonna be pimping, there's gonna be dealing. RAP needs to make it work *for* black people, make it help build a world without parasites like them." True and true, Beth had thought, though Susan's frown—almost a habit around Sugar now—meant she hadn't been buying it. "They're all over you, as it is," she said, "just waiting for you to fuck up." Meaning half the Boston cops, all the local FBI, their big game was Get Sugar. Didn't stop Sugar, though—seemed to give him energy, even.

The dealer came over then, right in her face, about her height but with federal-issue dead eyes, and this ridiculously tall red-and-white hat on his head about to topple sideways, something she'd seen before, like in a dream. Beth pulled her hood down around herself again, more worried about her identity than what he might do.

"How you doin', sister?"

Jesus, it was the Cat in the Hat—except this one, he was a black cat, with the longest scar she'd ever seen, all the way from the brim of his hat down his cheek to his jaw.

"Fine, fine," she said, the man probably certain she was a whore. "Night's over," she said, "gotta get the money back to the man." And if he asked who *the man* was? Use Shakur's name, maybe.

But he just walked away, a little extra rhythm in his step. A new drug coming from New York, Jacob had told her, cocaine you smoked. He'd tried it, asthma or no, said it made an orgasm for his brain. Maybe the Cat had the franchise.

She felt her heart pounding. What a life, she thought, afraid of blacks *and* Boston cops.

And the FBI? Olson had looked like an old man by the time of her hearing in 1978, her high bail maybe a retirement present for him. So probably he wasn't on the case anymore, and the truth was, without a little personal *impulsion* to goose it, who really gave a fuck about her?

She put her hood down, cold ears but better peripheral vision. Truth: she and her friends had blown themselves up, that's what they were famous for—not the Pentagon crapper or anything else.

But *then*, ah, in her salad days *someone* had cared enough to chase them all around the country. Down to fifty members, they'd become "mobile units," hooked up by phone for jobs, then scattered again, she always paired with Snake. But it already felt like postmortem effects. After the coup in Chile, they blew up the It Girl's golden rat hole on Park Avenue. Gulf Oil in Pittsburgh—solidarity with Angola. The AID office at State—her and Snake on that one. And for Victory in Vietnam, they'd boosted some champagne called Grande Dame. "Must mean Madam Binh," Snake had said. "Drink like her!" Then high, they'd done a spur-of-the-moment job on the DOD office in Oakland while across the country some comrades did the Banco de Ponce office in Rockefeller Center for the FLN.

Weathermen's Favorite Hits? Family Picture Album? Sad and lovely sepia-toned snapshots: like Kennecott in Salt Lake in union with Chile's poor. Or her and Snake at the INF in S.F. But she couldn't tell anyone about these swell days anymore, except for her Downstairs comrades. And they didn't give a shit for her war stories, trenches of Verdun to them.

And guess what? The Downstairs wasn't alone: *no one gave a shit, even at the time.* No one even noticed. The whole student thing had evaporated, the white kids just wanting to get on with their pig careers, like her former friends, who had started their "long march through the institutions," which really meant the institutions marched right through them. Like Jesse with his fine-point legal wrangling that only propped up the injustice system. Or Billy with his shit-pile comic book empire; Arkey become a teacher for spoiled suburban Jews; Jeffrey, an art pimp for the rich; and Laura, obsessed with penises, like do they matter and what do they mean? Jesus!

Beth and Snake had played married in the Southwest for a while. *A while?* Until what? *How long, Lord, how long?* Snake put a framed picture of martyred Che over their bed—sacred bullet wounds in his wasted chest. Lugubrious, but Snake said he would rise again. Meanwhile, Snake had got work as a carpenter, like his dad, and she'd clerked for a while in a bookstore. On a good day she would do Story Time for the kids at the shop or read to the kids at the Rez. She and Snake, they'd actually even played bridge with couples they'd met in their straight lives; and they'd also worked very hard at getting on each other's nerves, Snake making these horrendous grammatical mistakes she'd longed to correct—which impulse made her eager to throttle herself more than him. And sometimes they'd talked to old comrades about a job, where and with what, but nothing ever came of it.

Then Rudd had surrendered.

"Stay close," Snake had said to Bernadine, over the phone. The white kids had abandoned the movement, "but nothing's changed in the world situation." Black people fought in Angola and Mozambique. Soon the colonies here would rise. Things would tighten up for working-class people at home, and some white kids would want to stand with Weather again. "Our time will come." Then they'd get back to work, do some real damage. "Soon."

"Right," Beth had said that evening. "Soon. I believe that, Snake. But Rudd's right, too. The things we need to do now, organizing workers where we can, get them ready for when the imperial bennies disappear, that has to be done aboveground." The two of them had been forking up chili on wooden benches near the Zuni reservation, the hot meat cleansing the sinuses as it clogged the arteries. "I could make speeches," she'd added. A college stage? *Meet the Press?* Or some PBS tent revival, like *Unto This Light,* with her father and Marcuse?

"*You* could make speeches, Beth," Snake had said, "and I could make cheap chairs. Like I do now." She'd known what he meant: if they inverted, she'd be Beth Jacobs and he'd be . . . Beth Jacobs' friend.

But mostly what she'd wanted hadn't been *Meet the Press,* but a child. Use that college fund. "Jesus," he'd said the last time she'd brought it up in Arizona, "we can hardly take care of Mao-Mao. Imagine another helpless creature in the household."

They'd climbed back into the Jeep, the top-open rollover special— Beth certain then that the thing hiding inside his tight lips might be the name of one of those tough women who worked at the building site with him. That must be why he didn't want a baby with her. She felt sweaty, unattractive in a brown cardigan sweater, too hot for her even in the evening.

"We have to keep the armed struggle alive in the mother country," he'd said. "Bethie, the world *will* turn our way."

"Soon, right?" Beth a little ironic about it by then, thinking that she should just fucking surface ASAP. Snake could stay and fuck whoever his little heart and big dick desired—the man better endowed even than Wellesley College, but how did that make up for this pointless desert life?

"Right," he'd said, missing the irony. "Soon."

Soon, the two of them had been waiting for Snake's Trailways bus at the gas station near the highway, he on his long way back to Boston. Then she'd take an airplane to New York, get ready for her court date.

"You know too many people in Boston, darling," she'd said, still warm for him from their lovemaking the night before, and certain that she'd been wrong, there hadn't been anything else on his mind but the Revolution.

"The people I knew," he'd said, "they're in Revere. You're born there, you stay there, Roach Motel by the Sea. You hadn't broken my nose, I'd still be there myself." He stroked the top of her head. "I stay away from Wonderland, I'll never run into anyone I know." He looked nice today, his western shirt dirty, but his long hair over his cheeks clean from its weekly wash. He had picked up the porto cat jail from the swept sand in front of the gas station, their very Valiumed ball of fur lying prone now, whimpering softly. "And if they find me, sweetie, BFD, huh? Rudd gets probation. I'll get what? A parking ticket. I'm not Beth Jacobs. I'm wanted for like overturning trash cans or something."

They'd kissed, Beth looking over his shoulder at the scrub and cactus with its soft, inviting green flesh, its fierce prickles. And as soon as his black hair had boarded the bus, she'd missed him terribly. The bus had rolled slowly across the dirt to the asphalt road, and she'd run after, like in the movies, a woman in a long dress, her then red hair flying backward. But after a few steps she'd felt that her legs didn't mean it. She wanted to go home.

And then, a week later, in Laura's Manhattan studio, she'd felt crippled from missing Snake, from not sleeping in *their* own bed with *their* martyr overhead. And she'd felt suddenly terrified of spending even a day or two in jail.

And what if it turned out to be more than a day or two? Jesse, brokering the deal with the feds, had promised her that wouldn't happen. But then, if her deal was such plain vanilla, why was it taking so long?

Laura had been scared, but *of* her, not for her, much as she tried to hide it, like her friend just couldn't wait till Beth went to jail—temporarily, of course. Beth would look at Laura's trembling little chin, the same softly blinking eyes as when Beth had first asked to go on her boat, and her terror made Beth's own shivers much, much worse. She had even thought about going back to Great Neck to get away from her, hide under the duvet in her bedroom, her mother bringing her soup, her father bringing her big helpings of . . . analysis, probably, to show her that nothing she'd done made sense except as a symptom—though he, too, had been a Communist (she'd figured *that* much out), had known once what healing the world required.

And reciprocally, she would probably pretend he'd become a war criminal, when really he was . . . what? a coward? a minor American collaborator? A suburban husband and father, who looked smaller and older every time she saw him on television, telling folks to listen to their guilt, sounding like that cricket with the idiotic conscience song they'd played at the Rez's day care center.

Anyway, she'd stayed in the overstuffed Laura Ashley living/ dining/bedroom. While Laura worked, Beth had watched *Family Feud*. Things dragged on, the feds waiting, supposedly on confirmation from higher echelons, and Beth getting to be an expert on America's favorite breakfast food (survey says scrambled eggs) and what object most Americans had in the bathroom (survey says blasting caps), the first time in her life, really, that she'd sunk into this bland, comforting morass, like bathing her psyche in wet cardboard. She'd regretted leaving her violin for the Rez's school, that might have passed the time better, though she knew now that she played *very* badly, her father's *you're a wonder* all the more wonderful because it had been a sweet lie. Then she'd forgot about the violin, wondering what America's favorite snack food might be.

In the evening, she and Laura had watched yet more TV, ate Chinese food from little white cartons delivered sullenly to the door, Laura now afraid to be on the street any more than necessary.

Then, thank God, she'd started getting letters from Snake, a manila envelope to Laura and another sealed envelope inside for her, like Snake decided the FBI might not be brainy enough to open *two* envelopes, letters written in his terrible handwriting on scraps of paper torn from magazines. Zero punctuation and connectives, and, worst of all, no numbers on the pieces, either—that would fool the FBI, right?—so she had to piece the narrative together. It seemed like he'd seen Sugar Cane give a speech in a church basement in Cambridge, even the fluorescent lights looking dazed at Christ's total rout. Cane had lit Snake up, though.

She remembered Sugar Cane in his low boots and dark shades, pacing the stage at the Roxbury Strand a thousand years ago, a short, stocky man with a high voice, but everyone in that audience knowing even then that they beheld a prince of his people, the leader of the revolutionary movement in the U.S. B.C. had had the honor to learn from him, and Sugar surely had put steel into that white boy on his first farm vacation, made him ready to frag an officers' dance. Now Sugar would lift his community again, and when the time came—soon or Soon— they'd be ready to march the way they had that night at the Strand, when they'd streamed to the very school where she'd first met Harrison Baker. SDS *that* day had done slow circles to nowhere, snow settling on their uncovered heads, and only Frank's spectral arm had held her up. But Sugar, he'd known Frank, too, and he'd known the way to raise him: burn the rat trap down. Of course, the pigs would have found a way to put a black man like *that* in jail.

> bulls perforated one ear
> a rib through his lung
> slung into THE HOLE
> clogged slit for his crapper
> stone floor
> his own waste,
> he squats
> does push-ups

"*Der weiche Gang geschmeidig starker Schritte,*" Beth had murmured, giddy with it all.

"Is that something by your father?" Laura had asked innocently enough, as always.

"Christ, no," Beth said angrily, spitting out. She had laughed. "Or yes, maybe so." *Behold the man,* she intoned inwardly, spooning up some corn flakes. *The true black panther.*

> *Trays of crap*
> *He fasted*

In the Hole, probably. As far as she could piece out the pieces, Sugar had nearly gone mad in solitary, seen his own body lying in front of him, stabbed in his sleep by a guard, blood and shit mixing on the floor. He used some Buddhist thing Joshua Battle had taught him and it pulled his mind back together.

> *Now he studies all the world's religions*
> *taught me I have to lead all races*
> *whites can work with RAP the vanguard force for the colonized*
> *   worker*

Sugar had run things down that way he had, like he poured his thoughts right into your ear. He told them that the ORG. set-asides only skimmed the cream from the ghetto, poured them into suburban homes. But the lumpen, they got prison cells.

Sugar, though, had a program: the Roxbury Action Project. Jacob Battle, Susan Lems, two comrades from the past, they had run RAP while Sugar had been in prison, but he had guided their every step, setting up free breakfasts for kids, protection for the children being bussed, free rides for seniors. An ambulance service, and a screening clinic for sickle cell. Even a shoe factory, to make sure people had jobs. RAP programs would hold back the genocidal onslaught, raise consciousness among the lumpen. Then, when the last jobs for unskilled blacks moved offshore, *this* united community would be ready to fight back.

The fragments had cut through her stupor, made her giggle, made her miss her Snake, their life and what it might be. Snake had been right; the world *had* turned their way again. With Sugar Cane, their beacon, out of jail, the old mole, Revolution had surfaced once more!

Snake had signed up for a job in RAP's sickle cell screening clinic in Roxbury. And guess who else enlisted? Miss Priss, our comrade from SDS, hair cut short and dyed red, *"like you in Detroit*

Yeah, if I were a skinny ugly young hag.

Priss told Susan, "He should write a book about his life
like with all the great leaders you can just feel loneliness coming
*   off him, can't you?*
She wants to fuck

Sugar, no doubt. Beth could see Priss's skinny body curving toward
the Lonely Leader, her voice a mixture of fatuous sentiment and come
hither/don't touch me. How could Priss dream an anorexic hysteric
would be Sugar Cane's longed-for friend? Though Sugar, he'd have
wanted Priss to bend into him like that, he being a master of *come to me,*
and you'll be inside the charmed circle—which probably *had* been
Jesus', Mohammed's & Buddha's rap, too, now she thought of it, though
Sugar, like that night at the Strand, might suddenly dump you *outside,*
too—presenting *Miss Ann, the Girl Who Can Be Made.*

Still, RAP must be the real deal—or why would an adrenaline junkie
like her dear Snake feel that working in a clinic did as much good for the
Third World as blowing the windows out of a DOD office? Beth, not
thinking about how it might bring heat to Snake, swore that once her
trial got done, *she* would work with Sugar Cane, too. But what if this
plea bargain looked craven, what if Sugar and RAP wouldn't use her?

Laura must have seen her confusion. "Wha's the skinny?" she had
said, probably feeling Beth putting distance between them, the college
slang meant to reach out to her, like your mom buying some stupid food
you'd liked as a kid.

"Nothing," she'd said, just like that kid, Beth realizing by then that
Her Life So Far could only really make sense to comrades who had
shared it.

Then Jesse had finally closed the deal. Beth had surrendered to the
feds—only to find (mirabile dictu, eh?) that the Amerikkkan Government had been full of shit all along. Now they had her in custody, they
whispered in the judge's ear that the famous Beth Jacobs remained the
linchpin of "a worldwide terrorist conspiracy." They needed to hold her
without bail just a little while longer, Your Honor, so they could roll up
the rest of her dangerous "network."

And meanwhile they'd set this insane flute player to work keeping
her up nights. She'd skipped another period, and started throwing up
the prison mush each day. But Beth hadn't learned any Joshua
Battle–certified techniques to keep herself from seeing herself hemor-
rhaging, losing the baby, knowing even then that it would be, *had to be,*

a girl—which she was *not* going to give up, let someone else raise. Nzinga, the Queen Warrior. *Zing,* she'd call her. Her heart's lodestone.

Her parents visited. The baby growing inside her made her feel helpless. *Please care for me,* she'd wanted to tell her weeping father. And *that* also felt unbearable. Then the pigs had hit her over the head with that astro-bail. Well, thank God for Jeffrey Schell. Funny, he didn't share *any* of her politics, but he'd always been the one of her GN friends who got her. Adored her, actually.

Beth crossed the wide boulevard, empty now, which made it feel like a stage set before the play began. She strolled down the broad, freezing avenue whose sides looked like they'd been raked by a giant's claws, smashing windows, crumbling brick, turning whole buildings to mounds of rubble. Rush hour, some of the kids from the school would form up here for the Elderly Escort Program. Neat little boys like Buster, in jackets and ties, would help the old heads across this hooting desert, Sugar doing all a man could with the troops he still had. But the RAP shoe factory had closed down already; they couldn't keep the ambulance service going much longer; and things would have been even worse but for Shakur's shakedowns.

She passed the Stop and Shop. RAP would get something going there later, too. George, the addled bantamweight in a porkpie hat, would shout through his bullhorn, "We the people shop here, making the businessmen fat and rich. So we the people demand that this store donate to the breakfast program. Not to feed hungry children is low and rotten!" And a few pickets maybe—THIS STORE MUST CONTRIBUTE TO THE PEOPLE'S SURVIVAL PROGRAMS!—but all of it looking like one of those cheap movies where the extras run around changing hats to make the crowd look bigger.

Truth: RAP couldn't turn out the community anymore, not the way they had for bussing, RAP men there each morning to protect the kids from racist spit and baseball bats. Blacks had to fight to go to shitty schools where white racists hated them! Sugar had seen then that his people needed him to build the thing *he'd* always wanted most—a primary school of their own with an Afro-centric curriculum, on the very spot where the old one had been burnt down—so his life, he said to Susan, wouldn't just have left a hole in the ground for black people.

Sugar had harangued the city council at night, organized demos by day for the Malcolm X *Community Center*—which meant he'd got federal money to build a private school. It made Beth smile, the school underground at first, like her, or the hotel maids on their way home in their wigs. The place turned out to look like nothing so much as Cherry

Lane, plenty of glass and sunlight, a cheerful building, except for ghostly signs on the brick walls still where some kids had tagged it, tangled fauve initials that Butchie and George had spent a full day rubbing off, hard work for Butchie, whose left arm shook now. And the outline, she noticed, still there of "SUGAR," with a white smear to cover over "WILL DIE," work of the cops *or* the dealers, who knows? The pigs hassled him constantly, busted him for jaywalking, fucked with him about the inspection sticker on his car, like maybe they could annoy the black messiah into climbing onto the cross. So the cops could have left the love letters, but new Biggies had come to town, too, Jacob said, with new drugs, "and these men be," Jacob said, "like nothing you ever seen. Rip the living heart out of you with a *real* death palm." Beth had heard some, too. Ears taken, decapitations, whole families shot up. The little ones, too. These tags could be *their* warning.

She marched through the breezeway and down the hall, opening her parka as she went. Teachers had covered every inch of wall space with the kids' drawings of Great Moments in the Civil Rights Movement: Rosa Parks, M. L. King, Malcolm X, and Nelson Mandela, jailed leader of the ANC, all looking like members of the African branch of the Potato Head family, huge tubers with crooked, Martian-looking arms. Later today, in this big, sunny room, she would watch Delon lead his music class, little kids strutting around swinging their imaginary saxophones up and down like they were the Basie horn section, and the tall, wild-eyed man leading them the very one who had carried the drums of kerosene that SNAP used to fire up the old Pine Street school.

She marched down the stairs to the basement. What she saw in this school every day filled Beth's heart, the school and its teachers asking a lot of these kids, but acting always like they knew each one of them *could* succeed; so the kids all worked hard—and mostly for the same reason as her or Snake, they didn't want to disappoint Sugar Cane. Who sat now at one of their little desks, his legs stretched out in khaki pants, like he didn't have a care in the world.

Coming in late meant most heads pivoted toward her, but not—thank God—Shakur's huge melon, up by the green board, his back to them. The chalk stub in his mitt made him look more immense, and he was already the most powerful-looking man she'd ever seen, six foot seven maybe, and wide, too. But solid. "You should see the kind of people showed up this evening," Snake had said, first time Shakur and Bunchie had sauntered into the clinic. "These guys Sugar knew from jail, *real* lumpen prole. Stone-cold, selective killing machines for the revolution."

Well, he'd got that right. "Head shaved like a warrior," Snake had said to her that night as they spooned up their dinner peas, cleaned up Zing's strained ones from the walls.

"Yeah," Beth said, "or like a man doesn't want you to know he's going bald." But when she'd gotten to meet him, she'd felt the power in him, too. Hard to believe he'd once been called Baby—or ever been one, either, except that on that planet of a head he had weirdly tiny, shell-like ears.

"He was my hookup," Jacob had told her once, not exactly proudly, more like whatever happened now was on his tab. "After my mom died, I was so lonely, I rode this Greyhound upstate. See, a visit to Sing Sing was like going home for Thanksgiving dinner for me. I told Sugar how the man could have given me up, halved his sentence."

And Shakur had seemed like an answered prayer. The school already in money trouble—they needed new playground equipment, some musical instruments, books. Shakur, one day he heard Sugar complain how black people talk big but they don't put up diddly for their own organizations. Right off, Shakur came up with his plan to tithe the dealers and pimps. That day, Sugar had been the one *deciding,* Sugar the one in the front of the room: *the teacher.*

Not anymore. And those little squares and squiggles that Shakur made for today's lesson? Maybe they were the layout of the mall she'd cased. He scrawled a box and put some wheels on. Maybe the truck? The big man had bad small-motor control. She wedged herself as quietly as ever she could into a little desk with a bright-blue top. But she wouldn't be able to take her parka off now, would swelter soon.

"Sit right down, Miss Jacobs," Shakur said without looking back. "You're among friends."

"Better be," Beth said. "You just used my real fucking name."

No one laughed, but Sugar smiled over toward her, raising his broad eyebrows like he was about to pass her a note. Or the grin maybe meant to say *he* was in control of all this, just a generosity of his that Shakur seemed to be leading the group.

But for how long? Shakur, he always took the most dangerous role in the Downstairs jobs, left Sugar out of them—it not being a good idea to risk their very public leader. That was something Sugar clearly agreed with—which made some folks wonder if Sugar was scared. Which upped the ante. So Sugar *had* to go on the Big Dance—the most danger-ous job yet—or he'd lose face with the seven people scattered round this room: the Downstairs.

Priss had a box of shells open, busily knifing a cross on each one's tip, the way Shakur liked them. Jacob would drive from the Dance to Priss; she'd sashay to the van—the "white edge" all-girl on this job. Never one to miss a chance to play dress-up, Priss had put on a blue business suit, a curly wig with her straight hair tucked up under, and makeup that made her face look older, sadder, and even more pinched. She stacked the bullets back in their cardboard box, took a black 9 mm out of her attaché case, and handed it to George, grip first. He worked the action back and forth, maybe looking for a flaw.

Beth didn't want to, but she had to say something about that. "We shouldn't have guns here," she said, barely audible. "Anything goes wrong, we'll bring the school down." Not knowing if she should say this to Shakur or Sugar, she spoke to the white acoustic tiles of the ceiling.

It was Shakur who replied, though, turning back to her with a storm on his face. "I hear you, sister. Now you hear me, all right? Your friend Susan don't have to know nothing about this, not Susan and nobody else. You understand me?"

She nodded dutifully, while the others laughed at her, all of them probably strapped, of course, enough guns in this room to knock over, well, an armored truck. Shit, she couldn't help laughing at that herself.

Shakur had already started to talk again, and it turned out the dia-gram wasn't the mall, but their last job but one, the Wienie Man, a meatpacking plant. The wheels on the truck were supposed to be the stairs where Jacob had lost his wind, dropped some of the money, something about Shakur's tone making Beth feel Shakur hated Jacob, maybe because Jacob looked scared a lot of the time—now for instance, his shoulders curved forward, protecting his damaged lungs. The others wouldn't even look at him while Shakur dressed him down for how fucking long he'd taken inside, etc., the tale culminating in the bank-notes and Jacob's courage fluttering down the stairwell, in a haze of air that had—Beth knew—felt to Jacob thick as mucus, impossible to draw down. Jacob had fired his gun, too, for no reason, sending plaster frag-ments everywhere, then half slid down the stairs on his back to the steel door. Shakur had rushed up behind him, dragged him to the car.

"But it's not my man's fault," Shakur added, giving Jacob an alligator-smile. "It's those lungs of his. Man, I tell you, he's a hard case," meaning for acupuncture, another of Shakur's joint-honed talents. He had a clinic for addicts that met in this room twice a week, Shakur pok-ing them for withdrawal symptoms. After, everyone in the neighborhood saw people getting donuts at the corner, small silver needles still sticking out of their earlobes proudly—black people trying to get straight with-out that government shit that makes you a slave to the program, makes you sit in jive therapy sessions squealing like a baby to get more methadone. Meantime, though, irony of the dialectic, Shakur took a cut from the dealers whose clients he cured, and laughed to think how his counseling could dry up his own cash flow.

Might do, someday. Shakur had been an addict himself, really believed in his needles. Gifted, too; he'd helped Snake with his insomnia, even Susan with her migraines. But he couldn't seem to do jack for Jacob. Baba struck out, too, with his prayers, spiritual baths of mullein, comfrey, cherry barks. A hard case, like the man said. Beth looked past George and the other guys, trying to support Jacob with her glance, send him love. She knew he didn't think he could do it again. But he had no choice, he'd said a week ago at dinner—Zing asleep finally, Jacob having contributed several renditions of *Pat the Bunny*—Sugar had been a father to him and Shakur had saved his life twice now, last time by the Wienie Man's door.

"You can do it, man," Snake had said, the two of them in the entry-way. "After all, you had the courage to stand on the bridge in New York." Snake turned his hand into a pistol, ready for the Panther attack on the precinct house—Shakur having nestled dynamite by the station walls. "Bang! The pigs rush out, and you and Shakur were gonna shoot them from Harlem River Drive, right?"

"Right, brother. But the only bing came from the blasting cap."
Shakur's Panther group had been riddled with stoolies, "and one of
them switched oatmeal for our dynamite, can you fucking believe it?"

So no bing—but bango, two cop cars had pulled up beside the
would-be shooters. Jacob—all that work at the Dewey School track—
had got away, sprinting between the cars. Shakur, fat from smack and
sweets, ended up doing hard time for too much ice cream. "Shakur
could have traded me, gotten some time off," Jacob had told her once.
Instead, he'd traded *that* for Jacob's endless gratitude.

"And," Jacob had said to Snake that night, "the bomb had gone off,
the cops *had* come out, would I have had the guts to pull the trigger?"
He had smiled. "I tell you, I don't know. So far I've only wounded a
plaster ceiling."

"That's why we need Ifa," Beth had said from the hall room. "The
orishas'll put some steel in us."

"Your orisha, maybe," Jacob had said again. "Not Baba's, you ask
me."

But she hadn't gotten to ask why before he left.

The memory made her miss a beat. Shakur was standing in front
of Dreads now, and Dreads was screaming. Shakur—could this be?—
looked like he was pulling him to his feet by his ears, but Dreads, like six
feet tall, so Shakur could only get Dreads' head to chest level. He held it
there, Dreads stamping his feet on the ground, probably to keep himself
from kicking Shakur, getting himself killed. "Look at his motherfucking
eyes!" Shakur shouted. "I done told you, no motherfucking drugs when
you're on a job!"

Dreads, stoned, suspended by his ears, had the guts even then to
answer back, "*This* ain't a job, this is *planning* for a job." Man, but his
ears must have stung!

Shakur laughed at that, freed a hand to whack Dreads across the
face. He dropped him back down.

"Now this job," he said, "no room for error, you understand me?
We're going to get all of it, every damn dime. We take the guards the way
we planned, while they're loading up their cart. Then we march over to
the motherfucking driver, tell him to open up or we waste his friends."

Which had not *been the motherfucking plan.* She said that, though
she knew the reply: *So fucking what, the pigs die?* Right. But her stomach lurched anyway, that was the problem.

"And when the driver doesn't open it?" George said.

"He *does.*"

"Yeah, right, he *does.* But like when he *doesn't.*"

"Then we kill one of his pals, convince him we mean it." Shakur shrugging his shoulders wearily at the obstinacy of the world. "What can you do?"

George stood up. "I wish you guys the best, man, I really do. But you are all motherfucking crazy." He walked toward the door. Bunchie got up, started to go after him, but Shakur shook his head no and he stopped. George would be a real loss for Beth. He had short-order experience; Beth and Susan and Sugar, they basically did prep for him in the breakfast program.

Sugar rallied them then, talked about why they had to do this job to save the school, save the survival programs. And they had to show that the armed revolution was alive and well, even if pissants like Eldridge Cleaver had abandoned the masses.

Shakur, sitting on a gray teacher's desk, smiled, like *who gives a fuck about Cleaver.* Or maybe about Sugar either.

Then it was time for exercise, all of them staggering around and around the playground in the dark, parkas and wool coats open, doing wind sprints, Shakur running alongside them, shouting encouragement, like telling Prissy what a great comrade she'd turned out to be. Then push-ups, and Shakur squatted down by Dreads, sweet-talking the guy whose ears he'd just yanked, telling him "Get your arms in shape now, man, all that money we're going to have to lift," and Dreads, like an abused child, smiled gratefully over at him.

After, she went over to Sugar, him panting for breath worse than the others, said how she'd seen some awfully heavy bags that day, why did they need what was in the truck, too?

"Yeah, two heavy bags, and the school needs both, right? Give it an endowment. But then we got to have something for weapons, arm the community."

Harsh shouts of "Don't move! Don't move, asshole! Don't fucking move!" came from the edge of the yard. She jumped, made Sugar smile. It turned out to be the men screaming at the imaginary driver in the Toyota, everyone acting very grim and serious.

Shakur shouted, "So, listen, the driver don't open up, you waste the guard, you understand. You waste him!"

Maybe Sugar caught a look on her face. "The driver doesn't open the door," he said, staring over the long slope of bare trees that went to a hill behind the school, "he loves money that much? Then *his* greed turns them *all* into pigs, you dig?"

Anyway, why was she so bent out of shape that Brinks guards might be killed. Like, was the war over? Babylon in flames? The land free? No, just that heavy guilt tow pulling her under again. Which made Beth pretty sure she was wrong for the job—unless Baba could make her see straight so she wouldn't fuck up. Ifa, man, it *had* to know sometimes you had to offer a blood sacrifice, and the Brinks guard—black or white—he might have to give his life so the black nation might live.

By the Toyota, the guys swung twin-set wooden blocks, attached by hinges, pretend guns or something, cowboys and Brinks truck. She'd seen that wood shit before in Billy's comics, she thought, what were they called? Nunchukus? Damn, N.B. unable to remember *that*! Yeah, but *hers* had ferret heads on each end, magical mechanical animals with venomous bites, creatures made by Dr. Why?—i.e., her father made magus by the midget.

Priss came up then, even her hair grayed. "That Japanese shit," she said, jealous probably of Beth and Sugar talking together, "Ninja B. should be great with it," doubtless wanting everyone to see Beth hit herself in the cheek with a piece of wood.

"No," Sugar said sternly. "What Beth will be great at is driving the van."

Would she? Or would she send the van's rear end sliding who knows where, like in the rental car lot where she'd smashed up the brake light.

Rays from a distant star battered against the haze—and lost, for now. "We better get out of here," Beth said to Sugar, thinking of the kids with brightly colored canvas lunchboxes about to pour down that street, playing their own games of pretend. Panthers and Pigs? Or maybe Orishas and Witches.

Sugar shouted to the men to finish up, and they stopped—then glanced at Shakur, like orders had to come from him.

Shakur nodded. Beth turned toward the building, heard Shakur coming toward Sugar, croaking, "You sure she's gonna be all right? We could let the other one do that shit." Meaning Snake.

"I'll check her out later," Sugar said, his voice sounding even higher next to Shakur's. "I'll make sure."

Beth slowed, lifted her shoulders, trying to turtle her head, not at all sure she'd be all right.

"Yeah. Her or him, I don't give a fuck. Just send me one good offay."

Sugar gave a breathy laugh, formed little puffballs of frost in front of him. "A good white man's hard to find," he said, his voice no lower, but a little sharper when he spoke with Shakur, two powerful men slicing up the world. She heard one of them behind her, clapping hands together for warmth. Mirror image of the cops, she thought. Any White Will Do.

She closed the breezeway door. A few kids shouted in the halls already, and she scuttled into the big yellow kitchen so the kids wouldn't see her, taking off her parka as she went.

The kitchen, its gleaming silver pots on black wrought-iron ceiling racks, always cheered her up. Look what Africa can do! She got the egg cartons from the stainless-steel refrigerator, started cracking them into six bowls, making a game of it, this one then that one and back to the beginning, fast as she could. Then remembered she should wash her hands after, the hot water hurting her fingers. Back to the fridge then for more eggs she'd had to buy this time. The White Hen, last week, had only kicked in a carton, instead of its usual six, no excuse even. That night, the guy goes home, George puts a Molotov cocktail through the window. "Well," Beth had said to Sugar next day, "you can't make an omelet without breaking convenience stores." Sugar had laughed, head and chest tilted back. But his chuckle had been bullshit; the guy not kicking in right away, that meant something, the petite bourgeoise not so scared anymore, the breakfast program already only big enough now for students at the school. More reasons they needed to do the Dance.

Six bowls filled with frothy eggs, ready to go. George came in then— thank God!—put on a clean white apron, the man not willing to rob an armored truck, but still helping with breakfast. He had the griddles going in a jiff, working on the hash browns first—every place in Roxbury that made French fries donating at least a bag of skins—cooking them up in bacon grease, a beautiful odor. George flipped the taters, focused on his work, not like a lot of the Downstairs, the "nutrition counselors" and "martial arts teachers." Meaning that teenagers in their down jackets came once or twice to learn karate, but Dreads never showed; and just as well probably, the coke making a lot of the Downstairs edgy. Beth rinsed the bowls in steaming water, a job that bored her usually, but today it was okay, calmed her a little even.

She dried her rough hands on the clean white dish towel. Susan Lems came in, a simple black dress, but a lovely blue-green-red scarf on her head, Susan about forty now, round curls under the scarf, round breasts, her body and face all circles, but a mouth that might turn downward sharply, spreading devastation. Susan set to pouring gallons of milk into large silver cylinders, popped a flame on, to heat the milk for cocoa. Sugar came in, too, changed to a dashiki, and buttered the toast as it popped up, him and Susan side by side, but not talking.

Breakfast ready, Beth the school mouse couldn't even bring the food out to the long serving table. She peeked through the door at Susan and Sugar, behind the table, doling out treats, and at the laughing kids getting them, at least forty of their eighty this morning, the program a godsend not just for kids who went hungry otherwise, but for families where both parents worked. "Maybe we could charge a little for that," she'd said to Susan once, the two of them working in her tiny office, doing the books. "Like give them a means test, huh?" Susan had said, making her feel like shit—but also like she was the only one counting the pennies, the only one knew how bad things really were. Sugar ladled dollops of scrambled eggs onto their brown plastic trays, looking happy to feed others, bc connected to his flock. She heard him ask Zongar—this sweet kid with puffed-out cheeks—why he wasn't working harder at math. He told Buster—her particular favorite because he liked to spin in the playground with the girls, pretending they'd been possessed by an orisha— what a great sax player he was sure to be, like Bird, this eight-year-old nearly flinging his tray with joy, cocoa already slopping onto the eggs. Buster probably didn't know who Parker was, but he knew it was Sugar Cane saying something good about him—and in a way not just Sugar saying it, but *Africa,* as though Sugar, he spoke from that place, and showed everyone, too, what a man, his inner life grounded in Africa, could do, because he always had somewhere inside himself that belonged to him to stand on, a place *away* from this cold country that hated them, and where something was always being taken from them, like the house where they lived or their families.

Then the line bunched, some pushing going on in back. Xilixa, ten years old, stumbled, her tray clattering down, and Sugar, dropping his ladle, was *there,* grabbing a boy, holding him by the neck. The kids she knew gave coal-colored Xilixa a hard time—the truth being that the kids liked it best when Africa was words in Sugar's or Baba's mouth, not when it was a girl with a Nigerian mother. Maybe she should read everybody that book about the bears, how those hurt at home hurt others? Or maybe those bears, they didn't know Roxbury.

George saw her looking. "I leave here, I might miss this part of the day," he said, meaning, *and not much else besides.*

She turned. "Mississippi, eh? You going home?" George, he had gray hair, a former boxer, a former con, too.

"You don't believe me? It's beautiful country. The first place I ever flew."

That being a thing he swore on, and wouldn't back down from. Beth could never tell if he meant it or not.

"You can't help loving the place you grow up, you know?"

"Yeah, I know." Or the people you grew up with, more like it, even suburban kids who had no idea—or an utterly false one—of the revolution, what it would take.

George, not much taller than she was, stood on tiptoe, looked over her shoulder. "He's got a way with them," George said.

In the cafeteria, Sugar had settled the kids down. Marcus, a broad-shouldered boy who'd done the pushing, looked like he was apologizing to X. The two of them took their trays to one of the long tables, started to eat together in perfect amity.

"Anyway," George said, "I'm probably gonna go on this one. Save this place, right? Like Sugar says."

"Yeah?" *Me, too,* she wanted to say—if Baba would cast for her, give her guidance from her god, maybe even arrange for an orisha to possess her.

The kids started to scrape their plates into the big gray plastic buckets, put their cups in the bins, everything ready for washing—which would be her next job, another chance to calm herself a little before she tried to sneak into Baba's class, sixth graders this week. Maybe, if Baba knew she'd loved Frank, he would cast for her. Then she could go on the job. Not Snake. *Her.*

By the time she'd washed the last plate and scurried in, Baba was already seated in a heavy carved chair he must have dragged to the school. He wore a white robe—sacred color of Obatala, orisha of purity—and had his eyes closed. Sixteen desks in a circle around him, and the kids behind the desks quiet—for the blessed moment, anyway. She folded herself into one of the spare desks they'd pushed up against the wall by the door. When he opened his eyes again, saw her, he might fling the white girl into the hall. Or he might see how much she wanted to learn the way to life, let her stay.

Long strings of beads hung across his chest, and a wooden tray lay on his lap. *They cast the nuts there, right? Find out what the gods want you to do.* In his hand, Baba held the Osu staff of the Ifa order. *He is Babalawo,* Beth thought, *he carries the Osu staff*—hearing herself, so solemn, rhythmic, made her smile: Baba, he carried her back, or forward—anyway, *somewhere else.* And one of the kids too, apparently; Buster of the laughing eyes in his dark red sweater slowly walked to Baba; lay on his belly on the linoleum floor by Baba's feet, his tortoise-shell glasses falling off. "Mofobibale. I place my head to the earth," he said, the whole thing holy, maybe, but weird, too, this full-of-beans Roxbury kid on his stomach under fluorescent lights, the other kids watching, and not laughing; or not *yet* anyway.

Maybe never. A lot of families came to Baba's storefront on Tremont now, the Temple of the Mystic Path in a block of mostly boarded-up windows, getting readings, offering blood sacrifices to get right with their orishas; which meant Baba would become a power in the community soon. He could help them stop being long-suffering, help them build RAP to fight for their future.

Buster's small hands clasped Baba's ankles, swathed in silk socks, and Baba said some words, his hand on the boy's head, a woven *ide* on his left wrist, Orunmila's symbol that told Death: *this is a child of the prophet and should not be taken before his time.* They'd become a craze, mothers wanting the band for their children, crowding the storefront, until Baba chastened them with: *to die knowing is not like death to those who die unknowing*—like Mao's *to die for the people is light as a feather.*

Baba opened his eyes, sat his staff against the chair, picked up a white pitcher from the floor. He saw her then, but didn't say anything, just raised his brows, maybe because Sugar and Jacob came into the classroom, took seats against the wall by her. Sugar slumped, his eyes reddened-up since this morning. He snuffled. A cold, she hoped.

Baba poured a little water out on the formica. "*Omi Tutu, Ile Tutu, Ona Tutu, Tutu Eshu, Tutu Orisha,*" a few students mouthing the prayer with him, Baba adding, "Cool, fresh water, so our path may be cool and fresh."

Then Baba held up his *opon-ifa,* a carving of Elegba's smiling face taking up one side of the board, showed them his palm nuts, brown, uneven things, four "eyes" on each that could help see her future, bring answers from Orunmila, the special orisha in charge.

Marcus, a head bigger than the others, that much farther along on the testosterone express, shouted, "Do ya slit the hen's neck, Baba, like the way my grandma does?" Thing was, it hadn't been disrespectful, but *urgent.* He wanted to know. "For dinner, I mean, you know, not for Shango."

Baba turned his head aside. "Sacrifice means you give up something you love, and that shows your connection to the orisha is strong. Like you give up your Saturday to help others, that means you've *sacrificed* it."

Saturday—that meant *pleasure.* Which sounded, goddamn it, like something she might have said at her bas mitzvah—like, since the destruction of the Temple, we've found a deeper, more *moral* way to offer a sacrifice, we give up the Saturday dance instead of killing a flaw-less calf. And *that* was *not* what she needed to hear right now.

"Sacrifice means that instead of satisfying yourself you do what the orisha wants for you. You serve others." He directed this one right next to her, to Sugar. Seemed strange, the man had devoted his life to serving others, after all.

This thing tasted like horseradish—no, like bullshit. The fluorescent lights took the shadows from the room, the flavor from Baba's words. Baba didn't take his eyes off Sugar, and Beth peeked, saw Sugar smiling back at Baba, like *bring it on, sucker, I got your number.* "True sacrifice is about *your* blood," Baba said, "about your life force being used to serve your community."

Like Baba was saying, *the orishas in Africa were hungry; here, they'd all become luftmenschen.* Reform Ifa? She had to laugh; she finally got the courage to walk inside the room, and she found a Baba who sounded like a canned-goods drive at GN North. Was he changing this for her, like she didn't deserve the hidden, black meaning of things? But he never looked away from Sugar, who just smiled acidly back at him.

"Sacrifice is a way to pray that your orisha will make you a better person. And it shows you're becoming that person already. You renounce *your* greed, *your* appetites, *your* anger, and *your* violence."

Give up your appetites? Be a better, self-denying *person?* No, sacrifice *had* to mean blood offered, steaming *ashe* for the orisha. It *had* to mean the Brinks guard, need be, he didn't give up the money. Otherwise it was no good to her. Baba had nice robes, beautiful beads, but today he sounded like just another rabbi saying, hate your body, hate your appetites, sacrifice *that.* In other words: *Thou Shalt not.* How could she have gotten Baba so fucking wrong? Or maybe *he'd* got it wrong. Maybe if she could get back to the original, the African meaning? Right, but she had no way there but Baba.

"But, Baba, couldn't you kill one chicken or something?" Marcus asked, his voice skittering between registers. *So,* Beth thought, *Marcus agrees with me. Only blood will do.*

"Not here. Not now," Baba said.

Though before he finished, Marcus had gone wild, had his arm around Buster, choking him, "You're *my* chicken!" She smiled. Sixth graders, little gusts of hormones worked their wiseass mouths, budded their breasts, flinging them this way and that like untethered kites.

Baba banged his staff on the ground, once only. "Settle down!"

And the magic thing was, they did, Marcus falling back into his seat, and Buster looking like he had payback on his mind, rubbing his neck. She'd have to tell Susan to keep an eye out in the playground this afternoon.

"The sacrifice of your Saturday fun, putting aside your pleasures, that helps you find your way back to the path. Then you will always walk upright."

Those words, that measured tone: *not too much this, not too much that.* Beth started to sweat; inside the room had turned out to be definitely not as good as listening at the door.

"When you walk upright, your earthly existence becomes a

reflection of your orisha's power. *Ashe* shines from your face and is a light to show our nation the difference between right and wrong."

Like Glow Girl, Beth thought, this moral jive making Ifa about as thick as a BillyBook page. Beth couldn't help herself, moisture formed behind her eyes. Yeah, *Baba that is* surely equals *Chuck that was;* and like a topsy-turvy, he was the same Hebrew/Ifa thou-shalt-not man either way you turned him. Maybe she would ask him about that today—though she'd have to admit then that she knew he was Chuck Taylor because she was Beth Jacobs; and if his idea of righteous was the same as Waxman's then it might include turning in bail jumpers.

"In Yorubaland," Chuck said, "I found fathers to help me now and I found the fathers before time, the ancestors I needed to have if I was to grow up again, and properly this time—a decent, just, and upright man."

"Scrubbed, and clean," Sugar whispered. Beth smiled, hugely pleased that Sugar had made a joke to her, like they could be bad kids together, co-conspirators. It had passed like a current between them: this had been their reverse bar mitzvah, this the day they both had seen through the Ifa thing.

"Now you're *all* my godchildren. And my job is to help you do the same," but the kids had heard the bell, started running out already, recess next, the holiest time of the school day, when they could run, shout, *do,* and Ifa couldn't be what they needed either, this just Hebrew school to them, Baba getting the kids to say, *Abo ru, Abo ye, Abo Sise,* and *boray prie hagofen,* but all of it just repeating what somebody once told somebody about something.

Sugar walked into the circle, rubbing Marcus's head as he went by. Baba gathered his nuts and water vessel. Beth just sat by the door, hoping they wouldn't notice, wanting to hear, but Baba already saying no to Sugar. "If you're considering doing evil, if that's even one of your choices, Ifa can't advise you."

"Sometimes the elect have to descend into the badlands," Sugar said. "Force the prison doors from within," that being the way Sugar talked sometimes. But he and Mao, they got it right. Break out of the fucking guilt prison any way you can, *that* was the way to life. *But how?*

"You shouldn't talk about things you don't understand, Sugar."

"I understand."

"If you did, you'd know it's never right to do evil."

"Yeah, okay, not evil, Chuck. But there's a difference between killing and murder."

Right. Why couldn't Baba see that? But she heard the too-muchness in her tone; sure sign that she meant Dad. Well, whether Dad or Baba sees the difference, Che did. Mao did. Madame Binh did. And Sugar Cane *does,* thank God.

"Maybe there's a difference, Sugar. But what makes you think *you* can tell what it is?"

Sugar smiled. "Well, with Ifa's help, I could tell the difference, right? So you should cast for me."

Baba laughed then, shaking his head theatrically. "You're still the best. We always said, never argue with Sugar."

Sugar, he grabbed Baba around the neck, pulled him backward, the man choking. "Ought to break you like a chicken, Chuck, don't you think?"

Beat your staff on the floor, Beth thought—that won't stop Mr. Sugar Cane.

But Jacob Battle could. He put a hand on Sugar's shoulder, and Sugar gave it up. After all, what did Sugar need Ifa for? He always *knew* what to do. Then he fucking *did it.*

Jacob patted her on the hand, stared at her a second. "Not what you expected, huh?" He went into the hall, waited. Then Sugar walked past her, without looking she had thought—until he said quietly, "See you later, Miss Hunt."

Right. Her final exam—which brought all her own doubts back. Ifa said no to everything, just like Moses. But maybe *she* had to say no to *this,* not that it was wrong, but because it was too heavy for her without Ifa's help, her fantasy Ifa, it turned out. She would fuck up this safe-as-milk thing, get everyone busted—*which meant Zing's mom goes to prison too.*

Sugar closed the door. She levered herself up from the desk. "What happened to your Judaism?" she said to Baba, mostly just curious now.

She got a *how did you know* look—and a smile. Warm, too; it made Baba look like an illustration in a children's book. "My Sammy Davis Junior phase?" So it was true: Baba = Chuck, and Topsy-Turvy Turned Again. "Well, there were some personal reasons for that. If you're a smart boy from South Carolina, your family, the whole town, thinks you're going to be a preacher. Turning Jewish, that's definitive, you know?" He stood, put his things down on the teacher's gray desk. "Besides, I thought, that religion of theirs, it understands suffering."

"Doesn't it?"

He smiled again, warmly. "Oh, yes. It does. But its own first. And there's so much suffering there, it usually keeps everyone busy."

Unfair, she thought. *Frank Jaffe, he cared about the suffering of others.*

One by one, Baba carefully, almost caressingly, put the nuts in a beautiful leather bag, his nation sack. "And Sugar, he told you about my Judaism, Miss Hunt?"

"No. I was a friend of Frank Jaffe's." She had to tell more, let him see who she was. "His girlfriend." But that sounded so kid! "His lover."

"Yes? He talked about her. But I had it in my mind her name was Beth Jacobs?" He tilted his head back, a knowing grin—getting it, or more pretending that he'd always had it—like a *babalawo* who can see the future, he had to have already penetrated black hair turned blond. "When I would read about her in the paper, I used to wonder what Frank Jaffe would think about her now? Bombings—my, my!"

Beth couldn't help herself, thought, *You read about me!*—but managed to say: "I hope he'd think that that's what raising the sparks requires in this fallen world. Like Sugar said, sometimes you've got to use force to get the doors open." But this *babalawo,* he probably wrote articles for the *Orisha* version of *Commentary.* Listen to your guilt and listen to the pine nuts—same deal, as it turned out, both saying *don't do.*

"Sparks, Miss Hunt? Have you been talking about that with Sugar?"

"Sugar? No, I mean, Frank wrote us he heard about the sparks from you. And I was thinking that maybe he told you about *ashe.*" Which would mean what? He was *her* godfather? The sparks were real? Ifa was real? Someone, somewhere, knew if she should do the Brinks truck? Too late for that.

"Frank Jaffe? No, not that I remember. *Ashe* was Joshua Battle's doing."

"*He* talked about it?"

"No. He *did* it. He made the god. Once, in Washington, all of us squeezed into those little desks, like you and Sugar today, I saw Joshua Battle ridden, looking at us with an orisha's eyes. And I didn't even know that name then. Joshua, he told me he'd seen his own death, and everything that came after. Of course, I didn't believe him. But then, when it happened, I thought, *How could such a thing be?* I studied. And Oludumare led me to the right people. To Africa."

She'd been about to ask for a reading anyway, though, what the hell? But Baba had started for the door, his magic board under his arm. Besides, there had been no special connection, so he would say *no,* like *who knows what your ancestors did?* Another reason this stuff was no use to her: it thought the sins of the fathers got inherited in the genes.

Which was racism, wasn't it? So fuck him and his Ifa. For a moment, she felt furious with Baba. But unfair; *she* was the one who'd gotten it wrong, dreamt the Ifa she needed. That black people actually needed, too, come to that. She sat back down in her desk, waiting for the empty, angry feeling to pass, and the kids to get into their classrooms or out on the playground, so she wouldn't be seen. Anyway, she'd only lost an illusion, a friend she'd never really had.

Then, on her way downstairs, she stopped by a seventh-grade class, listened to a girl saying what X equaled. It equals equality, Beth thought, a place where the teachers think a black girl can learn algebra. It equals science, she thought. It equals a lot that Ifa isn't. If they needed to do a Brinks guard, then she *had* to somehow find a way to get her head around it, so this beautiful school she'd put in jeopardy could be saved.

Beth's furry gray back nearly pressed against the wallboard as she scurried unseen into her hidey-hole. Small shock when she opened the door and Susan already sat at the first of the two gray desks they'd pushed side by side against the wall. She looked up, lips pursed—which for her equaled thunder in her face. Susan's silk scarf lay on the desk, Beth could see now that she had some gray in her hair, from Sugar-worry, no doubt. "There's a problem."

Beth felt the guilt in her—and, as always with that toxin, anger too. "I already told you, I didn't tell the state about the drop in enrollment last quarter."

"Yeah, you should have. But if you'd told the state, we would have gone under then."

"And I'm thinking, before they find out, we'll find a way to pay them back, say we made a mistake. Here's the cash. All better. OK?"

"Pay them back? How?"

The question hung. Beth shrugged. *The Downstairs, that's something Susan don't have to know nothing about.* Just take the money, teach the kids algebra.

"Anyway, not that. Worse. The bank called this morning."

"Yeah? And?"

Susan handed the books to Beth, two large marbled ledgers, most of the entries penciled in Beth's own tiny handwriting. "Look at the last few pages."

"OK."

Beth pulled the calculator toward her, punched a few numbers. The phosphorescent glow too faint. "This needs a new battery. Maybe that's the problem."

Susan laughed. "Don't I wish." She reached over, got her big black canvas bag, as always took out the thing needed. "Sugar's new friends, they're the problem."

Beth snapped in the battery.

"You saw Sugar, right, before prison? You heard him, I mean, in person, in the day?"

"Yeah, a time or two."

"He was electric," she said, "wasn't he?"—the doubt in Susan's voice plain as pain: *he's fallen so far, could it be true that he was once what I thought?*

Beth punched in the first numbers.

"Like that night when we burnt this rat trap, the one that squatted here? You were there, right? You couldn't hear him without being turned upside down, could you? Agitated. You had to do something or burst."

Beth saw then—some of the entries had been changed, not her writing. Things didn't add up anymore. "Me," Beth said, "those days I mostly felt excluded and accused. But, yeah, no shit, uplifted, too."

"The world was going to change, right? It *had* to. By any means necessary. And he made you feel you had to be a part of that."

Beth marked her place, looked over at Susan, crying, but her face not puckering, not a line; round, smooth, circles only.

Beth walked to the filing cabinets, got her correspondence with the state.

"I'll tell you," Susan said quietly, "I prayed they'd put Sugar in jail, can you imagine that?"

"Jail?" And that other folder, the canceled checks.

"He ever tell you that thing Malcolm told him: *if a state wants to kill you, they will?*"

Beth brought the stuff back to her desk, spread it out.

Susan shook her head at her own foolishness. "Yeah, *of course* he told you. Well, they wanted to kill Sugar for sure, Hoover's nightmare, the black messiah, the one who'd set us moving in one direction. What we all thought then, me, David Watkins, everyone."

"Me, too, yeah. My comrades, we already looked to him for direction." There was a letter missing, too.

"So I'd be like people who make deals with God, you know? *Do this for me, and I'll say seven Hail Marys.* If he's in jail, I thought, maybe they'd stop. Like white people *ever* stop, you know." Reassuring to Beth when Susan did that—like she'd forgotten Beth was white. "I thought, if he gets a heavy sentence, they'll think he's out of the way, they don't have to kill him. So dear God, take him from me, go ahead, put him in jail, get him off the streets, shut him up. Let them forget."

"Someone took a letter from this file."

"Surprise, surprise. Letters, Beth, that's the least of our problems."

A game, really. Susan knew what had happened to their money, but she wanted Beth to find out for herself, so she'd believe. "I knew what harm his arrest would do to him and me, and to our movement. But I wanted it. I loved him."

And you do still, Beth thought. *Shit, we all do.*

"Well, God protect us from answered prayers, right? They put him in jail, they beat him like a drum. They stuck him in the soul breaker."

"Yeah, but it didn't break *him*, right?"

"The hell it didn't. This man, this Sugar who came back to me? I thought, the two of us we maybe didn't know how to be with each other yet, but he knows how to be with the people, he knows how to lead. And he made everyone stronger during that brutal bussing. Then he built this school. You can't imagine how hard that was. But we could never be together again. Not that Sugar wanted it, him always measuring me, looking for my weak spot, so he could play me down. He'd even use his supposed deep sadness, you know, he'd look at me like he wanted me to crawl, just to make him smile at how low I'd go for him." She stared at Beth.

Who tried to look sufficiently dubious. "Which you wouldn't."

Susan didn't say anything but pulled a wad of tissues from the bag, blew her nose. A confession? "Sugar, he has two ways now only: He can do you. Or you're the stronger one, and you can do him. Like some sick SM game."

"Tougher, though, eh?" Whistling in the dark, she punched the last few numbers into her calculator. But really, the trail had hardly been brushed over, a few pencil smudges, a missing letter, like the bank wouldn't actually call, find out why the state checks hadn't arrived to cover their letter of credit. Susan had called the state, found they'd been issued, cashed. An algebra problem, where X equals Shakur's people, for sure.

"Tougher?" Susan said disgustedly, with a look at Beth, like she'd turned white again. "Any con can work him, dare him like a kid. Shakur, especially. Then Sugar has to show how tough he is, like he's back in the can, Shakur's gonna make him his punk." She laughed. "It's that voice, you know, too high, like a woman's. He's fighting his voice."

"I should have seen earlier," Beth said, "the way they got into the bank accounts."

"You want to feel it's all *your* responsibility, huh? You're *that* powerful, it's you who failed the black nation. Ninja B., none other!"

But before she could take that in—or spit it out—a big-fisted rap at the door startled her. No one ever came to her hidey-hole. That was the point of it.

"I sent for him," Susan said, but before she said, "Come in," Shakur pushed the door open, Sugar behind him. Shakur wore a suit and tie now, held some needles from his clinic—*Doctor* Eatmore.

Susan stared at Sugar, said sharply, "*He* stole from us."

Shakur let the needles fall to the floor like stars, yanked her up from her seat, and slammed her against the wall, Susan not screaming, but the air coming out of her with a dull whooshing sound. Beth terrified, squatted behind her chair, like Susan's breath had knocked her down, too. Thing was, Sugar waited a two-count before he went over to Susan, knelt beside her. On the ground, Susan still shimmied with rage and terror. Sugar looked at Shakur, who stepped back, stepped out of the office, but didn't close the door. "Everyone's a little tense now, little jumpy, Susan. You got to think about that, before you say things, you know." He stroked her cheek, but that made her crying worse.

Her nose bleeding onto her nice white blouse, Susan crawled to her desk. She got some tissues from her purse, then dragged herself up and slumped down into a chair.

"Now, I'm not gonna let anything happen to this school," Sugar said, "am I? You think I don't love it as much as you? Me, Butchie, some guys, we'll go to some places, after-hours clubs, you know, haven't paid us in a while. We'll make this all right."

"Oh, Sugar," she said sadly, a lot of lost love in her voice, "you think that makes me feel better?"

"Yeah, I think it should. And Shakur, I'll see he doesn't have anything more to do with this," gesturing to the office, but not clear if he meant, *he won't come in here;* he won't *steal* from us; or he won't be part of the school anymore at all. Shakur, standing right behind him, didn't look too happy at that, like who was Sugar Cane to give *him* the law?

Susan laughed, said, "God, Sugar, you are so totally full of shit."

Sugar, though, he looked like that made him want to cry. He stepped past Beth, who looked out from the slats of her chair. "I'll see you later, Miss Hunt. Show you something better than that Ifa shit this morning."

Meaning what? Cocaine? She prayed not. Prayed to whom, though? Not Oludumare, for Christ's sake. Well, she hoped he had something that would work for her. She needed permission, guidance, strength from *somewhere,* or she sure as shit would fuck up the Dance.

Sugar left, Susan said, "Suge's become what you want now, Beth, hasn't he? The lumpen prole *leader,*" saving most of her sarcasm for the last word. She put some Kleenex up her nose, like a tiny Tampax. "Man, that's one thing we never get free of, what you people just have to have us be." She turned her face away. "I think you better leave me alone for a while, Bethie. I'm in a foul mood."

Beth picked up her coat, walked all the way out of school then, beat the rush, down the darkening hill to the avenue, toward a pay phone that maybe worked, near the restaurant with the broken sign.

The booth smelled like a urinal. She told Snake he had to hold on just a little longer. She had to go to a meeting later tonight.

"Look, couldn't you come home first?" he said, making her furious.

"Right. Then come all the way back here? You're fucking crazy." Then she remembered how he loved Zing, but a whole day, not going to the bathroom when you wanted, no reading a newspaper even, he was probably just tired. She understood. "It's with Sugar," she added. "He's like got to test me or something. You know, for the thing."

Sugar's name, that made everything all right with Snake.

"Don't worry," he said. "It's going to be fine." Yeah, she thought, *probably nobody will throw me against a wall.* She heard Zing in the background then, crying, Snake turning away from the phone, exasperated. "It's Mommy," he said. "She says she loves you."

Then poison ran through her veins to punish her for not having said that yet. "Okay, darling," she said. "Give Zing a kiss. Tell her I'm gonna look in on her when I get home, okay?"

All of it left her shook up, weeping when she went into Fried CH. to get some delicious greasy poultry pieces for her dinner.

And the chicken meat and fries not making her feel much better hours later as she walked up the path to Sugar's house. A neat two-story, bare trees all around. Roxbury had a lot of nice houses, the banks ever lent the money so people could true the walls again, repair the sagging foundations, resurface the streets, tear down the derelict shooting galleries. Some good schools would be nice, too. She strolled past two big guys sitting on a glider on the porch, B&B, everyone called them, Bunchie and Butchie, swathed in down and strapped for sure. Butchie, in gold-rimmed glasses, had these smart eyes, looked like he could have been a professor of hers from Wellesley, if any of her professors had been black, done time, carried a gun. Butchie had Parkinson's, dragged his leg already—on his way, Shakur said, toward being a living statue if his acupuncture needles didn't save him. They gave Butchie the shit jobs, so she didn't go off on him when he gave her a billboard smile that clearly meant *here comes nooky.*

And inside, Sugar, cross-legged on the floor on big crimson pillows, wearing white silk pants and a T-shirt, he had the same smile as Butchie, just waiting for Miss Muffet. Barry White–kitschy for sure, but the man good-looking, too, always. Deep-set eyes, strong brow, and his muscles, at least, bigger from his time in jail—all those push-ups in solitary, tell the guards they hadn't broken his spirit. But they'd done *something* to it, Susan had said. This setup tonight—like he was so melancholy, but she would provide the heat, unfreeze him? A version of a con she was all too familiar with.

Sugar had a small earth-colored ceramic teapot, and two handleless glazed cups. "I'm purifying my body," he said. "Fasting."

"So you can hear the pain of the world? Like in the comics, right?" The fasting thing, she meant, it sounded like the Bad Ears regimen; but Beth saying it, too, to make fun of Sugar—take the piss out of him. Also to remind him that *she* was different from Priss, Beth the incognito comic book star, the ORG.'s worst enemy.

"I don't read comics," he said all-too-precisely, his cold smile adding *you say that 'cause I'm . . .*

Which was ridiculous. "Oh, well, *I* do read them," she said sharply, to beat that shit away. "My friend draws 'em. And I'm even *in* them." *So there.* She decided not to sit down beside him yet. Besides, if he was flushing his system why was a guy in a baseball cap bent over a wooden table, the hand with a razor blade making a tight shuttle, *clickety-click, clickety-clack.*

"That right?" He gave her the BIG SMILE, laughing at her anger. "It's too easy to play you, Beth. You jump at any bait." He laughed. "Everyone knows you're *Deborah, AKA the Prophet.*"

"And Ninja B.," she said, trying to make the brag into a *you got me* joke on herself.

"Look, I know what you wanted from Baba and that Ifa shit. What I wanted once, too. Broke my heart when I saw it wasn't there."

She actually began to weep then, the horrors of the day washing over her, her disappointment, Shakur throwing Susan against that wall.

He gave her a sweet, sad smile. "So I went back to the old books. And you find that the old books, you work hard enough"—he scooped at the air, like he was actually digging something out of the text—"they *all* tell the same truth. Your people, and you especially, Beth, you already *have* what you need to become the one who can do the hard things."

My people? Meaning what? *Marxists?* "You mean I already have the ruby slippers?" But she wise-mouthed because she felt some excitement. He'd seen what she needed: some cure that would put steel in her. And he said *your people,* and *you especially,* like she was chosen. But how exactly?

"Snake told me about you and your friends in Great Neck. The letters. The divine sparks."

Oh, Snake shouldn't have done that, no matter how desperate to B. Cool he'd been! Serve the bastard right, she fucked Sugar. So she sat down, felt the power of his body bending her slightly toward him, the tight curls of hair on his face. What would his lips feel like?

"So I know you're someone, maybe the only one, who can understand where I'm coming from now. Chuck and his Ifa sure as shit can't."

The cutter handed him a mirror with a mound of blow on it as big as the Ritz. *A taste,* Jacob had said—lying to her, or Sugar a lot farther down the coke trail now than even Jacob knew. Still, this man wouldn't go farther that way than he could handle.

He bent gracefully, hoovering some up through a rolled C-note, looked back up at her, eyes alight. He held the mirror out to her.

"None for me, thanks," she said. "I've used it for housework, eh? Vacuumed the whole place four times without stopping. But it made me cranky the next day."

He laughed. "Cranky, huh? That's a nice word. Like a kid. Yeah, cranky."

"Yeah." Beth thought of Zing. Five o'clock precisely, you could set your timer by it, she'd wail like a banshee.

"You know Israel has been dispersed among nations to find the scattered sparks of divine light, right?"

"Sure," she said, because that much she *did* know from Frank's letters and Billy's sermons—all of it suddenly close to her again, like it had been yesterday. So *weird* that Sugar should be repeating it to her tonight.

"Then through prayer and pious acts they uplift them from their prisons. You dig it?"

"Right." Well, probably the rap was for her, but nothing mystical about that. The man knew a lot of things, gnosticism, sufism, kabala; another night, *another woman*, he'd be rapping about the *Bhagavad-gita*. Still it *was* strange, made her a little light-headed.

"But do you understand that's really talking about the Revolution. *Israel*, that means the most elect cadre—like our Downstairs."

"I can see that." And she could. Frank having set her going—into the movement, the Weathermen, the underground, the Downstairs; a natural progression; all of it intended for her by Frank, she felt again, his guidance from the first.

But she got off track when the machine in the baseball cap started back to work, *clickety-clack, clickety-clack,* toot-toot's coming back.

"But then dig this. Nathan, prophet of Zevi, he says sometimes prayer and goodness aren't enough to free the sparks from the *kelipoth*."

Kelipoth! Jesus, that was another blast from the past! "The shells that trap the sparks," she said, not thinking about it, but hearing that stuff *in this place* made her a little dizzy, loosened her tongue, made her Beth the Good Student again.

Sugar smiled, reached over, hooked a finger under the leather cord, pulled her nation sack out from between her breasts; fingered it and let it drop to her chest, not asking anything. Had Snake said what was in it until the end of time? She felt herself falling forward, leaned toward Sugar for support. Could he have really quick-studied this for a good line to reel her in with? No, Sugar's words meant he'd seen she would be the one who would understand him. They could do this thing together.

She felt sweat under her arms; excitement or the ungodly heat. She leaned back, tried to remain calm, but still feeling that she could be the one who got Sugar's soul, give him what he needed. Maybe even help him handle the coke.

"*You* know, then," he said, "that the cadre has to descend into evil's realms. Get right into the shit, and smash the prison doors from within. Like I reminded Chuck. But he can't understand anymore."

"Right." And Beth feeling, then, that she couldn't even halfway pretend anymore that this was just a seduction, no, his words formed a rope stretching taut now all the way from Frank's grave to Laura's bedroom in Great Neck to this coke-filled living room in Roxbury, Mass., the *kelipoth,* the sparks, all weaving themselves together around her. She, *in particular,* had been *destined* to hear this. This *was* her story, her *fate.* The Big Dance. She would do it. She would give her life utterly in his people's service.

"Chuck doesn't see anymore that when the world is a shit-pile, then healing evil means you got to reach right in, do some evil, bad-smelling things yourself." His voice got higher, more insistent. He put his hand on her arm, started to stroke it gently. She liked it, swooned a little, even. "To the world's eyes, maybe, the cadre *seems* to become evil. But in the end the truth and necessity of our acts will be revealed."

Revealed even to my father, she thought, a little hypnotized by his stroking, pretty sure that whatever else, Sugar was *also* coming on to her. Was ever woman in this humor wooed? *Wait, that's from* Richard III*! Watch out for this guy!* She took her arm away, but at the same time wanted to give it back, couldn't help saying, "I'm ready." Smiling, too, like it had a double meaning, the *kelipoth,* she thought, having made her a fool for him. "For the job, I mean." But she meant much more than that; she wanted to spend the night, feel his weight on her, be joined to his power.

He took her hand back.

She looked at her arm, its red-and-green snake tattoo glaring at her, and a phrase of Sugar's popped into her mind. "Anyone can be made, huh? Your mama, your sister, whatever." Not over yet, but the feeling definitely fading with that.

"I was younger then. Women, I didn't know them." Humble, eyes a little downcast, little-boy-charming. She hadn't known he'd have that in his repertoire, too. But a line, for sure. Which pulled the rest of it in its train, made this maybe *not* her fate. *Sugar, he has two ways now only: He can do you. Or you're the stronger one, and you can do him. Like some sick SM game.* Still, a little of the glow remained, enough to tease, maybe think about a future for them, another time. "Yeah, and what do you know about us women now?"

He laughed. "I know how I need them. How I need you."

"That's very flattering," Beth said, meaning it, too. "But I'm married." Meaning *not tonight. But show me you're serious. Ask again.*

He leaned over, snorted more from the never-diminishing mountain, Sugar kind of sloppy now, powder knocked onto the Oriental rug.

"Married, huh? I'll tell you, adultery is *nothing.* It's not even one of the worst sins, the ones the little godlings try to scare you with, tell you your soul's gonna get instantly severed from your body you do that. If you can't do a little sin like that to please yourself, if you can't accept what your own body needs, sweetheart, how are you gonna do the really hard things, like this job? The elect got to be able to taste *every thing.*" He let his hand go to his crotch.

She got up. "I got to get back to my kid."

He frowned. "So go. I'll have Butchie drive you." He looked to the guy at the table. "You fucking done yet?"

"How'd it go?" Jacob asked, he and Shakur coming up the walk, grim-faced, while she and a pissed-off, slow-moving Butchie crab-walked their way to the car. An acupuncture needle glinted in Jacob's left lobe, and he a little less friendly to her with Master Shakur around.

She shrugged. "He's angry I won't fuck him," unsure if that was true; or even what *had* just happened to her. Signs and wonders? Or cocks, *kelipoths,* and come-ons? She felt dazed. Had she seen what she *had* to do, the marks clear enough for sure, or had she just gotten scared again, run back to Great Neck, so to speak?

"What?" Shakur barked. He wore a down vest over a black T-shirt, the combo very macho, appealing even. Which meant she still felt hot from Sugar—and hey, Any Man Will Do. "You wouldn't fuck Sugar Cane? Then you *got to be* a racist." A beat or two; and he smiled. Thing she forgot about Shakur always, he was a comedian, like that Upstairs/Downstairs thing. But those cold eyes, they scared her. What if she drove that van, no god inside her for sure, fucked something up, and had to meet him later?

She slid forward a step on the ice, nearly took a dive. But she didn't reach out to grab Butchie's cloth coat, afraid she might pull him over. "One of you guys should put some salt down here."

Cold night, Jacob and Shakur rushed inside, Sugar waiting for them in a long leather jacket, hopping from foot to foot in soft black Gucci loafers. "She says you're bent out of shape, she won't fuck you."

"I told her that made her a racist," Shakur said. "She bit, too."

Fucking with the girl who wouldn't fuck them, Jacob thought, but Sugar not smiling this time. "They see a black man, they think—"

"Yeah," Shakur jumped in, looking at Sugar's white silk pants, "they see a black man dressed like Barry White, anyway."

Sugar snorted.

"Besides," Shakur said, "you *also* did want to fuck her, right? Those titties, man."

And Beth, it might be true: see a black man—a leader, anyway—she thought about sex, Jacob thinking how conventional even Beth was in so many ways, looking to the black side for a stylish response to all God's dangers, the knife supposedly already out, guilt not having slowed the black hand. Still, he liked Beth. She had those ideas, but they usually floated up above her somewhere; down here, on the ground, he and Beth got along fine; she saw *him*—more or less, anyway. And about the best he could do for her, too. But Sugar, he didn't really want to fuck Beth, or not *just* fuck her, and the thing he wanted there, the thing that would make it all right, make him all right, he never got from fucking. The man was a romantic or a monk, or the two in some uneasy combo, and actually fucking married Beth would bend him out of shape more than her.

"You better change those pants, man," Shakur said to Sugar, "you're gonna freeze your balls out there in that silk shit. Not like this fucking hothouse you got going."

Sending him upstairs—like an order? Jacob wondered. Or just a friend's good advice? Every moment like that now, a test of who's in charge. Like Sugar hadn't usually gone on these collections before, even a month ago; but now he had to show the Downstairs he was the smartest, most charismatic—which he was—and the *hardest,* too. Which he never would be.

Looked like they had a powdery mountain already on the table, but Artie busy making more, cutting, cutting, cutting, some kind of obsessive disorder in that man. Or a *Guinness* entry: most finely chopped coke. Pulverized. Reduced to quanta. For Sugar? Had it gotten *this* fucking bad, the man needed a pile like that? And whoever it was for, what was Sugar thinking? The cops rousted Sugar out of bed twice a month just to keep their hands in—what would happen to him they found *this*?

What was Sugar thinking? Man, a pile like that, he wasn't thinking anything but *more.* If there's coke around, a man will snort it all eventually—white people, black people, kids at the Dewey School, all the same that way. But the black man, he doesn't get a second chance. And for the black man, the coke is always there, no gates, no guardians to keep it out. Hell, the cops are shoveling it *in,* and skimming a nice profit, too.

Except that Sugar hated stories like that. Talking to whites, he said, "You people let heroin into the ghetto, to cull the herd." But to blacks he said, "Whites want to kill you. So what? That's a fact, like the weather. Doesn't mean you have to shoot their poison into your arm." So if Sugar took cocaine, it had to be it was *his* choice, Sugar doing it 'cause he *wanted* to, taking responsibility. Which, by the way, would make no fucking difference at all, if the man became a cokehead.

King Shango was a warrior, Baba told the class. *But the witches made him crazy with lust and rage. King Shango had to keep himself from going over to those enemies.*

Jacob looked around the classroom; Sugar and the kids mesmerized: *poor King Shango.*

"*To do* that," Baba said, "*he had to destroy his human body. So Shango hung himself.*"

Ah, they all sighed; and, hey, Jacob thought, pass the fucking popcorn.

But the people of Yorubaland, they still loved their king, saw how when he'd been their leader an orisha had shone from his face like a bea- con of righteousness for all of them. And they saw, too, that there'd been a great war inside him. He had been a great tree struck by lightning.

To honor their king, they called the orisha they'd seen shine from his face Shango, after him.

Happy ending? *And here comes our star now.*

Sugar walked downstairs toward his friends, his executioners, oh, what the fuck were they? And Beth another confusion—he'd mostly wanted to talk to her, but her knowing eyes, her shapely body, she gave him that warm feeling, cut through the coke and his troubles the way no whore could anymore. And those sparks he'd told her about, how they had to sin to free them, Snake had said she believed in that shit, too—which was strange, had to mean *something*. Like that she'd at least find it *inter- esting* what he'd told her, let him sit down beside her, eating her curds and whey. Instead, she'd run. Like no one saw that he might *also* be a man anymore, lonely even, needing someone to talk to. Okay, right, not *just* talk.

Good talk, though, huh? He'd known this shit forever, since Sing Sing, reading about Jacob Frank and Sabbatai Zevi in someone's gift to the prison library, and just what the cons needed—twenty volumes about Jews, no pictures of a woman not in an ugly wig. Some things there he could use, though. He'd swear she needed those things, too. Free her some if she bought in with him, help her cross the line. And he felt like if his rap worked on *her*, then it might work for him, too. He needed to cross some lines himself soon.

"The thing made me sick," he said to Jacob, "was that look on her face. You know the one I mean? Like I was going to force her." But he was bullshitting. What made him sick was he'd been sure she had wanted him as much as he had wanted her. She'd hit him hard. Been a while since he'd felt like this.

They stepped out on the porch, and shit, this leather jacket, it *wouldn't* be enough, a hawk wind slicing right into his chest already. "Same old, same old," Shakur said, just motioning to Bunchie with his head when they passed him, the guy getting up, following them, not asking Sugar. Bunchie not the brightest bulb; didn't seem likely he had a spark hidden under that shower cap.

"Yeah, change the hair color," Sugar said, "it's still Miss Ann." He should have teased her a little more, brought up her father. Snake had said even mentioning him knocked her off balance. He and Joshua had met the man once, and Joshua had thought he *was* all that. But when Sugar saw him on television later, arguing with some old German, he'd been a wizened thing, telling everyone to feel guilty, same as any preacher. Now whites, he might tell Beth, that made sense for them, they had lots of reasons to hate themselves. But Beth's father had it ass backwards when it came to blacks: they felt too fucking guilty already.

Or was it shame? Kinds of self-hatred, he could hardly tell them apart since his time in solitary. Naked legs lapped by his own feces, it made him loathe himself. He'd bit down on that feeling for a while—keep himself from disappearing. *I stink, therefore I am!* That faded, though, and he'd set to work scraping his legs with his nails, peeled swatches of his skin right off. The mess got infected—and that septic fever—not hunger strikes or push-ups, like people said, like *he* said—was how he'd really gotten out of the hole. How could any man stand his or anyone's body again after that? He'd bend toward Susan's cheek, smell that death coming off her, off him. Nowadays even a fart could make him dream of suicide. He wore cologne always, but *its* smell just reminded him of how prison had maimed him. "The hell of it is," he'd tell Beth, "civil rights don't mean shit. Being free, that ever happened, you'd still be *human*—which you damn well know is intolerable." He'd tell her, "And the thing is, beyond white people and their shit making a man feel trapped in this black body is the pure stone-cold horror a man feels being trapped in any motherfucking body at all."

She'd say, "Why so bad to have a body, darling? A handsome man like you." Or some such.

"Nothing wrong with a body, sweetheart," he'd say, stroking her thighs. "But we make it hell. We make it jail. Your pussy grows wet for me, you say, *don't do that now.* You tell yourself, *Remember those Ten Commandments Jehovah gave us.* But that guilt shit just can*not* be what the real God wants for your body, or he wouldn't have put these holes in it so you can fuck and eat in the first place. It all comes down to a body, Beth. Will you cherish yours or punish it?"

The point of *this* exercise, Sugar knew, being his trying once again to crawl out from under Christ's body—and get into bed with Beth's. He and Beth, he felt they were a lot alike, each thought Ifa would let them leap free, be what the people needed. *Blood sacrifice,* right? So Ifa must have a place for more than chickens in front of its altars, right?

Wrong. Baba had laid it out straight as could be that morning. Ifa was X-tianity redoubled, *thou really shalt not, sucker,* and in some Yorubaland language. Which made Sugar furious with Baba. Like he'd been betrayed by his own people this time, by Africa. So he took his gizmo out of his jacket pocket—a dose a day to push those thoughts away.

Sugar got out his little glass vial, a rubber stopper with a metal straw in it, and no matter how much Jacob prayed, up it went into his nose. Sugar's body gave a little shiver, Sugar, Jacob thought, needing a dose to stay on the edge, be street 24-7, make himself the Man of Steel for the troops. Enough cocaine meant a religious rap was sure to follow. What had Susan said about Sugar and Chuck, hope too long deferred?

"Like a raisin in the sun?" Jacob had said, he and Susan sharing sandwiches in the little office where they kept the files, Beth's mouse hole. But Susan had this way with smart-asses, namely she ignored them, let them come back to their better selves.

"David Watkins, he told me once how revolutionary fervor defeated becomes prophecy and madness. Maybe the two mixed together."

"Defeated, Susan?"

She'd just shrugged. "So Baba and Sugar Cane," Jacob had said, "they're like William Blake?"

"Exactly." Susan had smiled. "That's exactly what David said." Which had made her look more tired. "You must have been a good student. I heard you wanted to be a writer."

"Woulda been, I think."

"Could be again."

"Woulda shoulda coulda. That's my middle name."

Sugar finally dropped the vial in his jacket pocket, then, eyes glazed, like how many hours had he already been communing with the coke before they'd arrived tonight? Jacob's lungs started to feel tighter, the edge of pain, but he knew it would piss Shakur off he used *his* gizmo, his inhaler, that meaning Shakur's needles hadn't worked.

"She good for Tuesday?" Shakur asked Sugar, serious now, nearing the main drag, business to be done.

"Yeah, why not. She wants to play with the big boys, you know?"

"Big black boys," Bunchie mumbled.

Jacob saw this fat fuck of a drug dealer they had to collect from trying to press himself into a stone wall where the bank used to be. Dudley Street—the Land of Used to Be. Sugar put his hand on the gun in his waistband, but when Shakur and Bunchie walked toward the guy, he pulled a wad of bills from his jeans, held it out to them with his arm straight, like, *Please take this offering and come no closer.*

Good boy, Jacob thought, and a good sign for the rest of the night, things, after all, not always working out that smoothly anymore. Like that guy wore the clown hat last week who'd said, *"Fuck—"* and Shakur knocked off his Ringling Bros. stovepipe, had him on the ground before the *you* got out of his mouth. Then Shakur had carved his face from one end to the other.

Good enough. On the other hand, the guy had thought he *could* say no. Petty dealers like him felt they had people watching their backs now, guys more ruthless than Shakur. Jacob even heard about their taking ears, like in Vietnam. So could have been worse, right?

And at the blind pig things felt good, too, Freddy giving them all proper respect. Everyone knew that some pimps, some club owners, they'd been talking together, saying Sugar and Shakur not all *that* anymore, so why not turn to the cops or even let the New Bigs in, get protection that way? But *Freddy?* To see the fat fuck in his drooping brown suit was to *know* he was *not* a ringleader. Shakur and Bunchie talked to him in back, near the stage with the crooked pool table, and Freddy already had his serve-me-more-shit-please grin going, would reach for his wallet soon, beg them to take the money to build the school, all those good programs for the kids.

Jacob, drinking a warm beer, stayed with Sugar up front—part baby-sitter, part bodyguard, scanning the ten, fifteen mostly empty tables along both walls, the raised platform at the back, which was never used—unless some scag wanted to take her clothes off, free show. Sugar, he pulled up a chair at some asshole's table, started talking to a guy with short hair, a gray moustache, bow tie even—Jesus, Jacob hadn't seen a black man in a bow tie wasn't a Muslim since Al's Barbershop—but prison muscles on this one. His date looked like he'd better get her home fast, fuck her before she passed out. But the guy had something to say to Sugar first, how he'd heard some heavy things about Roxbury Action he didn't like the sound of, like he was a choir member happened to have wandered into a blind pig tonight. Nah, he was just showing off for the whore, talking back to Sugar Cane.

Sugar leaned in toward them both, a rush of his urgent words going already, and the thing being that no matter how it started, these coke sermons, once Rev. Blow got in the flow God would pop up somehow. "The warriors who follow me," Sugar said, "they've had to do some hard acts to change things around here, make the revolution for everybody, you know?" Sugar put his arms down on the table, leaned closer. "But I'll tell you, doing those things felt *good*. And that's shown me the way to life for all of us."

The way to life? Like Fanon said about the revolution, right? Violence squeezes the slave out of you. So maybe Sugar would be telling the truth but telling it slant. A line from that class Hartman had taught. *Had* that guy been after his ass—that question as always making Jacob space out a little. Hartman, he thought, already had that shaved head then, like the fags who wanted to suck him off a decade later. Did that mean he was one? Or had Jacob worried *that* bone to beat back what Hartman had really wanted him to become, not a butt boy but a bar mitzvah boy? Or a college graduate anyway, which was the same thing his mother had wanted, Hartman having died just before his mom, and Jacob surprised by how hard he'd taken it, like he'd always had it in his mind they might talk again in his *other* book-lined home, where he could be someone else, not Sugar's boy, not Shakur's either, but . . . a poet? And then with Hartman and his mom dead, all the people who expected something like that from him were gone.

He focused on Sugar, mouth moving, but the other guy quiet, no danger signs yet. So Jacob went back to his thought, remembered reading some of Hartman's book on the bus trip to Sing Sing after his mother died, like poems might make his mother's death better; or his sadness about it more solemn and appropriate. Worked, too. From the poems it seemed like Hartman's parents had died in a death camp. Or his sister, maybe. Hard to say—all deaths, when there are so many, they roll themselves into one mighty, indifferent river. Jacob knew that one. People said Hartman's poems were hard to understand, but those crazy sentences of his, they spoke right to Jacob's heart, Jacob sitting then where you talk like that—where the fellow sufferers sit, Hartman would have said—the place where everything's taken from you and even the words fall inside themselves like matter sucked into a black hole.

But what the man said on the back of the book, "the magical exhalation, something returned to us to cling to. And it is enough," *that* was bullshit. It wasn't enough or Hartman wouldn't have killed himself. Which made him feel like he'd failed Hartman, and both of them were losing out. Like it would matter to the man whether he had a little friend like Jacob? Like it would matter to Jacob if some poet said to stay away from the Brinks job? And now it turned out that Sugar and Hartman agreed, black or white, it was too shitty to bear being human. Shango the King's conclusion too, come to think of it; after all, the man hung himself in Baba's fairy tale, the story maybe having a darker purpose, telling its truth aslant, too, like it had been meant to remind Sugar he hated being human so much he was gonna become a cokehead, then maybe he should make like Shango and do himself.

"The *true* God," Sugar said, "He's not one of those naysaying little godlings, those orishas who fobbed the Ten Commandments off on you, try to stop you from doing the hard things."

Bow Tie suddenly had some blood in his eye, Jacob could tell. Jacob scanned the room, Shakur standing by the side of the stage, peering out, Freddy, the owner, on the other side, by the back door, looking sick. "The true God says you got to listen to what feels good to you and do it," Sugar said.

"Yeah?" the moustache said. "What feels good to me is drinking with this woman *alone*. I don't want to listen to your shit anymore."

Sugar smiled, thank God, or Shakur might have pulled his ears off. Then Sugar just stared, eyes glazed, coke circuits dead.

And next? Sugar wondered, staring at this asshole who he knew wanted to kill him now. But he had to finish his thought for Beth, that was the thing. For her, but it was lots more now than just a line he'd started to spin to get Beth into his bed, this flow so strong—like a god spoke through him, right? He jumped up, felt his legs already jiggling, like a god had put on his body. *This* must be truth. This would help her fuck him, help them both do the job. "You people have to learn that the Ten Commandments, they're laws for slaves. You follow some jive godling's Ten Commandments, then you're his fucking slave, right? But the real God, He doesn't want slaves. If you got it in you, He wants you to be like Him, be one with Him. And God, the real God is the one I'm talking about now, *He* does it all. He does things people call good. But He feeds the pretty lamb to the lion, too. Lion has to eat, too, right?" He felt his arms and legs shaking, pressed them down into the table and floor. "You people," he said, "you have to break every little rule. Then you do some big sins the way God does 'em, you fuck a married woman or kill a man with your whole heart, then you'll get the biggest rush of your life." Yes, that's what he wanted to tell Beth. Tell himself. And who knows, might be true, even. "Then the Lord God puts on your body, not some pissant orisha, and your whole brain lights up.

"A man like that, *he's* the one walks upright, Baba. A free man, he makes his own law. He sees what's necessary, he does it, just the way God does *His* business, right?"

"Baba," Bow Tie said. "Who the fuck is Baba?"

Sugar laughed, but at himself. Hearing himself say *we make our own law* reminded him of his singing *we are not afraid* when he'd been scared to death in Mississippi. Truth was, he'd been written on from the moment he first saw the light between his mama's legs and cried. First the priests had written on him; then parents; teachers; the guards. Then in the soul breaker the silence and the shit-soaked floor had washed all that writing away, and he had had to face the terror in his own mind without it. He'd been undone by that, become a repellent, shit-stained baby, no words, just babble. So who would give law to what? He couldn't even give himself the law to breathe then. Or not breathe. He couldn't give himself the law to kill. Or to die. He couldn't do even *that*. Pulling him out of the hole, finding a doctor or letting him die, everything had been up to his jailers.

"Whatever it takes to keep the world going," he managed to squeak out, "God just does it, right? So you got to be like Him."

Sugar sounding kind of thoughtful that last bit, Jacob thought, but his musing interrupted by Bow Tie saying he should stop staring at his woman and shut the fuck up. Sugar leaned forward then, whacked the man across the face with his fist. The guy swayed sideways and tilted backward, then started to right himself, blood dribbling from his mouth. Sugar must have had a pistol in his hand. Which made it a miracle when the man's head stopped bobbling. But by that time Shakur had a gun at his temple. Made a silence everywhere.

Sugar walked to the back then, like he wanted to talk to Freddy, who looked like he wanted to vomit, bound to go to the New Bigs now, beg them for protection.

Jacob handed the woman the money they'd taken off the dealer, which would make the night a wash. The guy stirred then, began to whimper. "You forget all this happened now, okay? You do that," Jacob said, "there's more money for both of you."

Tomorrow Shakur would go by, visit them both, put more fear of Shakur in them. And when he did, Sugar would be that much deeper in the man's pocket. Jacob could see days coming of Sugar getting more and more fucked up, doing more this and that, and Shakur always fixing things after. Soon Shakur would have twined himself around Sugar, around RAP, killing the tree. That thought made the air thicken into a hand crushing Jacob down to the asphalt. Fuck Shakur. He got his inhaler to his mouth, breathed as deeply as he could, felt the rush not just in his lungs but in his brain. *Jesus. Look,* he mind-screamed to the guy, to Freddy and the other juicers, *Sugar'll come back. He'll stop doing that white shit. Don't you go turn away from this man now, 'cause we still* need *Sugar. And we do this job, he won't need that coke anymore to help him step up, he'll have* proved *he's the Special Agent in Charge. And we'll have enough money for the school, too, so we won't any of us need Shakur anymore, you dig?*

Thirty more minutes, Beth thought, and they'd have enough for the school. Shakur would be out of it forever. She fiddled with the side lever, pushed the seat back, let them see more of her legs in her short skirt, it came to that. She put her tennis racket beside her on the front seat, unsure again if she should seem like a suburban mother, or would the cops treat her better as a babe? "Be both," Snake had said, "like what you are, a sexy mama," the intention sweet, but the corn of it sickening her. Anyway, no way to get a compliment through her anxiety before this job.

Four in the afternoon, rush hour just beginning. And the weather freezing. Tennis, anyone? *Indoors,* right. Her health club. Which was where? Shit. And "Panel van, Officer? Oh, you know, big family." *No.* "Hubby's a contractor." Rented? "Right. For a job."

More cars than she'd thought there'd be on the access road behind her. Rush hour must start earlier on Friday, the road running right along the Pike, and the trees not blocking the growing *thrum-thrum-thrum.* Hers was still the only car in this lot, though. Sore thumb? Snake had said there'd be nothing to worry about, "this the most carefully scripted job of all, and the others had no problems, 'cept for Jacob shooting that ceiling." By the time they got to her, he said, everything would be quiet. He'd been bouncing Zing on his knee, his only task for the Dance getting her from day care. "No cops will *ever* get to the white van," *white* because *she'd* be driving, Caucasian female, short skirt, tennis racket, sexy. Freezing.

More cars on Route 20 now—*for this,* she thought, *is the way to life,* the book having the very phrase that had popped into her mind once, thinking it meant Ifa. Sugar, he'd been right that she'd understand things with him, the sparks, the need to sin, because she'd been *meant* to understand this, the time from Frank's first letter until now forming a single path, and she the one chosen to walk it.

The engine purred. Gas needle on full. She adjusted the rearview mirror, made sure it had a clear view of the road, so she could see them coming, this being, she realized, the hundredth time she'd fiddled with it. She rolled down the window, felt a blast of cold air on her ridiculous blue sweater, something a flapper might have worn, eh? She twiddled the side mirror, too. Ready. Ready. Ready.

Ready if the driver wouldn't open the truck, and they had to drop the guard? Well, if they had to, they had to. *This is the way to Edom, to Esau,* Jacob Frank had said, *the way to life.* She could picture the guard, the gun against his head; short, like that kid not much bigger than Arkey who had the audacity to brush up against her in the halls though she was two grades ahead. *Johnny Ryan,* an implacable little shit, he slammed his cheek into her breasts, and she too self-hating then to know what to do. Now she did. The guy doesn't open the truck, waste him. But the other Jacob, Jacob Battle, could he shoot something that wasn't plaster, or would the way to Edom be too hard for this Jacob, too? Jacob didn't truly appreciate all Sugar had tried to teach those people at the nightclub. "Amazing rap," he said. "Like the man went almost as far as you could go along that line, you know?"

"And on the other side?" She knew the answer now: *you become a god.*

"The other side? Some drunk gets pistol-whipped, that's all that's on the other side. Weren't you listening?"

Him, clearly, the one not listening or not seeing, that supposed *Law is on the side of death,* like Jacob Frank wrote. *"But we are going to Edom, to life."* Four hundred years ago, Jacob Frank had been the most inspired follower of Sabbatai Zevi, the two of them messiahs for the elect only, *for the cadre*—which was why the rubes called them false saviors. But *her* comrades, the Downstairs, made hard by four hundred years of oppression, *they* were ready&steady for *the way to Edom*—the place of Esau, of true life, where its force and power are not subject to *any* restriction, where you're joined to the source of things, and you make your own rules.

She'd read those holy words in the main reading room of the Boston Public, this big volume of the Jewish Encyclopedia weighing down her lap, Zing whining, wanting to go, and the thoughts had nearly knocked her over. *This was it,* what she'd always been on the track of, the Weathermen and their fuck sessions, blue-plate cats, even the bombings. But that had been penny-ante stuff. The Brinks job: *that* would be the real deal, the top of the line. Zing had whimpered, and the musty reading room patrons glared at her. She'd taken her for a carriage ride down dirty Boylston. She shouldn't have been strolling a main avenue like that, but she felt desperate for Zing to sleep so she could read more.

Thank God, Zing's head fell forward, not even the busses waking her. "You understand, Zing, I have to do this thing," she'd told her sleeping child. "I have to save the school. It's me that fucked things up, not refunding the money, not seeing how people were dipping in the till. I don't do something to make it right, they'll throw me out of the collective. I'll be alone."

Zing hadn't said anything, head to the side like she had no bone in her neck. A panhandler looked at Beth, decided not even to try the crazy woman talking to her sleeping child. "Then I'd have failed. And, Zing, ten years from now, I didn't help make the revolution, if I was part of the problem, an accomplice in genocide, then I swear you'd have nothing but contempt for me. I couldn't bear that."

She wheeled back to the shopping cart lady, a young fat woman, hand out all day. She put in a dollar, looked over the garbage she rolled from place to place. *Christ,* she wanted to say, *this is pathetic. Don't you have the strength to go rob someone, take what you need?*

She wheeled Zing away. "And this thing, it's perfectly safe for me now, darling. Sugar, he's shown me how to do it a way I won't screw it up. He's turned me on to something that'll put the steel in me, so I can free the sparks from their prisons, waste the fucking guard we have to do that, eh?"

But saying that made her a little uneasy still. She raced the carriage back to the BPL, up the handicapped ramps, so word by word Jacob Frank could flow into her like black milk from the black kabala, the hidden within the hidden, the reviled denied *truth,* glimpsed by the Jews, but made real by another denied people. With her left arm she'd moved Zing's stroller back and forth on the smooth floor, psy-sending a zingaby and turning the encyclopedia pages with her right hand. She'd seen then that she *had* to do the job, the pages reknitting the golden chain from her to Frank. Hard to believe, she'd once wondered if Sugar meant something more than *fuck me* when he tried to tell her these things, when you had to see now that the man had found something he *knew* only she could share. That's what had attracted him to her. An African man, alive to what Ifa could have been—maybe once had been, and what Chuck couldn't see—the orisha who dances, the God who loves our bodies, wants to possess them, wants to be us so we can be Him. Sugar had gone back to the old stuff, found the secret doors. Kill a Brinks guard? Those acts, they're called evil by minor bureaucrats—the one the God of Creation put in charge to give his lesser beings the petty laws they needed to regulate their terrified suburban lives. Someday she'd tell this shit to her father, how that guilt he loved so much, it was *such* bullshit, the voice still and small because it was a tiny godling talking, not the one true God. Sugar saw through that. He did *evil* wholeheartedly. And *that* was the road to Esau, the source of Life, it made them one with God, made them God.

She adjusted the mirror one more time, turned around in her seat, forgetting that you couldn't see out the back door. She peered at the side mirror, the world going dark outside. A white guy in a running suit, big mittens on his hands, came toward the 7-Eleven.

After this job, Sugar and she would have a lot to say to each other, the man finally free from Christ's shadow now, and she from Leo Jacobs'.

A siren came toward her. *No,* the mall would be too far away for her to hear anything. The job would go off without a hitch, like Snake had said, and it would turn things around for all of them. An endowment for the school. And respect for RAP everywhere, if they could maybe let out a little of what had happened. Respect for her, again, too. When she'd taken Zing to day care this morning she'd blown her baby a kiss through the mail slot, and felt again that glow, Beth once more a soldier on her way to war, Nzinga her queen even, and Beth doing her part to free the land for her, for all the kids inside. After this job, Billy Green would have to wake up to who *she* really was, too, a woman who'd helped drive the stake into imperialism's heart, not that lunatic he'd drawn lately in her cunt-showing leotard, *that* woman just flying up her own butt!

Yeah, it had been a siren, for sure. Not a cop's screech, though, an ambulance, and going away from her to the west. She relaxed. Snake had it nailed, the white edge in the catbird seat, a cool no-risk deal for her, easily getting her back to Zing's side a few hours after day care let out.

But where the fuck were they? Jacob, he'd be driving one of the cars to the van. She loved him, but she suspected the boy was just *not* strong enough for the way to Esau.

Jacob, meantime, watched the skinny guard kneel in front of a short man in a ski mask and a green janitor's jumpsuit—none other than Sugar Cane, one of the first leaders of the Black Power movement, the chairman of RAP. The Brinks guard's brown uniform looked like a *kick me* sign; and even from here, Jacob could see the guy crying, face twisted up, snot running from his nose, a middle-aged white guy, thin hair in a corny comb-over. Behind him, Bunchie lifted the white canvas bag from the dolly.

Shakur—couldn't be anyone else, a mountain in a ski mask is still a mountain—handcuffed the guard, then yanked him back up, probably nearly shearing his muscles off, and dragged him by the arms, heels scraping the asphalt. He held him up in front of the driver, shouting, "Open the door, motherfucker! Open the fucking door!" Bunchie pushed a gun into the poor pullet's temple same time. Get it, asshole? An easy-to-win charade.

The Brinks truck must have had a loudspeaker, Jacob hearing a voice shouting, "Shoot him, you bastards. I'm not opening that door." *Oh, shit, he refused!* He fucking refused! Didn't the guy get it? His friend would die! "I can't open the door. That's it. Company policy," the guy sounding way too calm about it, though, like him and the comb-over *weren't* exactly friends, so company policy and bulletproof glass were good enough for him.

Plus only one hostage. That was bad. If they shot him to show the driver they were serious, then what? They had no one else to shoot—so what's the point? But Shakur, he pulled the ears off flies; and Sugar, he pistol-whipped drunks to become one with the whirl and swirl. *Comb-over,* Jacob thought, *he's a dead man.*

Armored truck looked like a tank, too; and the guy, Jacob pretty sure, still mouthing into his microphone now, but no sound coming from the speakers, which meant he had a radio phone. *Of course,* the guy was calling the police! No one had thought about *that.* Shakur saw it now, though. He threw the pullet aside, the guy rolling up into a ball while Shakur fired his rifle into the truck window. The glass crinkled, but didn't open up, so Shakur pumped another round, the driver gone now, ducked under the dashboard.

Then an old man in another kind of uniform, pistol out and hat flying off, came round the corner of *Sears,* must be a mall rent-a-cop who heard the rifle shots and snuck through the perimeter George and Dreads had set up. Jesus, duty calls, huh? Almost had to admire the minimum-wage moron. Shakur saw him, pumped a round into his stomach, knocking him backward on the ground, like he was sitting down to watch his guts spill out. Same time, Jacob could see around the edge of the building, two cop cars pulling in, sirens going, but Shakur turned back to the truck, so pissed he couldn't see that it was definitely time to go. Jacob leaned out of the window, like maybe Shakur didn't realize the shit-storm heading toward him, and a cop's bullet tore into Jacob's shoulder. He looked up toward the darkening sky, head out the window still, this the worst fucking pain he'd ever felt in his life, worse than an asthma attack. Bunchie ran toward him with a sack, and Jacob, not even thinking about it, floored the pedal, like he had to get away from Bunchie. The car took off, went up on the sidewalk as he made the turn, sending a shopping cart skidding. He glanced off the liquor store wall, and his head smashed into the rearview mirror.

Beth saw Jacob in her right side mirror, coming toward her *alone,* wearing a blue suit, white shirt, like for his bar mitzvah, but blood all down his side and dripping from his hand. He flung open the door. "Where's Sugar?" Beth said, scared.

"Who gives a shit? I need to get to a hospital."

Just then, another car came down the access road, the wrong way for the job, but one she'd rented. Right, with Drama Queen Priss at the wheel, everything always gets turned around. A cop car came off the thruway, lights on, saw the car coming past, the wrong way on a one-way, and nearly fishtailed. Priss's car went sideways, crashing into the railing, but the head smashing down on the wheel was Snake's. Fucking Snake, Jesus, no, how *could* it be him? Snake had to pick Zing up from day care if Beth didn't get back. Snake should grow up, she thought reflexively, not getting at first how serious this was. Snake *should* fucking die, she thought. How could she ever have gotten mixed up with someone so stupid, so irresponsible!

A cop ran up to Snake's car, gun out, and the lid popped open, Shakur coming out like the trunk had vomited a green and black elephant, his rifle already firing, blowing the side of the cop's head off. The side door opened same time, and she saw the edge of someone's head, a green jumpsuit, Sugar's maybe. The other cop got down behind his car door, shooting at them, and Shakur dove behind his, with Sugar. Jacob shouted at Beth, "Get the fuck out of here, Beth! Go!"

She couldn't go, Snake trapped in that car, Sugar probably too. Her job. The spark. Her head. Why didn't she see what she should do, the way God did? Beth looked at Jacob then, blood all over his chest, a gash in his forehead. Jacob saying something about Zing, getting out of town, hospital. *Now.* And Snake, what if Snake were dead? God, no one would show up at day care! That sweet, bewildered-seeming lady who ran the place, she'd start calling their contact, Priss. Had she been here, too, and was she already in custody now? The lady would follow procedure, then, call DSS.

More words from Jacob, not too clear, his mouth making a sound like a motor, sucking air.

Another cop car came up behind the first, stopped, side doors open, and rifles over the edge, aimed at Sugar's and Shakur's car. They would surely blow Snake's skull apart.

"Where's your inhaler?"

"Fucking Shakur, he threw it away. A crutch, he said, ruined his needles. Shit."

Yeah, shit is right. She started to put the car in gear to back up, get the men on the fly, then take off forward again, but Jacob put his hand on her arm.

"You go back there, we die."

Die? She stopped.

"The money's to buy drugs."

"Right. And for the school."

He didn't say anything, stared at her.

"Fuck that shit. It's for drugs."

"Don't be stupid. That's too much—"

"Fuck you, bitch, calling me stupid. You don't fucking get it, do you, Beth, you never fucking get it. Not drugs to snort. Drugs to sell. The Downstairs is gonna deal now. Cull the herd, Shakur says. Milk the weak ones, till they die, so the rest can be saved."

"What did Sugar say?"

"Look, I don't know. He said, make the spark bloom inside your cerebellum, and you the same as Him, some shit like that."

Beth stared at the big red stain on Jacob's shirt, read the message, the truth, like Baba would say, in the blood. *What shit it all had been!* Her life, her fucking life! All the air went out of her, Beth a broken balloon. *Culling the herd*—those words were the truth of all the crap she'd bought—no, *sold herself.* All that Esau shit, that's what it came down to. She wanted to throw up. No, she wanted to throw *herself* up. That's why they needed so fucking much money—not to save the school but to front a drug deal!

Then she realized she hadn't heard what else Jacob had said. "What did Sugar say?" she screamed, or had she already asked that, live rounds nearby, like a hundred yards away, and her bladder had already let go, soaked her panty hose, the seat. And "how many, how many died?" she said then, like that would matter. She began to cry, Jacob looking at her now like he hated her.

"Sugar," he lied, "like I said, Sugar said some shit about treading on the vestures of the Torah. Or loving God with the evil impulse." Or,

Shakur, get the fuck out of my face with that shit, you black, self-hating bastard. The money goes to the fucking school, which was what he'd actually said. Brave, too, 'cause Shakur had blood in his eye, might have taken Sugar's head off with a blow. Coke brave, maybe, but brave nonetheless.

Beth meanwhile thinking she had to get away from Jacob, too, the fucking murderer, get home. Where home? Zing, where her child was, that had to be home. That's the thing she felt guilty for all along, not the Brinks guard but her daughter. That's what she'd needed help leaving— that the truth of the shit she'd become, dressing herself in something gaudy and mystical-sounding to make her think it was ever all right to leave her child!

She had to go now, drive from this firefight, show up at the nursery school's red door on Green Street, the traffic not too bad, take her daughter back to Great Neck, leave Zing with her family. Beth would have to hide for a while.

But first did she have to go back *toward* the firing? And if she *died* doing it? Could they prove Mary Hunt equaled Beth Jacobs from dental records, fingerprints, notify her parents eventually, and oh, God, not leave Zing in some foster family. No, she couldn't go backward, had to get out of here, get back to Zing. She had wanted to be free of her guilt for wanting action and fame—to be a comic book star again! *That* guilt, Christ, she *should* have listened to it—the other half of love, of gravity. Now she longed to give every moment to Zing. Not just to be safe, Lord, but to be with her daughter. *Please God, just give me that chance again.*

Wait, she thought. In a moment, Shakur and Sugar would start running toward them, the two wearing bulletproof vests. She couldn't go back, but they could come toward her, dragging that bastard Snake, Jacob could open the side door for them from the inside, the car already moving, they'd dive in, and they'd all be out of here.

"You pick them up," Jacob said, reading her mind, "right off Shakur kills me for running. I'm not opening the fucking door." But then he started to cry, like a kid. "I don't want to die, Beth. Please don't let him kill me."

A helicopter, *whoosh whoosh whoosh* overhead, churned her brain waves. Was it too late now? Had they seen Jacob get in? If they had, that bug would follow them everywhere!

That van, Sugar thought, *had* to be where Jacob had gone, the little punk. Or had he just gone home? No, he wouldn't be that stupid, knowing the cops had the license from the mall. Still, Sugar *wanted* the van to

pull away with Jacob in it—after all, he'd promised Mr. Joshua Battle
he'd take care of the kid. And he and Shakur, they ever got to the van,
what good would it do, now that the helicopters were on them?

He fired at the cop car, the pigs there making it clear they moved,
they'd be able to nail them, but not shooting much until help came. The
pigs such morons, but eventually even they'd figure it, another cop car
could drive past the pickup point soon, have them boxed in on both
sides. He looked over at Shakur in his green jumpsuit, sweat pouring off
him, pumping another round toward the police car, Shakur his *Golem*,
like in that comic book he'd read in Mississippi. *Cull the herd*. Man, that
was too much, wasn't it? Fuck this skinless guy.

But look, if Beth wasn't smart enough to move, maybe they *should*
try to run, him and Shakur. *Who was not his creature*, face it, more like
the other half of his heartbeat these last years. Which made Sugar what
exactly, if the other half of his heartbeat had said *cull the herd*?

Sugar would *never* allow that. He'd kill Shakur first. Maybe today,
come to think of it. A big-ticket sin, right? When he'd whacked that
drunk's skull, it felt good. Good enough, anyway. So who knows? But
even thinking that wearied him.

Which meant what? That he should just let the cops shoot him? No,
that would be Christ shit for sure, what Malcolm warned him about, not
the way for black people. The Church, man, it had taught young Sugar
how to suffer and sacrifice, but not about what to do when the whole
world looked to you to know what they should do, Sugar everyone's
father, judge, protector—everyone on their knees in front of him, offering him some blow and a blow job, like he was a god.

"That bitch is too scared to come toward us," Shakur shouted. "We
got to run to that motherfucking van."

Shakur giving orders? Everyone at the job had been listening to *him*,
that had been *most* clear, not even looking to Sugar to see if he agreed.
And when Sugar said no again to his dealing shit—the man bound to ask
over and over like a kid who wanted a toy—then it would for sure come
to the knife between him and Shakur. Christ, all the struggle to keep control of RAP, to save the school, it made him so fucking tired.

Stop bullshitting yourself. The real wearying struggle for *him* had
become one thing only: get more coke, light up the circuits in his brain,
make the darkness go away, so he had the energy to get more coke, light
up the circuits in his brain again, world without fucking end. *How long*,
he thought, *O Lord, how long how long how long*, his mind stuttering.
Man, you want to know what Same Old was, get yourself a coke habit!
Pain forever, like Pascal said in that book the white boy had shown him

Christ is in agony until the end of time. And if he got *worse* instead of better, did more wigged-out things, like that insanity in the club, he'd *need* Shakur to clean them up. He'd be a messed-up baby, sitting in his own shit, and Shakur could use him any way he wanted, Sugar Cane and RAP the front for Shakur and the Downstairs, till the man bled it to death. He had to do Shakur *now.*

He fired his pistol at something out ahead of him, show he was alive still.

Which, Shakur thought, probably hit a tree. Jittery coked-up loon, the man just useless most of the time now, not the hero they'd all admired in the joint, the only man to go into the soul breaker and come out stronger. Now he was a fucking burnt-out case, yet he had the effrontery to see *him* as a monster, Shakur, who was the *real* fire under the breakfasts for kids, the people he scared into paying; while Sugar had the *effrontery,* yes, that was the word, to act like Shakur was his big bad black body, the smart man's Stagolee. Fuck him. He didn't like the dope deal, fine, he didn't have to give him that lecture like he was shit for black people. He'd thought the idea would please him even, all that *do evil* shit. This ends, he thought, the cops don't kill Sugar, he was definitely gonna do it himself. Right after he did Jacob.

No, shit *no,* that would be wrong—Jacob, yes, but Sugar would come back to them. He remembered him—funny, the guy was right next to him, but he was thinking about Sugar on TV—calling Johnson a cracker, shouting *Black Power!* to some terrified white reporter, making the man's pale face fall into itself. Black people needed him. The man saw far, would see far again, they ever got the fuck out of this.

Sugar reached into his jacket pocket, got his little friend out, lit himself up. Shakur looked at him disgusted.

"Come on, man, I'll go first," Shakur said, "you cover me, we'll drive back for you," Shakur having truly changed his mind now. He'd make it, he'd push the pussy boy out, put a gun to the bitch's head, and off they'd go. Fuck Sugar. The man *wanted* to die, had it written all over him. Shakur couldn't kill him, but the cops could if Sugar wanted, that was between him and his God.

Shakur ran toward the van, comical-looking, Sugar thought, slithering like a serpent; something he saw in a movie, probably. He looked back toward the van again, still there, and Shakur nearing it. He stood out from the car, then—*upright, Chuck, get it?* The cops, distracted by Shakur, didn't even shoot at him.

Then another car sliced down the exit, doors open already when it stopped, cops with rifles coming out, the morons still not thinking to box them in from the back. He turned, saw Shakur get closer to the van.

He put the gun across his arm, like the vets had taught them at the farm long ago, waited for the serpent to come back to the left, and aimed for Shakur's back.

Got him in the foot, though. Knocked him on his fat face. A definite rush, too.

"Come on now, bitch," Sugar psy-screamed at the van, "save that kid!"

Worked, too. The van took off down the access road, Shakur up again, dragging his leg, chasing the van, like he was doing it to make Sugar laugh.

So duck back down? And what? Go to jail, again? Sit in his own shit. Inconsiderable. Handled. Death at every fucking moment in there. That was the real shit smell, his life turning to waste in the joint.

So, do the thing all the godlings condemn, little bigger than shooting another foot, do the real double dare, the top of the *keritot,* the one gets your soul ripped right out of your body.

Or had that fucking Christ bit him on the ass again? Like he'd just reinvented the way that man became godlike when he let the Roman pigs shoot him?

So should I—

The bullets hit Sugar in the back, the shots right into the vest, knocking him forward. Then the van finally went past the ramp, as cop cars sped down. *Good,* Sugar thought, turning back toward the cops.

And the next rounds opened up his skull.

Beth looked up Arkey's address in a phone book at a booth near MIT, and Gail opened the door, like she'd been expecting them, not screaming either when she saw the bloody man. In fact, she'd actually touched him, put her arm around Jacob's chest and helped him in, blood going down her thin nightgown. She led him over to the couch, his head lolling already, about to lose consciousness for sure.

"Don't," Beth shouted at her. "Don't let him pass out," unsure anymore why it mattered, like maybe that was for a drug overdose?

"Jesus," Arkey said, not nearly so cool about things as his little girl-friend. How many coins would he have to eat after this? He wore those white pajamas from Brooks Brothers her father used to like. "Jacob," he said, pointlessly. "You."

"Me," Jacob said, about to conk. "Me."

"Right. Me, too," Beth said, losing it herself.

But Arkey had already gone to the phone, made a call. *Cops?*

"Beth's here, and she's brought this guy I knew from high school all bloody," like that fucking mattered. "Wounded, yeah." It sounded like Jesse's voice coming from the handset—like the asshole thought what they needed now was a lawyer, not a doctor.

"Call the police, Arkey," Jesse said. "Then call an ambulance." Not, Arkey thought, his comforting *I'll take care of everything* voice. Maybe that one was just for murderers. Not accessories.

"He's losing a lot of blood," Arkey said, like that would be relevant. Should be, though. Blood, it's the essence of things somehow; their condensed, glistening truth made him think nonsensically of that drop from Billy's prick, that bris years before.

"Okay, then," Jesse said. "Call the ambulance first, Arkey. *Then* call the police. It's over, Arkey. It's really, really over."

"Beth has a kid." Arkey saying *that,* he decided even then, because the blood had turned him into a babbling idiot. Gail had Jacob's jacket and shirt off, had gotten a towel, pressed it hard to this *big* fucking wound in his shoulder. "Help me," she said to Beth, smiling at her, not scared-looking—soft, really, like she was in love.

"Listen to me, Arkey," Jesse said in the emphatic, condescending tone Arkey had heard last in hospitals, surgeon to lowly nurse. "Call the police. *It's over.*"

4

1982: SENTENCES

Can't you see it's over for your friend? Bobby Brown wanted to psy-shout. *Don't let her fuck up our lives, too!* But this transmission alerted only him. *Our* lives? He grimaced at Laura, who innocently slurped the last of her coffee Fribble. Bobby knew that when he tightened his muscles, the square shape of his face, his thin skin made him look like a man who had a hard time restraining himself. Which, right now, was the case. A pigheaded woman wouldn't do in the life Bobby Brown had planned for himself.

But how would even a far more reasonable version of Laura Jaffe fit into that life? A white wife would be a deadweight for Bobby Brown in a black district. Or a white district, for that matter. So forget *that.*

Easy to say. But he felt the heat just being in the same room with her again. Not the most romantic place, either—molded gray-plastic benches, a back booth at an antiseptic unFriendly's. Her foot accidentally-on-purpose touched his. And Jesse Kelman, across from him, did her thigh touch his at the same time? Archie, Veronica, and, *gee, I don't remember the name of the black guy in those comics, 'cause there wasn't one.*

Kelman was about the same height as he was, but Bobby was wider, better muscled. Put Jesse on the line, he'd have run through him like a piece of wet tissue. But Laura had a tender edge with the Defender that made Bobby uncomfortable—like they shared a parallel comic book reality he couldn't muscle into.

Her head tipped toward Kelman, and her hair curved about her cheeks in two semicircles. She wore a white blouse with one string of pearls, and a long, straight skirt of a cunningly woven fabric that hid her amazing legs from Bobby, made him want them and the rest of her more. He wanted to talk to her more, too, mind you, Laura able to understand—even help him understand—the insane difficulty that people's projections made for him, like they were talking to some hologram alongside him, trying to please it, apologize to it, hurt it; meanwhile, *he* felt the pain.

And then last time she'd done just that, he'd swear; she'd walked out on *someone,* but Bobby Brown had felt the hurt. She had thought it was because he was a prosecutor, while the real reason was clear as black and white. That must have come crashing down on her; not her feeling about *him,* he was pretty sure, but the way the world would be toward them. Well, she had that right; but it was no reason they shouldn't make love again.

"Look," he said, too much exasperation in his voice, Bobby angry mostly at his own lack of self-control, wanting her so damn much, "you don't answer the DA's questions, you'll be in contempt. They'll put you in jail until the grand jury expires or you talk."

Laura carefully painted some ketchup on her last French fries and glanced at Jesse—like she couldn't trust Bobby Brown on this. Fair enough. Then he felt jealous again, pretty sure she and Jesse Kelman had done that thing, too, once upon a time. The Defender had anyway—with SheWolf. And that's what Bobby had here—this "you can't make me talk, copper" of hers—dialogue for a comic book.

"It's true, Laura," Jesse said. "They're impaneled another six months at least. And it'll probably get continued. You stay in jail as long as they're in session."

"He'd do that?" The unspoken: *to me?*

"Wergel? You bet," Jesse said, working hard and fast on his own fries. Bobby wondered how he'd lost that digit. And those long cat scratches across his cheeks, what was the story there? "Two people died," Kelman said. "Wergel satisfies people here, he thinks he can be governor," Beth's counsel, fortunately, reminding Laura how serious things had become. He couldn't help liking the guy. He had kindly eyes—but steel behind them, Bobby knew. In Mississippi, DA's got overturned like cards in a gin pile from Defender-discovered reversible errors. "You should have your own lawyer on this, Laura," Jesse added. "I represent Beth. Your interests and hers, they don't necessarily coincide."

Right, Dorothy, you're not in Great Neck anymore—where Bobby, too, had lived most of his childhood. 'Cept that Steamboat Road, Darktown, Maidville, that had been a whole other world from Kings Point.

"Okay." She paused. "Jesse," she said, "could you leave us alone?" Iron filings of command mixed in with the pleading.

Jesse looked reassuringly at Bobby, mournfully at his remaining fries. "Sure," he said, instead of *I can't advise that.* Or *I'm not done eat-*

ing yet, Princess. Kelman took ten bucks from a creased brown wallet, just enough for a squared-off hamburger, fries, and Fribble, tip apparently to be provided by the client. Maybe he lived on his earnings, which, given his clientele, couldn't be much. Which could be Bobby's own fate soon. Lately, he felt like a black beard for Reagan, thought he might leave Justice for defense work.

Laura's eyes followed Jesse out the door. "Bobby, I'm going to tell the grand jury that whatever Beth said to me is covered by doctor-patient privilege."

Bobby couldn't help himself, he barked a laugh at her, it was so damn foolish. "*Did* she say anything to you?" He made his face impassive.

"No. We talked about the past. We talked abstractions."

Laura bit her lip. Corny—but he liked it, wanted to reach out, stroke her plump, rosy cheek. "About her father, maybe, that's it."

"Then why go through this charade? Answer Wergel's questions. Go home with a clear conscience that you didn't help *anyone.*"

"I can't. Beth says she's a political prisoner. She says anyone who cooperates with this country's court system is a collaborator."

"You believe that shit?" He wanted to shout at her, *She's a comic book character, for Christ's sake.* Or should he say, *You're from Kings Point, sweetheart—you have* no *motherfucking idea what prison is like.*

She shrugged. "I believe that if I cooperate with . . ." She'd been about to say, *with you,* but maybe she decided that sounded too stark—like she saw a future for them, too. ". . . with the State, then she'll hate me. Then, if she goes in, she won't let me keep Zing."

"Oh, she *is* going in," Bobby said, but thinking, *This is all about a kid?* A new one on him—contempt charges to prove you'd be a *good* mother. "Well, you go to jail for a year, who's going to take care of Zing then? Your mother?" *His* aunt, it would have been not long ago at the Jaffe home.

"Look, you're telling me I'm in a box, Bobby. I know that. I'm asking you how I get out of it."

He could say, again, answer Wergel's questions. But she probably knew Beth's cinder of a heart; she talked to Wergel, she'd lose her chance at the grand prize: a baby, and Laura, he knew, scared to have any of her own, 'cause of that disease of hers. Was that sensible or neurotic? He'd have to check with some neurologist friends.

That future thing again! Could he possibly want Laura so much that he would be willing to raise Beth Jacobs' child, have that witch in his life forever? And not have a child of his own, if it turned out Laura was right to be afraid—or wrong, even, but he couldn't change her mind?

Anyway, he had a job to do that conflicted slightly with romance. If Laura went to jail on contempt, they could use it to squeeze Beth—supposing, that is, the bitch cared about any other human beings on the planet except herself and her "lumpen prole" playmates. They could get her to help wrap up the network she was part of, the soldiers that Baby—AKA Shakur—supposedly led now.

And look how their Baby had grown! Shot, he'd dragged himself through some woods, hijacked a Volvo—and disappeared. The woman he'd jacked, still hysterical when forced to think about it, didn't remember a rifle. Had he buried it in the woods? Olson thought so; had men combing it already.

"Look, Laura, tell me something small. Tell me how you and your friends supported Beth in the past. Sent her money, right? Lent her a sweater. Give me anything. It'll show we're working together. Then I can maybe get a deal for us."

She glared at him, much angry Princess in those almond-shaped eyes. Fuck that *us* shit, huh?

"Right," he said. "Thanks." For nothing. He gathered his yellow pads, put them back in his green book bag; a stupid affectation he knew, his not using a leather attaché case. Meant to say, he wasn't like the other Justice suits, supposing his skin color hadn't clued you in to that.

He couldn't help himself, though, he still had to have her. On the way out he turned. "Look, I'll tell Wergel you cooperated fully with us. We already have everything from you, and it's nothing. Maybe he'll let it go." Really, what he'd have to say was: *do me a favor,* when he had other favors he needed more.

"Thank you." She smiled. "Was ever woman in this humor wooed."

At least they each knew what was going on here. "Was ever woman in this humor won."

"How d'cha know that?"

An insult—for Bobby Brown, Dewey School '66, Harvard '70, Yale LL.D. '73! Et tu, Laura?

She looked bewildered at the pain on his face. "I thought that was just something Beth said."

"No. It's something the former queen says in *Richard III*," Bobby said, with too much asperity, Bobby still smarting from a slap that hadn't been delivered—not by her anyway. Or not today. "Ann, she's the widow of a king that Richard had murdered," he added for extra credit—the black man having to be that much smarter, do that much better.

"Oh," she smiled, sunny again. "You and Beth, huh, some ways you're like two peas in a pod."

That truly pissed him off. "She's a cop-murdering fool, Laura."

The smile flicked off. "Right," she said, eyes cold, but still getting a little teary anger into the word. "But like you, she's wonderfully well educated."

And that *when Beth goes inside* of his—truth was, Bobby couldn't be positive about it. He strolled round the block toward Wergel's office, his ridiculous book bag over his back. Nice-looking town. Like Great Neck, but with a big grassy square where the cows used to graze, and an old iron cannon parked in the middle for drunk high school kids to mark up. A lot of cops here, still, though not the battalions they'd massed when they brought Beth to the courthouse.

Wergel, he'd let the witnesses at that hearing go all over the place. David Watkins, the famous Harrison Baker, they'd made sure the scared suburban moms got all the cars and clothes wrong. And who could blame those women? They'd gone to the mall to get togs for their kids, found some little back eddy of history had spilled into their parking lot.

And the key witness, a Brinks guard, had been a mess. Wergel had to have him hypnotized—"regression therapy"—until he would parrot that a tall, thin black man—AKA Jacob Battle—sporting an earring but strangely not wearing a mask in this guy's account, had shot the mall cop with pistols in each hand that no one could find anymore, the guard obviously unable to distinguish between fantasy and memory. Well, Bobby thought, why should he? No one else in this case can.

"You're sure it was pistols?" David Watkins had said, innocently.

"Yes, sir."

When marked-up rifle bullets had been taken out of the guard's stomach. Jacob Battle hadn't smiled, though, just stared straight ahead, not looking at Bobby, his neck in a dirty white brace, the cops having broken it and the prison guards beaten on it. He would have to have surgery soon, make sure he could walk to his trial. Fucked-up witnesses or not, Wergel had put him up for murder.

Poor little Jacob. Still, important to remember that Jacob may not have pulled the trigger, but he'd sure as shit been there, probably driving one of the getaway cars. Important to remember, too, Bobby Brown couldn't ever be sure Jacob *hadn't* pulled the trigger. They'd done some turns around the track, long time ago, the time Jacob had tipped him to that Mississippi march, so he could hear David Watkins, not yet gray, tell Sugar Cane *drop it, drop the bomb on them now.*

A young cop stepped out from the side of the door, put a most unwelcome arm on his. "What you got in that bag?"

Wise precaution, nasty tone. Bobby handed it to him, but he wouldn't take it. "You open it."

Bobby did. The man looked in, his hand on his pistol. With his free hand, he moved the papers around carelessly.

Next time, Bobby would have a briefcase, make it *almost* all fit together, not make the next cop so uneasy. And Laura? With his skin, she would always be a green book bag.

"What's your business here?"

"Federal officer," Bobby said, on edge, patience thin, hard to keep the *fuck you* out of his voice. "I'm going to reach into my jacket pocket, Officer, get my wallet for my I.D."

And after that melanin-toning exercise, he decided not to wait for the elevator, took the wide stairs up to Wergel's office, work the nerves off. *Time to get out.* This building, this job. But not till Mr. Bobby Brown, Esq., had done one last thing, settling Jacob Battle in prison for ten years instead of life—a decade enough time for him to think about what he'd done. But how to get him the deal?

"No deal," Beth Jacobs said to Jesse Kelman.

That would be *Beth the Red,* Jesse thought. Always a question: which Beth he'd meet in the big room with seven or eight other tables, all unused today, that the prison provided for conferences. "They're not offering a deal," Jesse said.

"Copping a plea would be a skin privilege." Toneless, though; rote; the dead voice of *Beth the Penitent,* scouring her whiteness off with state-provided steel wool. Beth looked tired, pale, her eyes pouched and dark underneath; the gray prison smock the only garment he'd ever seen that didn't work for her. Like *that's* what she'd been hoping for all her life—*unsex me here.*

Behind her a matron looked in through the dirty plastic plate in the metal door.

Jesse smiled at Beth, best he could, repeated calmly, "Beth, they're *not* offering a plea." The pipes knocked, heat coming on, drying out Jesse's nose some more. *Put some Vaseline inside,* Carol had said at the airport. But first she had screamed and raked her long fingernails down his face. He'd had to change his bloody shirt in the airplane bathroom.

He rubbed his cheek; the marks raised still, scabbed over. A party and some young clerk for Justice Bubba had told Carol about Barkely, like it showed how fair-minded Jesse could be—"You know, even though the man had said he's the one who raped you, he put in this clever exception for him." Jew, of course, being implied.

Now David nodded at Jesse, but pursed his lips thoughtfully. "They're not offering a plea *yet*, Miss Jacobs. But we'll pressure them every way we can," as if Beth had never said she didn't want one. *Father Knows Best.* "There are demonstrations for you already. That might help us."

"Demos, eh?" That mixed memory with desire, stirred her dead flesh.

"Yeah, New Afrika flags everywhere, people shouting, Free the Land!" but David sounding even more like ArIsto when he mouthed that kind of thing.

"Judge Hurlbut you can't hide!" Jesse chanted, quietly, getting a nostalgic buzz from it—but the high cut with so much irony, it left a sour taste.

"We charge you with genocide," David finished, voice mildly raised—close as he ever came to shouting. This meeting was mostly so Beth could see more of David Watkins, maybe grow to trust him because he could chant slogans. David's being here was a kindness to Jesse—and for the memory of the beloved/hated Sugar Cane.

Beth smiled wanly and adjusted the glasses it had taken Jesse two court hearings to get for her. ("I have to touch the dress of the lady in front of me. Which, let me tell you, could get me shivved.") Now her mind's eye probably feasted on thousands of angry blacks with raised fists, when it had actually been maybe twenty tired people walking in a lazy circle in front of the courthouse. Several hundred cops and troopers looked on, though—local, MDC, state—the gang's all here and heavily armed.

"How's the school doing?" Beth asked.

"Susan Lems was subpoenaed, but she won't talk to the grand jury."

Despite my best efforts, David Watkins thought. "Susan," he'd said, trying not to be too avuncular, "it's over now. Sugar ain't looking down on us. You go to jail, it won't help anyone." He'd meant to sound frightening, but he knew it had come out condescending, even with the *ain't.*

He'd looked away. The waiters wheeled a cart around with samples, 'case you didn't know what porterhouse meant. Her eyes lit. She'd plumped up—more than *him*, he thought proudly, sucking in the gut a little. Always had curves, but now she'd added one to her belly, made the whole picture lose proportion. Still, she had her fine smile, one filled with knowledge and kindness, and just enough vinegar, if you turned out to disappoint, to keep you in the game.

"I'm not doing it for Sugar," Susan had said. "The things I might have to say to the grand jury, they'd be bad for the school."

"And your going to jail, won't that damn near close it down?"

"I know I'm deep in a hole, David."

Dug by Sugar Cane. Well, no one on the planet, not even Sugar, does time that hard and doesn't come out calloused, out of kilter.

David felt a dark, sharp stab of hatred for Beth Jacobs then, this fool the reason Wergel had jailed Susan, a woman so much wiser, more powerful, and decent than her. Not just that; he remembered how very wet her cunt could be—that most precious fluid—and felt her long fingers touching his lips. As she came, she'd go *oh, dear,* softly. It all comes down to a body; *a remembered one* ever the most powerful for him, purged of the anxiety of the moment, he could just take pleasure in her—as she was.

They must think Susan could be used to squeeze Beth. So Susan would get out if Beth came to her senses and pled. He didn't know how he'd get Wergel to offer her a deal, however horrendous. But he'd been through this before. The cards always got dealt and redealt along the way; he would find an opening; and he'd get Jesse to sign off on the deal, too—use *whatever* lever he needed to make him do it. David felt a surge that made him think of poker at the Kappa house, nice big pot, everyone sweating, but David sure that pluck, luck, and a good bluff would see him through. Thing about Jesse, though, he was smarter than David. The other thing, though, *he* also wanted to be more decent.

"And the school year?" Beth was saying to him. "With Susan in jail, what happens to the kids?"

Nice to see she could care about something besides her own sorry self. "The school named a new principal," David said. "Delon Sanders. It'll probably be able to finish out the year."

Talking to her felt like dropping messages down a well. But she must have taken that in. "Delon?" She smiled. "You know he's the one set the old place on fire that night? You were there, weren't you?"

He nodded. Did she do that to make him feel implicated in this story? *Worked, too.*

"Is Laura going to testify to the grand jury?"

"I don't think so," Jesse said.

"Good. We have to stand together," Beth said. "We've decided," she announced on behalf of the Fantasy Central Committee, "that we will put on a political trial. No defense until we make our statement at the end."

"Laura Jaffe may have to do time for contempt, too."

Beth turned her head to the side, tried to hood her eyes. Not so much hard, David would swear, as someone trying to make herself hard, though what she'd done said otherwise.

The *Boston Herald* opined that they should reinstate the death penalty for Beth Jacobs. And at the hearing David had been amazed by how beat-up their clients had looked; not that they'd been worked over—that was a given, a case like this, cops murdered—but the thing done so indifferently, so carelessly, that the marks showed. The one they called Dreads had his arm in a sling; Snake and George had huge bruises on their cheeks. And Joshua's little brother, Jacob, they'd broken his neck somewhere along the line.

"I need to see Zing." Beth began to cry—big, wailing sobs.

"We'll do what we can," Jesse said, his right shoulder moving forward, like he wanted to put his arm around Beth.

The matron came in then, hair pulled in a ponytail so tight it looked like it hurt. "Time's up, gentlemen," like her cue was to wait till the prisoner looked the most broken down, take her back to her cell then.

In the corridor David said, "Right now, she can't imagine taking a deal, can't imagine a life away from her comrades." A guard behind them, but David made a point of talking like he wasn't there. "Beth's father, he's our secret weapon. He won't want her to throw her life away. We have to find a way for him to see her more."

"Yeah, he tells her every visit how she has to get out for her child." For himself too, Jesse thought. His wife gone, he was an old man, alone in the world, though Leo Jacobs, walking morosely through Kings Point in his blue wool suit, all weathers, or even that once Jesse had seen him in his office, after Morris, he'd seemed alone already.

"We could try this one," Jesse said. "The appeals court might throw *all* the pre-trial testimony out. Tainted by hypnosis."

"You're dreaming," David said, brows raised, not smiling.

Jesse signed out at the front desk, got back a shopping bag with small gifts for Carol.

"Potential jurors," David said, "they called the defendants *garbage, fecal matter,* and *animals.* The jury consultant said it's the worst results she's ever gotten."

The guard behind the counter took David's pens and legal pads out of his briefcase, scattered them on the desk for David to put back.

"So we try for a change of venue."

"No, Jesse. What we do is, we work like hell to get a plea for her." He stopped, looked him full in the face. "I think you're having some trouble hearing me on this. Why is that, I wonder?"

Did he mean *Beth's an old friend of yours and that's got you confused?* Or, *you think you win this you'll get to be famous.* No, too much bite in David's tone—acid he reserved for one subject only: *race.* It was like a blow to his stomach. At the same time, he wanted to laugh that David thought he could work *that* particular mojo on him! Jesse stopped for a moment in the waiting room, looked over at his gray-haired mentor, one fucking eyebrow raised in theatrical wonder, like he was waiting for an answer. Fury came flooding over him.

David saw what crossed his face, but he couldn't possibly understand. "Why so angry with me, Jesse? Because I'm right?"

Jesse felt like an idiot. He couldn't say, *It's your fucking eyebrow.* In this mood, David would probably try to fold *that* back into race, too; like Jesse was annoyed to have a black man who was so much more aristocratic in bearing than he was.

Why did David want a deal so much that he was willing to play those cards? They got into opposite sides of the rental Ford, Jesse driving. He would take David to the airport himself, through that always jammed-up tunnel, maybe drop the rental off and go back, too. Or should he save the gifts for another time? Things had unfolded just like he'd imagined that night he'd dreamt of Mr. Voltage. So would Carol deliver the next line, say, *Give up this work or our marriage is over?* He threw some money in the corroded turnpike basket, decided he wouldn't go home until all the scratches on his face had healed. And until he knew what he wanted to say back to Carol when she delivered that next line. Could he stop being the Defender? Combing those transcripts, shaming those judges by getting their verdicts overturned, that was more than his work, that was *his worthiness*; probably his way to pay for the fantasy that he'd pushed Morris in front of the car.

Construction along this part of I-95 slowed things down to one lane, gave him time to think. But what came to mind was Susan Lems. *Was that what made David so desperate? Get a plea, free his ex?*

"No plea," Wergel said, Bobby barely settled into his leather chair, after ten pointless minutes in the waiting room. "Not for Battle. You can have the Jaffe woman, though." He smiled, so Bobby would know a favor had been done here. "I don't believe she doesn't know anything. But you can have her." Underlining: you are now in *my* debt. "But Battle murdered a mall guard and a cop. I wish we had the death penalty for that little shit."

Did Wergel believe he had the shooter? Made himself believe it, probably. A lot of outrage in the county about the cop's death. He'd better get a conviction for that, he wanted to be elected anything again, let alone governor.

"And we find the other guy, Shakur?"

"As my daughter would say, *I should care about that why?*" But Wergel smiled.

So he was full of shit, maybe even suspected who had done the deed. "And we find the rifle and the pistol Shakur used, his fingerprints on it? And it's his bullets that killed the cop?"

"Then maybe that's a different story."

"A better one, too. You should see this guy Shakur."

"Yeah?" Looking down at papers. "Why's that?"

"He looks the part. A nightmare. Give your jury a good scare." Already scared your witnesses, Bobby thought, so they can't remember him. "Much better movie with him as the heavy."

"When you have Shakur, the weapon, the bullets match," Wergel was saying, "then you talk to me. For now, no deal."

"It's not a done deal yet," the fat FBI agent said to Jeffrey—like he enjoyed saying it, too. "But look, we don't think you're in much danger anymore."

"Don't *think* I'm in much danger? Jesus!" Jeffrey stood on a street corner in Jackson, the phone pressed hard against his ear, like he wanted to crawl into it.

"The crew that shook you down, they were rogues. Your carcass belonged to another group. They'd been poaching. So no one's gonna do you on their behalf. And we've probably gotten all of them."

"Rogues?" What a jaunty musical comedy air this all had—*if you were in the audience.* "Probably?" That fucking word again!

The agent ignored that, or didn't hear it. Jeffrey looked around the suddenly menacing street. A pawnshop, glittery saxophones hanging in the window. No one about. Jackson not jumping at seven o'clock on Monday night.

"Yeah, it's probably safe to come back. You're gonna have to testify soon anyway."

Jeffrey hung up, fast-walked back to his empty bed at the hardly-a-Holiday Inn. The fight over how callous Johannus had been when Billy had robbed him of his subject had turned into Johannus saying, *I always feel you're judging me.* Plus *when I'm not hot for you, you think I don't love you anymore.* In sum: *I'm not sure I can put up with your particular combo of insecurity and judgment.*

They'd kissed and made up. But not really. Now Johannus was bivouacked with Jesse in Massachusetts. They talked almost every night, but Jeffrey was usually the one placing the call. And it had been weeks since the last *what are you wearing?* Johannus, after all, could oh so easily find others, probably already had.

He took a shower, stroked his cock while dreaming of Johannus taking him from behind. Afterward, in a terry-cloth robe, he ordered a club sandwich from room service. The Jackson night had nothing for him—other than biscuits, and he and Carol Kelman sometimes crying together about their fucked-up lives.

He liked the biscuits; liked Carol, too; sharp-eyed, witty; and she'd been more worried about Jesse than angry. "Trapped in the past," she said, "like all of you."

Jesse looked ashen lately, she said, haggard. "It breaks my heart, Jeffrey. You know he really is amazing. Doing good, protecting others, it's like . . ." She had laughed. "It's pathological with him. Look, no kidding, what he does, I know it really is the right thing to do."

Jeffrey had nodded. It always was. He had seen Jesse in front of a jury in Hellangone or some such place, a cracker who had killed a drinking buddy. While he spoke, Jeffrey longed for someone to care for him that much; but for that, he thought, he'd have to commit murder.

"You've seen him work a case. Well, I've met the others who do death penalty trials, and a lot of them have mirrors out, you know, to get a good look at themselves doing good. Not Jesse. He never, never makes himself the star of the show. Whichever guy he's trying to save, that's the one right at the center of his concern. He cares for those guys, which makes the jury think they should care, too. At least enough not to put them in the gas chamber." She looked into her glass. "I'm jealous sometimes."

"Who wouldn't be?" Jeffrey had been, in the sense that he wanted Jesse's concern. Or to be him, like when he'd seen Jesse talk to a committee of the Mississippi House in that mail-order suit of his—his costume that meant *simply true*—telling them it was plain wrong to execute the retarded, made them all lean toward his still, small voice. Impossible to hear him, Jeffrey had thought, and not agree—though the committee had managed it well enough.

"It's silly," Carol said. "It's like I can't get used to how wide his circle of care can be. I shouldn't be scared of what he does, Jeffrey,

I know that. I fight it. And I look at him now, too thin, his eyes some-times twitching uncontrollably, and I know that part of what he's wor-ried about is me." She shook the rue from her head. "But if I make him feel better, I'm helping *them,* and I can't stop myself, I *hate* them. I start to go to him, to stroke his cheek, and then I think, *No, don't. Maybe if he's upset he'll make a mistake and let one of them drop down the sewer.*"

"Wow," Jeffrey said, helping himself to more bourbon. "Carol Gins-berg Kelman, think of the power you have. *You* get to decide: Shall those men live or shall they die?" Like that might make her think it would be powerful of her to save them, too. Make the idea more attractive—save the marriage.

But that had all been before she'd found out about Barkely. *That* thought made the Jackson evening feel vast and empty, sucking every-thing good out of life.

He called Arkey, asked him to make one more try at getting Specs to broker a deal for him.

Two days and innumerable biscuits later, Arkey called back. Things were better for Specs. He thought he could help now. But he wanted the paint-ings Jeffrey had left, his Johnses, his Rauschenbergs and Hennessys.

"I can't do that, Arkey. I love them. They're going to be my career when I get back, the nucleus for my gallery."

"I don't get it. You love them? Or you want to sell them yourself? Anyway, Specs won't care. He wants to get even with you. He says you and Gaston fucked him over on prices."

"He says that?" Jeffrey said, stalling, sweating. They had, after all.

"I think Specs has already settled with Gaston. This guy told the cops that Gaston chained him up for days, made him piss in his pants."

"Probably true. But consensual."

"This guy lies probably, says he was forced—and I'll bet my brother-in-law made him rich for saying that. Your friend Gaston got charged with kidnapping. I saw him on Gabe Pressman, weeping. Which sur-prised me, I got to say. I thought Gaston would be a ferocious, macho hypnotist. But he looked like this small, plump, balding, *pathetic* man."

"I'll tell you, Arkey, things look different you have your hand on your cock," knowing damn well Arkey understood *that.* "A little Vase-line, a stiff dick, it makes the comic book come alive, right?"

"Gaston could get life, Jeffrey. You're lucky. Specs just wants your paintings. But he'll give you something for them, and he'll fix things for you, too, supposing there's something to be fixed. Otherwise, I'm scared for you, and more about Specs than those guys you set up. *He's definitely gonna get even.*"

"I thought you admired this guy."

"I was young. Specs was like a vacation from Grandpa Abe, from Torah ethics and guilt. Now I see more clearly. A killer is a killer."

But Arkey, buttoned up and down, was scared all the time anyway, maybe he couldn't judge this right. "You sure Gaston was set up?"

"How the fuck would I know?" Arkey sounded desperate. "Maybe Specs is taking credit for it to scare you. But it's your life. You wanna bet that?"

"No," Jeffrey said, trying not to scream. He had this image, Jesse Kelman in a suit whose pants hung too long on him, addressing a weeping jury, making a killer sound positively human. *His killer.*

"So, look, you want me to make this deal? Specs promises safe conduct back in the world. And he's gonna give you something for the paintings, after all."

"I do love them," Jeffrey said again. But he wanted to get to the trial. What would happen to Beth would be awful; maybe should be awful; but whatever it was, she knew he loved her—*he'd* bailed her, after all!—his presence there might comfort her. Mostly, though, he wanted to see Johannus. And he wanted to be sure when he did that no one would shoot him.

Arkey grew impatient. "Deal? No deal?"

No deal, Shakur thought, smiling broadly at the *Daily News. Those are my boys!* Even that skinny doctor with the floppy hands that they'd arrested for sewing him up, meeting Shakur had put some steel in him. But not the Betrayers, Beth Jacobs and Jacob Battle. They might stand with their comrades now, but it was too fucking late for them as far as Shakur and History were concerned.

He looked out the window toward the avenue, see if Priss had made her way back home yet. Nice street, cars both sides, small houses, little window boxes on some of them, geraniums and things, this the same block, Priss said, as the house Beth Jacobs and her idiot friends had blown up. "Better she'd blown herself up with it," Shakur had told Priss, "than have left me to die in the road like a dog."

But he'd settle with her. Maybe even order her boyfriend to do it. After all, Cane gone, Shakur had become the Supreme Commander. Or like Newton: Supreme Servant? That could be how he should sign the statement.

The statement had been Priss's idea—and a good one. "Let the oppressed know," she said, "the armed opposition is still alive in Babylon."

He looked over at those *troops* still sleeping on the couch, namely Butchie—you gave him a gun now, his arm shaking, probably he'd shoot his own dick off—and Monroe, smiling empty-eyed at the piles of newspapers these people had everywhere, Roe doped up as usual. Never any discipline to that man. Once upon a time, Monroe had sucker-rapped Jacob on the nose, that barbershop they'd hung out in. Would have gone on to give him a good beating, Shakur hadn't put a stop to it. Pity he had. Pity he hadn't given Jacob over when the little shit had scampered away through the traffic after that fucked-up Panther job. Shakur, people didn't think it of him, but he felt truly hurt by Jacob's betrayal. Jacob had helped him see the way imperialism fucked over Shakur, his family, his community. Jacob had been the first to let him in on Sugar's vision, too, see how if he joined the struggle, he had arms and legs fighting for him and his people all over the world, like one vein ran through all of them.

He'd always loved Jacob for dropping that knowledge on him, got the boy his first pussy, protected him from the cops, tried to cure his rotten lungs with his own skills. Shakur had felt that had made them brothers! But Jacob had run like a punk at the mall, no one even after him. He'd got a second chance, too, should have dealt with that bitch, made her come toward them when the police had him and Sugar pinned.

Shakur heard rapping on the door, peeked into that little spy eye thing. Priss it was, with bags of groceries. Looked like a fun house freak through the peep. Not only through the peep, for that matter. Tight little lips, no makeup, Priss not trying in a game she'd already lost. Probably jealousy made Priss such a snake with the other women. But she knew her place around the leadership, he thought, finally getting the last motherfucking lock to snap free.

"You get it?"

"The shit?"

Lord, that sounded stupid from her tiny mouth. "The *painkillers*."

He saw his words whip across her eyes: *Don't pretend you're one of us.* "Right. The painkillers. Yeah, I got them."

"Sack Eyes remembered what he owed me, huh?"

"Scared of you, too, I'd say." She smiled, proud of him.

"I'll fix later. We got to do that statement first. It's our priority." Because you have to prioritize, that's what Sugar used to say.

"Tell the world Beth Jacobs ran, huh?"

Jesus, he thought, have some perspective—Priss wanting to get Beth more than any other damn thing. But *he* couldn't be like that; he had to think about the future of the movement. Still, he saw the appeal there, too: tell everyone that whites, whatever they say, comes the time, they're motherfucking cowards.

On the other hand, he also wanted to frame Beth, maybe say she'd wasted the cop. Make her an example for whites, help them do better in the future. Put her and Jacob at the Brinks truck when the shooting started. Do them both that way.

He pushed Priss down in a chair by the kitchen table, with pen and paper. *Her* handwriting.

"*There will be no deal,*" he dictated.

"*. . . because we will never admit that the pig courts of the so-called Dis-United States have jurisdiction over the world's revolutionaries.*" Arkey gazed majestically around the wooden table, where the Band of Out-siders, like the English knights of yore, great trenchermen all, gathered to partake of ye British Pizza, renowned for its shitty Englishness.

"*We are deeply sorry for the families of the slain officers,*" he continued.

"Previously known as pigs and Bugs," Laura said, mouth full.

"*But this is no place for sentimental patchwork dolls.*"

"Huh?" Johannus said, turning his handsome head to the side. Gentle eyes, Arkey thought, narrowed now in theatrical confusion. "Whaz that? From an Oz book or something?"

"*Now we will free our imprisoned comrades by any means neces-sary.*" Arkey looked to Jesse, who shrugged—like maybe they would really try it, add to the body count.

"First time tragedy," Jeffrey said. "Second time farce. And third time, fourth time, fifth time equals what? Summer reruns?"

"You sound," Arkey said, "like their crime's against artistic tact. Shakur is . . . clichéd." He gave a fake grin. "Oops, I forgot. We all have to be nice to you now that you draw us."

Jeffrey, that is to say, had come back on the scene at just the right time, and with the right attitude. Warner had decided BillyBooks had "worn-out heroes." And worst of all, "it's sixties stuff." Also, *without Billy there, guaranteed, they weren't sure what they'd be buying.* But Jeffrey, the perfect Saint Paul, had gone to Mississippi to mock and had ended up the newest, last, only remaining believer in the Dead Letters and their suburban prophet—also the one with enough cash from Specs for his paintings to make a down payment on the company.

"It's what you should do, Jeffrey." Which, from Billy, had a certain force. After all, he'd seen their futures. "You'll be the new superhero who draws himself." General Gao's chicken, midtown Chinese. Billy as deft with chopsticks as with pens.

"If I could draw, I would be."

"You *can* draw," Billy had said. "I know. I taught you. But look, you know you don't have to do it the hard way."

Meaning *his way. The artist's way.*

"You can just write a story. We have people who can do the pictures. We have inkers to color them. Letterers to put in the words you write. Or mix and match, just do any piece of it you want."

You trivial dilettante. Still, Billy couldn't hate him, or he wouldn't be selling him the business, right?

Wrong, Sam had muttered. *He's selling* you *the business because you have the money to buy it, and Billy wants to make aliyah.*

Or do a geographical.

"And you don't feel like doing *any* of that, that's fine, too." Billy ran a piece of poultry through his tiny incisors. "Just manage the company."

"Then Billy," Jeffrey told the knights of the roundish table, "he went directly off to El Al and his new life. Though he writes me nearly daily, letters like lessons to me, Billy's Comics Correspondence Course."

"Why would *anyone*," Arkey said, voice ripe with envy, "go to Israel now?"

"Well, *that's* what made Billy go there, I think. Like not Israel triumphant, but Israel in difficulty, Israel self-doubting, self-critical."

"Israel rampaging through the Levant?"

"Right," Jeffrey added, "which means Israel reviled by American Jews like you."

"I can see it," Laura said. "You know, he once told me that same thing about his circumcision. The difficulty showed he really wanted to be one of us. He had a gentile mom, you know."

"Yeah? Anyway, it turns out they know who he is there, too. Billy Bad Ears AKA the Superhero Who Used to Draw Himself Before He Sold the Business to the Superhero Who Would Draw Himself If Only He Had the Talent. They gave Billy VIP privileges, let him go with the troops in Lebanon as a journalist. I think he dreams he might find a story there, you know, get his talent back."

Billy's letters from Israel had been pages from his sketchbook, with charming ornaments around the edges, like a corpse with a gaping wound in its chest, that black hole spiraling in and down . . . a blank-faced sniper in an apartment building window . . . a woman in European dress with blood dripping down her cheeks, her ear blown off . . . sleek Israeli jets dropping bombs on an apartment building . . . men pointing rifles at a family over an open cooking fire; and in the center of each page, small blocks of neatly lettered text, saying that what the IDF and the Phalangists, the Hamas and the Druse, the PLO and the Lebanese Army did in Lebanon terrified and repelled Billy. "Or maybe I just hate being pressed against the fence of the actual, hate anything actually *lived* and not just *drawn*. This war is too immediate, too confused and too brutal for *me* to make into art."

"How are you doing yourself, that department?" Arkey asked.

"Well, Billy's lessons helped me start this one thing." And heart a-pitty-pat, he took his mocked-up pages from the leather portfolio he'd gotten at Cross. Time to find out what his subject/audience, producers/consumers thought of his most lamentable comedy—

THE DEAD LETTERS
The Band of Outsiders
Confronts Its Greatest Crisis!

"And try not to get any pizza grease on the pages."
Arkey mimed carefully wiping his hands on his shirt.

> Long, thin fingers—
>
> A man bent over a page, writing with a long quill pen, his face barely visible in the dark.
>
> His eyes are closed! Yet his hand forms letters!!

"He's a Transmitter," Arkey said. "Right?"
Jeffrey smiled. "Just the way you imagined them, Arkey."

> Close-up on the letter:
> signed, BBE.

"Jesus, is Billy Bad Ears *dead?*" Arkey asked.

"Yes," Jeffrey said, "I'm afraid Bad Ears will no longer be with us. With the Band, I mean. Not in his papery form. My killing Bad Ears a contractual condition of the sale. Billy said the company couldn't be mine with that character hanging around. Really, I think he felt I wouldn't do justice to him."

"But will you do justice to *us?*" Jesse asked, smiling. Still, the word had a certain weight when Jesse said it.

They probably couldn't believe Jeffrey thought about *that* as much as they did; and maybe *more;* like heterosexuality and morality came in one package. "That clause in the contract," he said, "it makes me kind of uneasy now." There had been something in Billy's letters worse than whining, like Billy's grip on life had loosened, and he wouldn't be careful enough in that dangerous place. "The drawing lessons give me the shivers, too. Like Billy's in a rush to pass on his knowledge."

"Well," Arkey said, "he *is* in a battle zone."

"He foresaw other deaths, so why not his own?"

"He didn't *foresee* my brother's death," Laura said precisely. "He just guessed that he'd already been killed."

"But he also saw where he was buried," Jeffrey said. He didn't want to hurt her, but truth was truth.

"He said under tons of earth. I think you'd have to say it was likely my brother would be buried in the fucking earth, Jeffrey."

Jeffrey couldn't help himself: that was holy earth to him now. "But tons, Laura?"

Laura shrugged, poured herself another mug of beer.

"What does the letter from Bad Ears say?" Arkey asked. " 'How long, O Lord, how long do I have to march around northern Lebanon'?"

A candle next to the letter makes a halo—
enough to make out the writer's face:

It's the Sophist!

SheWolf pads through the door—

Her shocked face. "My God, he's transmitting!"

The blind Sophist addresses the envelope.
SheWolf reaches across the candles, and
THWACKS!!! him across the cheek.

He trembles like a man ripped from deepest
sleep.

SheWolf holds him close to her chest.

"So you're, I mean *he's*, like the first of the Band who actually transmits a letter himself?" Johannus said.

"And to himself? Or what?" avid Arkey asked.

"You'll see," Jeffrey said, savoring his first opportunity to wear the smug *artist's* smile.

> **Close-up on the envelope: For *Ninja B.,***
> *P.O. Box 111, Aspen, Colorado.*
>
> **The Sophist: "How did I know her address?"**
>
> **His thought bubble:** *Ninja B.—the first woman*
> *I loved! What has become of you? What are you*
> *planning now? Is this letter meant to guide you,*
> *to stop you?*
>
> **SheWolf's thought bubble:** *How will he bear*
> *being used? Will he drink like the others did? Or*
> *could he be that rare man who can stand being*
> *entered by a force stronger than himself?*

"After all," Jeffrey said, "not everyone can bear such an intimate relationship with death."

"An intimate relationship?" Arkey said. "I don't even want a first date."

"What's next?" Jesse said.

Jeffrey shrugged.

"Aw, man," Arkey said angrily—like a kid who wanted another bedtime story.

Success!

Or almost. Jeffrey had absolutely no idea what came next. Until he did, he guessed he'd just run the business—and do his shifts helping Harry Hennessy die from GRID. Or AIDS. Or who knows what. He had the feeling that Johannus—the two of them tenderly, gingerly, reunited—didn't like the way Jeffrey felt tied to an almost-corpse. Johannus was so vital, so healthy; and this disease was so strange, so Big City. He hoped anyway that Johannus would know how to arrange for the priest Hennessy said he wanted when the end came.

A black priest sat talking with a guy at the end of the row. Low voices, no other sounds, no monitors in a prison ward, like in a real hospital, no Mr. Ping and Pong to keep Jacob company in his pain daze. No nurses around either, except at drug time, when they walked the ward ladling out all the painkillers you wanted, keep you quiet, make you into a junkie. Then they could sell you the dope later, cull the motherfucking herd.

He didn't take anything, though. He'd told Beth that Sugar had gone along with Shakur's plan so Beth wouldn't go back for him. Really, Cane had told Shakur, a raging bull the day of the job, to fuck himself with that cull-the-herd shit. Then he'd begged her to leave them, to save his own life.

Which meant that I, Jacob Battle, killed Sugar Cane. That was the long and short of it.

So it *should* be agony for him to lie down.

Agony to sit up, too, it turned out. But in this position he could pass the time writing letters for the prison censors to black out—provided he didn't try to bend his head to look at what he'd written, provided, too, that he had anybody to write to, now that he'd killed Sugar Cane.

So he could doodle. *Was that like a curve?* He couldn't see past his own chin. *A crescent? Scimitar?*

Islam? *No.*

A machete, then? No, not another fucking weapon!

Well, that could be a tool, too—*Shango's tool,* Shango, draped with chains, carrying his curved knife, like in that picture in the Cuban place in New York. Shango, the protector and warrior. Kingly. Stately. Virile. *That* would have been the orisha who guided Sugar, if Sugar had deigned to have one.

Yeah, right. Hope too long denied, Susan would say, was making Jacob crazy now. That and the goddamn pain in his neck where the cops had broken the vertebrae, the process of mercy getting mighty strained with these people, it turned out. Eight fucking hours of surgery.

But this orisha shit, Susan, it's not what I believe, *it's what the people* need. Sugar become Shango. Sugar the hero, battling the cops at that crossroads.

No. No more of that gunslinger shit. Thing now is to save the school—what they'd been there for. And to save the school, Jacob had to save Sugar, change him from a coke-addled thug into a god. Which was what Sugar had wanted after all, with that *do a sin a day* shit, Sugar wanting that not from a big ego, Jacob would swear, but just to bear his life, like only a god was entitled to a man's ordinary appetites.

Shango the orisha, he'd once been Shango the Hanged Man, right? That's what Baba had said to Sugar with his eyes: *Do it, have some Shango courage, drop it now;* and the little kids listening not knowing this rap of Baba's a con job to lure their Sugar to his death.

And Sugar *had* stopped hiding behind that car door. He'd stood up-right, giving the pigs a clear shot at him. Why the fuck had he done that? To shoot Shakur? No, he could have nailed him just as well kneeling.

Did he do it to die at this crossroads, even in that janitor's outfit, put the lights out before he made a fool of himself one time too many? He wanted the kids to remember him a purer way, maybe. That stuff in blind pigs, that's not him, Jacob wanted to tell the kids, that was the coke talking.

So *good character* for Sugar, Shango-character, like what Baba hinted, it had become *no more character* for Sugar.

Sugar Cane knelt behind the car door, hiding from the police.

He stood upright. "*Ojo o buru, ebo nii gbe ni o,*" Sugar shouted.

He did that, yeah, just not in so many words.
Scrawl it down, your head fixed like a statue, not even seeing what you write, and go ahead, add:

I, Jacob Battle, heard him say that.

The man called Shakur grew furious at Sugar's words. But Sugar knew that "In days of turbulence it is sacrifice that saves."

So lift Sugar up into the pantheon. *With his brother Jacob?* Yeah, to build his school Sugar had gone into Roxbury, a more arid desert, he'd bet, than Mississippi, Sugar as much of a hero as Joshua. And Jacob had a big debt to pay to Sugar, the man who had folded him into his arms at his brother's funeral so Jacob wouldn't sink down into despair, folded Jacob right into himself and carried him out of there, to Africa and beyond. Then before he died, he'd saved Jacob again, shooting Shakur down before he reached the van. Sugar had done that, the man Jacob had killed with his "You go back there, we die."

She stopped.

"The money's to buy drugs."

Which it was *not.*

The man in the next bed moaned then like a son of a bitch, breaking Jacob's concentration. *He* probably needed more drugs, his chest swathed in bandages, but blood seeping at the edges, the guy barely patched together after a knife fight. "You can have my fucking drugs, you want them, you promise to shut the fuck up."

The man didn't say anything.

Hurt like a son of a bitch, but Jacob got the tablets over to the man's mouth, dropped them in. The man gulped, shuddered, but went quiet, eyes rolling up and closing. Jacob hoped he hadn't killed him, but he had work to do. He got back into bed.

It would be a terrible act, Sugar knew, to destroy the house that was his body. But he had been a great leader when his orisha had been strong within him. If he continued on an evil path, others might be misled by his example, and they, too, would use the witches' powder. Only by bringing his own house down could he keep his human part from joining with the *ajoguns*—and so save others who might follow him down this deadly path.

Sugar Cane, devotee of Ifa—not something the man would have liked, or not on that particular day anyway, those particular coke-circuits firing, Sugar then trying to be a Man of Steel, a Man Beyond Remorse. Another day, who knows? Anyway, he's gonna get to be a god, *Jacob Battle–style,* and that's that; an orisha for a good cause—to save that midget Basie horn section roaring around Delon's classroom, save that prig Xilixa and all the others.

Which makes me, Jacob Battle, the real power now, the neck-broken scholar, Jacob the artist, working with his words. The role Richard Hartman had planned for him, he'd bet, what he'd said, really, the two of them drinking that smoky tea, looking at pictures, talking about bar mitzvahs. Strange, but there'd been something good there for him.

Like dick? Well, now, he's had some experience, that didn't bend him out of shape the same way. He'd met other guys wanted to suck him off. Okay, *had* sucked him off. So what? Just not for him, not the end of the world. But fourteen, fifteen years old, what would he have said to the old man, *if* he'd asked? Thanks, but not for me? Nah, he probably would have kicked his ass downstairs. Just the way he had, come to think of it.

Which made him think of the time Hartman wanted to hit him, when Jacob had called him out on those lists of his. He could see Hartman had taken that harder than he had. He hoped it hadn't stayed with him. Given the number of people Jacob actually *had* hit, they could call it even. Thing about suicide, though, he couldn't tell him to call it even. He couldn't tell him to call it *anything*.

But he couldn't see any other way for Sugar to save his school. What a world, where the best thing you can do is let yourself be killed! But that had been the world Sugar had made for himself—with some white people's help, naturally.

So let's send little Sugar back to Ginen, the water beneath the earth that is also Africa, let him heal there, a year and a day, return to them as a spirit.

The bullets flew everywhere. Through bullhorns the police shouted to him, "Surrender!"

I, Jacob Battle, heard Sugar shout back, "Ka Maa W'orisa O! *Let us keep looking toward the orisha!*"

Jacob smiled, felt like he'd finally gotten to bring *his* warring orishas together here, Richard Hartman and Sugar Cane; used his Hartman skills to turn Sugar into Shango. This prose, though, he ever got to read it over, it might be a little too *plain* for Hartman's taste. *But it's the right tool for this job, Mr. Hartman, like your twisted sentences had been for yours.*

Nearby, I, Jacob Battle, saw Shango, machete hanging down beside his leg, his chest bare. Shango looked with fury from the police rifles to the policemen crouched behind the door of their car, their rifles firing at Sugar Cane. "It is not for *them*," Shango said, "to take Sugar Cane's life!"

And Shango, you better believe, he has some *big* muscles, like those paintings of a bald black man Jacob had seen in *Newsweek*, arms likely to burst the man ever used them, punk wet dream stuff. That painter, he could have been one of the guys sucked him off. Why not?

> Sugar Cane understood what he must do. He turned his back to the police rifles, turned toward the orisha of his head. Shango shielded him then, so the police bullets could not reach Sugar.

> Then Shango came toward him, and raised his machete. With one blow he severed the withered part of Sugar, the branches that the witches had snaked about. Shango did Sugar the grace of helping him offer this sacrifice to Shango.

Amazing how he could forget the agony in his neck for a while, making his own law like this, his own Sugar, his own history—close as Jacob would come to being godlike—or to speaking in a foreign language for *his* congregation.

> As Sugar started to fall to the ground, Shango opened his arms and gathered him up. He let Sugar's head lie against his chest. Shango breathed in the beautiful odor of Sugar Cane, breathed in Sugar's spirit, let him become part of Shango as he died, so he could return through Shango to help guide his people again, help them to make righteousness among the nations.

> The police stopped firing and wept to see this tragedy.

No, those sons of a bitches had taken batting practice on Jacob's neck.

> I, Jacob Battle, saw all this and was transformed. I saw that I had made a great mistake when I contemplated wicked deeds. Now Sugar in his sacrifice had made me see that it was the people of Roxbury, guided by their orishas, who will save the Malcolm X Community Center. *They* will make a world to nurture their children!

He wished he had the strength to do more drafts, make the language jump a little. But the guards saw this, they'd tear it up just to fuck with him, and if they ripped up his *masterpiece* it would hurt worse than their stomping his neck had.

So he had to find a way to get this the hell out of here. Maybe that priest, if he was still here?

"Catholic priests, too?" Bobby Brown said. His feet hurt already.

"Yeah," Olson said. "Babalawos, rabbis, priests, whatever." Olson having had the idea the Boston office should canvass all Roxbury residents in the God business, see if they knew where Shakur might be. "It's a God-loving community."

"I've heard." But the priests, Bobby bet, they would have heard precisely nothing. Anyway, this walk gave him a chance to talk to Olson about Jacob.

"You can still turn him," Olson said. They passed the storefront that had been the SNAP office in the long ago. A dry cleaner now. *Something,* at least. People stood in the street in clumps nearby, not moving much. So much dead-eye plywood on the windows everywhere meant nowhere to go. "You get something good, then we can give him a deal, maybe get a plea for him with Wergel, too."

"You're dreaming, you think Wergel will deal without Shakur in custody." Dreaming, or trying to con Bobby. Sometimes, when Olson talked, Bobby saw the younger agents rolled their eyes, like *Hoover's gone, but the people who believe that dwarf was six feet tall are still in charge.* Crew cut still, too. But Bobby's own boss deferred to Olson. The man had experience, he said, had weight.

"You just have to reassure Jacob," Olson said. "These guys, they say they've got principles, when what they're worried about is payback. Tell him his government will look after him. Tell him we have a special prison wing for informants. Most of all, use those sympathetic eyes of yours. Show that you know this is a hard choice for him. Show him you respect him for it."

"Right. I'll call him in the morning."

"And tell him you know he's doing this not just to save himself, but for his people." Olson turned, smiled back at him as he moved down the sunny, desolate block, showing the grin Bobby should use to flatter Jacob. But that shit-eating, condescending smile, Olson left it turned on just a little too long, like he was saying, *That's how we worked it on you, isn't it, Mr. Head Nigger in Charge?*

Bobby tried to return a *we're using each other* smile, but it faltered, Bobby not being so sure of that anymore. Anyway, that shit already hadn't worked with Jacob. Jesse Kelman had let him do one interview with him and Wergel, see what they could produce, Wergel naturally leading with "And we know you did that truck to buy cocaine to sell." You know, establish rapport, by saying, *Fuck you, you scumbag.*

"What makes you say that?" Jacob had said, polite in the best Dewey School manner, with its undertone of *you idiot.*

"Little birdie." Wergel witty as always.

"Little shit bird named George, right?" Jacob had made his skinny face look sour, like there was a bad smell in the room. "You know that man thinks he can fly? You put him on the stand, maybe my lawyer will ask him about that, huh?"

"Cocaine's a fact, though," Wergel had said. "Isn't it?"

Jacob had studied Bobby's face, like *what do I do with this man?* But Bobby had kept it smooth. His view: *Truth will out.*

"Yeah," Jacob had said. "It may have got mentioned. But Shakur said a lot of things, you know? He might have said we need money to make a black Disneyland, too, like Africaland or something."

The bad air had spread to Wergel's nose now, his big lips pursed in shit-smelling pose. "And you know where this Shakur is?"

"The fuck I do."

"It would be a good thing for you to know," Bobby said quietly.

"Yeah? Might be good to know. But I don't."

"You don't want to go down for those murders, Jacob, we got to have Shakur."

"That's not a promise, counselor," Wergel had barked at Bobby— fucking the play up royally.

"Somebody did those killings, Jacob," Bobby had said, staring at Jacob. "Shakur did them, he should pay. You didn't do them, you shouldn't. In a black world, a white world, a polka-dot world, that's how it should be."

"That man saved my life once," Jacob had said, mournfully, looking down at days of yore on the metal table, and Bobby had wondered, *like when had that been?* "And this ain't a polka-dot world," Jacob had said—the *ain't* not coming easily to him, though, drilled by Richard Hartman not *ever* to split infinitives, let alone throw that *ain't* shit around. "It's a white one. So y'all come see me when that's different, all right?" He'd stood up, hands shackled, but like it was up to him when the interview was over.

Bobby reflected how Baby still pulled a lot of loyalty with these people, while Olson headed across the street, toward a storefront soul cleanser—the very temple of African Bazzle-Fazzle Jacob had told him about, asking him to give a letter to the baba-who-hoo there. "And you give me?" Bobby had said.

"My gratitude."

Bobby had taken the envelope, forgotten about it until yesterday when Olson mentioned his God Patrol. Leave it to chance, Bobby had thought that morning, tucking it into his jacket. They run into Babaville, he'd give it up.

Olson strode off in this ill-fitting brown suit, white socks, made Bobby a little queasy to be seen with him, like back in this place, even his companions had to look *good.* Olson nodded and smiled to a woman pushing a folding grocery cart, like a politician working the crowd. The sign said TEMPLE OF THE MYSTIC PATH. Herbs? Drug deals? Bright reds and greens on the sign, secret handshake of the Republic of New Afrika. "What exactly is this place?"

"This? Used to be an after-hours club. My men say Willard Cane pistol-whipped a guy here, just to hear him yell. Not good for business, you can imagine. So now it's a church."

"Yeah, but what kind?" Bobby couldn't help it, these things embarrassed him; which meant, he knew, he had a ways to go.

"Santeria or something. Orishas, you know."

Bobby raised his eyebrows. He didn't know.

They entered a long dark room. Dusty streams of light fell from small windows set high in the whitewashed walls. A stage in front had five huge stone vases, turned on their sides, a little collection of things inside each of 'em, like kids' toys. Some colored gems or glass scattered up there, too. And could that be a dead chicken, feathers still on? A man knelt in front of a vase—really down on the ground, too, prostrate, flat as a snake. "Just a minute," the man said, not turning round, then something sounded like "*Ebo fin, Eru da.*"

Some African language? Afro-Am, when he'd done it, it had been about *here,* not enough in it about before the ships stole them—which absence made him feel like a perpetual babe sometimes. It's good, he thought, that his people had Africa now. He should find time, learn more himself.

The short man stepped down from the stage, long white beard and a mostly white dashiki, edged with green. "That means, officers, *the offerings are accepted, evil forces depart.*"

"I hope we're not the evil forces," Olson said, giving Baba the grin.

"You're Special Agent Olson," Baba said, most certainly not grinning back. He had a high, protruding forehead, made him look foreboding.

"We know each other?" Olson said—like he actually hoped it was true.

"I was in Mississippi, with Joshua Battle."

"I remember now. You still look like that kids' drawing. You know the kind I mean?"

"It's called a Topsy Turvy. Yes, I've heard that, Mr. Olson. A time or two, actually."

Funny, Bobby thought, on him the African clothes didn't look jive—or not *as* jive, anyway.

"We're here for information about a man called Shakur."

"I know." He crossed his hands over his dashiki—prelate-style. "You're asking all the men of God, I think."

"Look, I don't know if it'll matter to you," Bobby said, "but I think Shakur did both those murders."

The man nodded. His beard, a couple more feet, he could sweep the floor with it when he walked. But nothing Santa Claus about those eyes—piercing and sad at once, which mixed up to: bitter.

"So we find Shakur, it could help Joshua Battle's younger brother, Jacob. He's charged with the murders now." Bobby reached into his jacket pocket. "I forgot. I have something for you, from Jacob." He fished out the letter, noticed he hadn't bothered to reseal it.

Baba took the envelope, rolled his lips inward. "You read it?"

"That's part of my job, yes."

He went to a small wooden desk with a green phone on it, scribbled something down on a piece of paper, and handed it to Bobby. "I don't think you've checked there yet."

"Thanks," Olson said. "But look, I'm wondering. If we hadn't come by to ask you ourselves?"

"Would I have helped you?" The man looked over toward the—what were they—shrines? "I've been thinking about it."

"Casting the palm nuts, right?" Olson said. "And how much more thinking you think you would have done?"

Baba turned his head to the side a time or two, shaking that off. It made him look like a big-headed bird. "I hope I would have acted when the time was right. I think Mr. Brown's coming here to ask, bringing me that letter, means that it is."

On the way back to their car, Olson said, "I'll go with the agents and the local PD." Meaning he'd try to make sure Wergel got his live body, Jacob his chance. "Watch," Olson said, opening the door to the Dodge. "The street's gonna say the gods told him where Shakur was hiding."

"Really," Bobby said, opening his door, sliding in, "he probably knew it from when he and Shakur ran together."

Olson, driver's side, put the key in. "Yeah, except *really* I'll bet those two, they never ran together."

Not so mystical as all that—the address turned out to be the apartment of a white woman named, oh, a lot of things, but Priss most of all. Olson sent him a thick folder, supposedly with everything they got, to have a look at on the shuttle back to New York. A diary: the woman recording everything for history—or because none of it felt real to her till she wrote it down. Christ, *Upstairs and Downstairs*, wasn't that clever! Calisthenics before dawn. A diagram of the Wienie Man they'd robbed. Also a handwritten play about Joan of Arc, subtitled *The Virgin Who Trusted Her Vision*. "I am a woman who fights better than most men," she told the Dauphin, which must be French for Baby. "I am a girl who will struggle by any means necessary to save the oppressed." Which apparently mostly meant marking up Shakur's cartridges the way he liked, to add to the splatter.

Oh, good reading, all of it—especially the list of every one of her pals on the East Coast. He took out a ballpoint, made a note to call Olson, remind him he'd better be there with the cops for the arrest.

"Put your Social Security numbers there," the guard behind the Plexiglas said, shoving out two clipboards. Laura must have looked blank. The guard pointed to a black ballpoint on a chain.

They sank into anchored gray-plastic seats. The other people in the waiting room looked as strung out as Laura felt. Cigarette fog everywhere; probably people nervous about their adopted children visiting their bio-moms. Two battered vending machines offered jailed sodas and snacks for the visitors to bail out. This room was a dirty concrete-walled place that lay cut off from life, outside time; a special anteroom where the minor soul-sparks waited to return to earth, but mildly depressed instead of refreshed.

Stagflated, in her case; exhilarated that Bobby had come back into her life these last weeks, but terrified, too, by her own premature questions, like, would he accept Zing? Would he want a child of his own with her?

This go-round, though, the dread about the Imagined Child felt a little more bearable. What Bobby had said to her at their breakup dinner in New York had been all too true, she hadn't minded that he'd listened to the tapes of the warning call. Part of his job—and it had let him forgive her. So why had she gotten bent out of shape that he'd read her letters to Michael? Love and marriage and a baby carriage, that's why, all her worries that a child might harm her, that she would harm a child.

But life went on. No new attacks for years, and day by day she felt less worried about another one. Besides, she and Bobby were just dating again. She could see where it went . . .

"Kind of a train wreck, huh?" Arkey said.

"What?" She hadn't been listening for a while.

"Our relationship," Arkey said.

"More of a fender bender, I'd say." This room—the perfect *no place* and *no time* for them to admit that neither had cared that much about the other.

"Yeah, I guess I always felt I was a kind of placeholder for you."

True. She liked Arkey, but how seriously can you take a man who eats pennies? Still, a girl had to say *something*—not seem like a user. "And I for you, right? In between Gail . . . and Gail."

Arkey wore a black Stetson, even inside. Soon he'd probably cover himself with bandages all over, like the Invisible Man.

The white woman sat down opposite them, the shopping bag, it turned out, filled with shiny apples. Had she dreamed the guards would let them inside? Think what you can hide in an apple! Look what God had secreted there!

Arkey extended his legs on the worn linoleum—pretending they were long, probably. He wore corduroy pants, brown penny loafers, and brushed his hair across his forehead; except for the hat he looked like a perfect prep school kid—Semite subset. He had a sweet, inquiring gaze, too, truly interested in others, like they had clues for him on how to live, though he sounded a little too close to terrified bewilderment, like someone perpetually asking directions at a gas station in the Twilight Zone. Now, he looked around worriedly, then knocked on his forehead three times.

"Oh, Arkey," she said, fond again, "why so worried?" She rummaged in her purse for a candy bar. *Ah.* Arkey gave her a lean and hungry look, but the Baby Ruth was gone before the question could form. "It's Gail that's bothering you, I presume."

He hung his head. "Kind of, yeah. It was the weirdest thing, I mean she showed me this story she'd written about my grandfather, Abraham, and I told her it was full of shit, sort of."

Good for you, Laura thought. But she was trained to say, "Hmmm."

"In the story he's standing on the sidewalk outside this factory fire, the Circle Fire she calls it in the story. Really it was the Triangle Fire."

"Hmmm." Potato, potato, you ask her. But that wouldn't be Arkey the Historian's opinion.

"Anyway, there are women jumping from the window. And one of them, an old flame of Abe's, she floats down slowly and talks to him on the way. The floating woman, Anna, she tells my grandpa that she had wanted to sleep with him, he'd only had to ask. He wouldn't have had to marry her either. She would have done it for love."

"Ah, love."

"Yeah, love. Then she laughs dismissively at Abe, just the way you did. Which turns out to be the thing Abe and me fear most in the world, and the reason he'd never tried even to kiss her. She's still floating during all this, mind you. And then she looks at the ground and says, 'Well, what difference would it have made anyway?' "

"Is that it?"

He shook his head no. "Gail thinks that if you call the Triangle Factory the Circle Company," he non-sequitured, "that's a license to say *anything*."

"Yeah?"

"I called her on it, and she told me she changed things because she wanted to be there in my past, my family's past, the Jewish people's past, and if she helped things along, that made her feel like she was there. I went nuts. 'Help things?' I shouted. 'What help does history need? It is what it is. You're not helping things, you're just hyping them.' She just stared at me then, big eyes already tearing up. She said, 'I wanted to write stories for you, Arkey, about how you got to be the way you are. And it's never exactly just what happened that makes us the way we are, is it? It's our fantasies, too, right?' "

"Très freudienne," Laura said—to indicate that *she* would soon have the Institute imprimatur, while Gail remained an unanalyzed, uncertified child at this game. But Gail was on to something. Arkey recognized truth only in its Joe Friday *just the facts, ma'am* form. Gail's p.o.v. would be an affront to Detective Arkey; the buxom brunette saying history isn't economic rationality but people rushing about, moved by fantasies that transform and command them, make them flee or run forward, often not even knowing that they've dreamt.

A woman with lanky hair and a sharp nose came over then, to ask if they had a cigarette. Laura smiled, said, "No, sorry." To Arkey, Laura said, "What happened next?"

"Next she ran from the Pamplona. I think the waiter, you know, those guys in black pants, with their ties tucked into their shirts, he stared at her. Probably he wanted to follow her, get her number."

Ah, Gail the Irresistible. "Yeah, he melted inside but grew hard at the same time. Like an M&M."

"What?"

"Nothing. Look, I actually meant what happens next in the story?"

"Anna goes *kerplunk* on the sidewalk, naturally. Then Abe looks at this splayed and splattered manikin, and thinks how he could have fucked her without having to marry her. He decides he'll dedicate himself to the strike that's coming, show Anna that he can work as hard as she would have, make her regret not having slept with him, like it was her fault. Then he remembers he's talking to a dead woman and starts to weep."

"Oh," she said absently, having lost interest, like when you're ten and someone tells you a *Twilight Zone* episode; or, frankly, a dream—listening to such productions being her very own trade now.

"Abe did still feel special to me," he said, "still does. Like a floating woman *might* have talked to him or something. My fantasy Abe, part rabbi, part kindly Lenin, head of the fairy tale internationale based on Torah ethics, Abe the Allrightnick, a man as utterly convinced of his own fucking rectitude as our Beth. Thing is, I still compare myself to my fantasy Abe, and my life, Laura, it feels to me like nothing compared to his. Tawdry. Cheap. Unenduring. I guess I have to rededicate myself. The way he did. In the story, I mean." He smiled at her. "I haven't saved the workers from being forgotten. I'm not someone my grandfather would admire. Someone God would think He should save."

What should she say? *You are great?* Or, *Grow up, for God's sake?* So she tried, "Hmmmm."

"Right. Thanks."

"And the Talmud? That still help?" Laura asked.

Arkey shrugged. "The Talmud? Can't live with it, can't live without it." He looked over at her handbag. "Do you have another candy bar in there?"

"Sorry, no."

Recrimination poured from his eyes. "So it turns out she's the Story Teller, after all," Laura said.

"Right. And I'm OurKey, keeper of the kabala, seer of the future. Couldn't prove it by me, though, or I would have brought some quarters for the candy machine." He looked around for rescue. The woman handed some apples to two young black kids with round faces, short haircuts. Zing came out with the matron then, wailing, and the lady held out an apple for her, too.

As the car pulled onto Memorial Drive, Zing whimpered, woke up, looked over at Laura: *who's this woman and what's she doing here?* Then—as she so rarely did—Zing smiled. "I want to walk," she said, pointing across Laura and out the window at the river.

"Okay," Arkey said. "That okay, Laura?"

"Sure, that's great," though she felt drained from the visit; and from days when Zing was miserable because there would be no visit. Still, it was a sunny day, and a request for *anything* but a bedtime story was rare for Zing.

He pulled over to park, near Kirkland House.

"Michael Healy and I," she told Arkey, "we used to walk along the river near here. He'd explain physics to me." And to Zing, she said, "That's someone your mother and I knew before you were born." Which turned out to be a part of the historical record of no interest to Zing.

"Yeah?" Arkey said. "What's Michael doing now?"

"He's on probation and working with this company in Seattle. Microsoft, it's called. He doesn't do physics anymore." Or have visions. His, hers, theirs—oh, visions, they were scattered like mica on the sidewalks then. She looked out at the spangles on the river, the scullers floating by. "No more waves, no more particles. But lots of stock options."

"Yeah?" offhandedly, Arkey still in a mood, she knew, to think that money wouldn't be as good as the secrets of the universe. Or another big thick square book to hurl against the bourgeoisie, make justice for the workers, make him dream that Abe & God approved of him.

"And Gail," Laura said, speaking of hearts' desires. "I guess she wants you back, huh? I mean I see her at all of Beth's hearings."

"Nope. Gail doesn't even much want to talk to me anymore. It's Beth she wants."

"She *wants* her?" Well, she'd kissed her once. With tongue.

"Not like that. Well, like that, but different. She wants to write about her." He smiled. "What a time Gail would have with the letters, huh?"

"She knows about them?"

"Not from me." He had a loopy smile; probably it made him happy to hold Zing's hand. It would have made Laura happy, too. "She's even worked out some way to visit Beth in prison," Arkey said. "Gail, she'll get Beth to talk about the letters, and then you guys better watch out. She'll snatch your souls next."

"Snatch our souls or your material?"

"I'm not writing about that anymore. Never actually *wrote* anything except a hundred titles. When I got to *Send in the Clowns* I gave up."

"So you don't see Gail anymore?"

"Gave up on that, too."

He deserved a pat on the back, so she gave him one.

He smiled over at her. "I'm wooing Kate again."

Zing—could it be?—reached out her hand to Laura, that soft, sweet thing.

"Kate's forgiven you?"

"Not hardly. But sometimes she comes to synagogue with me, which

I take to be a good sign. She won't sleep with me, though." He looked down at Zing, strangely quiet still, but not seemingly unhappy. "Sorry."

"That's okay, I think. Sleep with means sleep with, you know?"

"Me and my mom sleep together sometimes," Zing said, stopping everyone's heart for a moment.

"We could sleep in the same bed tonight, Zing. You want to do that?"

She nodded. Laura's heart gave some loud thumps. "Yeah, well," she said to Arkey, "it could take a little while for Kate to trust you again, huh? One or two lifetimes, say?"

"But it's got to be a good sign she says she understands now about my wanting her to convert. She says she really sees how it's part of my fear. About my cancer, I mean."

Laura laughed. "Doesn't she know that everything you do is part of your fear?"

"Right. I'll make a point of mentioning that to her."

"Anyway," Laura said, "that could give her a way to convert without feeling she's giving in to the chosen people, mystical part. Instead, she'd be doing it to help you."

"Converting to Judaism from pity for the Jews. Or the Jew, anyway."

"What's cancer?" Zing said.

"It's something that makes people not feel good," Arkey said. "Like when you have a stuffed nose."

"Yuck."

Soon, Laura thought, Arkey would be tucked in beside Kate again, the difficulty of observing the mitzvahs substituting for Gail's fairyland whippings; the pain letting him know God exists—instead of Gail. Him and Billy and Jeffrey, they all liked it hard. And her? Would she be tucked in with Bobby? *That* would be hard, indeed.

"Zing me," Zing said.

"What's that?" Arkey asked.

"Swing your *arms*," Zing said, like, how stupid could these - people be?

Arkey got it right off. "One, two—" and on "three" the two of them swung her in the air. Laura was slow on the uptake, though, and Zing's body sideways swayed.

"No!" Zing shouted, her voice on the edge of tears.

They quickly tried again.

Success! "Again," she cried. And "Again!" And "Higher!" This the first relaxed time that Laura'd ever had with Zing. Maybe having a man around helped? Laura looked out at the river, Cambridge like a very heaven to her again, the way it had been when she and Michael had strolled here scattering quanta.

And look how that had turned out! "Kate'll take you back, Arkey," she said, as if wishing someone well might chase the bad luck away. "She loves you."

"Impossible. Why would she?"

What did men want to hear? The size of the banana, probably. "Underneath all those tics and lucky charms, you're a decent guy. Probably she thinks you'll make a good father." Then she turned to him and smiled over Zing's nearly backward-falling body. "I think you will, too."

And Bobby Brown? For the adopted daughter of Beth Jacobs? Like Beth would let her prosecutor raise her child! That made the air go out of Laura—heaven and hell, they were mighty close together since Zing had entered her life.

Arkey looked stung, too, like *good father* had been the booby prize. But he gathered himself. "Kate and me talk a lot after services, and I swear, it's like she's getting something out of it I don't. Like she could show *me* the value of this, I don't know, more daily Judaism."

And implied: *without such heroic messianic shenanigans as raising the sparks of someone's dead brother.* Like *that* had been her fault—all of them believing Billy so *she* wouldn't feel so bad about Frank's murder. Or to get in her pants. "We ought to go home," she said. Zing got cranky if dinner came after five.

"You're going to make a good mother," Arkey said.

Well, no booby prize there as far as Laura was concerned. "God, I hope so." But she couldn't believe it. There wasn't enough to her. She'd never found the Knowledge Stone.

Then they all seemed to observe a moment of silence, Laura thinking how her motherhood, good or bad as it might be, depended, after all, on Zing's own mother spending the next umpteen years in a cramped cell.

Priss prayed he'd come out alive. But Shakur would never allow that if it meant the pigs got to put him on display in a cell, like a zoo animal. She took a few more steps backward, until she pressed against the wall of the brownstone opposite, under a window ledge. FBI men—big white letters on their jackets, in case you couldn't smell the pork—counted off and swung the ram into the door. She heard the wood splinter. More pigs poured up the steps in bulletproof vests that looked like umpires' protectors, pump-action rifles forward. A frontal military assault—which was the least the man deserved.

The shots—hundreds of them, like whining metal balls slamming into a huge iron bucket—made her run toward the avenue. Lights snapped on, people probably calling the precinct to tell the police about . . . the police. Confused, she stupidly ran two steps back across the street toward the smashed door, like she had to see who they'd bring out on the stretcher. One of them, she knew, would certainly be that brave giant of a man. She wanted to kneel next to him, stroke his cheek, turn his face to the side.

She stopped, started back toward the avenue. Monroe if he hadn't been in the apartment tonight, then he'd be back at his place. She realized then that if her train had gotten in a few minutes earlier, *she'd* have been there with Shakur and Butchie. She trembled with relief, then felt like she'd done it on purpose, abandoned Shakur in his last moments, left him like Christ at Gethsemane.

She walked faster—to keep from falling apart with fear and guilt. Meanwhile, her fingers searched in her pockets for coins for the phone. Plans had to be made. Vengeance had to be exacted in response to this monstrous crime.

· · ·

"I told you," Wergel nearly shouted into the phone that morning, "I'm not *ever* giving Jacob Battle a deal. He did the crime—"

"He does the time. Yeah, I've heard that one." Bobby, in his New York office, looked down at the gridlock. He hadn't been notified about the raid, and he felt damn sure Olson hadn't bothered to be there—the man bullshitting him like the others. Olson must have figured it by now: the Downstairs had been a "network" of two junkies and a whacked-out Joan of Arc. So why save Shakur? To tell him what? Or Jacob—he had nothing to trade either. That morning he'd gotten a memo from his boss: *Battle's a county matter. Let's leave it alone until they're done.*

"Your Jacob Battle is a stone-cold killer," the Wyndham County DA said over the phone. "I told you that how many times? He did both the mall guard and the police officer."

"What if we find the gun, can link it to Shakur?"

"Yeah, sure," he said. "You find the gun, you link it to Shakur, then we'll have something to chat about." Cold day in hell, his offhand tone added. "I got to go now. My other phone's ringing."

Shoes rang in the the corridor now. The lawyers, probably; her father's footfall would be light, an aging luftmensch, a vapor walking. David Watkins had had him made part of her defense team, so they could visit more—but this open crapper, a single bed stuffed with straw; his seeing this place, *smelling* this place, it shamed her.

"*Der weiche Gang geschmeidig starker Schritte—*" her father said as he entered the tiny overheated cell.

"*Ist wei ein Tanz von Kraft um eine Mitte, in der.*" Then, all too quickly, she added—for the others' benefit supposedly—"He paces in cramped circles, over and over. Like a ritual dance around a center. That's it, more or less."

The test passed, they embraced. The other interviews had been through Plexiglas. This was the first time she'd felt her father's arms around her for eleven years. He had grown downward toward death, and his head lay at the level of her breast. She looked at his mottled scalp, his sparse gray strands, the years he had left, and she cried. *Like Zing would cry*—reminding herself she had a baby, couldn't be one anymore.

She picked up his hand in hers, started to trace the path of the blood through veins grown bulbous, rubbery, weak. The bull stuck her head in, shouted to let go of him. Beth felt the tremor in his body.

That left them with a riddle: all the people crammed in this shoe-box—Beth and her father, Harrison Baker, Jesse, and David Watkins—

how could they avoid touching each other? She and her father stood with their arms at their sides; the lawyers sat on her bed against the wall, like three monkeys.

"Shakur's death—" David said.

"His murder," Beth corrected.

"Yes, most probably so, his murder," David Watkins said to the air in front of him, "it means they'll want you that much more. If we have to try this case, then we've lost it already."

"On the other hand," Jesse said quietly, "if we go to trial, then without Shakur, you and Jacob don't make such convincing villains."

Her father tilted his face upward toward her. How cloudy his eyes had become! "You see, darling, Mr. Kelman believes you can win your case. Think about your beautiful daughter," he said—with a murmurous undertone only she had been trained to hear: *and why didn't you think of her before?*

"I did think of my daughter," she said. "I wanted her to be proud of me." She'd wanted *him* to be proud of her, too, insanely enough.

"Look, if we can plead this, get a reduced sentence for you," Watkins said, "you'll be with your daughter that much sooner."

She and her father, less than a foot from Watkins in the cell, looked at him then the way they'd probably looked at her mother: *What are you doing here? In our solitude?*

So the lawyers reciprocated in kind, talked about what to do with her as if she and her father weren't there.

"Even if we go for a plea," Jesse said to Watkins, "we have to at least threaten a defense, David."

Watkins raised a brow, but nodded curtly.

"They have a witness to her renting the van," Harrison Baker said. Cancer of the larynx meant a new voice box, made him into Mechano-Man. She tried to hear the remnants of the reedy Southern voice that had tried to dominate her at the SDS house in Somerville. He'd failed, though; she'd had the clearer vision of the future. Now, his voice gone, he would plan her fate. "The clerk remembers her because Snake said they were shooting a pet food commercial."

"Instant coffee," Beth said. Her father smiled at that—though he must really think her mad.

"Not good," the Machine That Had Been Baker whirred. He had lost his voice and most of his hair, too. "But Beth hadn't heard what her husband said."

Actually, she'd been grateful for it. Guilt had turned her into a stuttering fool that day.

"She might have thought they were going to move some furniture," Jesse contributed.

"She would have been surprised when Jacob showed up empty-handed," Harrison whirred.

"He was bleeding," Beth said.

All three lawyers stared at her—like surgeons, if an anesthetized patient had started talking after they'd begun handling her heart.

"Right. She'd be shocked when he showed up bloody," Jesse said. True, but a lie, too, when you put it that way. These obfuscations, they more than misunderstood her, they cloaked her past in acidic fog that ate away at it, made it and her disappear.

"She didn't think about why the police might be there," Jesse said. "She made a bad decision, but all she meant to do was get him to a hospital."

"You forget," David Watkins said, sourly clasping his hands across his chest, "that the other whites plan a political defense. Your construction, you'll have to get Snake to go along, say she thought she rented the van so they could pick up furniture, though *he* knew better. It is *very* unlikely he'll agree to that."

Actually, Snake *might* do it. For Zing. But most of all, so Beth Jacobs would become *the dupe who had lived with Snake*—the white man who hadn't broken ranks with his comrades. That would be the cost of being with her child and her father again.

And the idea of *not* being with Snake, *not* standing with the others anymore, it made her feel weak. Before reason even, there was this: she couldn't go through the trial and jail alone. And to be with people like these who didn't understand anything of what she'd done, why she'd done it, *that* was alone, for real.

That made her tremble. The way she felt this moment, it wouldn't matter if she got out of here. She couldn't take care of Zing like this, she couldn't even hold her pee, she couldn't feed herself.

"Look, David, worst case," Harrison twanged, "we say that once she fled, she wasn't part of the conspiracy anymore."

"They won't be able to say precisely when the man was shot," Jesse said. "Maybe it happened long after she'd gone."

"I saw him shot."

"We won't call her," Harrison said.

"It's my life," Beth hissed. "I'm not ashamed of it, and I won't let you lie about it."

That made the monkeys stare; and she could feel her father shrinking inside himself. But she had to set this right and stop the ferocious pounding in her chest. "I can't be part of this charade you people call justice. My comrades and me, we're going to do the only thing revolutionaries can. We're going to get in the world's face and tell the goddamn truth."

"Don't be too concerned by what she said yesterday," David Watkins said to Leo as they sat waiting in the conference room. Watkins' voice was soothing, instructive, slightly condescending—a tone Leo knew well; it was so often his own. "It's as if she's waking up from a trance. She feels bewildered, helpless. So she flails about, screaming, terrified of being alone. That's why it's so important that we see her again immediately. We have to become her new comrades, her new society, her new—"

"Family," Leo said, tired of the lecture. Besides, Watkins wanted her to plead her case. It would be a decade before she was released then. Kelman was the one who saw things more clearly, who knew she could go free, be with him now.

Beth, if infant, had language already, and began to speak even as the guard led her in. "You have to understand, Dad, I can't let them make a joke of everything I've done in my life."

She sat across a table from Leo, steely—but like a child, as Watkins said; his daughter at ten years old, accused of having been cruel to a teacher.

Accused of murder.

"You're right, darling. It won't be quite the truth. But don't you have to do whatever you can to get out of jail, be with your child?"

"I'm not ashamed of what we did," she said.

Not responsive. Which meant she *was* ashamed. Or so he hoped.

"What I did, Dad, is I worked to make justice for the oppressed. So there will never be another Auschwitz."

He took his glasses off, trying to keep himself busy, keep himself from shouting, *In what way could you possibly imagine that leaving two families without fathers would prevent another Auschwitz?* He didn't want to anger her. He wanted to show her she could be free again, so they could search out work for her that might help others and help her bear the remorse she'd soon feel. *That,* he knew, was the reason she needed to stand with her fellow conspirators; they needed to lie to each other, reassure each other that they had acted nobly, or she, at least, would be crushed by what she'd done.

"Can't bear to look at me anymore, eh?"

"Oh, darling, no." Hurriedly, he put his glasses back on his nose.

"My dearest wish is to see you every day for whatever life I have left."

"I tried to become what you wanted, Dad, can you believe it? The special daughter of a special father, a leader of the revolution."

This decaying room, he thought, this prison, *ah this is so very special, darling!* But the cream of the jest was that his insightful child had most likely gotten it right. He might have sent her out into the world in just that way—not in words, precisely, but with a thousand unconscious gestures, *be special for me, justify my having survived the camps.* He bowed his head—like one wolf showing his neck to another, wanting to put a stop to the battle. He'd lost her, he knew. She would go back to her comrades and their political defense, their certain sentences. He closed his eyes again, to keep from weeping.

When he opened them, she stood in front of his seat, holding out her manacled arms to him. But a guard came in immediately and yanked her away.

Back in her cell, alone, Beth hated herself for making her father cry. But she'd told the truth: *He'd* sent her to make justice—his Valkyrie.

So she was "just following orders"—not from the Reich but from her father?

Too true. Though what had made her understand *that* had been Billy Green's death. Billy hadn't been able to draw her father and the camps; so he had had to heal the wounds of the Holocaust by building the Zionist entity. *But it had been her father's wound, not his.* For her, too. Each of them set on a mission by Leo Jacobs.

Then, a rainy day near an abandoned village some soldier shouted, "*Not there!*" and Billy's hearing really had been Bad Ears quality; or thunder had blotted the words out; or he had been thinking about a drawing; or he didn't understand the Hebrew. Or maybe, like Jeffrey had said, the sheer pointlessness of it had overcome him, and he didn't want to live anymore.

She wept for Billy then, remembering their first night together among the moos. She'd been sure he would come like a rocket, but instead, before he entered her, he'd gazed at her and slowly moved his index finger along the edge of her chest, her legs, her face, tracing her outline over and over, drawing her for the first time. Now he'd died at the hands of the Palestinian Revolution—her hands, in a way.

But Billy's absence was a *disaster* for her. Jeffrey wanted to do right by her, but nobody would care what Jeffrey did; he'd never transform her, or any of them, in a way that got them more right than life did. So frame by frame, Jeffrey the Sophist would morph into Jeffrey the Nearly Bald, Jeffrey the Comic Book Entrepreneur; OurKey would wear chinos and loafers instead of his starry blue robes; all the Band of Outsiders would become ordinary suburban kids.

But that very diminution made them look so vulnerable, too, so fragile, Beth almost wanted to protect them. After all, a mine could rip a person out of life. Or a pipe bomb. Or a huge jack-in-the-box in a janitor's suit who pops out of the trunk of a car. Her father, a frail old man with monstrous liver spots on his spidery, arthritic hands, no one could say how much more time he had. Or how many moments *she* had, how many more chances to cook breakfast for Zing, read her one of those bear books, wipe her bottom, get her to bed at night. A few moments— that's what it all really came to.

So she had to get herself out of here, had to be with Zing, and the person she loved as much as Zing, the one who, when they weren't gnawing at each other's vitals, made her feel least lonely, most complete; and even, for as long as they talked, less guilty. She felt the full force of how much she wanted to care for him, nourish him; and she felt too, how utterly wrong that feeling was; how immature. Unhealthy. Inappropriate.

No. Yes. No. Beth rings the Beth gong.

The sink, the walls, her life, shook in front of her. She leaned against the wall for balance.

Jesse Kelman had seen Dr. Jacobs' face tremble as Beth shouted at him the day before—all her actions his responsibility somehow. He looked dizzy, battered. Today, though, Dr. Jacobs sat on the cot, seemingly at home in this little toilet of a cell. Jesse busied himself by the sink, so they'd forget he was there. Maybe her father could keep Beth from throwing her life away. Jesse didn't want her to "make a statement." He didn't want her to take a plea, either. David had it wrong. He could win this. So he hadn't told his partner about this interview. He wanted things to run their course between father and daughter, let her feel more how much she wanted to get out of here, be with her family again.

Though he hadn't exactly expected this seminar on gnosticism, Beth the Scholar saying, "The idea, Dad, is you start out eating lobster and you see that nothing happens to you."

Her father had crossed his stick-figure legs at that, actually smiled at her, brown stubs pointing every which way. "I've done that, yes."

With those teeth? Jesse thought. He looked down at a yellow notepad that he rested pointlessly on the sink, tried to pretend he wasn't there. Actually, to the two of them, he clearly wasn't.

"After lobster-size sins you're supposed to do adultery, but I couldn't manage that one." Like she wanted her father to know she robbed bank trucks, but she'd always been a faithful wife to the redoubtable Snake. "Then you're ready for the advanced course."

Her mockery meant to hide shame that she'd once believed this crap? Or that she still did?

"Which would be Brinks trucks?" He wanted to win her back, but he was still her father.

She nodded, eyes wide, younger somehow.

"So, it's only that wretched Moses who makes us weak? Without that Law, we'd be virile, decisive? I remember now. It's Jacob Frank, eh?"

Who was who when he was at home, Jesse wondered, though naturally Beth and her father both seemed to know.

"Sugar said the true God wanted the elite to do all the so-called sins."

"It's called climbing the *keritot*. Those are the worst."

Beth smiled, delighted that her father had been there before her, wherever it was. Company, Jesse guessed, that was the key here. David was partly right; if they were going to split her from her comrades he needed to find new companions for her, who understood her heart. Her father that would certainly have to be; Jesse had only a distant idea what they were talking about.

"Sugar said that if you can do the sins wholeheartedly, you know, unreservedly, a spark blooms inside your head. You and God become one."

"What a great responsibility! So much to oversee!"

Beth laughed. "Yeah, I guess so. Sugar, come to think of it, he sounded like you. God maintains the universe, Sugar said, and we should do the same. That's like you're saying we should tend the whole that made us, right? It means the elite have to be like God, have to do what people call sins, too. After all, God feeds the lamb to the lion."

So, Jesse thought, *I'll tell the jury that's what they'd been doing at the mall: feeding lions.*

Beth's father reached into his jacket, took out a pillbox. Should Jesse offer him some water? But that would mean incarnating himself. Dr. Jacobs shook a pill out, swallowed it dry.

Beth lifted a brow.

"The pill? For my heart, eh? Just mild angina."

Exacerbated by whacked-out theology. Still, angina or not, the two of them loved talking together. Like as long as they did it, they couldn't even smell the pervasive odor of Beth's shit that wove itself into Jesse's gray suit.

"Do you think Mr. Cane believed all this, dear?"

"I don't know. He probably believed for as long as he told me about it anyway. Or maybe he mixed it together *for* me. Like a tranquilizer. So I could do what needed to be done."

Needed? Jesse could have sworn Dr. Jacobs trembled from the effort of restraining himself.

"On the other hand, Dad, it's true what Sugar said, whether God makes sparks bloom inside you or not. It's true even if God is dead, eh? *Especially if He is.* I mean either you make your own laws, or the ruling class writes its laws on your body. Look at this place! Look at that horse collar they put around Jacob's neck. They can do anything they want to him."

"Or to you," her father said sadly.

"Exactly. Or to me, comes to that."

He smiled again with those hobgoblin teeth. "It's all so much spilt Nietzsche, darling." He rubbed his cheek with a withered fist. "Not much worse than the original, mind you."

"Spilt or still in the bottle, Dad, that doesn't change anything. The question is, *their murders or our killings?* To enslave people or to liberate them?"

Jesse had to admit, he was enjoying this a little. And he'd bet it would work toward his ends. Like, the two of them, they felt free to say *anything* to each other—*as long as the conversation kept going;* then the sentences meant they valued each other beyond anything else, no matter what they said. They wouldn't want the talk to end, would they?

But Leo *had* just stopped speaking; not angrily, Jesse would swear, but as if he were already listening—like he could hear what she couldn't yet: *the thing she'd say next.*

His calm, his silence, it seemed to let Beth fall inward for a while. "This is just a way of not having to feel things." A quiet voice, Jesse wasn't sure he'd heard her right.

"To feel what?" her father said, but as if he already knew.

"I left Zing. I left my child! What I did, right or wrong, it put me in this place, Dad. This place where *they* dictate to me, *on* me. I did this thing, and they do or don't have justice on their side, so fucking what? I did this thing where they can take my child from me!" She wept. He got up and put his arm around her; they even got to hold each other a moment or two before the bull came charging in, nearly broke the man in two pulling him off.

Beth screamed like she'd put a knife in her.

Jesse said, "Miss, that man is seventy-eight years old. He's no threat to anyone."

"You don't know what he might be passing to her."

"I promise they won't touch each other again."

The bull backed off a step.

"I want you to do it," Beth said to Jesse, not crying anymore. "I want you to put on a defense for me. Get me the fuck out of here."

Victory—which allowed him to have a voice again. "I will, Beth. I'll take care of you."

She looked at him, became the child he'd met a thousand years before on a sailboat in a place far away. She turned then, started to take her crying father in her arms, but before Jesse had to say anything she remembered where she was and let her hands fall helplessly to her sides.

After dinner that evening, Laura and Bobby Brown walked up Brattle Street toward Laura's apartment. Laura, her mind in Lebanon, felt utterly helpless and bereft. Five-foot-two Billy Green, she thought, with his ghastly school report and those talks of his about raising Frank, had formed her more than father or mother. He'd made her Famous Among Adolescents, had even made her feel what it would be like if her life mattered, if she made justice—comic book justice, anyway. Which had done what? Made her actual life feel like a somewhat shrunken thing!

She took Bobby's arm for comfort and protection, the Cambridge night filled with land mines, autoimmune diseases, and baby-sitters. This would be the third time she'd ever left Zing with anyone. A substitute teacher from her preschool, for God's sake, a Master's in Education! No, no one would take Zing from her except Beth—and the reason would be the very man on Laura's arm.

Billy's death, it made her see how important every decision a person made could be—and this one, Bobby and her, it had to be wrong. So everything had to be over between them. Again. And that felt like a foretaste of her own death.

Death? Come on now, after what had happened to Billy, that had to make her smile at her own melodrama—the Weepies her version of Bobby's annoying third person.

Bobby stopped, looking over at a huge house on Tory Row, pillars holding up a portico facing a wide, evenly trimmed lawn, lovely in the last light. Money made into grass, Arkey had called the golf club greens—a dig at his father, the salesman, the *successful* salesman.

"You know," Bobby said, "I used to play football."

"Yes, darling, you know I know *that*. It's Laura here, right?" Moods like this, she became a projection screen for him.

"I loved the game, but you get to college, even at Harvard, it's about doing some damage."

"Winning's not everything, it's the only thing, right?" she said. "I have this emaciated nervous bum, he dresses in surgical masks, you know, like the Haunted Desperado, and he always says that to me. Then he adds, 'Those are the words I live by.' " She'd had to take a long leave from the clinic, prayed the Desperado was all right. "The man's a homeless junkie, so I think the slogan didn't do him much good."

"Yeah, and it doesn't make much sense syntactically. But what I'm trying to tell you, you give me the chance, is that the game of football's not mostly about the highest score, it's about hurting someone. I was a running back, but even then, it's about the flat-out joy of humiliating someone, not just scoring yourself but running them out of a job. Best of all, though, was helping some lineman put them in the hospital." He stopped, looked at her. "I have that in me, Laura. I do."

Did he want to tell her he'd be going full bore after Beth? Like Laura had to respect him, accept who he was, where *he* decided to go? "Everyone has that, Bobby. It's good you know it's there, I think. Then you can look at it, use it properly." Not be vengeful to Beth, she meant, but *just.* Whatever *that* was, when your best friend's been part of two felony murders.

"Football, basketball," he said, "we're from Africa, so we play them our way. But the thing we're playing, it's American. It's like a baby with its mother, you just can't help loving her, right, and you can't help loving where you grew up, no matter how shitty it is. We're here, and what Beth did, all the guns on the other side, it doesn't scare anyone anymore—not to change anything, anyway. And it sure isn't overthrowing anything. So it has *got* to stop."

She took his arm—show she agreed. How could he doubt that?

"This job, I've been learning a lot. I've got a lot of places I can go from here. Defense work. Politics, even."

She could feel it: *Congressman Brown.* Senator even. He had that energy in him; charisma. Like another Bobby. But she'd bet he couldn't forget his past the way that Bobby could. She stroked his arm. Billy's death shadowed her still, suffused her chest with a melancholy seriousness. After all, who knows how much time anyone has? An unheard shout and your life explodes forever. Maybe she couldn't go all those places with him, but she longed for them to be together for however long they could.

But as they turned up Appleton, the feeling evaporated. *Be together for however long they could?* Those were always a woman's famous last lying stupid words before she fucked the guy. Really, she would sleep with him tonight, and then she'd want him again and again, had already fallen in love with him, would be heartbroken if he didn't call the next day, if he didn't want to be with her just as much as she wanted to be with him. For how long, Lord, how long? Oh, say, *till death do us part.* "Come back to my apartment."

"Thought that's where we were headed."

"Oh, right."

"Where's Zing, by the way? Seems like a sweet child."

Not much, but at least he didn't say the apple doesn't fall far from the terrorist tree. "The sitter will have gotten her to sleep. Zing always cooperates with sitters. The torment and negotiations, those she saves for me." She had this dream then: if she accepted Bobby's ferocity, maybe he would go easier on Beth. And Beth would let her keep Zing—even with Bobby in the picture.

Laura—analytically trained, after all—didn't miss how that dream made it fine, almost her duty in fact, to go to bed with Bobby.

So, soon after that, they lay precisely there, with Bobby softly kissing her breasts. She pressed his head into her body, but said, "It's a certain time of the month."

"Your period?" She heard that sound in his voice; like he'd been raised on the Talmud: *unclean woman.*

"No, not that time. I mean I might ovulate."

"Don't you take the Pill?"

"Not anymore. There's research that shows it might be linked to . . ." She couldn't say the word; it scared her; worse, it might scare him. "To my attacks."

"I could pull out."

"No," she said, decidedly, it being neither safe nor pleasurable.

"Okay, look, I have a condom." He walked naked to where he'd hung his jacket—that body, it probably *could* do some damage. He lifted the blue natural-shouldered jacket, like the ones Miles Davis wore in those pictures on Frank's record jackets, her brother's jazz period. He fished out his wallet. "Voilà," he said, gripping the packet tightly between his *long* fingers, like a genie that might get away before it granted their wish. Black and gold; lambskin that meant, kept moist by an odd medicinal liquid. Nicer for him, they said. "He gets out of *this,* we'll call the child Houdini."

The next morning at five, he woke her, said he had to get the shuttle back to New York. And maybe it would be best if he was gone before Zing got up.

Was that his way of saying, the kid isn't for me? You aren't for me?

"Your friend," he added, "we both know what she did was wrong. But I think the state rope is enough."

Relief flooded her. She put her arms around his neck, bent his head toward her to kiss him on the mouth.

"So I'll try to keep the federal government out of it. I'll try to get a fair deal for her from Wergel, too."

"Thank you." She meant that wholeheartedly. Beth had to give *them* Zing now, right?

"But when it comes to Wergel, you have to know there are other favors I need more."

"Jacob Battle?"

He lay down next to her, his arms under his head, an analysand, talking to the ceiling. "Yeah, Jacob's the boy I didn't care for enough at Dewey. The one I couldn't bring back from that Black Power thing. Truth was, I enjoyed Sugar Cane too much myself, his calling Johnson a cracker and all. That man told the *truth*. So this trial, it's my last chance to do things right for Jacob."

She kissed him on the cheek, no special reason, but Billy dead, her claws had become just ordinary, if nicely manicured, nails—but love, ah, that's practical magic, available to all.

"I do that, I can maybe reconnect myself with what was *good* about shouting 'Black Power' in Mississippi. *We will look out for our own.* I'll show myself I'm still the person that Sugar Cane, the heroic, the uncoked-up Sugar Cane, said would be a leader of his people."

Nice that he wanted to boast to her. But he sounded almost tearful, too. Would he be saying farewell to his dream if he married her? She put her hand to his cheek. "*He* said that? Perceptive man!"

"But look, Laura, if Beth gets out earlier, she'll want Zing back that much sooner. You okay with that?"

Laura nodded, crying now. She was *not* okay with that.

"Maybe you'll have kids of your own by then."

Too dangerous, Laura was about to say. But was it? And to whom? Her? Probably most of that worry about pregnancy and MS, that had been a way not to think about Topic A, that she'd be a fucked-up mother for any child, Laura too selfish, inconsiderate, irresponsible—or so her own mother had told her almost daily.

But what she wanted to say most of all was, *Is a child of ours something you want?* Billy's shadow fell over her again, then, reminded her of how near death might be. She needed more warmth and pulled him down toward her.

"I don't have another one of those traps."
She shrugged.

Later, when she heard the careful closing of the door, she tiptoed quietly to the kitchen, looking forward to the luxury of the newspapers before Zing woke. And which child would it be? Affectionate, desperate, furious? Ah, no matter what: desperate. Like her.

Still, Bobby *would* call. Whatever else, it surely wasn't over with them. And if they married? What happened in bed, how long could it be that sweet, imposing total? Long enough, she decided. After all, marrying him would have so many difficulties inflicted by the world that she wouldn't have to feel guilty for her happiness, could feel she deserved it—a kind of pay-as-you-go plan. On the monitor, the sounds of a stirring Zing. "Mama, I . . ." Zing said. Then Zing remembered, and began to cry.

Jeffrey pointed across the large floor to one of the drawing boards set against the back wall. "I just can't seem to use it," he whined to Johannus. "I don't believe I deserve to sit with the others."

"*Yet*," Johannus said. Sweetly. But truth would be, *Yeah, like when?* In six months he'd done only the six panels he'd already shown everyone. No failure in his life equaled this. A week before, he'd sworn that if he was so fraudulent, so utterly talentless that he couldn't even make something of a main character like Beth, then he deserved to die, might poison or gas himself, or try sex roulette. Then things got worser. Jeffrey had never been able to trust himself without the dream that some greater power, like Warhol or Hennessy or Billy Green, had chosen him, believed in him. Now Billy had gotten himself blown up, leaving Jeffrey *abandoned* here, alone, without lessons, without a mentor. Without *a master.*

An old man, left over from when Billy's dad had started the company, offered a big, if wavery, "Hello there, stranger!" His thick glasses gave him goggly eyes that made him look like—well, a comic book character.

"Hi, Matt," Jeffrey said. "He hates me," he whispered to Johannus as they passed. "He *worshiped* Billy."

"I mean, Billy called it again, right?" Johannus said. "Had you draw him dying in the Ninth Baby Colony War while he got himself blown up in Lebanon." Johannus saying that to be agreeable, like a date you had taken to the synagogue; *so that lovely oak chest is where you keep your special book.*

Anyway, tonight Billy's death felt more like a sour stomach than a prophecy fulfilled, meaning Jeffrey wouldn't have the strength to cruise with Johannus. Not much gaiety in that anymore; their m.o.—the two of them picking up a guy together—it only reminded him how tenuous his connection to Johannus felt. The short/fat/tall/thin stranger would come with them for handsome "Joey"—Johannus's *nom de nuit*. Now that "Joey" knew what places to go, and that the IRT ran on the West Side, what did he need Jeffrey for?

He felt faint from jealousy and longing; kissed Joey good-bye with melancholy finality, this the last few strains of their sonata, surely.

Maybe, he prayed, that sadness wouldn't leave him the extra oomph for fear. Matt shuffled out, and Jeffrey turned on Billy's hinged lamp. Try just one scene, though it would undoubtedly go nowhere. Maybe a whole page for a single frame:

The Outsiders have gathered at the oak Wisdom Table. The Sophist holds a letter.

OurKey looks down at a large open volume. "Yes, then we shall begin."

Then, some regular-size quanta?

"But can we," the Defender says, "read a letter addressed to another?"

"Yes," says OurKey. "For whatever has happened, whatever Ninja B. has done, she is still one of ours."

The Sophist doesn't reply, just stares at the letter.

And stares.

And stares.

His brows knot, his face a tormented mask.

Finally he reads: "*Hard banging makes goop in the pipes. Sparks cannot rise.*"

Bewildered faces turn to OurKey.

He shrugs. "Hell if I know."

Too true, he thought, stumped again. He heard the metallic shudder of the elevator cage, the doors creaking open. Considerate of Joey to have dragged the guy here—though Jeffrey didn't want the mouse tonight, however handsome. In fact, the more out of his price range, the more he would remind Jeffrey how gawky, bony, balding, and nosy he was, how unworthy of Johannus, how certain to be dumped soon.

He was alone, only a brown paper bag in his hand. Jeffrey's heart leapt, pointlessly. Still, for tonight, Joey had become Johannus again!

"I got you a sandwich." He peered down at the first page. "Goop? What does that mean?" He sounded avid; not quite at strange cock levels, but still.

"I don't know."

"*Yet,*" Johannus added sweetly. He opened up the bag. "I got you two half-sours," he said, taking out the precious white packages. "I've been thinking, Jeffers. I could finish law school here, if you're still willing to help with the tuition."

Could Jeffrey want that still, knowing that every day he would tip over into a ferocious disabling jealousy that made him want to kill Johannus just to know he wasn't with someone else? Too late to sort it all out, though, as Johannus leaned down toward his face, expecting joy.

And finding some, perhaps. Oh, yes, judging by his cock's response he *could* want Johannus in New York—*even if.* He and Johannus, Beauty and the Geek—still so infinitely impossibly wonderful. Okay, maybe not three times wonderful anymore; but once, at least.

> The Sophist lies on his back in his bare wooden room, deep within the Fortress. SheWolf puts a cold compress on his forehead.
>
> The envelope addressed to Ninja B. is on the table beside him.
>
> The Sophist's scalp is dotted with red pustules.

"What's wrong with Jeffrey?"

"He's insecure. Doesn't know what a prince among men he is." He kissed Johannus on the lips. "Actually, I don't know that yet, either. But that poor prone body, it reminds me, it's my shift tonight."

"Look," Johannus said, "why don't I join you?"

"It's grim, you know, right?" Jeffrey had become nearly phobic of Harry's loft, death not lurking invitingly in the shadows anymore, whispering promises of art projects, but disgustingly out in the open, promising pain. "But really, darling, I'd love to have the company."

"So it's like I'm marrying him, too," Johannus said, showing his big teeth. Hennessy's head lolled back to his pillow; nearly asleep, but pee still dribbled from his shriveled cock into the green ceramic bedpan in Johannus's hand.

"Yup," Jeffrey said. "Till death us do part."

"Which isn't going to be long, I think."

All right to say, Jeffrey thought, *if* you're the one holding the bedpan.

"Jesus, God, I can hear every word you bastards are saying!" Harry picked his wasted head an inch off a pillow soaked with his poisonous sweat. "Do you think I'm dead already?"

"Sorry."

His hand tremored on the sheet in helpless frustration. "I need . . . I . . ."

Johannus flipped the top off the morphine tablets.

"No," Jeffrey said, "he wants oxygen."

Johannus inserted the plastic clips under Hennessy's nose, and went to the kitchen to rinse the bedpan, still wearing clear rubber gloves.

Jeffrey put on a pair, wiped the red frothy spit away from Harry's lips with a tissue. He dropped it in the covered white cylinder marked MEDICAL WASTE.

"Wonder what a hand job would be like with these babies?" Johannus said.

"I think that's the kind of perversion they have in boys' schools in Transylvania."

Johannus went toward the bed, holding the bedpan aloft like an offering, the glowering self-portraits of the sacrifice/god observing him from the walls. Hennessy in full leather, Hennessy with a whip for a tail, Hennessy horned. Plenty of self-representation here, but meager accommodations otherwise: a narrow bed, a sink, a hot plate, an open toilet. Harry should have been in a hospital, but he'd demanded his loft; demanded his friends give up their days to keep him comfortable; and— most of all—demanded they sit ringside and watch the disease slowly and forever fuck him over. Suki especially—recalled to service for double shifts, *femme de chambre* of Hennessy, the AIDS king.

Harry wheezed in his drowse; a low rattle. Pneumonia. This shitty disease incited more diseases, like kids piling on in a schoolyard. Johannus put the bedpan down on the night table, next to the brown vial of morphine tablets. Jeffrey pulled Hennessy's pajamas back up around his stilt poles. Harry's neck had a thick, bulbous succubus all down one side; his scalp was dotted with pustules that looked like giant spider bites; and thrush grew in all his moist places. No one could safely touch any part of him without gloves on.

Death this close wasn't like visiting a condemned man in Mississippi, wasn't even like his father in the hospital. This was coming at the wrong time in Harry's life. *This* was someone Jeffrey had wanted to be. This could happen to him. Worse: it could happen to Johannus—all bright things come to confusion, come to sarcoma.

Oh, he'd be the one to confront death head-on, he'd told himself in Mississippi. What a joke! Jeffrey felt dizzy with revulsion and terror even this close to it; probably just the way Billy had felt in Lebanon. What deep knowledge does death offer but that a sane man should hate it? Death was too ugly, too awful, too painful; come within a mile of it, and you couldn't make anything of it or find any reason anymore to make a thing. Jesse had it right from the jump: Death is crap, and no SM game and no art could ever make it bearable. Death is intolerable. No one should ever die.

To get away from Harry's raspy moan, Jeffrey walked to the kitchen area and picked up one of Hennessy's drawing pads from the counter near the sink. Not that the man could ever draw; every page still a blank. The big sheets of paper made him think of Billy's decorations, the bleeding woman, the shards of glass, the terrified faces of refugees—and why not add the dead men walking in Mississippi, the dead cop at the mall, to that skeleton dance, that river of vengeance, death inside and outside him, anger and black, syrupy guilt, the world slowly drowning in pain, in agony until the end of time.

Beth's father had said we should listen to our guilt; and his daughter certainly had done just that. But it had been too loud inside Billy and Beth, too clamorous, an SM-style fucking, but endless, and nobody came. Well, how much guilt *should* a person feel? How *should* they atone? What is justice, goddamn it? Without the Talmud to tell you, the black goop becomes infinite, clogs the pipes.

Him and Hennessy not that much different from Beth either—all with a nearly endless supply of guilt, and no Book for any of them. So Harry and his confreres had turned the Hellfire into their Wailing Wall, made Gaston equal God. While Beth, she found her Gaston in Mao. Held in his fist, she was slave and killer at once, his Little Death Book positively ordering her to blow the shit out of some cops. Beth suffered death as guilt, and Beth wielded death as bombs. Beth Jacobs hardly existed at all; she was just a door, a flange, a gate that swung as death moved in and out, Beth nearly the Distinguished Thing itself, Beth = Death. *That* had always been her dark charisma, the pull that had nearly bankrupted him.

Johannus left the bedside, looked over Jeffrey's shoulder.

> OurKey: "Perhaps the Sophist will recover when
> he sends the letter to Ninja B."

Jeffrey looked up, saw Hennessy reach for his pain pills, rain them down into his shaking hand.

> "No," the Sophist says, "I *can't* send the letter!
> The ORG. would trace it! I can't risk that!! She
> still works for justice!"

> SheWolf: "You still love her, don't you?"

Did he? Or maybe Jeffrey *didn't* need that dream body anymore? Maybe, his actual body burnished by Johannus's affection, Jeffrey could stop taking vengeance on himself and rest content with his gawky lot. Maybe he didn't even need a master anymore. With Billy dead, no one would be looking over his shoulder—

> Nighttime. In the darkness, eyes still closed, the
> Sophist rises.

"How many pills is that?" Jeffrey shouted, but Harry had already thrown them in his mouth, reached for the water.

Hennessy's legs pistoned up and down, like the galvanic jolts of a dead frog. He knocked his blanket to the floor.

"Is he okay?" Johannus asked.

"Yeah, he does that when the morphine kicks in. I'll tuck him back in in a second. I'm on a roll right now."

> The Sophist walks through the metallic corridors
> of the Outsiders' quantum hideaway, and steps
> from Uncertainty into . . .

But Hennessy's wasted muscles had kicked his inspiration away; no more relief *there* from loss and judgment *here*. He looked over at

Hennessy, his eyes huge in his face, his lids fluttering closed. *Nothing is serious unless a body is marked.* Well, Hennessey's wasted chest, the savage snakes curling on his cheeks, this must sure as shit be serious, then. Really, though, everyone got marked up by the last frame of their particular comic book, no extra SM tattooing required; herpes, cancer, hunger, time itself, they all do the job.

That was it! Death itself did provide the vision by which this world could be judged; the judgment being: *there's too much fucking death in the world.*

> . . . Scarsdale. Wide green lawns, rough stone
> gates. The frames are circled, as if someone
> follows him through binoculars—

All that splatter on the pages of *Girls with Guns,* on the asphalt of mall parking lots, it had to stop.

Wait, Sam said. *You've already been stupid enough to sacrifice BBE, as per your idiot promise.* This *death will be financial suicide.*

Sam had him there. Could he really afford to ice Ninja B. now that he finally, fully owned the copyright on his first love in her most sublime, essential, and lasting form? It was his decision. His page now.

I don't know why I'm helping you, Sam said. *But she's definitely your only chance ever to make anything. She's what SM was to Hennessy, the thing that compels your adoration, the thing you simply love.*

And that's why, Jeffrey thought, he had to be the one to do this. Jeffrey *had* to lay down the law and draw a limit on his own idolatrous love, and on Beth's vengeance. And no decision in an artist's life is serious unless a drawing is marked, is it?

So he made some sharp, decisive strokes and—

> The zombie Sophist drops the letter into a post-
> box!

Wait. Revolted by death—so he would *kill?* Even in a comic book *that* made no sense. But his hand kept moving, making him feel a little lighter, too, as it did. Immoderate pleasure, actually.

> Through binoculars: A little post office in the deci-
> mated remains of Aspen, Colorado, ground zero in
> the war against Frananda. A woman with blond hair
> and dark roots trudges through the snow.

> Now it's nighttime: Ninja B., her head wrapped
> in a long kaffiyeh, arms cradling an automatic
> weapon with curved clip—

> leads six skiers down the mountainside past signs
> that say TO THE DENVER PLANETARY
> TRADE PALACE...

... providing an occasion for Jeffrey to experiment with superimposed images, get a new "quantum" feeling of motion into his frame...

> ... when out of the swirling snow, a battalion of
> Bugs emerges, the rabid Haunted Desperado at
> the fore with his deadly Fate Icicle—the real Big
> Chill—

Johannus walked over to Hennessy and tucked the thin blanket around what was left of his once beautiful wings. "Jeffrey?"

"Just a second." This was too much fun. For as long as his pencil moved, Jeffrey didn't have to be afraid of his anger, or his bottomless desire for pain. Plus, on his page good would always triumph, as per the *Ethics of the Fathers*? Or those of the Warner Brothers. Justified mayhem! His own *righteous* SM show!!!

He glanced over. Johannus had put a finger to Hennessy's neck. He had to remind him to put his gloves on when he touched Harry.

"Jeffrey, come over here."

"One minute." He made a few last shadings with the side of his pencil.

> "For truly," OurKey says when the dreadful news
> reaches the Fortress, "she had been noble once,
> but she had become part of the goop. Your trans-
> mission may have been His way of keeping her
> from doing more harm."

"Jeffrey, please?"

> "Or maybe," the Sophist says, crying, "I just
> helped the Bugs flush away my best friend."

Find the gun, the bullets match up, Wergel had said, *maybe I can do something for Jacob Battle.* Then two days ago, a ten-year-old discovers a rifle in a hollow tree trunk, and, thank the Lord, he doesn't kill someone with it. Or himself.

Wergel wanted a live body—but Priss's diary, the marked bullets, the rifle, what could he do? He looked around for the DA, this ye olde pizza hole pretty dark even at lunch, probably so you couldn't see what you were eating. What would they franchise next? Bobby wondered. Hungarian pies made from rat's milk cheese? He walked past a middle-aged serving wench, her breasts pushed up and out for him to look at.

He did, and she glared at him. *Beware of reckless eyeballing,* he thought. He saw Wergel in a booth, slid in across from him.

The DA had already started shoving slices into his face. But Wergy looked him in the eye as he chomped—a sure tell that the fat motherfucker would be lying to him. "You here to talk about the rifle? The rifle's useless. The bullet fragments we got were too partial." He stuck the whole piece in his mouth. Sauce dripped down his chin.

"Give them to the FBI," Bobby said. "See what they can do." He decided not to say anything about Wergel's tomato beard.

"Look, I'll tell you the truth, the way our guys did the test, you can't check them again. Not reliably, you know?"

He knew, all right. What bullshit! The *truth* was same as always: next election the county won't care if Wergel says a dead man did it. They want a conviction. Wergy needs meat.

A day later, the meat in question entered the conference room, hands pointlessly shackled. "I need to get the iron off him," Bobby said to the guard.

The guard gave him a *fuck you* look, but he did it. Jacob sat down opposite. Bobby gestured toward the door, and the guard exited.

"You got to trust me here, Jacob." He laid the papers on the table in front of him. "I'm bringing you a full grant of immunity on all federal charges. You just have to tell me you don't want your lawyers present for this, okay?"

"You know"—wiseass tone, tilting his body like he was looking under the table—"I was just wondering where my lawyers were."

"Thing is, if they're here, I can't do this."

"Okay." Jacob was as arrogant, finally, as Bobby himself, sure he didn't need any help. "But I'm not giving you anything."

"I'm not asking you for anything. Just your signature, okay? You're gonna have to trust me." Dewey School student; years playing street with Shakur and Sugar, but bang, Jacob bit on the *trust me* line, took Bobby's Waterman and signed.

Then he tried to hold on to the pen. A joke probably.

"Gimme that back."

He smiled, handing it over. "But I'm not giving you anything else."

"How's your mom? You think you can give me that?"

Jacob got a sick, is-this-a-trick look. Then: "She died nine years back. And I hadn't seen her for maybe two years before the funeral."

"I'm sorry. She was such a strong person."

"Yeah. But not strong enough for what I did to her."

A confession—but also trumping his brother's murder, which might, after all, have softened his mother up a little for Jacob's body blow. Weird how everyone loves their guilt. Must make them feel important. "I see my aunt once a week," Bobby said, "but she's had this stroke, sometimes she doesn't know who I am. Makes me feel like my past has disappeared, you know, like *I* don't know who I am anymore."

"I'm sorry, man. But Bobby Brown, *I* remember him, and he'll *always* know who he is."

Bobby put the waiver into a manila folder. "Thanks. And thanks for this. Now I can go about saving your worthless ass."

And flushing my career at Justice down the toilet.

He waited a week before talking to Wergel again, eager though he was to tell the man that Jacob Battle had talked to a federal lawyer about the case, and without—oh, my!—having in the presence of his attorney waived his right to counsel, said waiver being a state but not a federal requirement.

"You little shit."

"You know every time we come here, you get sauce on your chin, and you go back to your office that way."

"I'm going to tell everyone what you did."

"We expect good things from Jacob Battle. Wrap up the rest of the network. That's the department's main concern." Meaning Priscilla and Monroe, those two grave threats to the Republic. "You should know that Battle had already been fully apprised of all the defense strategies planned for his case," Wergel surely able to dot the *i*'s on that one. The appeals court would assume Justice had talked to the state prosecutors—compromising the defense. And Bobby Brown, he wouldn't even try to tell them otherwise, unless Jacob refused the deal Wergel would now be forced to offer.

"What do you want, you little . . ." way too long a pause there, "bastard. You want that murdering shit to get off?"

"No, I want you to offer him less than murder one. He didn't do it, and you know it. You have the bullets, you found the markings. You lied to me." *You sluglike piece of shit.*

Bobby walked out then, leaving Wergel with the check, and a grim view of his own political future. To his back, Wergel shouted, "You bastard, I helped you with that bitch you wanted to nail, and you stabbed me in the back. I will *never* make a deal!" Two bailiffs heard the anger in Wergy's voice, looked up as Bobby left, blood in their eyes.

The anger in the bailiffs' eyes must have been gratifying to Snake, or so Jesse Kelman hoped, Snake having given up the rest of his life, probably, to see it. Snake no longer his client, so Jesse sat with the reporters ringside for this extra-legal circus, Snake rising with tattooed face, shouting, "Death to U.S. imperialism!" The terrified young doctor who'd sewed up Shakur barely managing to add, "All the oppressors will fall!" The bailiffs didn't even try to restrain them, like they knew they'd burn out; sit down; and wait with the rest of them the hour it would take the jury to deliberate—just long enough for a free lunch to be served—before finding them guilty.

The doctor looked crushed at that, but the Snake Man rose again. "We are barely at the beginning of our historic task to build a revolutionary proletarian movement."

Thing about me is, Jesse thought, *to the end of my days I may not be sure—not absolutely sure anyway—that Snake is wrong.*

But that out of the way, Beth and Snake got to have a conversation—all Beth's lawyers present to hear Snake say that Beth had been a coward. Fighting the charges or pleading them meant you were cooperating with the storm troopers. He wouldn't testify that they'd rented the van to pick up furniture.

Or, basically, he was saying fuck her, and his kid.

David said, "You see, Miss Jacobs. We need a deal." He handed Snake the papers so Laura Jaffe could raise Zing, just in case.

But I will win this, Jesse wanted to psy-shout. *I'm the Defender, for God's sake.*

Which was pretty much what Carol had said the week before. "And I see that about you now." She hadn't been furious-sounding, either.

He'd managed a weak smile back, a potent combo of guilt and lust undoing him. "I never ever thought he was the man."

She put up a palm. "He wasn't, I think. But what's important is that I've discovered who you really are, that you'd do this thing." Carol had sat on their couch, a long way across from him, short skirt, gamin legs tucked under. "Your friend's death, it's made me think, Jesse. And I'm renewing our vows."

He'd begun to cry then.

"After all I didn't say till death penalty do us part. And I still love you—no matter how bad your doing good is."

Now, he'd wondered, Would she let him carry her up to bed? It had been weeks.

"Your work, it scares me. But that's my problem. I'll get help for that." She smiled, glanced round the shadowy living room. "Anyway, we'll need that paycheck, get some decent furniture. Build a nest for our child."

He'd suspected as much. And if a little extra forgiveness had come his way because a child needs a father, that was fine with him, too. He was thrilled. Pleased, too, that they'd finally have some decent furniture. But what he'd *also* felt, maybe a little *more* strongly than joy, was regret that she hadn't said, *If you want to keep me, you have to give this work up.* Instead, a ten-ton bag of felons had once again been hung right round his neck.

Now, carrying the spectral weight, he shambled off down another corridor to see the DA and Jacob Battle.

Wergel, though, he just stared at Jacob. "I'm going to offer you the deal of your life," Wergel said, as soon as Jesse walked in. "You can plead to a lesser charge than murder one."

Jacob, bent over like his chest had been caved in, managed a smile. "Thank you, Massa, for not charging me with a murder you know I didn't do. It's very—how shall we put it—it's very white of you."

"Yeah, whatever, shithead. But in return you got to do something for me. You put Beth at the scene, with the Brinks truck."

Jacob bent farther over, hard to do in the horse collar, his whole body curved, forcing his head to the desk.

"Do you need your inhaler?" Jesse asked. It had taken two visits to the appeals court to get the prison to allow it in. Jesse kept an extra in his briefcase for him.

Jacob shook his head. "I can't do that for you, boss," he said to Wergel.

"Your own . . . comrade, Shakur—he said she was there. The whole world knows it."

"Nope. Once again, the Supreme Commander is—was—supremely full of shit. That woman just was not there."

"Look," he shouted, "then we don't deal. You go down for the murder of the guard at the mall *and* the cop. We have witnesses."

"Trilbys," Jesse said mildly, just to fuck with Wergel.

Everyone, Wergel's face said, *is trying to make me crazy.*

"Svengali's subjects," Bobby Brown offered. "Hypnotic dupes."

"In other words," Jesse said, "reversals waiting to happen." But he was bullshitting. Anyway, Jacob had most certainly been at the scene. He needed this deal.

Wergel returned to staring at Jacob, whose wheezing had started to fill all their heads with twisted iron bars. "Look, you think about it." He motioned to a bailiff, who opened the door.

A matron brought Beth in, shuffling, handcuffed and manacled, but her green eyes already spitting poison darts.

"I've offered your friend here a deal, Miss Jacobs," Wergel growled. "He won't have to stand trial for murder if he admits that you were with him when the Brinks truck was robbed, the two of you armed."

"Can I sit down?"

"You can manage it in that outfit," meaning her shackles, "then sure." He gestured to the table. "You take the plea, you'll actually be better off. And Jacob here, he'll be a lot better off."

Complicated play, Bobby Brown thought, the dummy at this bridge game. Wergel worried that given the way Bobby had screwed him— which *so far* only the two of them knew about—Jacob might get off altogether. This way, Wergel made Jacob think he was offering him a good deal in order to get Beth. Meanwhile, Beth thinks she's doing something noble for Jacob *and* maybe getting some time off her sentence, too—so she gives up her chance to win the Get Out of Jail Free card.

"Look, Miss Jacobs, you two don't take this offer," Wergel said, eyes wide, face code-red choleric, "you'll be charged with felony murder, wherever the hell you were. Your able counselors, they've explained that possibility to you? You can say you left before the cop got shot, but the other officer there, he's gonna say otherwise. And I think your lawyers here know the judge will instruct our citizens that your having left the conspiracy is, in the legal phrase, a crock of shit. Instead, I'm offering Mr. Battle murder in the second degree and you an accessory charge. So it works out swell for both of you. He doesn't get life, and it shaves some time from what you'll most certainly get, you make me try it." He gathered up the papers he'd spread out on the table.

"But neither of you gets this blue light special unless you both sign on," Wergel said. He pushed a button. "Now I'll let you talk it over with your lawyers, Miss Jacobs." A bailiff came in, yanked Jacob up by his chain, made him look like a plucked pullet. "That hurts, Officer," he said quietly. "That really, really hurts." Then he just put his head down, walked out—like what fucking choice did he have? Bobby followed after.

"One more thing," Wergel said to Beth, over his shoulder. "Let me remind you, if you take this deal, Susan Lems can stop rotting in jail. So why not do the decent thing, Miss Jacobs, for once in your life?"

"The hypnosis stuff may not be allowed," Jesse said quickly, soon as the government had gone. "And the rest of the witnesses can't tell black people apart. It could blow the case open. And no one will ever put you at the Brinks truck, unless Mr. Battle decides to lie."

"He won't." She remembered Jacob on the floor for hours building spaceships with Zing; how protective he'd been toward Sugar, too—a younger brother's kind of protectiveness, like his arm on Sugar when he'd started to choke Baba and all that *don't disappoint me* in his large eyes. "Look," she said, "I'd trust Jacob Battle with my life."

"That's precisely what you'd be doing," David said. "And I think he will sell you. Once it sinks in how much time he faces, Wergel will come back to him and say, *Okay, the bitch didn't take the plea to help you. So you help me now, I'll give you a deal anyway.*"

"This plea, it's the best Jacob can do?" She looked to Jesse.

"It might be," Jesse said. "He's been wounded. There's a lot against him, if the hypnosis doesn't shit-can everything."

"And he's not getting the plea without me going down."

"I don't know," Jesse said. "That could be a bluff."

"No," David said. "He's not getting the plea without your being part of it, one way or the other."

"But the case against you is much weaker than the one against him," Jesse said.

David looked over at him sadly—which she knew from her father would be his equivalent of furious table pounding. "The case against you may be weaker, but you're Beth Jacobs, the famous radical bomber, the daughter of the famous Holocaust survivor. They want you much, much more."

Two weeks later, Beth, outside for the first time in months, was almost blinded by the winter sunlight. The other women in the yard talked, wandered about aimlessly like souls in . . . prison. The few times they'd let Beth out for exercise there'd been no other inmates. Probably a fuckup now; or maybe Wergel wanted to show her what a jolly place jail could be, ease her into the plea. Gynecocracy—out here, anyway. Hundreds of women, hair pulled back or in butch cuts; big shoulders and muscles, tank tops even.

Beth lit a cigarette—the mild addiction giving her a goal each day, a reason to live. *Oh, where were the Gauloises d'antan?* And why had no one hit on her yet? At night she could hear fucking—or maybe that had been a hallucination. Part of her repertory already—ten years back, the Weather Bureau had decided it was time for women cadre to make their bones with the women's movement so they could help move it toward the revolution. A curious cat, Beth had voted for it. Like now she *had* to fuck a woman, eh? But she'd only managed a couple of weeks with a skinny girl, Patricia, sharp features, flushed like crazy when she came. That had been . . . fun; but there'd been just as much bullshit as with Snake or B.C.

She watched a black woman, sweet eyes and breasts as big as hers, trying free throws. The ball didn't even reach the rim. Maybe she could join the game, make a new friend?

She'd need them here. She didn't have any comrades now. And the last time she'd seen him, Jesse hadn't looked like he thought he might win it anymore—or maybe that it would matter if he did. Bunchie, George, Dreads, they'd gone to trial already with Harrison at the wheel. "The identifications had been fucked up, like I said, years old, a total bag of worms," Jesse had said. "And Wergel didn't have Shakur to play the heavy. The jury only took two hours to find them innocent of robbery and murder."

"*But and so,*" David Watkins had said quietly. She had the feeling he'd gotten sick of the whole business, too. Of her, mostly.

"What's that?" she'd said, trying to give him her most winning smile so he wouldn't abandon her. Like Harrison Baker had; she didn't see much of him anymore. Or Jeffrey. All those professions of undying affection, and then he'd had the ORG. murder her—for the world's own good. What shit! And Laura? She still visited, but her motherhood depended on Beth in a box, so she couldn't be pulling so hard for the home team, could she?

"*But and so,*" David had said, "means *out of victory comes defeat.*"

"They got convicted as accessories after the fact, racketeering and racketeering conspiracy. Far from the heaviest charges."

"But the judge gave them a horrendous sentence for it, anyway," David had said, happily confirmed in his wisdom. "Forty years each."

"So, like, without the plea," Beth had said, about to weep, "Jacob, even if he beats the murder charge, if he doesn't get off completely, he's deep in the shit?"

"Yeah," Jesse said. "And they're gonna slice it up into different charges." He bent over, dragged down, defeated. "They get him on anything, they'll put him away longer than the plea."

"And," David said, "they will get him on something. Accessory after the fact, whatever."

"Basically," Jesse said, sadly, "Jacob will lose."

"And me?"

"I don't know," Jesse whispered.

"And," David said loudly, "I do. Jesse loves you too much to see things clearly, Miss Jacobs. It's the same for you or worse. They'll get you on something." Very matter-of-fact, the man holding the winning hand.

"But my father, he's *alone.*" Like the word would make the heavens weep. "He really needs me now." Taking the plea, it might help Jacob, but by the time Beth got out, he'd be writing her letters from the grave.

"The plea may not help you and your father, but it will let you see your daughter that much sooner. And you'll probably get parole, shave some years off that way. She'll be a young teenager."

Who hardly knows her mother. But if she gambled with Jesse—supposing he was still willing—and got off altogether? Then lucky Zing could be with Beth—a woman whose effect on people could only be compared to some slow-acting poison. Better not to have been born than to have her for a mother. Chances were, Laura would make a better mom than she had. Chances were, too, the shadows in Jesse's eyes had said, *I can't take care of you this time.*

Whoops, Sweet Eyes clanged another one. Man, being outside with people was freaking Beth out, too much space and all of it so empty. She wanted to run over to the nearest person, hug them, keep from flying off the streaming planet.

Bottom line: She went to trial, she'd almost certainly lose, be worse off than the plea. Maybe even convicted of felony murder and in for life. But if she cut the deal, she'd avoid the maximum risk, and Jacob wouldn't have to do the full boat for the cop and the mall guard. It would be known that she'd sacrificed for her black comrade, that she'd stood in real solidarity. So saving Jacob was the right thing to do from everyone's point of view—hers, Zing's, and even her father's.

"But Jesse thinks you still have a chance," her father had said when she told him that.

"He said it's a long shot, Dad. We have to look at this objectively, the way you taught me. Like scientists, eh? This plea, it's the best I'm gonna do. I take the risk, I probably end up in even deeper shit and I don't help anyone."

His eyes had been bleary then, tears on top of cataracts.

"And the hell of it is, you got one thing right, and Sugar, he was wrong. I can't give the law to myself. I do have something already written on my heart." Hard to say why or whose law—the Talmud, or her father's, or the Whole That Makes Us, but *this* particular mitzvah whipped round in her blood. "I can't sacrifice someone else to save my own life."

"And your daughter?"

"Laura will take care of her. She's a good person. And Zing loves her already." The way the state kept her from seeing Zing alone, that had been a solvent. Zing fell down now, she looked first to Laura to comfort her, and Beth even reached out her arms, the matron yanked her back. "They live in New York," she'd added to her father. "You'll be able to see Zing a lot."

"No, I'll move here. So I can be with you more."

My God, that kind of consideration, like he could turn his life upside down, it was so unlike him, it had wrung her heart. "Good," she'd said, not adding, *don't be ridiculous,* but pretending he'd meant it. "Then *we two alone will sing like birds i' th' cage.*"

"*When thou dost ask me blessing,*" he'd said, nearly crying, "*I'll kneel down and ask of thee forgiveness.*"

"But you should stay in New York, Dad. Zing will need you more."

He'd reached to his jacket pocket, probably for his pill. Then he stopped, like *why live?*

She had felt it, too. But she *would.* She had a daughter. She'd see her in prison whenever she could, and someday, they'd be together again.

She beamed her best smile toward the basketball court, offering life—whatever that meant in here—a brave, false welcome. The woman looked over, raised her thick eyebrows, then, grim-faced, went back to her game. Everyone in the yard knew Beth would be going back to a singleton in a block reserved for special treatment. Why waste time on her? No future in it.

Leo watched the man in the horse collar at the defense table bend his torso downward, not wanting to see his lawyers parse his future with the judge. The glint of Jacob's earring made an odd brightness in this sad spectacle. His brilliant daughter, Leo thought, had given up her last chance to raise her own child or to spend her father's last few years with him, in order to save this misguided man, following Leo's morality, she said, sucked from his breast—as if he'd convinced her that nothing could be worse than to sacrifice someone else to save yourself. And most probably, he had, not knowing how chance would have it end, for him, for her, here.

Jacob had the concave chest of the consumptive. And his beautiful daughter's face had become pale, round and soft—like someone taking anti-psychotics. Almost better than the truth: that prison food and a captive's lack of sun and exercise had done this to her. Beth looked uninterested in the proceedings, but Leo recognized his daughter at her most concentrated and anxious, her inward, preparatory look—before a spelling bee or a violin recital. Probably she thought her life would be summed up for History when she rose in front of the judge.

David Watkins remained behind with the defendants. This arrangement with the state, Watkins had told Leo, was the sensible thing to do. Beth would get a lighter sentence; and one of the government's lawyers—the black man who would raise Leo's grandchild—would ask for mercy for Beth. This plea, it was probably the right thing to do. Leo had no doubt been blindly selfish, wanting her to throw her life away on a dream of his. This way she'd get out earlier, be with her daughter that much sooner.

The lawyers stepped back from the bench.

Beth rose, her hands by her side. "I understand the meaning of a plea of guilty and I enter it of my own volition." She drew breath. "Only one thought has ever guided me," she said, speaking more slowly, her voice ringing now. "I am a white woman who does not want the crimes committed against black people carried out in my name. I will not be an accomplice in genocide." Her voice gained in volume, each word like a blow to his chest. "And that meant, that means still, that I must stand in solidarity with the black liberation struggle."

That is to say, she would not be an obedient citizen of the Reich. That thought, too, he must have poured into her ear. She looked over to him, smiling with half-closed lips. He nodded—drew back his lips, showing his mottled, broken teeth as he sometimes would when she played for him on her violin, though she had been mediocre at best, her tone shrill, her pitch wavering, her fingering atrocious.

The suntanned judge looked disgusted by her brief recital today.

Beth added a few words of regret—but too mild, Leo felt sure, for the judge's taste, Beth holding remorse at a distance because she found it too scorching; or so he liked to think. Her brief part over, she sat down, erect and focused again.

Leo looked about. All the seats in the courtroom were filled. One family group wept. A short-haired, tight-lipped woman in a suit glared furiously at Beth. Perhaps a victim's wife or daughter? A fat man, notebook out, had the amused expression with which one greets the always already known—a reporter, no doubt.

David Watkins rose to say that his client, too, would like to address the court before sentencing.

Then Jacob Battle stood up behind the defense table, like a man who wanted to faint out of life. He, too, said he entered his guilty plea of his own free will, though his eyes looked bewildered, hopeless, incapable of volition.

"But I want Your Honor to know," he said, "that I don't believe in this court."

Leo smiled. *Dear boy, look at the wood, the gavels, the guns— what's not to believe in?*

"Mr. Watkins," the judge said, "please tell your client that if he wants to continue to address this court, he will mind his mouth."

"You see what I mean, Your Honor?" Battle said. "You say mind *my* mouth, but no one told the cops to mind their motherfucking hands when they wrote your law on my neck. Was that justice?"

The judge offered a frighteningly mild gaze in reply, clearly waiting his turn, confident in his revenge.

"You people, you have these laws that are good for cowards like you, and you pretend God made 'em. Truth is, you make your laws out of fear of us. Sugar got it right. He knew we need laws that work *for us*."

Again, Leo thought, the madness his daughter had told him about. Well, *make your own law* had a grand sound, but it forever meant egotism disguised as rigor; and it always ended in murder.

"My people," Jacob said, "need laws according to the gods of Africa. Olodumaré, Shango, Yemoja. Names you don't know, Judge."

Jacob damn near had to laugh at himself then. He'd thought he'd made up a story in his hospital bed, godlike and free. Now, saying it here, all these reporters listening to this message in black code, his supposed freedom vanished; he had no choice but to fall in with what he'd made up, to fall right *into* it. *I, Jacob Battle, heard. I, Jacob Battle, saw.* Now, he had to *say* it, here, too, sentenced by his own sentences.

More ways than one, too. The judge looked like he couldn't wait to spit him out, his time probably getting heavier with each word. And knowing his speech would hurt him made him feel it *must* be true in ways he couldn't understand yet—like what he'd seen at the crossroads, it didn't look like that, but it *was* that. "Africa knows that the human body is holy, Your Honor. Our gods put it on themselves sometimes, like a beautiful suit. I myself, Jacob Battle, saw a true god, an *African* god, put on Sugar Cane's body. And Sugar Cane knew the orishas do that so we can be godlike ourselves and do what gods do: *make justice in the nations.* Then all people will know that life is holy. That's all I want to say." He sat down too hard, making his neck sting.

How very odd, Leo thought, distracted for a moment from his fear. What he had thought was mumbo jumbo had come out sounding like Torah law. But the judge had already started to speak. "I like to think that the still, small voice of conscience speaks in each of us," Judge Hurlbut said, "if only we will grow quiet and attend. But Jacob Battle and Beth Jacobs try my faith. They have shown a horrifying, icy lack of remorse for the people they helped kill during the course of this dreadful robbery. My only hope is that the harsh daily realities of prison will help to cleanse their minds of their vicious fantasies. Toward that end, I sentence both Beth Fanny Jacobs and Jacob Battle to the maximum sentence of twenty years to life."

Pain radiated down Leo's left arm, gathered in his chest. Jesse Kelman looked stunned, and even Watkins lifted his eyebrows. But his brave daughter turned to smile at him, to comfort *him.* Next to the district attorney a man laughed loudly—the FBI *kapo* who'd made Leo perform circus tricks to save his daughter's life. *Well, no one should be cheated of their triumph,* Richard Hartman sometimes told him. *Not even the world over us.* And that man with the military haircut, Leo thought, he must be the world.

Uniformed matrons snapped handcuffs around his daughter's wrists and walked her to the door beside the judge's bench. Beth, glancing back at Leo, saw him crying. Her cheeks shivered slowly, and she began to weep too, the way she would at seven when she thought she'd disappointed him in her German lessons. The matrons held her up on each side, kept her moving forward.

Was this justice—this vicious sentence? Well, hadn't he always known that there is no Judge, no judgment? And his little substitute religion, tending the whole, the logos that creates and re-creates us, wasn't that as sentimental as burying those sinews had been? There was no God, no whole, no logos. Leo had perpetrated a fraud on the public, sold them sugar houses.

How that nonsense must have sickened poor Richard Hartman! *Yes,* Richard had said to him once, *there is an order, Doctor Jacobs—but it excludes us, wants us gone.* Like Kafka saying, *There's plenty of hope. Just not for us.* But Richard and Kafka had been sentimental too. The No Order That Doesn't Exist wants precisely nothing from anyone. The world is chance all the way down, and a throw of the dice, a wonderful little girl, they never abolish chance, never, even when thrown in eternal circumstance, from the bottom of a shipwreck.

Sonorous, familiar words, comforting almost—for a moment, anyway. Then the reporters ran to their phones, their newspapers, their stories with beginnings, middles, ends. Leo rubbed his eyes, and his glasses fell to the floor, where Clerc could smash them.

He saw a short blur in a striped suit come near. David Weiss, no doubt, to help him steal another pair from a *muselmann.*

"Are you all right?" the blur spoke. More nasal than Weiss's voice.

"I'm sorry, I can't see your face clearly."

"I'm Arthur Kaplan. A friend of your daughter's from Great Neck."

"She certainly needs friends now, eh? But could you help me, too? I've dropped my glasses."

The young man knelt, then stood up triumphantly, Leo's spectacles in hand, to receive his *A.* "Thank you. And if you don't mind, I'll just sit here a little longer." Alone, he meant. But at that moment the fat beadle came over to tell them to clear the court.

Leo steadied himself on the young man's arm, and together they left the courtroom.

"What a triumph," Bobby Brown said, *con molto sarcasmo,* not a flavor he usually indulged. "They broke every fucking part of the plea agreement. And Hurlbut didn't listen to a word I said."

"Maybe Jacob made it worse for himself," Laura said, "that speech about Sugar and the African gods. And Beth, she probably didn't sound sorry enough." She needed to pee again.

"It doesn't matter what either of *them* said. A deal's a deal."

"Apparently not, huh?"

"No, apparently not." He didn't say anything for a while, concentrated on passing a truck in his vintage MG. Dashing till you found out it didn't have air-conditioning, and no imaginable way for a pregnant woman with an aching bladder to get comfortable in a bucket seat. She put a scarf over her hair, and rolled the window down.

"What you got Jacob, it's better than murder one, right?"

His jaw relaxed a little. "But thing is, I think it was partly my fault they did him like that. Wergel did me a favor, you and the grand jury. And then I fucked him. So he got Hurlbut to screw me." He fished some sunglasses from a soft leather case in his jacket pocket, though the sun wasn't that bright. "Gonna be forever and a day before they get out."

Which meant Zing was theirs. And soon she'd have a sister. "The kid," Bobby had said, laughing, the day she'd told him, "how did he get out of there? We're gonna have to call him Houdini."

"Not exactly," Laura said, mightily warmed by his laughter. That first time at her apartment, she meant, they *had* used a condom. But there had been a second time that night, and she hadn't insisted—which was all Billy Green's fault! She had stopped believing in the letters, or that her brother yattered at her from the grave, but she'd gone on being *Billy Green's* SheWolf. Then he'd died and the magic had leaked out of her life. But love and making new life, that had seemed a replacement miracle; all the more wonderful in her and Bobby's story, she dreamt, for the risk in it, black and white together. Then, after that first of the second times, it had became a romantic ritual with them: premier episode on any particular night, they used a rubber. But if there was a second time, Laura didn't make him suit up.

Still, with guys, you don't know *why* they do it; it could just be for the feel of skin on skin. Or maybe they do it to show they have power over you at that moment, or for more life in *that* moment. Then they change their minds, afraid they won't be strong enough for that life when it arrives—like her that way.

But Bobby's laughter when she told him had seemed filled with delight.

"And if it puts me in a chair?"

"Then I'm here to push the chair."

She believed him. But in truth, she didn't think anymore that she would have an attack. In remission three years now, not even a twitch. Before, she felt pretty sure, she'd scared herself, told herself she couldn't have kids to hide her real fear: that she'd fuck the kid up. A scared, unreliable, and selfish person, she might even kill her child carelessly, not watching the traffic or something, distracted by her own problems. No, MS had never been the real issue.

"Flushing his life away," Bobby said now. "That didn't have to be Jacob's story. He just got too close to Sugar Cane and Black Power. And maybe to me."

"Oh, my love," Laura said, putting her hand on his arm.

He swerved, almost overshooting their exit. The lurch made her stomach jump. Which made her anxious. And worry could be bad for the pregnancy and worse for her own myelin. She tried not to be anxious about the anxiety. Chance was on her side, but still, the pregnancy *could* put her in a chair.

"Look, how 'bout I drop you off, see some old places, then come back in an hour, you know, give you a chance to talk a little, plan the wedding and all."

"Probably a good idea, yeah. Then, on to your aunt's." Trying to put some Gidget in her voice. "Our royal tour."

"Ebony and ivory," Bobby said, with equally false heartiness.

Her father snapped a nitro vial under his nose. "I'll just leave you and your mother to decide on the dress."

Her mother gazed sadly at his slow climb. "This has been a shock," she said to Laura, but straightforwardly, without anger.

The two of them settled into the dark mahogany den, shelves of books, a new color TV taking the place of the huge old one that had shown her the Selma March in ebony and ivory. Her mother, in a long skirt, sat primly on the cold-looking Danish-once-moderne couch. "It's just not what we expected."

To put it mildly, Laura felt sure. A black man. The maid's nephew. "I'm sorry." In fact, for a moment she was. *A baby!* Which she hadn't yet told her mom about. *Could Laura care for a baby?* The dark light of an acidic *no* streamed from her mother's rheumy eyes, ate away half Laura's own face. She reminded herself of what Smerless had taught her: That No from her mom's eyes was Laura's own projection.

Laura looked toward the window and the tall inverted cone of the beech that had shed its coppery leaves. Her dad had helped her climb there. The tritest plot, really: *The Family Romance,* starring a little princess, the hero's daughter. So the child disparages her rival, the supposedly evil mother. That's why Laura had always *imagined* her mother disparaging *her* right back. Smerless repeated this truism for months, and Laura tried to believe it.

"Bobby Brown," Laura said, "he's the most wonderful person I've ever met. He's focused. Kind and strong. Completely reliable."

"Really, dear, he does sound wonderful. He must have worked so hard to get to Harvard, become a federal attorney. Like your father . . . but better schools." She smiled at that. "It's not him we worry about, darling. It's you. I mean, an interracial marriage, an adopted child, Laura. That's awfully serious for someone with your health. We worry if you really understand what you're taking on?"

Two children, actually. But today was perhaps not the time to tell her mother that.

Her mom picked up the pink oval glasses that dangled from a gold chain around her neck. Then she just let them fall back to her blouse. Laura had to talk to her mother soon about having her eyes checked for glaucoma again. "Do you know, darling," her mother said, "what was one of the worst moments of my life?"

"Frank's death?"

Her mother raised her brow, tilted her head—as if to say, *Of course, that's the lodestone of pain; like gravity, so reliable, so present, it's hardly worth mentioning.* "It was you with your brother's corpse, that autopsy room or whatever it was, the bastard who helped kill him watching us. You rubbed Frank's cheek over and over, shrieking, 'I'll remember you, I'll remember you.' It was horrifying."

"It was a confusing time for me, too, Mom." No need to say

altogether why, though, Frank communicating with her from his grave. She started to cry. Her mother's disparagement wasn't Laura's fantasy; and it was probably just. She shouldn't have a child.

"Oh, God," her mother said. "I'm sorry I sounded so mean."

Laura wiped her sleeve across her eyes.

"Wait. I'm sorry that I actually *was* so mean. It's your father I was really angry at that day. He always preferred you to all of us, even then."

Her mother had said that a time or two before, of course. But it always surprised Laura—pleasantly so.

"I think that jealousy has often kept me from treating you fairly, dear. But still, what I want to say is that it's always been grand opera for you, hasn't it? You like to have a drama in your life. I'd just like to be sure that none of this is about getting the world to watch you, even if they do it because they hate you."

Hysteria? After years of training with Leo Jacobs, her mother had mastered psychoanalytic typology, always a good way to curse someone. But she'd given Laura a twinge; her diagnosis sounded too much like Laura's *pay as you go* thing, her not having to abuse herself for her pleasure in Bobby, because the world would take care of payment in large and small ways. Like that afternoon walking down Middle Neck Road, the two of them on the way to *Jay's Drama in Footwear* for her new pair of flats, all those frankly curious looks, men and women both studying her face, thinking perhaps that the black man on her arm meant that Laura had an intriguing tendency to depravity, a masochist, a "nympho," a girl mad for black dick. Or were they thinking, *My how wonderfully far the world has come.* And, *What a handsome couple.* She'd never know. And the whole world would be like Great Neck.

"No, Mom," she lied. "It's not for the spectacle, I'm sure. It's love."

"Oh, darling, even so, how hard things can be between two people! And the world will add so much to your difficulties, won't it, make life harder than it already is even for the lucky ones." She got up, straightened her skirt, and, amazingly, opened her thin arms toward Laura.

Laura, so strangely eager, almost stumbled into them, nearly tipping her mother over, greedy for the feel of Ellen's lacquered hair near her cheek, that magical smell of her mother's perfume, roses and alcohol. God, she needed her now, she couldn't possibly handle all this alone.

"You know we'll help you," her mother said, reading her mind—the way moms are supposed to, right? "We'll do anything we can for you."

They pressed cheeks a moment longer, mingled tears a bit. Then her mother let go suddenly, long before Laura wanted. Well, they needed practice at this mother-daughter thing.

Ellen gazed out the window, toward the climbing tree. "You know the two of you used to play together, until you were five or so."

And *the two of you* didn't mean Frank, she realized, but Bobby. "Funny, I don't remember. And Bobby never mentioned it."

"Well, maybe he doesn't remember, either."

"Why did we stop?"

"It wasn't my idea," her mother said. "Ruth just wouldn't bring him over anymore."

Which was when Bobby rang the doorbell. Her mother smoothed her blouse down; one breast lopped off, she never felt her clothes sat right anymore. Then she produced a Loretta Young smile for the next scene of *All You Could Hope For in In-laws*.

Until Bobby scared her with a smile and "I've heard so much about you."

Meaning from Ruth? The dirty underwear everywhere? The sex toys in the dresser drawer?

And an hour later, Bobby's cousin scared Laura, rolling Aunt Ruth up in a new chrome job. Thin wheels, but it stopped on a dime. Ruth's withered face sagged terribly to the left, and the side of her body hung like an unused puppet's torso.

They all sat together silently in the Queen's parlor. Ruth wore a shawl despite the heat. She just stared at Laura. Finally, she made a gesture with her hand—more like a tremor, if a tremor could be imperious. It meant that Bobby and his cousin should depart so Ruth could stare silently at Laura for several more long minutes. Those eyes, though—not glassy but furious, darting, spitting poison.

"My . . . boy?"

Crystalline, actually: Ruth accusing Laura of theft. "I love him," Laura said, the defense offered by a heart that's simply true.

Ruth laughed—or rather, made a small declension of air that said *fuck that true heart shit*. Her face tightened, her eyes closed, so she could concentrate better on her pain. A white foam formed at the corner of her lip.

Laura, the Lady Saint, walked over, dabbed the drool with the edge of her bunched cotton sleeve. Ruth, barely perceptibly, turned her head to meet the cloth.

"You're . . . carrying."

A comic book talent? No, Bobby must have told her. "Yes."

She tilted her head toward the slipcovered chair, meaning: *sit*.

Laura collapsed on the chair, overcome by the stone-cold horror of her life. A child about to be born; a mother who could be crippled by the birth. And then this woman would come to live with them!

But maybe they could find money for a home to care for her? No, Bobby had spoken too often and too pointedly about how *family was better.* She wept then. And Ruth just sat there in her shawl, blue stripes and fake gold threads that reminded Laura of her lost brother's lost prayer shawl. Could she have chosen it to say something? No, the cousin had probably grabbed anything to wrap Ruth in, keep her warm that warm afternoon, Ruth now going "Cold . . . cold." Meaning she was cold? Meaning she was playing a game of hotter-colder?

And *that* would soon be Laura's life—guessing what a woman who hated her wanted from her. *Hated her*—when Ruth once-upon-a-time had been like a mother to her. A fantasy, of course, a substitute for the warmth she had needed from Ellen—like those monkeys who bond with a washrag and a stick.

And Zing? Could she do better for her, with her own on the way now and Ruth to care for? Panic rose from her womb. *Dear Beth,* she should say, *Please forget about all that pleading, I have my own bun in the oven.* She *had* to find a way out; that feeling taking her back to the dusty Fortress—that squalid little *attic*—when she'd realized that she would never be the infinitely resourceful and daring SheWolf. No, more like ShePussy, SheJerk.

But Zing didn't have anyone else to turn to, even if she might be mostly sticks and washcloths. She shook her head; the panic passed; and she knew herself already connected to that child by a thousand silken cords. Laura wanted to raise her, treasure her. And thank God for a kid's endless ability to dream, those mixtures of memory and longing that so comfort us. Laura would just do the best she could, and Zing could imagine the rest, make Laura into the best damn good-enough adoptive mother in the world!

Zing liked to push her adoptive mother in her new chrome wheelchair. Probably it gave her a sense of control, now that things had become uncontrollable. But Zing rarely pushed her in a straight line, and never without frequent stops. Today, though, she mustn't dawdle. One hour was all the prison allowed for a family visit.

Laura saw Beth in a line with the other con-moms, black hair in a sharp butch cut, expectantly scanning the approaching visitors. And even ten yards away, Laura could see the horror form on her face. Since they'd been here last, a wolf's head cane wouldn't do the job anymore. But Beth didn't look away; more measuring, really, like, *she's in a chair, and I'm in here.*

Yes, Laura thought, *but I've got no possibility of parole.* Though Bobby said in the current political climate, it would be a very long time before Beth got out.

Zing ran forward across the dirt, abandoning Laura's chair. Laura tucked the thin white blanket around Deborah, who lay, for the moment, asleep in her lap. Thank God Nzinga seemed eager, wore her biggest smile—enough to light the b-ball court for night games. Beth bent down, and zinged her up into her arms, kissed her daughter's face as if nibbling quickly all the bread of life.

"Mom, you cut your hair."

"Hard to keep clean here. Do you like it?"

"I hate it."

A few moments later, as usual, Zing looked down at the asphalt, said she had a stomachache, that she needed to go to the toilet badly. Not the work of a moment, either; you had to go through the gates to the waiting room, then get checked back in. Visiting time would be almost over. Usually she wouldn't come back.

"I'll see you later, sweetheart."

Beth, this gray prison sack around her, watched her daughter go off side by side with her former prosecutor. Laura pulled Deborah closer to her, to say to no one in particular that they couldn't take her child away.

Beth turned back, looked down at the gleaming wheels, raised her thick brows.

"You know, this clever disease. But the muscle tone in my upper body's still strong, thank God." Reassuring Beth, really, that she could care for Zing. And she *could*, she would.

With Bobby's help. Though lately she worried he might be pulling away. Almost daily he worked to reassure her, said he loved her, but she could see how they might all get to be too much for him to carry.

The other families spread into the corners of the court and toward the brick wall, left Beth and Laura alone under the basket.

"Zing seems really to like kindergarten," Laura said. "But she gets kind of wild at the end of the day."

"The apple not far from the tree?" But no oomph in the words. Beth lit a cigarette.

"*You?*" Laura said. "*You* loved school. Industrious, filled with stick-to-itiveness. You always took a project seriously. Even the Revolution."

Beth gave Laura a version of her father's closed-up smile: *Please don't try to amuse; it makes you seem trivial.* Then she switched off even that anemic bulb.

Laura spent long days sitting next to depressives, misers who thought each of their words a gold coin; or a hard stool. But Beth Jacobs, *her* down-turned lips lacerated Laura's heart.

"She's adjusted well to Deborah."

"AKA the Prophet."

"Also my grandmother's name." *I.e., the world doesn't revolve around you.* Of course, prison had probably already taught her that. It had certainly washed the luster from her once magnificent eyes.

Beth didn't ask any more questions about Zing, just stared up at the sunny sky.

"Arkey's brother-in-law, Specs, he's gonna join you soon," Laura said, looking for something neutral but interesting, get Beth back in the game. "The United States of Prisons. The American Gulag."

"The Mafia banker?"

"That's the one. Turned out Arkey's and Jesse's fathers let their business launder money for him."

"The scamps." Toneless, though.

"Well, Bobby says they didn't have much choice. Anyway, they're in big trouble with the government."

"Ah"—a mildly prideful *tell me 'bout it* in that *ah*.

"Arkey feels terrible."

"Arkey always feels terrible."

"Like if he hadn't been so contemptuous of Great Neck, had gone into the family business, his father wouldn't have needed a substitute son or something. But I think he's also glad Specs got his dad in trouble. He and his dad, they get along better now. Like he can admire what his dad made."

Beth laughed mirthlessly at that—to say, *the supposed radical historian is bourgeois to the core, or he'd be here with me.* Or was Laura projecting that denigration? Actually, it wasn't clear to Laura if Beth even remembered who Arkey was. This place, it dimmed your eyes, and probably your memory, too.

"Anyway, the feds used his father-in-law to squeeze Specs. Specs gave himself up to protect Mr. Kaplan, but he won't rat out his clients, which is what the feds really want. So he'll have to do some heavy time." Laura hoped she'd gotten the slang right—like she didn't want Beth to find out that under her fur, SheWolf was really just a crippled West Side psychoanalyst.

"Specs, he's a stand-up guy, eh?" Beth said indifferently.

Tough talk. But wrong—and a chance for unimprisoned Laura *not* to play the ingenue. "Stand-up? No, if he testified, his clients would kill him. It's made Specs see his life a different way, you know." Implied: *Like you should, Beth.* Maybe Laura could help her make an adjustment, get some therapy. Instead of "self-criticism," and political mistakes, bottomless remorse. That might satisfy the parole board. " 'These thugs,' Specs told Arkey, 'they love to play *men of honor,* that Godfather shit, but really they sell each other out in a heartbeat. I guess everyone prefers the comic book version of things.' He meant us, too, of course." *And Mao, probably.*

Beth said nothing, did a French inhale on her cigarette.

"Anyway, Bobby brokered him the best deal possible."

"Bobby the broker, eh?" Meaning: *look at me and Jacob, sweetheart. Hubby's deals are for shit.* Though the way she said it, she barely seemed to care. "But Great Neck?" she added. "They spit Specs out, eh?"

"Well, a lot of people at the Temple turned on him, yeah. A convert and all? But some members wrote letters to the judge before sentencing. His good character. His charities. Money for the new wing at the Temple."

"The judge gonna give a shit?"

Laura shrugged, offered up her husband to put some light back in Beth's eye. "Probably about as much as Judge Hurlbut did."

Beth sank back into herself, looked over at a little black girl, spinning round and round in a pink skirt. "I'm sorry," she said after a few moments. "I have no energy today. It's the anniversary of my father's death."

"Oh, God, no, I'm the one sorry, Beth. We just weren't thinking." Beth, she saw now, was shell-shocked with guilt today. The old man, he had come to the city almost every week since they'd taken Zing, would sit for hours on the floor with her, building with blocks, keeping Zing interested. *Do you think we can put this one here without toppling everything over?* He still had the knack, made Zing want to guess right. Heal the world, too, probably. After, he and Bobby would have a drink—schnapps, Bobby had taken to calling it—and they'd talk together at the kitchen table, sometimes for hours.

Then, after one ordinary visit, her father had gone home, put a plastic bag over his head. Beth had refused to go to the funeral shackled—which meant she hadn't been there. Bobby had sobbed, holding Zing in his arms. Someday, as far in the future as Laura could manage, Zing would find out *how* her grandfather died. And why? That would be one more thing Laura would never be able to explain to her.

"How's the school?" Beth asked.

"Bobby says things are good. The RAP programs, you know, free breakfast, free shoes, they're never coming back. But Susan and that African priest, Baba, they've made Sugar into this hero-god to save the school."

"An orisha, an emanation of the one God, Olodumaré. Like an angel." Beth's voice became younger, not so much teaching Laura as reciting *for* a teacher. Her father, that would be.

"Anyway, your friend Jacob Battle, you know he says he actually saw Sugar embrace one of those god emanations that day at the shootout." Laura, what she mostly remembered about Sugar was the lashing her family had gotten at her brother's memorial. "Did you see that transformation perchance?"

"There are more things in heaven and earth . . . Than are dreamt of in your philosophy."

"I don't doubt it, actually. Baba, he made this story, this *account* of Jacob's into a pamphlet. The gospel according to Battle, huh? It had this big black guy on the cover in reds and greens, no top on him. Thick chains and a machete. Looked like a painting by that guy Jeffrey used to live with. Anyway, they wouldn't let me bring it in here. Like you were gonna come looking at the guy. The god, I mean."

Beth barely lifted her brows. "I think it was probably the machete they didn't like."

"Yeah? Well, the Sugar/Shango thing really got people to rally to the school."

"That's great." The enthusiasm real this time, though Beth not quite on the basketball court with her; her mind with Zing, probably.

"Anyway, my dad, he helped get some foundation support for the place." *My dad,* she wanted to say, *he's an orisha, too,* whatever that is.

"Good."

No, Laura thought, a *miracle.* A wedding gift. Followed by congestive heart failure. Maybe he had a year more to go. "And the guy who set fire to the school way back when, the one who became a teacher there—"

"Delon. He used to get those kids marching around his class, playing pretend saxophones. It was adorable."

"Well, thanks to Baba, he just got elected to the Boston City Council."

That made Beth smile. "Delon and the long march through the institutions, eh?"

Laura knew the idea: radicals all get jobs, transform their workplaces. Buy summer homes.

"Me," Beth said, smiling quizzically at herself, "I'm marching through this prison."

Laura had heard: Beth did reading classes. *Yes, this is an "m."* Doing good, Beth's father would have said, mending the whole, it might help her bear her guilt for those dead cops. But damned if she'd say that to Beth.

"Believe it or not," Beth said, "me and my class are rewriting *Antigone.* We're gonna do it for the whole prison."

"What happens in your *Antigone?* She gets buried with my brother? Or gets letters from his grave?"

Beth actually laughed. "No more letters, okay. No *mas.*"

"You heard about Gail's book?"

"Arkey told me. He comes to visit sometimes. *Great Neck,* right? He said Arnie Golden is gonna make a movie of it. I think Debra Winger might play me, eh?" She smiled, kidding—but *not.* She'd been a comic book headliner, sure, but Debra Winger, ah, *she was a star.*

"Well, Arnie had a script done. But he said it wasn't 'a home run.' So that's that."

"Thank God." But Beth didn't mean it, quite. "Jeffrey, anyway, at least he got what he wanted from those letters. He's an artist, like he always dreamt, eh?"

And you're a prisoner. And I'm a cripple. But Laura flicked her eyebrows up slightingly. "In comics, yeah, and under someone else's name."

"But surely that's Billy Green moving a living hand from beyond the grave." Deadpan delivery. A joke? Or maybe she wanted Laura to pass that on to the True Believer (formerly known as the Sophist), to curry favor. Recently some cells from Ninja B. had been re-cloned by the Fizzyits. Now the Outsiders must vote on whether OurKey should do a living-to-dead kabalistic mind-meld between the departed and a Ninja B.C. (for clone, but with a tip of the Hatlo Hat to the dear departed Baruch Cramer), thus returning her to quasi life and the product line to profitability. Maybe, Beth thought that her believing like that would swing the vote.

"I saw Jeffrey in the flesh last week. Johannus had just passed the bar. He's going to join Bobby in practice."

No interest there. She stared at the basket.

"He and Jeffrey both had their heads shaved right down to their skulls."

"Two bald men, eh?"

"Yeah, well, on the football player it looks good."

"The haircut," Beth said, "that would look good on Ichabod Schell hasn't been invented yet."

"And Jesse, Johannus said he has a case coming before the Supreme Court. A guy named Ferris. Jesse says they shouldn't execute the retarded."

Beth stared up at the sky. Would she say, Jesse's a pig for cooperating with the fascist courts? "Well, they *shouldn't.*"

"Bobby says Jesse's a legal genius." Which, given how hard it had been for him to say it, must be true. "Jesse and Carol, they're going to have a second kid."

Beth cackled. "But he has all those murderers to take care of!" She stopped smiling altogether. "Like me," she added.

Hard work taking care of Zing today. As soon as they left her mom, her eyes had glazed over, like she needed a nap, but sorrow and fury, Bobby knew, lay just beneath that sheen. "She regresses at the prison," Laura had said, like the word would keep Zing from saying the air smelled bad in the bathroom . . . in the waiting room . . . in the prison . . . until she'd led them outside the walls to the parking lot.

"I want to go home."

"Soon, darling. Right now Laura needs to talk more with your mom. Tell her how great you're doing at school."

"I hate this place," Zing said. She looked up at the brick barriers, covered with barbed wire. Uniformed guards stood inside the towers at the corners, scanning the view inside and out, scoped rifles already in their hands. "I mean, it's not my *favorite* place. I don't *love* it." Like saying she hated the place had gone too far, had meant she hated her mother.

"Yeah, it's not very nice." He took her hand, wishing he'd brought a ball, or a book, some way to keep her distracted for a half hour. Brown the Clown. Like Arkey Kaplan had said to him the night before, "It's frustrating. I can only do nonverbal shtick with baby Abe. None of my A material."

Bobby had to admit he liked Arkey. He'd been decent to Jacob in the long ago at the Dewey School. And his thing with Laura, so past, so clearly insignificant, impossible to feel jealousy over that. Or triumph, either.

"Don't step on any cracks," Zing said.

"I'll be careful." He took comically high steps to avoid a seam's witchy power, prayed that might amuse Zing for a while.

The night before, Zing had cried herself to sleep in Laura's arms, while he and Arkey had talked in the kitchen—attractive hardwood floors, and so much more space than New York, too. Arkey had poured him a glass of white wine, to celebrate the publication of his new book. Something about the garment workers and a fire.

"You're conservative, huh?" Bobby having by now figured out the different flavors.

"Yeah, not too hot, not too cold. Just right. Or right enough."

"Gives a glow to things?" Meaning, it makes your life less tawdry— Laura having told him about Arkey's *narcissistic wound.* The Temple seemed to work for him, though. Arkey didn't wear scarves and hats anymore—not at night anyway, in the house.

"Try the wine," Arkey had said. "*That* gives a glow." But before they drank, Arkey had whispered some Hebrew words.

Bobby had swirled, sniffed, sipped; Arkey waited, deferring to Bobby's opinion. "Over-oaked, alas." Bobby flipped to the book's dedication: *To Kate and Abraham: Day by Day.* "That's an AA thing, isn't it?"

"Damn. Is it? I didn't know."

"It sounds kind of like a man saying there's some rain in his life."

Actually, he wished Arkey well, but he'd have been relieved if he'd said, *Yeah, there's trouble in paradise.* Bobby had wanted a chance to discuss his own unhappiness but had felt he couldn't go first.

"Trouble? No, just the usual corny daily joys and sorrows. But you know, it's like Kate's shown me that marriage, a career, raising Abe, it's not a glorious all-or-nothing thing. More like try, fail, try again."

"Sounds a little grim." Though Bobby's own life recently had been more like fail, fail, and fail again.

"The Messiah, the final victory, the end of history, that's for chumps," Arkey had said. "Sabbath candles, one night's illumination a week, that's enough. And if there was once oil for eight nights in a dark time, *that* was a miracle."

"You sound like a rabbi."

"You mean like it's bullshit?" He'd taken a sip of his wine. "Okay, the truth is, Bobby, I'm screaming with terror every goddamn second of the day. It gets so loud around this time, you listen closely at my temples, I'll bet you could hear it. And the mitzvahs, they help me a little. Or maybe they just distract me. And that's good, too."

Bobby thought he didn't share that feeling, and said instead, "We've been trying the Sabbath thing, believe it or not. Laura, you know, she looks at some phonetic spelling of the Hebrew letters." He had a drink. "We do the Kwanzaa candles, too, mind you."

He and Zing walked aimlessly around the parking lot, still searching for seams in the asphalt. She wouldn't tolerate this much longer. He kicked himself, bringing all that baby paraphernalia but forgetting even one book. Things could get hard, Zing wailing at him, and no way, really, to make it right or even to distract her. From her boredom, from her mom's incarceration, from Laura's legs.

And thinking of those lovely pins made Bobby remember that scream Arkey had talked about, almost hearing it now behind his *we do the Kwanzaa candles.* Like *that* could help with Bobby's fear of Laura's being crippled, when really what fucking good would Ron Karenga's candles be—a little homegrown thing, no different from their ridiculous dead letters. A new baby here, were candles gonna help him care for Deborah and Zing alone? Even caring for them with Laura—and caring *for* Laura—he wanted to scream because he felt his life being taken from him, the kids just making him feel how fast it went.

How much more time did he have? However much it was, he couldn't do a damn thing about it! Heart pounding, he looked at the barbed-wire walls, the ugly cars, feeling trapped. But they were *outside* the walls, so where was he trapped? *In this fucking body, that's where!*

He picked Zing up by her arms, hugged her to his chest. Strangely the warm pressure of her body quieted his heart for a moment.

"Too hard, Daddy. That hurts."

"Sorry, darling. You okay? You cold?"

She shook her head no. He hoisted her onto his shoulders. It hurt his back a little, but it might be enough amusement for a few minutes—their just walking from nowhere to nowhere, south.

But not getting anywhere wasn't sustaining enough for *him*. What had he thought? Adopt a child, have a child, take care of a broken relative, a crippled wife—*just put it all on my broad black shoulders.* He had to carry Laura now from the chair to the toilet, wait for her to finish, averting his head, for his sake, not hers, then back to the bed. And neither of them had much appetite for *that* anymore. Or much energy, Deborah waking them every two hours to suck a little. And that thought made the panic start up inside him again.

"Does that man have a gun?" a small voice said.

He couldn't see where Zing pointed, but she must have spotted the tower guard. "Yes. He's a policeman, darling, protecting everyone." *From your mom.*

"Why is Mommy here?" Zing said. She *always* asked that. At the prison every time they came, but at playgrounds, too, bathtubs, her bed. And he and Laura always answered as best they could—which wasn't ever good enough. So she asked again. As she did with all the big questions—where do we go when we die? who made us? why did they kill Martin Luther King?

"Your mother . . ." That question, it always made him try to reconnect with who he'd been—like if he could remember Bobby Brown shouting *Arm yourself or harm yourself,* then he could put up a decent defense for Beth. After all, your own choices always made sense from inside, seemed inevitable even; maybe understanding them could help him make a narrative of Beth, bring her back up the food chain. So he asked himself again, *I shouted that because . . . ?* From the overflowing sap of his youth? For the excitement? Because Sugar Cane said to? Or because there was so damn much truth to it?

Or because he had wanted to go on being the leader of the OBU, and he couldn't let his followers get ahead of him, had to be more militant than thou? Vanity and love intertwined for Bobby Brown, always; even now with his clients. Maybe it was the same with Beth.

But two men dead? Could Bobby ever have made that wrong a turning? Maybe, yeah, he could have. Laura, he knew, still dreamt him certain, decisive, always knowing where to go, but his life then, his life now, he saw, maybe wasn't so damned inevitable, even to him. Today, anyway, it felt more like, *you do this then you do that,* chasing one dream or another—like a rat in a maze who goes to an opening; that dead-ends, he spins around and scampers for another exit. That boy going round and round the Dewey track, he runs toward Sugar Cane in Mississippi who's shouting "Black Power," and he runs after that crowd burning a school, and he runs away from the flames into law school . . . *until you end up carrying a terrorist's child on your back, marching next to high brick walls with barbed wire on top.*

Zing began to beat on his head a little—a rainfall of Zing drops. "Talk to me!"

"I was thinking about your mom." A half-lie; actually he'd mostly been thinking about himself. But he'd *meant* to find the connection to her mom, use his own self-pity to find a vein of forgiveness for Beth.

"Why is my mom here?"

So what would it be? Ambition or love of his people, for him and Beth? Or dream-addled rats in a maze without exits? "Your mother," he said again.

Your mother wanted to stop a terrible war? Not to be an obedient German? Not be a racist? Not feel guilty anymore? Avenge what happened to *her* father? Make a world where such things never happened again to anyone? Star in a comic book? Be beyond human, one with the sempiternal upsurge of the world? *Your mother,* he stuttered inwardly, *your mother, Zing, your mother.*

"Just a minute, sweetheart." He put Zing down, felt the ache in his neck. She stared up at him out of her mother's big eyes.

"Are you okay, Dad?"

Dad? Extra desperation in Zing since Deborah arrived, for sure. Any port in a storm? Or the child saw his sterling qualities? But if she got too attached to him, would he *have to* gut this out, carry her and Deborah, Laura and Ruth for the rest of his all-too-short life?

But he already knew he would do it—a loving, *moral* rat in a maze. And that made him think of Zing's grandfather, his peppermint drink, his crooked teeth. Their talking each week, it had eased Bobby a little. A father thing, right? Leo Jacobs, the famous analyst, the Holocaust survivor, treated Bobby like a son, or better, like *a fellow sufferer*—and that, for the space of a drink with Leo, seemed the most honorable estate the world could offer. Like they'd both heard this blue note at the heart of things, that in the best world you could imagine people still died; and in *this* one they even hurried each other along—especially, mind you, if the victim's skin was a darker color. Why? Probably to get a jolt of power when they were really so utterly powerless, or maybe just to distract themselves from the shrieking. Now Leo's death had left Bobby burdened with a mixture of memory and longing, this dream that he should do a good job with Zing so she would help cure this septic, incurable world—or make up in some small way, anyway, for her mother's mistakes.

But now, the sweet drinks gone, the panic came back. He wanted to tell the old man that that was not *his* dream. He wanted his own life back. Still, he took Zing's hand, and strangely it helped a little—like doing right by her, living out that ridiculous story, might briefly quiet the awful sound the world made rushing away from him, the same thing that burdened him on the in-breath easing him even more on the out—if he did something about it. Crushing him, too, most likely, if he didn't.

He knelt in the prison parking lot to be at his adopted daughter's level, found himself staring at her green eyes, her long lashes, her down-turned mouth that was so like her mother's. He could see the woman she would become, could feel the very little time when he could still affect her, when she would care what he thought. "Your mother," he said.

But Zing interrupted him. "Daddy," she said, the word offering his burdened heart equal amounts of gravity and grace, "can we go home now?" Without waiting for an answer, she turned and walked toward their car, Bobby following helplessly after.

A NOTE ABOUT THE AUTHOR

Jay Cantor is the author of two previous novels, *The Death of Che Guevara* and *Krazy Kat,* and two books of essays, *The Space Between: Literature and Politics,* and *On Giving Birth to One's Own Mother.* A MacArthur Prize fellow, he teaches at Tufts University and lives in Cambridge, Massachusetts, with his wife, Melinda Marble, and their daughter, Grace.

A NOTE ON THE TYPE

The text of this book was set in Sabon, a typeface
designed by Jan Tschichold (1902–1974), the well-
known German typographer. Because it was designed in Frankfurt, Sabon was named for the
famous Frankfurt typefounder Jacques Sabon,
who died in 1580 while manager of the Egenolff
foundry. Based loosely on the original designs
of Claude Garamond (c. 1480–1561), Sabon is
unique in that it was explicitly designed for hot-
metal composition on both the Monotype and
Linotype machines as well as for film composition.

Composed by Stratford Publishing Services, Inc.
Brattleboro, Vermont

Printed and bound by Berryville Graphics
Berryville, Virginia

Book design by Dorothy S. Baker